DUST & FURY

First edition, published in 2002 by

WOODFIELD PUBLISHING
Woodfield House, Babsham Lane, Bognor Regis
West Sussex PO21 5EL, England.

© David Barnett, 2002

ISBN 1-903953-25-1

Dust & Fury

David Barnett

To

Keith n Daphne
Best Regards
David Barnett

Woodfield Publishing
~WEST SUSSEX · ENGLAND ~

Sultanate of Oman

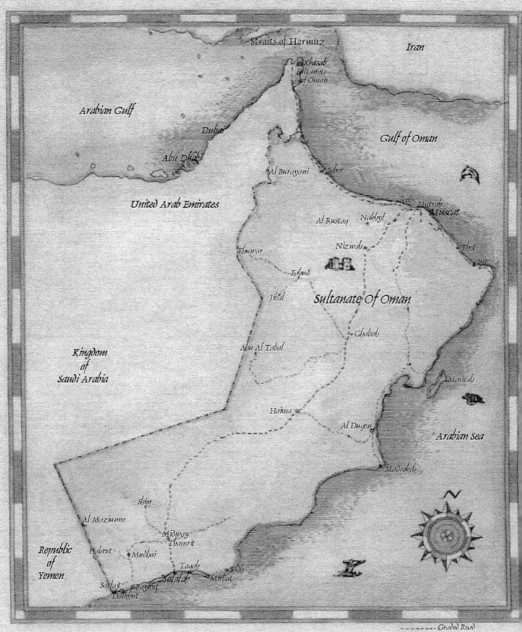

Straits of Hormuz

Iran

Khasab
Sultanate
of Oman

Arabian Gulf

Gulf of Oman

Dubai

Abu Dhabi

Al Burayami   Sohar

United Arab Emirates

Al Rustaq   Nakhyl   Seeb Mutrah
Muscat

Khawr   Nizwah   Tiwi
Sur

Ebrid

Jibdl   Sultanate Of Oman

Abu Al Tabal   Ghabah

Kingdom
of
Saudi Arabia

Masirah

Hanna   Al Duqm

Arabian Sea

Madrakah

N

Shisr

Al Maziunne

Midayay
Thamrit

Republic
of
Yemen

Habrut   Mudhai   Taugh   Sleh
Salalah   Mirbat

Sadah
Dalkhut   Raysut

———— Graded Road
———— International Boundary

This book is dedicated to my two daughters,
Karen and Jennifer, who make me very proud,
and, of course, to my wife Ivy, who is my inspiration in all things.

Tarqah Castle – see Chapter 7.

The road to Raykut from the West. – see Chapter 26.

Acknowledgements

My grateful thanks to the following people, whose help was invaluable in the course of compiling the background information for this story.

Airwork Limited [Shorts of Belfast] – who gave me the opportunity to live and work in the Dhofar area. Without that opportunity, I could never have begun this story.

Les Straw – a friend and colleague who as a young man spent some of this period in Salalah with the Royal Air Force. He was able to give me some feelings of what life was like during the Dhofar conflict.

Bakheit Bin Abdulla Bait Masen – For the wealth of information on the compilation of tribes and their traditional areas within southern Oman. Including some of their history, customs and unwritten laws.

An Unknown Shaffer – who one day, through two young interpreters, told me a story of a skirmish on Jebal Arum as we sat in Wadi Darbat beside a campfire and drank sweet black tea from plastic margarine containers. Much later, after reading Tony Jeapes book, I was able to relate that skirmish to the struggle to move the gun from Arum.

I would also like to acknowledge the work of the following authors:

Ahmed Hamoud Al Maamiry, *Oman and East Africa*
General Sir Peter De La Billiere, *Looking For Trouble*
Ranulph Fiennes, *Where Soldiers Fear to Tread*
Robin Hunter, *True Stories of the SAS*
Major General Tony Jeapes, *SAS Secret War*
Michael Kennedy, *Soldier I*

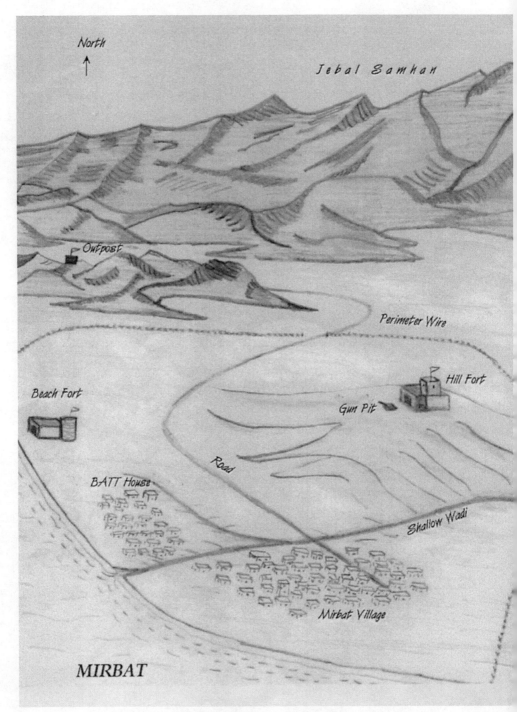

Hill fort at Mirbat – see chapter 18.

July 1968 • The Beaver dropped through the thick blanket of grey cloud at around one thousand feet. It continued its shallow descent to eight hundred feet and then banked sharply to starboard and began a one hundred and eighty-degree turn back towards the runway at Salalah. The single piston engine whined angrily at the strain applied, then as the aircraft levelled out its protest changed into a long noisy groan. With the sea on his port side and the towering mountain range of the Jebal Qara on his starboard the pilot flew along the Salalah plain and lined up the aircraft on the runway.

Halfway up the steep mountainside Mussalim sat in the mouth of a shallow cave overlooking the flat coastal plain. A cheap plastic cagoule kept his shoulders dry but the *dish'dasht* he wore beneath was wet from his waist down to his ankles. His head and the lower part of his face were wrapped in a *shamag* dampened by the fine spray of light drizzle. Only his eyes were not covered. Those dark eyes watched the aerial acrobatics unemotionally. They betrayed nothing of the resentment and envy directed at that pilot. He had not the vaguest idea who that pilot might be, but he saw him as a component of the elitist selective system that had educated him and had therefore given him the freedom of choice. Such opportunities were denied to the vast majority of the population. He compared his own circumstances of poverty with his perceived situation of the man in the aircraft and his stomach churned with rancour. The aircraft was much too far away for him to see the Oman national emblem of crossed swords beneath a curved dagger on the tail fin, but by its vintage age and the predominant white colour he knew that it belonged to the Sultan's Airforce. He watched it gradually descend until it disappeared from his sight behind a plunging peninsula of the jebal presumably to land safely on the runway.

He shifted his gaze to the deeply rutted track, which was the road from the jebal and across the plain to the town. It was badly muddied with many deep puddles scattered along its twelve kilometres. Two Qara Jeballys picked their way around these puddles as they led their camels, burdened with sticks and logs, towards the fortified town. At the end of the road they would join the queue of other woodsmen standing outside the concertina razor wire waiting their turn to be searched for concealed weapons before they would be allowed into the town to sell the wood.

His own camel, which really belonged to his father, stood nearby in the deep wet grass nibbling quietly at the soft wet leaves on the shrub like *Ghaf* trees. He had taken the camel without his father's consent. However, even though they had quarrelled he could not believe that he would have denied him at least that possession. He had far to go across the scorched barren waste of the *nejd* and over the border into Yemen. Without the animal he would have absolutely no hope of getting there and would probably die somewhere out on the rocky gravel waste of the Dhofar Desert.

The camel stopped its nibbling, lifted its head and stood perfectly still staring eastward waiting expectantly. Mussalim followed the animal's gaze and also waited. Eventually around a rocky crag less than a kilometre away another camel came into view its rider guiding his animal along a narrow goat track towards him. The motionless camel gave out a long throaty welcoming bellow to the approaching animal and then turned its attention back to the leaves. The rider guided his animal right up to the cave where Mussalim sat and then skilfully using his camel cane he made the animal kneel so that he could get off.

Mussalim got to his feet and waited in the shelter of the cave for his brother to come to him. When he did he greeted him wordlessly by kissing him on both sides of his face. After Juma had reciprocated they sat and silently stared out across the Salalah plain.

"I knew you would be here," Juma said after a while.

Mussalim nodded and thought of those days when they had played in and around this cave. This had been their 'secret place', but that was twelve or fourteen years ago and in much happier times. In those days as very young boys they had cared nothing for any comparison between the illusory privileged few and the deprived many. At that time they had more important youthful trivia to pursue and had no time consider the moral philosophy of wealth over poverty. In their childish ignorance poverty was the normal state because everyone they knew suffered the same daily struggle for their very existence.

"This is not a safe place to be." Juma added as he scratched the loose sand in front of him with his camel stick. "Any second one of the artillery batteries from the Air Force base or the Army Garrison could open up and pound this very spot."

Mussalim knew that was true. The Government forces at irregular intervals and at random choice selected a spot on the steep mountainside to pulverise. The purpose was to discourage the guerrilla forces of the Dhofar Liberation Front from setting up a mortar line and shelling the military bases.

"*Inshaallah*," he muttered allowing that it would happen if it were Allah's will. "I came to this place hoping that you would come and find me," he said, then after a pause. "Is father very angry?"

Juma shrugged. "He had not returned when I left."

"Father does not understand." Mussalim shook his head sadly. "He has lived his life in these mountains and knows little of what is happening beyond this region." He glanced sideways at his brother. " If he had seen the things that I saw during the year I spent in Bahrain, then he would understand."

"We are a poor nation. Bahrain is oil rich."

"I believe that this country is not as poor as this Sultan would have us believe. Do we not have oil also?"

Juma nodded agreement. "So it is said, but it is all in the north and none yet discovered in this region."

"But the oil companies drill all over this area so it can only be a matter of time before it is discovered. We must break away this despotic rule and set up an independent state. Then when the oil is discovered the revenue will belong to the people of Dhofar and will not disappear into Sultan Sayyid Said Bin Taymour's treasure chest."

They had had this conversation many times before and Juma recognised it as a futile topic. His brother's extremist view meant that no concessionary ground could be achieved. He sighed quietly recognising it as dangerous ground. He did not want to quarrel with his brother, so he changed the subject. "What will you do?" he asked.

Mussalim looked sideways at his brother. Although Juma was younger by more than two years they were so alike that they could almost pass for twins. His shamag was wrapped tightly around his head with the free end hanging loosely down the side of his face onto his shoulder. Both brothers had inherited their father's slight but tough physique and their mother's handsome facial features. Juma's vanity was such that he would not allow those youthful good looks to be hidden by a man's beard, unlike Mussalim, who possessed a full black beard clipped somewhat untidily at an easily manageable length. Both men's complexions were dark with eyes darker by far than their complexion. Those eyes now met as Juma waited for an answer to his question.

Mussalim shrugged. "I will go to Sheikh Mussalim Bin Nufl and join his liberation cause."

Juma turned away and looked sadly across the plain. "You are our father's eldest son and despite all of your quarrels you are his favourite. He will be saddened by the news."

"He will not be surprised!"

"No," Juma agreed. "But still, he will be saddened."

"Someday this region will be liberated from this poverty which Said Taymour uses to suppress the people. When that day comes, then the people of Dhofar will thrive and prosper. Father will then see the wisdom of what I do now and he will be proud that his eldest son was an active part of that struggle."

"He is proud of you, Mussalim. When you came back from Bahrain only a few short months ago and handed to him more money than he has ever seen I had never seen him so pleased."

"He was pleased to have the money."

"No," Juma shook his head. "He was pleased that you had succeeded."

"Succeeded!" he scoffed. "Juma, you do not know what I had to endure, what degradations I suffered, to get that money."

"I thought that you worked in the oilfields at Awali."

Mussalim was thoughtful a moment before deciding to make his confession. "Yes I worked at Awali. But I worked in the living quarters of the British Oil Field employees. The menial tasks which I had to do were humiliating."

"Menial tasks?"

"Yes, menial tasks. I swept the floors, cleaned glasses, tended gardens and other similar tasks. I did women's work and smiled while I did it. All the time the lazy British women seemed to do nothing except lounge around a swimming pool flaunting themselves half naked and be waited on by people like me."

Juma winced silently, embarrassed by his brother's confession. He could understand the humiliation any Arab would feel performing woman's work in those circumstances.

"And for this you got all that money?" he asked attempting an apathetic tone. He drew obscure shapes in the sand with his cane feigning some disinterest trying to moderate his brother's embarrassment.

"All that money was but a mere pittance compared to what the British and Bahraini technicians got."

"It was not a pittance here, there was enough for father to buy those twelve cows." Juma stoutly defended the significance of the gesture.

"Yes, it was and I hope it sustains you all for some time to come. But I fear that when this Khareef grass has once again been scorched away by the sun he will be forced to sell half to buy hay for the other half. Eventually the stock will dwindle away."

"Perhaps not. Father does have a plan."

Mussalim got to his feet and moved from the shelter of the cave into the fine drizzle. "Let us hope that it works," he said peering upward into the thick mist which covered the top half of the towering mountains.

"You should come home and help him to make it work. Forget this madness."

Mussalim looked at his brother and studied him for a few moments, and then he turned his attention back to the jebal mist. "I must go," he said disregarding the comments. "I want to be over the jebal and onto the *nejd* before dark." He didn't want to spend a night in the cold rain and mist among the peaks.

Juma shook his head sadly. "Where will you go to find Mussalim Bin Nufl," he asked with resignation and got to his feet.

"Just over the Yemen border to Hauf. I have heard talk of a guerrilla training camp there."

Juma nodded, he had heard the same talk. "Hauf is one hundred and fifty kilometres directly west from here."

"Yes," Mussalim agreed.

"Why then do you go north across Jebal Qara?"

He smiled at his younger brother's naivety and placed his hand on his shoulder. "Government forces are strong all along this plain and their patrols many, particularly so along that stretch of the border. Even if I did not get picked up for questioning on my journey almost certainly I would get arrested attempting to cross the border."

Juma nodded understanding. "Which way will you go?"

"There are no government forces on the jebal at this time of the year. They dare not venture into the thick blanket of the Khareef mists. So I will go northward over the jebal, then northwest across the nejd to Mudhai. From there I will turn west and cross the border at some desolate stretch south of Habrut. Once in Yemen, I will travel directly south to Hauf. *Inshaallah!*" he added.

"It will take you many days."

"Yes." Mussalim agreed. Then he looked at his brother sadly and said. "Come, let us pray together before I go."

Juma realising fully that his brother's mind was set sighed sadly and then unhooked his goatskin water bag from his camel's saddle. He tipped a little water into Mussalim's cupped hands and, unnoticed by his brother, he watched him gloomily as he splashed the water on his face. When he had washed Mussalim did the same for him. They then spread their prayer mats, roughly facing the direction of Mecca, and on their knees in the drizzle they quietly prayed.

Mussalim finished his prayers before Juma and he noiselessly moved away. He caught the rein of his camel and led it towards a flat piece of ground. He checked the animal's girth and after a precautionary tighten he made it kneel and mounted. Then he sat patiently waiting for his brother to finish.

When he had finished Juma picked up his water bag from the floor, a string of figs from his own camel and brought them to his brother. "The figs were sent by our mother," he said as he hooked both items over the saddle horn. Mussalim looked at him quizzically.

"She guessed that you wouldn't becoming back," Juma said with a shrug. He nodded slowly without replying and stared down at him. He had no words, but then they were close enough not to need any, each knew what the other thought. "*Masalaama*," he said and slapped his cane down the animal's shoulder. The beast moved forward instantly.

"*Masalaama*," Juma replied as his brother left. He considered the inappropriateness of the 'go in peace farewell' as he watched him make his way along the goat track. He continued to stand and watch his brother until he had disappeared from view behind the rocky crag and he brooded gloomily that it might be a long time before he would see him again.

He used the dangling end of his shamag to wipe the rain from his face and looked up to the thick grey mist, which shrouded the heights of the jebal. It was July in this year of 1968 and the Khareef only in its early weeks. It would be another seven or eight before the mists would gradually thin and disappear. When they did these mountains would emerge from this annual metamorphosis completely transformed. Gone would be the dry streambeds, the scorched shrubs and the sparse brown grass. Replaced by fast flowing streams hurrying down from the peaks gathering momentum as they tumble over rocks and waterfalls rushing ever downwards to form pools and rivers at the mountain's feet. The shrubs will be rejuvenated with thick green canopies and flowers and the grass lush and deep liberally interspersed with pink balsam and an array of other wild flowers.

Juma pulled on the reins of his camel to bring it to a kneeling position and climbed on top. A sharp slap on its rump from the cane got the animal to its feet and moving along the narrow track. It would take at least an hour to climb the steep valley to the top of the mountain and the village of Shair. There would be a further thirty minutes beyond that before he would reach home. He could anticipate that there would be a subdued and sad atmosphere in the home tonight after he had delivered the news. He did not relish his arrival home and he sought of ways to delay it. He thought of the pretty black eyed girl he had seen two weeks ago at the pool at Sahalnawt and he considered the chances of her being there today. It wasn't likely he reasoned, but even if she weren't it would be a pleasant place to spend an hour and it would delay his arrival home.

The waters tumbling down the steep Shair valley gather in a small lake on a wide shelf at the foot of the jebal. From there it overflows and cascades over a cliff sixty feet into the basin at Sahalnawt. After filling the basin it drains away as a small river across the plain down to the sea. Despite the almost permanent drizzle its waterfall spectacle make it a popular attraction. Juma hoped the girl would be there and he resolved that if she were then this time he would speak to her.

✳ ✳ ✳

Although the copse was concealed by the thick swirling mist Abdulla knew roughly its position and walked in that direction. Lailla, his daughter, should be close by the trees somewhere shepherding the small herd of goats, which belonged to him and his brother, Fiad. He wore a faded *futa* wrapped around his waist and legs while his feet were bare and in the long wet grass, cold. A ragged cloth hung draped from his shoulders and sagged over his bare chest while the ends hung loosely down his back. His scant clothing dripped, soaked by the rain, as did his mass of unruly frizzed hair. His stature was small and emaciated to a degree by almost fifty years of under nourishment, but toughened by an indomitable spirit to survive the harsh conditions living in the Qara Mountains. His face was thin and deeply lined, his nose slightly hooked and his teeth crooked. An untidy pointed beard on the end of his chin added to the stoical facial cast.

He came in amongst the goats, scattering them in all directions before he could see the copse. He called Lailla's name and she answered from somewhere to his right. He adjusted his direction and found his daughter huddled under a spread cloth cover beneath the canopies of the small cluster of trees.

"Is it time to go?"

He sat down beside her and as he did she lifted part of the cover over him. "You can take the goats home a little early today," he said.

She knew the appropriate time to return with the animals and she was normally left to come in alone. If there was to be any deviation from the routine then it was usually Jokha or Kathya, one of her father's two wives, who would come to fetch her. "Is anything wrong?" she asked.

"No," he said a little to sharply to be convincing. She was little more than a child and female too, therefore it was not fitting that he burden her with his present troubles. "Go," he instructed. "Gather the goats and take them home."

She got up and leaving him under the cover went to do his bidding. As she started to fade into the mist she let out a long and shrill piercing warble calling the goats to her. As he watched her go Abdulla acknowledged that she was not really a child any longer and at the age of fourteen was verging into a woman. He would need to talk to the girl's mother Kathya at an early opportunity about her puberty.

He took a long breath and sighed as he began to feel somewhat inadequate. It seemed that things were beginning to slide from his grasp. The autocratic control over the family and their circumstances that he had always firmly held was being challenged by events, which were beyond his control. Lailla was the youngest of his four children and the time was approaching when she would have to be husbanded and begin a new life elsewhere beyond the sphere of his regulation. Meanwhile Mussalim, his eldest son seemed determinedly set upon his own destruction and unable to hear any opinion of sanity. Indeed he had begun to treat his own father's opinions with a degree of contempt. He regretted the day that he had sanctioned his son's venture to Bahrain. At the time it had seemed a marvellous opportunity for not only Mussalim to transcend his limited expectations but the family as a unit would prosper with the not inconsequential extra income that would come with it. At first his return had seemed to fill all those expectations. Very soon after, however, Mussalim had begun to flagrantly voice his discontent and speak angrily of revolution. He had been a naive young man when he had left and therefore had been particularly vulnerable to the corrupting influences of the agitators with whom he had come into contact. Now fully convinced by the ideology of others and his passion fuelled by the impatience of youth his entrenched beliefs had taken him to the very rim of criminal actions against his own country.

"Oh Allah," he muttered appealing for some divine guidance which may yet show him the way to dissuade his son from joining those bandits which cavorted throughout the region adding more misery to the poor people in the name of Liberation.

There was, he acknowledged, a great deal wrong with a system that made a few rich beyond comprehension and the vast majority of the populace impoverished to the point of starvation. However, had it not always been so? But now with the advent of oil in the country this Sultan will eventually use some of the revenue for the benefit of his people, he felt sure. Patience was all that was needed. Somehow he had to make Mussalim realise this and to bridle his impatience a little longer. In the meantime with a dozen cattle, three camels and the small herd of goats he shared with his brother's family they were in a much better position than most in their tribe. He knew that his son's decision to leave was imminent, so tonight after the family had eaten and the men of the family were assembled to talk he would try once more to talk some sense into his eldest son. This time, however, he resolved that he would control his own exasperation and talk quietly and rationally to him. He sat a few minutes more in deep contemplation staring unseeing into the swirling mists. Then with a heavy sigh he pinched the cloth, which covered his head, tightly beneath his chin, got up wearily and slowly followed Lailla into the thick mist.

✳ ✳ ✳

After a few minutes Lailla found the worn track which led directly to the family home. She walked slowly allowing the following goats to meander casually in her wake. After a little while she came to the rustic wall, which served as a livestock pen. It was constructed entirely from stacked rocks and because no mortar bound these rocks together many had tumbled off giving an uneven appearance to the wall. She turned into the pen through the gateway and made her way towards the square one storey building, which was the house. She was perhaps a little apprehensive about the unknown reason which had permitted her early arrival home nevertheless she would be pleased to be out of the rain and cold mist of the Khareef weather.

As she passed a diminutive building, also constructed of piled rocks with bent and corroded corrugated iron sheets for a roof she heard sounds of activity from within. She paused and then ambled across to the small hole, which was the doorway then bent and peered in.

Hamed busied himself inside selecting suitable logs and kindling wood for burning then tossed them into a home made wheelbarrow. She stood in the entrance a few moments watching her brother work, then she ducked inside.

"Lailla," he said seeing her for the first time. "You're back early."

Hamed was her full brother and three years older. They had the same mother, Kathya, while her elder brothers, Mussalim and Juma, were from her father's number one wife, Jokha. Abdulla had put his stamp on this son in every way. Their slight, but wiry physiques, were identical and so were the stoical facial cast. Even Hamed's hair was massed and frizzed like his father's. There was, however, only faint evidence of a man's beard. His physical development was at comparatively early stage.

"Father came and sent me home."

Hamed paused a moment with a log in his hand and looked at her. "Where is he now?"

"I left him at the copse."

He tossed the log into the wheelbarrow, which was little more than a wooden vegetable box on wheels. He wiped the grime from his hands and looked at his sister. "There was another quarrel between him and Mussalim."

"I wondered what had happened."

"He left with angry words and he has been away all afternoon."

"Same topic?" she enquired.

"Of course."

"Where is Mussalim now?"

"He left too. Shortly after father left, he saddled a camel and rode away."

"Where to?"

"Who knows," Hamed said sadly as he turned and once more began throwing wood into the wheelbarrow. "Jokha thinks that he has gone."

"Gone?"

"Left home."

Lailla was silent reflecting unhappily on the disharmony that had come into the family since Mussalim's return from Bahrain. "I wish," she muttered, then did not voice her thoughts.

"So do I," Hamed agreed as he began to distribute the load in the rickety wheelbarrow. He looked at Lailla and sensed her gloom. "Jokha sent Juma after him so perhaps he will bring him back."

She hoped so. It would be a very subdued atmosphere within the family tonight if he didn't.

Juma forded the river below Sahalnawt. It wasn't deep at this point, not more than a foot, but it flowed fast and the camel was a little reluctant to step into the water. A short slap from the camel cane persuaded the animal to go on. On the other side Juma dismounted and left the animal to forage while he made his way on foot to the falls.

The rain here away from the jebal was little more than a fine spray on the wind raising hopes within him that perhaps there would be people about and in particular that black eyed girl. He approached the wide split of the canyon with river water spewing from its mouth. He entered the canyon walking along a narrow ledge six foot above the rushing water. The sheer rock walls grew taller as he progressed inwards. Stalactites hung in abundance along the cliffs faces placed there by the persistent dripping water of centuries of Khareef's. Faint sounds of excited cries mingled weakly among the roar of the rushing water as he neared the basin raising his hopes. He rounded the last sharp bend to view the annual spectacle of Sahalnawt.

Beyond the basin, water cascaded sixty feet from the cliff's lip crashing in spectacular fashion onto the smooth rocks below. From there it tumbled over the rocks and filled the basin to make a small sheltered lake. Near to where he stood that lake overflowed, the water fizzing down across the rocks to feed the river rushing along the canyon base. A small party of people sat on the ledge just above the lake watching five young boys shouting excitably as they swam and played in the water. Juma had no inclination to appreciate nature's vista, nor the happiness of the boys. Instead his eyes quickly scanned the party of people as he searched for the girl. She wasn't there.

For a while he sat on the ledge his legs dangling above the water watching it hurry past. His mind returned gloomily to his brother and the sad news, which he would have to deliver to the family tonight. Still seeking to delay his return he decided to leave the canyon and go up onto the cliff above for a different view.

He was on the top above the canyon making his way slowly through the thick brush and almost above the lake when he saw her. She was sitting with three other girls of similar age on a large cloth, which had been spread over the damp ground. His heart leapt with pleasure and surprise. Shuffling past slowly he muttering an embarrassed greeting. He stopped a few yards further on and half-leaned and half-sat against a large rock not sure what to do next. He glanced back at the girls and wondered how to make an approach.

The girls, sensing his desire and his dilemma, cast furtive glances in his direction, whispering among themselves and giggling frequently at his expense. Juma feigned an interest in nature's vista and looked down into the canyon pretending not to notice the amusement he was causing. The girlish giggles became louder demanding his attention. Eventually it became loud enough to give him complete justification to stare in their direction.

All were young girls in their early or mid teenage years and none had yet donned the black shroud that the Islamic religion demands. He studied the black-eyed girl clandestinely. She did not giggle like the rest, instead sat quietly demure and benign to the amusement around her.

She wore a long shapeless ornate gown buttoned tightly at her throat. Its length extended below her knees while the trousers she wore beneath the gown were buttoned tightly at her ankles. The sleeves of the gown were long and hung loosely from her wrists. The long gossamer veil that she wore draped over her head and shoulders completed the vision of blue. Just for a brief moment she held Juma's stare then she discreetly lowered her eyes and lifted the edge of the veil across the lower part of her face.

Juma, encouraged by that glance pushed himself away from the rock and walked over to where the girls were sitting. The giggles became a little more discreet then died completely when he was close.

"Peace be with you all," Juma gave the customary greeting.

"Peace be with you also," one of them muttered shyly.

"Where are you girls from? Salalah!" he suggested an answer to his own question.

One grunted agreement then added, "Al Dharitz."

He knew Al Dharitz. It was a small village attached to the very western edge of Salalah and inside its concertina wired protection.

"I am Jabally!" he said proudly dabbing his finger in his chest, "and my name is Juma." Then he introduced himself a little more fully. "Juma Bin Abdulla." The response was limited, just a couple of brief nods. Undaunted he pressed on, "what are your names?"

The names were given shyly. He looked at the black-eyed girl who had yet to utter a sound. She still held the edge of the cape over the lower part of her face. "And your name?"

"Khamisa," she replied softly.

"Khamisa, that's a nice name," he offered a compliment. She lowered her eyes in appropriate modesty. "And the rest?"

"Khamisa Bint Talib," she didn't raise her eyes.

He stared down at her and admired the propriety and elegance in her manner. He could feel the swell of hope and desire increasing inside. The veil partially hiding her face only heightened his curiosity and increased his interest. He had on previous occasions watched her from a distance clandestinely. Now he was closer to her than he had ever been and he took the opportunity to study her from close range. Even from her sitting posture it was obvious that her physique was petit. His impression from a distance had been that she had a strikingly pretty face, even though that veil now hid most of it he could tell that his impression had not complimented her enough. Her complexion was swarthy and flattered by long shining black hair, which hung heavily onto her shoulders and tumbled forward beneath her veil. He decided that without doubt this was a woman that any man would be proud and exalted to own.

"I have seen you here before, Khamisa."

"Yes," she raised her eyes briefly.

Her reply indicated to him that she knew that he had and his hopes took flight instantly. It meant of course that she had noticed him too.

"We come here as a family on most Friday's after mid-day prayers," one of the other girls informed him unwittingly reminding him that they were there.

"You are all one family?" he asked.

"Yes. I am Khamisa's sister and these are our cousins," she went on indicating the other two girls.

"Where is the rest of your families?" He addressed Khamisa, wanting her to speak to him again.

"Our brothers swim in the lake and our fathers and mothers sit by the lake side," she answered her eyes daringly meeting his.

A distant deep and heavy thump interrupted the conversation but not the eye lock as they listened intently for the hiss of the passing shell. Moments later another dull thump as it exploded somewhere on the jebal far to the east.

"It's a long way off," he said reassuringly. More thumps followed and Juma listened intently trying to establish whether the barrage was from the Air Force base or the Army Garrison. He decided it was the guns to the south. "It's the Army Garrison. Probably just routine," he added a little indifferently trying to dispel any alarm and in so doing keeping the contact with Khamisa from ending.

The routine for these barrages was that there was no routine. Their start was always unpredictable as were its duration. Sometimes they would pulverise a specific area, sometimes distribute the shells into three or four areas and sometimes just place the shells randomly. Always, however, the target was the south face of the jebal, sometimes in the peaks sometimes along its base but usually somewhere in between. In their current position on the plain just away from its foot the danger would be from a rogue shell falling short. But while the target continued to be far to the east that danger did not exist.

"Should we go down into the canyon?" one of the girls asked Khamisa.

She looked up at Juma seeking support.

He sensed that she too was reluctant to end the contact. "Nothing to be alarmed about," he said shaking his head dismissive. "At least not while they keep shelling over that way."

"If there is any danger our father will come for us," Khamisa answered the girl's question.

"Why do they have to spoil our day out. Wouldn't you think that they would at least take Friday off," the girl complained.

"It would be nice," Juma agreed with a grin.

A coarse shriek attracted all their attention and Juma turned to see a woman emerging from the thicket. She was covered from head to foot in the black *abeya* that Islamic women are obliged to wear and she hurried towards them waving her arms in agitation.

"Get away. Get away," she shouted at Juma.

He stood still and waited, not sure of what his reaction should be.

"Go away," she said. As she got closer she took hold of her black gown just above the knee and began to flap it in his direction with a herding motion.

"I wasn't doing…"

Go away," she cut him short continuing to flap right in front of him now.

Juma began to give ground and move backwards. "I'm sorry," he said staring at the beak-like black mask, which she wore. "I meant no harm."

"Go," she said without compromise. "Go."

Juma stole a glance over her shoulder at Khamisa. She stared back with hopeless sympathy. He continued to retreat slowly as she continued to crowd him. "We were only talking," he said.

She glanced back and decided that they were now the correct distance away from the girls. She stopped flapping her gown. "Who are you?" she demanded.

"I am jebally and my name is Juma Bin Abdulla."

"Well jabally don't you know better than to approach unchaperoned girls?"

"We were only talking," he repeated appealingly.

She was much calmer now that she had achieved proper space between him and her charges. "What tribe are you from?"

"Al Hamer."

"Then you had better not come here again. We are Bait Ruwas, from Salalah. Ruwas and Al Hamer do not mix socially."

"But both tribes are Kathiri!" he pointed out.

"Yes," she allowed. "But we are the Hinawi faction of Kathiri, Al Hamer is not. You must stay away."

These defined tribal boundaries were a handicap to progress and often harmony in the Dhofar region. On this he was in complete agreement with his brother's radical viewpoint. Each tribe jealously guarded its own rites and properties always taking inward looking parochial stands on all issues when meetings took place between the tribe Sheikhs. Consequently there were little or no compromises on issues and therefore little of any consequence came from those meetings. But with a sigh he nodded compliance, realising that in this instance there was nothing to be gained by not agreeing. He retreated back to the large rock and sat down.

She went back to the girls and spoke harshly to them. They began gathering their possessions and then followed her into the thicket and down the hill.

Juma watched hoping for a glance from Khamisa. She had used subtle delaying tactics in order to be at the rear of the party as they departed. At the last possible moment before she disappeared from his view she looked back in his direction. He waved briefly. She did not respond, but then he hadn't expected her to. He was just delighted that he had got his glance.

He sat there quietly on the rock waiting for the artillery barrage to stop. Although the target was a long way to the east it was still not a wise policy to venture onto the south face of the jebal and make his way home up the Shair valley. He passed the time thinking of Khamisa. He had made the contact that he wanted and he was both delighted and excited about that. But more than that, he knew also that her father's name was Talib and that they all lived in the village of Al Dharitz. So therefore, he now knew how to find this girl. All things considered he was highly satisfied with the progress that he had made and he even dared to hope that Khamisa was not displeased by his attentions. He was determined to overcome the inflexible insulated attitude of the tribal system and continue with the pursuit of the object of his desire. Then he remembered his brother somewhere on the jebal in the thick mist and rain heading into an uncertain future. A black shadow spread across his happiness like a thick night cloud obliterating a full moon and it deflated his buoyant spirits.

~ 2 ~

It had been dark for a while by the time Mussalim began the descent into the steep and narrow pass that would take him clear of the mountains. He had followed the muddied road, which snaked its way through the mountains, for the last six hours. He was thoroughly wet and more than a little tired as was the beast beneath him. Nevertheless, he had pressed on determined to clear the rain and mist before he made camp for the night. Just one more hour would see him emerge from the entrance to the pass and onto the rocky gravel plain of the *nejd*. He grunted several times at the weary animal urging it onwards down the steep incline and into the deep rocky canyon. The landscape around him changed dramatically. Gone were the heavily canopied trees and the deep lush grass, replaced by a rocky terrain where some shrubs did grow but only just eked out a bare existence in cracks in the rock. When he reached the bottom he followed the winding road until he came to the wood bridge which crossed a deep and wide wadi. Because of the season water flowed in the wadi bottom and after crossing the bridge he turned the camel down the bank to the water's edge. With a slap of his camel cane he drove the animal into the fast flowing water before dismounting. He stood knee deep in the water while the camel drank and he washed away the caked mud from its legs and belly. Then he unhitched both of the goatskin bags and filled them to the neck. His next water opportunity would not come until he reached Mudhai in at least two day's time and between then and now there was a flat barren desert scorched by a blazing sun to be crossed.

The rain stopped and he left the thick mist behind him when he emerged from the pass. Above him millions of stars seemingly punctured every inch of the clear night sky. He turned and looked back at the murky greyness, which shrouded the higher ground of the mountains and he wondered a little gloomily when, if ever, he would live among its peaks again.

He travelled on a few more minutes before he turned off the road and along the bed of a shallow dry wadi. He found a suitable place to camp for the night beneath a shallow overhang of the wadi wall. He sent the camel to its knees and dismounted. Then he snatched the vintage Martin Henri rifle from its pouch in the saddle, laid it down close by and then unsaddled the animal. He bent and tied one of the camel's front legs so that it would not wander too far then he turned it out to forage for itself. There was plenty of dry wood to be found and he soon had a fire burning. He pulled off his wet clothing and draped it around the fire to dry. Next he took a blanket from his pack and wrapped himself in it then with the old rifle laying across his knees he sat nibbling figs and staring hypnotically at the fire's flames.

He was more than just a little apprehensive about the liberation cause that he sought to actively get into. It was not the justification, of that there was no doubt in his mind at all. He firmly believed that the region would be much better off independent from the rest of Oman, or even in the worse scenario not any worse off. Obviously the Sultan would not give up the Dhofar easily. Indeed he liked it so much that he had chosen to live in his Salalah Palace with his Dhofari wife instead of the northern capital of Muscat. Armed resistance was the only option open for people to break free from this despotic rule. But it was the very act of resistance that made him apprehensive. The armed struggle was not only against the Sultan's forces but the British also. Because of the strategic value of the country, particularly in the north where Oman guarded the narrow entrance into and out of the Gulf, Said Taymour could command the support of the British government. This was a formidable force, which had to be reckoned with. Loaned British officers and soldiers starched the Sultan's ground forces, while the Air Force base at Salalah had a large contingency of the Royal Air Force with modern aircraft and weapons. It was on the face of it a very unequal struggle. However, the Dhofar Liberation Front movement did have the active support of its Yemeni brothers. They had proved that by determination and perseverance victory was possible by making the British presence in Aden untenable and forcing them to withdraw. But in every war there are casualties and this was the point of uncertainty that made him apprehensive. After some deliberation he arrived at the same conclusion that he always did, if it were his fate then it would happen. "*Inshaallah*," he muttered committing his fate to Allah's will. He decided then that it was an appropriate time to make his last prayer of the day, ask Allah's protection and then to get some sleep. Tomorrow he intended to make an early dawn start and get as far into the *nejd* as he could before the sun became too hot.

It was still dark when he gave up attempting to sleep and sat up. He had slept well enough for the first part of the night but the last couple of hours had been cold and although wrapped in his blanket he had shivered constantly making sleep impossible. Still with the blanket wrapped around his shoulders he shuffled over to his clothes still draped across the ground. If they had dried around the fire it hadn't mattered because they were once again wet with heavy dew. Slightly irritated he aimed an exasperated kick at the clothes and turned away. A few yards away he squatted down and relieved himself. A half moon in the northern sky provided only a minimal weakening of the darkness. But close by he could see the camel squatting with its long legs wrapped out of sight beneath its body. Mussalim shuffled over to where his pack still lay on the ground. Using his water supply conservatively he washed his hands and face crudely, and then cleaned his teeth using his finger. He then turned to face westward stood quietly for a few moments and then he sank to his knees pressed his head against the ground and made his morning prayer.

Thirty minutes later dressed in the damp clothes and his camel loaded he was ready to move on. The road, two hundred yards to his right, led directly north. The angry red patch beginning to scar the night sky indicated where the sun was about to rise in the east. He chose a point roughly northwest and with a slap on the camel's rump from his stick urged the beast on.

Early progress was slow. The terrain in the closer proximity to the mountain range was etched with an endless labyrinth of deep dry wadis causing him to constantly turn from his northwest course as he meandered left and right trying to pick out the easier route. Often he was forced to wander wadi lips for a very long way in wrong directions before he was able to find a crossing place. Then when he had made a successfully crossing he found himself confronted almost immediately by yet another wadi with precisely the same problems. It was mid morning before he finally got clear of this gigantic and endless quarry. He looked back at the mountains with its peaks hidden in low thick clouds. It could not, he estimated, be more than ten kilometres away.

The sun was high and already mercilessly hot, but it was yet to reach its zenith and was therefore going to get hotter. His clothes had dried quickly when the sun had first risen, now they were once again wet, but this time from his sweat. He used the end of his shamag to wipe the sweat from his face and decided that now it was time to find a place to hide from the uncompassionate heat through mid-day.

He looked forward at the terrain ahead. It was flat rocky ground covered liberally and randomly by enormous pointed mounds like tall slagheaps of rock and gravel as far into the distance as he could see. Here and there low frankincense shrubs deformed to be flat-topped and slanted by the persistent wind from the jebal dotted the arid landscape. Only the heavy breath of the desert wind interrupted the deathly quiet. The unforgiving parched land seemed to be watching and waiting to see if he dared challenge the awesome potency of its desolation entirely alone.

The only possible shelter from the fierce midday sun would be beneath one of these sparsely leafed shrubs. He went on a little further looking to select one that had at least a reasonable canopy. When he eventually found one he dismounted, unsaddled the animal and turned it loose. Then he crawled beneath the low growth, spread a blanket and made himself as comfortable as he could. For the next five hours he lay there in the dappled shade.

When he rolled out from beneath the shrub it was mid afternoon and the sun was still ferociously hot. However, from this point on it would become progressively cooler. The camel had stayed close by. At first it had nibbled at the leaves and after that had squatted, patiently waiting for its human companion to reappear from his cover. The animal got to its feet in anticipation when he saw Mussalim. He gathered together his belongings and made ready to move on, then before continuing his journey Mussalim once again dutifully offered his prayer.

Those giant mounds seemed to be endless and a serious handicap to progress as he weaved his way around and in between to avoid climbing them. His course, however, always returned to northwest as soon as it was possible to do so. As the sun set those slagheaps had become more spaced and less lofty and he was able to follow a more direct course. Now that his rate of progress had improved he was reluctant to stop and he continued on into the deepening darkness. Even the sore red spot, where the sun had set, had disappeared from the night sky when he finally left the last of those rock and gravel stacks behind. Now the landscape was flat and completely featureless carpeted profusely by black volcanic rock chippings.

Although he had perhaps progressed no more than thirty-two or thirty-three kilometres into the *nejd* he calculated that due to the endless tacking he had probably done close to sixty. He decided that was probably enough for the beast beneath him. He reined in and on the exposed flat rocky plain he stopped for the night. Since absolutely nothing grew there, there was no material of any sort that would do for a fire. He drank water warmed by the day's sun from the goatskin and ate the last of his figs. Then he cleared a small area of volcanic chippings to make a more comfortable resting area and spread out his blanket. After he had made his last prayer of the day, he wrapped himself in his blanket and lay sleepless on his back staring up at a million stars.

Once again he was travelling before the sun had even started to rise. He hoped that by the day's end he would be several miles to the west of the great wadi Ghadun. If he was, then he should be able to arrive at Mudhai sometime late tomorrow. Once there he would perhaps be able to buy enough food to last him until he reached Hauf. More importantly he should be able to rely on inter-tribal benevolence and replenish his depleted water supply from the village well. He had used his water as conservatively as he could but even so he had emptied one goatskin this morning. He planned to ration the last skin to half today and half tomorrow.

The rocky plain with its black rocks stretched out before him as far as the eye could see. As the hours slipped by the skyline neither changed nor became any nearer. The beast beneath him plodded on relentlessly, gently jarring him rhythmically with each step of its big feet. On this exposed plain there was no shelter, nowhere to hide from the sun's blistering heat so there was no point stopping. For protection he had covered himself completely from the sun leaving only his eyes staring out from beneath the bundle of cloth. He kept those eyes to the front staring hypnotically at the skyline and continually fixing a point around northwest. The area below the skyline quivered and shimmered with mirages of lakes of water making it difficult to concentrate on his agrarian navigation point. The day grew to its hottest and sweat trickled profusely down his back soaking the clothes beneath his buttocks making the riding sore. Around noon the covering of black volcanic chippings came to an end abruptly, leaving the hard baked sand beneath exposed. An hour later the skyline had changed subtly, it now had become less flat and much more uneven.

It was early afternoon when he reached Wadi Ghadun. He came upon it suddenly, its presence masked from a distance because of its geographical construction. A giant crack a kilometre wide and a half kilometre deep had been opened in the ground by centuries of underground water flowing from the mountains into the desert. The water relentlessly eroded the substratum lowering the wadi bed by a centimetre or two in a man's lifetime. Mussalim stopped on the lip and stared down into the wadi. Its sides were steep and sheer, with shallow caverns where enormous chunks of sandstone had slipped away from the face into the bottom. The bottom was covered with large white boulders bleached white by the sun and smoothed by fast flowing water, which had many centuries ago disappeared beneath ground. Desert shrubs and cactus sprinkled the bed managing to eke out some moisture from beneath the boulders. This would be a good place to rest he decided.

It took a little while but eventually he found a way down into the wadi. Selecting a suitable site to camp with a shallow cavern in which to shelter he unsaddled his camel. Using a little water in the palm of his hand he wet the animal's muzzle and allowed it to lick the remaining moisture from his hand. Then he turned it loose to graze. It would graze upon the greenery and in so doing extract fluid from the leaves.

He carried his pack to the cavern and laid it in the shade. He had noticed in the soft sand around the edges of the boulders animal footprints indicating a wild life haven. He drew from his pack the old Martin Henri rifle and primed and loaded it. Perhaps there would be an opportunity to shoot something, which he could eat; also wolves were not uncommon in these type of wadis.

Travelling through the hottest part of the day had been expensive on his water supply and he had already used this day's ration. He decided to make a still and use nature to get himself a little back. He found a sandy patch of ground in full sun and using only his hands and a knife he dug a hole about three feet deep and three feet square, then he filled it with foliage and greenery. After compacting it down using his foot he placed a tin pan in the middle. Next he covered the hole with a small sheet of polythene and weighted the edges down with boulders. To make it sag he placed a smaller one in the middle. The sun would make the greenery transpire, the polythene would catch the rising moisture and turn it to droplets. These rivulets would run down to the lowest point of the polythene and drip off into the can.

Satisfied that within about four hours he would have about half a pan of water he decided that he could afford to make himself a little soup. He didn't have to look for very long before he found a patch of purslane, a succulent plant, which grows freely in these kind of wadis. He snapped off lots of the reddish stems and when he had both hands full he carried them back to the shade of his camp. Then he gathered dry wood and soon had a fire burning. He placed a pan of water in the middle to boil and broke up the purslane into small pieces and dropped them in the pan.

There was nothing he could do now until the soup was ready so he stripped out of his sweaty clothes and laid them in the sun to dry. Then he made himself a rough bed at the back of the shallow cavern and placing the old rifle within easy reach he laid down to wait.

His thoughts wandered and overtaken by weariness and the heat he drifted towards sleep. However, he remained conscious of the soup brewing on the fire and he disciplined himself to only cat napping until after he had ate it. His rudderless thoughts drifted to his home in the mountains and what his family would be doing at this moment.

Although it would be cool up there they too would be resting. The Khareef made not a jot of difference to the fixed routine that was followed throughout the year. His father would be taking his afternoon nap and perhaps he would have taken Kathya to his bed with him. For certain Hamed would be sleeping, that boy could sleep eighteen hours every day if given the opportunity. Of Juma he wasn't so sure, compared to Hamed he was positively hyper active. His own mother, Jokha, would be busy preparing the family main meal, for when his father, Abdulla, eventually stirred, as she did each day. Lailla, pretty little Lailla, she would of course be out with the goats.

Not trusting himself to remain at a low level of sleep he sat up and went over to the fire and sat staring at the bubbling green fluid in the pan. After a while he took it from the fire and placed it to one side to cool a little. His camel he could see had in its foraging wandered to the middle of the wadi and now that too rested motionless in a squatting position in the shade of an Acacia tree. Everything was as still as a painting without even a slight breeze to stir the leaves. He felt completely isolated and frighteningly alone in the middle of an environment just waiting for him to make a slip so that it could award its ultimate unforgiving sentence. His bitter soup finished he stretched out on his makeshift bed, covered himself with the blanket and this time, without any restrictions, he passed into unconsciousness.

His sleep was rudely interrupted by a hard kick on his thigh. He awoke with a start, his nerves jangled and stared up into the barrel of an automatic weapon with two men standing behind it. It seemed an age before anyone spoke.

"Where are you from?" the one holding the rifle in his face asked. He wore faded military camouflage speckled green brown and sand. A heavy black moustache, a long nose and deep brown eyes were the only features visible from beneath the brown and sand coloured shamag that covered his head, chin and neck.

"Jebal Qara."

"What are you doing all the way out here?"

Mussalim was at a considerably disadvantage. Not only due to the rifle less than six inches from his face but also he had no way of knowing who these men were. "Who wants to know?"

The barrel was jabbed into his cheek and stayed there. "I do."

"I'm on my way to Mudhai."

"What for?"

Mussalim didn't want to give too much away. It was likely that these men were government soldiers. He shrugged. "I have Bedouin blood, it is my nature to wander."

"Are you alone, Bedu?" The Bedu was emphasised with contempt.

"Yes."

"Liar," he screamed and thrust the barrel even harder into his face. "Even Bedu are not stupid enough to wander out here alone without a very good reason."

"Let Suhayl take care of him." The other man spoke for the first time. He was similarly dressed in faded camouflage, his shamag wrapped tightly around his head like a turban. Under his foot he had Mussalim's old Martin Henri and he too pointed an automatic weapon at him.

"The other man thought about it for a moment then withdrew the barrel from Mussalim's face. "On your feet."

Mussalim obeyed still clutching the blanket.

"Move," the moustached man demanded, indicating that he should move out from the shallow cave. As Mussalim moved past, the blanket was snatched from him leaving him naked. He was driven down and into the middle of the wadi with a series of prods from the gun barrel. There he was made to sit on a rock.

"You go up there," the moustache instructed his partner indicating the top edge vantagepoint of the wadi face. "And keep your eyes open, he may have friends around somewhere."

He tossed down the Martin Henri at the other man's feet and then without a word, did as he was instructed. Mussalim watched him as he went and made the climb slowly up the face. Once on top he found a position, which gave him a clear view of both directions in the wadi and the high ground on both sides. All the time the other man sat on a nearby rock and watched Mussalim with his rifle pointing directly at him. Then they waited.

"What are we waiting for?" Mussalim asked.

"I will ask the questions," the flat reply.

But he didn't and the time passed slowly. After a while Mussalim could feel the fierce heat of the sun tingling his skin but still they waited in silence. Mussalim had noticed that his own camel had been joined by two more presumably belonging to these two men. He began to wonder about them. As far as he knew Government troops moved around the *nejd* in a convoy of Land Rovers. It was still possible that these two could be a scouting party but using camels to scout ahead of the much faster vehicles made no sense. Perhaps they were Special Forces on a special mission, it was possible. Or perhaps they were guerrilla forces of the Liberation Front. The more he thought about it then the more convinced he became that this was the most likely. His guard was in no mood to give him even the slightest hint, so he decided that there was nothing to be done except to continue to wait. The wait continued in silence.

The shadows in the wadi were lengthening as the sun slipped down the western sky. There remained only about one hour to sunset when the man on the top lip of the wadi gave a shrill whistle, shouted something inaudible to his partner and waved.

The man on the rock sighed and eased himself to a more comfortable position. It was obviously the expected signal. "Won't be long now," he said speaking for the first time in almost two hours.

Before they came into view Mussalim could hear the whistles and cries of the drovers. A caravan of camels was coming down the wadi from the north. It was still just out of Mussalim's sight around the rocky outcrop but by the pink dust that rose into the air he could tell that it was quite sizeable.

Soon they began to come into view one by one around the rocky bend. Mostly camels burdened by large bulky packs overhanging from their backs onto their ribs. Drovers walked alongside the animals their faces masked against the dust growling and shouting at the laden beasts. They swished their canes frequently occasionally bringing it down with a slap on an animal's rump. Not all the camels were weighted by packs – some carried men. These men were armed with automatic weapons slung diagonally across their backs and a bandoleer across their chests. It was obvious that this was a supply caravan and judging by the presence and size of the armed escort very probably the cargo was arms. At least thirty camels had come into view and still they continued to appear from behind the rock outcrop. Three men near the head of the column split from the group and hurried their camels in the direction of the rock where Mussalim and his guard were sitting. When they neared the guard, for the first time, diverted his attention away from Mussalim and slowly got to his feet.

The three reined their camels to a stop only a few feet away and then sat on their beast looking down at the pair, quizzically. They too were dressed in speckled camouflaged shirt and pants with shamags covering their heads and most of their faces.

"What have you got there, Ziad," the one on the left asked leaning forward slightly and staring directly at Mussalim.

"Found him up there." He waved his rifle in the direction of Mussalim's camp. "Might be a Sultan's spy."

The mounted man continued to study Mussalim thoughtfully in silence. Then after a pause said tersely, "take him back up there and shoot him." He began to turn his camel away.

"Wait!" Mussalim jumped up in alarm.

He waited.

" I am Mussalim Bin Adbulla from the Jebal Qara and I am not a Sultan spy. I am travelling to Mudhai, from there I go west to the Yemen border. Once into the Yemen I intend to turn south and make my way to Hauf. There I hope to join the Liberation Front and train to fight for the freedom of the Dhofar region."

No one spoke. All four continued to stare at him.

"Could be saying that to save his neck," the man standing on the ground said.

Beginning to panic a little Mussalim realised that he needed to convince the man on the camel if he were to live longer than just a few more minutes "That is my camel, in the middle of the wadi for all to see." He turned and waved in the direction of his camp, "I camped and lit a fire up there in full view. Are those the actions of a man who is spying?" Still no one spoke. He looked at his old rifle still lying where the other guard had tossed it. He pointed towards it. "That is my weapon. Is that old rifle the weapon of a man working as a Sultan's spy."

"Just a moment," one of the other men said and kicked his camel forward. When he was close to Mussalim he stopped and peered down at him. What tribe are you?" he asked.

"Al Hamer!"

"Did you go to Bahrain?"

Mussalim nodded. "I returned a few weeks ago."

He turned towards the man who had pronounced sentence. "I know of this man. He is of my tribe and lives near the village of Shair. At tribal meetings I heard talk of the Jabally son of Abdulla who had gone to Bahrain to work."

The other man sat motionless just staring at him. Mussalim held his breath full of tension knowing that in the next few seconds this man would decide his fate. After what seemed to be an age he nodded very slowly.

"Had your eyes opened in Bahrain did you? Saw the difference between the have's and the have not's." He turned and looked towards the sun moving towards its setting. "In thirty minutes we will stop for the night." Then he turned back and looked at the man standing. "Let him put some clothes on. Then bring him. Don't let him out of your sight and if he makes a wrong move kill him." He hauled the head of his camel around kicked his heels into its ribs and went back to rejoin the caravan. The other two riders followed.

The guard turned to face Mussalim and levelled his automatic at him. Keeping the barrel pointed at his midriff he stooped slowly to pick up the old rifle, then as he straightened he gave a brief flick of his head motioning him back towards his camp. Mussalim glanced briefly at the three departing riders and wondered with a great deal of apprehension about the man who held his life on a personal inclination. He had a reprieve for the moment but there was no certainty that it was not just a temporary situation. He looked at his guard, nodded agreement and then led the way back to his camp.

The second man came down from the wadi edge to join them and now went to collect their camels. Mussalim took his time to dress then sat sipping water while his belongings were scattered in a crude search. Even though it had been the later part of the afternoon it had been hot and dehydrating sitting out in full sun in the middle of the wadi. Satisfied that he had no weapons Mussalim was then allowed to repack his bundle and load his own camel. Thirty minutes after the last of the long caravan train had disappeared, the three set off in pursuit with Mussalim leading, a rider on each flank.

The light had all but gone when they rode through the posted guards and into the camp. Campfires were scattered about randomly in small sheltered leas. They continued on until they came to the fire surrounded by the armed escort. Mussalim was ordered to dismount and marched into a circle of about a dozen men and the light of the fire. He looked around at the indifferent faces staring mildly curious back.

"So jabally you want to join the Liberation cause!"

He recognised the voice and looked at the man who had spoken. He wasn't looking at Mussalim his concentration was centred on the weapon in pieces on his knee. He had removed his shamag and Mussalim studied the man who had the power of his life or his death in his hands. His thick hair was shoulder length, unkempt and tied with a headband above his ears. His face narrow and his nose hooked. A scar ran from the corner of his mouth across his left cheek so deep that the flesh both sides folded over it giving the impression of a hideous crooked smile from the side of his face.

"That's right."

"Why?" he demanded as he began slapping the parts of the rifle together.

"To help take this region to its own independence and free the people from the yoke of poverty."

"Poverty!" he paraphrased with mild surprise. "And how will that be accomplished?"

"By sharing the wealth that this Sultan keeps for himself."

"What wealth?" He looked at Mussalim for the first time

"Oil."

"Oil? There is no oil here. It's all in the north."

"They will find it."

He turned his attention back to the rifle and slammed in the last piece. "What if they don't?"

Mussalim shrugged. "Then we will be no worse off."

"What about help from other nations?"

"Other nations?"

"Yes Russia, China, Korea. Our Communist friends. They can help in this struggle and after independence has been won then they can help with trade."

"Whatever it takes," Mussalim agreed. "I am content to leave such politics in the hands of Mussalim Bin Nufl."

"Mussalim Nufl?"

"Yes. Mussalim the Liberation cause leader and Sheikh of all the Kathiri tribes."

He cocked the rifle and pointed it directly At Mussalim's face then squinted down the sights.

It wasn't loaded. Or at least Mussalim didn't think so. He hadn't seen him load it, but then it could be. He held his breath and waited. He flinched and heaved a sigh of relief when the hammer dropped and a loud click echoed around the campfire. Many of those seated around the fire watching laughed at his ordeal.

"Bin Nufl betrayed the cause by his weak and conciliatory leadership. He was thrown out and to save his own skin he fled across the border to Saudi. He is under a sentence of death by the Front and wanted by the Government Forces too, so he will never return. So much for your tribal Sheikh, Mussalim."

Mussalim was confused, this was all news to him. "When did that happen?"

"A few weeks ago." He picked up the magazine and began loading it.

"Then who is the leader now?"

He paused from loading his magazine and gave Mussalim his full attention. "A man with much more vision and higher ambitions than your Kathiri Sheikh." He replied sneering of the tribal leader. "Muhammad Bin Ahmed Al Ghassani. We are no longer content to free only this pathetic little region of yours. It is only the first step on the long road to free the whole of the Arabian Gulf. After we have taken control of this region we sweep onwards to the north and complete the destruction of Said Taymour's regime. Already there has been sporadic insurrection in the north and it is common knowledge that the Sheikh of the vast Sharqeeya region has no love for this Sultan, so we can expect support from the people. Then when we have secured Oman we will control the narrow Straits into the Gulf and we will have a stranglehold on all those elite oppressive regimes that sell their nation's oil, pocket the revenue and keep the Arab people destitute. We no longer call ourselves the Dhofar Liberation Front. We are now the Popular Front for the Liberation of the Occupied Arabian Gulf."

Mussalim listened dubiously to the rhetoric. It sounded almost like a madman boasting of his intention to conquer the world to him. His life was still hung in the balance, therefore he still needed to be circumspect about voicing his opinion. "How will all this be achieved?" he asked.

"With support from our Communist friends in Russia, China and Korea."

"What about the British? Won't they do something to stop you?"

He laughed derisively. "The British," he scoffed. I am Yemeni. In Aden we harassed and killed the British until they had no stomach for the fight and they were all too relieved to withdraw from our country. We will do the same here in the Dhofar. And when they have withdrawn from here also, then the region will fall like a ripe olive from a shaken tree. Then we will go on northwards, unstoppable. By the time the British realise their mistake it will be too late." He paused and waited for a reaction from Mussalim. "What say you now jebally? Do you still want to join the cause?"

Mussalim was thoughtful for a while. "Your ultimate ambition seems a little fanciful to me." He waited for a reaction wondering if he had already said too much. The seated man only stared back. "But the first step to make this region independent is what I am willing to fight for. So – yes I will join your cause under Al Ghassani until this region is free. After that, well I don't know. I would have to see."

The scarfaced man considered his answer a few moments then his mind made up said. "Jebally, you're alright. Welcome to the cause. I am Suhayl from the Yemen of the tribe Manahil. Come sit with us. In a little while food will be brought" He motioned towards a vacant gap in the circle of seated men. Mutterings of approval came from all around the campfire.

Mussalim grinned with relief. He was, it seemed, in the cause and out of danger of execution. He went and sat next to a man who moved over and made a little extra space. He offered his hand to be shaken.

"I am Ali and I am of your tribe, Al Hamer."

Mussalim took the hand, recognising the voice of the man who had spoke up substantiating his story an hour earlier. He was a young man of around his own age and beardless, except but for about five day's growth. His shamag was now balanced on the top of his head in a tight turban with black greasy hair hanging in ringlets from beneath. "Thank you Ali for speaking on my behalf."

He flashed a ready grin showing even and white teeth. "No problem."

He dismissed it lightly but Mussalim appreciated fully that his intervention had contributed to his survival at that crucial point. Whether it was to a minor or major extent he wasn't sure, it was enough that he had spoken. "Nevertheless I am in your debt." Ali's response was a simple shrug. "Where are you travelling to?"

Ali hesitated a moment before answering. "Jibjat."

"Jibjat! Why I live less than forty kilometres from there."

Ali nodded. "Hmm. I live a little further away at Hajif close to our tribal area." He handed Mussalim a grimy plastic cup.

Mussalim took it and looked into the darkness at the other fires dotted around the wadi estimating roughly the size of the caravan. He wondered why its destination was a small village in the southeastern part of the Jebal Qara. "What is happening at Jibjat?"

Ali shook his head. "Only Suhayl knows."

"Suhayl," he looked at the man once more. "He is your leader!"

Ali looked towards Suhayl also. "Yes, he is a very determined man and ruthless too. Take care not to cross him. Out here he has the power of life and death and he carries the responsibility lightly."

"How does a Yemeni come to be a leader in our cause?"

"Because of his experience and training! Three years ago he was selected for special training in Russia and spent six months near Moscow studying Guerrilla tactics. After his return he was very active fighting to free Aden from the British. Now he uses all his experience in our cause. He is well regarded by our leaders including Al Ghassani." He filled the cup with water from a goatskin.

Mussalim said nothing sipping his water and pondering silently about "our cause" and the different agendas. Mostly the Dhofaris, including himself, wanted their independence and freedom from poverty. This man Suhayl, however, furthered the cause of Communism and his fight would never be ended unless the whole world eventually succumbed to its ideology. He wondered how many others in position of power within the movement shared that agenda. He wondered just who was manipulating who? Still their first objective was the same so for the moment he was prepared to sup with the devil.

Four black shrouded women wearing the grotesque black plastic beak over their faces emerged from the darkness carrying large round tin trays piled high with rice and goat meat. They placed them strategically at four points around the campfire and then withdrew as silently as they had emerged. The camp circle now split as each man moved to the tray placed closest to him and made himself comfortable. Suhayl motioned that Mussalim should seat close to him.

"Come sit here jabally and talk to me about your days in Bahrain," he said

"It will be my pleasure, Suhayl. But first I must pray." He stood to leave.

"We do not pray and any man that does is not welcome to our campfire." Suhayl raised his voice and the social chatter died as each man sensed another confrontation.

"I am Muslim and therefore I must pray five times a day."

"Who says?"

"It is written in the Koran."

Suhayl scoffed. "The Koran is written by the wealthy few who cleverly use it to convince the poor that it is noble in God's eyes to have nothing. This makes the poor content and in effect they become no threat to the riches which the wealthy possess. I suppose you believe that your reward will be in the afterlife when you sit at Allah's side!"

"I do."

He laughed derisively. "Muslim, there is no after-life. This everyday existence is all there is, so you need to take your reward now."

Mussalim stared back at the Yemeni and held unflinching eye contact. "You have your belief and I have mine," he replied with a slight shrug. Then breaking the eye contact he turned away.

"You will not sit at our campfires, you will not drink our water nor eat our food until you stop praying," Suhayl called after him as he moved towards the darkness.

Mussalim found his camel with its front leg tethered to a tree stump. He angrily pulled off his pack from the animal's back and dropped it close by. He was becoming more and more disillusioned with the Liberation cause – it was turning out to be nothing like he imagined. He sank to the ground by his pack and staring into the starlight sky tried to appease the anger inside. He could not to pray to Allah with wrath controlling his thoughts. Eventually he laid the blame for the whole situation squarely at the feet of Suhayl. These were his thoughts, his ideas, his actions entirely and not necessarily the philosophy of the rest of the movement. He decided that tomorrow he would leave this caravan and continue his journey to Mudhai and eventually on to Hauf. The solution now resolved the ire left him and he was ready to make his prayer.

He used a little of his water to prepare himself. He shook the skin; it was about half full. He planned to leave early tomorrow, well before dawn and then to shelter through the midday. When the fierceness had left the sun he would push onwards riding non-stop into the night until he reached Mudhai. Providing he could reach Mudhai before dawn then he would have sufficient water. He found a sandy patch among the smooth boulders a little way from his pack and spread his prayer mat towards the northwest. He then emptied his mind of all his earthly woes and devoted himself to Allah.

His prayers ended and a plan of contingency in place he felt composed and once more in control of his destiny. He picked up his mat and returned to his pack intending fully to get some sleep in anticipation of an early start tomorrow. He had no intentions of unpacking and making himself comfortable opting instead for the least delay after rising tomorrow. Dragging his pack into position to use as a pillow he discovered that it was wet. He picked up his goatskin. It had been slashed and all the water gone.

In abject disgust he threw it to the floor and glared back towards the campfire of Suhayl's. He now had absolutely no choice he would have to leave right away. He began to gather his possessions and to load his camel.

He was tightening the girths when Ali approached out of the darkness.

"What are you doing?" he asked.

"I'm leaving."

Ali shook his head, "you can't."

Mussalim picked up the empty goatskin for him to see. "I have no water therefore I cannot stay." He continued to tighten the girth.

"You don't understand. If you try to leave you will be shot."

He stopped what he was doing. "Why?"

"You have seen too much and know too much. If the information you have were to finish up with the government forces this caravan would be ambushed or maybe attacked from the air. Probably both. You also know its destination. The whole operation would be compromised. Suhayl will never let you leave." He shook his head sadly.

"But I am on your side, I would never tell."

"He can't take the chance. And why should he? He cares nothing for your life."

"But without food and water I will die if I stay. He will not let me have either, unless – ." He didn't finish.

"Unless you agree not to pray." Ali finished for him.

"Yes."

Ali placed his hand on his shoulder. "What is the act of prayer? Is it so important?"

"To me it is."

He looked around nervously. "Then pray in secret. In your bed at nights or on your camel's back, wherever, but do not make it obvious. Allah will understand," he said in a lowered voice.

"Is that what you do Ali?"

"Come to the campfire tomorrow morning tell Suhayl that you will pray no more and that you consider the cause to be more important to you than religion. In return he will give you food and water." He waited for Mussalim's reaction. "Will you do it?"

Mussalim considered his situation a moment. To pray in secrecy or death. By bullet if he attempted to leave or lingering death by thirst if he stayed. "What choice do I have?"

"Good. I will tell him that you are considering your situation. But be very careful if you do intend to secretly pray because you will be closely watched for a while."

"He knows you are here?"

"He sent me!"

Mussalim glanced down at the curved dagger in his waist belt and wondered if he had been instructed to destroy his water supply. He watched him disappear once more into the night realising the awesome power of the caravan leader and his own vulnerability. He turned to his camel feeling that this animal was the only one that he could really trust. He patted its nose affectionately and muttered quietly with a sigh. "Well ugly beast, it looks as if we're on our way back to the jebal and Jibjat."

✳ ✳ ✳

The mist on the jebal was much thinner this day and it drifted in the stiff wind. Sometimes visibility was more than a quarter of a mile sometimes only a few yards. There was no rain today either and even the sun kept offering a watery presence. Jokha had seen forty Khareefs in her lifetime and her feelings never altered. She was always delighted to see the rain and cloud at its onset because it provided relief from the daily unrelenting frazzle of the sun. However, as the weeks wore on and everything became increasingly wet and damp it percolated into everything. There was no escaping from the underfoot mud conditions, the persistent trickling water nor the damp shroud of the mist. Always from about its halfway point she longed for its end. She was at that point now.

She filled the battered tin jug from the milk barrel. Because of the long rich grass the cow and goat yield of milk was high and there was a surplus. Even though they distributed it freely among their neighbours a lot was poured away. When the Khareef eventually cleared and the sun reappeared then she could use its heat to turn much of the surplus to cheese and whey. But then as the sun once more scorched the grass to dry straw the milk yields would also decrease.

A little distance to her right and beyond the square dwelling house was the derelict remnants of their original circular home. It had been typical of all the jebal homes at that time and built from the inexhaustible supply of rocks that covered the mountains. The rocks carefully positioned in a tight circle and mortared into place with wet sand were stacked at around head height. The roof comprised only sticks, grass, and palm leaves tightly thatched to a raised centre point, like some giant beehive. The thatch had many years ago broken up and blown away while many Khareef rains had washed away the sand mortar leaving the rocky walls wobbly and collapsed. For Jokha that old ruin held memories of her youthful days and happier times past. Sometimes when she had opportunity she would covertly spend time in the disintegrating ruin indulging in nostalgia. She walked over to it now and sat in the space where the doorway had once been. She looked out across the rugged terrain.

Despite the inconvenience the Khareef weather inflicted, there was no denying the side benefit of the green beauty it bestowed on the landscape. When the mist was thin as it was today then those making the time to appreciate its vista could enjoy its spectacle. These afternoon rest periods were periods of recreation to her. She rarely laid and rested like the rest of the family. Instead she busied herself with the family chores working at her own sedate pace and enjoying the quiet solitude in which to work.

Juma had left early that morning for Salalah attempting to trade some of the surplus milk and some firewood in exchange for rice. He had surprised the whole family by performing this task entirely at his own suggestion. Even more startling, he had invited Lailla to accompany him. To Lailla's delight Abdulla had agreed that the goats could remain in the compound for today and that she could go with him. Hamed as usual slept and Abdulla was taking his rest with his younger wife Kathya at his side.

Abdulla never took Jokha to his bed anymore only Kathya. Jokha had once been very attractive but forty years of hardship living in these mountain regions had taken its toll on her physique. Her role as wife and mother had demanded that she ensured the welfare and comfort of all the family before attending her own needs. Food had on many occasions been sparse and usually low in nutrition value also. This meant as she was always last in line to eat, she often did not, and when she did there was barely enough. Her body now showed obvious evidence of many years emaciation. Her ribs protruded through taut skin almost offensively as did her hips. Her breasts once full and large now hung like flat leather purses and her legs once young and shapely now spindly like old dried rope. There was no pleasure left in her body for her husband to ravish and his physical attention was now non-existent. She didn't mind too much, however. Sex to her had always been a thing of duty. She had suffered the barbaric ritual of the Grandmother's razor blade when she was very young to ensure that she took no pleasure from the act of intercourse. Consequently she knew little of carnal pleasures.

She had listened with curiosity to Kathya's moans of pleasure as she lay close by in her own bed and wondered what it was like to enjoy the act so much. In privacy she had questioned Kathya many times, desperately wanting to understand the experience of an orgasm. Her explanation was always inadequate, tinged far too much with sympathy for her older companion's situation. Kathya could not comprehend how the parents of a small child could condone such inhumanity. Even now Jokha could vividly remember the pain that she suffered during the crude operation and the fact that she almost died. She bled profusely and later became dizzy and light-headed. Then after being put to bed she hovered for two days in a semi-coma state. Gradually the coagulants in her blood did seal the wound and she eventually made a recovery. But she realised many years later that it must have been a pretty close thing. In those days there were no doctors or hospitals to appeal to for help. Even today the only hospital in the whole country is nine hundred kilometres away in Muscat.

Despite the fact that no demands were made on her body by Abdulla she still maintained the position as number one wife and Kathya's role in all other things was secondary. She had given Abdulla two fine sons. There had been a third and a first daughter but both had succumbed to some illnesses and had died at very early ages. There had been miscarriages too, induced to a large extent by her own undernourished health condition.

She pulled up her long robe and scrutinised her thin legs. She wondered that if by some miracle she could obtain a few full meals could she even now still recover some of her past comeliness. It was a forlorn thought and she dropped her robe. For her there was nothing left except to grow old with dignity. She could look forward to a life of perhaps twelve or fifteen more years and if Allah was truly merciful maybe twenty. It didn't seem a lot of expectancy she thought gloomily. She could understand the anger in her eldest son directed against the incumbency, which deprived the people and made them old before their time.

She held up the jug and took a long drink, then continued to gaze pensively out at the craggy terrain. He mind slid back to another time, another Khareef when she had been young and her two boys' little more than babies. The sound of the young boys laughter and excited cries echoed from around the corner of her mind and rolled back the years. In her mind's eye she once more relived a day and a time when they had played hide and seek in the mist. Abdulla, distracted by the noisy frivolity had paused from his labour of building this rustic home to watch with benign amusement. She smiled to herself warmed by the happy memory. Poverty it seemed was much less important then. Perhaps, she concluded, it is easier to accept when you have the exuberance and energy of youth. Then she thought of her eldest son and the smile faded. He was young but poverty was not easily accepted in his case. She sighed with a mother's worry and wondered where he was at this very moment. She estimated that by now he would be at Mudhai. There was no doubt in her mind that he would survive the *nejd*. He had been well taught the craft of Desert survival by his father's brother Fiad, who even today still clung to the nomadic *bedu* ways. No, she did not fear for his safety from that aspect. But the thought of her son, very inexperienced in the ways of armed conflict, pitting himself against the trained soldiers of the Sultan's Army filled her with trepidation. Her eyes filled with tears as in her thoughts she tried to prepare herself for the worse possible news sometime in the future.

❊ ❊ ❊

Juma sat on the ground in the shade of his standing camel. He tapped the ground with his cane impatiently as he waited in line for his turn to be searched. Behind him the double row of concertina wire stretched into the distance. To his front the graded road and the military manned gate into Salalah. Beyond that the concertina wire fortification continued. He glanced towards Lailla, she had followed his example and was sitting close by in the shade of their second camel. He gave her a reassuring smile falsifying the impatience that he felt. He was anxious to get into the town and quickly complete the day's business. Then with the free time he could make his way to Al Dharitz where he hoped to catch sight of the dark eyed Khamisa. His ulterior reason for bringing Lailla with him on this trip was to pose her as a fortuitous chaperone should he see Khamisa and that old crone make an undesired appearance. He hadn't of course taken Lailla into his confidence. The encounter, which he hoped desperately would happen, was to appear accidental and spontaneous and not at all contrived.

Eventually he was called forward and he led his animal into the small wire compound by the side of the gate. He then withdrew a couple of yards away while two armed soldiers searched the thick bundles of sticks which burdened the beast.

A third soldier sauntered across to him, his rifle hung on his shoulder by the webbing strap. "Peace be with you, Juma."

He turned and looked at the man who had called him by name. "Khaleef!" he replied recognising the man as a casual tribal friend of many years. He held out his hand to be shaken in a gesture of friendship. "I didn't know that you had joined the Sultan's army."

He nodded, "more than a year ago," he replied as he shook his hand.

Juma remember the last time they had met and assumed, somewhat surprisingly, that the occasion must have been more than a year ago. He hadn't until this moment realised that he hadn't seen him for that length of time. "A year ago?" he echoed. "That explains why I haven't seen you for so long."

"I have been away for most of it," Khaleef confirmed. "I was sent north to the garrison at Ghubra for twelve weeks training. When I finished training I stayed in the north at Bidbid garrison near Nizwa for about eight months. Then four or five months ago I was posted back down to this region."

"What made you become an *askar* of the Sultan's army?"

"Money!" he replied firmly. "Not a fortune perhaps, but I get paid every week. And it is a lot more than my father and brothers make added together. I am able to send money to my family regularly, which helps considerably."

Juma could appreciate how it important that was. It probably meant the difference between meals and hunger.

"And," he went on, "I manage to save around half of my wages. I even have a bank account. I am the first person in my family to have a bank account," he boasted. He leaned closer and lowered his voice. "And...I still have a little left over to visit the local Philippino ladies in their boudoirs once a week."

Juma had heard talk of such places. "You seem to do well Khaleef. What does the army pay?"

"I get one hundred rupees every week, soon to go to one hundred and twenty when I become corporal."

It was true that perhaps in general comparison it was not a fortune but to someone like a Qara mountain man it was a considerable amount and Juma was impressed. "Ah...but what dangers do you face for that amount of money?" There had to be a snag.

Khaleef shrugged. "Of course there is an element of risk, particularly in this region. But so far my duties have amounted to mostly routine boring stuff. Like this gate search and routine guard duties in and around the garrison." He waved his arm in the direction of the Umm Al Ghariff garrison standing less than half a kilometre away.

Juma glanced curiously at the long high walled garrison with its two octagonal towers at each of the front corners. He had never seen inside its walls but judging by the activity and movement that seemed to move through its gates ceaselessly he imagined it that was a vast and busy place.

"Quite boring really," Khaleef went on. "Once a week, just to break the monotony, I volunteer for escort duty and if I'm lucky I will get on the convoy taking supplies to our garrisons at Taqa and Mirbat. That sometimes takes a couple of days."

"Two days?" he queried. Mirbat was a small fishing village about forty kilometres along the coast to the east of Salalah and once many years ago his father had taken both Mussalim and himself there. It could be done very easily within two days by camel from his home in the jebal. However, as the convoys consisted of military vehicles and the journey shorter from Salalah he wondered why it should take so long.

"Landmines on the road," Khaleef explained. "Particularly around Taqa. We hardly ever drive along the road and try never to use the same route twice. Often we make wide detours and sometimes we are reduced to following men on foot waving mine detectors in front of them."

The money aspect did not sound quite as attractive to Juma now. "That sounds dangerous to me."

"*Inshaallah,*" Khaleef replied in a casual manner. "We are at our most vulnerable on the return journey."

Juma cocked his head with interest.

"We never make the trip on the same day so that no one can predict when the supply convoy will leave. But when the rebels have seen us go through then they have a pretty good idea of when we will be coming back."

One of the searching guards motioned that the search was finished and that he should collect his camel. Juma moved forward gathered the rein and led the camel to the gate. He waited with Khaleef at the side of the lowered barrier while Lailla's beast was searched. She glanced at him a little apprehensively and he smiled at her reassuringly.

"Your sister is growing," Khaleef muttered, his eyes riveted to the girl.

He glanced at the man by his side and then towards Lailla, he knew precisely what he meant. Her small young breasts pressed against the thin material of her long gown imprinting clearly the nipples. The time had arrived when she would have to start hiding her physical personality beneath the Islamic shroud so as not to provoke lewd thoughts in men.

The two soldiers pulled the camel to its knees and opened the lids of the two battered milk churns fastened to its back. One of them pushed a stick inside and stirred the contents around. Satisfied that it contained only milk he repeated the operation on the second tin and then nodded his approval for a pass.

On foot Juma guided his sister and the camels through the uneven narrow streets of the old town between the dilapidated flat-topped sandstone buildings. Each house fronted directly onto the dirty streets. The heavy wooden window shutters were pegged back against the walls admitting a semblance of light and air inside the houses. The dust and sand kicked up from underfoot wafted through these glassless windows also. Each street had a warren of thin alleyways leading off, barely wide enough for two to pass.

Eventually Juma emerged from this labyrinth onto a wider road. Here the twentieth century had begun its inevitable creeping invasion into the ancient and static habitat of the town. The road was tarmac and the sidewalks paved. Vehicles flowed in both directions in front of full glass windowed shops and stores. Modern western commercialism in the form of garish advertisements assaulted and bombarded the eyes from all directions. This road too was liberally sprinkled with those thin alleyways, which exposed the whole facade with glimpses of the ghettos behind the fascia.

Halfway along this busy street Juma turned off and into the exposed area of the souk. Here was a miss match mixture of ancient and modern. The ground was even and paved and some conventional wooden market stalls lined the perimeter. The centre, however, was filled with a seemingly myriad confusion of people. Vendors had laid out their wares on cloths spread over the ground or on wooden boxes. The range of these items was endless from homemade sweet smelling scents to traditional clothing, from fresh gathered fruit to fish, exposed to the sun, reeking and covered in flies. Potential buyers meandered casually through the maze peering inquisitively at the goods seeking the lowest price for the items that they sought. When they had they then bartered demonstratively attempting to reduce the price further.

Juma found a small vacant corner, unloaded the camels and laid out the bundles of sticks to be sold. In the front he placed the two battered milk churns, then leaving Lailla in charge of their wares he led both camels away to the end of the street. There he turned them loose onto the beach.

He glanced up at the sun. It was hazed behind a thin mist but nevertheless it was hot. There was perhaps one hour to noon. In less than three hours the people of Salalah would disappear taking refuge from the heat of the afternoon and would not re-appear until early evening. He didn't want to be still trying to sell the goods when they went. It didn't suit his plan to be still in the souk at the arrival of the evening. He wanted to be in Al Dharitz sometime during the afternoon respite period. He decided that he would tour the souk, clandestinely compare the milk and wood prices of other vendors and then undercut his competitors to achieve a quick clearance.

His plan worked. When the people had begun to dessert the souk and some of the traders had began to gather in their possessions Juma and Lailla had only couple of bundles of sticks and half a churn of milk left to sell. It was, he decided, close enough. He went to the beach, collected the camels and brought them back to the souk. He gave Lailla a few rupees as a deserved reward so that she could buy herself some of the perfumed powders, while he loaded the camels. He finished loading the animals but was obliged to wait while his sister made her careful selection from a seemingly endless range of jars and tins. The souk by now was thinning rapidly of both sellers and buyers and the vendor attending Lailla was becoming a little impatient at her dithering. If she sensed his impatience she chose to ignore it and continued to sniff the different powders unhurriedly. Eventually she made her choice and ambled back to where Juma had settled to wait. They made their way down the street and onto the beach.

They sat quietly on the sand and watched the agitated Khareef seas hurl its breakers relentlessly at the shore while they sipped milk and ate coconut. After that they each made their own short prayer and then Juma cautiously raised the subject of his intentions.

"We don't have to go home straight away," he said. "We could spend a little time here." He paused and waited for her to comment but she remained quiet. "I think perhaps we will go east down the beach. It should be a nice ride past the coconut palms and then when we get to Al Dharitz we can spend a little time on that beach. Then when we are ready to go home we can always go out through the east gate."

Lailla looked around the beach where they now sat. Apart from two small groups of children playing not too far away it was deserted. The ocean's roar suppressed all sounds except its own and lent a pacifistic air to the scene. The long golden sands stretched as far as she could see in both directions, the fine sea spray hanging over the sands fogging the distance. "This is nice here. Why do we need to travel four miles to Al Dharitz?"

"Yes it is nice here," he agreed. But it's nicer down there. Besides," it was time to let her into the secret just a little," I might see a friend down there."

"A friend?"

"Yes," he got up to leave effectively imposing his will and hoping to avoid further questions.

But her curiosity was aroused and she wouldn't be put off. "Who do you know at Al Dharitz?" she asked as he helped her onto her camel.

"A girl," he said as he slapped the animal's rump for it to get to its feet.

They rode along the deserted beach close to the sea in silence. The ocean's roar made conversation from even a small distance difficult. Juma was quietly thankful, he didn't want to be pressed by Lailla's curiosity. The animals plodded along at a sedate pace just beyond the reach of the breaking waves as they collapsed fizzing and frothing on the beach. After a few minutes the fatigued sandstone buildings that backed the beach and faced out to sea were replaced by rough grassed dunes. A few minutes more and the dunes themselves were replaced by groves of tall coconut palms with their long fronds bent acutely subservient to the strong wind off the sea.

The flat topped dwellings of Al Dharitz came into view and soon they approached the fringe buildings. Juma slid down from his camel and proceeded on foot leading both animals. His eyes scanned the beach ahead hopefully. Fully four hundred yards ahead he could see a large group of young people sitting in the sand in an extended circle. He strained his eyes as they got progressively nearer searching the group for a female form, which could raise his hopes. He optimistically identified three or four possibilities, which might be Khamisa. But his optimism withered and died as he neared and could see that she wasn't in the group. He tried to placate his disappointment by telling himself that it had always been at best only a slim chance right from the start. Still he approached the circle to make absolutely certain. All eyes turned to watch as he neared.

"Peace be with you all," he greeted when he was close.

"And with you," some muttered in reply. The group was a mixture of young boys and girls their ages ranging from children through into early teenage years. With the energy of youth an afternoon siesta was only tedious and a gathering of kindred spirits much more desirable.

Juma hesitated before the group not sure what to do next. As the faces stared back silent and expectantly he decided the only thing to do was to bluntly ask. "Does anybody know Khamisa?"

There was a lot of reaction. Some grinned, some giggled and some openly laughed.

"Everybody knows Khamisa," one of the older boys replied.

"Do you know where she is?"

He leaned back and pointed towards a small figure much further down the beach at the sea edge.

"She's over there with her brothers."

Juma's insides gave a wild lurch as his eyes followed the direction of the pointing finger and realised that she was close and that once again he might talk to her. He thanked him, wished the peace of Allah on the rest and continued further along the beach until he got to within a few yards of where she stood. Today she wore the full length black *abeya*. Her head however was uncovered and the strong wind savaged her long raven coloured hair. She had her back towards him and his arrival had gone unnoticed, her concentration centred on two young boys who paddled in the demarcation line of sand and sea.

He halted the camels and brought the one on which Lailla sat to its knees and then helped his sister off.

"Who is this girl?" she asked.

"It's a girl I have met. Come and meet her, you'll like her she is nice."

They came up behind her all sounds of their approach obliterated by the noise of the crashing waves. "Hello Khamisa," Juma had to raise his voice.

She turned quickly startled by his voice. "Juma," she gasped with relief. "What are you doing here?"

"Looking for you," Lailla answered for him.

Juma glared at his sister. "This is my sister Lailla."

"Hello Lailla," Khamisa said and she lifted her black veil over her head but she did not cover her face. Her face was oval shaped with high cheekbones and a thin straight nose. Her lips were full, suggesting some distant African ancestry and eyes almost as black as her hair. Juma stared unabashed, revelling in the privilege of his first sight of her full pretty face. Embarrassed by his stare, she lifted the corner of her veil to cover the lower part of her face.

"We were in the souk today," Juma said in a voice raised trying to be heard over crash and splash of a wave that broke just as he spoke. Khamisa shook her head indicating that she hadn't heard.

"The souk," and he pointed down the beach towards Salalah. "We were at the souk."

She nodded understanding and pointed across the sand away from the ocean and its boom. She called to the two young boys and bade them follow. They all made their way to the pile of rocks and boulders which acted as a sea break and a crude line of defence for the bucolic dwellings, which lined the rough road separating the beach from the village. They settled on the soft sand in front of these boulders and with the ocean's roar now reduced to the background they were able to talk without raised voices.

The conversation to begin was stiff and polite. The two young boys, however, soon loosened the nerves. With the intense curiosity and uninhibited characteristics of children they posed direct questions at both Juma and Lailla. The barriers breached, enquiring questions crossed back and forth rapidly. At first the topic ranged only the basic family circumstances. Juma learned that Khamisa was the oldest child in a family of six, a father, one mother, two brothers and two sisters. Her father and his three brothers owned a small boat and that they fished off shore for a living. In return Juma, aided and punctuated by Lailla's comments, revealed his own family details.

The two young boys soon became bored and broke away from the small circle to play in the sand close by. The conversation went on without them and the questions gradually became more probing and more personal. Opinions and viewpoints were given on a wide spectrum of topics ranging from the common everyday struggle to survive to trivia. Juma held a question, which burned his inside but he was afraid to ask. He feared the personal nature of the question might be inappropriate at this stage but more than that he feared the answer. So he continued with the superficial topics and waited for an opportunity. But the opportunity did not come and time was passing so he decided that there was no other way than to ask the question outright. He waited for an appropriate pause then he asked, "Khamisa, are you promised?"

"Embarrassed by the question she once more took refuge behind the corner of her veil and shook her head slowly.

Juma could hardly believe her answer and his hopes soared. Ignoring his sister's huge smirk as she read his mind he sought confirmation. "You are not promised to anyone?"

"My father says that it is time and he is considering two or three suitable husbands."

His heart was in his mouth. "Do you have a preference?"

"Not particularly. Two already have wives. My own preference would be the third, a young man in our tribe. But my father will decide for me soon."

His hopes were in orbit and he felt the crushing urgency to have his own bid submitted; he would talk to his own father this very evening.

Lailla produced the perfumed powders she had purchased in the souk and invited Khamisa's opinion. She dropped her veil once more to smell the perfumes; the talk became feminine and Juma was temporarily excluded. He was quite content, however, to sit in silence and secretly study Khamisa's profile. He concluded that she was truly a goddess and would be a prized possession for any man. She propped herself up with a straight arm in the sand as she sat by his side, facing Lailla. He allowed his fingers to slowly slide across the sand and touch her hand. She snatched it away as if it had been stung. For a moment she held her fingers in her other hand as if easing some pain and then put it back in the sand. He allowed his hand to cover hers once more and this time she didn't take it away. Lailla grinned with benign amusement as she witnessed the mutual bonding.

~ 3 ~

There were still three hours left to sunset when Suhayl halted the caravan train. He waved his arm and pointed towards the mouth of a short rocky canyon indicating to the drovers that all the camels should be assembled in there. He sat astride his camel and watched the herd pass until the choking dust became too thick then he turned his animal and retreated twenty-five metres further up wind. He sat still and straight backed with one leg curled across the saddle, his dark eyes watching the activity from beneath the rag which wrapped his head and face

In little knots of twos and threes, the armed escort joined him. They waited in silence for his instructions. The last animal had entered the canyon before he spoke. "We rest here until after dark."

This unexpected stop was in complete contrast to the previous day's forced march and it left Mussalim more than a little baffled. He made no comment, neither did anyone else

"I want two guards up there," he said and pointed to top edges of the canyon. "Another up there," this time he turned and pointed behind him to the top of a high slagheap of rock and sand. "You, you and you," he selected three, "and stay out of sight. Come down one hour after dark," he added as the three prepared to leave. "The rest of you make camp over there. No fire." Then he roused his camel forward to go and issue his instructions to the head drover.

"Why do we stop?" Mussalim took the opportunity to ask Ali as they moved towards the spot indicated to camp.

"Because we are near the road and we don't want to cross it in daylight. We will wait for the cover of darkness." Mussalim nodded understanding. He knew the road.

It was the country's artery. Graded perhaps, but the only road from Salalah across Jebal Qara eighty kilometres to Thamrit and the Air Force base of Midway Onwards then another nine hundred kilometres to Muscat in the north of the country. Sometimes there was troop movement along this road between the Salalah and Midway bases. A long cumbersome caravan train crossing it would take time and be particular vulnerable to attack if caught in the open. He glanced upwards seeking potential threat from the skies as he realised also that they were probably under the flight path of shuttling aircraft between the bases. Campfires would act as beacons to passing aircraft and would betray their position so it was easy to understand Suhayl's instruction.

It had been an early rise long before sunrise both this morning and the previous day. Breakfasts' had been brief and frugal consisting of stale bread, dried figs and water. Even so by the time the drovers had loaded the camels and were ready to move two hours had passed.

When the drive had got underway yesterday Mussalim had kept himself a little apart from both the escorting guerrillas and the drovers. He was not at all sure of his status within the caravan so he thought it prudent to do so. He was neither soldier nor drover therefore without an active role to play. He was just a new and untrained recruit to the cause and as such was, for the time being, just excess baggage. He determined that if he couldn't be useful then he had better keep out of the way. His self-imposed isolation, however, suited his petulant mood. He was still irritated about the previous evening's episode. He could not understand the atheist attitude of the dictatorial leader nor could he accept that it was anything more than this man's conviction and therefore not mandatory in the movement. He was convinced that when he did eventually manage to get to the training camp at Hauf and away from Suhayl's predominance things would be different.

For almost two hours he had stayed in isolation keeping wide on the flank and a little behind the small bunch of armed lead riders. Eventually when Suhayl considered that he had perhaps sulked enough he dropped off the pace and joined him out on the flank. The conversation at first was a little strained but amiable and superficial, centring mainly on Mussalim's personal circumstances. It gradually turned more probing as Suhayl's subtle questions pressed him more for his political opinions and his motivation for joining the fight for independence.

Satisfied with Mussalim's answers he became more open about his own background and experiences. He told Mussalim that as a reward for some defiant and determined actions against the British occupation in Aden he had been selected to go for special training in Russia. He had travelled by ship to Egypt and then flown direct to Moscow. From there he had journeyed by road to a specialised training camp where he spent six months training in guerrilla and disruption activities.

He outlined how the Russian people had many years ago thrown off the suffocating yoke of imperialism. Mussalim learned how the poor people of Russia had fought and died in their thousands in a war against the Germans for no better reason than the

Tsar's woman was related to the King of England and at that time her relative needed all the help he could get. He learned about a man called Lenin who opened the eyes of the downtrodden people and made them realise that they fought only to protect the Tsar's riches and their own abject poverty. Lenin rallied the people to revolt and cease fighting in a war, which although the aristocracy promoted, they themselves took little or no participation in it. Where they did it was always from a safe distance. He went on to relate how the people in Moscow then rose against the criminal oppressor Tsar Nicholas and executed him for crimes against his own people.

He explained that since that day the Russian nation having freed itself from the rich sucking leeches had used the wealth for the benefit of all the people. He described the lifestyle that all the Russian people enjoyed now that the country's wealth was distributed fairly amongst all. Every home had a television set, a fridge, a machine that did their laundry and every family had its own car. It was a lifestyle which the American's and British envied so much that they were forced into false propaganda and lies about the nation in order to keep their own people subjected. Russia had in only fifty years, Suhayl told him, become the leading power in the world.

He made comparisons to the Russian people before the revolution and the present day Omani nation both shackled in the same suffocating yoke of imperialism. He identified Sultan Said as the Tsar Nicholas of Oman and pointed out that the way forward for the development of the nation and its people was clearly mapped in the history of Russian revolution.

There were very few schools in Oman and Mussalim had had no schooling worth a handful of sand, consequently he had never heard the story of the Russian revolution before and he had listened with interest. On the last point, however, Suhayl was singing with the choir because he understood completely that the only way the people could escape from their poverty was to take from those elite few who stole the nation's riches and kept it all for themselves. Mussalim had agreed and empathised by relating his experiences in Bahrain. He told Suhayl how his already discontented beliefs had gradually hardened into resentment when he made comparison between his own living situation and the way that the rich Arabs and their imported western lackeys lived. He had confessed his shame to a stranger that he had undertaken women's work. For this daily degradation he had been paid a pittance compared to others, but even that at the end of one year amounted to more money than he had ever seen before.

All the time they talked Musslim's eyes kept drifting, as though magnetised, to the deep scar elongating one side of Suhayl's mouth. He wondered what had caused it but did not yet feel secure enough to ask. Instead he made a conscious effort to try and ignore the mutilation.

Suhayl, more relaxed about Mussalim's convictions had extended his confidence a little. He told Mussalim that this caravan was the last of three carrying arms of Kalachnikov automatic rifles, grenades, mortars and landmines to Jibjat. They had journeyed as one from Hauf to a point south of Habrut. There they had been split into three and crossed the border at four day intervals bound for Jibjat. Each caravan train had been given a different route but with a time limit to arrive at the destination. That time limit in Suhayl's case as the last to leave was seven days.

Mussalim had enquired casually why so many arms were being assembled at Jibjat, which was after all only a small village. On this point he had become evasive and replied only that a raid was planned that would rock the Sultan and his troops to their very core.

Realising that it was not a point to press further Mussalim had changed the subject and asked about his own uncertain future. Again the answers were vague and only possibilities suggested. This time, however, Mussalim sensed that it was not evasion on Suhayl's part – he genuinely did not know. He suggested that perhaps he would be allowed to go to Hauf with the returning drovers as soon as the raid had started. Or maybe, he would wait at Jibjat until after the raid and then go to Hauf with any troops assigned to return. More senior leaders would he was informed, decide his future after they arrived at Jibjat. Shortly after that Suhayl had left him alone again to deal with the routine problems of ensuring that the caravan progression continued smoothly. As he left, however, his parting question had been about the old rifle slung across Mussalim's saddle and if he could shoot it.

His answer must have been acceptable because an hour later he was tasked to ride one of the flank positions at about the halfway point of the camel train. However, he had been posted to ride that position with Ali and it was not lost on Mussalim that it was the only position doubled. Suhayl, it seemed, still took no chances and he was in no doubt what would happen should he try to slip away.

The rest of yesterday they had pressed on relentlessly across the open plain of the *nejd*. Mussalim and Ali were on the downside of the strong hot wind, which without of any kind of obstruction skimmed across the desert completely unhindered. As it tore through the caravan it picked up the sand kicked up by the camels' feet and hurled it into the air in clouds of dust. To protect themselves from the flying sand's sting and the choking dust all the flank riders on that side had covered themselves completely leaving only narrow slits in the bundle of rags for their eyes to see out.

Because of its vast open exposure it had been pointless to stop, there was no shelter from the midday sun's singe. Mussalim suspected that they would have driven on regardless anyway. This suspicion was confirmed when they had continued through the heat of midday today even though by now they were in amongst the giant mounds of rock and gravel and shelter could be found.

He halted his camel at the foot of a steep bank of shale, which led to a sheer sided rock wall. He slid down from the animal gingerly. He was beginning to ache and become stiff from the time spent on its back. Following the example of the others he didn't unload his pack taking only his goatskin of water and his old rifle. He slapped as much of the dust from his clothing as he could then removed his shamag and shook it. He draped it casually across his shoulders and followed the others up the bank of shale. There he found a space among the seated men and joined them huddled in the sliver of shade provided by the natural wall of rock. Conversation was almost none existent, it consisted only of muted and abrupt exchanges among the weary men. Dates were passed around and eaten mostly in silence. Then all but two or three stretched out to sleep.

Mussalim stayed awake and stared tediously across the rocky valley. Both sides towered at least a hundred feet above the twisting and uneven valley floor. These sides were steep and rugged and completely covered with a deep blanket of loose shale. Large embedded craggy rocks protruding through this blanket their contours chiselled into strange shapes by a desert wind funnelled down the valley. These irregular patterns continued up into the very top ledges where the purple brown of the rock contrasted vividly with the bright blue of the sky. The scene was unnaturally tranquil belying completely the presence of more than sixty men and seventy animals. Only the hot wind with its monotonous low whine and short blasts disturbed the silence. Weariness it seemed had overtaken almost all and they had quickly settled into a sleep mode.

He watched with curiosity as a drover led a black shrouded woman across the valley floor and up into the privacy of some rocks. Then he smiled to himself when he realised the purpose. It seemed as if the black shroud and beaked mask had not had any deterring effect on that man. He would have to seek Allah's forgiveness in the evenings' prayer, he thought. But then perhaps he followed Suhayl's decree and didn't pray. Certainly he would be very brave to do so openly. He stole a glance around him – all now slept. Seeing his opportunity he closed his eyes and clandestinely prayed. He begged Allah's forgiveness for not going through the physical motion of his prayer and for his weakness at obeying another man's will above that of God.

The sun had set and twilight overtaken the day when Suhayl summoned a counsel of his troops. He drew diagrams in the sand with his cane as he laid out his instructions. Twelve men were detailed to set off immediately and go due east ahead of the caravan to the road. There they were to split into two groups, one group to go a kilometre north and the other a kilometre south. They were then to find appropriate places and set up ambushes. The road was to be mined and for the next two hours after that absolutely nothing was to be allowed to pass those points. In the caravan train itself the last ten camels would drag brush behind them. This would obliterate any give away tracks that a camel train had crossed the road. After crossing the road the caravan would then continue due east until it arrived at Wadi Dhahabun. Once there it would then rest for what remained of the night.

He selected the twelve and they began making their preparations to leave immediately. Counting himself and Suhayl, Mussalim counted fourteen men left, excluding the three guards still out. Suhayl detailed two others to scout the route ahead of the caravan when it was ready to move out and the rest were assigned accompanying posts around the train. Mussalim was detailed to ride at the head with Ziad and Suhayl. Once again Mussalim suspected that he had been placed under close supervision.

Suhayl then went among the drovers and instructed that all things that might rattle and carry sound were to be padded and tied down. He then gathered everyone together and impressed on all the need for silence and speed.

One hour after dark and with Suhayl softly cursing the clear moonlight sky the caravan was on the move. It turned due east along the northern edge of the maze of wadis that lay between them and the jebal and an hour after that they approached the graded road. They were met by one of the scouts who reported that nothing had moved on the road nor had there been any sounds of any problem from the two ambush parties. The night was too clear and the moon too bright. The tension showed clearly on Suhayl's face as he signalled the camel train forward to cross the road.

He stayed on the road nervously policing backwards and forwards, all the time urging the drovers to more speed. Eventually the last camels dragging the brushwood crossed the road. After relieved glances up and down the road he galloped his camel back to the head of the train. With every step adding distance from the road and vulnerability decreasing he permitted himself a huge grin.

A little over two hours later they again met the vanguard scouts who had waited for them at the lip of Wadi Dhabahun They stopped at the very edge of its precipice and stared down into its depths. It was a half a kilometre wide and its sheer rock sides towered at least a hundred metres above its base. A fresh wind still blew from the south teasing the spindly branches of the scattered shrubs growing down in the wadi bottom. In the eerie shadowy pallor of the moonlight Mussalim could almost imagine that these branches waved in aggravation discouraging anyone to descend into the wadi this night. He felt uneasiness and glanced quickly at his companions to see if they experienced the same foreboding feelings. If they did they did not show it. Suhayl questioned the scouts about a suitable way down and just for a moment Mussalim's hopes rose that they would have to camp on the top and in tomorrow's daylight find a way down. But his hopes were never really born because only half a kilometre away they had found a wide and well-worn track down the side of the cliff face.

The caravan turned south towards the distant jebal and after a few minutes they arrived at the descent place. The downward track was steep, the surface underfoot loose and the burdened animals struggled to keep their footing as they made their slow and cautious descent. They protested noisily as they slid and slipped, their anxious bellowing unsettling the animals waiting their turn to make the descent. It took an hour of pulling, cursing and swishing canes before the overworked drovers got the last animal to the bottom.

They soon found a track winding its way south down the middle of the wadi and followed it toward the jebal. After only a few minutes they began to pass ancient Bedouin graves on both sides their low piles of rocks placed in narrow rectangles. In the bright moonlight these rocks, deliberately positioned with the sharp ends pointing upward, cast low unnaturally shaped shadows across the ground. The more they progressed down the wadi the more numerous these graves became until the whole wadi bottom seemed to be filled with these abnormal uneven pilasters of rocks. Even the sheer walls of the wadi had been utilised. Each crack, crevice or shallow cave had become natural sepulchres, their entrances sealed with rocks and boulders knotted into place by packed wet sand acting as crude makeshift mortar.

An unnatural eerie quietness had gripped the caravan train. Whether it was from uneasiness or out of respect for the hundreds dead the conversation was decidedly muted. Even the camels with their loose equipment padded and tied firmly down moved noiselessly through this valley of the dead likely ghostly apparitions.

After a mile they came to a flat clearing with a rough mausoleum crudely constructed from an assemblage of rocks and boulders where the dead were prepared for burial. By its side a well with three scaffold poles pyramided above and dangling a pulley on a chain to draw water. It was now close to midnight and it was here where Suhayl called a halt to rest.

The drovers drew water from the well and poured it into a nearby stone trough and then brought the now unloaded animals forward six at a time to drink. The bellows of the waiting camels echoed eerily off the wadi walls as they smelled the water and protested with impatience.

Mussalim watered his own camel but did not drink himself. He had some paranoia about the purity of the water drawn from beneath a wadi of a thousand dead. Instead he carried his pack a few yards to the wadi wall climbed the few feet of scree and settled between two sepulchres with his back to the rock face and his old rifle across his knees.

After a few minutes he was joined by Ali, he did not speak only nodding tersely and settling silently at his side.

Although Suhayl had still maintained the no fire's precaution he was obviously pleased with the progress and had declared that since they were now little more than half-a-day from Jibjat then tomorrow could be a late start.

The night was still bright and the jebal was much closer now. Little flecks of mist that had been teased free from the main bank by the wind drifted across the clear starlight sky just above the wadi. At times these thin shadows filtered the moon's light as they moved silently across the sky changing shape slowly and ghostly as they did.

"This is not a good place to stop." Ali broke the silence.

Mussalim did not answer instead looked across the developing camp. Guards had been posted and the remaining soldiers had split into several small groups of threes and fours. The drovers, however, more gregarious had formed two larger circles on the flat ground to the front of the mausoleum. It was unnaturally quiet and if anyone did speak it was with a reverent low voice. Such mutterings as there were did not carry as far as Mussalim and he surveyed a camp of around fifty souls and an abnormal scene of noiselessness. Ali's uneasiness it seemed was shared by many.

"When do you think the others will catch up?" Mussalim said referring to the ambush parties and seeking to change the subject.

Ali shrugged, "maybe soon. Maybe tomorrow if they can't find the way down into the wadi in the dark."

"What do you think is happening at Jibjat?"

"Something big," Ali replied with a shrug. "We will know in a couple of days."

"Suhayl said it would be something to shock the Sultan and his troops."

Ali looked around and after deciding that he wouldn't be overheard said, "Rumour is that the target is the Air Force Base out at Juffar. It is only a small base isolated and on an open plain with only a scattering of temporary buildings. In the Khareef mist we can get in close without being seen until it's too late. While the buildings are attacked another party under the cover of the mist can destroy the runway with explosives. It's only graded so not difficult to blow great holes in. And if there should be any aeroplanes on the ground we can destroy them too. They don't have many they can afford to lose, so that would be a bad blow to them. It is more than eighty kilometres east of Salalah and the road bad. It would take the whole day for any reinforcements to get there after the alarm was raised. By that time they should find nothing but smoking ruins."

"What about air strikes?"

"In a thick mist they will be flying and striking blind." He shook his head dismissively, "It's a soft target and perfectly achievable."

Mussalim was quiet for few moments while he thought about what Ali had said. The idea seemed to be perfectly credible. To attack and destroy a government base would truly send shock waves to the very core of the despotic institution. Even a partial demolition of the base would be a victory and a tremendous boost to the Popular Front and many more would join the Liberation cause because of it.

Screams and shouts interrupted his thoughts and he looked towards one of the drovers' circles. Men leapt to their feet in alarm and scattered putting some distance between themselves and a man who hopped from one foot to the other as if he were on hot coals and screamed unintelligibly as he did. He then collapsed to the floor and rolled around with arms and legs thrashing the air. Within a minute a second man close by had copied this bizarre behaviour and another fearful stampede of close bystanders began. As if the behaviour was ragingly contagious a third man suddenly sank to his knees and grabbed handfuls of sand and then with arms outstretched above his head opened his fists and allowed the sand to drain over him through his fingers loudly chanting something incomprehensible as he did.

Mussalim had involuntarily jumped to his feet and his grip tightened on his rifle as fear and hysteria began to spread.

"It's the *djinns* of the dead," Ali muttered. "We shouldn't be here."

Suhayl walked quickly into the midst of the drovers and stood over the man rolling on the floor and shouted down at him but it had no effect. He cocked his automatic weapon and fired a short burst into the thrashing body. The body ceased to thrash and after a few abrupt twitches lay perfectly still. Then he turned his weapon to point at the man who poured sand over himself. He stopped his chanting and sheepishly got to his feet. The effect was the same on the remaining case of madness. He suddenly regained control when he became more afraid of Suhayl than his superstitions. Suhayl glared slowly around at all the shocked faces looking for more hints of lunacy. Then without a word he turned suddenly and stomped away coming in the direction of where Mussalim and Ali stood.

As he walked away the drovers began to approach the still body slowly and with caution almost as if they half expected the man to suddenly leap once more into his quivering madness. Mussalim stood fixed to the spot stunned by the rapidness by which death had overtaken the man and the indifferent way that it had been delivered.

Suhayl looked up at Mussalim and Ali when he got close. He stopped at the bottom of the pile of scree and briefly glanced back over his shoulder. "Sambo's," he spat when he faced them once more. "Two, three generations and they still believe in their mumbo-jumbo superstitions." By Sambo's he referred to those of African descendant previously brought into the Arab world as slaves and now for the most part living as integrated but easily identified by their inherited African facial features.

Ali shook his head. "It was the *djinns* of the dead. They took possession of those men's minds and bodies."

"It was hysteria," he replied sneering. "Nothing more. It was spreading and it had to be stopped before half the camp ran away." He shook his head sadly, sighed and asked himself aloud. "What chance do we have of winning this struggle if our fighters are afraid of the dark and old bones?" Then much more assertive he said. "Be more afraid of me than those *djinns* of yours. Didn't I just chase three away? Just my Kalachnikov, and me" he waved his automatic rifle to emphasis the point.

Behind him the first of the ambush party began arriving in the camp and he turned to watch. "Get some sleep," he said turning back briefly. "I've changed my mind, tomorrow will be an early start." Then he left to greet the new arrivals.

"It was the *djinns*," Ali muttered as they watched him go. "They haven't gone, they can't be harmed by bullets. They're still here among us, looking for new victims."

Mussalim didn't reply. Instead he went and sat down pressing his back nervously against the rock face between the two sepulchres. He gripped his old rifle firmly and laid it across his knees. He watched two drovers take a leg each and drag the dead man away.

Sleep was only fitful. Part of his mind was intent on staying alert and subconsciously roused him when second level sleep began to overcome him. He continually jerked to full consciousness and then stared quickly around him wondering if something had awoken him as it stalked from the darkness. Always however the situation was placid. Most men slept huddled beneath their blankets, but here and there some sat on the ground talking quietly in small groups. Ali's fear of the spirits of the dead seemed to have been appeased because he slept soundly. Still sitting with his back to the rock but slumped right over to one side. Eventually tiredness won the battle over Mussalim's subconscious and he too sank into a decent level of sleep.

Movement around the camp was early beating the sunrise by about thirty minutes. The dark red patch in the eastern sky gradually changed to pink and then golden yellow dismissing the night shadows and with them the disquieting fear of the ancient graveyard. In the cold light of day the piles of stones, which marked the graves, looked decidedly innocuous and all previous trepidation seemed just childish hysteria.

The first problem to be faced, however, was that four drovers had disappeared during the night deserting their belongings and their camels in their anxiety to get away from the wadi graveyard. Suhayl quickly dispatched two armed men on camels after them and Mussalim was in no doubt what the fate of the deserters would be when they eventually caught up with them. It was patently obvious that their only chance on foot to survive the desert would be to make their way back to the road and seek help from chance travellers. The likelihood of that was that the most likely travellers on that road would be government forces. Mussalim could imagine that in their gratitude of being rescued what a story those deserters would have to tell. He found himself hoping the riders would intercept them in time as he watched them gallop their camels down the wadi.

The caravan was loaded quickly and soon on the move heading towards the mountains and the safety of the mist. As they began to gradually climb Mussalim halted his camel and paused to look back into the valley of the dead harmless and benign in the early morning sunshine. He thought of the fresh grave and the hysterical comrade that they had left in it. In the light of day he now believed that Suhayl's action although extreme was probably correct. It may have avoided a situation, which could have jeopardised the security of the whole arms shipment and possibly the success of the raid on Juffa. "Inshallah," he muttered conveniently excusing Suhayl from the murder and he kicked his camel forward once more.

✳ ✳ ✳

The logs in the small fireplace hissed and poured thick smoke as the heat and flames beneath rapidly dried the moisture soaked in them. Most of that smoke was sucked up the crudely constructed chimney but not all. Traces loitered in the small austere room smarting eyes and irritating throats. The room would have been bare but for a large and tired old mat constructed entirely of faded goatskins in the centre and a liberal quantity of hand made cushions positioned around its edges. The room was dim, the only light was the firelight inadequately supported by an old paraffin lamp hanging from the ceiling. The fumes given off from this lamp mingled with the thin veil of smoke adding additional discomfort to respiratory tract.

Hamed sat on the mat close to the fire and lolled across two thick cushions. His brother Juma sat cross-legged next to him while his father sprawled opposite on the other side of the fireplace. The three women sat at the back in the shadows whispering among themselves and waiting to give their opinions if they were asked.

Abdulla opened the small plastic bag once more and took another pinch of the wet green pulp inside. He rolled it into a small ball in the palm of his other hand and then placed it carefully under his tongue to suck. The operation required some degree of concentration because his senses were becoming confused.

Hamed watched concerned at the slow and deliberate way that his father re-supplied his personal intake of the madman's grass, *sweeqa*. He had a tendency to use it but not often. Sometimes at tribal meetings when all the serious discourse had ended then in the company of others he would suck just a little to inflate his spirit and relax his inhibitions before the tribal dances. Sometimes he would use it privately and more heavily, as he did now, when his spirits were low and depressed. But tonight was the third consecutive night and that was unusual. Hamed knew well that the reason for his depression was the defection of his eldest son from the family. He also knew well the sequence of events. His mood would gradually improve to a point of good humour and then as the drug took effect he would become sullen and tired then he would gloomily retire to his bed to sleep off the effects. He was starting to move into that phase now and if Juma were to achieve his approval then he would have to accomplish it soon.

Lailla had pre-empted Juma's subject on their immediate arrival home from Salalah when she had announced to all that Juma had a secret girl friend. Juma's despair and embarrassment had been obvious as curiosity packed questions poured from all the family members. Eventually Abdulla had silenced everyone by declaring it was a topic to be discussed in the *dirwain* after the evening meal. It took an extensive stretch of imagination to consider this room a *dirwain*, a place where men sit to discuss topics. It was the communal family room and the only room of three in the house which wasn't a bedroom.

Now settled after the meal had been cleared away, Abdulla had invited Juma to talk about his 'secret girl friend'.

To Hamed and all that had listened, the depth of his excitement and desire to possess this girl was patently obvious. From his description of her physical beauty and her correct shy disposition, this girl sounded not only admirably suitable to be his wife but a veritable possession to be prized. Initially Abdulla had showed some pleasure that Juma had at last found himself a potential wife and from Juma's description of the girl's propriety, Abdulla's provisional approval seemed a formality. However, when Juma had revealed that Khamisa was from a different tribe that perceived formality evaporated.

"Father?" Juma pressed for an answer.

Hamed looked at his father waiting for him to speak.

Abdulla sighed heavily. "Forget this girl. Choose one from your own tribe." His words were slurred.

"I can never forget this girl."

"You can," he grunted. "Select another from our tribe. Select two! Select three! Imagine three wives to pleasure you," he raised his eyebrows insinuatingly. "That has to be better than just one Ruwas woman."

Hamed was inclined to agree with that statement. Fleetingly he imagined three women in his own bed.

Juma shook his head sadly and stared into the fire. "Father you do not understand. Khamisa filters into my every waking thought and when I sleep she fills my dreams. One hundred women cannot replace her."

"You feel this now," he paused his befuddled thoughts forgetting what he was about to say. "You are young," he recovered his track, "one week from now you may feel exactly the same about another girl." Exasperation was also showing. "Hamed. Tell him."

Hamed was embarrassed and firmly on the spot as everybody waited for his opinion. His sympathies were with his half-brother, his obedience with his father. He sought a way to diplomatically appease both. "Father I do not know this girl but the way Juma describes her she is a jewel. Even though she is of another tribe and all the difficulties and problems that such an alliance will present perhaps you should meet with this girl's father. Perhaps he won't mind so much that that Juma is Al Hamer." He shrugged and pulled a face, "What can it hurt? Maybe you and he can find a way." He waited for some reaction, but none came. "If anybody can get around it then you can," he added flattery.

Abdulla still didn't reply, he just stared glassy-eyed through the gloom towards him and then spit the spent *sweeqa* into the fire. "Jokha?" he invited a mother's opinion.

She was a little surprised at being asked for her opinion and she hesitated. "Hamed may be right. What can it hurt to speak with her father."

"What can it hurt?" he drawled. "He may not welcome an approach from an outsider. And it would not be received too well in our own tribe either when it becomes known that we look elsewhere for Juma's wife."

Jokha glanced at her son with his back towards her and sensed his mounting dismay. "Abdulla, you and I have grown old together. Little by little each day that we have lived the mysteries of life were destroyed until now we forget what it was like to be young, inexperienced and excited by expectancy. Anticipation is always more exciting than the event. Juma stands at the anticipating stage, you stand at the other side of events. This makes you wiser by far. You and I can see that perhaps he could be just as happy with another woman. But he doesn't, this Ruwas woman excites him and it is excitement that makes life worth living. When that's gone then what is left? He should be allowed to taste all of life's excitements and disappointments for himself and not be disillusioned at a young age by cynical experience."

It was a bold answer and Hamed hoped that his own mother would be as daring on his own behalf when the time came.

In his inebriated state, however, such intellect was wasted on Abdulla. "You talk in riddles woman," he slurred.

"Tribal difficulties can be overcome and once two are married then what difference will it make anyway. I think that you should go and talk to the girl's father," she persisted. Then held her breath fearing that perhaps she had gone a little too far with her persistence.

Abdulla only scowled and got to his feet with some difficulty. He stood there unsteadily, "I cannot decide tonight. Tomorrow I will make the decision whether to go and see this man or not." He looked at his younger wife, "Kathya come," he said then led the way with a stumble into the bedroom behind him. Kathya got dutifully to her feet and followed Abdulla. A few moments later Jokha got up and took Lailla's hand and led her through the door at the opposite end of the room leaving the two brothers alone.

"Will he do it?"

Juma shrugged and then smiled at Hamed ruefully. "Eventually! It may take a little more persuasion but I think he will."

"What about the girl's father, will he agree?"

"*Inshaallah*."

Hamed stared into the fire at the hypnotic dancing flames and wondered about this girl he had yet to meet. She would have to be something special to account for his half brother's obsession. With a seventeen year-old's perspective he pondered with some curiosity about Juma's preference for this single girl instead of three which his father had suggested. When his own time came, he wondered would he choose one over three? He doubted it. But then he could and there was nothing to stop him adding a second and a third in the future assuming of course that he could support them. He glanced sideways at his brother and wondered if this thought had already occurred to him and he decided that it probably had. Then he tried to imagine what disruption might be added to the family with the introduction of an adult sister. There would have to be many changes, he realised and he found himself suddenly hoping that it would not after all happen.

❊ ❊ ❊

Lailla sat on her low cot at the end of the narrow room and took an old cardboard shoe box from beneath it. From inside the box she took out the small tin of spices, which she had bought that afternoon in the souk and dropped a tiny pinch of the brown powder into the small clay incense burner. It began to smoke profusely giving off a highly aromatic vapour of sweet smelling spice.

Jokha drew the old heavy curtain, which divided the room and gave Lailla some privacy from the other cots where her brothers slept. She lit the old paraffin lamp, which hung by a small rusty chain from the ceiling. Then she poured a little water from a bucket into a small and battered tin bowl and indicated to her to undress and bathe herself. Lailla started to pull the thin cotton dress over her head and then found herself tied arms and head into the blind side. Jokha smiled briefly at her dilemma and then came to her assistance with guiding tugs and pulls until she was free. For a moment the adolescent girl stood dressed in only baggy knee length shorts and then with a slight shiver went to the tin bowl to wash. Jokha paused a moment and watched the girl. She was lithe and youthfully slender and her development still at an early stage. Nevertheless, it was very apparent, even in the poor light that a woman was beginning to emerge from a child's body. It was time for her to be made aware of the effect that she could have on a man's mind and for her to learn the ways of fitting demeanour.

Abdulla would have to be told that she would very soon need to be dressed in a manner more appropriate to modesty. As she busied herself arranging the blankets on Lailla's bed into a more comfortable position she decided that at an early opportunity tomorrow she would talk to Kathya and then together they would approach their husband.

When her toiletry was complete, the girl stepped out of those baggy shorts and pulled on her nightshift. It was little more than an old tee shirt worn out and discarded by one of her brothers. She sat on the cot and waited while Jokha looked for her comb among her private possessions in the shoebox.

"Do you think father will go and talk to Khamisa's father?"

"I don't know," she said shaking her head. "We will have to wait and see." She found the plastic comb and momentarily studied its dilapidated condition with almost half its teeth missing. Lailla's hair was long and thick which accounted for the poor condition of the comb. She dropped it back in the shoebox and fiddled in the deep pocket of her own robe for her own comb. "You should have bought yourself a new comb with the money that Juma gave you instead of those spices," she gently chided and began to slowly comb the girl's hair. "Do you like Khamisa?" she queried.

"I would be pleased to have her as my sister," Lailla replied. "It would be nice to have another girl of my own age around here for a friend. You would like her too. She would make a fine daughter for you."

"How old do you think she is?"

She shrugged, "I'm not sure. I think that perhaps she is around the same age as Hamed."

Jokha took her time grooming the girl's hair while she encouraged her to talk freely about the object of her son's desire. Lailla revealed as much as she could, satisfying some but not all, of a mother's natural curiosity. Eventually when she accepted that there was nothing more to be learned she stopped combing and gently instructed her into bed. She took from the basket at the foot of the cot Lailla's only other dress and hung it above the smoking incense burner to become seasoned by the aromatic fumes ready for her to wear the next day. She dropped her own comb into the shoebox and took for herself the worn one. Her own hair was now thinner and short, this comb could easily cope, she decided. She picked up the discarded dress then turned down the paraffin lamp and turned to leave. Abdulla would have spent what little had remained of his energy gratifying himself with Kathya and would by now be asleep, she reasoned. She could go to her own cot now in the same room and would not have to lay and listen to the sounds of *jig-jig*.

"I wish Mussalim was here," Lailla's voice from the darkness. "He would have persuaded father to go and talk with Khamisa's father. Where do you think he is now, Jokha?"

Jokha paused, her hand on the curtain. "I don't know." It was now the sixth night since he had been gone and she tried to calculate where her eldest son would be at this moment. "By now, far away. Somewhere between Mudhai and the Yemen border, I imagine. Now go to sleep," she said as she ducked under the curtain.

✳ ✳ ✳

But in fact Mussalim was only forty kilometres away in the small jebal village of Jibjat having arrived there early in the afternoon of that very same day. Now after having slept poorly the night before in wadi Dhabahun, he slept soundly rolled in his damp blanket under an open sided large tent.

"Hey jabally," Suhayl said prodding his legs with his foot. "Wake up. Are all jabally's as lazy as this."

Mussalim looked out bleary eyed from his blanket cocoon. "What?"

"Get up. Things to do."

The sun had risen bringing the light but had not percolated the mist and the day's expectation seemed to be grey. Mussalim sat up and looked around him. Prostrate forms of men still slept on all around him in mish-mash distribution. He looked up at Suhayl with an enquiring expression.

"Here put that on," he said, tossing him a faded sand coloured shirt streaked with smudges of green dye.

Mussalim, still sitting and more asleep than awake, put it on. It was a passable fit and as he pulled it straight he discovered two ragged holes to the left of the midriff section. He poked his fingers through and examined the red blush of blood still contaminated the edges. He looked up again at Suhayl.

"It belonged to a hero of the revolution," he said and then tossed down a similar faded shamag.

"This too I suppose?"

He nodded agreement. "These are new." The pants were still in the wrapper and the contrast in the sand colour was striking. "The hero probably shit in the old ones as he died."

Mussalim got wearily to his feet and dressed. Although fitting around the waist the trousers legs were too long and draped over his bare feet.

"You almost look the part," Suhayl said. "Almost! Find yourself a woman somewhere in the village to shorten the trousers for you. And who knows," he went on with a smirk made hideous by the deep scar, "maybe you can get her to do something else for you while you have the trousers off."

"What about some boots," Mussalim ignored his ribald suggestion.

"Boots?" he said as though shocked. "No boots. You will have to get them off a dead man, sometime."

He slipped his feet into his old flip-flops wondering just who and when someone with the same sized foot would obligingly die for his benefit.

"Here catch," and with both hands Suhayl forcefully threw him a rifle. "If you can shoot it then it's yours."

Mussalim caught it cleanly and turned it in his hands. It was a single round bolt action reload and not a fully automatic Russian weapon like the other regulars possessed. Nevertheless, it was much superior to his old Martin Henri. "Suppose this too belonged to a hero of the revolution?"

Suhayl laughed out loud. "A hero? Maybe! But he would be a misguided one. That is a standard government issue soldier's weapon. Come, let's see how good you are with it."

As they walked out of the campsite Suhayl paused at a trash pile and sorted through it gathering an assortment of bottles and cans. Then he led the way away over the flat featureless plateau on which Jibjat stands.

It was still early and very little stirred in the camp nor, abnormally, in the small village. Since their arrival yesterday the village Mosque had been silent. There had been no Muezzins lament from the Minaret to call the faithful to prayer. This morning too the call to pray, which precedes the rising sun, had also been absent. Consequently few, if any, of the villagers had stirred from their homes. Perhaps the large force gathered on the very edge of their village also inhibited them and kept them hidden in their homes. The significance of the silence from the mosque, however, had not been lost on Mussalim. He had now begun to fear that perhaps the atheist attitude of Suhayl was a general policy within the insurgent movement after all. It rather looked as if he would have to continue to pray in secret for as long as he remained actively committed to the cause.

The grass was wet and deep and the mist damp and clinging with visibility no more than a hundred metres. When the camp behind them had disappeared into the mist Suhayl looked back and then paused. "This will do," he said dropping the trash. Then he held out his hand for the rifle that Mussalim carried. First he pointed out the safety catch and then he demonstrated how to work the bolt action to arm and cock the weapon. He passed it back for Mussalim to practice. After that he explained the sighting and settings and when he was satisfied that he understood he selected five smaller pieces of trash and placed them as targets twenty-five metres away. Then he handed Mussalim a magazine with twenty rounds.

Mussalim lay in the wet grass and made himself comfortable and laid the rifle on the hand of his propped arm. He pressed the stock to his shoulder and squinted down the sights lining up the target. When he was ready he began to shoot. The rifle was more finely balanced and easier to use then his old weapon and Mussalim quickly adapted. He scored five hits with eight shots. Suhayl nodded with satisfaction and then picked up the bigger pieces of trash and wandered out again, but this time almost to the edge of visibility.

"Go ahead," he said when he had returned.

Mussalim adjusted the sights and then took careful aim. When he had exhausted all the remaining twelve rounds he had scored only one hit on a target.

"What does that tell you?" Suhayl asked.

The answer was too obvious but Mussalim rolled onto his side and replied patiently with a shrug. "That it is easier to hit a target when it's closer."

"Hmm. Why? Those second targets were bigger."

He peered back into the gloom towards the targets not sure how to explain.

Suhayl didn't wait for him to answer, instead answered for him. "If you are a fraction of a degree out at close range then you will probably still hit the target. But if you are far away then you will miss it and the further you are away the wider will be your miss margin."

Mussalim only nodded. It was a lesson taught many years ago by his father when teaching him to use the old Martin Henri.

He handed him a second magazine and stooped down at his side. "Try again. This time take more care with your aim, don't fire until you are absolutely ready and hold your breath before you pull the trigger."

This time Mussalim hit the remaining targets with five of the twenty rounds to spare.

"Finish off the magazine."

He then selected a rock at around the same distance as a target and exhausted the magazine.

"You'll do jaballi!" he said patting him on the head. "For the time being get used to shooting from that distance. The target maybe harder to hit, but it's easier to kill a man. At that range he's just a target when he gets closer in then he becomes a man and it is much more personal, you will be inclined to hesitate. And that can be dangerous." He ran his fingers along his face scar slowly. "I know all about that. But after a while you'll get used to it and if you're worth an olive to our cause then you'll learn to kill the enemy from any range."

Mussalim moved to a sitting position glanced at the man by his side and felt confident enough to ask the question now. "What happened?"

"What happened?"

"The scar."

He touched the scar again a little consciously. "A British bullet. It was my first real action and almost my last. I took part in an ambush in Aden that didn't come off. We picked the spot, got in position and waited in hiding for a British convoy taking supplies inland to Dhala to come through. Before it arrived a vanguard force of infantry scouting the route ahead of the convoy attacked us from behind. It became every man for himself and in the confusion to escape I came face to face with a Jundhi," a native soldier fighting with the British for money. "I hesitated and he fired. Lucky for me he was a bad shot. His bullet took away the side of my mouth and a few teeth. Then I fired and took off his face. Never have I hesitated again."

"You were lucky! Another inch and it would have gone down your throat."

He flashed his twisted grin. "Maybe I was unlucky another inch the other way and he would have missed me completely. But heed what I say, keep your distance for a while, if you can." He stood up. "The rifle is yours. You will need it tomorrow. You're assigned to my group and you will see action tomorrow with the rest of us."

Mussalim jumped up, he hadn't expected that he would be allowed to take part in the raid on the airfield. "Is it the raid on Juffar?"

"Juffar? No not Juffar. Be at the briefing four o'clock today in the *Dirwain* tent."

✳ ✳ ✳

The tent was a large marquee about sixty feet in length and without sides or end fittings. There was no ground sheet, instead the grass had been covered by many old and odd carpets appropriated from the homes of the villagers. The mist which had thickened during the day had brought with it drizzly rain. That rain driven by a southerly wind invaded into one side of the marquee wetting everything down that side. The place hummed with expectant chatter as late arrivals came in and sought vacant space. The wet southern side was not a particularly desirable sitting area and these late arrivals now caused some disruption as they made their way carefully through the seated congregation to squeeze into small vacant spaces.

At one end of the tent and sitting on pillows of silk and a fine Persian carpet four men impassively surveyed the confusion before them. These men of the council sat quietly patient and passed occasional quiet comments between themselves as they waited for the gathering to settle.

Accompanied by Ali, Mussalim had been one of the earlier arrivals and had squatted close to the front. Now as more of the late arrivals squeezed into the space between them their position became less favourable.

"That's Al Ghassani," Ali had muttered to him and had indicated the only one of the four that didn't wear some kind of uniform. Mussalim quietly studied the man who now led the movement and whom until three days ago he had not even heard of. Al Ghassani sat quietly composed with a definite air of assurance while his eyes continuously raked around the assembling crowd. His face was partly hidden by a grey streaked beard but it did not hide a complexion that was much paler than was normal. He wore a full length white *dish'dasht* beneath a long flowing *basht*. The dark coloured *basht,* was decorated around the edge of the collar and at the sleeves end with threads of silver. His head was covered by a white shamag that hung down onto his shoulders.

The assembly was becoming more orderly as the latecomers began to settle into suitable niches and the busy chatter began to quickly fall away. Those that were still to settle soon became aware of the spreading quiet and glanced around. Realising that the briefing start was imminent most settled for the position that they now occupied and squatted down. An expectant silence spread across the assembly as everyone waited for the movement leader to speak.

Al Ghassani didn't hurry and his gaze moved slowly through the audience, his eyes seemingly taking in every man in attendance. The man on his left leaned towards him and quietly muttered. Without taking his eyes from the crowd before him he leaned over just a little to catch the quiet comment and then nodded slightly.

"Welcome to you all," he said eventually. "For those of you who do not know me I am Ahmed Al Ghassani.

I am the elected Secretary of the new General Command." He paused and then indicated the man on his left. "This is Commissar Abdel Tahir, he is a man that most of you who live in this area will already know as the main organiser of the disruption activities of the eastern section of this region." He then turned to his other side and introduced the other two. "And these two Commissars are Salim Al Mushani and Mohammed Bin Talib. Not many of you will know either of these men yet, but in the coming months their reputations will spread."

He paused, either waiting for comments or gathering his thoughts. "There have been some significant developments within the party recently," he went on. Before we proceed with the main purpose of our gathering I will take a few minutes to outline the structure and policies of the new PFLOAG.

Earlier this year the previous committee of eighteen was dissolved and with it the Dhofar Liberation Front organisation too."

Two or three members of the audience began passing quiet comments to each other. Al Ghassini paused and stared in their direction. His prolonged and sterile stare silenced their mutterings.

"The full congress then elected a new committee of twenty-five members and formed the General Command," he went on. "I was appointed General Secretary of this new command and the first order of business for the Command was to pass a proposition to rename the movement to, the 'Popular Front for the Liberation of the Occupied Arabia Gulf.' This, in effect, raised the profile here from just a small regional insurgency to a movement with a far wider recognition and allied us to all other brother Arab strugglers. This alliance is not restricted to just the mass of our brothers throughout the Arabian Gulf who suffer poverty while their rulers live in blatant luxury. The PFLOAG allies itself to the struggles of all our Arab brothers and that includes such national struggles as the thousands of Palestinian refugees who have had their traditional homelands taken from them. The Jordanians, who had their West Bank annexed. The Egyptians, who have had their land of the Sinai seized and the Syrians who also lost the Golan Mountains. All vast quantities of land taken by force and occupied by the American backed Jew." He spoke with a great deal of confidence and composure, his words unhurried and although quiet, easily carrying to the far ends of the *dirwain*.

"So with this higher ideal of allying ourselves to all our repressed brothers we can also count on much more practical and significant support from our friends in Russia, China and North Korea.

The previous objectives of the movement had been 'civil disobedience.' This really only amounted to some quite ineffective sabotage, some sporadic shelling towards Salalah, sniping and some half-hearted ambushes. The main reason for these comparatively ineffective tactics was of course because of the lack of funds. However, now that we have elevated our status we have been able to negotiate better financial support from our sympathetic supporters. And the second decision from the new command is that the strategy should now be escalated to that of organised revolutionary violence." He paused a moment while his eyes raked the congregation quickly looking for signs of dissenters before continuing.

"This is the reason why we are all gathered here today. We now move into this new and much more effective phase in this struggle. You will have the opportunity to begin this new campaign and shock the decadent bourgeois right out of their complacency. After tomorrow they will definitely have to seriously consider our claim to a rightful inheritance to the regional wealth. At the same time your victory tomorrow, when it is announced throughout the Arab world, will encourage other strugglers to increase their own efforts." He stopped a moment and nodded slightly to Abdel Tahir. He got up immediately and went to a nearby blackboard and easel covered by a large cloth. He glanced back to Al Ghassani. "Comrades your target for tomorrow!" Abdel Tahir pulled the cover away.

Mussalim stared at an outline drawing of a small town flanked by the sea on two sides and protected by concertina razor wire on the other two. Inside the wire two forts, one on the beach and the other on the higher ground protected the houses between them and the sea. His own reading ability was poor and he had only just started to piece together the word written at the top when an excited murmuring swept through the gathering. "Mirbat!"

~ 4 ~

Early August 1968 • Abdel waited for the murmuring to cease. "Yes comrades, Mirbat! The objective is to take this fort," he pointed with a camel cane at the blackboard indicating the fort on the high ground. Then to destroy it." He let the cane fall and waited for some reaction. None came, so he carried on. "This target has been carefully selected because it is considered to be perfectly achievable. And because by its nature, as a government stronghold, it will stun and alarm the Sultan and his supporters when it falls. The element of surprise is with us too. We have never made a full and open attack before, therefore they will not be expecting it. And because they are not expecting it then they will have made no special defensive preparations. We on the other hand have planned and prepared carefully." He paused a moment turning the cane horizontally in his hands. "If all goes as well as we expect then we will have time to turn our attention to the secondary target." He raised the cane and pointed briefly at the other fort. "Which is this second fort. However, there are time limits. We can expect re-inforcements to be summoned from the Salalah Garrison so we need to have achieved our objective and to have withdrawn safely and victoriously before they arrive.

As we speak two teams are at this moment on their way to the Salalah Mirbat road to blow deep holes at strategic places and then to mine other stretches," Abdel continued. "After that those two teams will set themselves in a couple of skirmish places to engage and delay the re-enforcement's. These tactics should prevent the relief arriving at Mirbat before dark. The attack is planned to start before daylight tomorrow, so we will have about ten hours to achieve the objective. The leader of this attack will be Commissar Salim Al Mushani." He paused allowing the attention to momentarily fall on one of the seated commissars.

"Commissar Mohammed Bin Talib meanwhile will lead another force to the jebal foothills overlooking Salalah. After the garrison has been depleted by the despatch of forces to Mirbat he will then attack the airforce runway with rockets and 3-inch mortar. Our intelligence is that there are at this time three of the Sultan's aircraft on the base – two Provost fighters and a Beaver spotter. We expect that they will be airborne as soon as they receive the distress call from Mirbat. If Mohammed's rockets are accurate then they will not have a runway to land on when they come back to re-arm and will have to divert to Midway. With luck they will not have shells for their cannon up there. In which case they will effectively be out of the battle." He looked around the attentive faces. "Any questions before I hand over to Salim Al Mushani to describe the attack on the fort?"

"What about the British Air Force on the base at Salalah?" somebody asked.

"We will take care not to shell their particular area," Mohammed took the question. "If we don't attack them then they will see it as an internal matter and will take no active part."

"What about the artillery?" another questioner. "Won't they blast the mortar positions?"

"Yes undoubtedly. We can't prevent it. But what we can do is to confuse their target by splitting into two teams and firing from one position only until they measure it. When they do that team will move to a new position while the other team takes over the shelling. The Khareef mist will make it difficult for them to pinpoint our positions anyway."

While Mohammed was answering the question Al Mushani had got up and taken over from Abdel at the blackboard. He waited a few moments. When he was sure there were no other questions he took up the brief and began to outline the attack plan. Mussalim listened with excitement growing from the pit of his stomach as he became increasingly convinced of the plan's success.

The attack on the primary target would start before daylight with a mortar bombardment from two sides. In the north from the mountain foothills and in the south, with the aid of cause sympathisers, from within Mirbat itself. At the same time a small force would attack and neutralise the small outpost outside the perimeter fence. The main assault force would gather on the eastern perimeter fence and when the shelling ceased would attack from that side. Attacking up the eastern side of the hill on which the fort stood it would be completely out of sight from the second fort down on the beach. Poles with crosspieces hammered in and pre positioned in a nearby gully would act as crude ladders to scale the walls if that became necessary. A smaller force would assemble on the northern perimeter wire with the sole objective of engaging the beach fort and keeping its defenders inside. Salim finished his brief and then stood with his arm resting on the top edge of the blackboard surveying the listeners waiting for questions.

"What is the strength of the forts?" the first questioner stood up and asked.

"From our intelligence from within Mirbat, not very strong. Around twenty-five *askars* in each fort armed with single bolt action rifles. We, on the other hand, will be around one hundred and forty – most of you armed with automatic Kalishnikov's so you will seem to be more like three hundred to those inside."

"What about machine guns in the forts?" another questioner stood.

Al Mushani shook his head. "None," he answered briefly.

The questioner was not convinced. "No fifty calibre Browning?"

"No none!" He pointed at another questioner dismissing the last.

"How do we get through the razor wire."

"Wire cutters to cut away sections and then ropes to drag it away."

"What about replenishment ammunition?"

"No problem! It is all pre hidden and stored in and around Mirbat. You will be re-supplied." Al Mushani permitted himself a grin. "You will have plenty, unlike the defenders in the fort who may run out after a while."

"Why do we have to withdraw after we have taken the fort?"

"I will answer that," Ahmed Al Ghassani said softly and then took an effective pause waiting until he had all the attention. "We will take and then destroy this fort and then after we have withdrawn we will claim a complete victory. Can you imagine just how stunned the Sultan and his followers will be? We can proclaim our victory not only in this country but also throughout the whole Gulf region. But if we to try to hold Mirbat after we have taken it then it would be only a matter of time before the government forces took it back. With the amount of armament that they can muster on the ground and in the air we couldn't hope to hold it. The previous victory would then be greatly neutralised." He shook his head slowly. "Far better for our cause if we withdraw and keep our victory intact. Besides there is no real strategic value in holding what is after all just a small isolated fishing town on the eastern edge of the region."

Shortly after that the meeting was dismissed with a request from Abdel Tahir for each section Commissar to remain behind for the detail assignments of their particular sections.

Mussalim waited for the early exiters to leave. Then he got to his feet and slowly shuffled out with the rest of the crowd into the mist and drizzle. Excited chatter surrounded him as the men discussed the merits and possible flaws of the plan. He made his way away from the village towards a small tree where he knew Suhayl's band would gather beneath its canopy. Several had arrived before him and the campfire was already in the early stages of some regeneration with a large pan of water squatting in the middle.

He listened in silence as one by one the more experienced guerrillas gave their verdict of approval to the new initiative and its leaders. There was a unanimous air of satisfaction that at last the movement was taking a much more aggressive and positive role and would therefore become a more significant threat. Tea leaves and sugar was tipped into the now boiling pan of water without any pause to the conversation. An excited feeling of optimism pervaded the conversation and potential future targets were suggested for discussion. The widespread opinion was that the success of this attack would be a prelude to further successes and would therefore signal the beginning of the end for Sultan Said Bin Taymour and his regime. Only the time, which remained before the Sultanate would topple, was in dispute. Tin jugs were dipped into the boiling tea then dispensed into small handless cups and passed around. Morale was high and reverses tomorrow, or even in the future, were not even considered.

Mussalim sipped his tea quietly listening to each opinion gathering confidence in the movement's ability to win this bid for regional independence. Al Ghassani impressed him and he felt assured that he and the cause leaders could obtain the financial support needed to see the campaign through to its liberation success. The wider issue of liberation for the whole of the Gulf, however, did not particularly inspire him and he would make the decision on his future role after the Dhofar was liberated. At this particular moment he could not see himself continuing to fight on behalf of others in distant lands. But for the time being as long as the PFLOAG objectives included his own he would welcome the support that it seemed to guarantee.

The conversation was becoming exhausted by the time Suhayl arrived. He paused for a moment surveying the expectant faces then settled down in the circle. He pulled off the rag wrapped around his head and wiped his rain soaked face. His long black hair hung like strands of greased string onto his shoulders. Someone filled a cup from one of the jugs and handed it to him, he nodded acknowledgement briefly. "Listen carefully," he said and went on to explain the detail for this particular group.

The first objective was to eradicate the outpost on the high ground outside the northern perimeter wire immediately the first exploding mortar signalled the start the of the attack. After that the company was safe to advance to the perimeter wire and engage the beach fort to keep its occupants sealed within. There was to be no advance on that fort until signalled by Al Mushani to do so. That signal would not come until the first fort had been taken. After both objectives were achieved, or at Al Mushani's signal, all companies would withdraw and make their way to designated dispersal points. No pursuit was anticipated, however, as a precaution several different dispersal points had been allocated. From there further instructions would be issued. "Our own dispersal point is back here at Jibjat," Suhayl said.

"How do we get to Mirbat? Ziad asked.

"By truck tonight."

"By truck?"

"Yes, two trucks. Loaned by a couple of villagers," his grin suggested that they had probably been loaned under some intimidation. "They will carry us to a spot just outside Mirbat and from there we will move forward on foot before dawn. The trucks will shuttle backwards and forwards into the night until everybody has been moved. Then after that they will carry the Salalah attack team to their position."

"When do we go?" Ali asked.

"As soon as we have been fed. His voice relaxed a little, "tonight the villagers feed us. Even as we speak they slaughter goats and prepare a feast."

Mussalim considered in silence what that feast must be costing the impoverished people of Jibjat. Everyone would be expected to contribute something and that would probably mean some families would have to go hungry for a while. Including the drovers there were over two hundred mouths to be fed. His face must have betrayed his thoughts

"Don't feel sorry for them, it's the least they can do. Tomorrow you could die fighting for their liberation." Suhayl said looking directly at Mussalim.

"What about the drovers?"

"They are going back to the Yemen. They leave tonight in two separate parties and by two different routes." He grinned, the scar twisting his face. "If you want to keep your camels," he said addressing the group, "find a villager to look after them while you're away. When they go they're likely to take with them any loose camels they can find."

Mussalim considered that was probably good advice then he thought about Suhayl's previous remark. For the first time he began to consider the personal danger associated with the coming attack. Later tonight after he had made all his arrangements he would leave the camp find a concealed place and then make secret prayers for Allah's protection

* * *

Abdulla bent and picked up another thin staff from the pile at his feet. His head throbbed mercilessly when he straightened making him groan quietly. He stood still for a moment until the throbbing receded to a more bearable ache. Then silently pledging that never again would he touch the mad man's grass, he laid it horizontally into the top edge of the rondaaval fence he was creating and wove it tightly through the upright sticks.

He had risen late this morning attempting to sleep off the effects of last nights over indulgence. When he had eventually got from his bed Jokha had dutifully, but disapprovingly silent, laid before him a bowl of cold rice and goat meat for his breakfast. It was re-cycled from last night's meal and the grease thick set. The very sight of it made his stomach churn but trying to disguise his afflicted condition he had attempted to eat some of it. His deception must have been a little convincing at least, because it was at that point that both Jokha and Kathya had judged it as the suitable time to raise the subject of Lailla's emerging maturity. In no mood for a protracted discussion and since he had previously arrived at the same conclusion himself, he gave in easily. He agreed to an early trip into Salalah to purchase the material so that more appropriate dresses could be made for her. Then he made a quick escape to suffer his agony in private with the excuse that he needed to continue the work on the new rondaaval.

He bent tentatively and selected another pole. With well-practised swings of his khunjar he trimmed the sappy side branches and then lopped off the end at about the right length. This was pushed in on top of the other except it was woven into the upright sticks on the opposite sides. He gave the fence a brief shake to test its durability and gazed absent-mindedly across grassland into the mist as he did.

The day was nearing noon and a heavily filtered sun glimmered white and pale through the mist. The persistent drizzle had for the moment stopped, but everything around him lay sodden and heavy with rainwater. He had seen more Khareefs than he could count, but each one seemed to have been just that little bit colder and that little bit wetter than the preceding one. There was in all probability very little difference, but to him it seemed as if they got just that little bit harder, particularly in recent years. He was getting old, he acknowledged and he wondered just how many more Khareefs there would be for him. His age he didn't know for sure, perhaps somewhere around fifty, he guessed. Whatever the accuracy was, he knew that he was within a mere handful of years of the expected life span for a jebally. Perhaps he would survive another ten years, perhaps not. That was in the hands of Allah.

He sighed heavily and wished that Mussalim had not left. His duty as the eldest son was to be here easing his burden and taking on more and more of the family responsibilities, until eventually he would become the family head. Perhaps, he would soon learn the futility of the quest, which he now pursued and quickly come home. But that was a delusive hope he concluded, and he dismissed it almost instantly. Mussalim was a proud and stubborn young man and would not give in until all hopes of success were gone, or he was dead. The burden of family responsibility would fall more and more onto the second son, Juma. Perhaps if Mussalim had, like Juma, found himself a woman that he wanted he would be more concerned with developing his own home and less concerned with this sterile struggle for the illusory better life.

In an instant he saw Juma's desire for the Ruwas woman as a method of guaranteeing that he at least would stay loyal and close to the family. If he could get this woman for him, he could then use the money that was left from that which Mussalim had given him and build Juma a marital home close by. That should ensure that he did not follow his brother's example. However, the problem of differing tribes still remained, but it was not an impossible situation – perhaps something could be worked out. Even if it couldn't then the plan was still good. All that was needed would be to find Juma an alternative woman from within Al Hamer. Abdulla knew, however, that Juma would not be content with another until all hopes of possessing the Ruwas woman had gone. So he would have to go through the motions even if it would prove to be a completely fruitless exercise.

He decided that this coming Friday he would dress himself in his best jebally outfit and find Khamisa Bint Talib's father and present his credentials. At the same time he would take both wives with him and leave them in Salalah where they would enjoy buying material for Lailla's more suitable dresses.

It was an astute plan he thought smugly and its shrewdness made him feel quite pleased with himself. Feeling just a little bit better, he turned his attention back to the pile of poles at his feet and selected another.

* * *

From a few yards behind him Kathya paused and watched her husband gazing into the mist lost in contemplation. She smiled to herself, it would take a very long time before the fence would be finished at that rate, she thought. She didn't disturb his meditation. She turned instead and continued along the path towards the copse where she would find Lailla and the goats.

Abdulla was a good man and a good husband. He could not be considered a particularly good-looking man by any stretch of imagination, but he never beat her or Jokha, nor did he make them work too hard. He demanded only obedience and servility and in return they were well treated. She appreciated the sufficiency of her marital situation and she did not intentionally intend to do anything that would jeopardise her place.

Thoughtfully she pressed her hand on her stomach trying to detect through her fingers if there really was a child within. She was more than three weeks late with her period and if she did not start within the next four or five days she could be certain. Physical agonies of the last two childbirths still burned fresh in her memory. Both babies were born dead and on both occasions she had almost died with them.

Within the first year of her marriage she had given Abdulla his third son, Hamed. She had failed to carry their next child the following year but the year after, Lailla had been born. On both occasions immediately after those births she had used salt in her vagina; she had been told by the older tribal women that it caused contraction and that would please her husband and keep him interested. She didn't know whether or not that was true but she feared that Abdulla's loss of interest would result in the dreaded trip to the local *Mullah*. His simple declaration of divorce would then leave her with neither shelter nor support. So in case it was true she had done it. After all what harm would it do? Since then, however, she had heard a different opinion that the salt treatment caused scar tissue to form and subsequent babies would find their exit blocked by inflexible tissue. Now she feared that this might account for the agonies of the last two failed births.

Her last pregnancy had been almost five years ago and she had become complacent mistakenly believing that either Abdulla had become sterile or perhaps she had suffered some sort of womb damage which now prevented her becoming pregnant. She now feared that perhaps she had been mistaken and she was racked with indecision. Should she tell Abdulla? He would probably demand that she have the baby despite the risk to her own life. Perhaps she should keep it from him and find some method of starting a miscarriage. However, if he were to find out then he would probably be furious and the consequences too alarming to contemplate. However, she did not have to make the decision just yet and she decided to wait one more week and see what would happen. Perhaps the problem would resolve itself. "Please Allah," she muttered.

She was nearing the copse and she let out a shrill piercing warble. A similar reply came from the trees to her left as Lailla indicated her position.

✳ ✳ ✳

It was dark by the time Mussalim led his camel on foot into Jibjat village. The mist had thickened as soon as the sun had set and now it clamped the village in a cold and wet cover. The narrow streets and alleyways were quiet and deserted with only an occasional tiny chink of light leaking through the wood window shutters. To leave the guerrilla camp, he had used the valid excuse that he needed to place his camel in the care of a villager. Hidden in thick mist between the camp and the village he had made his secret prayer to Allah. Now, with his new bolt-action rifle hanging on his shoulder, as a prestige symbol, he wandered aimlessly along the slender paths between the crude shanty buildings seeking a potential caretaker. With the villagers either observing some curfew, which he did not know about, or simply taking refuge in the comparative security of their homes, it was not proving to be an easy task.

He stopped a moment absent-mindedly patting the animal's neck while he pondered what he should do. As he stood in the dark alleyway between two tall sandstone walls he heard a tiny sound of movement and he listened intently for it to be repeated. He had almost dismissed it as his mistake when it came again but this time more pronounced and he was able to place the sounds to the other side of one of the walls. Tugging on the camel's bridle he moved a few paces down the wall until he came to a solid and heavy old wood gate. He looped the reins through an iron ring bolted into the wall for just that purpose and pushed open the gate. The rusty hinge creaked fiercely as it swung open and he stepped inside. Goats scattered to all four corners of the small yard as he did and his instant reaction was disappointment as he attributed the sounds he had heard to simply goat movement. However, a voice demanded, "Who's there?"

At the end of the small yard was single storey sandstone building with two shuttered windows either side of a heavy roughly constructed door. Just to the fore of this door stood an old man. He wore a *dish-dasht*, which had once been white but now grey and grimy. His white hair was long and unkempt, as was the beard which hung right down onto his chest.

"Peace be with you." Mussalim said as he moved towards him and held out his hand to be shaken.

The old man looked at the rifle slung on Mussalim's shoulder and nervously muttered the customary reply. "And with you."

It was obvious that because of the rifle he was recognised as one of the PFLOAG. "Are you well?" Mussalim continued the Arabic protocol of politeness trying to appease the old man's fear and suspicion.

"Praise be to Allah."

Even in the darkness Mussalim could see the alarm that immediately came to the old man's face as he realised his verbal slip. "Praise be to Allah," he replied. At the old man's feet was an old dilapidated prayer mat and the thonged flip-flops placed neatly by its side indicated to Mussalim that he had interrupted his prayers. "Please continue your prayer. I will wait over there." He indicated back towards the gate.

The old man shook his head vigorously. "I wasn't praying!" he hotly denied.

Mussalim placed a sympathetic hand on the old man's shoulder. "*Shaffer,*" he used a title of respect, "It's alright. I will not tell, please continue." Then he turned and went over to the gate sat down and waited.

The old man stared after him a few moments trying to decide if it were some kind of perverse trick and then, dubiously at first, he went back to his interrupted prayer. When he had finished he pushed his feet into the flip-flops came to where Mussalim sat and with typical Arabic politeness invited Mussalim into his home. After a moment's hesitation he nodded acceptance. He looped the rifle from his shoulder and after removing the magazine he propped it against the door.

It was dark inside, lit inadequately by a single paraffin lamp hanging from the low ceiling. In the corner an incense burner smouldered and the air was heavy with the pungent odour of frankincense. The stone floor would have been bare but for a worn carpet constructed from goatskins in the room centre. Two women sat cross-legged on this carpet and they looked up with surprise at Mussalim when he entered. The old man following closely on his heels spoke reassuringly and both women covered their heads and then getting up silently from the carpet they retired to the gloom of a corner and sat on an old wooden chest.

Then the old man with a motion of his arm invited Mussalim to sit on the carpet. When both men had settled the old man introduced himself as Ghulam of the tribe Mahru. Mussalim then introduced himself and although he was impatient to find a carer for his animal he restrained himself and proceeded unhurriedly through the polite and practised protocol. As the pleasantries were exchanged a jug of goat's milk was placed on the carpet by one of the women and a small tin cup was offered to Mussalim. He took it and held it out while she filled it from a small ladle, which she dipped in the jug.

"This is my only daughter, Jumaia." Ghulam said.

Mussalim looked up and offered Jumaia a smile and a brief nod.

"She has now reached the age of child bearing and I must find her a husband," he went on. "Do you have any wives?"

Mussalim shook his head, "no."

"She is a pretty girl," Ghulam said and instructed her to lower her veil.

Her face was square with high cheekbones, thin lips and a small narrow nose. Her brown eyes stared downwards with modesty at the milk jug. Although very young, probably only just into her teenage years, Mussalim had to agree that her father was right – she was pretty. "Yes, she is," he agreed. Then still looking at the girl said. "Your father will soon find a husband for you Jumaia."

Her eyes met Mussalim's for the first time and for a few moments held. Then she lowered them and muttered a polite, 'Thank you.'

"Are you looking for a wife," Ghulam asked.

"No, not at the moment," Mussalim laughed to cover his own embarrassment. "But what I am looking for is someone to take care of my camel until I return," He cleverly changed the subject and arrived at his objective.

"That's no problem. I'll look after your camel while you're away," Ghulam said dismissing the task as if it were inconsequential. "How long will you be away?"

Mussalim shrugged, "Should be back late tomorrow or early the day after. *Inshaallah*," he muttered as an after thought.

The old man stared at him thoughtfully and then nodded agreement. "If what I have heard today is true then truly that is in the hands of Allah."

Mussalim offered no comment instead he changed the topic and offered to pay Ghulam for his service. Despite the impoverished surroundings in which he lived he seemed to be offended at the offer of money. Mussalim hastily apologised and expressed his gratitude at his host's kindness.

The girl returned with pieces of coconut on a wooden platter and offered it to Mussalim and, as courtesy demanded, he took a piece, but tactfully he selected the smallest.

His objective achieved Mussalim was now anxious to rejoin his comrades before they left for Mirbat without him, however, he was once again careful not to let his impatience show. He sipped his milk and ate his coconut while the old man talked about his life. He had taken three wives and two had succumbed to some disease and had died, as had four of his nine children. Of the remaining five, four were now young men with families of their own and Jumaia, the only surviving daughter, was the youngest. Mussalim listened attentively, making occasional nods and comments where it was appropriate. He understood only too well the under nutrition which made the poor particularly vulnerable to illness and disease. As soon as it was polite to do so he began to make excuses to leave. Ghulam as the perfect host appeared genuinely sorry that he had to leave and as they made a departing handshake he covered Mussalim's hand with his other hand in a gesture of affection and then he said. "You are not like those other men. Why are you with them?"

"But I am *Shaffer*. I believe in the same things as they do. We must free this region of Bin Taymour and claim our own independence."

"Is this Sultan any worse than the masters you serve?"

"This Sultan cares nothing for anybody but himself. People starve and he does nothing except extend his own extravagant life style," Mussalim replied hotly.

"Maybe so," the old man said quietly. "But he does not impose his will by cruelty and threats like the people you serve."

Mussalim could feel his temper rising but he did not reply. Instead he pulled his hand from Ghulam's clasp and turned to go.

"Jumaia, see our guest to the gate and bring his camel into the yard," the old man instructed. Then he turned towards Mussalim who by now was in the open doorway and said. "Go in peace my friend and may Allah protect you."

Mussalim hesitated recognising that his anger was probably misdirected. There was truth in Ghulam's remark and it was probably that truth which had irked him. "And with you *Shaffer*," he said quietly, turning to face him. "In the future when you pray lock your gate."

Outside the cold and damp mist had not thinned and he wondered if it would be just as thick at Mirbat early tomorrow. It would be much to their advantage if it were. Jumaia shyly handed him his rifle, interrupting his thoughts. He smiled took it and slammed the magazine back into place. After hooking the weapon over his shoulder he fiddled in his pocket then taking her hand he thrust in a few rupees before closing her fingers over the notes.

She shook her head. "Father will be angry," and she offered them back.

"Then don't tell him," he replied, ignoring the outstretched hand.

They walked slowly to the gate. "How old are you Jumaia," Mussalim asked as he unlooped the rein from the iron ring.

She shrugged, "I don't know for sure. I think I may be around fifteen."

Mussalim doubted that she was even as old as that. "If it is Allah's will that I don't return then tell your father that he may use my camel as part of your wedding dowry."

"I will pray for your safe return."

"Thank you." He handed her the reins. "I should be back late tomorrow or early the day after. *Inshaallah.*" He hesitated, a little reluctant to leave, then finding no excuse to stay he said, "*masalaama,*" turned on his heel and walked into the mist.

Twenty men huddled silently together in the darkness behind the large square mausoleum of Mohamed Agyl, Mirbat's famous pirate son. The other side of the tomb a hundred metres up a steep hill was the forward outpost of the town's defenders. Sometimes its black pill box shape would be visible silhouetted against the night sky and sometimes it would be swallowed completely in the swirling mist. Mussalim sat cross-legged with his back to the tomb and his propped rifle leaning against his chest. He listened to the agitated sea, just metres away, throwing itself around in a cauldron of agitation before it hurled itself fizzing onto the beach. Now as he waited for the attack to start he was ice calm in complete contrast to the tension he had experienced when he had climbed into the back of the truck at Jibjat.

Both trucks had begun to ferry the men to within close proximity of Mirbat a couple of hours after dark. The small trucks overloaded with men and equipment and handicapped by a road which was little more than a rough and winding track had taken almost three hours to make the thirty kilometre round trip. The movement was handicapped further when one of the overloaded trucks had dropped into a deep rut and had broken a half-shaft just before it reached the destination the second time. It was at least an hour after midnight before Mussalim and the others in Suhayl's section had climbed aboard the remaining truck. His stomach churned with nervousness and the blood pounded in his ears and despite the jarring and jolting ride he found himself hoping that the journey would not end. But end it did when it descended the steep mountainside onto the plain one and half hour later and still some four or five kilometres north of the town. Suhayl led his team on foot along the beach until within a kilometre of the outpost and had then taken Ali and scouted forward. Ali had returned alone and led the rest forward quietly to the tomb where Suhayl was waiting. Wasting no time he immediately took four men forward to new positions and now in the dark and dank mist and listening to the ocean's sounds of anger they waited in tense silence for his return.

He appeared suddenly from around the side of the mausoleum and gesticulated that all should rise. He waited until everyone was ready then indicating silence by putting his finger to his lips he led the way quietly forward. They skirted beach side of the hill until they came to a shallow wadi little more than a ditch. Then, crawling in the water trickling in its base, they made their way along the bottom of the hill until they were less than forty metres from the outpost. Suhayl now began to disperse the party in twos at intervals of a few metres. Half of the force had been dispersed before he indicated that Mussalim and another should remain at this particular spot. He watched the rest crawl away into the darkness then gingerly he peered over the edge at the outpost.

For the first time he had a clear view of the heavily constructed pillbox perched on the very apex of the short steep hill. It was perhaps six or seven metres square with narrow horizontal slots from which the defenders could shoot with comparative safety. To the side of the concrete construction, a heavily sandbagged sangar protected a formidable looking machine weapon. The weapon itself lay backwards on its tripod with its barrel pointing idly skywards. Mussalim peered hard into the darkness attempting to confirm in his mind that it was in fact a machine gun. At the briefing Salim Al Mushani had quickly dismissed the suggestion that there would be machine guns. He now confirmed in his mind that it was and that Salim had been badly mistaken. Lower down the slopes protecting the outpost were two double rows of concertina razor wire. Nothing visible moved within its compound suggesting perhaps that it were deserted. However, the very sight of the skyward pointing gun barrel indicated otherwise. It was, Mussalim feared, not an easy objective and the nervous churning returned to his stomach. He took his rifle and pumped a round into the breach and waited apprehensively.

He looked for the first tinge of redness in the eastern sky but the mist reduced visibility and blanked out even the distant towering jebal. His clothes were wet from the crawl up the ditch and in the cold morning mist he began to shiver. The waiting continued endlessly and his tension increased with every minute until he began to ache with a fervent desire to hear the first mortar explode and signal the start of the attack.

When the action did begin it took him completely by surprise making his whole body jerk with shock. It didn't begin with the expected burst of a mortar shell. Instead it came close by in the form of automatic rifle fire, shouts and screams from above him in the outpost. The shouting ceased and the rifle fire became sporadic until after two or three minutes it ceased completely.

At first Mussalim kept his head down in the ditch until his curiosity could be contained no longer. Cautiously, he raised his head and peered into the gloom. Nothing that he could see moved and, except for the background noise of the nearby ocean, silence had once more settled all around him. Everything seemed just as it had been before. Mystified he glanced at the man lying in the ditch close by. He caught his glance and responded with a simple baffled shrug. In the darkness he waited, peering towards the pillbox trying to find some clue and apply some reason to what had just occurred. Eventually a shadowy figure emerged from the vicinity of the concrete building and moved towards the concertina wire.

"Come on. Come forward," he shouted waving his arm in a beckoning motion. "Come on," he called again.

One by one and cautiously at first men began to stand up and then move slowly up the hill towards the wire. Mussalim glanced around at the wary advance and then followed their example. When the first men reached the wire they were directed along the wire and around the side to the chicaned entrance into the small compound.

Inside, five men stood casually beside a narrow upright sentry box while behind them completely disregarded a figure lay prostrate on the ground. Suhayl stood with them and greeted the arrivals with a self-satisfied grin, his facial scar twisting it out of proportion on one side. He turned and prodded the motionless form behind him with his foot.

"This was the guard. The lazy bastard was sleeping. Well now he can sleep forever."

Five or six men shuffled forward to stare down curiously at the body. Mussalim at the back of the group peered over their shoulders to get his first sight of a dead enemy. There wasn't much to see, the body lay face down and it looked almost as if the man slept.

"We killed him in his sleep with our Khunjars. There are another five in there," Suhayl said and nodded towards the pillbox. "We burst in on them and woke em up and then put them back to sleep with bullets," he laughed derisively. "And that my friends is our first objective secured. Easy!"

"But," someone tried to frame a question.

"Yes?"

"Wasn't we supposed to wait for the mortar bombardment."

"If we had then they would have all been alert and it would have been long and difficult to get them out.

"But now both forts have been alerted."

"So what? They're going to know very soon anyway." He pushed through the circle. "Let's move on down to wire and to Mirbat," he said his voice raised in encouragement. "And on to a glorious PFLOAG victory." Even as they turned and began to shuffle along behind him, the first mortar shells exploded somewhere inside the town's defensive circle.

The ground immediately in front of the concertina wire was flat and exposed so they took position among the rocks at the foot of the small hill and waited. The mortar shells continued to fall indiscriminately inside the defensive compound with deep and muffled thumps. Whether it was because of the limited vision of the mortar operator's firing from deep positions in the jebal foothills or just poor aiming Mussalim wasn't sure. But as far as he could see all the instantaneous fountains of sand and stone seemed to be erupting in the harmless sterile area.

The first glimmers of daylight in the eastern sky began to weaken the darkness and Mussalim peered through the gloom at the defensive positions. To his front and less than two hundred metres away was the beach fort. It was perhaps ten or eleven metres high with two stubby towers both on the western wall protecting the gate beneath and facing out towards the sea. Forty-five degrees to his left more than three hundred metres away and occupying the high ground a much larger and more substantial fort with one tall tower on the northeast corner. Its strategic position commanded a full clear view of the whole defensive wire. Deeper back behind the forts and towards the rear of the compound were the simple brick and mud houses of the Mirbat inhabitants. Unlike the sketch on the blackboard at the briefing these forts now looked formidable objectives to Mussalim.

His study of the defensive positions was interrupted by a slap on the shoulder from Suhayl. He thrust a pair of canvas gloves and a pair of wire cutters in his hand. "Go with Ziad and cut some gaps in the wire," he said.

He glanced at Ziad and the two other men crouching behind Suhayl. He nodded and reached for his rifle. Suhayl's hand grasped his arm. "Leave that here it will only slow you down."

They left the cover of the rocks and crouching over they moved forward cautiously. When they reached the wire they lay flat on the ground while Ziad took the time to study his options. Just lying there exposed as he was Mussalim felt particularly vulnerable and with every passing second he expected to come under fire from the nearest fort, but still Ziad waited. The swirling mist moved languidly over the ground drifting lazily from the sea in small banks. When he judged the mist between them and the fort was thick enough, Ziad leapt to his feet with a cry of, "Now," and he began to furiously cut at the circles of razor wire.

Mussalim followed his example and standing at Ziad's side he too began frenetically cutting the thick strands of wire. Expecting at any moment to feel the thump of a bullet his haste was desperate, consequently the care to avoid the wire's sharp barbs was non-existent. While they cut the wires the other two men looped a rope through the coils. As soon as the last strands were cut they hauled frantically bending the free end back at a sharp angle and creating a four metres gap in the wire defence. Their task completed they took off back to the security of the rocks at a sprint.

Back in cover they lay panting heavily, trying to recover from the taxing sprint. Mussalim, still breathing heavily raised his bloody arms slowly to inspect the ugly slashes. He rubbed each sore arm carefully and then apathetically let them drop, thinking that it was perhaps a small price to pay for a speedy escape which may have saved his life.

Suhayl appeared as if by magic "How many gaps did you make?" he asked Ziad raising his voice to be heard above the exploding thumps of the mortar shells.

"One," Ziad gasped.

"One?" Suhayl said derisively. "What do you think will happen when we try to go through that gap?"

Ziad stared back without replying.

"They'll concentrate fire and cut as down like dogs. That's what will happen. Now get back out there and cut at least two more." He glared at Ziad a moment and then turned towards the rest. "All of you," he demanded aggressively.

Barely recovered they got wearily back to their feet and set off for the razor wire once more. This time they split into two pairs with Ziad going down the wire towards the beach and Mussalim in the opposite direction. Just when it seemed that once again they might be able to achieve the task undetected the rapid rattle of machine gun fire came from the beach fort.

Mussalim froze then glanced hastily around for evidence that the bullets were coming in his direction. Not seeing any he looked towards the fort and followed the lights of the tracer speeding towards Ziad and his partner. The sharp repetitive cracks installed even more urgency into Mussalim as he realised that any second he too would become a target. He had almost cut right through when the tracer started in his direction and the ground around him started to erupt with dull thuds into little dust fountains. Dropping the cutters he dived to the ground and on his hands and knees he scrambled into a shallow ground indentation which gave him barely any cover. He covered his head with his hands and pressed himself down attempting to make himself as small a target as possible. The wire started to hum as some of the flying projectiles clipped and severed it on their way through. He could do nothing except wait in dread for the inevitable bullet to find its mark.

The wire stopped humming and little dust fountains around him stopped erupting but the rattle continued. Could it be that the gunner thought he had hit him and passed on to a new target? He lifted an elbow and glanced around. His partner had, in blind panic, taken flight back towards the safety of the rocks and because of his exposed situation he had become the gunners new target. It seemed it would be only a matter of seconds before he would be cut down but, miraculously, his luck continued to hold. From the cover of the rocks, Suhayl and the rest of the company now opened fire on the fort with rapid firing automatic weapons. The intensity forced the machine gunner to hesitate and then to change his target once again and spray the rocks. The fleeing man made the sanctuary.

Mussalim, for the moment at least, was ignored and he looked around for the wire cutters which he had dropped.

With his heart pounding like a jackhammer he crawled on his belly as fast as he could to the partially severed concertina wire. When he got there, still on his belly, he reached up and continued to snip through the remaining wires. It took very little imagination to realise that the air just above him would be full of criss-crossing lead missiles so he worked keeping his body as low as possible. When he had cut the last wire he looped the rope through the coiled wire and crawled away dragging the ends with him. Then turning onto his back he pulled on the ropes. With a series of gut wrenching pulls he fed the rope over his body moving the free end of the wire fence just a few inches at a time. He had opened only a small gap of a couple of metres when he decided that he had pressed his luck to its extreme and that he should attempt to get to the sanctuary of the rocks. He jumped to his feet and stooping low he ran as fast as his panic motivated legs would carry him.

He threw himself down behind the first suitable piece of rock that he came to gasping for breath and muttering breathless prayers to Allah for his deliverance. He lay for a couple of minutes on his back looking up and listening to the deafening cracks of the rifle fire all around him. The mayhem of noise from the weapons hurt his ears and made them whine at high pitch. At some point the day had taken charge and now it was light, the mist still swirled but because of the improved lighting it was less dense. When he had recovered sufficiently he began crawling back to the rock where he had left his rifle.

He got back to his original spot and found the man who had gone to the wire with him. He crouched over in terror with his arms locked around his automatic Kalachnikov. Mussalim's anger exploded and he grabbed a handful of his shirt and hauled him towards him intending to berate the man for his desertion. However, one glance at the man's terrified expression and rolling eyes and his ire evaporated. He let go of his shirt and placed a consoling hand on his shoulder instead. He eased himself slowly upwards to peer over the rock lip.

The beach fort was under intense fire from Suhayl's section here in the rocks. However the return fire, aided by that Browning, was just as intense and the air all around was full of the thuds of bullets and whining ricochets. The mortars continued to rain down inside the defensive compound mostly in the vicinity of the larger fort on the high ground. The fort walls bore scars that at least some of the mortar fire had been accurate. However, several fires burning in among the melange of Mirbat houses further behind indicated inconsistency. The fort was also under intense fire from the main strike force gathered at the bottom of the hill on the eastern perimeter wire, but by the tracers streaking towards the attacker's position its return looked to be at least comparable. The battle was in its early stages and even at this point it was furious.

Mussalim slid back down behind the rock. Many men would die here today, he thought pessimistically and he wondered if there was after all perhaps some other way to free the Dhofar from this despotic Sultan. Theories, however, didn't matter at this precise moment – victory was all that was important. Only a handful of such victories might be all that was needed to make Said Bin Taymour retreat northwards and abandon this region to the Dhofari people. He reached across the still cringing man for his rifle, got to his feet and added his own fire to that of his comrades on the beach fort.

He peered down his sights through the grey mist waiting for shadowy targets to appear in among the battlements before taking hasty aim and snapping of a quick shot. Suhayl was right, at this range it was impersonal and unemotional – all the targets were abstract figures. He continued to concentrate his attention on the fort repetitively seeking, aiming and firing having no way of knowing if he had managed to hit any of his targets. His concentration was absolute until he felt Suhayl's hand on his shoulder. He slid back down under the rock's cover.

"Out there at the wire! You did well, jebally," he said. Then he looked unemotionally at the other man still skulking in the safety of the rock's cover. "Give me your rifle," he said to Mussalim.

Mussalim a little puzzled handed it to him.

He raised himself up a little and appeared to be examining it. Then, suddenly, using the stock end he butted it forcefully into the side of the man's head. "Coward," he spat.

The man toppled onto his side closing his eyes and holding the side of his head.

Suhayl snatched the automatic weapon from his grasp. "Such a weapon belongs in the hands of a soldier not a coward." He tossed the weapon forcefully at Mussalim. "Here soldier take this."

Mussalim stared down at the Kalachnikov and then back with surprise at Suhayl.

Suhayl still glaring at the other man settled at Mussalim's side. "Safe," he pointed at the small lever, "single shot and rapid-fire." He indicated the three positions. He pushed the lever fully over to the rapid-fire position. "When you fire, say one two then stop. One two, stop," he repeated. "You will have fired five or six cartridges in that time" He then showed him how to unclip and re-clip the magazine. "OK then jebally go to it and welcome to the cause." He glared at the other man still prone and holding the side of his head, he stared sheepishly back. "You use that 303," he pointed at the discarded rifle. "And you had better use it well, because I'm going to see you later." He got to his feet, tossed Mussalim a spare magazine, and hitched his own automatic weapon more comfortably on his shoulder. Then waiting for a suitable opportunity he prepared to make a dash for the next rock.

"Suhayl!"

"Yes?" he waited.

"Ziad?'

"They made it back. Ziad caught one in the arm but he'll be OK."

Mussalim nodded.

Then keeping low Suhayl dashed to the next covering rock.

He watched him dash from cover to cover, then looked at the man by his side. "What's your name?"

"Yaqub," he replied.

"Come, Yaqub," he said encouraging the man to stand and fire at the fort.

Nervously the man got to his feet and followed his example.

The status quo of mortar bombardment, fire and return fire continued without abate until the expected aircraft arrived. The drone of their engines could be heard long before they came into view. A pair of piston engine Provost fighters appeared suddenly out of the mist coming in off the sea. They swept in side by side and passed low over the forts and on towards the jebal. One banked sharply left while the other continued on for a little way before following its example. They both disappeared into the mist and Mussalim strained his ears and searched the misty skies for their re-appearance. The engine drone started faintly and became increasingly louder until one appeared out from the mist from precisely the same direction as before. As it passed low overhead Suhayl leapt to his feet and began spraying the sky in its direction. The second aircraft followed close behind and Suhayl then turned his attention to that one shouting something inaudible as he did. Mussalim followed his example, as did several others. If they inflicted any damage at all it wasn't evident as both aircraft swept on towards the jebal where they strafed the mortar positions. They swooped low over the positions with their cannons blazing then climbed steeply to disappear into the mist only to re-appear moments later to repeat the operation. Mussalim could not see the results of the attacks because the hill at his back blocked his view, but he could plainly hear the loud drones of the engines as each aircraft dived into attack. Again and again those dives were repeated and Mussalim could imagine the destruction and mayhem being delivered by those two planes. The shelling from the jebal had ceased under the weight of the aircraft's repeated attacks and only sporadic shells now burst inside the defence compound discharged from somewhere within the town precincts. Eventually, the aircraft disappeared into the mist and did not return, their cannons, presumably, exhausted.

Now providing Mohammed Bin Talib has done his part with the attack on the airfield those aircraft won't be back, Mussalim reflected as he settled once more to put the nearest fort back under fire.

The mortar bombardment continued after a short pause but much more sporadically. Whether that was because of damage inflicted by the aircraft or that the supplies were beginning to run down Mussalim could only guess, however, it was noticeably less intense.

The stalemate continued with very little change and with no sign of any significant progress by the attackers. From behind Mussalim and Yaqub two men hopped from cover to cover cautiously making their way towards them. When they eventually arrived they handed the pair a generous re-supply of cartridges. At the same time they passed a message reminding them that their particular objective was to keep the beach fort defenders locked inside and that although they should keep the beach fort under fire they should conserve ammunition. Then they continued onwards dodging from cover to cover to re-supply others. Mussalim switched his weapon to single fire and then he and Yaqub took spells of around ten minutes each to fire at the fort.

During one of his rest periods, Mussalim, sitting with his back to the rock and refilling his spare magazine, looked skywards and through a hole in the mist caught sight of the white Beaver of the Sultan's Air Force circling above the battle zone. It was obviously carrying out reconnaissance duties and reporting the situation. He wondered if it was the same aircraft that he had watched from the jebal above Salalah only seven days ago. He reflected that so much had happened in that short period. He wondered what his father's reaction would be if he knew that at this moment his eldest son was taking part in an open attack on the fort at Mirbat. The fort was inconsequential, he recognised that it was only a symbol of the Sultan's authority. The mere fact that an attack of this nature was taking place forcefully registered the anger of the Dhofari people directed at the Sultan and that their tolerance to his imposition of poverty was at an end. It was not an attack on Mirbat, it was an attack aimed directly at Said Bin Taymour. He picked up his canteen and took a long drink of water, then after replacing the stopper he got to his feet tapped Yaqub on his shoulder indicating that it was time to change over.

The Provost fighters returned sweeping in low in single file from out of the mist on the sea. This time they passed directly over the high ground fort before wheeling and diving at the main assault force assembled on the eastern perimeter wire. Mussalim watched in helpless silence and listened with mounting anger to the cheers from the occupants inside the forts. The aircraft were by modern standards vintage equipment, nevertheless their effect was devastating since the attackers had absolutely no defence. Time and again they wheeled and passed low above the heads of the attackers with cannons ablaze distributing mutilation and death among the mass of his comrades. When their cannons were spent they broke off the slaughter and headed once more for base, presumably to reload. One headed for the sea flying directly towards Mussalim's position. He stood upright, leapt onto a nearby mound in rage and pointed his weapon directly at the brown and sand coloured approaching aircraft. He could see clearly the two men sitting side by side in the wide cockpit as it passed low and almost directly overhead. He squeezed the trigger and shouted to Allah to guide his bullets. He fired one round only. He pulled harder on the trigger with no results and then the plane was gone. In frustration he threw the weapon down as he realised that it was in single fire mode.

He stood and stared across the battlefield towards the eastern wire not noticing that he was an exposed target and the thuds of bullets all around him. He could only guess at the carnage that had been dispensed, but by the cheers which were still audible from that fort's defenders he assumed that it must have been significant. Angrily he recovered his weapon, at least he could do something about silencing the cheers. He pushed the lever into automatic fire position and without taking particular aim blasted away in the direction of the larger fort until his magazine was empty. He ducked back behind the rock's cover and picked up his spare magazine. He was slamming it into position on his weapon when Suhayl arrived.

"Calm down Mussalim Bin Abdulla you will only get yourself killed," he said with a grin. "You're no use to us dead and we need men like you."

"Those planes wasn't supposed to be back. What happened to Mohammed's attack on the airfield?"

"I don't know… could be a hundred things. Maybe this time they won't be back."

"It was a slaughter!"

"Perhaps not. We can't tell from here."

"They must have been caught defenceless."

"Perhaps. Be thankful that you were not over on that side."

Shaking his head sadly Mussalim said. "Are we achieving anything?"

"Listen," Suhayl said cocking his head. "What do you hear?"

Mussalim listened expecting to hear the drone of those aircraft engines again. "Nothing only the sound of gunfire."

"That's right," he said getting to his feet and peering over the rock's lip by Yaqub's side. "The mortars have stopped."

Mussalim stood between the pair and gazed across the battlefield wondering what the significance was.

"Don't you see?" Suhayl said. "They're about to make an assault on the fort."

They waited in silence looking through the mist towards the fort trying to glean some clue as to what may be happening. After what seemed an age, they heard the sound of massed yelling voices followed instantaneously by intense gunfire from the fort defenders. The direct attack had, it seemed, started out of their sight up the steep hill on the eastern side of the fort. The intense defensive barrage was led by the daunting cracks of a fort machine gun from the fort tower as it sprayed its lethal payload of indiscriminate death across the advancing men. Mussalim stared numbly across the battlefield, his impassive expression belying the horror which was mounting inside as he imagined the probable carnage being inflicted on that hillside. There seemed to be no respite from the merciless salvos inflicted on the attackers as they attempted to advance up the exposed hill towards the fort. The fusillade eventually eased and once again cheering started inside the fort and this time jeers accompanied the cheers.

Suhayl turned away with a shrug. "Driven back," he said with indifference.

"It's those blasted machine guns," Mussalim spat angrily. "Al Mushani assured us there wouldn't be any."

"So he was wrong!"

"No. He lied."

Suhayl paused in his stride. "What did you expect him to say?" he replied angrily. "Yes there are machine guns everywhere. Would you have come if you had known?"

"Yes I would. But I had a right to know, and so did those who have just died over there."

"Right! What right? The only choices you have are to live in servile poverty and die before your time or to be here today and change things. Those that have died over there this morning – are they any worse off than those living out a shortened life of abject misery? At least there is some dignity in their death. They died protesting." He stared hard at Mussalim then turned and stomped away.

Mussalim turned and in angry frustration smashed his fist against the rock with a grunt. At this instant his hatred for the defenders in the forts, who in their ignorance propped this corrupt regime, knew no bounds. He went back to peering down his sights seeking human targets at the beach fort but this time with compassionless intention.

Eventually the massed yelling voices were heard again through the din of the surrounding gunfire indicating that a second assault was beginning. The defensive barrage was just as murderous. However, this time a handful of shadowy figures appeared at the foot of the northern wall indicating that the sterile area had been crossed. Mussalim's hopes began to rise that perhaps this time there would be some success.

The sudden sound of the aircraft's engine startled him as it passed low directly over his head and sped on towards the fort under siege. "No, he cried with dismay, "no, no." He pushed the lever to rapid fire and sent a speculative shower of bullets in pursuit of the Provost. The aircraft passed unhindered over the barren stretch between the fort and the eastern perimeter wire, its cannons spattering continuously as it did. Then it banked left and climbed steeply to disappear into the mist. The second followed moments later in hot pursuit following precisely the same path and the same strategy. For a while the men at the fort's wall held their ground, perhaps waiting for more support. Both aircraft swooped once more out of the mist and, in single file, passed again over the area with their guns blasting those unfortunates caught in the open sterile zone. As soon as they had disappeared for the second time the men under the wall broke and fled back towards the wire and the safety of any cover that might be found outside the wire's perimeter. The aircraft swooped three more times along that wire with blazing cannon before they climbed into the enveloping mist and did not return, presumably their cannons exhausted again.

Mussalim stared gloomily towards the hill fort. It was not going well. Because of its deadly machine gun the fort seemed to be invincible and those aircraft lethal. It was clear that the whole offensive was approaching the point of collapse, something needed to be done and done quickly otherwise the mission would fail. The battle lapsed once more into the stereo strategy of attackers and defenders sniping at each without further incentive from the attackers. Time wore on and as it did it seemed to Mussalim that the attack motivation was dying.

He became aware of movement behind him and watched quizzically as a number of his section began withdrawing carefully through the rocks.

"Are we withdrawing?" Yaqub asked.

Mussalim bewildered, shook his head slowly and shrugged fearing that probably they were. Eventually Suhayl appeared bobbing quickly from rock to rock and heading towards their position. He was panting hard when he reached them but took no time to recover.

"You fall back with the others," he gasped pointing at Yaqub and then indicated the direction of the retreating men. "You stay." He said to Mussalim.

"What's happening?"

Suhayl pointed along the wire. "We are taking up new position there." Mussalim waited for him to catch a breath. "The plan is to simultaneously attack the fort from both the north and the east." He blew hard. "That way we split their fire. You have an automatic weapon so you stay here." He pointed a finger towards the beach fort. "Keep their heads down," he said in a low meaningful voice. "Because when we start to advance from there we will be caught in a cross fire if you don't."

Mussalim glanced towards the fort and then along the wire towards the chicaned guard post entrance into the protected compound. He appreciated completely the consequences of not keeping those heads down. The attackers would not only face fire from directly in front when they advanced but also from the beach fort to their right.

It took a while for the force to assemble in a shallow wadi north of the overlooking fort. Its depth gave only scant cover so each man moved into position cautiously, keeping as low as possible while the fort defenders sniped at any unwitting targets that became exposed. Suhayl's small group were joined by others from the eastern wire increasing the strength to around four dozen men. Mussalim continued sniping at the beach fort keeping an eye cocked on the men in that wadi who lay waiting in its meagre cover.

The sudden loud rattle of machine gun fire close at his back startled him making him flinch involuntarily. He spun round in panic and stared up the rocky hill towards the top. Two men had mounted a Browning in amongst the rock's cover and they sent its deadly projectiles hurtling at the beach fort. Mussalim turned and, with a grin of satisfaction, watched the lines of tracer whiz towards the fortification. He glanced back to re-assure himself that the gun was truly in the hands of his friends… it was. For a moment he wondered how they had managed to get hold of it. His curiosity was only momentarily when he remembered the Browning inside the outpost compound lying back on its tripod pointing at the night sky. Of course why hadn't someone thought of it before, he mused. With encouragement now boosted he turned his concentration once more to sniping at targets within the fort on the beach.

Mussalim glanced upwards into the mist at the heavily filtered sun above. It was, he calculated, approaching midday and there had been no significant breakthrough. The successful achievement of both objectives at this moment certainly seemed remote. Even the primary target still stood resolute and the attacks so far launched had been impotent. Time was running out but still the attackers waited.

The machine gun behind him clattered in short bursts causing a similar response from the gun inside the fort in a tit for tat argument. Mussalim, staring down the rifle sights, squeezed the trigger on another potential target. The hammer clicked on an empty breach. He slid down under the cover of the rock, propped his rifle and began replenishing both of his magazines. He froze for a moment in his task and cocked an ear listening intently. Above the rattle of gunfire and steadily growing louder, he heard the unmistakable drone of those aircraft engines again. The machine gun on the ridge above him began to chatter urgently in a prolonged burst.

He scrambled to his feet and looked across the battlefield. A lone aircraft came in from the south skimming the housetops on a path between the two forts bearing straight at them. Even as Mussalim located it the pilot opened fire with his cannons and two trails of eruptions cut through the sandy ground approaching towards him rapidly. He threw himself back beneath the rocks cover and buried his head beneath his arms waiting impotent and terrified as everything around him erupted. The ground beneath him vibrated and the air was filled with choking dust and flesh tearing splinters of rock as the cannon trails passed right over him. Moments later the aircraft itself with its engine screaming at maximum revs skimmed only feet above his head rattling his nerves further. Quietness spread quickly and he slowly lifted his head from beneath his arms and listened to the rock splinters rolling into their new niches. Cautiously he got to his feet and looked around him. The dust hung thick in the air but he could see some stirrings in amongst the rocks as his stunned comrades slowly recovered. Ominously the machine gun on the ridge had fallen quiet and disappeared from Mussalim's view. Cheering began in the fort, but this time Mussalim was too dazed to react instead he pressed his fingers to the pain on his neck. He inspected his red fingers sticky with blood and assumed that he had been cut by one of the flying splinters. Still stunned and acting on instinct he began to look for his rifle and the magazines. He found them all close by and was on his knees gathering them together when he heard the aircraft's engine once more.

This time it came from the west, off the sea and zeroing in once more on the hillside. With its cannons blazing it passed along the length of the hillside. The aircraft swept on towards the men in the shallow cover of the wadi. They were completely exposed to the aircraft above and its effect was devastating as its double trail of exploding cannon shells ripped along the wadi and the exposed men huddling in there. Some, in understandable panic, leapt to their feet and began to blindly run in any direction that they happened to be facing. The aircraft, however, belched a trail of black smoke in its rear, indicating that perhaps one shot at least had found a critical working part. The pilot pulled back on his stick climbed high into the mist and wheeled away.

The damage, however, had been done. From his position Mussalim had a clear view along the wadi length and could see the effects. Men who had escaped injury crawled around trying to help those not as fortunate. Though he could not tell how many had died, or the extent of the injuries to the wounded, he estimated, by the numbers that were moving, the fighting capability of that force had probably been reduced by almost half. He wondered again about the casualties among the main attack force assembled on the eastern perimeter. That force had borne the larger responsibilities for the main attack and as such had sustained the heaviest retaliation and therefore probably the greater casualties.

He was appalled and for the first time he began to question the wisdom of the attack in his mind. It had seemed so straightforward and achievable back in the *Dirwain* tent at Jibjat. However, it seemed that nothing was going as planned. Those aircraft had not been taken out early in the offensive and they kept returning regularly with deadly consequences. In between the Browning machine guns in each fort had a devastating effect on any exposed attack and if the defenders were going to run short of ammunition at some point, as was anticipated, there was no signs of it yet.

A spray of the hillside from the machine gun in the beach fort served as a sinister reminder that it was not yet over and that his own position was exposed to their guns. He scrambled around the other side of the rock and started once again to recharge his magazines.

Before he had finished the massed yelling voices started again. He realised immediately that another fresh attack on the high ground fort had begun, he rammed the magazine in place and leapt to his feet. He couldn't see the advance up the hill on the far side but to his left those men that were still able rose from out of the wadi and advanced towards the deserted guard post which protecting the chicaned entrance into the wired compound. Mussalim pushed the lever on his Kalachnikov to automatic and sprayed the beach fort battlements with short bursts.

Despite the overworked machine gun switching alternately to fire on the advancing men from both the north and east this attack fared better and several of the attackers made it under the fort wall. The crudely constructed ladders began to appear as more men made it safely to the fort. The defenders now were forced to boldly stand and fire down on the attackers beneath, exposing themselves to snipers from the wire as they did.

Now that the smaller force attacking from the north had cleared across the area vulnerable to the crossfire, Mussalim altered his weapon sights and began to fire on the exposed defenders of the hill fort. However, he was soon forced to cease firing as the attackers began to climb the ladders and the risk of hitting his own comrades increased. The struggle had now become close range as the defenders worked desperately to prevent the wall getting breached. They used their rifle butts to push the ladders away from the battlements far enough to achieve the over balance point and then fired down on the attackers beneath feverishly. The fierce face to face struggle continued and Mussalim could only watch frustrated from his position and completely impotent to help with the struggle in the slightest. It was impossible for him to see if there had been any successful penetration from the attackers but by their persistence to continue replacing the makeshift ladders and re-attempt to scale the walls he guessed that nothing that represented any sort of toe-hold had been achieved. He turned away dejectedly slid to a sitting position behind the rock and began to recharge his magazines preparing for a time when he could once again be useful.

Several fires burned around the wall's base when next he looked, but who had started them and for what purpose he could only guess. Some attackers had moved around to the western side of the fort to attack the heavy wooden gate on that side and instantaneously they came under fire from the beach fort opposite. Mussalim saw his opportunity to be useful once more and concentrated his attention back to bringing that fort under fire attempting to give his comrades some relief.

What caused the attack to eventually falter and then break Mussalim did not know. It started with a trickle of men retreating back down the hill and rapidly increased as the fear of being left weak and stranded beneath the walls spread. As the retreat became pronounced an aircraft swooped from out of the mist and with the fort defender's loud jubilant cheers it began to pulverise the retreating men. Turning tightly at the end of each pass it swooped again and again along the eastern side of the fort blasting the attackers positions until its cannons were exhausted. Its intervention was so timely that it could only have been above the mist circling and waiting for the opportunity to distinguish defenders from attackers.

With the aircraft's departure the firing became more and more sporadic until it had almost ceased. Mussalim could see men now fall even further back deserting their position along the wire and retreating right back towards the jebal. He glanced around wondering what he should do. His comrades around him were also beginning to withdraw back up the hill towards the outpost. Whether Salim Al Mushani had ordered that the attack should cease or whether the attackers had decided that that was enough Mussalim didn't know. He glanced in turn at both forts scarred and charred, but both still stood intact. The defenders of both forts now stood erect on the battlements their arm upraised shaking their rifles and cheering. Anger burned his inside once more. 'Those ignorant fools did not realise that they stood in the way of their own independence.' But, there was absolutely nothing else that he could do except to follow his colleagues and retreat also. With tears filling his eyes and the triumphant cheers and the jeers from the defenders ringing in his ears he too began reluctantly to withdraw back up the hill. His spirits utterly depressed he clambered, none too cautiously, upward back the way he had come some eight hours previously.

As he neared the top of the hill he heard his name called. Ali, close to the top and nearby waved him towards him. Mussalim altered his direction and scrambled over to where he waited.

Ali stared at him wordlessly his body language displaying his own disappointment. He shook his head sadly and lifted his arms slightly then he let them fall in a gesture of hopelessness.

Mussalim didn't speak, he dare not. His voice would have betrayed just how close to tears he was. Instead he looked away through the thin mist back towards Mirbat, avoiding Ali's gaze in case his face betrayed him also.

"Give me a hand," Ali said. We'll take the Browning with us at least."

He had turned away and began clambering upwards towards the hillcrest. Mussalim silently followed.

The grisly evidence of the aircraft's superior power lay before him in the shape of the two prostrate and pulverised bodies that had been the two brave men who had operated the captured Browning machine gun. The gun lay close by on its side still mounted on its now bent and twisted tripod.

Ali put his foot on the tripod and attempted to pull the gun free from its stand but it refused to come apart. Mussalim moved towards him intending to help and as he did he passed close to one of the prone bodies. The body lay twisted half on its side and half on its back. He glanced down at the lifeless frame which less than two hours ago had been full of vibrant existence. Now it was just a carcass with a stunned expression, open mouth and sightless staring eyes. Disturbed by Mussalim's close proximity, a mass of flies took to the air from the dead man's chest with an angry buzz chorus. As they did they exposed a wide and deep laceration across the width of the corpse's chest. Its inner contents exhibited in a mass of varying shades of reds and pinks. An involuntary retch detonated from the bowels of Mussalim's stomach. He managed to control it by clenching his teeth and clamping his lips tight. However, there was no controlling the second more impelled retch and he vomited violently. Ali induced by Mussalim's physical revulsion tossed the gun aside and vomited also.

They dragged the gun complete with its tripod a few yards away from the mutilated bodies. Now clear of the repugnance, both men were much more composed and were able to release the machine gun from the tripod easily. Ali then handed Mussalim his Kalachnikov heaved the Browning across his shoulders and set off down the hill away from Mirbat. They followed the identical route along which they had come with such high expectations. When they reached Mohamed Agyl's tomb they left the beach and turned inland towards distant jebal. After a few minutes they crossed the muddied Mirbat road and made their way across the flat land heading directly towards the steep jebal slopes and comparative safety.

The mist was thinner now than at any previous part of the day and the visibility had greatly improved. The defeated PFLOAG forces streamed in small-scattered groups across the flat land towards the sanctuary of the mountains. Mussalim and Ali trudged on in subdued silence only exchanging muttered words when they swapped loads. Eventually they reached the foot of the jebal and the thick protective shroud of the *Ghaf* trees and shrubs. They began the laboured climb upward towards the top some two hundred metres above. The trees blanketed the whole hillside and the growth beneath was thick. They tacked left and right continually as they worked their way through the tangled undergrowth. Sometimes they were forced back downwards when nature's barriers became impassable. However, they kept on a basic ascending route and after an hour they had reached a point about two-thirds up the hillside. The lack of sleep from the night previous had been more than adequately compensated by the excess of adrenaline throughout the battle. Now with the battle ceased the adrenaline was replaced by tiredness and demoralised morale. The energy-sapping climb soon became exhaustive.

At a small clearing Mussalim stopped and allowed the heavy Browning to slip from his shoulders then he sank tiredly to the ground. "We should rest," he said.

Ali looked down the steep hillside, across the tops of the trees and shrubs to the distant Mirbat road that cut between the flat land and the beach. From their high vantage point any organised pursuit could be easily observed. Also the hillside's rugged terrain, coupled with its thick covering of low tree canopies, offered potential for ambush every few yards. It would be sheer madness for the Government forces to pursue the vanquished PFLOAG into this terrain.

"There's no danger of pursuit," Mussalim said, reading his thoughts.

Ali sank to the ground without argument and freed his shoulders from both Kalachnikov's. Then even though the light drizzle at this height had dampened the ground he lay on his back and let out an exhausted sigh.

Mussalim gazed through the thin mist over the flat land below and out to the sea. The scene was deserted. It seemed that even the last of the stragglers had made good their escape into the trees' refuge. He glanced around and listened, seeking some evidence that the hillside was thronged with men climbing the hill and retreating away from their humiliation. Although he knew that they must be all around, there was neither sight nor sound of a single human being. He gazed across the placid scene to Mirbat and could make out the crudely constructed houses stamped a darker grey than the enveloping mist. The imposing hill fort, their primary target, still stood resolute and seemingly undiminished in the foreground. From this distance and this vantage point the scene seemed pastoral and peaceful, almost as if nothing significant had even taken place. No attack, no battle, and no deaths. But there had and there had been carnage. There is no glory in battles. It is only gory with hell added, he concluded.

"It was those damned planes," he said thinking aloud angrily. "If it hadn't been for them, then it could have been so very different." He shook his head sadly and shrugged. "We had no defence against them and nowhere to hide. They absolutely destroyed us time and time again." He paused for a moment his anger returning as in his mind he sought someone to blame. "So much for Bin Talib's attack on the Salalah airbase," he retorted bitterly

"*Inshaallah*," Ali replied quietly.

He glanced sharply at his still prostrate companion. The significance of the remark was not lost on him and he recognised the bond of trust growing between them. He glanced back towards Mirbat and could just make out the Sultan's flag hanging limply from the top of the flagpole of the fort's tower. "*Inshaallah*," he agreed cementing that trust.

Juma had heard the distant deep booms of the heavy guns soon after he had started the descent down the Shair valley towards Salalah. Now, after an hour the valley was widening indicating that he was nearing its mouth onto the open plain and still those deep rumbles continued. He had expected that the firing would have finished long before he reached this point, but it hadn't. However, the concentration was far away to the west and while it continued to stay there then there was no imminent danger so he had continued his journey.

Despite the mist and the persistent drizzle it was not an unpleasant journey. The rocky road, pooled and muddied, wound snake-like through the lush greenery as it descended the valley. Endless tributaries had swelled the trickle of water on its descent until it had become noisy flowing rapids. It coiled itself alongside the road and in several places rose from its bed to submerge the road and cross to the opposite side. Constantly, however, it rushed downwards tumbling and frothing over the rocks until it eventually spewed out of the valley mouth onto the plain to cascade and fill the basin at Sahalnawt.

Juma urged his camel, with a kick and a slap from his cane, to climb the sharp rise above the watercourse. From here he could just see the mouth of the valley, the mist masked the plain beyond. He adjusted the waterproof sheet over his head and gathered it a little tighter around his shoulders. Leaning back he grasped the load of kindling wood tied on the animal's back and then with a brief shake he tested the load's security.

After his father had announced yesterday evening that he would seek out Khamisa's father and present his credentials, Juma had suggested that he should make another journey to the market in Salalah to sell wood. It was transparently obvious that the wood sale was an excuse and his primary intention was to find Khamisa at Al Dharitz and inform her of the pending meeting and its intention. However, since the few rupees that the wood sale could bring would always be welcome Abdulla had no reason not to agree.

Juma had left this morning as daylight had started to break the night sky. His thoughts and aspirations had been completely dominated by thoughts of Khamisa throughout his journey. So much so that he was hardly aware of the surroundings through which he travelled. He hoped fervently that Khamisa would welcome his attentions and the memory of his hand wrapping hers a few days ago gave him some cause for optimism. He recognised the tribal difficulties and the parental influence that threatened his future happiness but he preferred not to dwell to much on those problems. There was of course the primary need to satisfy her father's terms but on the issue of different tribes he was determined not to allow any petty parochial conditions to jeopardise his happiness. Instead he concentrated his contemplating mostly on happy speculation of a future with Khamisa as his wife and making plans for a marital home.

Emerging from the valley and onto the plain he realised that at some point within the past few minutes the guns had at last stopped. His deliberations turned to the possible terms which Khamisa's father might set. The terms depended on the status of the families concerned, but even at the poverty level they were usually in the region of four thousand rupees, paid in cash or livestock value. Often a mixture of both. In which case, although it would not be easily raised, it ought to be within the bounds of his father's capabilities. Particularly in view of the gratuity which Mussalim had contributed to the family benefit. That thought of his brother made him wonder where he might be at this very moment. It was now eight days since Mussalim had left and he supposed that he should be in the Yemen by now, perhaps even in Hauf. Wherever he might be Juma wished deeply that he were here at his side right now to share with him his hopes and jubilant aspirations.

As he neared the road, gunfire started once more, but this time it was the lighter rattle and sharper retorts of smaller weapons. It was still, however a long way to the west and so it gave him no concern for his own safety. The exchanges had been much more prolonged than he had ever heard before and he wondered, without too much concern, why? He returned his thoughts once again to his own more important and genial concerns.

He joined the Salalah road and shortly after a rider emerged from the mist travelling towards him on an overburdened donkey. As he neared he looked up towards Juma, flashed a toothy grin, waved and shouted something. Juma didn't hear what it was that he said and looked back over his shoulder waiting for him to repeat it. But the man didn't look back, instead he continued along the road to become a darkening shadow until he gradually disappeared into the mist. Juma permitted himself a slight shrug and then dismissed it as not important.

He continued along the muddy puddled road, the ungainly plodding of the camel gently rocking his body making him drowsy and hypnotically assisting his flights of fantasies. He was more than just hopeful that after he had sold the wood in the Salalah *souk* then his trip onto Al Dharitz would be rewarded and that he would find Khamisa somewhere on the beach. In his mind he rehearsed for the umpteenth time how he would break the news to her and yet again prepared suitable reactions to all of her possible responses.

Voices from somewhere ahead slowly getting stronger aroused him from his reverie and he peered into the mist ahead. At this distance from the jebal the persistent drizzle had stopped and visibility had increased as the mist thinned a little. Shadowy outlines of several camels began to emerge from the mist ahead. As the distance narrowed Juma could see the men on foot leading the animals and he could clearly hear their voices gruffly urging the animals onwards. There was at least a dozen animals four or five abreast and filling the breadth of the road. He tugged on the reins turning his own camel's head and guided it to the side of the road. There he waited patiently for the group to pass.

One of the men slowed as he got closer. "Are you heading for Salalah?" he asked stopping close by.

"Yes," Juma replied.

He shook his head. "You won't get in," he said wheeling his animal off the road to allow others to pass. "The gates are closed."

"All of them?"

"Yes."

"Why?"

"Can't you hear the guns?"

"Yes," Juma replied dubiously.

"The Liberation Forces attacked the airfield this morning and the battle still goes on."

"They have attacked the airfield before, and if they did close the gates then it was only for a short time." Juma didn't want to believe that the gates would stay closed.

"This time is different."

"How?"

"Today's attack is a big one. A follow up to yesterday."

"Yesterday?" Juma slid down off his camel.

"Haven't you heard about Mirbat?"

Juma pulled a bewildered face and shook his head.

" Early yesterday, it seems, the Liberation Forces launched a surprise attack on Mirbat and scored a great victory. They attacked and destroyed the main fort," he said with a deal of ebullience in his tone. "After a fierce battle the fort was overrun and the Sultan's soldiers surrendered."

Juma was bewildered and he stared at the man's face seeking any sign of insincerity.

"They laid down their arms," he went on, "and then most of them deserted and joined the new Revolutionary Army. They even helped their Dhofari brothers to raze the fort and reduce it to a smoking ruin. Then this morning there was an attack on the airfield and who knows what is happening over there in the mist." He paused staring in the westward direction as if trying to see what was happening. "Anyway it's certainly shook things up and Salalah is sealed up. No-one goes in, nobody comes out."

"How do you know this?"

"Everybody knows. Its telling is all over Salalah and the jebal." He paused and studied Juma. "If you don't believe me then just go to the gate and try to get in." He turned his camel to follow the rest. "It's true! We now have a proper revolution. This Sultans day's are numbered." He hesitated a moment then muttered, "*Masaalama*," as he began to drag his camel away.

Juma watched him go. Then he turned to look the opposite way towards Salalah peering into the mist and willing the gates not to be closed. He pulled his camel to a kneeling position and re-mounted. He had come this far he may as well at least approach the gate, he decided. Besides, it just might open a little later, or it could even have opened since those men had left. The gunfire stopped and Juma cocked an ear listening and hoping that it didn't start again. Seconds turned to into minutes and the hills remained silent, encouraging him that perhaps the exchanges were now finished. He kicked his heels into the animal's ribs and urged it forward perhaps the gates would soon open.

The further he got from the jebal the thinner the mist became. By the time he neared the perimeter wire visibility had improved to over one hundred metres. From that distance he could see the search compound and that it was empty. There were no traders or travellers waiting their turn to be searched. In fact there was no activity at all. Reluctantly, he now accepted that what he had been told was true. Nevertheless, he continued on slowly towards the gate. Twenty metres away he was challenged by one of the guards to come no nearer. He reined in his camel and waited. Intimidating Browning machine guns pointing directly at him from behind two sandbagged sangars each side of the gate.

"The gate is closed today." One of the guards standing just the other side of the concertina razor wire called.

"When will it be open?" Juma called back. When there was no reply, "It's important that I get into Salalah today," he called again. Still no reply. "Is Khaleef there?"

One of the guards emerged from behind the wire and with a pistol held loosely in his hand he walked towards him. When he has within five metres he stopped. "The gate is closed today."

Juma nodded. "What about the east gate at Al Dharitz?"

"Closed! They're all closed."

"When will they be open again? It is important that I get in."

He shrugged. "Maybe tomorrow. *Inshaallah.*"

Juma stared helplessly at the man, it was not the answer he wanted. He sighed with frustration and slid down from his camel. "I really wanted to get in today."

The guard made a face. "You can sell your wood another day," he said with the merest hint of sympathy.

Juma glanced at the wood piled on the camel's back and then shook his head. "That isn't the reason why I wanted to get in."

He shrugged again. "Try tomorrow or the day after," he advised.

The helplessness weighed heavily on Juma as he accepted the situation. "Is it true there was a battle fought at Mirbat?" he asked.

"It's true," he confirmed.

"And the fort was overrun by the insurgents and destroyed?"

The guard laughed allowed. "No. In fact quite the opposite," he said derisively. The attack was held easily, and the *adoo* suffered lots of casualties for their actions. They won't try that again in a hurry."

Juma thought of the gunfire exchange that had ceased only a little while ago, but he decided not to pass comment on that. Both sides were claiming victory at Mirbat and he wasn't sure who to believe. Certainly the government forces would never admit to a defeat which would result in a humiliating loss of face. The truth, he concluded, was most probably nearer to the Liberation Forces claims, although those claims were probably exaggerated also. He gave the guard a good-humoured grin, took the strain on the reins and began to pull the animal away. *"Masaalama,"* he said as he disappointedly began his long trek back home.

✳ ✳ ✳

Little more than five kilometres away Khamisa stood alone on the beach watching the rolling surf bursting noisily on to the sand. The strong wind billowed her full length black gown and snatched at her long hair flapping it horizontally like whiplashes. Her mood was melancholy. The news that had been reported from Mirbat was not good and from what she had overheard her father and his two brothers discussing, in the family *dirwain* the previous evening, the consequences for the region spelled out open and bloody civil war. All of her life she had lived within the social climate of discontent and poverty. But this general discontentment had so far revealed itself only in malcontent voices and by weak token attacks on government bases and vehicle convoys. Most Dhofaris reluctantly and resentfully excepted their meagre existence, concerning themselves with the more immediate problems of day to day survival. This latest attack, however, constituted a sinister turn in events. There was now an army of discontents no longer prepared to tolerate the imposition of poverty and two armies in the region with conflicting interests meant that one would have to destroy the other.

She contemplated the effects such a war might have on her own family. Her family circumstances were tolerable. Not affluent by any stretch of imagination but perhaps just a little better than average. Her father along with his two brothers owned a small skiff. It was nothing more than an old four-metre rowing boat but it enabled them to make a meagre living from fishing the seas. Their family diets was not extensive but at least there was always seafood to put on the platter and the surplus was sold on to provide essential family extras. The Khareef season, however, did impose an interruption on the family income since the high seas prevented all but the foolhardy going to sea in a small boat. This war, she supposed, would actually have very little impact on the family routine activities. Her father would still have to go out and catch fish, her mother would still carry out the household chores and her younger brothers and sisters would continue to play on the beach. However, of her own circumstances she was not so sure, in a perverse way such a war may even be her salvation.

The family males had also discussed the subject of finding her a husband last night. She had listened intently without the opportunity of an opinion or preference. Her heart had sunk when her father had declared a preference for Mustafa Bin Ahmed, the eldest of the three suitors. He was fat and more than twice Khamisa's age with two wives already. Her mother, also listening, had sensed her dismay and had silently and sympathetically squeezed her hand. Mustafa was a comparatively well off tribal merchant and his business was trading livestock, cattle, camels and goats. But if there was to be war on the jebal than his business would almost certainly be effected since most of his trade was with the jeballys. This point was not lost on Khamisa's father and it was only this single doubt that prevented him from declaring a betrothal. The reprieve though was in all probability only temporary. Khamisa had little doubt that Mustafa's powers of persuasion would eventually convince her father that his wealth would continue unaffected by war. Her salvation, it seemed, was only a thin possibility.

She swallowed hard fighting back the tears as she considered the cruel circumstances of life that would make her the third and youngest wife of the fat merchant. She thought of the handsome young jabally with the ready smile and white teeth who had boldly held her hand on the beach the other day. She thought of his dark eyes that seemed to stare at her and pierce into her very innermost thoughts, embarrassing her and causing her to avert her gaze lest he see her exact feelings. She stroked the back of her hand reliving the touch of his fingers as his big hand had slid over hers. She considered if the size of his hand suggested in way the size of his penis and she shuddered as she felt a slow and deep pitch of desire in her stomach. She swallowed hard and quickly regained control of her wayward thoughts. Then she muttered a brief apology and plea of forgiveness to Allah. Of all the suitors Juma was easily the one that she would choose, if only she had the choice. But at this time she had nothing more than a remote and fervent hope that his interest was anything more than flirtatious. Perhaps he wasn't particularly interested in her as a wife. There had been no indication thus far of an approach to her father so he was completely unaware of a fourth possibility. Consequently the jeballi had not even entered into consideration. If Juma were interested and all her hopes of becoming his were to come true, then he would have to declare very soon or it would be too late and she would be betrothed to the fat merchant.

✳ ✳ ✳

From his position high above the pass Hamed sat and idly watched the small band of men making their way along the winding and twisting track below. They had first come into view away to his right some thirty minutes previously. Now directly beneath him he could see clearly that these men were dressed in an assortment of combat clothing. Except for three camels, these men were mostly on foot, which confirmed in his mind that they were members of the Liberation forces. Government soldiers would be much better equipped with vehicles.

The road beneath his position turned directly away from him and as the band of men moved slowly along that stretch their backs were exposed to his position. He lifted an imaginary rifle squinted down the sights and easily picked off three men. He considered the strategic value of his position. If he were armed and opened fire those men down below would be forced to seek whatever cover they could find. They could not scale the rocky face up to his position it was too steep and too exposed so the location was impregnable from frontal attack. Because of his high commanding position it would be extremely risky for them to move from cover. They would be comprehensively pinned down and would have to stay right where they were until dark. After dark they would have to retrace their steps back out of the pass and onto the jebal and circle around behind him. Even then there was an approach across flat exposed land to his rear to be negotiated before a short steep climb, which would gain them access to the table top area overlooking the pass below. That would take about a couple of hours by which time he would have long since made good his escape. He decided that it was a position of strategic dominance even for a lone sniper.

He wondered where those men were going. After the road emerged from the pass it went directly northwards across the open desert to the government Air Force base at Midway and eventually onwards a further nine-hundred kilometres to Muscat. He could, however, guess where they were coming from.

Juma had arrived home around noon with accounts of today's attack on the Air Force base at Salalah and yesterday's attack on Mirbat. These men were probably a fragmented section of today's attack. He had listened to Juma with an amount of incredulity. All of the discontented, it seemed, had effectively mobilised and organised into a significant force. Up to this point he hadn't concerned himself very much with the political circumstances of the region. The endless day to day activities of working their modest family farm occupied most of his waking hours. Now as he considered the situation he wasn't sure if he should be for the liberationist or against them. There was a great deal of poverty it was true, but had it not always been so? Certainly during his own comparatively short lifetime nothing had changed. However, now it seemed that things were becoming ominous and he was apprehensive about the effects that the developing situation would have on his family circumstances. Already the signs of change were apparent. First his brother Mussalim had left with angry words to join the liberation forces. Now his other brother Juma wanted to bring a wife into the family and his father had agreed. Only who it was to be and the arrangements were so far undecided. For seventeen years now Hamed had lived in the sheltered family environment with the same faces around him every day. He perceived that each family member understood their place, their role, and the expectations placed upon them. Despite all the hardships the routine was familiar and it was mentally a comfortable situation. Now the impending threat of a new face invading the family seclusion he saw as an intrusion and an unwelcome change. This, added to the developing war situation, posed a threat to his current comfortable situation. He feared that a great deal of changes was imminent and that the effects would greatly alter his own circumstances in the not too distant future. Today at the afternoon rest period Hamed had too much on his mind to sleep, so he had taken the camel and made the three-hour ride to this spot, his favourite place. He had a special reason to come to this place today.

Behind him in the mountain peak's the drizzle continued and the mist drifted slothfully, but here on this very edge of the jebal it was dry. From his elevated position he commanded an incredible view northwards over the barren wastes of the *nejd*. The sharply peaked and scorched hills stretched far into the distance as far as his eyes could see. Scattered greenery in the wadi's meandered between these hills, clearly indicating the paths of the underground watercourses draining off the jebal. In this narrow corridor between the two extremes of nature's awesome barren beauty and the lush mountain greenery he felt the presence and great power of Allah. All of human tragedy and affliction that it imposed upon itself amounted to the grand total sum of insignificance in comparison to this unaltering timeless vista.

The sky was still clear and very blue but the sun was turning red as it neared its setting. Very soon he would have to start the journey home but not yet. First he would watch the sun set. From up here it would be spectacular, it always was. This place at sunset, where the power of Allah was patently evident, he had decided would be a fitting place to make a special prayer.

As the last tip of the sun slipped from view on the western skyline he began his prayer. Spreading his prayer mat roughly in the direction of Mecca he sank onto his knees and pressed his forehead to the ground. Then standing with his head bowed he made his special prayer. He prayed fervently and begged the almighty that he bestow his protection on all of his family members and deliver them from any unwelcome imposed changes and the ravages of this coming conflict. To finish his prayer he sunk once more to his knees and again pressed his forehead to the ground.

His prayer finished he remained on his knees for a few minutes in quiet contemplation and watched the western sky slowly change from a variety of deep pinks to reds. Breaking his contemplative mood he got slowly to his feet, he was still three hours from home and tonight he would be absent from the family meal. No one would be concerned, however, because it would not be the first time. He bundled his rolled prayer mat under the camel saddle and pulled the animal to a kneeling position. He mounted the animal and turned it towards the bank of mist on the jebal. Despite the wet and the cold the grass over there was lush and the mountain flowers now in abundance. He thought of Kathya, his mother, it seemed to him that she had been very quiet and withdrawn these past couple of days, almost troubled. Perhaps she too felt apprehensive about the family's future. On the way home he would take time to gather a few of those mountain flowers for her. It may help to cheer her up.

※ ※ ※

It was early evening on the day after the battle when Mussalim and Ali wearily arrived back at Jibjat still humping the captured machine gun. They made their way to the same tree just outside the village where Suhayl's section had gathered before the Mirbat attack. Half the section was already there congregated around a large fire. The pair were greeted with huge grins, warm handshakes and a genuine show of enthusiasm when they arrived. With a deal of relief they unceremoniously dumped the Browning and then sank tiredly to the ground. Tea and chapatti were quickly thrust into their hands.

Despite his hunger, tiredness dulled Mussalim's appetite. He ate fastidiously as he looked around the faces making a mental inventory of the survivors.

"Is this it?" Ali asked mirroring Mussalim's thoughts.

"No there are more. Some have gone into the village." He was told. "There are only seven or eight missing now."

Mussalim thought of the two men on the hillcrest mutilated by the aircraft canon and in his mind reduced that figure by two. "What of Suhayl?"

His question was greeted by grins. "Suhayl?" in a surprised tone. "He's alright. He came back with Salim Al Mushani in his Land Rover."

Mussalim shook his head sadly. "It was a disaster," he said quietly.

He was hotly denied by several. "No, no. It is hailed as a great success by our leaders. We have struck a great blow for independence and we definitely now have Bin Taymour's forces worried."

Mussalim stared at the faces all around him looking for some evidence of fallaciousness but saw only conviction. He thought once more of the carnage wrought by the aircraft. Was it possible that the devastation had looked far worse than it was? Maybe! What of high the ground fort which had been their main objective? There had, it seemed, been only one occasion when it had looked in any sort of danger. Was he mistaken and had misinterpreted the evidence of his own eyes? Perhaps, but he didn't really believe so. However, he was much too tired to argue, or even to think right now. He slipped into a weary detached mode slowly sipping his tea and nibbling his chapatti indifferent to the chattering voices all around him.

Despite the cold and the percolating damp he soon fell into a deep sleep, but confused dreams disturbed his slumbers. Aircraft swooped from the skies and blasted the bucolic houses of Mirbat with rockets leaving great tongues of fire reaching upwards to the skies. In the chaos of unconfined hallucinations those Mirbat houses became his own home on the jebal. In dreams he watched in horror and helpless impotency as the gluttony of destruction on his family home went on unrestrained. Someone called his name and shook his shoulder and he tried to ignore it, but the offender was persistent.

"Wake up jebally."

He came awake with a start and sat up quickly. It was now dark and he tried to focus his bleary eyes on the figure above him, then he recognised the twisted grinning face of Suhayl.

"Welcome back Mussalim Abdulla." Still more asleep than awake he took the congratulating offered hand. "This is the man I spoke of who performed bravely and with passion," Suhayl said to the man behind him. "He will make an excellent recruit to the cause. See he has even brought a souvenir of the battle with him," he said pointing at the Browning.

Mussalim looked at the man behind Suhayl and recognised Al Mushani. His senses still a little fuzzy he wordlessly rolled to a more comfortable sitting position as Al Mushani settled cross-legged opposite him.

"I have had good reports on the way that you handled yourself at Mirbat, he said offering his hand to be shaken.

Mussalim shook the offered hand and glanced sideways at Suhayl, who continued to grin.

Al Mushani spent a few minutes talking quietly allowing Mussalim to recover his dazed wits. Then he began posing questions encouraging him to express his own opinions on the plight of the common Dhofari. He invited his personal thoughts on what he believed would be the best methods of gaining independence for the area and influenced him to talk frankly of his own background. All the time he listened attentively while Mussalim talked. Eventually satisfied with the responses he pulled out an envelope from the chest pocket of his shirt and held it up in front of him.

"This is my recommendation," he said. "Do you know the pools at Ayon?"

Mussalim nodded, the village of Ayon lay far to the west of Jibjat, at least a day's camel ride away.

"Go to the pools and take this letter with you. There you will find a man called Samir Mohammed, he will be your guide. He waits there for all new recruits to assemble and in three days from now he will leave for Hauf." He handed Mussalim the envelope. "Welcome to the PFLOAG," he offered his hand once more.

Al Mushani got to his feet and glanced at the twenty men sitting cross-legged around the blazing campfire. The chattering started to die away and twenty faces lit by the firelight stared expectantly back. He moved further into the circle of light and waited until he had all the attention.

"Yesterday," he said. "We scored a great victory for the cause. Because of that, this Sultan sleeps uneasily in his Salalah Palace tonight. He knows now that we will no longer tolerate his poverty imposing administration and that we are deadly serious about his expulsion from the region. He knows also that there is now a significant army in the region with the capability to take the Dhofar away from him." He waited for the mutterings of approval to die away. "But Mirbat was only the beginning and the offensive is being stepped up on several fronts. Tomorrow you men move to the village of Akhara where you will be based." Again he had to pause and wait for the murmuring to cease. "For those of you who don't know Akhara, it is a small village on the top of the jebal almost overlooking the Salalah Tarqah road." He turned and indicated Suhayl standing close behind him. "You keep your section leader, Commissar Suhayl. He will lead you, and your purpose for being there is to harass government forces moving along the road. You will carry out guerrilla activities." He paused briefly for thought and then to clarify went on. "Mine the road, make hit and run attacks, snipe and generally make it hazardous for any of the Sultan's forces to move along the road. The mines will be arriving from the Yemen sometime soon and they will be delivered direct to Akhara. The mines will be British anti tank mines, which they left behind in plenty when they left Aden. Suhayl has already asked if he can have mortars. I think that's a good idea and I will arrange for some to be sent also." He paused for thought a moment and spread his hands. "Everything that you need will be supplied. The Akhara villagers are sympathetic to our cause so you will be quite comfortable there." He stopped glanced once more at Suhayl before saying, "any questions?"

Mussalim waited a few moments allowing other more senior soldiers the opportunity. But there was a shy pause and a reluctance to be the first. "Yes," he said quietly. "What happened at the airfield at Salalah? Those aircraft kept coming back to Mirbat and they pulverised us every time. Did the attack take place?"

"Ah yes that! That was unfortunate. But first, those aircraft certainly did not pulverise us. Yes they drove us back into cover and kept interrupting our progress. But they definitely did not pulverise us." He stared intimidatingly hard at Mussalim, daring him to contradict. Then when Mussalim did not respond he turned his attention back to the main group. "The truck, which was to carry Mohammed Bin Talib's team to Salalah, broke down. The other truck had broken down previously carrying men to Mirbat and so he couldn't move until we got one repaired. Eventually we did, but they didn't leave Jibjat until yesterday afternoon. However, the attack, I believe, took place this morning."

"This morning, what was the point of that?" Ali queried.

"Harassment!"

"How can we claim a victory at Mirbat when we didn't take our first objective?" Mussalim asked earning another look of disapproval.

"But we did. The Sultan's soldiers where out of ammunition when we breached the wall. I ended the attack at that point to stop the slaughter of our misguided Omani brothers."

Mussalim stared at Al Mushani. Was it possible? He thought back to the battle and the men scaling the ladders on the fort walls. Certainly at that point there had been bitter hand to hand fighting. The far side of the fort was, of course, hidden from his view so perhaps the wall had been breached on that side.

"What about our losses?" someone else asked.

"No more than was expected!" He glanced at his watch, "I really have to leave now," he sought to cut short the questioning. "All of you men should be proud of what you achieved yesterday. It was a glorious victory and a remarkable start to the campaign. There is a long way to go and many hard battles to be fought, but so long as we stay united and show the determination of yesterday we will be victorious in the end." All the men stood and Al Mushani started to move around the campfire smiling pleasantly, shaking hands and embracing each man in turn.

Soon after he and Suhayl had left, a man produced an *aoud* from somewhere and he began strumming its strings. Whether it was because of relief at their delivery from the previous day's battle or the feeling of optimism at the final outcome Mussalim wasn't sure but the mood became light and happy. Soon men began to bang on tin trays accompanying the *aoud* player while others simply clapped. He sang songs of *bedu* legends, of the lost gold city of Ubar and the city of the Moon God Sin at Khor Rourri. He sang of the great frankincense caravans, which had journeyed from the coast of Salalah across the empty quarters of Saudi and onto the West Bank. When he had exhausted those he began to invent. He sang of the battle at Mirbat and related the deeds of the men around him. He sang about Mussalim who had stood on a rock and shouted insults at the aircraft that had bore down on him with its cannons blazing. The tune was indiscernible, the words didn't fit and the deed was embarrassingly over exaggerated, nevertheless Mussalim was secretly pleased with the complimentary remarks. Several men got to their feet and in a line began to shuffle their feet dancing and chanting the Arabic way.

Mussalim moved out of the circle of firelight and stood quietly watching for a few minutes. These comrades with whom he had stood shoulder to shoulder in battle would tomorrow go eastward to the village of Akhara while he went in the opposite direction to Ayon and eventually across the Yemen border to Hauf. He wondered how many, if any, he would ever see again and how many were destined to die in the struggle for the independence of Dhofar. "*Inshaallah,*" he muttered committing the future to Allah's will and turned to make his way to the village to collect his camel.

In the narrow alleyway Mussalim paused at Ghulam's gate before giving it a tentative push. After catching the old man in the act of praying just a couple of nights before he had expected to find it locked as a precaution, but it swung open. The goats scattered as he stepped inside. His camel was tethered in the corner, it looked around and gave a welcoming bellow when it recognised him. Mussalim picked up a small piece of cardboard and went over to the animal. He affectionately pulled the ears on its ugly head while the animal greedily snatched the cardboard from his hand and ate.

"Who's there?" a female voice demanded.

He turned, Ghulam's wife stood in the open door with Jumaia standing close behind watching him. The dim light from within silhouetted their shapes in the open doorway exaggerating greatly their size by the long shapeless black robes that they wore.

"It's only me, Mussalim." He moved closer to the light to be recognised. "Is Ghulam at home?"

The two women spoke quietly to each other. "No he's not here. But he will be back soon." The older woman said. "Would you like to come in and wait?"

Mussalim hesitated – it would be polite to wait and thank him personally for his kindness but it may be improper as a comparative stranger to wait inside his house alone with his wife and daughter. "Thank you, but no I won't. I have only come to collect my camel." He still hesitated. "I will wait for a little while here in the yard, if I may." It was a sound idea.

Both women went inside and shut the door.

Mussalim stared at the closed door a moment and then moved over to the rickety veranda and sat down. The mist had thinned a little and although it coiled around slowly at ground level the stars above his head were clearly visible and he passed the time studying the stars. He had heard it said that the stars that actually twinkled were really suns and the others that did not were planets that orbited those suns. He marvelled at the sheer mechanism of the heavens and he muttered a brief prayer to Allah and his divine power. His reflections were interrupted when the door opened and Jumaia came towards him carrying a platter containing a jug of water and dried pieces of *feta*. She laid the platter at his side and sat down. He watched her as she poured water from the jug into one of the small handless tin cups. She was robed from head to foot but her veil hung loose on her shoulder and clandestinely he studied her face. He decided that his previous impression that she was a pretty girl was fully justified perhaps he had even been a little unappreciative. Given time she would probably grow into a beautiful woman. Her high cheekbones and thin lips gave an impression of emaciation and Mussalim could imagine that as she became older that youthful impression of leanness would leave her features and in its place leave only loveliness. She picked up the cup slowly and offered it to him.

He looked into her dark brown eyes as he took the cup from her. "*Shukran*," he thanked her. Then he took a piece of *feta* that she offered.

"What was it like?" she asked.

"Mirbat?"

She nodded.

He took a bite of *feta* while he thought how to answer. Should he tell it the way he had seen it, or should he tell it the way everyone else had seen it. He glanced sideways at her, she looked back childlike and expectant. He decided to spare her the gory details and tell her only that which would not upset her. He gave her a brief account relating only the main events of the attack and then selected the more favourable accounts of each outcome. He left out completely the carnage wrought by the machine guns and the aircraft. When he had finished he fell silent while his mind relived some of the more unpleasant memories.

She sensing that there was much that he hadn't told her, touched his arm sympathetically and quietly said. "I prayed to Allah and asked him to protect you."

He looked down to the hand on his arm and then into her face full of sincerity. "*IlHamdu lillaah*," praise be to Allah, he said, holding the eye lock. He slid the platter further back, moved close to her side and boldly slid his arm around her shoulders. She did not move away, so taking encouragement he rested his other hand on her breast. Through the flimsy material he felt the swell of a young girl's developing breast before she lightly tapped the back of his hand and pulled it away. He laughed out loud in a cavalier manner, trying to mask the embarrassment of his clumsy approach. She did, however, place his hand to rest just above her knee, but took a precautionary firm grip of it with her own hand.

"Mussalim Bin Abdulla Al Hamer," she used his full formal title, "why don't you take me for your wife?"

He was taken by surprise and once again to cover his embarrassment, he laughed.

Jumaia was not too discouraged by his reaction. "You would then have a husband's right to caress my body."

"Hmm," he nodded agreement, "Yes I would, and that would be really nice. But I can't. Firstly you are tribe Mahru and not even one of the many Kathir tribes. Secondly tomorrow I leave for Hauf in the Yemen and I don't know when, if ever I will ever return to Jibjat."

"You don't have to leave you can stay here."

He shook his head. "No I can't. What would I do here at Jibjat!"

"You could help my father. He likes you. He said so after you had left the other night."

"What does your father do?"

She shrugged. "Anything he can. He buys bits of scrap and sells it at a profit."

Mussalim glanced around the yard at the impoverished surroundings. "Is it a living?"

"Barely," she admitted. "But if you were to help him he would do much better. And we would be together."

He audaciously squeezed her knee. "It's a nice thought Jumaia, but I am set on a different path." The disappointment on her face was obvious. "I'm sorry," he said.

She looked down. "Will I ever see you again?"

"*Inshaallah*. Only Allah knows what my future is." He leaned close and kissed her lightly on the cheek. He tried to move his hand along her thigh but she held it firm. "Perhaps it is my destiny to die in this war," he tried a new tact. "Maybe tonight is all we have. Perhaps this our only chance of a little happiness together." This time he used his greater strength to move his hand further along her thigh.

"No," she said and leapt to her feet. "You don't have to go to war. If you really want some of that happiness then you will stay."

Mussalim stared at her a moment then sadly shook his head. "Jumaia, I can't, really. This is something that I have to do."

"Why?" she demanded.

"Why? he echoed. "Because we need to break free of this Sultan's despotic rule and obtain a better future for all Dhofaris and for future generations."

"Will we really have a better future?"

"Of course," he replied his temper rising.

"How do you know? Have you even bothered to ask the people if they think it will be better? If you do, you may find that they prefer to leave things as they are rather than go through a war and then find out that at the end of it all the only thing that was achieved was to replace one oppressor for another."

Mussalim stared at her for a moment then wordlessly got to his feet and went over to his camel and began to untether the halter.

She came up behind him. "I have made you angry," she said.

He paused and sighed, bridling his temper. "When this war is over and independence has been won then these PFLOAG leaders will move on. This struggle here in this region is merely a stepping stone towards their main objective, the liberation of the whole of the Arabian Gulf. We will have our own Sheikhs democratically elected to govern us. All these harsh restrictions which are now imposed will be lifted and then we will all be so much better off. You will see."

"What of you Mussalim Abdulla? Will you go with them?"

He shook his head. "No. If Allah is merciful and I survive then I will go home to my father's farm near Shair."

"I will continue to pray for his protection for you."

"*Shukran*," he said softly. Then he leaned forward and kissed her lightly on both cheeks. He stared into her brown eyes then gently they rubbed noses. Boldly and impulsively he kissed her full on the lips and she responded.

He turned and gathered the reins on the camel. "Tell your father that I am sorry that I didn't see him and thank him for his kindness." He took her hand and wrapped her fingers around a couple of ten rupee notes. "I know that he will be angry that I have left payment for his deed, nevertheless I insist." Their need was transparently greater than his. He raised her closed hand and lightly kissed her fingers.

"*Masalaama*," she muttered as he began to pull on the reins.

In the alleyway he brought the animal to its knees and climbed onto its back. When it was once more standing he looked down at Jumaia standing framed in the gateway staring sadly up at him. "May Allah bestow only good fortune on you all of your life Jumaia," he said and slapped the animal down the neck urging it forward into the gently swirling mist.

~ 6 ~

Mid August 1968 • Abdulla leaned forward and took a date from the wooden platter, which Talib held out towards him. He didn't have to look into Talib's face to see the intense curiosity burning within, he could almost feel it. His host, however, was much too polite to ask him to state his business at this stage. Instead he politely asked if the rainfall on the jebal had been a heavy one during this Khareef. After considering the question for a moment Abdulla replied that he thought that it had perhaps been around normal.

Talib's wife entered and laid a tray bearing an upright coffee-pot and two small cups between the two men, who were seating cross-legged on the floor. Abdulla took the opportunity to glance around the room while she fussily adjusted the objects around the tray.

The room was small and basic. Two diminutive windows with their wooden shutters open let in the early afternoon light. The walls were lime-washed blue to give an impression of coolness but the bright multi-coloured carpet, on which the pair sat, contrasted vividly with that perception. Several handmade cushions were tidily placed out of the way along one wall but still handily placed for the evening *dirwain*. A frankincense burner had been lit as soon as Abdulla had been shown into this room and it had been placed on one of the three wooden chests in the room. Despite its strong odour, however, it had not yet subdued the strong smell of fish drying somewhere in another part of the house.

Talib picked up the gifts that Abdulla had given to him and showed them to his wife. A pouch of frankincense and a hand-stitched shamag made by Jokha. She made polite and complimentary comments as she examined the broad embroidered motif round the edge of the shamag. Then after graciously thanking Abdulla for his generosity she prudently left taking the gifts with her.

It was one week since Juma had been turned away at the closed Salalah town gate. Abdulla calculated that enough time had elapsed to calm the situation a little and that today being Friday, the holy day, the gates may have re-opened. So early this morning, without mentioning his intention to Juma, he had put on his best traditional outfit, his ceremonial belt with its silver Khunja and made his way to Al Dharitz. He felt reasonably sure that due to the tribe difference then this visit would prove to be a fruitless exercise. However, for Juma's benefit he was, at least, prepared to go through the motions of proposing a marriage between his son and Talib's daughter. He was hopeful that when Juma at last realised that there was no possibility of this marriage then perhaps he would be more receptive to alternatives. Then Abdulla could execute his plan and arrange a more appropriate in-tribe marriage, thus anchoring Juma to the family homestead.

He had calculated correctly and the Salalah gates were once again open. When he arrived at Al Dharitz he had sought out Talib and had been directed to his door. The surprise in Talib's manner and facial expression was plainly obvious when a strange jebally bearing gifts had confronted him on his doorstep. He had, however, recovered quickly and with customary Arabic politeness made his unexpected guest welcome into his home.

Abdulla took the cup, which Talib held out towards him, and then waited while he filled it from the coffee-pot. He slowly took a sip and made a polite comment. Satisfied that his guest's needs was catered for Talib then filled his own cup

"I am Abdulla Bin Salim, Bait Al Hamer," he introduced himself formally. "I am a first generation jebal farmer. My father was traditional Bedouin as was his father before him. I have two wives, three sons and a daughter."

Talib nodded acknowledgement. "And I am Talib Bin Ali, Bait Ruwas. I am a fisherman of many generations and I have one wife, two sons and two daughters "

There was a pause while Abdulla considered his best method of approach. "Talib, one of your daughters is of marrying age?"

He looked at Abdulla warily. "Yes," he guardedly replied. "Khamisa."

Abdulla nodded. "Is there an arranged marriage for this girl?"

"Er Well," Talib hesitated. "No, not yet but I am considering offers. One in particular."

"I see." Abdulla hesitated. "I am here to make a proposition on behalf of my second son, Juma."

"For your son?" The relief was evident on Talib's face and Abdulla realised then that Talib thought that he was proposing on his own behalf.

"Yes for my son," he laughed.

"But, what of the tribal problems? Your son is Al Hamer while Khamisa is Ruwas of the Himawi Kathiri."

"Yes I know," Abdulla said adamantly. "I understand all the difficulties and I have explained to Juma that there will be many problems. I even tried to persuade him to choose another, but he will not even consider it. It seems that his heart is set on taking Khamisa for his wife."

"How does he know Khamisa?"

Abdulla shrugged. "I am not sure, but I think he first saw her at Sahalnawt."

"Ah! The young man at Sahalnawt," Talib replied.

"You know of him?"

Talib nodded. "Yes, my brother's wife told me of a young man who dawdled close by the girls one day at Sahalnawt. She sent him away, but she said he would be back. He had big wishful eyes that hardly left Khamisa."

Both men laughed at the suffering of the young. "I hope that he was not too forward."

Talib shrugged. "No problem, he left when he was told. He did make an impression on my youngest daughter though. She enthused over his handsome looks," he said studying Abdulla's rugged face and wondering from where the young man could have inherited good looks.

"What about your eldest daughter, did he make an impression there also?"

He shook his head. "Khamisa didn't pass any remark, but then she wouldn't. She has a very reserved nature." He poured more coffee into Abdulla's cup. "Tell me about Juma," he said.

Abdulla then spent a few minutes relating the virtues of his son. He gave accounts of some of Juma's past youthful deeds and misdeeds using both becoming and humorous examples to create a mental portrait. When he had at last finished Talib appeared to be reasonably satisfied. He then asked about Abdulla's eldest son. At first Abdulla was embarrassed, then deciding not to fudge the issue he gave a brief account of the true situation. When he had finished he tempered the circumstances in Juma's favour by saying that although the two brothers were physically very alike they were very different in their opinions and behaviour.

The conversation from there moved naturally on to the conflict between the dissidents and the incumbent Sultan and his Government. They found themselves in complete agreement over the current situation. They agreed that although there was great deal wrong with the present situation a violent rebellion was not the best way to alter things. They both expressed some doubt also that the Dhofari people would fare any better under a communist inspired regime, if the rebellion were successful. As they sipped coffee the topics of the conversation diversified throughout the next hour and as the two men talked they found more and more common ground on which they shared the same view. Abdulla judged that he had just about reached the point where he should make preparations to leave and that to stay very much longer would be impolite.

He waited for a suitable pause in the conversation and when it came he said. "So, will you give the marriage proposition consideration?"

Talib looked at him thoughtfully silent for a moment. "The tribal difficulties are many," he said slowly.

"Yes they are," Abdulla nodded agreement. "And of course we would have to get both of the tribe Sheikh's permission also."

Talib stroked his beard thoughtfully. "First, I will meet your son and you should meet Khamisa. Then, if all is satisfactory, we can both consider the situation after that."

It seemed a sound plan to Abdulla. "Yes," he agreed.

"Can you bring Juma here one week from today?"

✳ ✳ ✳

Very soon after Abdulla had left that morning for Salalah, Jokha and Kathya left the farmhouse. They walked westwards over the high rocky knoll and down the other side into the rugged Wadi Theydawt. Once there they turned north and made their way along its base between the towering rocky faces on either side. It took more than an hour before they came to the waterfall which cascading noisily fifteen metres off a high lip into the wadi's base. They spread a cloth over the long wet grass and sat to rest by the side of the pool beneath the waterfall. Despite the shrouding mist this was a spot of great beauty of which nature itself could be justifiably proud. However, the beauty is annual and only temporary. The water drains away rapidly down the wadi and when the Khareef is ended and the rains stop so do the cascading waters that replenished the pool. Nature's splendour, however, was lost on the two women they had come to this spot for a more insidious purpose.

It was Jokha who broke the long silence. "Do you still want to do this?" she asked raising her voice to be heard over the noisy waterfall. Kathya glanced at her a moment then slowly nodded. She then turned away and stared sadly across the pool into the rolling mist.

Behind them backing up onto the rock face was a derelict goat compound roughly constructed from many large fifty-gallon metal oil drums. Jokha got up wordlessly, went over to the compound and began to inspect each drum. Eventually she found one suitable. Its top had been cut off and unlike most of the others had not rusted into holes. She tipped it over onto its side and rolled it to the edge of the pool. Then she hunted around, gathered suitable sized rocks and placed them into a circle roughly about the size of the drum's base. Before she had finished Kathya came to help her. The pair then hunted around trying to find some dry kindling. It took a while but eventually they had a fire burning inside the circle of stones. When she was satisfied that the fire would not go out Jokha placed the drum onto the stone circle, then using whatever they could find to hold water the pair began to fill the drum from the pool. When it was a little over half full they stopped. Next they gathered more rocks and piled them by the side of the drum taking care to lodge them together into a secure pile. There was nothing more to be done so they sat down on the cloth to wait for the water to get hot.

Conversation was difficult because of the noise from the waterfall, so for the most part the two women waited in silence. Occasionally Jokha got up to feed the fire with more wood. It was burning so hot by now that even wet wood soon dried and began to burn. She no longer returned to sit on the cloth, instead she remained by the drum and kept testing the water temperature.

"It's ready," she said after a while.

Kathya hesitated then got to her feet. She moved closer to the drum and peered in, and then she tested it for herself using her fingers. It was hot and she looked at Jokha dubiously. She gave her a reassuring smile and nodded encouragement. Then as Kathya removed her clothes she doused the fire. With Jokha's steadying arm Kathya got to the top of the pile of rocks by the side of the drum. For a moment still holding Jokha's steadying arm she stood there naked, steeling herself she jumped in.

She gasped with pain as the hot water enveloped her to just below her chest. It was too hot, she couldn't stand it and she struggled to get out. When she did, Jokha immediately made her submerge herself in the cold waters of the pool. She alternated regularly from the hot water in the drum to the cold waters of the pool gasping with shock as she subjected her body from one temperature extreme to the other. As the water in the drum cooled she was able to spend a little more time in there on each occasion. After a while the hot water was little more than tepid and Jokha ended Kathya's ordeal.

They left the poolside and made there way back down the wadi. When they came to the steep incline where they had come down and entered the wadi Jokha went on alone and when she got to the top she sat down and signalled to Kathya. Urged on by Jokha the younger woman began to run up the steep incline as fast as she could. Soon her breath came in short gasps, her legs felt like lead, and her back ached, but still she struggled upwards as fast as she could. By the time she reached Jokha she was staggering and exhausted almost to the point of fainting. She collapsed face down by Jokha's side gasping for breath and unable to speak.

Jokha stroked Kathya's hair sympathetically and waited until she had recovered a little then said softly. "Tonight you must coax Abdulla into *jig-jig* and then tomorrow perhaps your juices will flow."

"Will they? Will all this work?" Kathya asked when she had recovered enough to speak.

Jokha looked at the prone figure by her side and shrugged. "*Inshaallah.*"

"Do you think Allah will forgive us?"

"Kathya, we are all in the hands of Allah. If it is his will that this pregnancy end then it will. If it is not then it will go on. So the end decision will be his, therefore we have done nothing that needs his forgiveness." She said it and she hoped that was true. To avoid Kathya's scrutiny she looked down the incline into the wadi and caught a glimpse of Lailla in among canopy of the shrubs. She waited for her to re-appear but she didn't.

✳ ✳ ✳

Abdulla had revealed his news last night at the family gathering and after the initial surprise the mood had been one of cautious optimism. Only Hamed had greeted the news impassively. He passed no comment nor showed the slightest emotion, betraying nothing of his thoughts. There was, as Abdulla himself had said, still a very long way to go and many problems to be overcome but at least the proposition had not been instantly rejected. This morning the mood in the family had continued – even the weather, it seemed, had temporarily relented and the mist was only scant allowing sunlight to filter through and raise the temperature.

Lailla leaned on the compound gate and watched the goats inside milling around enthusiastically as they anticipated that she would soon open the gate. Kathya came out of the farmhouse carrying the old and battered tin jug and went to the rustic store shed. Lailla thought of the strange ritual that she had witnessed the two women performing yesterday.

She had not meant to spy on the pair. From a distance she had seen them leave the house together and her curiosity had been aroused. She had decided to follow them intending, fully, to catch up and perhaps they would allow her to go with them, wherever it was that they were going. However, as the distance between them decreased some instinct warned her that perhaps she would be intruding. Maybe it had been the unusual direction they had taken or perhaps it was their preoccupied attitudes. She had, however, continued to follow keeping a discreet distance without particularly concealing her presence. When the pair had reached the waterfall she had stopped also. Too embarrassed to reveal her presence at this stage, she had made her way around the other side of the pool and hid herself among the thick undergrowth of bushes there. She had watched with incredulity as her mother had alternated countless times between the hot water in the barrel and the cold waters of the pool. Baffled, she had supposed that it must be some kind of beauty treatment, perhaps for the skin. When the women had eventually left she had gone to the site to see if there were any clues to account for the strange behaviour. But there wasn't. So still puzzled she had followed them out of the wadi and almost stumbled into them when they stopped and rested at top of the incline. Once again to hide her embarrassment she had remained hidden until the pair left. If it were some kind of beauty treatment that she had witnessed, then since she was almost a woman herself, perhaps she ought to know about it. She decided to go to her mother and ask.

Kathya was filling the jug with milk from the barrel when she entered the makeshift building. Deep in thought she did not hear her enter and for a few moments Lailla stood in the small opening and watched her mother. When she eventually spoke her mother visibly jumped then recovering quickly she laughed off her fright. Lailla came straight to the point.

"What were you doing in wadi Theydawt yesterday, mother?"

Kathya looked around with surprise. "You were there?"

Lailla nodded, "yes she said."

Kathya didn't answer instead she turned her attention back to the jug.

"Was it some sort of beauty treatment?"

She finished filling the jug and turned around. "I didn't see you. Where were you?"

"I followed you and tried to catch up with you. Then after a while I didn't think you wanted me there, so I stayed some way off and watched."

"Come," Kathya said and led the way outside. She set the jug down and sat down just outside the building then she indicated that Lailla should sit by her side. When she had settled she gently stroked her daughter's hair. "Perhaps you will understand a little bit better when you get a little older," she said. "But what you saw yesterday was woman's business and should never be mentioned in the presence of men. Do you understand?"

She didn't. "Was it some kind of beauty treatment?" she asked again.

To Kathya it offered the easy explanation option. "Yes it was."

"Was it some kind of skin treatment?"

Kathya nodded and continued to stroke her hair.

"I thought it must be. What does it do?"

"Well… it sort of cleanses the skin pores and makes the skin soft."

Lailla nodded. "I thought it was something like that."

"Remember," Kathya said. "It's woman's business and nothing to do with men. So don't mention it to anyone else."

Lailla nodded agreement.

"Good girl." Kathya slipped her arm around her waist and squeezed her daughter affectionately. "Now I have a little surprise for you," she changed the subject. "Next Friday we are going to Salalah."

"We are?"

"Yes, you, me, your Father and Juma. Your father and Juma go to Al Dharitz but before they do they will leave you and me in Salalah."

"Are they going to meet Khamisa's father?" she interrupted.

"Yes they are. But you and I are going shopping in the souk to buy some material for more suitable dresses for you. You are becoming a young woman now and your father has decided that you should start wear the longer robes of an adult. After we have finished shopping we can spend some time on the beach while we wait for your father and brother to return from Al Dharitz."

Lailla thought of Jokha's needle skills. "Will Jokha make the dresses for me?"

"Yes she will," Kathya said and gently touched the side of Lailla's face. Her daughter was growing up much too rapidly she thought sadly. "Now, I think you should go and take the goats out before your father comes," she said becoming assertive and getting to her feet.

∗ ∗ ∗

Late August. Juma sat cross-legged on the mat next to his father. Directly facing was Talib, Khamisa's father, flanked on both sides by his two brothers and their father. Two young boys, Talib's sons, sat on the other side of Juma. All the male members of Talib's family were there, three generations. The exchanges had been pleasant and polite, nevertheless Juma was nervous. He knew that he was under close scrutiny and he badly wanted to make the right impression, everything in his life depended upon it. The conversation to begin had been superficial and he had tried to actively take part and to give his own opinions intelligently. Now they had passed that phase and the questions had started to come in his direction. They had started insignificantly but gradually had become more personal and demanding. He tried to answer each one as openly and honestly as he could. He was receiving a good deal of support from his father as he expanded points where Juma's answers might have seemed to be a little inadequate. Despite his nervousness Juma felt that things were going in his favour and that he had, so far, made the desired impression.

The conversation was interrupted when Talib's wife entered shrouded in the traditional black *abeya* and carrying a large flat tray piled high with steaming rice. The edges were decorated with strips of fish, while on top of the pile and in the centre a whole fish lay. She laid the tray on the floor in the midst of the seated men and left.

Talib politely indicated that his guests should start the feast. Abdulla acknowledged the invitation with a nod of his head and using his right hand only he took a handful of rice. Then while everyone watched he squeezed it into a ball in the palm of his hand and then working the ball between his fingers he pushed some into his mouth. He chewed it a little then swallowed.

"The food is truly excellent," he said.

Talib smiled pleased that his guest was satisfied and that was the signal for everyone else to start.

Juma was thankful for now the centre of attention had switched from him to the food. His nerves had affected his appetite, but realising that if he did not eat eagerly then he risked offending his host he forced himself to eat. Nevertheless, he ate fastidiously taking great care that his eating manner should not appear inappropriate. He took only small handfuls of rice and made sure that as he pushed it into his mouth none of it spilled down his chin. He took only the tiniest strips of fish, which were nearest to him on the tray and chewed it slowly. In the event he need not have concerned himself so much because everyone else ate with enthusiasm and was so engrossed in the food tray that it was doubtful that anyone noticed Juma's seemly manner.

Talib invited Abdulla to break open the whole fish in the centre. After acknowledging the politeness of his host Abdulla raked the side of the fish with his fingers and tore a generous piece off. Talib then indicated that Juma should go next. Juma took a smaller piece and passed a suitable comment. Then just like everything else on the tray that fish also became fair objective to all. Eventually the contents of the tray were decimated and after fingers had been licked clean of food remnants and then dipped in small water bowls the expected complimentary comments were made.

As if by magic Talib's wife appeared to remove the tray and as she left the room Khamisa entered carrying a smaller tray of sliced fruit. Juma's heart leapt into his mouth increasing his tension tenfold. His eyes were riveted to her as she slowly approached the circle. She wore a long and brightly coloured dress beneath a long black cloak and although her head was covered her face was not.

Abdulla glanced at the girl and recognising her appropriate age he wondered if this girl could be the object of his son's desire. He glanced sideways at his son and by the inane expression frozen on Juma's face he knew instantly that it was. He to studied her as she demurely laid the tray in the midst of the seated men. She kept her attention and her eyes on the task in hand seeming to ignore the presence of all the men around her.

"This is my daughter Khamisa," Talib said to Abdulla as she straightened up.

She stood perfectly still looking down on the seated men silently waiting for further instructions.

She was without doubt a very pretty girl and Abdulla could immediately understand his son's desire. "You are to be complimented Talib on having such a pretty daughter," he said.

Talib nodded politely at the comment.

Partly through embarrassment and partly through modesty Khamisa lifted the corner of her head cover and pulled it across the lower part of her face and with her right hand held it in place. For the first time she glanced at Juma. Her left hand hung down by her side out of sight of her relatives and she waggled her fingers. Abdulla glanced sideways at his son and from the big grin on Juma's face he could tell that he had caught the secret signal which had passed between the two youngsters. Undoubtedly this girl wanted this marriage also, perhaps even as much as his son, he decided. There and then he approved fully and decided that it would perhaps be a pity if all the associated problems could not be sorted out.

Talib dismissed Khamisa and the conversation about nothing in particular protracted throughout the next hour. Eventually Talib declared that it was time to make a decision and that he would like to discuss the proposition with his family before making that decision. He asked Abdulla if he could return in two hours and he would then tell him what had been decided. Abdulla agreed and assessed that two hours would be enough time for him to go into Salalah to collect Kathya and Lailla. Juma meanwhile was given permission to spend time with a chaperoned Khamisa.

＊ ＊ ＊

Talib sat alone in the room awaiting Abdulla's return. After more than an hour's discussion his father and brothers had left, leaving him to consider the points made and to make the final decision. His father had passionately advised against the inter-tribe marriage arguing that tradition should always be upheld. His brothers were more constructive pointing out the undoubted difficulties and then emphasising the one and only advantage. He had even taken the unprecedented step of asking Khamisa if she had a preference from all the would be suitors. Her reply at first had been that ot a dutiful daughter and that she would rely on his wisdom to make the decision for her. However, when pressed she had admitted a preference for the young mountain man. Now, with only a few minutes left before Abdulla's return, he thought through his decision once more and rehearsed what he was going to say to the old jebally.

He had been impressed by the polite and honest manner of Juma. The fact that he had previously sought Khamisa's company without prior permission should have counted against him, but to Talib it did not. He allowed that it was probably motivated by genuine feelings of affection for Khamisa and that he had allowed the impetuousness of youth to influence his behaviour. On the evidence at hand so far he did not doubt the sincerity of the young man and that if fondness alone was the only consideration then he would make a suitable husband for his daughter. However, his abilities to provide for her would have to be taken very much on trust. His elder brother had, by Abdulla's own admission, joined the rebel forces and therefore had communist tendencies. It was not so much the communist tendencies that concerned him, it was more the fact that he had deserted his family struggling for existence in order to pursue his own ideals. It was therefore possible that the generics in one full brother were the same in the other. These potential situations added to the fact that he would be surrendering his daughter to a different tribe meant that Khamisa would need the protection of a significant dowry. A monetary dowry was probably not the best option, because it may finish in the hands of her husband anyway. That would of course, be Khamisa's choice and her right. So he decided that gold and silver would be a far better alternative. She would be more reluctant to easily surrender valuable trinkets and in addition they would appreciate in value over time. A large dowry was essential.

Then there was the consideration of the marriage ceremony. With two tribes involved it would be much larger than normal and therefore much costlier. As is the custom many relatives would donate some token towards the celebrations, nevertheless the bulk of the expenses he himself would have to be shoulder.

The price that he would have to ask for his daughter's hand would reflect more than these considerations. Even if an inflated price were agreed there was still the embarrassment of seeking the tribal Sheikh's approval. He would be much more likely to agree to the match if the price quoted reflected a too good to be refused offer.

Here was the advantage of which both of his brothers had expressed. Talib could expect to receive a great deal more under these circumstances than he could in a conventional tribal marriage. Even in an agreement with the wealthy fat merchant he could not demand as much. There would be a handsome surplus. Easily enough to be able to buy a new and power driven boat for the family fishing business. With a bigger boat and an engine they could venture further off shore into deep water and stay out longer where the fish is more plentiful. In addition they could still keep the old boat and continue to fish close inshore. The potential increase in the catch would contribute significantly to family prosperity.

Inversely, however, it was doubtful that this jebally family could afford to pay that sort of price and Talib recognised this. If they could then so be it and if they couldn't, then he would personally be spared the embarrassment of an inter-tribal marriage and all the criticism from within his own Ruwas tribe which it would inevitably bring.

His wife entered the room and announced the arrival of the Al Hamer jabally, Abdulla.

✳ ✳ ✳

With the arrival of the rest of his family Juma's presence had become pressed right into the background. Khamisa greeted Lailla like a sister while the younger girl in turn excitedly presented her own mother, Kathya. Almost before the self-introductions had finished, Khamisa's mother returned from showing Abdulla to where Talib waited. The two older women recognised common ground and easily identified with each other as mothers and therefore kindred spirits. Women's stimulated chatter filled the small room as Lailla showed off both the brightly coloured floral material and the more sombre black that she and Kathya had purchased from Salalah. For the moment neglected, Juma was content to remain in the background and clandestinely study Khamisa.

Her dark eyes sparkled with benign amusement as she indulged Lailla's excitement and at her insistence she deftly felt the quality of the material. Remembering Juma she glanced in his direction and for a moment their eyes held contact. She gave him the briefest of smiles, quivering his insides, before turning her focus back to the attention-demanding Lailla. Juma continued to watch her and he decided that no man on this earth could aspire to anything better than owning this vision of loveliness. As far as he was concerned she possessed poise and elegance in abundance and a singular beauty that was without comparison. There was nothing that he would not do to have this woman for his wife and if only Allah would allow it then he would cherish her for the whole of his life and he would never consider any subsequent wives. He glanced towards the door through which his father had a short time ago disappeared and he wondered what precisely was being said between him and Talib. Those two men in the privacy of a closed room were determining the very structure of the rest of his life without any contribution from him. He wondered if they realised that it was far too important for them to get it wrong.

He stayed on the fringe of the activities adding the occasional comment at the appropriate time while all the time he kept a wary eye on the door watching for his father's return. He was undecided whether a quick return or a delayed one would be in his favour. As the minutes extended he began to convince himself that all was well and the two men were probably discussing the finer details to the arrangement. His conviction evaporated the very next second when he imagined that perhaps his father had to re-present his case attempting to reverse Talib's decision. He wondered if

Khamisa was feeling the tension too and he studied her face. If she were then there was no sign of it there.

Eventually both men emerged solemn faced from their meeting. Juma's hopes sank, there should have been smiles all round. He watched anxiously, trying to extract a glimmer of hope, as both men politely indulged the women's chatter for a few moments. Neither Abdulla nor Talib betrayed the slightest hint of the situation as Abdulla then began the process to leave his host. Eventually Talib stood before Juma and offered his hand. Juma took it, earnestly searching his face for the smallest sign of encouragement. Talib's expression was warm and sympathetic and his handgrip, firm. He held it longer than he needed to and then covered Juma's hand with his other in a gesture of geniality as he bade him goodbye. Juma gleaned a fragment of encouragement, at least it seemed that Khamisa's father did not dislike him. He glanced towards his father hoping to propagate that encouragement further but he was too busy with his own farewells to notice. Perhaps the situation was not hopeless, perhaps it was that no final decision had been reached, he thought. He brought up the rear of his family group as they shuffled towards the door making their good-byes. Close to the door and the last of his family left inside he came face to face with Khamisa.

"*Masalaama*," she said softly, holding eye contact.

Juma nodded, there was much he wanted to say but he could feel the eyes of the rest of her family watching the pair closely. He shrugged slightly indicating to her that he didn't know what the decision had been. "*Masalaama*," he replied.

Outside with both camels on their knees Kathya climbed on behind Abdulla, while Lailla behind Juma. As the animals got to their feet and began to move away the final farewells and arm waving began. A few yards down the road and just before he turned out of sight Juma brought the camel to a stop and half turned it around so that he could see back down the road. Khamisa stood alone and motionless outside the house staring up the road after him. The sea behind her formed a backdrop of blue, while the fresh breeze fluttering her long gown. He paused for a few moments committing the picture to his long-term memory fervently hoping as he did that this wasn't the end of his aspirations. He decided that he would never allow it to be and that he would see her again, most definitely. He waved in her direction. She continued to stand motionless staring in his direction. He wheeled the camel around and hurried after his father.

They had cleared the Al Dharitz gate and joined the road leading northwards towards the jebal when Juma decided to force the issue. He moved his camel up alongside his father.

"What was the decision, Father?"

Abdulla glanced sideways at him and then returned his attention to directly ahead. "The Ruwas man values his daughter very highly."

"How highly?"

"Too highly."

Juma stared at him apprehensively and waited for him to expand.

Eventually feeling that he had to fill the silence Abdulla looked back at his son and said. "We will discuss the matter tonight after we get home." There was nothing more to be said, so Juma dropped his camel back to plod on the heels of the leader.

It had been a clear day promising that the Khareef was nearing its end and by the time they arrived home the sun had set leaving spectacular colours of reds and pinks in the western sky. Nature's resplendent display, however, was lost on both Juma and Abdulla as both men removed the saddle from the animals in silence each wrapped inside their own thoughts. Abdulla finished first and with a slap on the animal's rump he turned it out to forage for itself in the long green grass. He picked up the saddle and blanket and carried it over to the crumbly old store shed nearby. After tossing them just inside the doorway he sat on a nearby rock and watched his son. Immediately Juma freed the animal of its yoke it bounded after the other camel. He watched the animals for a moment then he picked up the saddle equipment and carried it to the old shed too. He dropped them inside and stood looking inwards, then he thumped his palm a couple of times against the wooden cross member above the door sending showers of dust to the floor.

"This old shed is soon going to need some attention," he said.

"Before the next Khareef," Abdulla agreed.

Juma moved to sit by his father's side and for a while the pair sat in silence. Eventually it was Juma who broke the silence. "What did you think of Khamisa?"

"Very beautiful and very virtuous. I can easily see why you are so obsessed with the girl. Such a possession would add greatly to any man's prestige."

Juma was elated. "So you approve?"

"Oh I approve, but…"

"But?"

Abdulla sighed heavily as he sought a way to mediate his son's pending disappointment. There was no way that he could think of that would soften the blow, he placed a consoling arm around his son's shoulders. "Talib values his daughter so highly that the price asked is just impossible."

"What does he ask?"

"Ten thousand rupees."

Juma gasped, "Ten thousand rupees?" Six thousand could be considered exorbitant and even allowing for the inter-tribal consideration seven thousand maximum.

"That's not all. Seven thousand of it is to be cash with the remaining three thousand in either cash or livestock. Two and a half thousand is to be payable at the start of the agreement and that is not refundable if the details are not worked out."

Juma could instantly see the advantage to Talib in that. If the tribal Sheikhs did not agree then the two and a half thousand rupees were forfeit. With a family windfall of ten thousand rupees then the Ruwas Sheikh would almost certainly have to agree, however, it was unlikely that the Al Hamer Sheikh would sanction such an expense for a poor jeballi family. "Is there any room for bargaining?"

"None. Those are the only terms that Talib is prepared to accept before he will permit his daughter to leave their tribe."

Juma stared away towards the reddened sky thoroughly dejected there seemed to be no hopes of finding that sort of money.

"Three thousand in livestock value is not a particular problem," Abdulla went on. "We would have one year to improve our stock. We could do that by breeding our cattle, our camels, and our goats and still maintain our present levels. Nor would cash around two and a half thousand rupees. I have a little more than that left over from what Mussalim brought from Bahrain."

At the mention of Bahrain a glimmer of an idea came to Juma.

"For around four thousand rupees," his father went on, "you should be able to find a very suitable woman from within our own tribe." He squeezed his son's shoulder sympathetically. "Choose another," he said.

He ignored his father's advice. "What if I raise the other four and half thousand rupees father?"

"How are you going to do that?" he asked a little derisively.

"I will do as Mussalim did, I will go to Bahrain. In one year I should be able to earn a lot more than that.'

"No," Abdulla said firmly removing his arm from Juma's shoulders. Allowing his first son to go had been a grave mistake and the thoughts of his second son being exposed to the same affluent community and the same radical opinions filled him with alarm. "I absolutely forbid it." He did not want to lose Juma to the liberationists too.

"But it's an obvious answer father. I should be able to obtain the whole ten thousand rupees in a little more than a year and the family prosperity would remain untouched also."

"Definitely not," he was adamant.

Juma was silent a moment. "Then what if I can raise the outstanding four and half thousand some other way?"

"That will depend on exactly how you intend to do it," Abdulla said with an exasperated sigh.

"I will go to Salalah. I will find work and I will save all my money."

"You are the eldest remaining son and your place is right here helping your family with this farm," he replied firmly.

"Yes. I know. But one year father, just one year. I am sure I could get the money in that time. On the day's off then I can return here and begin to build a house close by for Khamisa and myself to live in. Then after we're married I can return to be with Khamisa and work the farm."

"Four and half thousand rupees in one year? Is it possible?"

"I don't know! But at least let me try."

"Work is difficult to find in Salalah."

"But not impossible."

Abdulla stared at his son. Could he do it? He could not in all honesty prevent him from at least trying. "I have one month to give Talib my answer. In one month you will have to have work in Salalah and be earning at least enough to save those four and half thousand rupees within one year from that date. If you are then I will go to this Ruwas man and agree his terms." He held out his hand to be shaken.

"What about the Sheikh?"

"Leave that to me."

"Tomorrow I will go to Salalah," Juma said with a huge grin and aspiring hopes. He grasped his father's hand and the bargain was agreed.

Juma left his home early the next morning and he was in Salalah well before noon. He began his search for full time work in the eastern area of the town amongst the many small fruit farms. Apart from one instance, where he had been offered one week's casual work harvesting bananas for a few rupees, his enquiries were greeted with either a rude flat rejection or a sad shake of the head. By mid afternoon he had been forced to accept that he wasn't going to achieve his objective amongst the fruit farms and he gave up and made his way into the town centre.

He sat in the shade of a large Bedam tree, ate a few figs and drank water from his goatskin while he waited patiently for the town to recover from the afternoon recess and come to life. When it did he began an endless round of shops and stores which might be able to offer him something. He wasn't at all sure precisely what he had to offer in this kind of work but if someone was prepared to give him a chance then he was prepared to accept almost anything. In the event it proved to be another futile exercise. Ex-patriot Asians seemed to have monopoly of all the shop positions from managers through all grades down to cleaners and every one of them appeared to be better qualified for the work than he was. Eventually with the evening turned into night he made his way to the beach and hugely disappointed he settled down to sleep and await the morning. Tomorrow would be another day

He was up early and tried his luck with the local fishermen as they prepared to launch their boats on the early morning tide. He knew nothing of fishing skills, which did not help his cause, and even if he had it probably would have made no difference because each fishing boat was family owned and manned by the members of those families anyway. He wandered into the gold and silver souk offering his services to the skilled craftsmen established there but no one was interested in a callow jabally.

By noon he was well to the west of Salalah on the docks at Raysut trying his luck there. Once again without any particular skill his opportunities where strictly limited and although one manager did take his name and promise to let him know if anything did come up, he was disappointed. Tired, hungry and discouraged he decided to make his way home.

He spent the next three days in a very subdued mood helping his father around the farm. With the Khareef into its last throws and the hot weather about to return Abdulla had pressed all family members into cutting down as much as possible of the long mellow grass which covered the mountains in abundance. After it was cut it was then spread across the ground to dry. His plan was then to sheaf it and store it beneath a large and heavy canvas. When the sun had once more scorched the mountains barren of animal grazing fodder and a bale of hay was at an exorbitant price he would have a supply of his own to use defraying the cost of feeding his cattle greatly.

On the fourth day Juma deserted the family task to continue work seeking and journeyed once again to Salalah. This time at mid-morning he presented himself at the gates of the Sultan's Air Force base. He reasoned that there must be many types of jobs inside and of varying levels of skill. The gate guards, however, would not let him onto the base, but one did use the telephone and spoke to someone on his behalf. He was told that someone would eventually come to talk to him, but in the meantime he was instructed to move away from the gate and wait nearby. All the rest of the morning and into the afternoon he sat beneath a palm tree watching and waiting. Twice he watched the guards change and twice he re-approached the gate to be informed both times and with a non-committal shrug that someone should come soon. Eventually, he realised that no one was going to come and that no one had ever intended to. The blatant dismissal irritated him and he resented the time that had been wasted. In bad humour he mounted his camel and rode the five kilometres to the Army base Um Al Ghariff.

Twenty-five metres from the barrier, he dismounted from the camel and left the animal to nibble on a nearby acacia bush. He approached the guards on the gate walking slowly, very conscious of the guns pointing at him from the sandbagged sangar. Two guards stood in the centre on the opposite side of the barrier watching him approach. As he neared a third man emerged from the sangar and began walking towards the other two guards. Juma was close enough to speak now but just as he was about to open his mouth he heard his name called. He diverted his attention to the man who had just come from behind the sangar and he recognised Khaleef.

"What are you doing here?" he asked as he ducked under the barrier and came to greet him.

Juma shook the offered hand warmly. "Hello Khaleef. I am looking for regular work."

"You and three-quarters of all Dhofaris," he replied sardonically. "But why here?"

Juma shrugged, "I hear tell that there are lots of workers on these bases."

"Yes there are some. What kind of work are you looking for?"

He shrugged again, "Anything."

"Unless you have a particular skill the only work that you're likely to get would be menial. What can you do?"

"Well," Juma didn't know how to answer. "All I know is farming."

It was Khaleef's turn to shrug. "Don't think there is much need for farmers on an army base."

Juma looked wistfully past the barrier at the roadway inside the base. "There must be something I can do. I'll consider anything."

"Cleaning?"

Cleaning was perhaps not very honourable but to possess Khamisa he was quite prepared to bury his pride for a year. "Hmm," he nodded.

Khaleef stared at him hard. "Why do you sell yourself so cheaply? Cleaning is not for proud Al Hamer jabally's like us."

"I need the money."

He stroked his beard thoughtfully for a few moments then he said. "Have you thought about joining the army? Become an *askar* a soldier of the Sultan."

Juma shook his head, that thought had not occurred to him.

"Due to the heightened tensions there is a recruiting drive going on. The money may not be that good, but at least it's regular and it's as permanent as you want to make it."

Whether Sultan Said Bin Taymour's regime fell or stayed in power did not particularly concern Juma. Until this very moment he could think of no reason why he should take either side in the current conflict. However, perhaps this was the opportunity to obtain the income that he needed which in turn would enable him to achieve his greatest desire. Also there was a far more dignity to being a soldier than a lowly cleaner. "Tell me more," he said.

"Well, the biggest number of recruits are needed for the Firqats. They're looking for a lot of young men who have a good knowledge of the jebal areas, just like you have, to train as anti-guerrilla squads."

"You are not in the Firqats?"

"No. I'm not. I am a regular in the Sultan's Army. Our duties are much duller, mainly security. We occupy and guard government posts and key installations."

"Are they recruiting for the Army too?"

"Yes, more guards are needed. So there is recruiting for the Army. Not as many as for the Firqats, but some. Are you interested?"

How could he not be? If the pay was right it seemed to provide the complete solution to his problem. Khaleef had told him once before about the rate of pay but he felt a need to get confirmation. "What's the pay?"

Khaleef sniffed and pulled a face. "Oh, I don't know exactly. I suppose starting pay around eighty rupees a week rising to about ninety after training. I get a hundred but then I am qualified to corporal."

"Yes I'm interested. What do I have to do?"

Khaleef glanced at his watch. "Well," he said. "I'm afraid that you are too late to see anybody today. I will mention to my Sergeant tonight that you are interested in joining the army and I'll ask him if he can arrange an interview for you tomorrow. I'll be guarding this gate tomorrow between ten and twelve so if you come back then I may have some news for you."

* * *

Abdulla bound a piece of twine around the bundle of cut grass and then stacked the sheaf on its end to dry. He straightened up and pressed his hand against his aching back while he surveyed what they had so far achieved. Sweat stung his eyes and blurred his vision. Using his fingers he rubbed his eyes vigorously but a haze still fogged his sight. He closed his eyes tightly for a few more moments and when he opened them again there was some improvement. He blinked a few more times and the haze cleared. Now he was able to survey their achievements.

Clumsily tied sheaves stacked randomly littered the hillside, so far he was satisfied with what had been achieved. Jokha and Lailla worked together close by, while further down the hill Kathya and Hamed worked alone. In his mind he balanced what had so far been accomplished against what was still left do. They were still a very long way from finishing the gathering and after that was finished all the sheaves would have to be collected and stacked. There would of course, be a few day's respite while the sun dried the grass to hay before they started stacking and he anticipated that by that time everyone would welcome the rest that the respite provided. He glanced towards the sun in the western sky filtered through a misty haze of the day and estimated that it would be setting within about two more hours. It had been a long day and he decided that at sunset he would bring an end to the day's labour

He bent to gather more of the cut grass and as he did he wondered how Juma was faring. Today was the third day since he had left for Salalah and he had expected him back last night at the latest. He didn't know what to think of his absence, perhaps it was that he had discovered a prospect and was still actively pursuing it. Or, more probably, it was directly the opposite and that in desperation he was extending his stay. In either case he wished he were here, his help was needed. Personally he felt that Juma couldn't succeed and that he was wasting his time, however, he could not deny him the chance to at least try. Eventually he would be forced to give up and when he did no resentment could be levied against him. Then he would find him a wife from within his own Al Hamer tribe side-stepping completely the complications attached to the marriage with the Ruwas woman. Juma's new concubine responsibilities would then anchor him to the family homestead. Even though he felt that his son's place was to be here right now helping in this task he was prepared to indulge his futile trips into Salalah anticipating that in the long term it was a wise policy.

Hamed called out. He didn't hear what he had called and he looked down the slope towards him. Hamed waved and then pointed along the hillside to the south. Abdulla followed the direction of his pointing finger. At first he saw nothing and then movement caught his eye and he could just make out a camel rider moving in their direction.

"It's Juma," he heard Lailla say. He squinted his eyes but the rider was just too far away for him to make out clearly. Lailla's eyes were younger and sharper than his were, therefore it probably was, he allowed. The rider, however, was still a long way off and would take a little time to reach them, so he silently turned his attention back to the gathering setting the example for the others to follow.

It took fully twenty minutes for Juma to reach them and when he did it was obvious that he had some good news to relate. He greeted his family boisterously and jumped down from the camel without waiting for the animal to kneel. His whole attitude was jubilant, in complete contrast to his previous return from Salalah. As the family gathered around to greet him he moved to each one in turn and cheerfully kissed them on both cheeks. Then while he generally related trivial items about his trip he distributed presents of small tins of spices to each female in the family. Abdulla watched his son's exuberance impassively and waited for his news with a degree of apprehension. Juma had not immediately shared the news that had placed him close to euphoria so he suspected that it was perhaps not all good. Eventually Juma ran out of trivialities and fell silent, the time had come.

"Well?" Abdulla said.

"Well, I have managed to get the regular income that we need, father. So you can go to Talib and agree the marriage contract between Khamisa and me." His mood had become less buoyant. "The pay is not a fortune," he went on, "but it's enough to achieve the target of four and half thousand rupees. Perhaps not quite within a year, but not very much longer than that. I will be paid eighty-five rupees each week to begin, rising to ninety-five after about twelve or thirteen weeks."

The women were impressed and in the background they chattered excitedly. Abdulla was less impressed. "And what do you have to do to earn this money?"

They had come to the very crux of the matter and Juma shuffled his feet uncomfortably while he tried to find the words. There was no easy way to tell him. He stared directly at his father and said quietly, "I have joined the Sultan's Army." His words were greeted with stony silence, even the women's excited chatter stopped. Juma felt the need to fill the silence and nullify his news to a large degree. "After I have finished training then I am going to be based in Salalah, so I won't be far away. When I have some time off then I can come home to help work the farm, work on a house and of course to be with my wife. It won't be for very long."

Abdulla stared at him quizzically. The plan that they had agreed was for Juma to return to the farm straight after his marriage and not to return when he had some time off. "How long is not very long?"

Again Juma squirmed uncomfortably and ran the back of his hand across his nose. "Three years," he said softly behind his hand.

"Three years," Abdulla exploded. "You want to go away for three years? Definitely not, I absolutely forbid it. All this nonsense for one Bait Ruwas woman," he said derisively. "I will find you a suitable wife from within our own tribe and you will stay, here raise your own family and help to work the farm and there's an end to it."

Juma shook his head, "No I can't, even if I wanted to, I can't."

"You can and you will."

"No I can't, it's too late, father, I have signed a three year contract. I leave in seven days for Salalah and seven days after that I leave for the training camp at Ghubra in the north."

Abdulla stared at his son. His carefully laid plan had all gone wrong. Instead of a marriage tying his son to the farm he had succeeded only in creating a situation which had actually driven him away.

"It's only for three years, father," Juma said sympathetically as if reading his thoughts, "and I will be home as often as I can, especially if Khamisa is here waiting for me."

Abdulla didn't doubt the last statement. Perhaps under the circumstances, three years was not such a heavy penalty to pay. But then in these uncertain times a great deal could happen in three years and he was filled with foreboding. After all being a soldier in a war situation was not without a great deal of risk. He recognised, however, that the situation was beyond his ability to alter and not for the first time he experienced feelings of inadequacy and that his head of the family autocratic control was slipping away from him.

~ 7 ~

December 1968 • Rocking very slightly in the calm waters of the enormous bay the Dhow tugged lazily at the bow anchor chain. Less than an hour previously she had continually tacked left and right of the chain yanking and wrestling against its restraint. Her wood timbers had creaked and groaned complaining against its bondage, as the rapidly retreating tide demanded that she follow. Now the tide had gone and it seemed as if the sixty-foot vessel had reluctantly accepted that she had been left behind. On her deck, seven of her eight-man crew slept. A piece of tarpaulin roughly tied across the port and starboard rigging provided shade from the heat of the mid-afternoon sun. The eighth man, left on watch, passed the time boredly repairing one of the fishing nets.

Mussalim standing in the bow looked across the benign sea to the golden beach little more than a kilometre away. Immediately behind the beach and in front of the towering green hills of Jebal Sayq the bucolic square and flat roofed dwellings of the Dalkut villagers. Any moment now a small boat would put to sea and make its way to the Dhow, which was the communal village fishing boat and the unloading procedure would begin. The catch had been good and it would provide the villagers with full bellies and even a little income from the surplus.

He peered over the gunnel into the clear water and through the distorted transparency he could see the sandy bed beneath. The boat's keel could be only just clear of that bed, he thought. But he knew that these crewmen knew these waters well and probably knew precisely how much water remained beneath them. He decided not to wait for the shore boat.

From the catch he selected two decent sized kingfish, this was his reward for his two-day voluntary assistance. He waved farewell to the watching fisherman then leapt over the side into the water. It was deeper than it appeared and still holding the kingfish by the tail fins he swam awkwardly for two hundred metres until his feet touched bottom. When he reached the deserted beach he stood a moment allowing the water to drain from the *futa* which wrapped around his waist. He moved from the water edge just a few metres before sitting down facing out to sea. He closed his eyes and quietly and clandestinely he made his prayers to Allah.

It was mid December and the Muslim holy month of Ramadhan had begun. This presented Mussalim with additional problems. Not only did he have to keep his prayers secret he now had to somehow disguise his observation of the daylight fasting obligation. So far he had been successful. Trips like the one he had just made with the local fishermen helped. As a soldier of the PFLOAG they regarded him with suspicion. Therefore they didn't openly pray when he was around and he pretended not to notice when they did. They pretended all day to be too busy to eat while Mussalim, diplomatically, did the same. An unspoken and cautious treaty was perceived. When he was required to do his duty to the liberation cause and stand his watch he would make his way to the observation sangars high in the jebal above the village and he would stand a voluntary double watch carrying only water with him. In other off duty daylight hours he would find excuses to avoid his comrades company, by sleeping all day in his quarters or disappearing into the jebal hunting or patrolling. So far it seemed that no one had noticed but the fear existed within him that at any moment one of his colleagues might become suspicious. If that happened then, despite the regard that his comrades held for him there would an immediate danger to his welfare perhaps even his very life.

His brief prayer finished he got up swung the two fish across his bare shoulders and made his way to the mish-mash of roughly constructed sandstone dwellings, which was the village. At the only two-storied building somewhere close in its centre he paused. It was old, flat fronted and flat topped and its best days long passed. Once, however, and perhaps until quite recently, it had been the grandiose home of the village senior. There were two rooms downstairs either side of double iron doors and three up. At its rear was a spacious compound, which was surrounded by single storied rooms. Its multiple rooms had made it ideal for billeting and the PFLOAG forces, who enjoyed unchallenged occupancy of the village, had impounded its use. Mussalim looked up to the centre widow on the first floor, which were his quarters. Its old wooden shutters were wide open and from one of the three horizontal bars the room carpet hung. Shamel was at home!

Sea-salt covered his body and he turned his head and sniffed his shoulder, the pungent odour of fish was upon him also. He looked forward to a refreshing wash down. A twinge of excitement stirred his stomach as he anticipated the touch of Shamel's hands on his body helping him wash away its grime and stench. But first he would report to the Shibam.

He pushed open the heavy iron door and went into the corridor that led through to the rear compound. He waited just a moment allowing his eyes to become accustomed to the darker surroundings before pushing open the door to his left and calling out, "Hemal." From the opposite room Hemal called a response. As befitted his rank as Commander of the Dalkut detachment he occupied the two reception rooms at the building front. Mussalim turned about kicked off his sandals and entered.

Hemal dressed only in a *futa* sat crossed legs on a carpet with his concubine at his side. "Crazy man Mussalim," he said greeting him. The woman lowered her head and retreated immediately into the darkened corner of the room.

'Crazy man Mussalim' was the name that the instructors had given to him at the Hauf training camp. Tales of his hot headed action on that day at Mirbat, when in blind anger he had leapt to his feet and attempted to shoot down that aircraft with his weapon in single fire mode only, had preceded him. There had, however, been some gross exaggeration and the story completely rewritten. Now the accounts were that he had stood in the open fully exposed throwing only rocks and shouting defiantly at the aircraft while the ground all around him erupted with the exploding shells from its cannon. It was therefore not surprising that he had been so named, insane actions such as that could belong only to a man that was indeed crazy. At first embarrassed, he had denied the actions. However, courage such as the story described suggested a high calibre of bravery amongst the soldiers of the cause and was good propaganda for recruiting. Its exaggeration therefore was not allowed to be reduced. It did, however, have side benefits for Mussalim, it singled him out for some favourable treatment during his training. So involuntarily he tolerated the 'crazy man' tag.

He took the hand offered by Hemal and sat opposite him on the carpet. Hemal was a short, heavy man with a plump round face and a neatly trimmed beard. He came from the Hadraumat region of Yemen from the historic town of Shibam. During the many evening *dirwains* he would dominate the conversation relating, ostentatiously, legends of Shibam and its historical and unique tower block houses seven, eight storeys high. He was proud of that heritage and as a perceived status he openly encouraged others to refer to him as Al Shibam. Mussalim offered him the larger of the two fish as a present and enquired of the news during his two-day absence.

"The news is all good," Al Shibam said with a satisfied grin. "We control all the jebal areas from east to west. Government forces no longer venture into the mountains for fear of ambushes. They are more or less encircled on the Salalah plain with their backs to the sea. On the *nejd* beyond the jebal we continue to ambush and harass, so much so that they dare not move around in companies less then sixty strong. Dissension is also growing in the north of the country. There is news of a new anti Sultan movement started, The Revolutionary Movement of Oman and the leaders of our own movement are offering them encouragement and support." He nodded with a degree of gratification. "Yes all the news is good."

Mussalim greeted the report with mixed feelings. He was of course delighted that all was going well for the PFLOAG but was somewhat resentful that he was obliged to carry out mundane sentry duties in the far south western corner of Oman far away from the impressive progressive action.

At the end of September he had finished training at Hauf and had been sent to supplement the small force occupying the Omani village of Dalkut less than twenty kilometres from the Yemen border. Dalkut was shielded on both its northern and eastern perimeters by the rugged and towering Jebal Sayq and, except from the sea, the only easy way in or out of the village was from the west along a rugged track that passed for a road. That road led directly into the Yemen passing directly beneath the escarpment on which the elevated border town of Sarfait sat. From there it looped northwards around the end of Jebal Sayq to cross back over the border into Oman. Since the Oman government had itself closed the Yemen border they had effectively surrendered both Sarfait and Dalkut to the PFLOAG forces. It was a safe and secure situation without threat. However, such a situation was not what Mussalim had joined the cause for and he was restless. He wanted to ask once again when he would be allowed to join the main action to the east, but he feared to. During the past weeks he had asked the Shibam frequently and he could sense the man's growing exasperation.

"When is my next duty detail?" he asked instead.

Hemel picked up a notebook from close by and thumbed through its pages. "Tomorrow six till midday, then six till midnight. Up on the point."

The point was high on the jebal at the eastern end of the bay. The sandbagged sangar up there had a strategic and unrestricted view inland to the north and of the seas to the south. Although it was extremely unlikely that any government forces would cross the rugged jebal to mount an attack on the village or even attack from the sea, Al Shibam was taking no chances and sentries were posted round the clock. Similarly too, at the other end of the bay on the high ground above the road.

"I will do the twelve daylight hours straight through." Mussalim volunteered. "It is a long climb up there and once I am there then I may as well stay there and complete my shift."

"As you wish," the Shibam said and began making alterations in his notebook with a pencil.

It was far more convenient to do it that way and covertly it would also enable Mussalim to complete another clandestine fast day. He looked past the man sitting cross-legged opposite him to the woman in the corner. She was preparing water and dates on a wooden platter to lay before Al Shibam's guest. It was not yet sundown and therefore not time for Mussalim to break his fast. He decided that he had to quickly make some excuse to leave.

He held up his arms and sniffed loudly. "Hemel, my body smell is offensive. I will leave you now."

"Nonsense, stay."

"No I must go," and he got to his feet.

The Shibam studied him for a moment then nodded and got up also. "Will you join us this evening in the *dirwain?*"

Mussalim nodded, he recognised that it was not an optional invitation.

The old wooden stairs, which led from the interior compound to the upper balcony, creaked as he climbed them. He dropped the kingfish outside the door directly at the top of the stairs and then went through into his allocated quarters. The room was dark and very sparsely furnished. From the only window the room carpet hung airing in the late afternoon sun. In the corner was a grubby cot, which he shared with Shamel and at its foot a bundle of rags on which her six year-old son slept. Behind the door was an old upright chest that served as a cupboard and wardrobe and by its side a rickety old table. Shamel it seemed was out somewhere. Mussalim was both disappointed and irritated. She must have seen the Dhow anchored in the bay for the last hour or more, he thought. Therefore she should be here, it was her duty to be here to tend his needs.

Shamel was a second widow of an elderly villager who had died. The burden of looking after the dead man's two widows and four children had fallen on the man's younger brother. He, like most of the Dalkut villagers already impoverished and with a family of his own to provide for, found the additional burden crushing. They survived barely above the starvation level. So he had offered up both widows to the Shibam for his soldiers comfort. The arrangement where surplus women were traded out to the PFLOAG soldiers for a couple of hundred rupees was a convenient and common arrangement. It not only brought a financial gratuity but it also relieved the man of his responsibility to clothe and feed her and her children.

One week after his arrival Mussalim had been given the choice of the two widows and had chosen Shamel. Not only was she the younger of the two, she only had one of the four children to bring with her. He had paid three hundred rupees to the Shibam and the woman was his until she pleased him no more, or he left the village.

On the table in an old and battered tin bowl Shamel had left water for him to wash, at least she knew that his arrival was imminent. He unwrapped the *futa* from his waist and tossed it into the furthest corner of the room. Then he set about washing away the salt and fish smell from his body. He opened the cupboard and took a clean *futa*, momentarily he held it to his face to smelling the odour of frankincense. Shamel always perfumed freshly washed clothing with the fragrance of frankincense by putting the laundry above a burner for a few minutes before putting it away.

He had just finished dressing when she swept hurriedly into the room muttering apologies for her absence. She removed the veil part of the full length black *abeya* and began to busy herself clearing up after him.

"Where have you been?" he demanded harshly.

She picked up the discarded *futa* and turned to face him. She was slightly built, due mostly to a degree of emaciation, and more than a foot shorter than Mussalim. She was older than he was but only by two or three years. Her facial features were pleasing to look at and her mass of light brown hair, frizzed. "I took Ali to my brother's house. I didn't think that you would want him to be here for a little while after you got back," she said quietly.

Mussalim understood instantly the reasons motivating the removal of her infant son for a little while. She had anticipated his desires and as always trying so hard to please had cleared that obstacle. He smiled gently at her and nodded, pleased by her actions. "Come," he said indicating towards the cot behind him.

* * *

The dark sky showed not even the first hint of daylight when Mussalim left his quarters to make the forty-minute climb to the observation sangar high on the jebal. At the very same instant his brother Juma stood in line waiting to receive an issue of ammunition from the armoury at the Um Al Gharriff Garrison in Salalah. This was to be his first sortie outside the Salalah precincts since his arrival back from camp Ghubra in Muscat.

He had completed his training and had been posted immediately back to the Dhofar regiment in the hard pressed region. On his arrival at the Garrison just three weeks ago he had been granted a five days leave of absence. He had spent most of that time with his family and the time was pleasurable. However, by far the most pleasurable time of that leave were the two chaperoned sessions he had spent with Khamisa. She was as keen as he that all should proceed towards their wedding smoothly. She had asked anxiously how the accumulate of assets and funds that would satisfy her father's terms was going. She empathised completely with Juma's plight agreeing that her father asked a very great deal. But she could do nothing that would help, except offer encouragement. But that encouragement helped and stiffened enormously Juma's already determined resolve.

On his arrival back at the Garrison after his short leave he had spent most of the following two weeks carrying out the somewhat dreary duties of guarding gates, installations and other potential targets. Today, however, there was the promise of a break from the mundane. Thanks to his friend Khaleef's influence, who was now a corporal, he had secured a place in the convoy bound to re-supply the outposts at Tarqah and Mirbat.

Through the barred issue window he received his supply of sixty rounds in four magazines from a moustached British NCO. He slapped one of the magazines onto his rifle and stuffed the rest inside his shirt, then he made his way slowly towards the row of convoy vehicles standing in the darkness a few metres away. Other soldiers hung around in small groups muttering quietly amongst themselves or wandered aimlessly around as they waited for someone to organise the assignment. He walked along the line of vehicles until he found Khaleef sitting in the rear of a Land Rover. He motioned that Juma should climb in. He climbed over the side and sat opposite his friend

There was no covering tilt on the vehicle, no windows, no passenger doors, not even a driver windshield. The Land Rover was stripped to its bare essentials. It was a cold morning and Juma blew hard onto his cupped fingers trying to generate some warmth. Then he rubbed his cold nose vigorously attempting to revive some circulation.

"It is a bit," Khaleef grinned and then wrapped his shamag tight around his face and neck leaving only his eyes visible. "It'll be even worse once we start rolling."

Juma copied Khaleef and adjusted his own shamag looking down the convoy line as he did. Two Land Rovers headed it, one with a Browning machine gun mounted in its rear. Then two Bedford one-ton trucks and two more Land Rovers, one in which he now sat. There was another truck behind them and yet two more Land Rovers brought up the rear, one of these had a mounted machine gun also. Briefly he wondered if those guns would be needed at some point during this trip.

"It's a milk run," Khaleef remarked as if reading his thoughts. "We should be back around sunset."

"Do you think we'll need those guns?" Juma asked.

"We often do," he replied with a slight shrug, leaving Juma a little apprehensive about what he had volunteered himself into.

As if by some silent signal the men now began to clamber aboard the vehicles and engines began to roar into life. Two men climbed into the vehicle beside Juma and Khaleef muttering a brief acknowledgement as they did. A sergeant sat in the front passenger seat and he now glanced back over his shoulder. Satisfied that he had the full compliment he gave the word for the driver to start his engine. A British officer wearing the uniform of the Sultan's Army, including the shamag, walked unhurriedly along the length of the convoy and paused at each vehicle to pass last minute instructions. Then he climbed into the lead Land Rover and after a short pause the convoy began to roll.

They left Salalah and headed east. As a precaution against planted land mines the lead driver ignored the road and led the convoy along the uneven ground between the road and the beach. It was slow going as the vehicles bumped and jarred along the crated and rocky surface. To maintain a safe distance from the vehicle in front drivers would sometimes be forced to stop halting the rest of the convoy behind when they did. It was important to maintain a the distance from the vehicle in front just in case it should be unfortunate enough to roll over a mine. The sun rose dead ahead glowing the skies above it an assortment of angry reds. Its low and blinding light added greatly to the drivers problems of visibility. With the British officer standing in the lead vehicle inspecting the ground immediately to the front, the convoy's progress was little better than walking pace.

It was mid morning before they neared the fishing village Tarqah only twenty-five kilometres from Salalah, and when they did they skirted around behind it and continued eastward towards Mirbat. They crossed the mouth of the Wadi Dharbat fronted by the spectacular Dahaq escarpment. Fully a kilometre wide Dahaq's sheer wall rose two hundred metres across its entire length. Still ignoring the road they ascended from the wadi onto the cliff tops and onto a stony plain. From this point on their progress improved. It is difficult to bury a mine in solid rock so there was a little more confidence in the under wheels conditions. Nevertheless, it was nearing noon when they descended from the cliffs into a wide sand bay and viewed the twin forts of Mirbat on the opposite side. Here for the first time they used the road and with clouds of choking pink dust spewing from the wheels, the convoy now sped towards Mirbat.

The guards dragged away the chicaned barrier as they approached and they sped unhindered inside the concertina wire's barbed protection. Once they were inside the leading Land Rover pulled over and the British Officer standing on the seat directed traffic. One truck and two Land Rovers to the fort on the high ground while the rest headed towards the beach fort. The convoy came to stop on the sea side of the beach fort in front of its enormous wooden doors. Wasting no time one of the two trucks was reversed up to those doors and unloading operations began immediately by the eager fort personnel.

Temporarily surplus to requirements the escorting soldiers took the opportunity to attend to their own personal needs. Juma sat on a nearby rock with his rifle resting across his knees watching the unloading until he became bored. Then mildly curious, he got up and went to examine some of the bullet scars on the fort walls before he wandered aimlessly onto the beach. He looked across the enormous bay towards the steep rugged cliffs on the opposite side from which they had descended a little while ago. The sun was high, the sky cloudless and in complete contrast to the early morning the day was now hot. The distant vista shimmered in the heat haze while the sea in between was like a millpond with barely enough energy to lap at the beach. It was a scene of natural pacifistic beauty disguising completely the strife that raged between the belligerent human factions in the area.

It didn't take very long for the truck's contents to be unloaded and the re-assembly of the convoy sluggishly began. Juma climbed back into the Land Rover and took his seat. "Quick turnaround!" He remarked.

"Hmm, the quicker the better," Khaleef replied.

Juma looked at him quizzically waiting for an explanation.

"It is not likely that our journey here went unnoticed and perhaps even at this very moment the *adoo* are preparing some kind of reception for our return trip. So the sooner we return the less time they will have to get ready."

A few minutes later the truck and Land Rovers from the other fort took their position in the convoy then without further delay the return journey began. They were about halfway across the stony plain when they came under fire from somewhere on the jebal hillside. The leading Land Rover peeled off to the sea side of the convoy and the British officer waved the vehicles through. He signalled to three Land Rovers that they should head towards the jebal and engage the enemy while the vehicle in which he stood fell in behind the last vehicle and followed the rest of the convoy. The three detailed Landrovers, including the one in which Juma sat sped across the rough terrain towards the foot of the jebal.

Khaleef pumped the bolt of his rifle and worked a bullet into the breach. Juma noted his lead and followed his example. The sergeant, sitting in the front, signalled that they were now close enough and the driver turned the vehicle side on and stopped. The very instant it stopped all the men leapt out and took cover rapidly behind the vehicle. One of the three Land Rovers was one of the gun ships and the mounted Browning in the back soon began its car shattering cracks in random short bursts. Juma looked across to see the gunner standing fully exposed behind the gun blindly firing short bursts before swinging the weapon to a new position and repeating the burst. He cautiously peeped above the Land Rover's cover and looked up into the thick brush on the jebal hillside, but could see nothing to shoot at. He sank back to sit on the ground at Khaleef's side.

"What's he firing at?" he shouted above the dim.

Khaleef shrugged. "Nothing."

"Nothing?"

"Just trying to keep their heads down while the convoy escapes."

Juma looked across the flat stony plain in the direction the convoy had taken and could see only the cloud of dust that followed in its wake. The sergeant meanwhile coolly stood with the upper part of his body exposed above the Land Rover's cover, searching the steep hillside with a pair of binoculars.

'Ninety-nine, ninety-nine,' Juma kept repeating in his head, keeping time with the bursts of the machine gun. He was not even sure if they were actually under fire as the close presence of Browning's deafening cracks blotted out all other sounds.

Suddenly the sergeant gave out a cry of pain staggered backwards and fell to the ground clutching his arm. He writhed around on the ground trying to relieve the agony, shouting incoherently all the time. Any doubts that Juma had were cleared completely, they were indeed under fire. Khaleef reacted instantly, he leapt to his feet, grabbed the man's collar and dragged him unceremoniously behind the Land Rover's cover.

The sleeve of the man's left arm was sodden with blood and spreading quickly. Acting instinctively, due in no small part to his recent completed training, Juma ripped off his own shirtsleeve and tied it tight around the man's arm just above the rapidly enlarging blood stain. Then he removed his bayonet from its scabbard, a round pointed pig-sticker, and twisted it in the sleeve rendering an instantly effective tourniquet. Khaleef grasped Juma firmly by the shoulder and nodded in an approving gesture.

A fusillade of bullets ripped through the aluminium skin of the Land Rover only inches above their heads causing them instinctively to flinch and indicated that their existing cover was both flimsy and vulnerable. The machine gun ceased its deafening retorts as its operator, under the onslaught of fire from the hillside, was forced to abandon it and dive for cover.

"How many are out there?" Juma shouted in alarm as the thuds and splashes of the bullets spattered the ground all around the three vehicles.

"Don't know. But it's time to go," he said and he shook the driver by his collar. "Let's go." He shouted the same instructions to the others crouching and huddling behind their vehicles. No time to pamper to the wounded man's comfort Juma and another bundled the sergeant awkwardly and unceremoniously into the back of the vehicle then clambered aboard themselves. "Go go go," Khaleef screamed at the driver as he climbed over from the back to the front seat.

The driver didn't need encouragement, he set off wheels spinning under heavy acceleration and the engine screaming in low gear. Now that they were moving they had become a much harder target to hit and the swirling dust they left in their wake added a covering screen to their retreat. The wounded man in the back screamed continuously as every bump and jar resonated agony through his injury until he mercifully fainted. Juma glanced back to see how the other two vehicles fared but the cloud of dust blocked his view, he could see nothing.

"What about the other vehicles?" he shouted.

"They're coming."

He looked back again and wondered how Khaleef could tell.

At that speed they quickly placed some distance between themselves and there would-be ambushers. Khaleef took a long look back studying the distance they had covered. "You can slow down now," his calm voice instructed the driver. "Take the road."

"What about mines?" the driver queried.

Khaleef shrugged and peered over his shoulder again this time trying to catch a glimpse of the other vehicles. Perhaps he wasn't as sure as he had sounded moments ago. But they were there, just a little way back and on either flank. A kilometre down the road they stopped and regrouped taking a damage assessment. Surprisingly they were in pretty good shape. The only injury was to the sergeant and although there were several jagged holes in all the vehicles the only disabling damage was to one vehicle that had taken a hit in the radiator and was now boiling up. They quickly transferred men and equipment to the other two vehicles, abandoned the crippled one and set off to catch up with the convoy.

By using the graded road and travelling at speed they soon caught up to the convoy which had continued to pick a cautious course running parallel to the road. Khaleef held the present course until they were a little ahead, then he instructed the driver to angle towards the convoy's front. As they neared he flagged down the lead vehicle.

"Sir, we have a casualty," he called standing upright in the vehicle when they had stopped.

The British officer stared at him a moment then slowly made his way across to peer over the vehicle side at the stricken sergeant. The man had regained consciousness a little while earlier and suffered in silence sometimes staring up to the sky and sometimes with eyes screwed tightly shut with pain. At this moment he stared back at the man peering down on him.

"Who put that on?" the officer asked quietly pointing at the tourniquet.

"I did."

"Good. When did you last ease it?"

Juma shook his head.

"Then do it now. And ease it a little every few minutes " He glanced once more at the wounded man and gave him a brief reassuring smile, then deciding he could do no more at this stage he went towards the front of the vehicle. "Corporal, you press on ahead to Tarqah," he instructed Khaleef "I will radio Salalah and arrange for a cas-evac helicopter to meet you there and to evacuate the casualty. You wait for us there, we will join us as soon as we can."

"Yes, sir," Khaleef acknowledged.

The officer took a step back and waved the two Land Rovers past.

As they moved away Juma looked back curiously and watched the officer walking back to the convoy. He wondering why a man like that would volunteer his services to a conflict that had absolutely nothing to do with him. He glanced down at the man stretched out by his feet, his arm soaked and sticky with blood and eyes screwed with pain tightly closed. Today was proving to be a considerable experience and his first real taste of what precisely he had got himself into for just a few rupees a week. This was not a game, the possible consequences were severe indeed and more than just a little frightening. The reality of the situation was impressed upon him hard. But then he had his own personal reasons for being here and in this situation. Primarily he had a woman to win and secondary this Dhofar region was where he lived anyway. But the British man? His region was four thousand miles away and this war was no particular concern of his. So what was his purpose for being here? He glanced back to where he had last seen him, but the swirling dust behind the moving vehicle hid everything. That man was still in the British army. However, just like all the British that were presently serving in Sultan Siad Bin Taymour's Army, he had put himself forward as a volunteer to be loaned. Juma re-lived those few minutes under fire. It had been quite terrifying but now that he had come safely through he admitted to himself that there had been a high degree of excitement also. Could it be that this excitement was the very reason why the Britisher was here?

Travelling at speed along the graded road it didn't take very long to reach Taqah and just outside the village Khaleef instructed the driver to stop. He looked back and waited for the following Land Rover to catch up. When it had he twirled his wrist upward with a pointed finger signalling to the driver behind. The driver signalled back indicating that he understood that he wanted him to stay close now.

He glanced at Juma and said with a grim face. "Not many people in this village are friendly towards us, so stay alert." He looked around once more making sure that everybody was ready and then gave the driver the word to continue. They proceeded at high speed into the village with the second vehicle very close behind.

The road entered the village from the east and routed right through the centre westward towards Salalah. On the left as they entered and separating the road from the wide beach, rough wattle shacks constructed mostly from recycled scrap materials. On the other side the buildings were more substantially constructed being made from coarse sandstone blocks. These dwellings, small and square with flat roofs and one storey only, could be considered superior to the wattle shacks but not greatly. Their crumbling and shabby appearances indicated various stages of decay.

It was by now mid afternoon and only a mere handful of villagers, who had not taken cover from the baking sun, witnessed the arrival of the army Land Rovers. Some stared silently with hostile expressions while others shouted some indiscernible abuse or waved their fists. All were left enveloped in thick clouds of dust disgorged from the wheels of the speeding vehicles. They retreated hastily from the choking grime. "That would do nothing to temper their hostility," Juma concluded.

Somewhere in the middle of the village they made a sharp right turn cutting through a narrow alleyway between dilapidated houses and into a wide uneven clearing. Here Juma got his first sight of the old castle of Taqah, which the Sultan's forces had now occupied and fortified. It stood on the top of a steep rocky incline some seventy metres above the clearing and faced seaward. A fat prismatic shaped tower separated the high castellated fascia walls in the middle. Squatting inside this tower, peeping over the edge of its castellations, was yet another identically shaped tower. A double row of tangled concertina wire protected the approach to the castle walls, even up the steep incline. Positioned as it was on the highest point in the village, it presided over the whole tangled composite of the village with austere autonomy. They drove past and turned along a rough track that wound steeply upward behind the imposing citadel. As they neared the top they were confronted by a guarded barrier, which provided the only easy access inside the concertina wire's protective palisade. The guards pulled away the barrier admitting the two vehicles inside the compound and onto a large flatish area at the castle's rear.

They drove up to and stopped under the shade of the tall featureless walls. A small group of soldiers had appeared on the building corner a few metres away and stood silently watching the new arrivals and making no attempt to approach. From the vehicles men began to wearily uncoil themselves and stand around aimlessly. At Mirbat the welcome had been cheerful and cordial, as one would expect towards a convoy bringing in supplies. Here, however, the welcome was definitely restrained. The Dhofari soldiers leaned nonchalantly on the vehicles or found some menial task on which they could conveniently busy themselves. Juma still sat in the rear of the vehicle and stared towards the men waiting for something to happen. Nothing did, then he too became a little embarrassed and sought something to preoccupy himself. He glanced down at the wounded man who lay there motionless with eyes tightly closed. Juma loosening the tourniquet on the wounded man's arm, permitting a little blood flow.

"How is he doing?" Khaleef asked leaning over the vehicle's side.

Juma was pretty sure that the man was conscious but was trying to drift into the world of sleep, which might provide some relief from his pain. , "I think he's OK," he replied unsurely and shrugging non-committally. Glancing over Khaleef's shoulder towards the men standing on the building corner he remarked. "Not very friendly, are they?"

Khaleef glanced over his shoulder. "No," he agreed. "It's always the same here."

"What's the problem?"

"The problem is that they are not Dhofaris. They are from the northern tribes around Muscat and they resent having to be here. This conflict is more than a thousand kilometres from where they live and they don't see this war as any of their business. Then the locals don't help to sweeten their attitude either. They are not particularly sympathetic towards government forces, so they don't welcome us into their village. Then when the soldiers turn out to be from northern tribes anyway." He snorted ironically. "Well then, that makes them positively hostile. These men are virtually prisoners inside this compound," he added with a hint of sympathy.

Juma looked around the wired compound trying to imagine what it was like to be imprisoned within such a small area and not daring to venture very far from its protection. A major and a sergeant pushed their way through the northern men and walked towards the vehicles. "Somebody is coming," he warned Khaleef who had his back towards the approaching men.

Khaleef pushed himself up from the Landrover and turned to face the newcomers. When they were close enough he saluted the major. He returned the salute and then offered his hand to be shaken.

"*Salaam alikum*," he greeted.

"*Alikum salaam*," Khaleef returned the greeting.

The three of them went through the usual polite customary Arabic greetings and replies. When the protocol was completed the major then instructed his sergeant to welcome the visitors and to take them inside to the coolness of the castle and then to offer them water. Although it was Ramadhan a soldier or a traveller is permitted to drink if they so wish. Only now, on their sergeant's loud verbal instructions, did the northern men begin to make their visitors welcome.

"You have a wounded man?" the major asked.

Khaleef indicated the vehicle behind him where Juma still sat.

The Major peered down thoughtfully at the injured man and then asked, "What happened?"

Khaleef gave him a brief report on the events.

When Khaleef had finished his account the major looked down once more at the stricken man. Although he still had his eyes tightly closed he nevertheless squeezed his shoulder and said re-assuringly. "You'll be alright. A helicopter is on its way from Salalah."

Almost on cue Juma could hear the distant heavy thump of a helicopters rotor blades and he searched the western skies trying to locate it. As it approached it grew from an indiscernible dot to the recognisable shape of a Whirlwind from the British Royal Air Force contingency at Salalah. It slowed and then came to a stop hovering above the flat area behind the castle. It sent everyone scurrying for cover as the giant whirling blades lifted clouds of dust and stones and hurled them outwards with ferocity. The pilot lowered the aircraft gradually until it dropped with a jar onto the ground and then he shut down the engines.

When the loud swishes of the free wheeling rotor blades eventually stopped, a door on the helicopter's side slid back and two medical orderlies leapt out. Acting on a signal from the major they hurried across to the Land Rover. Juma jumped out making room for the two orderlies and then stood back idly watching the pair work. They took a few moments to examine the injury before professionally applying an effective dressing. They then immobilised the man's injured arm by securing it alongside his body. One of them obtained a stretcher from the aircraft and then they carefully helped the casualty onto it with words of encouragement and guiding hands. The helicopter was back in the air within five minutes of touching down.

The major and Khaleef hurried away and disappeared around the corner of the castle as the dust and grit once more flew. Juma who had taken cover behind the Land Rover now stood and watched the helicopter as it passed over the castle heading seawards and then did a wide turn heading west towards Salalah.

Finding himself alone he picked up his rifle and slowly followed the direction all the others had taken. He emerged on the sunny fascia side of the castle facing seaward and overlooking the village. There were no imposing gates or wooden doors into this castle, just a small standard metal pedestrian door. The rest of the Salalah soldiers were sitting around this door talking cheerfully and passing around water bottles. Juma paused and studied the impoverished village houses below for a few moments before wandering off a little way to sit on a rock in the shade of a stubby Acacia tree. Despite the shabby appearances of the human abodes beneath him the overall view was not unpleasant. A thin line of greenery divided the crude shacks from golden sands and a blue sea beyond.

"The sea is very beautiful," a voice suggested. He turned to see one of the northern soldiers standing by his side holding out a water canteen towards him.

Juma glanced back over the village and out to the sea. "Yes it is," he agreed taking the offered canteen because it would have been bad manners not to do so. He took a drink, but did not swallow. He swilled the water around his mouth and then leaning slightly spit it out.

"Are you from this region?"

"Yes I am from Jebal Qara and of the tribe Al Hamer."

"A mountain man," the other man said sitting down by his side. "I am from a fishing village, not unlike this one, in the Batinah region of northern Oman. I am tribe Beni Amr."

"You are a long way from home my friend." Juma handed back the canteen.

"Yes and my family," he agreed.

There was a long pause in the conversation with both men staring silently seaward before Juma asked. "What brought you into the Sultan's army?"

"My village is very poor and the army pay regular. It keeps my family from starving."

He went on to describe conditions throughout the Battinah region and the hardships of poverty. Hardships that were almost identical in every way to those that the Dhofar people were experiencing. Juma's attitude had been parochial and he hadn't considered very much the people's plight outside his own Dhofari region. He had some vague belief that his fellow countrymen in the north were so much better off than those in the south. He couldn't account for the reason why he had believed that but he had. As he quietly talked this Batinah man was dissolving those misconceptions and acquainting Juma to the reality of the situation. The problem of poverty was nationwide.

They had been talking for a few minutes when the main body of the convoy emerged from the narrow alleyway and came into the clearing below. It crossed beneath them and headed towards the track that led up to the castle.

"Our supplies and your comrades have arrived," the northerner remarked getting to his feet.

✳ ✳ ✳

Hamed moved to help his father but two men standing shoulder to shoulder used their Kalachnikovs like staffs across his chest and barred the way. Helplessly, he looked past the two men at Abdulla staring up from the ground at the man who had just thrown him there. He could see no fear in his father's eyes only defiance.

These eight men leading three camels loaded with mortars and mortar shells and armed with Kalachnikov AK47's had arrived at the farmhouse a little more than thirty minutes ago. Hamed had seen them coming from a distance and had alerted his father of the approaching visitors. Abdulla had squinted hard straining his old eyes in the direction that he had indicated trying hard to find them. It was not until they were much closer that he managed to spot them. He waited a while and then moved a few metres away from the homestead in their direction and with customary politeness waited to greet the visitors. When they eventually arrived he greeted them as guests and good-naturedly invited them to rest in the shade of a tree inside the farm compound. Then with regulation courtesy he offered water to the travellers. He ordered Jokha and Kathya to bring a jug of goat milk in addition to the accepted offer of water.

Everything was pleasant and cordial giving no hint of the malevolence to come as the men sipped their drinks and talked cordially. After a few minutes, however, the men demanded that they should be fed. Taken a little aback by their abruptness Abdulla pointed out that they were only a very poor jebaly family with very little to offer. However, if they were prepared to wait until sunset when the day's fast could end then they would welcome them to share in the family's modest fare.

It was at this point that the leader of the group became angry accusing Abdulla of attempting to avoid his obligation to soldiers of the PFLOAG who risked their lives fighting to free people such as he from the Sultan's yoke. He had tried to deny it only to be cut short and accused further of being a Bin Taymour sympathiser. Once again he tried to placate the belligerent man claiming his reason was simply that this was the holy month of Ramadhan and that they observed the fasting obligation. This served only to enrage the man even further. He leapt to his feet grabbed Abdulla by his beard and lifted him close to his glaring face. He cursed him loudly before spinning him around and then cast him roughly away leaving him stumbling and then falling to the ground.

"Ramadhan *Zift*," he shouted standing above Abdulla. "There is no such object as Allah. It is a figment of a fool's imagination. Right now at this instant there is you and there is me holding this AK47." He held up the Kalachnikov. "And it is I who hold the power to end your life or not. So who do you fear the most?"

Hamed held his breath fearing his father's defiant reply.

"You may have the power to kill me. But it is Allah who will guide your hand. *Inshaallah*." Abdulla replied calmly.

The man bent the weapon down and because his left arm was straight and stiff he cocked it a somewhat awkwardly. Then he pressed the barrel hard onto Abdulla's forehead.

"No," Hamed cried out and struggled unsuccessfully once more to pass the two men confronting him. He could see the expression of terror on his father's face, but still he made no plea for his life. The man holding the AK47 stood above Abdulla motionless, except for some facial nerve slightly twitching in his heavy black moustache. His face was a mask of fury. To Hamed the moment seemed frozen in time as everyone stood motionless watching and waiting to see if the man would jerk the finger that would end Abdulla's life.

"Ziad," one of the other men said with a calm voice.

The word seemed to hang in the air for a while having no immediate impression on the situation. Then the man lifted the rifle from Abdulla's forehead and fired a round into the ground by his side making him flinch fiercely. He put a foot into Abdulla's chest and infuriated, pushed him backward. Then he stomping away some four metres and stood with his back turned staring across the jebal hills.

"Go to your women and help them prepare some food, old man." The man whose steadying voice had probably saved his life instructed Abdulla. By sending him to work with the women it demeaned him further, it did, however, remove him from further confrontation. To Hamed's relief his father obeyed.

"You stay," he pointed at Hamed and everybody once more began to settle beneath the shade of the tree. Still with a surly expression Ziad was last to join them.

"You must forgive Ziad, he was recently wounded in a battle with the Sultan's forces and his arm will now be forever stiff. So, understandably, he is not very amiable to those who are not prepared to do their part in this struggle."

"Don't you make excuses for me Musabbah," Ziad retorted with a glare. "I should have shot the son of a whore." He turned and stared at Hamed. "You're a young man. Why aren't you fighting alongside us?"

Hamed could feel the fury turn towards him and the questioning looks all around the group "Since my brothers left there is only myself and my father left to run this farm." He realised immediately that he had slipped and he wished that he had left the "brothers'" remark singular. Whilst it would probably placate these men to know that

Mussalim had left to join them, it would be no help at all if they learned that Juma was in the Sultan's Army "My first duty is to my family and as you have seen my father is old and cannot manage alone," he carried on trying to bury the remark under more information and realising at the same time that he had slighted his father also.

"This struggle is for your benefit and much more important than your poxy farm," Ziad snarled. "Leave the old goat to suffer in his squalor since he isn't prepared to help to change it."

"I would, except his mind is going and my two mothers and sister would suffer also." He slighted his father further not sure whether he did so to make excuses on his own behalf or to temper Abdulla's defiant remarks earlier. Beyond the tree he could see Lailla returning with the goats.

"Where did your brothers go?" Someone picked up on his previous remark.

"Brother."

"You said brothers."

"No," Now he denied Juma. "Brother."

"Where did your brother go," the man rephrased the question accepting his lie.

"He left last summer to go to Hauf." He was relieved that he could now establish some relation to these men and perhaps in so doing reduce the threat.

"Hauf?" Musabbah sought confirmation.

"Yes. He left to join your cause."

"What's his name? Ziad enquired.

"Mussalim."

"Mussalim. Not crazy man Mussalim?" Masabbah asked.

Hamed looked bewildered and slowly shook his head. " No. Mussalim Abdulla."

"Crazy man Mussalim," confirmed Masabbah grinning at Ziad. "It is as well that you did not kill his father. He would make a bad enemy."

Ziad made a scoffing sound and looked towards the nearing herd of goats. "Then Mussalim won't object if we take some of his goats to feed some PFLOAG soldiers." He pointed towards two of the sitting men and indicated towards the goats. They picked up their weapons and left.

"When did you last hear from your brother?" Masabbah asked.

"Not since he left." Hamed watched as one of the men stooped, grabbed a goat by its back leg and dragged it away so that the other could shoot it. The loud retort scattered the goats.

"Well he did go to Hauf and the last I heard he was still there. But before he went he covered himself in glory at Mirbat. Didn't you know?"

Hamed shook his head, only half listening. He still watched the men as they chased the goats and slaughtered any they caught while his sister, Lailla, watched terrified from a short distance away. These men did not even bother to kill the animals by the Islamic demanded *Hellal* method and therefore the meat would be unclean to eat, he thought. But then, of course, these men have turned their backs on Islam and probably didn't care.

"He is a worthy recruit to our cause. Even Ziad will admit that." Masabbah went on grinning at Ziad.

Lailla fled towards the house where Kathya, now very obviously pregnant, placed protective arms around her daughter.

~ 8 ~

May 1969 • Jokha plunged her hands wearily into the old tin bowl and for a few moments stared down at the water turning slightly pink as the blood on her fingers dispersed. She was tired, dispirited and very worried. Kathya had started in labour yesterday afternoon and now twenty hours later the baby still hadn't been born. Something was very wrong. For a woman who had two previous successful childbirths and two stillborn then it should not have taken half that time?

Dilation had taken place and contractions had occurred at regular two or three minute intervals. At that stage, all seemed to be normal. But that was twelve hours ago and since then no progress had taken place. She had continually urged Kathya to keep pushing and she had responded time and time again. As evening turned into night and then night into day her strength had gradually ebbed. Now completely exhausted Kathya had no strength left and had sunk into a semi-coma state just lying on the cot groaning and moaning in agony. Blood had now begun to flow freely and Jokha suspected that perineal tissue had begun to tear and rupture. And still the baby's head had not appeared. Jokha had guessed a long time ago that something drastic needed to happen. But she was no surgeon and she had delayed the decision to cut, waiting and hoping that the birth would still occur naturally. Now clearly she could wait no longer and perhaps she had already waited too long.

She dried her hands on a cloth and standing in the veranda's shade she looked out sadly across pacifistic jebal hills. Abdulla sat close by using a sharpening stone to put a fine edge on his khunja. She indicated with a nod that she was ready. He put down the stone and ran his finger along the blade's curved edge. Satisfied that it was as sharp as he could get it, he got up slowly and then handed it to her without speaking. Nervously, she examined the knife. She had never done this before and in her ignorance she feared that she might kill her sister. The alternative, however, was to do nothing and if she did nothing then Kathya would certainly die. This was her only chance. Jokha looked into her husband's dark eyes silently begging support. He looked back expressionless, then without a word of encouragement turned away and walked slowly over to Hamed, who sat waiting tensely beneath the tree.

Jokha nervously washed the knife in the bowl and then used the cloth to dry it. She could find no other reason to delay the inevitable, so she returned inside the house.

Ragged curtains shut out the sunlight, nevertheless, the room still seemed to be very hot. Perhaps it was just her nervous tension. She stood anxiously in the doorway and peered through the gloom, wishing that she were anywhere but here. With only her instinct as a woman and her personal experience of childbirth as qualification she felt completely incompetent to carry out this operation. But there was no one to help her. For a moment she was seized by panic and thought to run away. If she escaped across the hills and spent the afternoon enjoying the peaceful tranquillity of the mountains far away from this awesome predicament then perhaps she would return to find that someone else had resolved this situation. Gloomily she dismissed the thought, there was no one else. She had been selected by Allah to be the instrument of his will.

She held the knife loosely and with her finger felt the sharp tip at the end of its curved blade. Across the room Kathya groaned loudly and twisted first this way across the cot and then back as she tried to find some relief from her agony. Spurred by desire to relieve her sister from further suffering Jokha crossed the room quickly to her side. Although she doubted that still heard, she spoke softly and sympathetically to Kathya as she once more peered into the vulva hoping to see the baby's head. It was a forlorn hope and her last prospect of avoiding this operation evaporated. With a heavy sigh she repositioned Kathya's legs and stood poised with the knife.

"Stay very still," Kathya she instructed more in prayer than in any hope that she had heard. Slowly and carefully she inserted the khunja into position. Then taking a grip on the handle with both hands she hesitated and steeled herself against the cut. With pulse beats throbbing loudly in her ears Jokha took a deep breath and jerked the knife upward. She felt the pressure of Kathya's insides against the blade.

The pain reverberated through her coma state and Kathya let out a heart-stopping scream impulsively bringing down her hands to press on her stomach. Jokha reacted instantly withdrawing the knife dropping it to the floor as she moved back. Blood was now seeping more freely than it had before. She watched helplessly and began to weep uncontrollably as Kathya began once more to writhe in severe pain. Far from relieving her agony it seemed she had succeeded only in adding to it. She began to pray to Allah begging for her sister's relief from the pain. Kathya's moans changed to grunts as God's mercy pushed the baby's head into the birth channel.

Her distress now forgotten and into an area of which she was more familiar Jokha leapt to action. Using two wooden spoons she assisted the infant with little prises until she could get a handgrip on its head. Then she pulled with all her strength and non too gently until a shoulder appeared a few more tugs and the baby was born. She retrieved the khunja, cut the cord and held the baby up. Despite urgent little slaps and shakes she could not get the infant girl to take her first breath. As seconds turned into a minute and the minutes began to gather she became more and more frantic until eventually forced to accept that the baby had not survived the ordeal. She laid her on the floor at the foot of the cot and turned her attention back to Kathya.

She cleared away the placenta and then used cloths pushed tightly between Kathya's legs to control the free blood flow. She was very weak and very tired but at least the agony twisting contortions had stopped and Jokha's hopes that things would now turn out to be all right had risen. Feeling much more optimistic she talked softly to Kathya as she bathed the blood and sweat from her body with cool water. Getting no response she eventually gave up the conversation and began instead to hum and sing softly to her. It was sad about the stillborn baby, she thought, but at least it was over now. Now it was time to tell Abdulla the news. She brushed Kathya's hair gently preparing her for Abdulla's visit. Then she began to hastily tidy the room. The dead infant she washed before wrapping it in a cloth and placing it beneath the cot. She glanced around and satisfied that all was ready she gently shook Kathya by the shoulder to rouse her for her husband's visit. There was no response. So she tried once more this time a little more firmly. Still there was no response. She became alarmed and tried again, this time forcefully. As she looked down at her trying to decide what she should do Kathya's breathing became loud and erratic. With the back of her hand she gently touched her face, the skin was cold and damp. Jokha lifted the blanket and peered down at the blood soaked cloth between Kathya's legs. Panic welled up once more inside her, Kathya was now bleeding to death.

She dashed outside in alarm and shouted for Abdulla. She did not wait for him but went instead back inside. When Abdulla arrived she had removed the blood soaked cloth and was pressing another in position desperately trying to stem the seep of blood.

"She's going to bleed to death if I can't stop the bleeding," she said with dismay.

At first he didn't reply. Instead he looked around somewhat bemused trying to understand the situation. "What happened to the baby?"

"Born dead," she indicated the tiny bundle beneath the cot.

"Boy or girl?"

"Girl."

Abdulla nodded slightly, then came to look over Jokha's shoulder as she worked.

She had pressed the cloth firmly in position and now there was nothing more that she could do at this stage except hope. She pulled the cover back over Kathya. "I had to cut her," she said appealing for sympathy.

Abdulla lifted Kathya's limp arm and felt for a pulse.

"I had no choice." Kathya's dark complexion was now greying and her breathing was quick and shallow. Jokha watched her husband apprehensively not sure what his reaction might be. Would he blame her?

He let the arm fall and stared thoughtfully down at his wife before glancing at Jokha. "*Inshaallah*," he muttered with a shrug and left Jokha alone to continue her struggle for Kathya's life.

Thirty minutes later Kathya died and Jokha sank to her knees in dejection and exhaustion. She rested her arms on the cot and wearily dropped her head onto the back of her hands. Her tears slid through her fingers and wet the cloth beneath. Twenty minutes passed before she could compose herself and muster the courage to go and inform Abdulla that his wife was dead. She got to her feet slowly and stared down despondently at Kathya's lifeless body. She turned away and began to shuffle towards the door, kicking Abdulla's khunja along the ground as she did. Subconsciously she picked it up, then paused at the door preparing to convey the sad news to her husband.

When she came out he was sitting by the door again and he looked up at her. Leaning heavily on the doorframe she looked back and shook her head sadly. No words passed between them as she raised her arm and handed him back his knife. He took it instinctively and continued to stare into her face. Then he bowed his head and looked down at the knife in his hands. After a few moments he stood up and with a resigned sigh and a swing of the arm he stuck the knife firmly in a wooden support post. Without another glance at Jokha he walked across to the rudely constructed wood shed. By his reaction she guessed that he had expected this and had prepared himself.

He emerged a minute or so later carrying a shovel and a pick. He walked towards Hamed, who still waited beneath the tree and he indicated that he should come with him. The pair walked up to the hilltop and Jokha still standing in the doorway watched as, silhouetted against the blue cloudless sky, they began work scraping out a shallow grave.

She went back inside and working mechanically she began to prepare both Kathya and the infant's bodies for burial. When she had finished she laid the infant in her mother's arms and wrapped them both in a blanket. She stitched the blanket together crudely and waited for Abdulla and Hamed to come.

Abdulla looking old and tired and Hamed ashen and crestfallen came shortly afterwards to collect the bundle. They carried it outside and laid it on a sheet of corrugated tin. It bowed in the middle when they lifted it but slowly and carefully they carried it up the hill to the grave. Jokha sat outside the house and gloomily watched from afar as they lifted the bundle from the tin into the shallow grave and then began to backfill. She thought of Lailla who had left this morning expecting to have a new sibling on her return. Soon she would return to find instead that she no longer had a blood mother. The girl was going to be distraught and once again Jokha would need all her courage to comfort the child. She felt completely inadequate and groaned with dismay. She had failed abysmally and had let everyone down very badly.

Anger suddenly rose in her stomach like bile and resentment twisting her inside into tight knots. There should have been a hospital in Salalah instead of a thousand kilometres away in Muscat. Abdulla could have taken Kathya there last night when she had first realised that all was not well. In which case mother and child would still be living, of that she was convinced. It was a criminal waste of two lives. She now felt outrage against a Sultan that attended his own comforts with the country's wealth instead of providing a hospital in the region. She cursed Said Bin Taymour and his uncaring government and hoped now that her eldest son Mussalim and his friends would after all succeed in deposing him from the Dhofar region. He deserved to suffer at least that, she thought embittered. She had long ago disassociated her son and the cause that he followed from that small band of thugs that had come to the farm five months ago. There were good and bad in everything, she had allowed. They had just been unfortunate to have that particular small band of thugs descend upon them.

The two men on the hill were close to finishing their task and now they began to half bury rocks in an upright position marking the grave in the traditional Bedouin way. She watched them finish their labours and for a few moments stand silhouetted against the sky staring down at their work. Abdulla was first to move. He picked up the tools and made his way slowly down the hill leaving Hamed standing alone head bowed at the graveside. When he reached the wood store Abdulla tossed the tools carelessly through the door and then for a moment he stared across in Jokha's direction. She got to her feet nervously and tried to read his expression from the distance. She feared that his wrath was about to descend on her for not doing better? But he turned away, pulled the crude door shut with a slam and walked away to continue the routine chores of running a farm.

She watched him go wondering apprehensively if his retribution would burst upon her later. But that night for the first time in ages Abdulla took Jokha to his bed.

✳ ✳ ✳

When Hamed descended from the hilltop both Abdulla and Jokha had disappeared. Jokha inside the house to attend her chores while his father off somewhere probably to tend the stock. Not wishing at this moment to face either he quickly saddled a camel and set off across the jebal to retreat to the seclusion of his favourite place.

Barely a few minutes from the farm he saw his sister Lailla at a distance making her way slowly back towards the house with the herd of goats. He was instantly ravaged by dread, she would be demented with grief when she was told the awful news. Shrinking from the thought of being the one who would tell her, he angled the camel in a different direction and made a wide sweep to avoid her.

His heart was heavy with sorrow and his thoughts full of his mother's memory as he allowed the animal to plod along slowly at its own pace. Inattentively he guided it towards his intended sanctuary where he would be able to do his grieving in complete privacy. The landscape changed gradually from the short thick shrub canopies to bare rolling moors that is the *gatn* as he neared Jebal Qara's highest points. Thirty minutes later he reached the steep northern edge which overlooked the *nejd*. He ignored the road winding down into the pass and crossed instead to make his way along the rocky barren lip. When he reached the foot of a steep incline, which would put him on the flat plateau high above the pass, he spurred his mount up a narrow winding goat track. The black volcanic scree was sharp and loose and made underfoot conditions difficult for the camel. The animal bellowed with reluctance as Hamed, with hefty kicks and slaps from the cane, urged it to climb the track. Gradually it became less steep until it petered out onto the flat expanse. Here he relaxed and allowed the animal to wander at its own pace across the tabletop plateau to the opposite edge which directly overlooked the pass. He made the animal kneel so that he could dismount before turning it loose to forage among the cracks and crevices for any fragmented scraps of greenery that it might find.

For a while Hamed stood gazing pensively northwards across the vast expanse of sterile desert absorbing its awesome magnificence. The sun still emitted a fierce heat even though it was getting low in the western sky. Its lowering angle cast growing shadows of the countless hills across the ground, painting the vista of pastel browns with large patches of dark. Here was nature timeless and utterly indifferent to human vulnerability. A life of a mere mortal was as a single breath of wind passing over the desert, gone almost instantaneously and leaving no imprint of its passing.

He slid the goatskin of water from his shoulder and took a long drink before leaping over the edge to the narrow shelf four feet below. With his back against the rock face he settled in melancholy mood to watch the sun sink towards its setting and to contemplate human insignificance. It mattered not what personal tragedy befell human kind or its magnitude, the sun would still rise the next day with complete unsympathetic indifference. He watched as through the next hour its blinding light passed to an orange glow then a resplendent red before it disappeared from sight below the barren horizon.

As if awoken by some in-built alarm clock a large golden brown scorpion emerged from beneath a nearby rock and unaware of Hamed's presence it crawled slowly past his foot. In this instance he empathised with the insect's vulnerability and its right to life and so he did not kill it.

The light was fading fast and the temperature dropping rapidly when he stirred himself from his morose reflections. He decided that he would not journey home through the darkness this night but would instead remain here and wait for sunrise. He began gathering kindling for a fire. Here on the very edge of the jebal this plateau was subject to the rain and damp Khareef mists and with its arrival the dormant seed sheltering in the rocks cracks and crevices would spring to life. The shrubby plants would grow rapidly and complete their life cycle of growth, flower and seeding before dropping the seed to shelter in those same crevices to await the next Khareef. With the passing of the Khareef and deprived of moisture these small shrubs were then subjected to the baking sun and their life very quickly scorched away. All that remained were scraggs of knee high branches pointing skyward in tinder-like condition. With the evidence of years of this cycle all around him there was no shortage of burning material and Hamed soon had a fire burning. However, he could not stop gathering fire fuel and worked feverishly to feed the hungry flames. He progressed it to a roaring monster of a bonfire illuminating the immediate vicinity and creating a massive beacon which from its high position could be seen for dozens of kilometres. He imagined it as some sort of tribute to his mother's life and he worked feverishly to keep the monster fed. As the nearby fuel was spent he was forced to harvest further away until with the fire burning so hot and the distance increasing he could no longer keep pace and it began to get smaller. Eventually exhausted and with his face and clothes blackened by smoke he gave in and sat staring into the diminishing flames. It rapidly dropped to split into little pockets of idly flickering flames then to ash, first glowing red then grey.

Hamed lay on his back staring into the dark night sky and its millions of stars. Tonight the moon was new and just a mere sliver. Tomorrow would therefore be the first day of *Muharram* and a new Islamic year. With both Mussalim and Juma deserting their family duties in order to pursue their own interests and now his mother's death the family had been decimated. It had, he decided, been a bad year and he hoped that this new one would be better. Pessimistically, however, he could not see how it would improve. The likelihood of the conflict between government and rebels ending soon was remote and therefore he could not rely on either of his brothers' early return. His father was getting old and clearly his eyes were rapidly getting worse. Humouring his father's pride he pretended that he hadn't noticed, however, he knew that it would be a future problem. Now with Kathya's death he could also anticipate that Lailla would be expected to help Jokha much more and therefore contribute less to the goat care. He felt the crushing responsibility of the family's welfare was descending on his young shoulders more and more. He felt trapped and a little aggrieved. Everyone silently expected and no one considered that he had personal needs also, or so it seemed. He could only anticipate a new year with an increasing burden of responsibility. Towards the end of it there was also the probability that Juma would bring that Ruwas woman to the family farm and then return to his soldier duties leaving him with an additional unwelcome responsibility. He had not yet met Khamisa, but already he resented her.

✳ ✳ ✳

After thrusting the last of his personal belongings roughly into the old duffel bag Mussalim looked at Shamel sitting across the room watching him. The infant on her knee reached up clumsily to her face forcing her to bend her head away from his clawing fingers.

"Will you be back? She had asked that question before.

"I don't know," he said with a shrug and could see the disbelief in her eyes. But it was true he didn't know.

Early this morning Commissar Mohammed Bin Talib and two Officers of the Egyptian Army had arrived in a truck. The sound of slamming vehicle doors and unfamiliar voices had drawn Mussalim to look from his window. As one of the commanders from the Mirbat attack he immediately recognised Bin Talib and by the earnest attitude of the arrivals he had suspected that something significant was about to happen. They had gone immediately into conference with Hemel Al Sheban in his quarters. A little over one hour later they had left and the Shibam had summoned an immediate meeting of all PFLOAG soldiers in the compound. Mussalim's suspicions were confirmed when he ordered that everyone should be ready to move out in four hours. Then he abruptly left without explanation to make his own preparation. For a little while men had hung around in small groups speculating on the possible reasons until one by one they drifted away to get ready.

"What shall I do?" Shemel asked.

It was inevitable that this day would eventually arrive and he had previously considered what Shamel's circumstances would be when it did. Occasionally she had smuggled a few rupees of his money to her family and he had pretended not to notice recognising her charity as a probable solution. Her contribution albeit modest, had probably guaranteed that she would have a place to go. Or at least, she would have until the next time her brother in law sold her out once more for a soldier's comfort. "Perhaps you had better return to your husband's brother and his family," he suggested. She looked back dolefully obviously believing that his departure would be permanent. "If I come back then I will look for you," he added consolingly.

"*Muharram Wahed*," she said ruefully. "I had planned a small feast for us."

He felt a sudden spasm of guilt. For her this departure was certainly not what she wanted and her future had suddenly become very uncertain. While for him it was filled with anticipation and tinged with excitement. The way things were shaping it seemed that he was likely to get his wish and become more actively involved in the cause objectives. He crossed the room and sympathetically touched her face. "You don't have to leave here right away. Have your new year celebration and leave tomorrow."

She reached up and for a moment held his hand on her face. "You have been good to me, Mussalim. May Allah, the Almighty, protect you."

"And you Shamel." He withdrew his hand and fiddled in his pocket. For a moment he looked at the money in his hand trying to decide how much he could afford to leave. Then deciding that her need was greater than his, he put it all on the table and picked up his bag. With only a brief backward glance he left.

"*Masalaama*." He heard her say as the door closed behind him.

Outside the front entrance a small crowd of people had gathered. Soldiers, making their preparations to leave. Women, watching their men preparing to desert them. Villagers, brimming with curiosity, watching idly. The Shibam attempting to bring some order to the chaos paced around agitatedly and bellowed bad tempered instructions at everyone. Mussalim at first stood back watching the confusion until he too received the verbal lash of Hemel's tongue. Motivated by his stinging rebuff he moved to assist two men who were tying ammunition boxes to the back of a donkey. In fact the pair had the situation well under control and didn't particularly need his help. However, it appeased Al Shibam's humour to allow him to believe that he was doing something useful. It took another forty-five minutes of disorganisation before the pack animals were finally loaded with mortars and ammunition to the Shibam's satisfaction. Shading his eyes he glanced up at the sun high overhead gauging roughly the amount of time wasted and the amount left in the day. Then after another very brief look around to make sure everything was ready he set off leading the party towards the steep jebal incline.

Mussalim waited at the back as twenty-six men, two camels and four donkeys slowly unwound into indian file and following the Shibam. He stole a glance up at the window that had been his quarters for more than seven months. Shamel was framed behind the horizontal bars holding her infant son and looking down at him. She summoned a smile and waved and then holding the baby's arm she waved for him also. Mussalim smiled back and nodded then hitching his Kalchnikov more comfortably over his shoulder he picked up his bag and followed his comrades.

The sun's heat was blistering and it took an energy-sapping hour to reach the top of the steep jebal. The march continued at forced pace and pressed on northwards into early afternoon and the hottest part of the day. Only the growls and whistling of men urging and bullying the animals on broke the silence. Most concentrated on conserving energy. Al Shibam kept the company on the high ground following the winding upper edges of the wadi's electing to take the long route to avoid steep descents and energy-draining climbs. Following the high contours they snaked in all directions but always returned to a basic northerly course. Mussalim could feel the sweat trickling freely down his back saturating his shirt and making it stick uncomfortably to his skin. The dust and grime swirled up from underfoot stuck to the sweat that streaked his face turning his dark complexion grey. After about another hour the Shibam relented and satisfied with the progress made so far signalled to stop and rest. The animals still fully loaded were turned loose and allowed to forage among the scorched jebal grass. Thankfully and wearily, men shed their loads and began stretching out in the shade of a large Bedam tree preparing to snatch a few minutes sleep.

Al Shibam seated himself cross-legged in the midst and surveyed the crumpled heaps around him. "No doubt you are all wondering where we are going," he said and then waited until he had everybody's attention. When he was certain that he had it he went on. "There have been reports of a massive troop build up at Deefa army base and the assumption is that the Sultan's forces are preparing to launch a cross border strike at our Hauf base. So, all the forces we have in the area are being mobilised. Most are being pulled back to form a defensive barrier around Hauf." His plump face split into a grin and with a satisfied nod he added. "They won't be expecting it and that should give them a nasty surprise. We, however, have a different mission." He opened a map and laid it on the ground in front of him. "Along with the men stationed at Sarfait and Raykhut we are ordered to report to Salim Al Mushani for further orders. He waits for us in Wadi Khazart," he tapped a finger on the map indicating its position. "and we must to be there by dawn. So we will rest here two hours until it's a little cooler, then we will march through the night to Kharzart."

Mussalim eased forward and looked over his shoulder at the map. "Where is Deefa?" He had heard mention of it several times but had little idea of its location.

"Right there." The Shibam pointed at a spot some eight or nine kilometres north of Jebal Sayq.

Without taking his eyes from the map he sank down to sit at his side. "And Hauf?"

Al Shibam indicated the PFLOAG base in Yemen.

Mussalim studied the map thoughtfully. The distance between Deefa and Hauf, he estimated to be some forty kilometres in a south-westerly direction. With the element of surprise, government troops, presumably in vehicles, could move out of Deefa and taking the direct route across the *nejd* strike at Hauf in little more than an hour. Two hours or so to create mayhem and destruction then be back safely in their base inside five hours. He could well understand the urgent need by the PFLOAG leaders to get their forces in position. "Do we know how many troops are at Deefa?"

He shrugged. "Reports estimate between five and six hundred."

"They can't cross the border." Someone said from the little knot of men that had gathered round the map. It was a naive statement typical of a guerrilla attitude demanding the opposite forces stay within the rules, but nonetheless valid.

Al Shibam laughed out loud. "Write'em a protest letter," he said derisively.

"If they want to attack Hauf then why don't they use their aircraft?" Mussalim asked with his head down still studying the map. It seemed to be a more practical alternative to him. Commit three or four aircraft in three or four sorties instead of hundreds of troops in a cross border raid.

"Probably because ground forces can do a more thorough job," he replied and began rolling up the map indicating discussion was at an end. "Now get some rest. We have a long march through the night."

With the cooler temperature progress was quicker and they descended into Wadi Kharzat just after midnight. It took another hour walking northward along its base before they arrived at Al Mushani's camp. The camp was quiet and with the exception of the posted guards all slept. Not wishing to disturb the mounds of sleeping men Al Shibam halted his party on the camp fringe and they began to unload the pack animals. Al Mushani himself was roused from the tent where he slept and came to greet the new arrivals. He introduced himself to Al Shibam and then he moved among the Dalkut men slapping backs and shaking hands. When he came to Mussalim he recognised him instantly and greeted him with a huge grin. "Crazy man Mussalim, welcome. It's good to have you here." He then spent a few minutes exchanging recollections of the Mirbat victory while the Shibam, for the moment reduced to background importance, watched grudging his rapport with a cause leader. When he had finished his greetings Al Mushani leaned his back against a tree and addressed the group.

"Sometime soon, probably within the next couple of days we expect the force gathered at Deefa to move out cross into the Yemen and attack our headquarters base at Hauf. But unknown to them we will be ready for them. At this very moment a large number of our forces along with a full company of Egyptian soldiers are moving into defensive positions to stop them. But, our orders are that we are to wait here until we receive word that the Sultan's forces have moved off their base. When that happens we are then to disperse over the area between the border and Deefa and set up ambush positions. Then, when they return fragmented and demoralised, we hit them again." He thumped his fist into his palm to emphasise the point. "You men from Dalkut are the last to arrive and we now number almost a hundred. That gives us enough men to set up seven or eight ambushes. We ought to get a few returning stragglers stumble into some of the traps, especially since they are unlikely to be expecting it." He paused checking through his mind that he had covered everything. He looked at Al Shibam. "Hemel, come with me I have an additional task for you. Then glancing around at the weary group he said. "Now I suggest that you get some rest."

Mussalim stretched out on the ground and lay on his back staring up into the night sky. With no light pollution millions of stars were visible and he thought of another night at Jibjat when he had stared up into a starlight sky. That was nine months ago and much had changed since then. He thought of Jumaia and remembered the feel of her young breast that night beneath the flimsy material of her *abeya*. He wondered if her father Ghulam had found a husband for her. Almost certainly he decided, any man would be pleased to lay with her by his side. But then, what of Lailla his own sister? For all he knew she too might be married. Smiling to himself he quickly dismissed that thought. His father would have some stiff opposition to overcome from the girl's mother Kathya, at least until she was a little older. He thought of his brothers, Juma and Hamed, and assumed with a degree of surety that they continued to steadfastly do their family duty. With the wonders of the night sky above his head he made his secret prayer to Allah and included a fervent wish that he extend his protection to all of his family.

Al Shibam returned and began picking his way quietly through the prostrate forms sleeping on the ground stopping occasionally to wake one. He made his way towards Mussalim and seeing that he was awake motioned that he should collect his belongings and come with him.

Mussalim got up and followed him. When they were a little way from the camp the Shibam stopped and waited for the other seven to join them. "We are moving on to Deefa," he said in a low tone. "We are to place the camp under observation and when the troops move out we are to let Al Mushani know." He pointed at three radio backpack sets which lay against a nearby tree trunk. "These have a range of more than a hundred kilometres," he said then he distributed them to be carried. "We need to be hidden in observation positions before daylight. So let's not waste any more time."

They continued northward along the base of Wadi Kharzat until after two hours its high steep sides gradually petered out completely and they emerged onto the open *gatn* moorlands. A few minutes later they crossed the graded road that led westward to the border. They found a road that led northwards which was filled with many tyre tracks suggesting that it was the road to the base itself. They followed it, gradually climbing all the time until just as the dark sky in the east was just beginning to brighten they came into sight of Deefa.

The camp commanded the highest ground of the *gatn's* treeless rolling upland and was protected by a chain link fence eight feet high held in place by concrete posts topped with barbed wire. Before that a double row of concertina razor wire guarded the approach to the fence itself. The whole complex enjoyed a strategic uninterrupted view across four hundred metres of ground clear, except for low scorched grass.

Here Al Shibam handed Mussalim a map and one of the radios. Then leaving instructions to radio him the very minute any troops left the base he left him and two other men, to find a suitable hidden observation place. Before he left, however, he aired his opinion that it was unlikely that any movement would be southwards. The likely movement would be south-west in direct line towards Hauf and that was the position where he intended to station himself while the other three men would swing to the west of the camp just in case.

Mussalim and his two companions found a shallow cave in a rock wall a kilometre away from the base. It faced south and therefore did not afford any strategic view at all, but it was an ideal place to set up a base. From the top of a nearby hill they established an observation post which although a distance away gave an excellent view across the grassy area right up to the compound wire.

There were few buildings of a permanent nature inside the army compound but several long rows of tidily spaced tents. Behind this myriad of tents were the parked vehicles. Mostly they were Land Rovers with mounted machine guns in their rear, ideal for quick strike situations. Some were larger freight trucks and troop carriers indicating that plentiful supplies and troops had been brought to the base. The number of water tankers seemed to confirm that a large complement of men was presently on the base. While fuel trucks suggested that at least some of these vehicles did have a distance to travel. The presence of several ambulances ominously confirmed that they were indeed preparing for a strike and that casualties were expected.

Mussalim lay on the brow of the hill a kilometre away with his two companions and reviewed the assembled equipment. They talked in whispers, conscious that sound can travel a long way on barren landscape and they agreed that these forces were indeed well equipped for a quick and effective raid. There would, however, be a titanic clash when they unexpectedly stumbled into the waiting PFLOAG forces.

All through the long hot day they watched taking turns of four hours each. By sundown other than considerable movement of men within the compound, they reported to Al Shibam that the day had been uneventful. They continued with their four-hour shifts through the night reasoning that although in the darkness at the distance they could see nothing, any movement out of the camp would be alerted by the sounds of vehicle engines. Still nothing happened and by midday on the day following Mussalim was beginning to get concerned about the water situation. A radio contact established that it was a situation shared by the other two observation teams and the Shibam agreed that after dark each team should send a man back to the camp in Wadi Kharzat to replenish water supplies. As soon as it was dark one man left leaving Mussalim and Tariq to continue the watch.

It was a couple of hours after dark when Mussalim was woken by Tariq's hand over his mouth. He indicated that he should be quiet before he removed it. "Listen," he said and intimated that he should follow him out from the cave's shallow cover.

Mussalim stood in the cave's mouth and listened. At first he could hear nothing except the wind crossing a silent desert. Then gradually he began to establish alien sounds. The merest hint of a voice, a faint metallic clink and occasionally the rattle of slipping shingle.

"At first I thought that I imagined it. But the sounds became more frequent and more unmistakable."

"What is it?"

Tariq shook his head.

"Let's go and find out." Mussalim picked up his Kalachnikov, worked a round into the breach and led the way down the hill to the desert floor. The night was ink black and the new moon not yet risen and when it did it would be only the merest sliver and give very little light. They progressed about two hundred metres towards the sounds and the nearer they got those sounds not only increased in volume but began widening into stereophonic.

Mussalim's night vision had been improving with every metre until he could now discern varying shades of black. He saw the black shapes of the convoy's line against the dark sky two hundred metres ahead and he sank quickly to the floor. They watched the endless line of troops on foot moving southward across their front, some leading pack animals, donkeys and camels.

He had no way of knowing just how much of the convoy had passed through before they had arrived but by the amount that crossed in front of them now Mussalim estimated that it was probably the full complement. He stared into the darkness perplexed, this made no sense. They were moving out on foot and leaving the vehicles behind. The element of speed was being ignored. On foot it would take them very much longer to reach Hauf and equally as long to return after the strike. What could have been accomplished in around five or six hours would take around forty-eight hours this way and more curious they were unexpectedly marching south. Something was not as it should be. In any event he needed to alert the Shibam that the troops were on the move. He indicated to Tariq by a series of hand signals that he was returning to the cave to use the radio and that he should stay here and watch. Tariq nodded that he had understood.

Back inside the cave he turned on the radio and held down the switch and used Al Shibam's call sign. There was no response, perhaps they are all sleeping he thought and tried again. He tried a twice more with the same result and was beginning to become impatient when the Shibam himself answered.

He reported that the government troops were on the move unexpectedly on foot and unexpectedly in the wrong direction.

Al Shibam responded seemingly unconcerned, predicting confidently that when they got as far as the road they would turn west towards the Yemen border.

Mussalim wasn't convinced and emphasised that they had left their vehicles on the Deefa base.

Still unconcerned the Shibam offered that this may be an advance party which was to be in position by tomorrow and when they were then the main vehicle strike force would probably follow. However, he would immediately relay his report on to Al Mushani, he allowed.

Mussalim dubiously shut the radio down. It was he supposed a feasible conclusion but he was not convinced and was very uncomfortable with the situation. He reached for the map and spread it out on the cave floor. Considering the cave's position in relation to the moving convoy he knew that it was unwise to use a light but he considered the situation important enough to take a chance. Placing his body as a shield to the entrance he struck a match and hastily scanned the map. With his finger he traced the route of the convoy if it continued south. It would move into Jebal Sayq. His poor reading abilities was a handicap but painstakingly he worked out the names of places. Through Sayq further to the south lay the small town of Sarfait and villages Dalkut and Raykut, which until a couple of days ago were occupied by PFLOAG fighters. It came to him in an instant, but the match burned his fingers making him hastily drop it. He struck another to confirm his notion and arrived at the same conclusion. The Sultan's forces had not been assembled for a cross border attack on Hauf, their intention was to re-occupy those coastal locations.

He shook out the lit match and in the darkness thought about his theory and the probable implications. The more he thought about it the more convinced he became. Clearly the reason why they had left behind their vehicles and were using pack animals was because it would be very difficult to cross Sayq in vehicles. The bulk of the PFLOAG forces were assembled in the wrong place forming a protective shield around Hauf and were effectively right out of contention. Only Al Mushani with around ninety men stood between the Sultan's forces and total success. Suddenly he thought of Al Mushani's current position camped in Wadi Kharzat, in about two or three hours he could have an army force considerably outnumbering his stumble into his camp.

He radioed Al Shibam once more and reported his convictions.

Despite his convincing argument and the urgency in his tone he failed completely to persuade Al Shibam that Hauf was not the objective. He stubbornly clung to the belief that the force would turn west when it reached the road. He expressed staunch confidence in the tactical competence of the cause leaders and became quite scathing that a mere inexperienced soldier, as Mussalim, should have the audacity to question the tactical abilities of his superiors. Then he shut down.

Mussalim tried to prolong the communication desperate to have his theory at least considered but the radio was dead. Exasperated, he replaced the receiver and wondered what he should do. He wondered just who would be the most surprised when the southward moving troops moving through the woods at night stumbled across a sizeable liberationist camp. Not only would Al Mushani's men be greatly outnumbered, but also unless the sentries could raise the alarm in time then most men would be sleeping and therefore further disadvantaged. He feared for his comrades and decided that he must do something. He considered the personal repercussions if he by-passed the Shibam and contacted Al Mushani direct. If he were right and those forces were in fact moving into the jebal then he would probably save many of his comrade's lives. If he were wrong then he would look a complete fool and incur the wrath of Al Shibam and possibly Salim Al Mushani also. Right or wrong the Shibam's displeasure would certainly descend upon him. Far better to suffer wrath and look a fool than allow comrades to die, he concluded.

He radioed the camp and almost instantly established a contact with a radio operator and he asked to speak directly to Al Mushani. At first the radio operator was reluctant to have him disturbed from his tent, but on Mussalim's insistence that the matter was very important he agreed to send a messenger to get him.

Alone in the darkness of the cave and waiting for the operator to call him back Mussalim began for the first time to have doubts. Perhaps he had got it all completely wrong and perhaps after all Hemel Al Shibam was right. Most certainly there were a lot of vehicles inside the Deefa compound and what would be the point of gathering so many together if there was no intention to use them?

The radio buzzed and Al Mushani himself was on the other end. "What do you have that is so important, crazy man?" He asked.

"The Sultan's men are moving south in force."

"Yes I know. Hemel has already reported. They will turn west at the road." He sounded irritated.

"I don't think they will. I think they will cross the road and move into the jebal."

"Why would they do that?" It definitely sounded derisive.

Perhaps this was a mistake after all. "To move against Sarfait, Raykut and Dalkut." There it was, he was now fully committed. There was a long pause and he could imagine the comments taking place on the other end.

"It would be extremely difficult to move vehicles through these mountains." Now there was a hint of sarcasm.

Vehicles? Could it be Al Shibam hadn't reported that the soldiers were using pack animals? "There are no vehicles. The forces are on foot and using pack animals."

There was a delay. "Repeat!"

"The forces are on foot and using pack animals. And if they continue south they could be on top of you within two hours."

"Standby."

Mussalim waited in the darkness with hopes of justification. It seemed that perhaps Al Mushani didn't know the soldiers were on foot and he too considered this information relevant. Seconds went into minutes and he imagined a scene of hurried consultations and map studying at the other end.

Eventually they responded again. "How large is the force?

"Five-hundred or so," he guessed. More delay.

"Follow the enemy to the road and report which direction they take. And well done Crazy Man, out."

He gathered up the radio and their belongings in the cave and went to find Tariq. He found him waiting exactly where he had left him. He reported that the tail of the convoy had passed about fifteen minutes before and since then all had been quiet. Mussalim briefly outlined the developing situation and what they had been tasked to do. Then after allowing the convoy a few more minutes start they set off in its wake. They moved slowly taking care not to overtake it and cautiously to avoid stumbling across any errant stragglers or drop outs.

It was well after midnight by the time they reached the road and of the troops ahead of them there was neither sight nor sound. In the darkness they cast around in circles studying the tracks in the stony sand. It was clear that the column had at this point split into three. One party had continued directly south and another had angled south-east. Since Dalkut lay directly south and Raykut to the south-east then this was consistent with Mussalim's theories and he enjoyed a few moments of smugness. However, the rest had turned directly west causing him momentary concern. He found a shallow ditch and in its moderate cover risked a match to briefly study the map. It was, he concluded, probable that the westward moving contingent would continue west and at some point before the border turn south through mountains towards Sarfait. He radioed his findings direct to Al Mushani and suggested that he should follow the westward moving force to confirm its intention. Al Mushani agreed and he and Tariq set off once more, this time westward.

They followed the road for almost three hours before the tracks turned off to the left and bent into the jebal in a south-westerly direction towards Sarfait. There was now little doubt what the objectives of the government soldiers were and Mussalim reported to Al Mushani. After his report he shut down the radio feeling fully vindicated for his presumptuous actions of bypassing Al Shibam and even though that man would be far from pleased, in the light of subsequent events, his open wrath would have to be somewhat restrained. However, Mussalim appreciated that his commander would feel aggrieved at the loss of face that he had caused and that there would be a future price to be paid. He realised also for the first time that although probable confrontation was about to take place in the Sayq Mountains, the Shibam was still in hiding around Deefa, spying on an almost deserted base. He thought to contact him, but decided that it would serve no purpose except to aggravate him further, so he decided against it.

With their immediate mission accomplished and feeling weary Mussalim and Tariq decided to move into the jebal, find a suitable place and allow themselves a well deserved rest before deciding how best to rejoin their company. An hour later and with the dark eastern sky beginning to tinge red, they stopped in the dense canopy cover of the trees and rested.

They rested throughout the morning until midday. During that time they exhausted their already depleted water reserves. Their first priority therefore became to obtain more. In a green mountain region such as Sayq it was not a desperate problem. Bountiful supplies lay beneath the surface, the trick was to find the wells. Mussalim consulted the map and established that a small village lay a few kilometres to the south. Using a syllable at a time he slowly built the name Hatel. Where there is a village then there must be a well. Both men were experienced enough not to go seeking water through the heat of the day and so they elected to remain where they were until it was cooler. To ease their thirst in the short term they chewed on grasses and leaves and squeezed moisture from succulent plants. To obtain some water in preparation for their journey later they dug a hole and using the masses of greenery all around they created a still.

It was while they were creating the still that the sounds of gunfire drifted from the east. Both men looked at each other knowingly and without comment continued with their task. All through the afternoon gunfire could be heard from that direction, sometimes sporadic and short in duration and sometimes heavy and prolonged.

When the day eventually lost its heat Mussalim and Tariq prepared to start their journey to Hatel. The still had yielded a half pan of water and the two men shared its bitter tasting contents before setting off. They made their way southwards doing their best to stay off skylines and out of the wadi depths trying to remain as covert as possible. By the time they reached the top of the hill overlooking the hillside village Hatel it was getting dark. They descended the hill towards the village and as they approached the outer precincts they came to a group of village men sitting cross-legged beneath a large tree talking quietly and enjoying the cool of the evening. These men greeted the strangers with the customary politeness and invited to them to sit. Mussalim and Tariq thanked the villagers for their courtesy and joined the circle. Immediately the pair settled, water and figs were offered to the guests.

At first the conversation was of trivia then, as the villages became more confident and having noticed their Kalachnikov weapons at the very onset, they began asking question about the sounds of gunfire in the east. Mussalim shrugged away the questions with only outline or vague answers. Which in truth was just about all that he knew. He did, however, learn that until only three hours ago a large force of government soldiers had camped in the valley beneath the village. They had arrived in the morning, sought permission to drink from the village well and when the day got cooler had moved on heading in a southerly direction. He questioned further the force's number and after more discussion and some disagreements he received an estimated figure of about one hundred and forty.

The village head graciously offered the pair shelter for the night in the village and the freedom to use the well. Mussalim thanked him for his generosity, accepted the well offer but declined the offer of shelter. Instead when the *dirwain* eventually broke up he and Tariq filled their water bags and quickly left the village. As soon as they reached high ground Mussalim used the radio to contact Al Mushani. The radio operator responded and Mussalim reported the last known position of the force moving towards Sarfait. Al Mushani must have been close by because he replied to the transmission giving praise and encouragement to Mussalim. Mussalim volunteered a gloomy forecast that if the Sultan's forces continued on through the night then they would be in Sarfait by the morning.

Al Mushani accepted the forecast unconcernedly and reported a jebal victory for the PFLOAG fighters. They had, he claimed, stopped the forces moving to Dalkut and sent them back towards Deefa in some disarray.

Mussalim grinned at Tariq welcoming the news, and then he asked Al Mushani what he wanted them to do next. He instructed them to continue following the troops ahead and to report their progress.

They continued southwards until after midnight and then decided to abandon the pursuit for the night and rest. Neither of them could see much sense in earnestly pursuing a force when they knew precisely where it was going and roughly at what time it would arrive.

The morning sun had comfortably cleared the skyline when fierce and prolonged gunfire started in the south. Both men looked at each other in surprise. Who was firing at who? Al Mushani had fought his battle in the east and now seemingly somehow had overtaken the forces in the south. It was not possible! They spread the map on the floor to consider the possibilities. One by one they eliminated each possibility until they were left without a credible answer. The only thing to do Mussalim decided was to use the radio and report the gunfire exchanges.

After first reaching the radio operator and making a report, Al Mushani himself came on air his tone jubilant. He asked for their position. Mussalim gave it. Then he asked for confirmation that the gunfire was indeed directly south of where they were. Mussalim confirmed it. This was good news, he said. It meant that the force from Hauf had arrived at Sarfait and then had moved northwards in time to successfully engage the advancing enemy. He was once more congratulatory to Mussalim for his initial action when he had recognised the situation was not as had been expected and on his initiative to report those circumstances quickly. He signed off in good humour by instructing the pair to report back to the camp at Wadi Kharzat.

✳ ✳ ✳

A fly crawled on Juma's face disturbing his sleep. He wafted a lazy arm but irritatingly it returned buzzing to land in precisely the same place. This time he turned over but the tormenting insect landed on his neck. He gave up trying to sleep and with eyes now open he rolled onto his back. He glanced down the long barrack room, of the twenty cots his was the only one that was not empty. He glanced at the large pendulum clock hung on the end wall. It hung askew the only angle that would keep the pendulum swinging. It was nine ten but since the clock was not accurate and gained considerably throughout a day Juma guessed at the time.

Yesterday he had received message of Kathya's death four days ago and had been given a seven-day leave of absence to return to his family and join in the mourning. He had no more information other than his second mother had died in childbirth. He thought of Lailla, she was so close to her blood mother and he imagined that she would be distraught. He sat up, swung his feet to the floor and slipped them into thonged sandals thinking then of his brother Mussalim. He couldn't know what had happened and since he had not the vaguest notion where he might be there was no way that Juma could think of even sending a message. 'Strange how two so close could now be so detached,' he thought sadly with a sigh.

Turning his thoughts to consider his more immediate plans he decided that he would visit the *Jundhi* mess hall and take breakfast before he began the long journey home. Unless he were lucky enough to find some jabally trader returning to the mountains with an unladen camel then he would have to walk all the way.

He wrapped a *futa* around his waist, picked up the towel that hung on the end of his cot and walked out into the morning. The wind was strong tempering the temperature considerably and it ravaged his long shoulder length hair as he made his way towards the tin shack that was the ablutions building. He mumbled a brief greeting to a cleaner who sloshed a dirty mop around the floor and went to the nearest hand-basin. As he ran a tap he stared in the mirror and watched the callow cleaner behind him. These roles he thought, might have been reversed but for Khaleef's timely intervention, '*Inshaallah.*' He turned his attention back to his ablutions and prepared to shave his face. Not particularly desirably to hide his handsome features behind a beard he shaved regularly, not every day but regularly. When he had finished he went into the shower chamber. A long slatted form lined the wall on his right faced by an aluminium screen on his left. Juma hung his *futa* on one of the hooks above the form and went around the other side of the screen. His mopping task finished the cleaner now used a worn knife to slice up a long bar of red soap into small blocks to replenish the soap holders. He handed a piece to Juma as he went behind the screen. A row of ten showerheads lined the wall facing the screen, he selected one close by and turned on the tap.

A shower easily accessible and available at all times was a novelty of which he had so far in nine months not tired. In his thoughts he had tried to design something similar to fit in the farmhouse that he intended to build for Khamisa and himself. With a large water tank on the house roof then he had reasoned it should be possible. The only hardship would be keeping the tank topped up. He worked a lather on the soap block agitating a strong pungent carbolic smell and began spreading it over his body. He didn't particularly mind being contaminated with its strong smell, in the normal daily routine among his comrades it didn't matter. However, in those circumstances that were special, such as his chaperoned visits with Khamisa, he disguised it heavily with aromatic spices and perfumes. Today, however, it didn't matter it was likely to be a long hot and sweaty walk up the mountain.

His ablutions finished and dressed in a long white *dish'dasht* and a red chequered shamag wrapped tightly around his head he made his way to the mess. It was crowded with soldiers on duty taking the standard nine till ten breakfast and prayer break. With a bowl of porridge and a mug of tea he slipped in between two of his friends sitting on a form at a long table. The table topic was dominated by the scant reports of a series of battles in the west between the combined force of soldiers and Firqats against the *adoo*, which seemed to have gone disastrously wrong for the government forces. Juma listened to the various accounts and speculative opinions with interest.

His breakfast finished he made his way back to the barrack room and hastily gathered the things that he would need for his journey home. Taking a minute to check that he had all that he needed he snapped the padlock on his bedside locker and made his way to the main gate. He reached it just as the vehicles carrying the battle casualties arrived. He stood by and watched as vehicle after vehicle rolled by with casualties. First the ambulances and then supply trucks which had been hastily improvised to position stretchers inside the covered freight area. Bringing up the rear the troop carriers came with the gaunt and weary-faced walking wounded.

"The hospital is going to be swamped," the barrier guard said gloomily.

Juma glanced sideways at the grim faced guard, it was true. The base hospital was nothing more than a glorified dispensary with probably no more than twenty available beds. Some improvisation was going to be needed to cope with numbers that probably exceeded sixty. "At least they will get treatment," Juma said thinking of the unfortunate Kathya. "And the more serious cases can be flown north and be in Muscat hospital within four hours," he added.

"Not so the *adoo* casualties," he thought aloud.

"The *adoo*? Who cares about the *adoo*?" He guard demanded tersely. "The more of them that die the better."

Juma thought of those men, Dhofaris just like him probably still lying somewhere near the battle site, wounded perhaps dying and unable to get treatment that even if it wasn't able save their lives could relieve the agonising pain of their last few moments. One of those casualties, for all he knew, might even include his own brother, Mussalim. He glanced once more at the adamant barrier guard, wished him Allah's protection and started his journey home silently praying as he walked away that his brother had not been within a hundred kilometres of that battle.

It was the evening on that same day when Mussalim and Tariq arrived back at the camp in Wadi Kharzat and they were greeted with huge grins and handshakes from their jubilant PFLOAG colleagues. They were given no opportunity to even sit as they immediately became surrounded by a mass of happy faces and all with eager stories to tell of how the Sultan's forces had withdrawn in complete disarray and confusion. Several fires had been lit and were in their infant stages as preparations for a celebratory feast was beginning. Mussalim was rescued from the vivacity by one of Al Mushani's aids and taken directly to the Commissar's tent. Al Mushani's greeting was a little more restrained, nevertheless, he piled verbal accolades upon him for the vital part that he had played in the resounding victory as he shook his hand warmly. Mussalim was embarrassed and tried to reduce his actions to more modest and realistic proportions. Al Mushani, however, would have none of it as he ushered him inside the tent.

He went straight to a dog-eared kit bag suspended from the centre pole and fiddled about inside until he found a bottle of Indian whisky. He turned and indicated that Mussalim should sit on the ammunition box while he arranged two tin mugs on the top of another box which served as a make shift table. "We have scored great victories these past two days," he said pouring generous amounts of whisky in both. "And you should be well pleased with the part that you played." He handed one of the mugs to Mussalim and then sat on the camp bed behind him.

He took a mouthful from the mug while he collected his thoughts. "Throughout yesterday we ambushed and harassed an enemy superior in numbers to our own until they split up and became separated into smaller groups. Then divided and confused they lost the plot completely. Some groups continued south while others lost the stomach for fighting and turned back. Eventually those that continued to fight their way forward realised that half the force had gone back and so they turned back also. We had only to hold our ambush positions and they came stumbling in fragmented groups through our traps once again. In the end they ran in panic and in all directions as fast as they could. In their haste to get away and back to the sanctuary of Deefa they even deserting their pack animals." He allowed himself a satisfied grin then took a long drink swilling it around his mouth before swallowing.

Mussalim copied his example. The whisky scorched his mouth and throat and then ignited his chest making him cough violently. The fire started spreading and increasing in ferocity until at the very point of explosion it stabilised and began easing back to mere pain. It was the first time in his life that he had tasted whisky and at that very moment he decided that it was also the last.

Al Mushani laughed at his discomfort and got to his feet. "You haven't tasted whisky before," he said accusingly as he began pouring water from a canteen in Mussalim's mug. "Try that but sip it," he said sitting once more.

"What of," Mussalim tried to speak but it came out indiscernibly hoarse, he tried again. "What of the battle this morning?" he eventually managed at little more than a whisper.

"By all reports! Stopped in their tracks and they too retreated back towards Deefa."

Mussalim tried a small cautious sip. The results were similar except this time he was prepared and controlled the cough. The Islamic law forbidding alcohol was one he could very easily obey, he decided.

"The forces advancing towards Raykut we couldn't find," Al Mushani went on. "We must therefore assume that they are now in Raykut." He shrugged. "We are content to let them stay there for the moment. When we are ready we can get them out by making their position untenable." He took another generous swallow of the whisky. "Now, tell me about Deefa."

"Deefa?"

"Yes, You have seen it?"

"Yes."

"Tomorrow we are ordered to press home our initiative and attack the camp."

Mussalim stared at him in horror. "No," he said shaking his head. "It will be suicide."

Al Mushani stared at him a moment. "Those are our orders."

"How many men can you muster?"

He shrugged non-committaly, "eighty, maybe."

"Deefa stands on the top of a hill with exposed ground all round. It is well fortified with high wire and razor wire. Even allowing for their recent casualties there could be more than four hundred men inside. And you intend to attack with just eighty. We could lose half that number just crossing the exposed area. We could lose more on the fence. If we were to get inside then we would find ourselves so hopelessly outnumbered that we would be forced to retreat. When we did they could chase us in their vehicles and slaughter us as we ran." He wondered perhaps if he had been too frank and should have tempered his opinion. But he was in too deep to stop now. "Then who would be left to stop them crossing Sayq to occupy Dalkut and perhaps Sarfait too. We could turn a marvellous victory into a defeat."

"What if we were to place the camp under fire from a distance and not attempt an open assault?"

"That would be better, but we would need to be careful when we withdrew. We would still be vulnerable to their fast moving vehicles."

Al Mushani studied him in silence for a few moments. "Hmm, he said. "You really think it's that tough?"

Mussalim nodded. "It's a bad idea," he regretted that statement instantly wondering just whose idea it was and who precisely he had just slighted.

To his relief, Al Mushani didn't flinch. "OK," he said. "Don't speak of this to anyone. I will contact Al Ghassani and give him your opinion." He stood and offered his hand to be shaken. "Now go and enjoy the feast. We will talk again."

His opinion would be given to Al Ghassani! Mussalim felt both astonished and exalted that he rated that amount of consideration. He stood up a little dazed and shook the offered hand. "I am sorry, I can't drink this," he said apologetically as he passed the tin mug back.

"Leave it," Al Mushani laughed.

A dark patch of red where the sun had sunk still tinged the night sky when he left the tent and sought his companions from Dalkut. He found seven or eight of them including Tariq inter mingled with a group of other men who he didn't know. He greeted them all in turn and joined the circle around the fire.

Two men in the centre held up, examined then broke open cardboard packages. There was a great deal of humour as the pair behaving like clowns first tasted the pack contents then spit it out in a great show of disgust before emptying it into a large iron pan which dangled above the fire.

Having little idea with what precisely was taking place Mussalim looked quizzically at Tariq. "It's soldiers rations that was found on some of the pack animals," he informed him with a deal of amusement. "We have no idea what are in those packets but it's all going into the pot anyway."

Mussalim glanced around the campfire, without exception the faces displayed a lot of merriment. Having arrived in the middle of the joke he did not readily share their humour. However, he did recognise the situation probably had more to do with tension release than any particularly funny situation. "Where is Al Shibam?" he asked Tariq.

He shrugged unconcerned paying more attention to the two clowns than the question. "Probably still sitting in the hills at Deefa."

If that was true then he was going to be absolutely furious when he eventually rejoined the unit. A roar of laughter erupted around the circle as the pot contents now subjected to boiling water swelled enormously and began to spill out of the pot. This time Mussalim experienced his own release of tension and joined in with the hysterical laughter.

Before he had rolled out of his blanket the next morning Al Mushani sent for him. Still not fully alert he shuffled across the campsite following his aid towards his tent. The aid lifted the tent flap and indicated with a flick of his head that Mussalim should lead the way in.

Al Mushani had his back towards them and peered into a tiny mirror dangling from the tent roof. With his fingers he smoothed his beard then adjusted his shirt collar. He stared hard at his reflection and satisfied with his appearance, he turned and greeted Mussalim inviting him to sit on that same ammunition box.

"Whisky?" he teased, dark eyes twinkling. Mussalim grimaced. "Coffee then," he grinned and instructed his orderly. They then passed a few moments in polite pleasantries enquiring about each other's health. The conversation then lulled giving Al Mushani the opportunity to come to the point. "The attack on Deefa goes ahead," he said flatly.

Mussalim stared dumbly back at him with dismay.

"However, because of your report, it will only be a token attack."

"A token attack?"

"Yes. Its intention is entirely to satisfy the Yemen government."

Mussalim was baffled. "What has the Yemen government to do with it?" he queried.

He sniggered briefly. "Ah my young friend, you have so much to learn. You think that we are the complete masters of our own actions."

Mussalim shrugged without reply.

Seeing his confusion Al Mushani sighed and then said. "I will try to explain." He paused choosing a starting point. "You know, of course that our leaders and operations operate from the shelter of Yemen. You know also that Hauf our main base is there. You also probably know that all our arms and supplies are shipped into their ports from China and Korea or overland from Egypt from our Russian allies. Obviously, we therefore rely entirely on the goodwill of our Yemen friends. Politically, however, they don't recognise us – they can't. Internationally, they deny having anything to do with us.

The British government for one doesn't accept those denials and they find methods to retaliate. One of the methods they use is to employ guerrilla forces that masquerade as independent mercenaries. In fact these independent mercenaries are trained and led by British Special Forces. Officers and NCO's disguised thinly as retired ex-servicemen. These terrorists operate from camps in Oman and Saudi Arabia along the Yemen border. They work cross border sorties into the mountains attacking and murdering not only Yemen soldiers but also their Egyptian trainers who are invited guests in Yemen. They mostly target overland convoys attempting to restrict supplies reaching our and Yemen forces. It is strongly suspected that Deefa is one of the camps from which they operate."

Mussalim cast his mind to the vehicles that he had seen on that base. This perhaps would account for the unusually high number and different types that were there.

"The Yemen government forces can't cross the border and carry out an attack without creating an international incident," Al Mushani continued his explanation. "But we can. So in return for their continued goodwill they want us to do it for them. The sole intention of the attack is to make the point by the Yemen government that they are fully aware of just where these guerrilla operating bases are."

Mussalim could understand how the Oman Sultan would approve guerrillas operating cross border raids into Yemen. But Saudi Arabia? They seemed to have no stake in this "What has this to do with Saudi Arabia and why would they approve these raids?"

"Because they fear us."

Mussalim looked at him with a frown. "No," he disagreed tentatively. "They sheltered Mussalim Bin Nufl when he was leader of the cause. Therefore, they must support us"

"They sheltered Bin Nufl when he was the leader of the Dhofar Liberation Front. That movement posed no threat to the wealthy families of Saudi. It was a local issue and as such no real concern to them. However, things have now changed drastically. To obtain more support from our Communist allies we have elevated our sights to liberate all Arab countries in the Arabian Gulf. Peoples Front for Liberation of the Occupied Arabian Gulf," he reminded him of the cause title.

"The Arabian Gulf obviously includes Saudi Arabia and therefore when we win this war we will become a major threat to those wealthy few in Saudi. Saudis have no particular love of the western countries, except of course they crave their money from oil sales. They see them as bourgeois and decadent and are concerned about the influence they may have on their own deprived people. But they fear Communist people-power even more. While the Western powers continue to get Saudi oil they see no reason to interfere with their unequal autonomous class system. However, our communist friends most certainly will, if they ever get the opportunity. So the Saudis cultivate favours from the west and hope to receive an assurance of protection. That is why they allow these guerrillas to operate from within their borders. But just like the British government they firmly deny having anything to do with any terrorist activities."

Mussalim struggled with complicated double dealing politics, shaking his head slowly in amazement.

Al Mushani chuckled seeing his bewildered expression. "Never mind, our duties as soldiers are much simpler. Leave the politics to Al Ghassani and his team who are well suited to the political role."

The aid returned carrying a tray Al Mushani glanced up and indicated that he should set it down on the wooden box. Then with a brief "thank you" he dismissed the man. He picked up the pot and poured coffee into one of the small handless cups and handed it to Mussalim. He took a sip and made a suitable polite comment.

"The raid on Deefa will take place tomorrow immediately after sundown," he went on as he filled the second cup for himself. "We will drop a few mortar shells, hopefully in amongst their vehicles, and spray the camp with a lot of automatic rifle fire. Then as soon as it is dark enough we will melt away into the night. Even with vehicles they won't dare to follow us in the dark." He set the pot down and picked up the cup. "Afterwards we will probably exaggerate the success of the raid a little just to satisfy our Yemen friends and everyone will be happy." He gave Mussalim a self-satisfied grin.

"However, for you Crazy Man Mussalim this raid is of little concern. On my recommendation you are to return immediately to Hauf. From there you will be sent to Egypt, where you will undergo continuation training to become a junior Commissar in our cause."

He watched Mussalim's astonished reaction with amusement over the edge of the coffee cup as he took a sip.

~ 9 ~

July 1969 • The day was about as hot as it ever gets. The wind that moved over the barren *nejd* did nothing to ease the searing temperatures. Instead it lifted great clouds of pink dust high into the sky in spiralling thermals driving dense twisters across the flat and exposed land. Leaning idly between castellations of the fort wall Juma watched one of these dust devils pass along the shallow wadi between the two forts. Its density and width was such that for several seconds it masked completely the Yemeni fort just a kilometre away. It passed on its way northwards leaving the whitewashed fort beneath the flag of the Aden Federal Army once again contrasting vividly with the black volcanic hills in its background.

There was movement below him inside the compound. Juma turned and looked down on the handful of men unhurriedly assembling for the next guard shift. Very soon this tedious duty would end and he would swap it for an eight-hour rest period that was equally as tedious. The Habrut detachment was an assignment that all the Salalah Soldiers dreaded. However, it was a detachment that all must take a turn and Juma had just completed his first week.

The fort at Habrut was an isolated Omani outpost on the border and faced a larger and more formidable looking Yemen fort directly opposite. Both forts were backed by crude mud and stone built houses occupied on both sides of the border by people of the tribe Mahra. The Mahra people did not particularly welcome the Sultan's *askars* in their midst because the Sultan's men were made up mostly from tribes within the Dhofari Kathiri and the Mahra was a tribe in the Quaiti group.

Fifty years ago the great Sultanate of Kathiri was a semi-independent state. Its territory included the inland Hadhramaut region of Yemen down to its southern coast and extended eastward deep into the Dhofar *nejd*. An uprising by the tribes of the Quaiti Sultanate inside its southern region of Yemen challenged the domination of the Kathiri tribes and a ferocious inter-tribal war was fought. In the interest of restoring peace the occupying British came down with a heavy hand and annexed the southern region. They handed semi autocracy of the region to Quaiti tribes and in so doing effectively cut off the Kathiri people from the southern seacoast and the seaports of Mukalla and Shihr. For many years resentment between the two Sultanates bubbled and often flared into a series of tit for tat camel steal raids and village burning. Both Sultanates were incorporated into South Yemen in 1968 when independence from Britain was gained. The recent closing of the eastern border by Oman further eroded the Kathiri territory by dividing the tribes east and west of the border. The Mahra tribe also suffered from this border closure when its own region within Quaiti territory was split by the line drawn upon a map. Consequently the Mahra chose to ignore as much as possible this imaginary geographical line which attempted to keep them out of their traditional region and they resented the forces which now tried to implement border restrictions.

The fact that the Aden Federal Army from within the Quaiti region manned the Yemeni fort and its soldiers were made up mostly from other Quaiti tribes produced an amicable affinity between the two. This manifested into a tolerant and lenient attitude to cross border offences and turned a heavily biased slant against the unfortunate Salalah soldiers attempting border control. Resentment against them from all round was only thinly veiled.

Because of this resentment the soldiers stayed mostly in and around the fort's compound. Only the possibility of an occasional patrol thirty or forty kilometres along the border north or south promised to interrupt the monotony. Juma reflected gloomily that he could look forward to at least another twelve weeks of crushing boredom and he consoled himself with the thought that when the detachment did eventually end then he would be due some leave.

While he waited to be relieved he considered the strategic value of the fort's location. Eighty kilometres to the south lay Deefa on the edge of Jebal Sayq and in between only an expanse of flat barren desert. Its exposed and featureless landscape interrupted only by the wadis Diffan and Sheetah cutting deep scars in the terrain. Sixty kilometres to the north the small border post at Almaziune. Beyond that nothing but the awesome Ramlet of immense sand mountains which stretch more than six hundred kilometres well into Saudi. He compared Habrut to a gate without fence or walls isolated and pointlessly guarded in the middle of nowhere for that was precisely what it was. Its strategic value was due entirely to the water that was plentiful here. A sizeable oasis of date palms flourished around the pools and in amongst the web of *falajs* that the villagers had cut in the ground to irrigate the area.

The guard commander began somewhat apathetically to assemble the men into some sort of line for inspection. When he was satisfied that he had some comparison he barked a curt "Attention" instruction. The response was somewhat ragged but effective. Then he wandered down the line casually inspecting each man, occasionally stopping to mutter some words that Juma could not hear. The deficient inspection eventually complete the sergeant then wandered to the front to face the line and began detailing each man to a post.

Habeeb a grey bearded man almost as old as Juma's father climbed the rickety wooden steps to the castellation level and came to relieve him.

"*Sallaam Ali Kum*," he muttered as he approached Juma wishing him a peaceful day with the traditional greeting.

"*Ali Kum Salaam*," Juma responded and in no particular hurry to depart stayed a few minutes to talk. The older man told him that he was more than halfway through his detachment here at Habrut. He talked freely and used the soldier's prerogative to unsparingly complain about all things from food to pay. He blamed the local Mahras for all the boredom blaming their resentful attitude for imprisoning them inside the wall precinct. Juma glanced across the barren expanse of nothingness and wondered vaguely what it was that he would do if the Mahra people were not here anyway. Habeeb continued complaining bitterly this time citing the duty as a whole and went on to say that for him it could not end soon enough and he looked forward impatiently to getting back to Salalah. Which was where he lived with his two wives and five children when he was not on duty. Juma tiring of the old man's depressing complaints made his excuses to leave.

As he began descending the steps the sharp crack of a rifle shot split the desert stillness, its echoes repeated back and forth across hills. Another soon followed and then another as almost instantaneously the air was filled with an all out exchange of fire between the two forts. The rapid retorts from the Browning machine gun positioned in the squat tower just above his head added its own ear shattering contribution as its operators also opened fire from their elevated position. Juma turned quickly and leapt the steps two at a time back onto the ramparts. He peered cautiously out between the castellation across the shallow wadi towards the Yemen fort. Streams of bluish smoke drifted away from the whitewashed fort walls indicating intensive small arms fire was being directed at the Sultan's fort.

Juma stooping beneath the wall's protection ran along the rampart towards Habeeb. "What happened?" he gasped as he sank down at his side.

Habeed leaned in a well between the castellations his rifle propped on an elbow too busy pumping and firing his single action rifle to do anything more than shrug.

Glancing around him Juma could see that the fort had become a place of frantic activity. Those already in position concentrated hard on pumping as many bullets at the distant Yemeni fort as they could. In the compound below soldiers in various states of dress poured from their off duty resting places and ran to positions where they too could add the weight of their firepower to that of their colleagues. Juma twisted away into the next castellation and began firing on the Yemeni citadel also.

From this distance human targets were not readily identifiable only an occasional glimpse of some moving shape. So he contented himself by aiming roughly at the area around the castellation relying purely on luck for his bullets to find their way in between and perhaps score a hit. He could hear occasional dull thumps as incoming missiles thudded against the fort wall close by. It should have served a warning but with adrenaline now flowing through his veins at overdose level it didn't. Instead, he disregarded the thumps completely and concentrated entirely on the continuous sequence of load, aim and fire. Caught up in a wild fervour of excitement the nonsensical absurdity of the situation was lost upon him. Gradually the shouts around him that he been hearing for a few seconds began to penetrate his totally engrossed brain and he realised that the order to cease firing had been given. He was further shocked to find that in his complete absorption he had at some point risen to his feet and was standing exposed. Quickly, he dropped down behind the wall's cover. With his breaths coming rapid and shallow he sat with his back against the wall and knees bent to his chest. He blew hard through puffed cheeks has he began recovering composure realising too with some shock that he had no idea of how long he had actually been firing. The shots from the other fort, however, were still coming in and with the same intensity.

He glanced further along the ramparts towards the steps where the fort's Commanding Officer, a young *Raa'id*, crouched and peered through binoculars across the wadi. He turned back the other way and looked at Habeeb sitting close by. He wordlessly grinned back exposing crooked and gapped teeth.

It took a few minutes before the fire from the Yemeni side began to decrease and then finally stop as they realised that they were no longer under fire.

"What started that?" Juma asked staring at Habeeb.

He snorted. "Who knows!"

"They fired first though?" Juma sought confirmation.

He didn't get it. Habeeb just shrugged. "The first shots could have come from anywhere. Perhaps from the Yemen fort, but then perhaps not. From one of the Mahra houses maybe, or even from among those date palms."

By his matter of fact tone Juma suspected that there had been other similar incidents. "Has this happened before?"

"That's the third time since I have been here." He showed his crooked teeth in another grin. "Breaks up the monotony though doesn't it?"

Juma didn't share his off-handed attitude. "This is serious stuff," he said concerned.

Habeeb used the end of his shamag to wipe the sweat from his face. "Don't worry as long as the youngster remains CO here it'll never get out of hand," he said nodding towards the *Raa'id* still peering down the binoculars. "He is always first to submit," he added with a hint of derision.

"And if he didn't?"

He shrugged once more. "Well… it would go on and on until one destroyed the other, I suppose. Those Yemenis would never stop. They have a larger force than us, better weapons and probably more munitions too. It would be a considerable loss of face if they were to submit first."

Juma was thoughtful, considering a probable conclusion if the exchanges protracted. The probably end result would be the destruction of this fort. He glanced once more at the young *Raa'id* CO with some regard for the man's good judgement. He hoped also that an officer with much more vanity and far less prudence would not replace him, at least not until his tour of duty here was ended.

"Another hour when the fingers are off the triggers and the tempers cooled," Habeeb went on. "He'll be out there in the middle of the wadi under a white flag and he'll be joined by the Yemen fort commander. They'll sit down out there for an hour or so and accuse each other of firing first and then both lodge an official protest."

＊ ＊ ＊

Abdulla watched helplessly as the small band of men made off with the full supply of milk and another six goats. This was the third of these unwelcome visits and the goat herd was shrinking at a rate much faster than he could ever hope to sustain.

"What are we going to do, father?" Hamed asked.

He glanced sideways at his son. "I don't know," he said dejectedly and moved to a nearby rock. He wiped his hand across its flat surface and removed some of the moisture lying there before sitting down. Each morning the thin mantle of mist lasted a little longer and came back a little early each afternoon. The new Khareef was getting a little stronger each day. Perhaps when it clamped in fully and shrouded everything in thick fog and endless drizzle the men of the PFLOAG would stay away, he thought. It was unlikely though, because this particular group had established a base in the village of Raythut little more than a dozen kilometres away. The burden of feeding those men had fallen onto the already impoverished jeballys in the area.

"We have to do something." Hamed persisted.

Abdulla nodded wearily. "Perhaps we could move the goats to my brother's house at Haluf."

"Don't they have PFLOAG men there?"

"I don't know, Perhaps they do."

He knew that it wasn't the answer anyway. If there were no goats then these men would simply take cattle. They carried their Kalachnikovs as intimidation and did not listen to his plea of the additional hardship that they imposed. Abdulla was impotent to prevent them from systematically plundering his farm, as indeed were his neighbours. These men were nothing less than thieves taking what they needed and probably more besides.

He thought of his eldest son and in his mind imagined him acting in the same callous manner in some other part of the region. Instantly he rejected the thought, despite Mussalim's association with such men he could not believe that he would be so base. But he could not reject the feelings of anger and shame that his eldest son was allied to such men. Juma at least was enlisted on the side opposed to anarchy albeit perhaps for his own personal reasons. Nevertheless where he felt a degree of shame for his first son's actions he felt a degree of pride for his second.

With the PFLOAG contingent strong in the area it would be sheer folly for Juma to even visit his family. Abdulla had no doubt at all what would happen if they were to find and capture a soldier of the Sultan. He could also anticipate that their attitude towards the family would be severe if they even discovered that a son served in the Sultan's army. Tomorrow he decided that he would go to Salalah and pass a warning to Juma that he must stay away from his family home for the foreseeable future.

The drain on the livestock was a serious handicap in his bid to achieve the wedding targets set by Talib and because he had already paid the unrecoverable two and a half thousand rupees he was now fully committed. Briefly he wondered if he should sell all the livestock in an attempt to raise his three thousand rupee's target. But he soon rejected that because that would leave the family without meat, milk or any kind of resources. Gloomily, he contemplated that by the time these PFLOAG men had finished that might very well be the situation he would find himself in anyway. Involuntarily he groaned aloud.

Hamed glanced at his father. "Perhaps we should move away father," he offered as a suggestion.

"To where," he scoffed.

"Salalah plain, perhaps."

Abdulla stared at his son. Perhaps there was some possibility of a solution within that suggestion. He might be able to move the livestock onto the plain then place Hamed and Lailla down there to tend the stock. There would be much hardship for them both because they would have to live in primitive conditions in roughly constructed canvas shelters. But living that way and tending livestock, that was the traditional way of the Bedouin, so it was not impossibility. At least it did safeguard the existing stock and since nearly half the cattle and two of the three camels were in calf it seemed a desirable solution. He looked aimlessly in the direction that the men had disappeared with his goats and wondered if Hamed could manage it. Perhaps he would be asking too much of a man so young. He decided to say nothing at this point but definitely give the notion more consideration.

The next morning he rose early, loaded a camel with kindling wood and set off alone for Salalah. He made good time descending from the jebal and within an hour he emerged from the steep valley onto the open plain. As he crossed the plain heading towards the military gate at Umm Al Ghawrif he examined the growth around him considering its ability to provide fodder for his animals. The ground was tinder dry and dusty and grazing matter sparse. The animals would need to forage hard, but the rapidly approaching Khareef would soon stretch its fingers down the mountains to touch Salalah and provide enough moisture to encourage new growth. The plain would never have greenery as thick and lush as the mountains did during the Khareef.

However, he considered that if the campsites were moved to different areas as soon as the grazing was exhausted then there would probably be enough fodder for his animals to survive. But once the Khareef had finished and the searing sun once more scorched the plain dry that then would certainly be a different matter. It was a dilemma. Perhaps the easiest solution would be to tackle one problem at a time he decided. And the first problem was to find a safer haven for the stock and removing it down here was probably the solution, albeit temporary. The bigger part of another hour passed before he reached the queue at the gate waiting for loads to be searched.

The soldiers that manned the gate where in no particular hurry to progress the searches and the queue moved only painfully slowly. When at last it was his turn, Abdulla led his camel to the search area and stood aside while two guards checked through the woodpile tied on the animal's back. While he waited he approached a third guard manning the barrier and identified himself as Juma's father. After enquiring if he could either speak to his son or pass a message he learned that Juma had been detached to an outpost on the Yemen border and would not be back for about three months. Satisfied that for the time being at least, Juma would not be visiting home and stumbling into those PFLOAG bandits Abdulla returned to his camel and waited for the search to be completed.

His main objective achieved he decided to sell his wood quickly and return home. So he didn't bother to go to the souk. Instead he found a trader and sold the lot at knock down price. It was when he was leading his camel back through the narrow alleyways that he saw the sign. It hung a little askew above an old gnarled door.

He paused in front of small flat-topped sandstone building staring at it. The crudely painted shapes of stars and crescents indicated that this was a place where fortunes were told. Although he believed that the whole map of his life was pre-determined by Allah he did not particularly believe that any human had the ability to foretell Allah's intentions. But then what did he know? Perhaps there were those that were granted such privileges by Allah. If it were so then a little information might give him some indication on what his best course of action might be. The camel at his side fidgeted, pawing the stony ground impatiently. The animal was right, he decided, it would be a waste of money and he began turning away.

"Peace be with you my friend."

Abdulla glanced back in the direction of the voice. The heavy shutters were tied back and between the flat but warped pieces of wood, which barred the window an old man watched him. "And to you also," he replied.

"You are troubled, my friend come in, I can help you."

"No," he said shaking his head.

"Come," the man insisted.

Abdulla hesitated. What could it hurt other than waste money?

The face disappeared from the window and the old man opened the door. "Come in it's cooler inside."

He was dressed in a grubby glibbya that had once been white. His red dyed hair indicated that he had made the pilgrimage to Mecca and it contrasted strikingly with a silver beard which hung to his chest. One eye was white and grotesquely opaque while the other black as night stared piercingly at Abdulla.

He shrugged slightly then looped the camel's rein through one of warped pieces of wood in the window. Still he hesitated. The old man indicated with a wave of his arm that he should enter through the low doorway. He kicked off his sandals at the door and went in. Inside it was dark and except for an old carpet in the middle of the small room and half a dozen mangy cushions it was bare. He stood waiting to be invited to sit, dubiously wondering what he was doing there.

The old man ordered a shrivelled old crone to bring water before pointing towards the pile of cushions where Abdulla should sit. "You are a much troubled man but I can give you peace of mind, my friend."

Abdulla sat cross-legged on the dirty cushions where the old man indicated. "How much?" he asked sceptically.

"What price do you put on peace of mind?" He sat on the opposite side of the carpet. "Ten rupees," he suggested.

"Ten rupees?" It was exorbitant, he hadn't got very much more for the wood that he had sold. "No, too much."

He stared back at Abdulla with his one good eye seemingly piercing into his very thoughts. "What I have to tell you will be worth at least that." He paused, "but I will take eight."

"No," shaking his head. "Five is all that I will pay."

The woman arrived with two glasses of water on a brass tray and placed it in between the two men. The old man spoke to the woman in a language that Abdulla didn't understand. She hesitated a moment then nodded briefly and replied.

"Very well," the old man said turning his attention back to his guest. "Give your five rupees to the woman." She left wordlessly with his money.

"When were you born?" He asked handed him a glass.

Abdulla had no idea.

"You don't know which part of the year?"

He shook his head and sipped the tepid water. "I don't even know which year."

The old man stroked his long beard thoughtfully before reaching over and took the glass from Abdulla's hand. Deliberately he placed it to one side before reaching back once more and grasping both his wrists tightly.

"I know that you are feeling very alone and vulnerable at this time," he said squeezing his wrists sympathetically. "You are a kind hearted man who is suffering great hardships. Hardships that are made much harder by others close by who are uncaring. These others pursue their own ambitions with no regard to the increased burden they put on you and others like you. But do not despair, help is on the way. Someone is coming from the west, a man. A man who will pursue his own mission tirelessly and as he does the results will be that he will ease not only your burden but also of others just like you. You also carry the great weight of guilt. You see yourself as having failed others who are close. But you should not torment yourself with this guilt because the failure is not yours. Instead it is due to circumstances beyond your control and none can ever say that you did not do your best. You also have much sorrow locked inside but I fear that you have much more yet to come and a great ordeal to endure. That man that comes from the west will unintentionally add a great tragedy to your load. However, you must never give up because there are happier times ahead for you. One day you will prevail and it will all have been worthwhile. A bright sun will one day rise on a new Oman and it will bring peace and prosperity not only to you but also to all. Then you will know happiness and contentment such as you deserve."

Abdulla allowed his camel to plod up the Shair valley on its way home at its own leisurely pace. Inside he was feeling very irritated for allowing himself to be duped out of five rupees, which he could ill afford. He realised fully the old man had said much while cleverly saying nothing. Through the experience of many fortune tellings he had used simple powers of observation to state the obvious and disguise it in mystique. Then he had added in some vague prophecies that could be attributed to everything or nothing and ended with the essential happy ending which every fortune-teller's client wanted to hear. He had been as foolish as a silly superstitious old woman and had attempted to pay for a little sympathy and some nebulous words of encouragement. He decided that to avoid embarrassment he would not mention this little piece of stupidity to anybody. He made a second decision also and that was to go ahead and move the family stock down onto the Salalah plain.

✳ ✳ ✳

Mid August 1969 • Lailla sat on the lip of the *falaj* with her feet dangling in the cool water. She looked around hoping to catch sight of the young Bedu boy, Gheer and wondered if he would come today. Most days he wandered aimlessly to the Arzat waters and most days he would just happen to find her in the area grazing the goat herd on the lush greenery of the water's edge. Neither she nor he would yet admit that they came deliberately to the area in hopes that the other would be there.

The Khareef season had taken a strong grip on the mountains and shrouded the upper peaks in thick wet mists. Down on the plain the mist hung higher as low cloud and cast a grey pallor over the flat lands. Depressing, as this greyness was, it was still much more desirable to Lailla than being amongst the cold and wet jebal peaks. Here on the plain it was at least reasonably dry with only occasional rain instead of the unrelenting drizzle in the mountains.

It had now been six weeks since Abdulla had moved the whole family and stock from their jebal farm down to the coastal plain. He had gone to the east of Salalah and selected a campsite in the Ma'murah area at the mouth of the Wadi Arzat. Here the waters tumbled down from the wadi and formed a shallow brook along the base of the mountainside. A man made *falaj* carried the water twelve kilometres across the plain and into the grounds of the Sultan's beach farm. Abdulla had deliberately selected a campsite fully two kilometres from the water supply for reasons of safety. He was fully aware that the water supply was vulnerable to frequent sabotage attacks by the rebels as they attempted to interrupt the flow of water to the Royal Farm by bombs.

During the first week Abdulla and Hamed had worked feverishly to construct an animal compound. They had foraged the area for anything they could use and the end result was a crude and marginally effective mixture of poles, sticks, corrugated tin and rocks. Jokha and Lailla meanwhile had worked to construct a rough living shelter. Stout poles had been driven into the ground while more flexible ones had been tied along the top. Across these poles a large cover, consisting of many cloths sewn together had been stretched to give shelter on three sides and over the top.

Since then Abdulla had alternated his time between the campsite and the farm. His length of stay or absence usually amounted to five or six days and his periods of absence delegated a good deal of responsibility to Hamed. The spin off benefit of this responsibility was a high degree of independence and Hamed revelled in it. As family head in his father's absence he had complete autonomy and was free to come and go as he pleased providing his obligations were satisfied. He had become friendly with other young men of his age from the nearby Bedouin camp and a good deal of his evening time was spent in their company, mostly, when his father and Jokha were absent, beneath the shelter of their rough tent.

The group of young boys would sit well into the early hours, earnestly discussing the trivia that concerns the young and immature. During this time Lailla, suitably dressed in her black, all-covering *abeya,* would sit quietly listening in the background. From time to time some attempt would be made to bring her into the conversation and although polite with her replies she avoided being brought into the circle of young men. It would not be appropriate. There was a great deal of posturing among the boys – entirely for her benefit, she knew – but only the good-looking Gheer sought her company during the day.

Today he came from the wadi mouth, emerging from the dense shrubs two hundred metres away from where she sat. Although she felt a ripple of pleasure run through her she turned away quickly pretending not to have noticed him. Instead she peered down into the *falaj* checking her appearance in the water's reflection and adjusted her head covering more becomingly. This day she wore a full length green frock with a brown floral patterned head scarf that not only covered her head but most of her upper body also. Gheer, barefooted and wearing only a *futa* wrapped around his waist and legs greeted her brightly as he sat by her side. He placed a small bundle between them. "Are you hungry?" he asked

Lailla shrugged noncommittal and watched as he began unwrapping the bundle. When he had finished he offered her the choice of dried strips of lizard meat. She hesitated and glanced at him but he indicated that she should take a piece. The gesture was not lost on her. Whether he had brought the food especially for her was doubtful, however, he had unselfishly offered her the first choice and therefore he desired to please her. She felt herself blush so she took momentary refuge behind the cloth that covered her head.

They talked cheerfully about nothing in particular as they ate the dried meat. It was heavily salted and when they had finished they used cupped hands to scoop water from the *falaj* to wash away the salt taste. Gheer then lowered himself into the water and sat facing her with his back resting against concrete wall. The slow flowing water lapped gently across his shoulders. He invited Lailla to join him, but she declined. Without the hot sun, her clothes would dry only very slowly. But she watched a little enviously as he allowed his outstretched arms to float on the surface.

"I saw Prince Qaboos today," he said casually.

Lailla knew of the young prince and heir apparent to Sultan Said, but doubted that she would recognise him if he were to sit next to her. His public appearances were almost non-existent. She knew from what she had been told that since his return from England, where he had been educated, he lived a recluse existence in the Sultan's Salalah Palace with his mother.

"Where did you see him?"

"Over there," he replied nodding in the direction of the palace farm.

Lailla glanced across the plain to the island of dense green trees encompassed by a double row of high chain link fence and wide concertina barbed wire. "How?" she asked puzzled.

"I know a way in," he replied nonchalantly.

She looked at him dubiously. The fence was guarded every few metres by an armed guard in a tower. It would be a very dangerous thing to do to attempt to breach the fence.

"I can get in down by the beach."

"Why would you want to?"

"To steal fruit," he grinned. "Anyway I was in there early this morning stealing papaw fruit when I heard voices. So I had to hide. That's when I saw him. He was walking along a path between the trees talking with three British soldiers."

She stared at him amazed and not entirely convinced that his story was true. "What were they talking about?"

He shrugged. "I don't know, I think they were talking English. He is half Dhofari, you know," he went on after a short pause. "His mother is from Darbat," he waved his arm over a shoulder indicating roughly the direction of Wadi Darbat.

Lailla continued to stare at him thoughtfully without replying.

"You don't believe me, do you?" he said noting for the first time her sceptical expression. "Tonight I'll bring you a papaw fruit," he said with another grin.

✳ ✳ ✳

Hamed had never had so much fun in his entire life. He had a circle of teenage friends barely a kilometre away and lots of free time to spend with them which was in complete contrast to his existence on the farm. The responsibility of tending the livestock that he had been handed by his father did not trouble him at all. The high degree of independence that his current situation provided outweighed the burden of responsibility. He had quickly dropped into an effective routine.

He turned out the animals from the compound early and, except when a trip into Salalah for supplies was necessary the rest of the day was his. Even those trips into Salalah were enjoyable and hugely more desirable than working the jebal farm. The goats he didn't have to worry about too much, Lailla effectively looked after them.

By late afternoon the cattle would have made their way back to the compound to be milked usually bringing the camels in their wake. Before that Lailla had usually returned the goats to the pen and had then begun preparing food for the evening. It was the evening milking that took most of his time but for a little free goat milk a couple of his friends were prepared to help him. After that he would take the camels the couple of kilometres to the pool at Arzat and fill the skins with water to fill the compound trough. Even this was a task that he didn't need to do every day because the cattle would usually wander in that direction and drink their fill before returning in the afternoon, so the water trough did not become empty very quickly. After the daily work routine was finished then there was once again free time to spend with his new friends, usually at his campsite. It was only when his father and Jokha were on site that his movements were a little more restricted. Not too much, however, because even though his father always found extra work, the tasks were shared. It was the mostly the evenings that upset his social routine, while his father was there then he was unable to entertain at his campsite. It was only minor inconvenience, however, because he would then visit his friends at their Bedu camp instead. To Hamed life had never been better.

Today, he found four of his friends sitting with their feet dangling in the shallow brook that flowed from the Wadi Arzat. They greeted him with calls and grins as he approached. He removed his thonged sandals, hitched up his *futa* and waded across the brook to join them on the opposite bank.

They were in good humour and teenage banter crossed backwards and forwards, often at the same time. Eventually bored with the chaffing two of the boys, Ayud and Fiaz began wading upstream until they arrived at the point were the waters tumbled down the wadi and fed the brook. They then began scrambling up the rocks and stones amid the splashing waters. It looked much more interesting then just sitting on the water's edge so Hamed and the other two soon followed. The water force got stronger as the climb got progressively steeper until at a point around halfway Ayud and Fiaz gave up and waited for the others to catch up.

The pair were sitting on a bank of concrete when the other three caught up. At this point both banks of the cascade had been artificially reconstructed to ensure that water continued to spill downward on its original route. It was not very wide and the three new arrivals hauled themselves onto the bank directly opposite. By its dark colour Hamed guessed that the concrete had not been laid very long probably within the last three days.

"What happened here?" he asked.

Muftah by his side shrugged and then said. "Probably blown up by the rebels then repaired by the soldiers. It happens all the time."

"Waste of time fixing it, if you ask me." Ayud offered his opinion from the opposite side. "Even if the rebels do manage to block it, eventually it will overflow and find its way down there." He nodded towards the plain below.

"Sometimes they set booby traps." Muftah said again. "To catch the soldiers when they come to make repairs," he added for Hamed's benefit.

"Or wait in ambush." Fiaz contributed.

Hamed glanced up the steep mountainside towards the bank of thick mist that hovered only a hundred metres above them and considered the suitability of an ambush. The stubby tree canopies were thick and so was that fog. There were decidedly big cloaking advantages to intending ambushers.

"Is that Gheer down there?" Obiad changed the subject.

All eyes turned in the direction where he looked. A herd of goats and two figures looked minuscule on the plain far below.

"That could be Lailla with her goats," Obiad said again.

"If that is Lailla then almost certainly it is Gheer." Muftah said.

Hamed glanced sharply at the boy at his side and then turned back and peered hard down onto the plain. The figures were just too far away to be certain. He had not been at all concerned that Gheer seldom came on these leisure rambles, he assumed that he simply had other duties to perform. Now it appeared that it was not so and that instead he spent time unchaperoned with his sister. He wondered if he should be concerned. His father would be. He would also be very angry with him for irresponsibly indulging himself in his own enjoyment while he had been blind to the developing situation. Starting tonight, he resolved, he would adopt a much more supervisory role over Lailla's activities.

The deep thud of a splash and a descending shower of water made him gasp with surprise. Ayud stood and roared with laughter at the shocked faces of the three boys on the opposite side. Hamed understood immediately what had happened. He had deliberately tossed a large rock across to splash in the water at their feet. It now developed into a tit-for-tat exchange with the boys on one side throwing rocks across to the other trying to wet each other with the splashes. With each boy soon wary of the splashes no one was getting wet until Obiad turned traitor on his bank and pushed Ayud into the water. With a roar Ayud leapt from the water and began to chase him seeking revenge. Hamed and the other two watched and laughed as Obiad ran away up the hill throwing verbal taunts over his shoulder to Ayud. He had gone only a few metres when there was sharp dull thud and sudden fountain of earth and rock erupted from where Obiad had been less than a second before.

The three boys stared in stunned silence at the dust cloud as debris started to rain down and spatter the ground and foliage with light slaps. Slowly the cloud of dust cleared, revealing Ayud writhing slowly and silently on the ground whilst of Obiad there was no sign. Soon, however, screams of pain and panic began from a thicket several metres down the hill from where the explosion occurred.

"Mines," Fiaz muttered breaking the stunned silence and looking around him warily.

Muftah leapt onto the concrete. "Get on here!" he instructed the other two.

"We have to do something to help them," Hamed said, after following his example. "How?"

Hamed looked at him blankly his thoughts racing. "You two go to Ayud. Step only on any footprints that you can find. Then get him back here to where it's safe. I'll go and find Obiad."

Both boys looked at him somewhat dubiously, unsure of the situation and more than just a little afraid. Deciding that an example was the best way of prompting action Hamed turned and began scrambling back down the cascade. After a few metres he left the water and stepped onto some large rocks. Pausing a moment he glanced back up the hill. The other two had already begun a cautious and faltering journey towards Ayud. Obiad still shouted from the nearby thicket and Hamed studied the ground before him choosing a route. Slowly and guardedly he made his way to the thicket, stepping wherever he possibly could on rocks.

Obiad stopped shouting when he saw Hamed, but still moaned and writhed in agony, clutching at the remnants of his leg. Hamed stared in horror at the blood soaked limb and struggled to control the nausea rising in his stomach. The thigh ended abruptly, leaving only strips of bloodied skin dangling like tattered red rags. Blood gushed freely in pulsating squirts from the between Obiad's fingers has he clutched despairingly at the stump end that had been his leg.

Hamed pulled off his *shamag* and fighting back the retching from his stomach tied it tightly over the end. Before he had even finished it had become soaked to dripping point. Then using Obiad's own *shamag* he tied it as tightly as possible around the remnants of the thigh. It seemed to slow the bleeding but only marginally. Beginning to panic he pulled Obiad up by the arm and hauled him across his shoulders. Paying no regard now to the possibility of other mines he took the most direct route back to the cascade stumbled and staggering beneath the weight.

Muftah and Fiaz had already started on their way down and made their way toward him supporting Ayud between them. At least Ayud was on his feet and apart from looking a little bloodied and groggy he seemed to have escaped any serious injury.

It took an age for the party to reach the bottom of the steep hill, or so it seemed. When they did Muftah ran to catch a couple of camels that grazed on the shrub greenery at the brook's side. It took more precious minutes to man-handle Obiad face down across the animal's back as it, smelling blood, pulled and shied at the halter in fright.

Hamed climbed on behind and drove the animal at a canter across the plain towards the Salalah town gate. Fiaz and the injured Ayud followed on the other camel, leaving Muftah standing staring after them.

When they reached the chicaned entrance it took only a glance from the guards before they quickly waved them on through and directed them toward the Um Al Ghariff gate. At the garrison gate they were halted and not allowed through. Instead one of the guards used a telephone to summon an ambulance from somewhere within. Hamed jumped down from the camel's back and carefully lowered Obiad, who mercifully had lapsed into unconsciousness, to the ground. The ambulance when it arrived was no more than a fitted and extended Land Rover and with military efficiency both injured boys were quickly loaded and despatched to the base clinic.

Hamed and Fiaz watched it disappear back inside the camp precincts and they were then escorted into the gate guardhouse by two soldiers. They were shown into a small windowless cell with only a single cot along the far wall. To show that they were not actually arrested the cell door was left open. Dejectedly they sat on the bed speaking only occasionally as they waited to be questioned. Soon after they had arrived they were given mugs of tea but it took another hour for anything else to happen.

Eventually they were shown into a room by a burly Army sergeant that was specially laid out for interrogation. The room was featureless without windows and had brick walls painted a depressing brown and cream. A large square table had been placed in the middle directly beneath fluorescent ceiling lights. Three chairs lined one side of the table and two on the other. Ayud now patched up with plasters and bandages sat in one of the three chairs directly opposite a British man wearing the officer's uniform of the Sultan's Army. Ayud gave them a welcoming grin when they entered. The sergeant saluted the officer and then directed Hamed and Fiaz to the two vacant chairs.

For the next thirty minutes they were questioned closely by the Officer with the Sergeant acting as interpreter. They were made to describe the precise position where Obiad had stepped on the mine and in order that there were no misunderstanding asked to point out the position on a map. They were questioned about their activities during the day and asked if they had perhaps seen any *adoo* in the area laying more mines. When asked if they had seen or knew of any location of any *adoo* forces in the jebal Hamed was greatly tempted to reveal the parasitical group that had based themselves at Raythut. But he didn't, he was afraid to and besides it would do no good. The army would, he reasoned, launch a raid and possibly a successful one too, but when it was over they would return to Salalah back inside the safe confines of their fortifications. When they had gone the PFLOAG forces would simply return once again. If ever they were to find out who had betrayed their location the consequences not only to him but also his family would be severe.

Eventually the questioning came to an end and the boys were free to leave. Before they did, however, they were praised for their actions. They had, they were told, saved Obiad's young life, albeit now severely disabled.

The sun had set when Hamed slid off the camel's back at the campsite and found his father waiting. He waved tiredly to his two companions as they turned the camels in the direction of Arzat to return the animals to the area from which they had taken them. His daily tasks still undone Hamed turned expecting to face his father's wrath. Instead his father, sensing his son's despair asked simply, "What happened?"

Hamed thought dejectedly on the day's events and wondered how he could tell it. Even now he could hardly believe how such a genial day had turned to tragedy in just an instant. How could it have happened that a young man barely sixteen with expectations of a full and active life before him had gone so quickly to a one legged cripple with a bleak future as a street beggar. Hamed had started this day thinking how wonderful life was here on the plain in comparison to the dull existence on the jebal farm. Now he craved the security of that quiet life.

"When can we go home?" he asked slipping into his father's arms.

Abdulla had seen the riders approaching while saddling a camel. His eyes were not good enough to see who they were but he guessed it would be Hamed and his friends. Who else would it be approaching the camp? He tugged at the blanket beneath the saddle to remove any creases that might chafe the animal before tightening the saddle girth beneath its belly. Satisfied that all was well he turned and watched the approaching riders. Now he began preparing himself to hand out a verbal blasting to his son for neglecting his duties.

The rider brought the camel right up to him before Hamed sitting behind the rider slid off. Abdulla could now see the dried and matted blood that streaked the animal's shoulder and leg. He watched the camel carefully as it began moving away without sign of injury or discomfort. If the animal was not injured then something or someone had been on its back that had bled profusely.

He looked at Hamed and sensed his despondency realising that something traumatic must have happened. "What happened?" he asked.

Hamed stared at him a few moments without answering. Then he put his arms around him and simply said. "When can we go home?"

Abdulla placed his arms across Hamed's shoulders and led him towards the makeshift tent where Jokha and Lailla where waiting. Hamed slumped down heavily opposite the two women. Abdulla glanced at Jokha and made a sign to bring water before sitting by his side.

"What happened?" He asked again handing him the tin mug of water

Hamed sipped the water then began his account slowly. It gathered pace quickly until it tumbled out so rapidly that it was difficult to follow. Abdulla had to keep interrupting him to clarify points. Eventually he felt that he had the full story and once again placed a consoling arm over his shoulders. He was thoughtfully silent for a while then he got to his feet and went over to his camel saddle. From the pack he took a small plastic bag containing the wet green pulp *sweeqa*, the mad man's grass.

"Try sucking a little of that," he said tossing the bag in Hamed's lap. "It will help to raise your spirits." Then he left to finish the chores.

Most of the work he had completed during Hamed's absence and the only task of any significance that remained was to replenish the water supply. Three camels including the saddled one squatted on the ground and did not move as he approached. He attached a halter around the neck and over the nose of one of the unsaddled beasts and then he attached the end to the tail of the saddled animal. He then hung several water skins across its back before prodding it to its feet with his camel cane. He climbed into the saddle and with a slap down its neck made that one rise also. Then he set off in the twilight for Arzat. Unwilling to be left behind the third camel bellowed noisily and true to its gregarious nature got up and followed the other two.

Abdulla's body rocked with the rhythmithic plodding of the camel's leisurely gait as he pondered the situation. Last year's plan of collecting grass and storing it had gone well and had enabled him to keep his stock fat and healthy long after he normally could. Last year, however there had been six of them to cut and gather it. This year with only Jokha and himself left to harvest, then the amount that they could store would be greatly reduced and the plan not as effective. Hamed had so far done well managing the stock and he was pleased with him. Today's incident, however, had certainly shocked him and might have dented his motivation to continue living and working on the plain. Certainly it was inconvenient and considerably more work to maintain the farm on the jebal and the stock campsite down on the plain, but despite that and the anticipated restricted grass harvest then up to this point things had been working out reasonably well. All the cattle were carrying calves, as were the three camels. If Allah were good to him then there would perhaps not be many bulls among the calves. Even if there were, then they could be slaughtered for meat as soon as they were big enough but it was among the cows, both cattle and camels, where the most sellable assets lay.

The goat herd was once again on the increase and by the end of the Khareef might have even recovered to the level it was before those PFLOAG bandits had started their regular plundering. However, even at this current increase rate the three thousand rupees value of stock that he needed to give Talib looked as though it might be out of reach. If he moved the stock back to the farm then it would be subjected to plunder and the target become even more remote. He wondered if Talib might take less at the marriage time and allow him to pay the balance at a later time. He instantly rejected the thought. His pride would never allow him to request such a dispensation from a Ruwas man. It would reflect a bad loss of face not only for him but to his tribe also. But then what were his alternatives if he had a fall short at the deadline time? He would have to seek assistance from somewhere else, which would also be an affront to his personal pride. Momentarily he felt greatly irritated that he had allowed Juma to place him in such a predicament. Why couldn't he have simply selected a woman from within his own tribe? As it was the whole family was suffering hardship and disruption to satisfy his desire.

He had reached the *falaj* and he slid down from the camel's back. He knelt by the man made stream and dipping a cupped hand in the slow flowing water took a drink. He watched as the three animals followed his example then turned his gaze up to the towering jebal. Somewhere up there on its darkening slope an innocent young man had this day had his life ruined by self-centred uncaring men who followed some remote doctrine which was supposed to be for his benefit. He wondered just how much more good they would manage to do for him and others like him before it was ended.

~ 10 ~

Late October 1969 • It was only yesterday that Mussalim had returned and now he sat waiting nervously outside Al Ghassani's office. His return journey had been a long one. Ten days ago he left the Russian training camp, which had been his home for four months and travelled north to Moscow. From there he had flown to Cairo and after a couple of days waiting he had been attached to an overland Egyptian supply convoy that took a week to trundle slowly southwards down to Mukella. In Mukella he had been met and after resting overnight he had been driven to the PFLOAG headquarters at Hauf. On his arrival he had been billeted in comfortable quarters with the instruction that the General Secretary himself wanted to see him at nine o'clock the next morning.

He had no idea why Al Ghassani wanted specially to see him. He still found it incredible that he had somehow, without particularly seeking it, achieved favoured status and had now begun to move within such exalted circles. He wanted to make a good impression and he pulled anxiously at his trousers relieving the stretch across his knees trying to protect the sharp creases. He wore the sand coloured uniform of a PFLOAG regular and displayed the red epaulets and cap badge of the rank 'Commissar.'

The door opened and Al Ghassani himself came out and bade him enter. He issued a brief instruction to his aide for refreshments before following Mussalim into the room. The room was spacious with a polished floor and a large desk in front of the window. A Persian carpet with an ample supply of cushions was placed in the corner and although there were chairs in front and behind the desk, Al Ghassani indicated to Mussalim that he should make himself comfortable on the carpet. He sat down legs crossed and studied his host as he settled opposite.

Al Ghassani wore a white *dish'dasht* trimmed at the collar and cuffs with gold thread. His head was bare revealing short-cropped greying hair. His beard was trimmed and also streaked grey while his eyes were dark and piercing.

"How was your training?" he asked when he was comfortable.

"It was good," Mussalim replied. "I spent the first two months in Cairo, where I was sent back to school to improve reading and writing. With teacher trainee ratio of only three to one the tuition was intense and I have improved a lot. I even learned a little English."

Al Ghassani nodded approvingly.

"From there I went on to Russia where I spent four months training in the use of different weapon systems."

"What kind of weapons?"

Mussalim shrugged slightly. "The Kalachnikov AK47, RPD's and Shpagin machine guns," he began listing. "Katyusha rocket launcher, eighty-two mill mortars, anti tank and anti personnel mines, hand grenades and grenade dischargers. A wide range."

Al Ghassani then began a series of exhausting questions establishing the depth of Mussalim's knowledge. He did his best to answer the questions wondering all the time if this was normal practice for the General Secretary to concern himself with the depth of each new Commissar's training. A possible clue to the line and depth of the questioning came when Al Ghassani asked Mussalim if he felt competent to instruct in the use of these weapons. Satisfied with his answer he then turned the questions political and asked for his view on the spread of communism.

Mussalim quoted the indoctrinated message of the inevitable spread of communism as more and more of the world's poorer classes became aware of the deceit carried out by the wealthy. He expanded the party belief that even in the powerful western countries the communist creed was gathering momentum and would soon begin to threaten the very foundations of capitalism. The power of the people would eventually become irresistible and there would be equality for all. He quoted it almost word for word as he had been tutored, believing that was what Al Ghassani wanted to hear. However, inwardly he felt that what happened beyond the borders of Oman was of little concern to him. Before he had finished recounting the indoctrinated rhetoric the aide arrived with a tray of refreshments and laid it on the carpet between the two men.

Without interrupting Mussalim, Al Ghassani poured the tea and offered him a cup. "And do you believe all that?" he asked quietly when he had finished and his piercing eyes studied Mussalim carefully.

Mussalim took the offered cup and considered the question carefully. He was not sure whether to give the safe reply or to boldly give a more honest opinion. "Er – ," he suspected that his hesitation had already given him away and therefore he decided to offer a veneer of his inner most feelings. "It may all be true but it is in this little corner of the world where we need to concentrate."

Al Ghassani raised his eyebrows. "Go on," he said.

Before him was the most powerful man in the PFLOAG and a man that he knew very little about. He needed to proceed very cautiously or he could find himself in a very dangerous position. "I believe in the ideology of communism," he prudently confirmed. "Why should a privileged few by an accident of birth or other fortunate circumstances have wealth while the vast majority has poverty and starvation? But my immediate concern is not so much the plight of the world's downtrodden but the suffering of my Dhofari brothers. In my opinion that should be our first objective. After that is achieved then the next progressive step can be decided." He had no intention of revealing that personally that was his only objective. That would be to foolishly invite trouble.

Al Ghassani stared at him silently for a few moments then began to nod slowly. "And the next progressive step?"

"To spread northwards to Muscat and to control the Hormuz Straits. Then what oil passes out of the Gulf or to which country will be ours to dictate. The whole of the western capitalist system will be in a stranglehold and that is a prize well worth winning whatever your political belief."

Al Ghassani's serious expression turned to a brief smile and he saluted with the teacup. "Indeed," he said. "Commissar Mussalim, I believe that you are a jebal man from Qara." He changed tact.

"Yes."

"How well do you know the Qara area and its people?"

"I am a Qara jebally as are the people, therefore I am one of them. I well understand the problems that they face everyday simply to exist. I share with them their fears and their hopes. He nodded emphasising the point. "Yes I know the people well. The area? Well, I probably know that even better."

Al Ghassani sipped his tea and studied him over the rim. Then he placed the cup on the tray and sat staring at it while he thoughtfully stroked his beard. After a few moments he looked directly at Mussalim and said, "Commissar Mussalim, you seem to be well suited to the task that I have in mind for you. Come," he said getting to his feet and leading the way to a large map on the wall.

"The war is going well and there is no doubt that we are winning. We control all this area," and he indicated the mountain regions from the Yemen border in the west right across to Sadh well beyond Mirbat in the east. "The *nejd* behind the mountains we can wander freely and have only to avoid the scattered government posts at Midway, Deefa, Maboosh, Manston, Habrut and Almaziune." He tapped each position in turn as he named it. "The Sultan's forces are trapped on the coastal plain with their backs to the sea. And even there they are attacked and harassed when they try to move outside their secure areas. Yes, undoubtedly, we are winning this war.

The Sultan's men are reduced to sneaking out, under the cover of darkness, from behind their barricades at Salalah and taking up ambush positions in the mountains. They wait around in hiding for days then usually they sneak, once again under the cover of darkness, back behind their barricades. Sometimes, however, they are lucky and some of our men stumble into those ambushes. More recently though they seem to have been more successful than just lucky. We have reports of patrols moving through the jebal handing out sacks of rice and medical supplies to the jeballys. It is probably that this is in exchange for information about the locations of our own forces."

He indicated that Mussalim should sit in the chair in front of the desk while he went and sat behind it. He rested his elbows on the desk and steepled his fingers. "Our main problem," he went on, "is that our forces are stretched too thinly. If we had a larger force then we would be in a better position to counteract these sorties. Unfortunately we don't have the financial resources to increase the strength of our regular forces. So I intend to create a large reserve force of militia. This militia will be made up from the local jeballys themselves. They will be trained in weapon use and then left in reserve until needed. When they are needed they will be called and while on active duty they will be paid on a daily basis. When they are not needed then they will be sent back to work their farms until the next time. This is where you come in." He leaned back in his chair and surveyed Mussalim.

"You are to return to Jebal Qara and put together a small team. Then you will move through the villages, passing the message of Communism and convince the locals that they will be far better off under our regime. While many are already convinced there are some that are not and I fear that we are not winning them over as quickly as I would like. So by sending one of their own with the message I think that they will be more inclined to listen. Then I am hopeful that our support will increase. As you gather the support you will also enlist volunteers to form the new militia and train them to use the weapons. You may use whatever methods you see fit to convince these people and to recruit them to our cause. Also you will forcibly discourage the passing of information to government sources with warnings that the penalties will be severe. But on the other hand any information given about government soldiers on the jebal will be rewarded."

Mussalim felt a pitch of excitement at the prospect of returning to Qara with such an exalted role to play in the struggle for independence. "How big will this team be?"

"Well that would be up to you, but I wouldn't imagine you need more than four."

"Where would this team come from?"

"The team selection will be your choice. You are to report to Commissar Mohammed Bin Talib in the village Raythut, do you know it?"

Mussalim did. It was within a dozen kilometres of his home. "Yes I do."

"Good. He is expecting you and while you will be under his command he is instructed to give you a free rein on this issue and to give you all the assistance that you need. Your team will be drawn from men under his command." He paused. "Any questions?"

"Only one. When do I start?"

"Do you know village Haluf?"

"Yes I do. It is the very heart of my tribal area, and I have close relatives there. It sits just on the *nejd* beneath the shadow of Jebal Qara's western end."

"Good then you start right away. Early tomorrow you will join two supply trains leaving for the caves in Shershitta and Kharfat."

Mussalim forehead creased in thought, he didn't know where they were. "I don't know either of these caves," he said dubiously fearing that perhaps he was expected to.

"No reason why you should," Al Ghassani said as if reading his thoughts. "Shershitta caves are about half a days camel ride from here on the coast side of Jebal Sayq while the Kharfat caves are further on in Wadi Kharfat. We have arms stored in both. You will press on to the second location in Kharfat where you will find a small party including two Chinese explosive experts waiting there for a guide. You will be that guide and take them to Haluf. After that you are free to make your way to Raythut and join up with Commissar Bin Talib."

The next morning early, the large caravan train of camels and donkeys and a hundred drovers left Hauf for the caves. They journeyed east along a well-travelled road and by midmorning had skirted beneath the Sarfait cliffs. Each step east took them towards Dalkut stirring memories within Mussalim of Shamel. The nearer they got to the village the stronger the urge to see again grew. He was curious to see how she had fared since he had abandoned her more than six months ago. Whether it was a need re-assure some guilt complex of her well being or simply a lustful desire to lay with her again he was unsure. Probably a mixture of both he decided.

Around midday they arrived at the Shershitta caves. Set close to the bottom of the steep hillside the enormous cave mouths gaped across the gradual sloping land out toward the sea. Still sitting on his camel Mussalim watched the confusion dispass-ionately as the drovers attempted to sort the pack animals that were to stay from those which were to press on. That would, he decided, take a little while, so surrendering to the urge to find Shamel, he decided to abandoned the train and press on ahead.

As he neared Dalkut he came under close scrutiny from the guard in the sangar high above the road. Mussalim glanced up and briefly waved his cap in his direction and wearing the uniform of a Commissar was not challenged Dalkut, it seemed, had not changed at all and he made his way first to the two-storied building that had been the PFLOAG billeting. It still was and as he dismounted he wondered if Al Shibam still commanded the Dalkut post. If he did what kind of reception could he expect?

He did and if Hemel held any bad feeling towards Mussalim for any loss of face that he had caused in the eyes of Al Mushani then he hid it well. He greeted him with beaming smiles and warm handshakes before inviting him in. Mussalim sat on the same carpet in the same room and was served dates and water by the same comfort concubine as he had some six months previously. The two men exchanged news and views for a while until Mussalim felt enough time had passed to make his enquiry about Shamel seem casual and unimportant.

Hemel shook his head and making an expression of indifference. "Haven't seen her for a long time. She must have gone back to her brother's family. He never offered her back for re-sale, so I don't know what became of her. So," he said turning to more interesting topics. "Tell me about Russia."

In the interests of politeness Mussalim stayed another hour before making the excuse that he must re-join the caravan train. As he rode away he looked back to see Hemel standing in the doorway watching him and he wondered if the meeting had really been as sociable as it had seemed. He must have lost a considerable amount of regard from the cause leaders because of his blunder at Deefa while his own standing had grown.

He guided his camel through the narrow streets to where Shamel's brother-in-law lived and was disappointed to find the house empty. An enquiry at the house next door only brought a blank stare and a vague opinion that he thought the family had moved to further east to Raykut. There was nothing for Mussalim to do except rejoin the caravan. He left the village and retraced his steps down the road until he found the place where the caravan train had left the road and turned north towards Umbaraaf in the Jebal Sayq.

Just south of Umbaraaf the train swung more westerly and entered the deep Wadi Kharfat. From this point the going got progressively more difficult as a series of escarpments barred the way. The caravan moved into single file and with a deal of bullying and swishing camel canes the burdened animals were forced to follow narrow goat paths up the steep wadi sides to arrive at the top of these sheer rock walls. Eventually, after negotiating six or seven of these escarpments the train arrived at a long but narrow flat area surrounded on three sides by towering steep rock faces. At the far end were a number of crudely constructed tents and behind those with enormous mouths gaping wide, the caves of Kharfat.

Men emerged from the caves and tents and stood watching the approaching supply train. Mussalim guided his camel towards the cluster of tents before making it kneel, then thankfully he slid off. Gingerly he straightened his spine and rubbed his sore back. It was moving towards sunset and apart from the hour he had spent with Hemel he had been on the animal's back the entire day. He gave the animal a poke with his stick getting it back onto its feet and then unbuckled the saddle. Hauling it from the camel's back he growled at the beast driving it away to forage for itself. Glancing around he searched for a suitable spot to drop his gear. A nearby space between two of the agrarian tents looked suitable. He picked up his gear and hauled into the space. He could now relax the but for the drovers work still remained.

Three or four organisers from the Kharfat men began working methodically through the now standing animals inspecting each load. After identifying the contents they directed each drover to the appropriate cave for unloading. Mussalim sipped water from his goatskin and watched as the animals were led to the yawning cave mouths. As soon as each animal was unloaded the drover then led it away up a steep narrow incline up the wadi wall to the top and out of sight.

It was a busy area and probably the main arms supply in the area, perhaps even in the whole region. Realising the site's importance Mussalim studied its defensive positions. The basin was defended by a series of heavily constructed sangars along the top of the high rock walls, probably with RPD machine guns. Any assault force coming up the wadi from the south would find itself beneath those guns and hopelessly vulnerable. The caves were geographically protected on three sides by the sheer rock walls so any attack from the air would also have to come up the wadi. Even then unless the pilots had rockets that could turn sharply left or right then that attack would be ineffective. The caves faced each other across the wadi. He studied the top of the sheer sides. The only chance for a successful attack would have to take place up there he concluded and supposed that the PFLOAG tacticians had already considered that and would no doubt have taken precautions up there too. It was a good place to defend, he concluded.

"Peace be with you, Commissar," a voice addressed Mussalim.

He turned to see a young man with negroid features standing behind. "And to you," he replied getting to his feet and offering his hand to be shaken.

The man took the hand and stared quizzically at Mussalim. "You must be the guide that we have been told would be with this supply train."

Mussalim looked at the man before him. His hair was short and frizzed and whiskers that was more likely a week's stubble than a beard. He wore only a *futa* wrapped about his waist and a necklace of animals teeth hung round his neck contrasting vividly with the black skin of his chest. "Could be! Where do you want to go?"

"Haluf."

"Then I'm your guide."

He grinned easily revealing uneven but white teeth. "Good we have been waiting here almost a week now. I am Beni."

After Mussalim had introduced himself Beni led the way casually across the front of the tents asking polite social questions as he did. Eventually he stopped in front of one that was no more than canvas draped across poles and little more than a sunshade. Four men sat beneath its cover and Beni introduced each one in turn before inviting Mussalim to sit. It was not quite what Mussalim had expected.

"I was told that I was to guide two Chinese explosive experts to Haluf."

"Yes, we are their escorts."

"Then where are they?"

Beni shrugged. "Somewhere." Then seeing Mussalim's quizzical expression went on. "They don't speak a word of Arabic we don't speak a word of Chinese so we can't really communicate. They wander off. Have a good look around the caves and then discuss things together. Often they walk up the ramp out of the wadi and disappear for hours on end. But always at night they return here to sleep in that corner." He inclined his head.

Mussalim sighed this might prove to be more of a challenge than he anticipated. "OK," he said dubiously. "Why do you have to escort them to Haluf?"

Again he shrugged. "My orders are to simply deliver them and their explosives to Mohammad Ishaq at Haluf as soon as possible."

"As soon as possible?"

"Yes."

"In that case we had better leave at first light tomorrow. Make sure everything is ready." He took charge of the situation. "When these Chinese men return keep them here and come and find me. I'll be over there where my bundle is."

Before he returned to his bundle, however, his curiosity demanded that he at least take a look in the caves. Men busied themselves unloading the animals and placed the newly arrived stock at the entrance. Others picked it up from there and carried it further inside stacking it in the appropriate place. Mussalim took care to keep out of the way of all the activity and other than casual glances from the workers was virtually ignored. Each cave was different but all were deep and spacious. Even the smallest was stocked with an astonishing amount of cases containing weapons and ammunition. Rows of boxes in depth heaped from the uneven floors crookedly upward to the uppermost reaches of the chambers. The weaponry range was extensive from the basic Kalachnikov AK 47's to RPD 7.62 light machine guns. From Katyusha rocket launchers to RPG7 short-range weapons. From 82mil mortars to grenade launchers and from small plastic anti-personnel to large anti-tank mines. Mussalim had never before seen anything that could even begin to compare with such a large and capacious arsenal and underlined comprehensively that which he already knew. The communist governments of the world were determined to bring Oman beneath its standard. He made his way back to where he had left his saddle enormously encouraged that the insurgency would not fail through lack of armament support.

He took a regional map from his pack and studied it closely, mapping out the best route to Haluf. He wanted to do well in this his first command assignment. He recalled the instructions given to Beni 'as soon as possible,' already a week had been lost. With this in mind he decided to take the most direct route along the ancient Dehodoba frankincense trail. But as a precaution against stumbling into government patrols he intended to follow the example that he had learned from Suhayl and use outriders to scout the land ahead. That way he anticipated that he could arrive safely in Haluf within three days.

His plan decided he lay back just staring at the deepening blue sky as the sun withdrew its light gradually from the heavens. He wondered why two Chinese explosive experts were needed in Haluf. It was after all only a small isolated village on the *negd* with no obvious strategic value that he could think of. There was a road that was little more than a rough track behind the village which climbed the hill in a series of tight hairpins onto the jebal. This road was very definitely minor compared to the main Salalah to Midway road only twenty kilometres to the east.

Beni appeared above him blocking his view of the skies and looking down apologetically. "Commissar, the China men have returned," he informed him.

Mussalim got up and followed him back to the makeshift tent. The two China men stood to greet him when he arrived and both briefly bowed their heads as they shook his hand. Both were short men with typical round-faced eastern features. They wore the dark green uniform of the Chinese army complete with peaked caps. While those dark and heavy uniforms might be just about bearable here in the mountains they would be completely unsuitable for the scorching heat of the *nejd*. Besides that, Mussalim had already decided that no scrap of a uniform would be worn by anyone on the journey. If they were to stumble across a government patrol then it was very likely they would be challenged anyway but if there were uniforms in evidence then they would be challenged for certain.

He spoke to the men in Arabic who just looked back with puzzled expressions before giving some reply in their native tongue. Mussalim shook his head indicating that he didn't understand and then he tried a Russian greeting that he had learned while staying in that country. Once again it was greeted with blank expressions and then followed by a conversation between the two men. In desperation he cut through their conversation in English. This time there was some understanding and a reply. Mussalim's English was limited and he suspected so was that of the Chinese men. However, he successfully managed to make them understand that they must be ready to leave early the next morning and that they would have to discard their uniforms in favour of *dish'dasht* and shamags. After that both men became quite animated talking excitedly and pointing towards the caves. Eventually, one took Mussalim by the hand and led him into one of the caves. He guided him around the caves occasionally pointed at items and muttering, 'this.' Mussalim nodded understanding that he wanted to take those cases with him. They returned to the tent and Mussalim after asking Beni to find the two Chinese more suitable clothing for the journey set off to find the quartermaster in charge of arsenal to request the items that the China man had asked for.

Before it was properly light the next morning the small party of eight men and five additional supply camels left Wadi Kharfat for Haluf. Mussalim guided the party north east until he cleared Jebal Sayq then continuing in the same direction, he crossed the open *gatn* to overlook the *nejd*. By this time it was well into the early afternoon and the soaring temperature oven-like, so he called a halt. They sheltered beneath a rocky overhang on the north face of the escarpment to wait out the hottest part of the day.

Mussalim instructed the camels be left loaded and well tethered before he withdrew a few metres and quietly studied the map. The army camp of Deefa lay about fifteen kilometres due west while the smaller one at Marboosh lay twenty kilometres to the northeast on the *nejd* itself. There was now a danger of stumbling across army patrols or traffic between the two bases so this next part of the journey was particularly vulnerable. He decided not to even attempt to slip past Marboosh during daylight, even with outriders it would be risky. Instead he would keep the party together and use the cover of darkness to pass south of the base. His plan decided, he ambled back into the shade of the overhang.

The men had seated in a circle and were eating dry rations and drinking water when he drew near. Good humouredly they shuffled around to create some space for him to sit. As Beni handed him dry feta, dates, and water he declared his intention to remain under this cleft until sundown. Relaying his intentions to the two Chinese, however, proved more difficult but eventually he was reasonably satisfied that they too understood. He shook his head ruefully wondering just how much use these two would be to the front if no one could communicate properly with them. He was glad that it would not be his problem once the party reached Haluf.

With nothing else to do they stretched out to sleep through the afternoon leaving one man on look out. Mussalim could not sleep, his mind was far too active so after an hour he gave up trying and relieved the guard. The guard flashed him a grateful grin and within minutes he too slept as soundly as the rest. Mussalim's eyes probed the sleeping men for signs of consciousness. All slept soundly so he took the opportunity to make a clandestine prayer to the almighty.

He had continued throughout his time abroad to follow his religion. In Cairo he had been able to follow it openly, even his tutors were good Muslim's. In Russia, however, the concept of religion, any religion, was considered self indulgent and weak and was discouraged, forcibly. He had been forced to pray in secret and the opportunities for that had been limited. Nevertheless, he felt sure that Allah understood his predicament and made allowances.

Throughout the rest of the afternoon he gazed silently at the vast and awesome desolation of the *nejd* thinking about his home on the Qara. It was now well over a year since he had deserted his father's farm to fight for the cause and in that time his own personal circumstances had changed drastically. He tried to imagine what changes might have taken place at home in his absence. He smiled to himself believing that in all probability very little. He thought nostalgically of the Qara hills. The Khareef would have ended about a month ago, but even so he imagined the whole jebal would still be a picturesque rich green. The tree canopies would be thick, the grass still long and even though the wild flowers probably had gone over by now there would still be ample evidence of their elegance. He experienced an ache of homesickness and looked forward with great anticipation to his return. Almost instantly a shadow then passed over his thoughts. He wondered what his father's reaction would be when he once again presented himself before him. Would there still be some animosity between them? After all they had parted with a quarrel and on bad terms. Surely not, he concluded, though not too confidently.

Soon after sunset they moved on, this time travelling directly east along the upper level of the escarpment. It was only as dawn was breaking and Mussalim felt that by now they were well clear of Maboosh did he drop down onto the *nejd* and called a short rest for both animals and men. Within the hour, however, they were riding once more and back in a north east direction. From this point on, however, they were travelling through particularly deep and rugged wadi country and were forced to meander in whichever direction the geography of the land dictated. The terrain also lent itself to a myriad of ambush opportunities so it was at this stage that Mussalim posted his outriders to scout the trail ahead.

By midday the temperatures in the base of these ravines had soared to around one hundred and thirty degrees and both men and animals were visibly sagging. Satisfied that the rate of progress was good Mussalim called a halt to wait out the heat of the day. They took shelter from the blistering sun beneath a small clump of Qassis trees that somehow managed to find moisture below the baked surface and eke out an existence. This time hidden in the labyrinth of deep chasms and towering sheer bluffs, he felt secure enough to allow the animals to be unloaded and a campfire to be lit.

It was a good campsite isolated and well hidden with plenty of dried wood around. The ground hugging desert shrubs that were scattered around made good camel fodder and the fallen needles beneath the trees made a soft bed to lie on. Besides that to wander around in this maze of deep ravines in the dark was to tempt providence. He might get lost, so he decided to remain there until the next morning.

By mid morning the next day they had emerged from the labyrinth of wadis onto flat open *nejd* and because they could now travel directly northeast their progress improved. It was nearing noon when the two outriders returned and reported that there was a large herd of camels and attending herdsmen at the Abrun well, just ahead. From the well Mussalim knew that Haluf was little more than fifteen kilometres away and for a few moments he considered giving it a wide berth. The scouts reported, however, that nothing they could see suggested anything other than day to day normal existence. He decided to trust their judgement and approach the well.

They breasted a short rise and looked down into a wide sandy basin. Scattered greenery littered the basin while a hundred or more camels wandered slothfully or just lay staring apathetically at the new arrivals. Five scaffold poles pyramided and dangling a pulley revealed the well's position while at its side was an enormous raised water sump crudely constructed from concrete. On the opposite side of the basin beneath enormous fig trees were four large curved Bedouin tents with open fronts. Mussalim scanned the basin keenly for any sign of danger, but could see none. Two herdsmen bathed in the sump taking relief from the midday heat while the remaining seven or eight sat beneath the fig trees gazing towards the new arrivals warily. He indicated to Beni that he should leap down and throw a handful of sand into the air indicating a friendly visit. When the watching men waved acknowledgement Mussalim slapped his cane down the camel's neck and drove it down into the basin.

The herdsmen welcomed them warmly and invited the travellers to drink from their tribal well and to water their animals at the sump. When they had drunk Mussalim and Beni pleased their hosts by passing suitable compliments about the sweet water from the well. The men were all of the tribe Gidad from the nearby village Ghayl and with typical desert hospitality they insisted that the travellers should now eat with them. Because it would be impolite not to Mussalim accepted their hospitality. The Gidad men produced a large tin tray of heaped rice with strips of stewed camel meat placed on top. Then hot melted grease was generously poured over the platter. Sitting beneath the trees and around the tray the visitors grabbed a handful at a time and ate copiously to satisfy their hosts whilst taking care not to show greed.

Although they were too polite to ask outright the herdsmen's gaze wandered continuously to the two Chinese men dressed in Arab garb who were unable to take any part in the conversation. Mussalim did not want to be impolite but he had no intention of satisfying their curiosity, after all the next visitors to the well might be a government patrol. So he guided the conversation topics in a different direction when he felt that it might lead to the question. Despite the heat of the day and as soon as it was polite to do so Mussalim made excuses to leave.

There were still more than two hours to sunset when the party rounded a bluff and the small village of Haluf came into sight. A villager lazing in the shade of corrugated tin veranda directed them to where Mohammed Ishaq's PFLOAG HQ could be found. They found the HQ in a stone built single storied building on the edge of the village. The building was dilapidated with one corner already collapsed and a door which hung askew on one hinge. Mussalim halted his camel and made it kneel gladdened that he had accomplished his first assignment without incident. Prompted by the sounds of the new arrivals, two men wearing only *futa's* appeared in the doorway and watched curiously. Mussalim approached, shook hands with the pair and gave the customary greeting before introducing himself. He was informed that Mohammed Ishaq was not there but one of the men left to find him. The second man then led them to a nearby enclosure constructed entirely of sticks, where the camels could be unloaded and corralled. Before the task was finished the first man returned with Mohammed Ishaq.

"Commissar Mussalim," he said warmly shaking Mussalim's hand. The man before him was tall and grinned through a thick full beard, showing large and yellowed teeth. He was bareheaded with a shock of black shoulder length hair grimed with sand dust. The tan coloured uniform he wore was creased and wet with sweat and on his shoulders were the red epaulets of a commissar. He enquired politely about their journey before turning to the two China men and speaking to them in their native tongue.

"You speak Chinese," Mussalim stated the obvious.

"Yes I trained in Peking. Didn't you?"

Mussalim shook his head. "No, Russia."

He nodded and then led Mussalim and the two Chinese towards the coolness of the dilapidated house leaving the others to finish the work of unloading of the animals.

Mussalim now asked the question that had bothered him the whole journey. "Why do we need two Chinese explosive experts in a place like Haluf?"

"In Haluf?" he replied ramming the hanging door back against the wall with a couple of hefty pushes. "We don't particularly need them here. We do have a mission here which they can help us with, but primarily we need then to blow up drilling rigs."

"Drilling rigs?" Mussalim followed him inside with the Chinese close behind.

"Hmm. We intend to stop the Sultan's search for oil in the region by attacking and destroying all the drilling sites. Why should we allow him to steal our oil?"

The room was dark, painted a fading blue, and except for rubbish tossed in the corner, was bare. The floor was no more than sand compressed hard by countless feet and in preference to sitting on the grubby floor several large rocks had been brought in.

"Choose your seat," Mohammed said with a grin and a wave of his arm. From a box on the thick window frame he produced tin mugs and handed them out. "Your reputation proceeds you Crazy Man Mussalim," he said handing him a mug.

Mussalim groaned inwardly. He had hoped that during his prolonged absence that the "crazy man" tag would have been forgotten.

"I was at Mirbat that day too," he said beginning to pour goat's milk in each mug from a goatskin. "Some day we'll go back and next time we'll destroy both of those forts," he promised.

They talked about the Front's progress and with a communication link through Mohammed the Chinese were now able to join the conversation. As they talked other men drifted into the room and after settling down they too added their opinions to the topics. After a while Mussalim asked about the mission that Mohammed had briefly mentioned. "Come, I will show you," he replied.

They left the village on foot and followed a road, which was no more than a wide track, towards the foot of the nearby jebal. This desert side of the jebal was barren and craggy with a steep escapement towering above the *nejd*. They entered a deep ravine with sheer walls on either side and at the end the dusty crumbling road snaked up the steep hill in a series of tight hairpin bends.

"We are going to lure an army convoy up here and then destroy it." Mohammed said. He pointed towards the hill. "We will let them get half way up there and then we'll open fire from the top. They will have to reverse all the way back down and under fire all the time. If something happens to the last truck then the others won't be able to pass and they'll be stuck on the hill. If they should manage to get off the hill then they still have to run through that ravine." He turned and indicated the deep valley through which they had just walked. "We'll have men up there on the top armed with shpagins and just for good measure lots of grenades to toss down too."

Mussalim examined first the exposed hill with its tight bends and then the ravine with its sheer rock walls. It was a good plan and certainly it would be a deadly place to get caught in an ambush. "What happens if they come from the other direction?"

"They won't. But even if they do it will still work," Mohammed replied. "Perhaps not as well. We will have to close in behind them when they on the way down the hill and drive them through the ravine."

Mussalim nodded. "OK. So how will you get a convoy to use this road when the main road is only twenty kilometres away."

Mohammed displayed his yellow teeth in a grin once more. "That is where the Chinese men come in. They are going into the pass between the *nejd* and the jebal to plant charges in the cliff faces. That will bring hundreds of tons of rock down onto the road blocking it. So then, they will have to come this way."

The plan seemed sound to Mussalim. "When do you intend to blow up the pass?"

"As soon as we have finished our preparations. Tomorrow maybe or perhaps the day after."

"Then I will leave you tomorrow because I want to go through that pass before you do," Mussalim said.

"You are most welcome to stay in our humble quarters tonight," Mohammed said.

"Thank you but my father's brother lives in this village and he would be greatly annoyed if I didn't stay with him while I am here." Whether Fiad would actually be found at home was doubtful, however. He was born Bedu as was Mussalim's father but unlike his father he had been unable to bridle his nomadic genes and even now he still wandered the barren wilderness for days on end with his friends. Fiad's wife would be there for certain, however, and perhaps some of Mussalim's cousins too.

✳ ✳ ✳

Juma stood on the edge of the Parade Square at Umm Al Ghawarif watching angrily as the succession of dust covered Land Rovers rolled to a halt on the square itself. As each vehicle stopped tired and grim faced men, clinging to their rifles uncoiled themselves and climbed from the back. Some tried to beat away the thick dust from their clothing while others didn't even bother. A soldier from the base mess hall passed among the demoralised men from Habrut dispensing tea mugs which he filled from a bucket that he carried.

The news had broken only this morning that the fort at Habrut had yesterday been reduced to rubble by artillery fire from the Yemeni fort. A cross border incident had escalated until the Yemeni's resorted to their recently positioned artillery guns. The Omani soldiers having no answer to the guns had been forced to abandon the fort as it was progressively destroyed. They watched helplessly from a nearby hill as it was systematically reduced to a pile of rubble. There had been casualties too, some fatal. But thankfully considering the brutal and callous nature of the attack, comparatively light. When the demolition was complete the soldiers had gone back in and salvaged what they could. Then they piled everything and themselves into any vehicles that were still mobile and to smiling faces of the Mahra locals had ignominiously retreated from Habrut.

Juma could guess that the incident had probably started with a single gunshot and expanded to one of those contagious hot headed exchanges. His three-month tour of duty at Habrut had finished a little over a month ago and during his time there he had witnessed two such incidents. He should be thankful that he had left before this particular attack he reminded himself. But he wasn't, far from it – he wanted revenge!

After a few moments he turned and walked away seething with outrage against the Yemenis arrogance. However, all soldiers had been confined to barracks, leave had been cancelled and those already out had been recalled so some kind of reprisal action seemed to be imminent. He went to find Khaleef, he might know what was happening, and perhaps he would be able to get him assigned to be part of the revenge team.

✳ ✳ ✳

Abdulla peered through a crack in the shutter at the four men standing in front of his house. A jolt of despair walloped his insides. From the bits and pieces of faded uniform that they wore they were easily identifiable as PFLOAG thugs. Cartridge belts wrapped their waists and hung across their chests. Each man carried a Kalichnikov either casually looped under arm or held nonchalantly resting over a shoulder. The weapons intimidation was deliberate and the four guerrillas waited arrogantly for the homesteaders within to emerge in servility.

Just for a moment he considered remaining quietly inside and pretending that no one was home but he decided against it. They would, in all probability, simply kick down the door to plunder the place anyway. He glanced balefully at Jokha and then resignedly moved towards the door.

"*Ali Kum Salaam*," he greeted the men.

A couple muttered an unenthusiastic reply.

Abdulla invited them to sit beneath the shade of the crudely constructed veranda then he went back inside to prepare some refreshment for the visitors. Jokha poured a little camel milk into a jug and placed it on a platter along with four small handless tin cups. The milk was from last night's milking of the solitary camel that remained on the farm. It was not fresh and in the heat of the day had already begun to curdle a little. She added a little water.

"What do they want?" she whispered as she stirred it vigorously trying to dissolve the tiny floating lumps.

Abdulla shrugged. "I don't know yet, but I can guess." He picked up the platter and carried it outside.

All the men had moved to the edge of the veranda but remained sitting on its edge and had taken no advantage of the shade that it provided.

Abdulla stood before each man in turn and filled his cup then waited until it was empty. When it was, he refilled it until the man shook the cup indicating that he had had enough. The first man he recognised as Masabbah a pillaging visitor on more than one previous occasion. The next two he had not seen before but when he stood before the last his heart gave a wild lurch. Despite the rag that wrapped his head and covered most of his face he recognised the man Ziad who had pressed the barrel of a cocked AK47 hard against his forehead some months before.

He poured a little milk into the cup that he held out pretending not to recognise him.

Ziad took a drink then stared down surly at the cup while he swilled the milk around his mouth. His thick moustache was stained white by the dregs. He turned his head and spit out the milk. "It's sour!" He retorted glaring at Abdulla and tossed the cup back on the tray.

"I am sorry," Abdulla apologised. "It is from last night's milking, but it has been a hot day."

"Then send your boy to milk another."

"He is not here."

"Then you do it."

Abdulla wasn't sure if it were a suggestion or an instruction.

"Don't bother old man," Masabbah came to his rescue. "My friend Ziad is just a bad tempered and ungracious guest." Amusement twinkled in his eyes while Ziad only scowled without reply. "The milk was palatable. However, we do need food." The twinkle disappeared.

"You are welcome to share what we have," Abdulla replied pretending to believe that these men expected only the customary guest meal.

"That's gracious of you. But that's not what we are here for," Masabbah said.

"No more games." Ziad said getting to his feet. "He knows exactly what we are here for." He turned to Abdulla. "Ten goats. Bring us ten goats."

"I don't have ten goats."

Ziad stared back impassively. "You have a herd. Now go and get us ten goats."

"The herd has gone."

"Then we'll take five cows."

Abdulla shook his head. "They have gone too."

Ziad seized him by the beard and hauled him close to his face. "You've hid them. Ten goats or five cows, now go get them."

"I can't, they are not here."

"Then we'll take your wife." He twisted the beard in his fingers and hauled Abdulla down to his knees. "Ria," he addressed the man at his side. "Go get his wife."

The man at his side glanced at Masabbah for confirmation.

"Go get his wife," Ziad repeated firmly seeing his hesitation.

He passed his weapon to Masabbah then wordlessly got up and went into the house. Moments later he came out dragging Jokha by the upper arm.

"After you Ziad," Masabbah said with an easy laugh.

"Not that one you idiot. The young one," Ziad growled.

"There is no one else," Ria said.

"So, old man, you have hid her too. Have you?" he turned his attention back to Abdulla.

"My number two wife died earlier this year."

"You liar."

"Before Allah, it's true. She is buried up there on the hill." He waved an arm in the direction.

"Someone's coming," Ria said glancing in the direction that Abdulla had indicated.

* * *

The wild flowers had faded but the lush greenery that the Khareef leaves behind when it has gone still remained. Mussalim rode casually and unhurried allowing the camel to stop frequently and nibble on the choicer bits of grazing. When it did he took the opportunity to enjoy the Qara vista and savour the sweet smell of the grass in his nostrils. He hadn't realised until this moment just how much he had missed these mountains. During his time in Russia he had in his mind often compared the flat featureless land and cold weather of a Russian summer to these Qara peaks. He had readily dismissed the Russia environment as completely unable to compare in any way. Now as he absorbed the fresh greenery complimented by the dark grey rugged landscape he felt that even that ready dismissal had been complimentary to the Russian countryside.

He was nearing his home now. On the other side of the hill the old farmhouse would come into view. Instead of taking the long curving pathway around he drove the animal up towards the hilltop preferring his first view to be panoramic. Balsam grew tall and thick on the hillside. It had long since dropped its flowers but the seedpods were full and ripe, and as the camel brushed through they exploded scattering seed to lay dormant until the next Khareef.

He was still anxious and unsure of the reception that he would get from his father. When he had left the homestead it had been immediately after an angry and bad tempered quarrel over his insurrection convictions. He had decided to wear his Commissar uniform hoping to impress not only his father but also the rest of the family with the esteem that he had achieved during his time away. Now he wondered if that might prove to be a mistake and serve only to exacerbate him further. Still undecided if it was the right or wrong decision he crested the hilltop. Halting the animal he gazed down on the family home.

He recognised his father immediately but the four strangers with him he did not. As he watched one of the men grabbed his father by the beard and then hauled him down to his knees. Moments later another went into the house. Something was not right. He leaned forward and pulled his Kalichnikov from the saddle and cocked it. Another glance down the hill and the man emerged from the house dragging his mother by the arm. He kicked his heels into the camel's ribs and slapped it down the neck. She responded at an easy canter down the hill.

He pulled on the reins halting the camel a just few metres away in the flat area in the front of the farmhouse. He didn't wait for the animal to kneel as soon as it had stopped he leapt off and walked purposely towards the group. They watched him approach and stood silently waiting. He recognised Ziad almost instantly, but the others he did not. By the pieces of uniform that they wore and by the weapons that they carried, however, it obvious that all were PFLOAG regulars. He held his own Kalachnikov casually under his arm but tactfully took the precaution to point the muzzle downwards. He was outnumbered and realised that if it should come to a shoot out then his single weapon against four would be no match. Nevertheless he didn't intend to be intimidated.

"What are you men doing here?" He demanded.

"We are collecting food for our liberation forces, Commissar," one of the men replied

"And is this how you do it?" He asked helping his father to his feet from the ground.

"He is a Sultan sympathiser," Ziad said brusquely.

"Why do you say that?"

"Because he has hid his stock so that he doesn't have to donate towards the cause."

"This man is my father." He searched Ziad's face for any sign of contrition, but received only a bland stare. "Did you offer to buy?"

Ziad scoffed. "Why should we buy? After all we fight to make a better life for him."

Mussalim squared face to face with him. "Then you are worse than the Sultan. He keeps the nation's wealth for himself but you! You keep your own money in your pocket and then you steal from those worse off than you."

Anger blazed in Ziad's eyes and he instantly levelled his weapon at Mussalim's midriff. Mussalim reacted quickly doing the same. Both men glared silently at each other with fingers poised on triggers.

"Ziad," Masabbah's calming voice. "Would you kill one of our own Commissars and a hero of the revolution at that?" He allowed time for the thought to germinate. "If this old man is the Commissar's father then you have your gun pointing at Crazy Man Mussalim."

"I know exactly who he is," Ziad said coldly. "Once before I had my gun pointing at him. I should have killed him then."

"Perhaps! But now it's too late. If you kill him now then a slow and painful death sentence at Hauf awaits you."

His eyes betrayed a shadow of doubt and he glanced quickly at his colleagues for support. The other men watched impassively not wishing to get involved. His moustache twitched nervously as he sought a face saving way out.

Sensing his predicament Mussalim provided it by lowering his Kalachnikov and stepping back. Ziad paused a few moments then realising that a way out had been offered slowly lowered his automatic also.

Mussalim turned away from Ziad and addressed the other three. "Where are you men from?" he questioned firmly.

"We are part of the central Qara regiment under the command of Mohammed Bin Talib and based at Raythut."

"Then return there and tell him that I will report there myself tomorrow morning."

"We'll tell him alright," Ziad caustically remarked from behind him.

Two men shuffled their feet unsure what to do until Masabbah indicated with a nod that they should leave. He hesitated himself a moment before saying. "Welcome back to Qara, Commissar Mussalim." Then he sauntered after the other three.

Mussalim watched the men walking away then turned towards his mother and father. His mother greeted him eagerly with a beaming smile and a warm hug. Then she laid welcoming kisses on each of his cheeks. When he untangled himself he turned to his father who stood impassively close by. Still a little unsure of his welcome Mussalim offered his hand. "Father," he said reservedly.

Abdulla hesitated a moment then took the hand and in the same movement threw his other arm around his son's neck. *"Il hamdu lillaah,"* he said praising his God.

~ 11 ~

Early November 1969 • With a tinge of disappointment Abdulla watched his son ride away into the morning sun. On his unexpected return yesterday he had cherished hopes that he had turned his back on this revolutionary folly and returned home to stay. But it quickly became clear that this was not so. He consoled himself however, that even though he was still associated with the PFLOAG bandits he was at least going to be in and around the Qara Mountains. He still held hopes that when Mussalim had witnessed with his own eyes the brutal methods used by the liberationists then he would soon become disillusioned and leave the movement of his own accord. His actions yesterday had proved that he at least was not like the others. He felt a father's pride at the way that his son had fearlessly stood up to the four armed men and was impressed by the way that he had asserted authority. In particularly over that thug Ziad.

Last night it had been good to have his number one son beneath the family roof once more where he belonged. The evening had been enjoyably spent exchanging news and although the subject of insurrection could not be completely avoided its discussion had been carefully shallow and impartial.

Abdulla was not at all impressed by the malevolent company that Mussalim now kept but nevertheless he was impressed by Mussalim's quickly acquired esteem in the organisation and also by his recent trips to Eygpt and Russia. He had been curious about the "Crazy Man Mussalim" tag that had been mentioned during the afternoon confrontation and questioned him closely. Although obviously embarrassed by the exaggeration that had been made of his action that day at Mirbat, Mussalim was undoubtedly pleased that he had taken part in the action that had signalled the escalation of the conflict.

For his part Mussalim had been surprised to learn of Hamed and Lailla's detachment onto the Salalah plain with the stock. He urged his father to bring them both back to the homestead giving his assurances that the circumstances would be changed. The sadness and sorrow that he had shown at the passing of his number two mother had been evident. He also showed a flash of anger and was in full agreement with his mother that it was a needless death and if there had been a hospital in Salalah it would not have happened. This news coupled with his astonishment that his brother Juma now served in the Sultan's army probably had marred the whole evening for him. He had listened to his father's account that the reasons for his brother's enlist had been entirely to acquire possession of the Ruwas women, Khamisa. After that he had gone to his saddlebags and produced a bag of *riyals* in the form of Maria Theresa dollars, a form of universal currency throughout the Gulf nations. It was PFLOAG money due which had accumulated during his time in Egypt and Russia. He had kept a few for himself but gave the rest to his father donating generously towards the target and then urged him to persuade Juma to leave the army of the despotic Sultan. He promising that if he did then he himself would somehow find the outstanding balance. Calming a little he had enquired curiously what it was that was so special about this particular woman when a woman from his own tribe, Al Hamer, would probably have cost less than a quarter.

With Mussalim's intention to leave the next morning clearly established they had been reluctant to end the discourse and both men had talked right through into the early hours long after Jokha had tiredly retired. Eventually with both news and topics exhausted they too went to bed.

From the crude veranda Abdulla watched squinting hard until Mussalim disappeared from view sinking gradually beneath a hillcrest. For a little while he gazed sadly at his disappearance point. With a sigh he eventually turned away to begin the daily routine tasks. At least number one son was once more in the region. With his return and the unexpected influx of funds together with Mussalim's promise there was reason to hope that number two son Juma might be persuaded to return to farm also. Perhaps, he thought optimistically, things would after all work out and the situation would once again be restored to as it had been before Mussalim had left.

Tomorrow, he decided he would go to the campsite on the Salalah plain and bring back his family – that would be a start. Perhaps Juma would be there too. If he was then he could also begin work on persuading him to leave the army.

✳ ✳ ✳

Where the head of Wadi Raythut started and was surrounded on three sides by steep hills the rudimentary stone and rock built village dwellings nestled languidly. About half of these dwellings were constructed in the traditional round beehive style with crude thatched roofs, while the rest were the larger square style with corrugated tin roofs. They had all been built on the lee side of the valley sheltering beneath great glaciers solidified hundreds of centuries ago into dark grey rock. Across the dry dusty base the hills opposite were much less steep and fully exposed to the strong winds that funnelled up the wadi. These winds forcefully skimming over the surface and swirling at the end had over a myriad of centuries patiently abraded these hills into unnatural looking terraces. Thick stunted shrubs of *Ghaf* thickly coated with wind borne dust blanketed the hills on all sides and clustered together in large clumps in the wadi base. A wide and well worn track wound down from the hill top to the bottom passed close to the dwellings and then meandered its way down the wadi to disappear behind a far bend.

Mussalim altered his position to kneel in the saddle and survey the village. If there were a sizeable PFLOAG force billeted in the village then he could see no evidence from his advantage point on the hilltop. Not even look out posts on the surrounding hills. He compared the Dalkut location where Hemel Al Shibam had posted guards in a situation where any surprise attack by government forces was extremely unlikely to this position just a few kilometres down the wadi to Sahalnawt and the Salalah plain. Perhaps the low-key presence was a deliberate tactic by Mohammed Bin Talib he allowed. Nevertheless, he could not help but wonder how much this sort of incautious approach had contributed to the recent reported success of the *askar, firqat* ambushes.

He slapped the camel down the neck and drove her down the track into the village. Someone must have monitored his approach and by some unseen signal alerted the house occupants because as he approached each abode men emerged to stand in the doorways silently watching as he passed. When he reached the village well he couched the camel to its knees and unhurriedly slid off. Still no one approached him. Unsure of the situation he hesitated then acting a lot more unconcerned than he felt he busied himself encouraging the animal to drink from the trough while he waited for something to happen. No one was going to approach him, he decided, therefore the first move had to be his. So there could be no mistake he changed his shamag for his cap displaying the badge rank 'commissar' just to reinforce the smaller badges on his epaulettes. Then he pulled the Kalichnikov from its sheaf in the saddle, just in case. Feeling slightly more confident he selected a nearby '*beehive*' and moved towards it. Two men in the doorway watched his approach.

"*Salaam Ali Kum*," he greeted.

A slight nod and a muttered reply were all the response he got from one of the men.

"Where can I find Mohammed Bin Talib?"

The man stepped out into the sunlight and pointed towards a large square house a few metres away. "There," he said.

He walked slowly across to the building where Ziad stood in the doorway regarding him surly. Mussalim guessed the reason for his less than hospitable welcome might have something to do with Ziad's report on yesterday's incident. He stopped in front of the doorway. Ziad made no effort to move.

"I am here to see Commissar Bin Talib?"

"Mohammed," Ziad called leaning his head back slightly.

Moment's later Bin Talib appeared behind him and looked over his shoulder. "The Crazy Man is here," Ziad informed him.

"Then let him in," he said. "And ... Ziad, assemble the men, I have an announcement to make in fifteen minutes." Then he turned and disappeared into the darkened interior.

Ziad stood aside slightly leaving just enough room for Mussalim to pass then waited until he had squeezed past him into the short narrow corridor before he slowly sauntered away to assemble the troops.

After the brightness of the day the inside seemed dark but gradually his eyes became adjusted and he followed Bin Talib to the door at the end.

"We can talk in here," Bin Talib said opening the door to his private quarters and indicating that Mussalim should enter.

The room was a decent size with a sand floor baked hard. For light it relied on a small single window. Its furnishings were Spartan, containing only a cot, a mat, cushions and a box on which facilities for refreshments were placed.

He invited Mussalim to sit on the mat while he went over to the box and brought back a jug of water and a tin mug. "You don't believe in starting quietly, do you?" He handed Mussalim the mug.

Assuming he was referring to yesterday's incident, Mussalim didn't reply but took the mug and held it out to be filled. When it was he thanked him for his hospitality and then took a drink. The water was warm and slightly brackish but to be polite he held the mug up to be refilled then placed it down at his side.

Bin Talib sat down cross-legged opposite.

"I have my written orders for you," Mussalim said and reaching inside his tunic he took out an envelope and handed it to Bin Talib.

"I already have a pretty good idea of your assignment from Al Ghassani," he said taking the envelope. "I am instructed to give you full independent authority to carry out your task and to give you as much assistance as I can without disrupting my own operation." He paused and stared at Mussalim hard. "Yesterday, however, was not a good start."

"You didn't see what was happening."

"I can guess," he said in a matter of fact manner. "What you perhaps do not understand is that firmness is the best method of ensuring these people support us. They expect us to fight to achieve independence for them, therefore they should show a little gratitude. That's not too much to expect, is it?" The question was rhetorical and he didn't wait for an answer. "They want this independence and therefore they must realise that it can only be gained at a price. And they must be prepared to pay the price, if not by fighting then by other sacrifices. Of course there are those who want independence but they want others to shoulder the complete load. Well, they have to be made to contribute their bit also, even if it happens to be your own father."

Trying to ignore that last remark aimed as a personal affront Mussalim stared at the man before him. Did he believe all that rhetoric himself? He had managed to make himself, and all the other PFLOAG regulars, sound like unpaid mercenaries employed by the Dhofari people and for that they should accept the additional hardships with gratitude. That theory might even have had some foundation except for two important reasons. First they were not unpaid. Communist money filled all their pockets and secondly the Communists wider goals were the ultimate target.

"Yes, Commissar Bin Talib there is no denying that we do fight for the Dhofari people's independence and it is true that they should be grateful to us. However, we are paid and therefore we can afford to buy food from the impoverished jebally instead of taking what little he has and adding greatly to his hardship.

Part of my assignment is to improve relations between us and the Qara people which should in turn improve their support." He paused considering the best way to present his next intended mandate. There was no tactful way that he could think of so he pressed on bluntly. "I have Al Ghassani's permission to use any means that I think suitable to achieve those aims. Our soldiers have money in their pocket therefore they can afford to pay for the food they take from the people. I will be grateful therefore if you will instruct your men that they are to offer to pay for any food that the people can spare."

Bin Talib scoffed loudly.

Mussalim ignored the derision and carried on. "Another part of my assignment is to organise and train a militia that can be used as a reserve back up at any time to support our regulars. This will in effect increase our numbers and our strength. It's not likely that I will find many volunteer recruits for this militia if there is widespread resentment against us. Improved relations between us and all the jebally's are a must. Al Ghassani appreciates that fully, Commissar." He dropped the leader's name once more to influence his argument.

"Then Commissar," Bin Talib carried on in the formal manner introduced by Mussalim. "You must do what you see fit to achieve your mission. But remember this, although you have your brief direct from Al Ghassani, you will still be under my command and three months from now I am directed by Al Ghassani to submit a full report on your achievements. So you see Commissar I also have the ear of the General Secretary."

This news eroded Mussalim's confidence somewhat. He understood fully that this report would undoubtedly influence his future good or bad. Bin Talib still held the whip.

"Anyway," he went on. "Your assignment may already be irrelevant. There are more important events taking place."

Mussalim looked at him without speaking and waited for him to explain.

"It seems that a couple of days ago the Sultan's *askars* fired on the Yemeni fort at Habrut. The justified retaliation by the Yemenis was severe and they reduced the Oman fort to rubble. Last night this Sultan used his new Strikemaster jet fighters to bomb the Hauf base. The Yemen government has protested at International level and even as we speak Yemeni forces mass at the border preparing to invade. War is coming which can only aid our cause. We are ordered to move out and set up positions in the mountains to ambush and harass any troop reinforcements coming down from Muscat. If all goes well then within a week this area could be under Yemeni control and Sayid Said Bin Taymour gone."

Mussalim stared at him aghast. Was it possible? Were the goals as close as that? If it were so then the end had come suddenly and the Sultan's removal much more easily achieved than he had dreamed possible. Somehow it seemed just a little too easy. "Are you sure of this?"

"Reported by radio only a few minutes ago by Al Ghassani himself," he replied smugly. "I am about to assemble the detachment now and break the news. So Commissar you may stay here and feed pinches of sugar to your jeballys. Within four hours we will be leaving to carry out more significant actions." He began to get to his feet indicating that the discussion was at an end.

"Commissar. I need four men," Mussalim said.

"I will ask for volunteers. Meanwhile I will get someone to find you suitable quarters. Now I have much to do."

The quarters turned out to be a village house deserted and bare. It was a typical small family dwelling and as he tethered his camel outside he wondered what had become of the people who had lived there. A single doorway at the front admitted into the main room with three smaller ones off. It smelled rank of goat that had probably regularly wandered in through the open door to shelter from the hot sun. He went through each room throwing open the wooden window shutters as he did. He stood in the middle of the main room and surveyed the place which was to be his base. It was a long way from comfortable by any standards but since he intended to spend most of his time circulating around all the Qara villages the time that he would actually spend here would be minimal. Perhaps he could pay some of the village women to clean it for him he thought. Then he realised that he hadn't yet seen any women, or any villagers for that matter.

He went back outside and unsaddled his camel before turning it loose to forage for itself. He carried his saddle and bags inside, then with very little for him to do he sat outside on the shady side of the building watching the intense activity as men hurriedly prepared to leave.

He thought of the other detachment waiting in ambush at Haluf. The pass on the Midway road would probably have been blown and sealed by now. Everything it seemed had conveniently slotted in to place almost as if reinforcements from the north had been expected. Could it be, he wondered that the whole crisis had been manipulated? If that were so then the PFLOAG leaders had been consulted and forewarned so that they could play an integral part. Once again he marvelled at the deviousness of politics and politicians and it placed into perspective the very minor role that he personally played in the struggle for Dhofar independence.

When the detachment left Raythut in mid afternoon they left behind three men to man the radio station and two volunteers assigned to Mussalim. One volunteer was his comrade in arms from Mirbat, Ali. Mussalim was delighted to see him and to renew his association in this venture. He knew that Ali was a man on whom he could rely and trust. They greeted each other with hugs and handshakes. The other volunteer was Musabbah and the greeting to him more restrained. Mussalim had reservations, he suspected that possibly he wasn't even a volunteer but a Bin Talib man detailed to watch and to secretly report. Nevertheless, Mussalim gave him the benefit of the doubt and welcomed him to the duty.

* * *

Hamed was pleased to be going home. His stay on the plain had lost much of its attraction when Obied had stepped on that mine and blown off his leg. Since that day Hamed had stayed mostly close to the campsite venturing onto the jebal slopes only rarely. His friends from the Bedu camp he still saw but didn't spend the same amount of time in their company. The happy nonchalant attitude that the boys had shared had instantly evaporated beneath the shadow of Obied's injury. A wedge had been forcibly driven between the halcyon careless attitude of unsuspecting young and the need for mature cautious responsibility. He had visited the Bedu camp just once since that day. The sight of the one legged Obied hobbling pathetically around on a makeshift crutch had ravaged him with both pity and anger so much so that he decided as a personal defence mechanism that he could not go back. However, this only compounded feelings of guilt in him that he had turned away from his friend because he was now crippled. The fact that he was now going back to the farmhouse provided a blameless escape opportunity relieving him somewhat from this guilt. He could not be expected to remain in close contact once back on the jebal farm. It had been inevitable that one day he would have to return and his desertion now only fulfilled that predicted inevitability.

He helped his father pull down the cover from the makeshift tent that had been his and Lailla's home for three months. The cover was large consisting of many smaller pieces sewn together. Deciding that it may have some future use they began carefully to fold it ready for taking back with them. The pull down and folding proved to be far easier than getting the cumbersome cover draped across a camel's back even though the animal was crouched on its belly. Eventually it was loaded and all that now remained was to collapse the poles and the site would be ready for desertion.

Yesterday afternoon his father had arrived at the site in an elated mood with the happy news that his eldest brother Mussalim was once again in the Qara. More than that, he had returned as a man of some influence among the Liberationists and had promised his family personal protection. His father had decided to trust that promise hoping that his influence extended to all the robbing thugs in the PFLOAG. Hamed hoped that he was right. His other brother Juma, had been a regular visitor to the campsite after his return from Habrut adding his own labours to family welfare in his off duty periods. Abdulla said that he intended to remain at the site until Juma came, intending to relate the news of his brother's return. At the same time he would begin to persuade him that because of Mussallim's promise of financial help towards his wedding he need not stay in the army. Unfortunately, Hamed informed him, he had missed Juma by a full day. He and his company had been sent to the western border to intercept any possible Yemen invasion. Abdulla had been unable to hide his disappointment at having missed his son or his concern for the even more dangerous situation in which his profession had now placed him. As far as he was concerned it only illustrated the point and made him more determined to influence him to leave the army. There was now no reason to wait so he had decided to pull down the campsite and return the stock to the jebal farm this very morning. Because of the condition of the stock with pregnant animals and young calves the start was to be early and the drive slow and leisurely.

Hamed looked across the plain towards the towering mountains. Huge gorges carved out gigantic slices from what otherwise would have been steep and sheer rock. These gorges formed deep valleys penetrating inward and upward providing an easier access to the upper reaches of the jebal. More than a month after the Khareef the jebal still remained green and the early morning sun cast shadows on the shaded sides of the valleys creating a graphic contrast of light and dark greens. The mountains at this time of the year were a picture of breathtaking scenic beauty that only Allah could fashion. What a shameful indictment of humanity it was that men sought to kill each other in Allah's garden, he thought with a sigh.

He identified the gorge above Sahalnawt that would be their route to Shair and home. The remnants of the Khareef would ensure that there would be plenty of animal fodder to be nibbled during the climb through the valley and there would still be water trapped in large pools not yet evaporated by the sun's intense heat to provide drinking water. It would be a casual and unstressful journey for animals and humans alike.

Anxious to be on his way he looked round to see if everything was ready. His father moved from camel to camel carrying out last minute checks on the loads and girths. From the direction of the Bedu camp he saw the figure of Gheer approaching, When he got a little nearer he waved and grinned cheerfully in Hamed's direction.

❊ ❊ ❊

Unlike Hamed, Lailla was not so gladdened with the intended return home. She had enjoyed the higher degree of liberty that the remote campsite had given her. The responsibility of maintaining a home albeit nothing more than a makeshift tent had to her signalled the approach of womanhood. But most of all she had enjoyed the attentions of Gheer. With the imminent return to the jebal farmhouse all these things would come to an end.

Although sympathetic to Obied's plight she had not been as affected by his misfortune, as had been her brother. She didn't consider herself callous though, after all he was Hamed's friend and not hers. If it had been Gheer then the circumstances would have been entirely different. So by using that viewpoint she could appreciate her brother's feelings and his visible change of attitude. The news of Mussalim's return however, was good news and in a cluster of disappointments she saw one ray of consolation and looked forward to seeing her eldest brother in the near future.

All the preparations were now nearing completion and the journey would soon begin. She looked around hoping to see Gheer. He had said that he would come and that he would walk part of the way with her and her family. Then she saw him approaching and struggled to keep a silly grin of pleasure from her face. She did not want to betray her feelings to the others. Their relationship had continued to develop steadily despite the more recent closer attentions of Hamed. He never seemed to be very far away when they met anymore. When there were opportunities of privacy she allowed Gheer to touch her in some of the more personal places such as her thigh and bare upper arms. It was not so much that she allowed him to but more truthfully that she wanted him to. However, she would admit that to none but herself.

Tactfully Gheer approached Hamed first greeting him and offering his services to help with the drive for at least part of the way. Hamed was not fooled for an instant and glanced at Lailla, but he said nothing. Instead he referred the offer of help to his father. To Lailla's delight Abdulla gratefully accepted and graciously thanked him. He then organised Jokha and Lailla to herd the goats while he would himself look after the camels. Hamed and Gheer he put together to herd the cattle mistakenly believing that was what both boys wanted.

Progress was very slow and deliberately so. By midday they were less than halfway up the Shair valley. They had reached a place where the cascading Khareef waters had flooded and forcefully rushed over the road washing away a large part in the process. By now though the waters had ceased to gush and its flooding had receded completely. Although greatly scarred by deep trenches excavated by the floodwater, what remained of the road was still high enough to dam a significant amount on the up side into a large still pool. It was an ideal place to stop, rest and water the stock then to shelter from the heat of the day.

By the time Lailla and Jokha had caught up Abdulla and the two boys had guided the animals towards the pool. Now they stood watching idly as the contented animals stood in the water lapping their fill. Jokha identified the camel carrying the bread and dates and disturbed Hamed's tranquillity by ordering him into the water to recover the food from its pack.

Lailla spread out a cloth beneath the canopies of *Ghaf* trees and stood back while everyone settled down cross-legged to eat. Then doing her best to appear nonchalant she calculatingly sat in the space next to Gheer. The animals quietly foraged while they ate. As they ate Gheer declared his intention that this would be as far as he would go. Lailla sensed his reluctance to leave, but except for this instance and in the presence of all of her family there had been no opportunity for she and he to talk. The prospects for them to talk intimately during the remainder of the journey looked equally as unlikely. As always eating was a leisurely affair protracted by conversation.

Eventually Abdulla and Hamed withdrew and after preparing themselves by washing in the pool they found a suitable spot to pray. Almost immediately after they had finished they both stretched out a few metres away and in the leafy shade went to sleep. Jokha, Gheer and Lailla remained where they had eaten quietly talking.

Lailla guessed that Jokha had no intention of leaving them alone. Attempting to bring about a situation where she and Gheer might at least be able to talk privately she got up and wandered away towards the nearby pool. The water was the colour of mud with thick scuds of greeny brown moss floating on the still surface. She knelt down and scooping up the water with her hand she splashed a little over her face washing away the dust and grime. Then she sat with her feet dangling in the pool waiting for Gheer to escape from Jokha. Soon he did and Jokha contented herself to remain a little way off with her back resting against the tree trunk watching from a distance.

✳ ✳ ✳

Like Abdulla, Jokha had initially believed the young Bedu boy to be Hamed's friend but during the final preparations to leave she quickly noticed the silent signals that passed between him and Lailla. They glanced at each other just too frequently. With so many of these clandestine glances their eyes met often and when they did shy smirks spread across both their faces. When the journey got underway and they made their way slowly across the plain towards Sahalnawt the boy herding the cattle ahead regularly looked back just to satisfy himself that they were all right. He waved often and both she and Lailla waved back. However, Jokha soon realised that those waves were directed entirely towards Lailla, so she stopped responding. Instead she half watched Abdulla comparing the number of times he looked back to concern himself over his woman folk. It didn't compare at all favourably. He glanced back strictly occasionally just to satisfy himself that they were back there somewhere still in pursuit. She was curious about the situation wondering how it had developed and perhaps more importantly to what stage. Lailla was a young girl obviously becoming aware of her sexuality and the curiosity to her bodies' reactions definitely aroused. Jokha smiled to herself for a moment remembered only too well her own adolescence and those awakening feelings of excitement when young boys had shown interest in her direction. From here onwards any contact with Lailla and young boys of her own age would need to be carefully guarded, she decided. The opportunity to talk with her stepdaughter at this moment, however, was non-existent. She brought up the rear on one flank of the goat-herd while Lailla was a few metres away on the other side. Certainly Lailla was developing into a very pretty girl and Kathya's resemblance in her facial features and mannerism's was becoming increasingly evident. Jokha was pleased that she was returning to the jebal farm where she would be able to bring her under her protection much more and keep a closer eye on her.

Her thoughts turned to her own two sons. Both entirely devoted to each other, as good brothers should be. But by a sardonic and cruel twist of fate both placed on opposite sides in a conflict that, with the new threat of invasion by the Yemenis, threatened to degenerate very much more into bloody contention. Allah certainly works in mysterious ways she thought considering the irony.

Unmistakably Abdulla was pleased to have his elder son back in the Qara mountains and had even been a little proud that he had returned with a deal of influence albeit among the uncompromising liberationist hoodlums. He even had hopes that Mussalim's influence may be strong enough to be able to temper some of the hard line activities of the PFLOAG. If that were so then it would indeed be something to be proud of. Jokha, however, had some different concerns. It was common knowledge that through a network of spies and tiny bits of information received government forces kept dossiers on the PFLOAG leaders. The intent was that one day when the Front forces were defeated then these leaders would be brought before their authorities to answer for the activities which they interpreted as criminal treason. If Mussalim's influence and reputation grew enough then his name too might find its way into one of these dossiers.

On the other hand, if the Liberationists were to be successful what then of Juma's future? As a common soldier of a defeated army then it would perhaps not be as severe. But the PFLOAG forces were definitely less forgiving so perhaps that was something upon which nothing could be relied. In view of recent developments maybe Abdulla would yet persuade Juma to leave the army and return home. She certainly hoped so. That at least would be one mother's worry of which she would be relieved.

About midway up the Shair valley and at a suitable place Abdulla called a rest halt. When she and Lailla caught up to them the three men were standing watching the stock, now joined by the eager goats, drink from a large pool residue from the Khareef rains. The pack in which she had stowed bread and dates was on the back of a camel standing knee deep in the muddy pool. After Hamed had waded out and recovered it she and Lailla then laid out bread and dates on a cloth beneath the thick canopies of *Ghaf* trees. When they had finished all settled down around the cloth to eat. Jokha did not miss the way that Lailla manipulated her position to sit next to the Bedu boy and she hid a smile of amused tolerance.

As she sucked the stone from another date she looked back down the valley over the low tree canopies across the plain and to the distant blue sea beyond. Their progress had been slow. She turned and glanced the opposite way towards the higher ground. From this point on the going would be very much steeper and therefore slower, even so they should still be home before dark, she estimated.

After Abdulla and Hamed had retired to sleep away the hottest hours of the day, Jokha took the opportunity to subtly question Gheer. She learned that he was of the tribe Masan, a brother tribe closely allied to Al Hamer within Kathiri. His own family was traditional Beduin and they all dwelt within a nomadic tribal group of Bedu. Mostly they wandered on the *nejd* driving their large camel herds between the wells at Bithnaw, Shisr and Dawkah moving on to the next well when the grazing became exhausted. Every year before the Khareef they drove their herds through the mountains and down onto the plain to fatten their stock on the green plenty. Soon, however, they would, as they always did, move back into the mountain greenery to graze their animals. Later they would once again descend down the *nejd* side and move slowly up the great Wadi Ghadun back to their ancestral area.

Now she leaned with her back against the tree resting but nonetheless watchful of the two youngsters sitting side by side at the pool.

✳ ✳ ✳

Late November 1969 • For ten days now Juma had been part of the remote detachment of a hundred men that manned a temporary post on the top of the deep wadi Sheetah. Somewhere just a kilometre or two to the southwest was the Yemen border. However, there was no obvious physical evidence that Juma could see. Immediately behind him in a barren shallow valley were the orderly row of twenty tents and the line of trucks and other vehicles that had brought the soldiers to this place. Beyond that an expanse of nothingness altered only by slight variations in the brown colour and an uneven rocky skyline contrasting vividly against the cloudless blue sky.

He sat on the low wall of a stone and rock sangar and peered down into Sheetah. The sides were steep but not sheer and in many places deeply indented forming giant overhangs which looked precarious and as if they were about to collapse. In its base, some three hundred metres below a narrow dried sand bed meandered haphazardly around the rocky outcrops and disappeared around a sharp bend. Sheetah's origin began high in the Jebal Mahrut deep in the Yemen and it fell away gradually in a north-east direction. Paying no regard to man made boundaries it crossed the border cutting deep valleys in an otherwise featureless landscape until it eventually petered out on the stony *nejd* of Oman.

This wadi had been identified as one of the likely invasion routes by the Yemeni forces and this outpost was established to prevent any such advance. Rows of sangars had been built along both sides to establish effective ambush points while anti-tank mines had been laid in the sandy bottom. After three days the Salalah soldiers had been strengthened by the arrival of a small artillery unit from the Muttrah area of northern Oman. These gunners had laid out a row of four twenty-five pound guns along the top lip of the bend so that they pointed directly down the wadi. But since then nothing had happened.

Each endless day and night copied the one previous with repeated long spells of lookout duties punctuated by boredom relieving sleeping sessions. Only the evening meal times relieved the monotony and that to only a small degree. Occasionally they would be treated to the spectacle of a pair of Strikemaster jet fighters flying at almost zero height patrolling along the border. These aircraft mostly flown by British ex-Royal Air Force pilots skimmed along the wadi tops banking and rolling seeking the potential targets of invading Yemenis. But still the expected invasion did not materialise.

News was non-existent and therefore rumour rife. One rumour had it that the Yemen forces had advanced in the north past Alamaziune and already had reached Mudhai. Another reported fierce fighting had taken place around Habrut. But none of these rumours had turned out to be true. To Juma the Yemeni forces were turning out to be as remote and faceless as the PFLOAG forces which seemingly controlled the mountain region of his home.

Bored he looked down at the barrel of the GMPG machine gun by his side. Its ugly snout poked out from a gap between the rocks and he cautiously touched it. Exposed to the full glare of the sun he found its black metal to be as hot as he anticipated. A camouflaged net was draped over the low walls of the sangar and he peered through at the sleeping man with whom he shared this particular duty. He lay fully prostrate taking advantage of the dappled shade that the net provided. Should he wake him, he wondered? After all they were supposed to be on watch. He took a long slow look around. Thermals of heat rose from the baking *nejd* distorting the horizon into shimmering mirages floating above lakes. The wind whispered unceasingly and apart from a distant buzzard wheeling lazily overhead nothing in the landscape stirred. Let the man sleep, he decided.

As he often did in these quieter moments he turned his thoughts to Khamisa and his forthcoming wedding. As far as he knew everything was proceeding smoothly towards the event. Soon it would be Ramadhan followed by Eid Al Fitr, which had been the original target. However, although good progress towards the ten thousand rupee's target had been made it was proving to be difficult and his father Abdulla had requested a little more time. The new and conclusive date was to be the Eid Haj ten weeks later. There was to be no more extensions and if the money were not found six weeks before that then the arrangements would be cancelled and the bond deposit lost. The last time he had seen his father, about three weeks ago at the plain campsite, he had been a little dubious that livestock target would be achieved. The cattle had begun to drop their calves and the camels were heavily pregnant with three or four months of their term still to go. All was going well there. The goat herd, however, had been severely reduced due to the PFLOAG plundering. After more than three months on the plain it was once again on the increase and close to the level it had been six months previous. However, that did not achieve the significant planned increase. But his father had told him not to worry, he would find an alternative to bridge any fall short. Instead he was to concentrate on the more significant amount of four thousand rupees cash that he had set himself to accumulate. With the ten-week extension he was confident that he could now achieve it. Crushingly boring, as exercises such as this were there was no opportunity to spend money and they assisted greatly in helping him to save.

The afternoon leached away painfully slowly and when the sun had slid down in the western sky the round of watch changing began. Men sauntered up from the campsite below unenthusiastically. On the wadi rim they sorted themselves into pairs and wandered along the row dropping into any sangar that had not been relieved. Juma thankfully gathered his kit from the walled pit where he had spent the last endless six hours and watched the new arrivals lay out their own equipment preparing for an equally long stay. He hitched his pack, his water bottles and his belt of spare magazines over his shoulder, picked up his rifle and then made his way slowly over the loose scree down the hill.

He ducked through the vestibule of one of the twelve man tents and tossed his kit down on the ground in a corner that was his. Three men slept further down the tent, while two others sat on their bedrolls talking quietly. They both nodded to him briefly and then continued their conversation. He responded vaguely without speaking. There was nothing really to say. His clothes were wet and heavy with sweat and clung irritatingly to his body as he pulled them off. He spread them out carefully to dry. There was to be twelve hours before he would be back in one of those sangars but tonight he preferred to eat and then sleep rather than wash away the stench of human sweat from his clothes. He wrapped a *futa* around his waist and went back outside. Several rubber buckets lay just outside the doorway. He picked one up and made his way over to the large water tanker a few metres away.

Several men from the same watch were already at the tanker when he got there. He waited his turn to fill his bucket. After that he found a place aside and began to swill away the sand, grime and dried sweat that covered his body. He ended by tipping the remaining water over his head attempting to rinse away some of the thick dust that matted his hair. Reasonably content that he had as far as possible cleansed himself he pacified himself turned roughly in the direction of Mecca and made his prayers.

Two hours later he awoke hungry as a desert fox. It was dark and probably by now the food trays would have been laid out. He sat up and looked down the tent. It was empty and that strengthened his suspicions that his comrades were probably already eating. He wriggled from his bedroll, wrapped himself in a *futa* and put on his sweat-dried shirt. He wrapped his head tightly in his shamag leaving only his eyes uncovered. The nights on the exposed desert were very cold at this time of year. Then he went to find food.

As usual when the food was laid out, men were seated cross-legged on the ground in small circles of seven or eight around a campfire. The food trays were placed within easy reach and using their 'clean hand' only they helped themselves to handfuls. The only exception to the small groupings was among the gunners. Invariably a group numbering upward of fifteen or more set themselves apart even from their northern colleagues. These men that gregariously hung together were all Baluchistan immigrants. Baluchistan was a region east of Iran and north of Pakistan that had, until sold by the Sultan for one million pounds, been a province of Oman. However, even though they were now technically Pakistanis the impoverished Baluchis still flocked into Muscat in their thousands seeking work. The Sultans Army in the north traditionally had been and still was a major source of employment for these immigrants. Considered as little more than mercenary foreigners by the Omani *askars* they were prudishly regarded to be somewhat inferior. However, it was their own closed communal attitude that contributed most to the psychological barriers that existed. Probably this attitude had something to do with their dialect, which was different to all the other Arabic speaking countries.

Despite this they were not unfriendly and most grinned and waved to Juma as he went past. He found a suitable place in a ring of his own company and after greeting them all he settled into a gap. The warmth from the stoutly burning fire warmed his front agreeably while the raw wind chilled his back. Several men had brought blankets and had wrapped them across their head and back cheating the cold wind. Juma wished that he had done the same.

The current conversation he joined in the middle but very quickly took an interest. The northern gun teams had, it seemed, received orders to withdraw back to Thamrit one hundred and twenty kilometres away.

"But what about us? Are we to withdraw too?" Only head shaking and shrugs answered his question.

"What if a battery of Yemeni tanks come rolling down the wadi?" He tried again to install some concern.

"*Inshaallah*," the only fatalistic mutterings.

Someone courteously offered him a slice of the goat's liver. He took it mechanically muttering thanks and withdrawing into his imagination of Russian built T62 tanks in the wadi blasting unchallenged at the upper lips.

It was too cold to stay very long and soon after eating he retired to the shelter of the tent and the warmth of his bedroll.

He need not have worried, however, for although the artillery unit moved out soon after daylight, the Salalah soldiers also received withdraw orders before midday. Anxious to leave this desolate site they very quickly cleared the campsite, recovered the anti-tank mines and knocked all the sangars flat. By early afternoon they were on their way back to Salalah speculating amongst themselves that the border crisis had probably passed.

It was not until the next day and back at Um Al Gharriff that he learned that on the insistence of the Council of the Arab League both factions had been brought to the negotiating table and it was only through this arbitration that war had been avoided.

~ 12 ~

February 1970 • Mussalim hunched over a little closer to the gas flame trying to thieve some of the surplus heat. A tin coffee-pot balanced precariously on the wire frame over the small heater. The flames licking around the bottom edges of the pot cast flickering shadows on the bare walls of the darkened room. A winter evening in mid February had the temperatures outside plummeting downwards to a point a little above freezing. The house in Raythut that was Mussalim's base headquarters had little or no capability of heat retention and the only source of heat, the flame from the pocket sized heater. Ali sat opposite with legs crossed and tucked beneath him just staring hypnotically into the flames while the dancing shadows distorted his facial features.

It was four months since Mussalim had returned to Jebal Qara and so far the programme that he had been detailed to carry out had gone better than he could have even hoped. He reflected with justified smug satisfaction that in the face of severe criticism and even undisguised hostility, his methods had proved an unqualified success.

But, it had not started out very promisingly. As he and his two assistants visited each village they had been greeted mostly with sullen suspicious silence. In view of the cool reception he had proceeded cautiously doing nothing more than sit and talk quietly to groups about the generalities of day to day existence in the mountains. Only when he felt that the ambience was relaxed and a bond had been formed would he move the topic towards his objectives. Then he outlined the advantages that independence would bring and the important role that all could play in supporting the freedom fighters. His non-threatening attitude had gradually won confidence and soon lists of grievances and of PFLOAG abuses were laid before him.

The anti religion restrictions were a major grievance and the policy of land confiscation to make model farms with forced labour, another. These policies, however, were decided at congress committee levels and beyond Mussalim's power to reverse or even mediate. Inwardly he empathised completely. Outwardly, he hypocritically quoted the party line as his position as Commissar dictated he should. There were also too many cases of extreme reprisals and sanctions brought to his attention. Some of the reprisals were horrific and inhumane. Bare feet had been plunged into fires, lit cigarettes stubbed into held open eyeballs, lashings using barbed wire had been carried out and women raped. Sanctions that impounded almost all possessions were not uncommon either. PFLOAG soldiers had carried out these atrocities, as punishments on people considered to be disobedient. This disobedience often amounted to nothing more than minor misdemeanours, such as praying or expressing disapproval of the liberationist movement. Sometimes the evidence had been flimsy and no more than reported hearsay. It was easy to see why Al Ghassani's hoped for support from the jeballys was not forthcoming. There was much to be done before Mussalim could even begin to form the militia. His first priority he decided was to do something about reducing some of these sadistic acts.

His first meeting with detachment commanders had proved turbulent. While some actually welcomed his initiative others resisted vigorously. The resistors petitioned the necessity for strict control of the jebally populace backed up by the fear of retribution for discipline breaches as the only method to ensure loyalty. Mussalim, however, suspected that many of them had different and more sinister reasons. Some of the acts of sadism may have been motivated by tribal conflicts and a misdemeanour had perhaps given the opportunity to gratify some deep-seated prejudice. Also confiscating a man's possessions in the name of the PFLOAG provided an ideal opportunity to rob him and then to skim off a portion for their own benefit. In the end after much argumentative discussion Mussalim had been forced to fall back on the support of the General Secretary by announcing that it was his proclamation that better relations had to be achieved and that he had his full and unconditional mandate to achieve that objective. Though some were disgruntled, from that day on the abuses had been reduced significantly, though not disappearing completely. Bin Talib had also endorsed Mussalim's original instruction and the Front forces no longer took food from the villagers without offering to pay. This in effect provided a trading opportunity for jeballys to sell some of their surplus without having to make long trips into Salalah.

Things did not improve overnight however, but at the end of two months Mussalim felt that there had been enough progress to begin recruiting for the new militia. His small team by this time had swelled to four beside himself. He personally took charge of recruiting volunteers and used the same basic communication techniques of casual informal talk before moving to his main objective. When he had his volunteers he then left two members of his team to do the necessary arms training while he moved on to the next village to begin the process anew.

At the end of these four months he had militia situated in several Qara villages. In some there were as many as eighteen while in others as few as six. But overall he could claim additional support for the regular Front forces numbering around one hundred and forty and just as important widely dispersed.

Bin Talib had quickly recognised the strategic significance of this and had placed two or three regulars in each of the villages where a militia had been established. These men had been supplied with a cache of arms and ammunition suitable to the size of the militia and equipped with backpack radio sets. With this radio contact Bin Talib had a quick response force established in many parts of Qara. He could quickly send a body of armed and trained men to any destination close to their particular area. Now, when information was received of Government troops on the jebal he could mobilise a quick reaction force to outflank the ambushers.

No one could deny that Mussalim had so far carried out his mission with enviable success. Even the hard line Detachment Commanders, who had at first opposed his methods, grudgingly admitted that his strategy had so far worked very effectively. Bin Talib's first day antagonistic reaction to him had over the weeks mellowed and by now had even warmed to friendly as the benefits of his programme to the PFLOAG had become apparent. He had not discussed with Mussalim or even intimated the contents of the report that he had sent to Al Ghassani at the three-month point. However, the very fact that he still continued the project and without interference suggested that the report must have been favourable.

The water in the pot reached boiling point and overflowed making the flames beneath hiss angrily and turn yellow. Ali roused instantly from his hypnotic like trance and using the end of his shamag lifted the coffee-pot from the flames. From a small bowl of discoloured water at his side he took a small handless cup, shook the remnants of water from it and handed it to Mussalim. He took it and held it out while Ali filled it with boiling coffee. Three sips and it was empty and he held it to be refilled.

"You should not go," Ali said as he filled the little cup.

"I must. It's my brother's wedding."

The rest of his team knew that he intended to go into Salalah tomorrow and attend his brother's wedding. All had spoken against it fervently advising that the risks were too great. But only Ali knew the full extent of those risks. He alone knew that Mussalim's brother Juma served as an *askar* of the Sultan. Mussalim trusted him enough to have confided that to him, but the others he did not. Sulieman and Nazir were recent recruits and although they had fitted into the programme admirably he was still wary of revealing such sensitive personal information as that. Nor did he completely trust the other original member, Musabbah. Although he had so far given him no cause to doubt him, having proved fully committed to the programme, he still suspected that he was really Bin Talib's man.

"What of your brother's friends?" There are bound to be some of his soldier friends there. They may recognise you." He filled a cup for himself.

"How?"

He shrugged. "I don't know. Maybe somebody will point you out. After all many of our Al Hamer relatives will be there and you are well known. Particularly now that you are the Commissar that tours the villages recruiting."

What Ali said was true. Almost certainly someone would recognise him. "At the wedding my brother will be my *Rabia*," he said with a shrug.

"How can you be sure? You haven't seen him for nearly two years." He emptied his cup in one swallow.

"I know my brother."

He shook his head sadly as he refilled his cup. "He may be powerless to give you a *Rabia's* protection. British officers who do not understand our ways control that army. They will not regard for a moment a *Rabia's* pledge if they have a chance to capture a Commissar."

Mussalim smiled and held out his cup to be filled once more. "Don't worry. I'll be careful."

The conversation was ended when Musabbah swept in from outside. He muttered the traditional greeting, "*Salaam Ali Kum*," sniffing the coffee as he did. Then he settled down cross-legged between the pair and fished a cup from the bowl of murky water. "Mohammed wants to see you," he said to Mussalim as he held up the cup for Ali to fill.

"What about, do you know?"

"Yes I do. But I'll let him tell you himself."

Mussalim stared at him for a moment then decided that there would be no point pressing him. Instead he got up slowly and went to find him. The night was dark, there was no moon. Tomorrow a new one would rise and coincide with the start of the Eid Al Hadja. He wondered if he would ever get the opportunity to make the pilgrimage to Mecca. Not while he was a Commissar in the PFLOAG that was certain, he concluded. He paused outside Bin Talib's quarters pondering the dilemma. While the communist influence, for which he worked so hard to promote, remained in these mountains he would never be free to practice his religion. In this respect he worked to his own disadvantage. Perhaps when independence was won the communists would move on to their next and more important objective and lose interest in Dhofar. He hoped so and not for the first time.

He walked down the short corridor and knocked softly on the door at the end before pushing it open. Bin Talib was alone sitting in front of a log fire smoking a cigarette and staring absent minded at the flame. The room was light by two paraffin lamps hanging on rusty chains from the ceiling. Mussalim muttered a greeting.

"Mussalim! Come sit," he said motioning a place opposite by the fireside.

"You wanted to see me?" He came straight to the point when he had settled.

"Yes." Bin Talib offered him a cigarette. He shook his head. "Cold tonight." He started with trivia.

Mussalim agreed with a muttered, 'yes.' Not assisting with the trivia.

Bin Talib was forced to the point. "Commissar Mussalim. Despite my early reservations I am forced to admit that the work that you have done so far has been invaluable to our cause. But you already know that, he added after a pause. "Your methods have been unorthodox and not particularly popular. However, no one can say that they haven't worked."

This was rare praise from the overall Commander of the Central Dhofar region. Mussalim nodded his gratitude.

"But your work is not finished. There is still much left for you to do. We still need you." He stopped and took a draw from his cigarette. "So what is this nonsense that tomorrow you intend to put yourself in danger by attending your brother's wedding in Salalah?"

"Musabbah!" Mussalim said. "Musabbah told you," this confirmed in his mind that which he had always suspected he was Bin Talib's man.

"He did. He came to me because he is concerned for your safety and he wants me to stop you."

"I have to go."

"You will be recognised for certain. Four months now you have wandered these hills moving from village to village – your face is well known."

"Nevertheless that's my brother who is getting married and I should be there. Besides that I have another reason to see him. A special reason."

Bin Talib waited for him to explain

"After he is married I am going to persuade him to return to our father's farm."

"And leave the Sultan's army?"

Mussalim stared at him.

"You think I didn't know," Bin Talib said with a smirk. " Jeballys just love to sit talking. News and stories spread as easily as the wind blowing across the hills. You should know that, after all these are your mountains." He flicked his cigarette into the fire. "Do you think you can convince him to leave?"

Mussalim shrugged. "Perhaps. The only reason he joined was to save the money that would buy the bride he wanted. Once she is his then there is no longer any reason for him to stay a Sultan soldier."

If he does leave do you think he could be persuaded to join us?"

Mussalim hadn't even considered it. But that was not what he wanted anyway. He preferred him to be at their jebal home with his family and his new wife out of danger. "I don't think so."

"You don't think you could persuade him? I have seen your powers of persuasion."

Mussalim shook his head.

Bin Talib sighed. "I fully intended to forbid you to go tomorrow even to the extent of locking you up. But if you could influence your brother to leave the army and join our cause what a piece of propaganda that would be for us. It would be a tremendous incentive to not only jeballys to join us but other *askars* too." He paused letting the point settle. "We need the Dhofari men to desert Bin Taymour's forces. That would send him a loud clear message that the Dhofari people do not want him here."

"Do you think he would heed such a message?"

" Probably not," he agreed with a slight chuckle. "But it would weaken his position in the eyes of other nations.

If we can just get one or two to desert, it might then become a trickle. After that, who knows, perhaps even a flood? Your brother might be the one to start it. If he were to join your militia then he could still be at home with his woman, but the propaganda effect would be the same. Even if he were never called to action."

Mussalim was in a cleft stick. If he didn't agree to try then he would be physically restrained and miss the wedding event completely. "I will talk to him," he agreed but secretly not prepared to try very hard.

The next morning wearing a white *dish'dasht*, a red and white chequered shamag and the ceremonial silver belt complete with Khunja around his waist he set off for Salalah. For an hour he travelled south down Raythut Wadi until it merged into the wider and deeper Wadi Sha'ab Al Sheikh. Another hour and it emerged onto the plain above Sahalnawt at the Shair valley. He pointed his camel along a well-worn path gradually angling in towards the road. It was midday by the time he arrived at the gate.

As he waited his turn to be searched he scanned apprehensively for familiar faces among those around him. A small group of men a little way off were dressed identically to himself and were obviously attending the same ceremony. He experienced a moment of panic when he recognised three or four of the group. Two were actually members of the militia. Calming himself he realised that they were hardly in position to give him away so he moved towards them and conveniently latched himself to their party. If they were surprised to see a PFLOAG Commissar sneaking into Salalah they didn't show it, instead he was welcomed readily with grins and handshakes. When his turn came he was frisked by one of the guards while his camel was searched by two others. From the way he was dressed the guard guessed the purpose of his visit and informed him that he had missed the marriage procession by at least two hours.

Mussalim had planned it that way. He didn't even want to attend the religious ritual. The less time he actually spent at the wedding then the better it would be for his safety. He reasoned that a short time at the celebrations would be enough to achieve his purpose and at the same time satisfy protocol. Hopefully everybody would be pre-occupied eating dancing and socialising to notice background faces.

Inside the compound wire he stayed with the small group on the short journey to Al Dharitz. People tend to be less observant of faces in a group than the face of a single traveller. In a large clearing in the midst of the closely packed Al Dharitz stone built house and beneath the shade of circle of tall palm trees, two large marquees had been erected. The celebrations were well advanced. Drums beat relentlessly while groups of men all similarly dressed in white *dish'dasht*, danced, stamping their sandalled feet and swinging ceremonial swords with perilous exuberance. Further back women, clad in their black *abeya's*, also danced but much less precociously. Their feet remained rooted, swinging only their shoulders and bending their knees to the monotonous drum beats. Away from the tents and beneath the palms several fires burned, the flames just touching the spits of roasting carcasses. Behind the fires several carcasses of slaughtered cattle and goats lay still awaiting butchering.

Mussalim led his camel onto the beach nearby then crooked and tied its foreleg to ensure that it didn't wander far. From his saddle pack he took a small parcel containing modest wedding presents then, just a face in the crowd he went to join the celebrations. He walked casually through the throng of happy faces to the first marquee. At the entrance he slipped his feet from his sandals kicked them among the many dozen's of pairs to a place where he might be able to find later and went in. Inside was less boisterous than out, men reclined casually around the sides resting against large and brightly coloured cushions talking. His father and his brother Hamed he saw at the far end of the tent among the positions of honour. Selecting the most discreet route up the side he made his way slowly and casually in their direction. However, before he had got to the top of the tent he had been recognised and acknowledged twice. Unnoticed by both his father and his brother he sat down close behind them.

"Father," he said softly.

Both turned and the shock of seeing him registered on both their faces. Hamed started to blurt something but his father's restraining hand touched his arm silencing him.

"Why have you come? Don't you know it's dangerous?" Abdulla asked.

"Juma is my brother. How could I not come?"

Abdulla nodded approvingly. "Nonetheless it was foolish. And what if someone reports that you are here and the soldiers come to arrest you. Have you thought on how that will spoil your brother's day?"

"Yes I have. That is why I don't intend to stay long. I need Juma to see that I came and to spend a few minutes with him."

Abdulla stared at him thoughtfully for a few moments. "Hamed. Take your brother to Jokha and let her introduce him to his new sister."

As the pair left the marquee Abdulla's brother, Fiad was about to enter. He greeted Mussalim with a roar of delight and a bear like hug.

"You look well my uncle," Mussalim said when he freed himself.

"You too my nephew," the old man said grinning through a mass of wild grey beard and showing the many gaps where teeth had once been. He was five years or so older than Mussalim's father with similar wiry physique. However that was where the similarity between the brothers ended. Abdulla had as a young man settled and built for himself the farm on the jebal and scratched out a living raising his own family in the process. His brother, however, had never given up the traditional Bedouin life. Although he had settled his wife and children in the Al Hamer village of Haluf he himself had wandered the *nejd* and *ramlet* freely throughout his life. As a young man he had earned himself a reputation as a fearless warrior riding in the great Kathir raids stealing camels from the Mahru in the east and the Rashid tribes in the north. Even though those days had by this time just about faded into history it was well known that if he and his travel companions came across poorly guarded camels during their wandering they would, as a force of habit, be compelled to steal them. Never happier than when he was being chased by other tribesmen to recover their stock or chasing others who had the audacity to steal Al Hamer camels he had been and still was a figure seemingly larger than life.

"You do well," he said approvingly. "I hear only good things about you." He glanced at Hamed. "Perhaps you should be a little more like your brother and a little less like your father," he suggested.

"Hamed is a dutiful son and does what he should," Mussalim defended.

"Maybe so, maybe so," he relented. "But life is richer with adventure, isn't it? He said grinning again. "You and Juma are much more like me. And my father before me," he added. "We don't stay home with our women when there is a fight to be fought."

Mussalim smiled indulgently. "This war, uncle, is a little different to a tribal skirmish."

He shrugged. "Its still experiencing danger though isn't it? Fear you can taste at the time then massive elation and celebration when you prevail. This is what makes you feel alive. Really alive."

He had managed to make the terror of facing death sound desirable. But then wasn't it always somebody else who got killed? Or at least it was only the living that voiced an opinion. "I have to find my brother and to meet his bride. I will see you a little later, uncle," he excused himself.

As he walked away with Hamed he placed an affectionate arm across his shoulders. "Don't worry about what our old uncle says. He is an old fool who lives in an age now past," he said when out of earshot. "By stopping home unselfishly to help father you show much more responsibility than both Juma or I."

Hamed led the way to the second marquee which was predominantly occupied by women. Temporarily freed from the expectations of servitude and composure and in an environment of female privacy the women in the tent behaved less restrained than the men he had just left. They called to each other as they happily laughed and sang.

Jokha and Lailla occupied a similar position of honour in this tent and Hamed led the way walking boldly up the centre aisle. Uncharacteristically the woman on both sides called out flirtatiously to the men, one or two even called out Mussalim's name unsettling him further that he had again been recognised. As the new centre of attention walking boldly up the centre it wasn't long before both Jokha and Lailla saw him. Both were on their feet before he reached them and delighted to see him. Both hugged and kissed him. Through excitement and perhaps not immediately realising Mussalim's perilous circumstances Jokha began to proudly present her number one son to his new relatives. When at last he stood before the bride he understand instantly the motivation for Juma's actions. Up to this moment Mussalim had considered that his younger brother's eagerness to subject himself and his family to extremes and hardships to possess a woman from a different tribe to have been both irrational and bewildering.

Khamisa sat straight-backed and very still among a bank of brightly coloured cushions. She wore a black *abeya* with a loosely draped head cover. Her long hair shining like burnished ebony framed her oval face and cascaded onto her shoulders in abundance. Heavy gold earrings dangled amidst these tresses while on her head she wore a matching gold tiara with pendants hanging down to her eyebrows. Her father it seemed had not stinted on a dowry to his daughter. Her demeanour though calm and reserved was obviously shy.

Mussalim gazed down in admiration on this vision of enchantment and instantly envied his younger brother. No sacrifice that had been made or any price paid would have been too much to possess this girl. She was, he concluded, truly worth a King's ransom. He looked into her eyes as he bent forward and gentle took her fingers. Just for an instant her eyes betrayed the facade of poise and slipped revealing to him the very tense child within. He smiled at her and gently kissed her fingers wishing to wrap her within a brother's protection and reassure her that she captivated all and had no need of anxiety.

"Truly my brother must be one of Allah's favourites," he said staring deep into her dark eyes. After holding the eye contact a moment he straightened and fiddled in the parcel which he carried. He pulled out three silver bangles that he had bought in Cairo. In truth there were six and he had bought them to give Lailla, but the new circumstances had forced an adjustment to his intentions. One at a time he slipped them over her hand aligning them with two gold ones already on her wrist. In comparison they looked inadequate and tacky, but Khamisa smiled graciously accepting them with gratitude as if they were of equal value.

Suddenly remembering the rest of his family standing at his elbow he widened his attention from the divinity before him and generalised the conversation. "Where is Juma?" he asked of no one in particular.

"I will go with you to find him," Hamed replied.

A little reluctant to leave, he glanced wistfully at Khamisa. "Welcome to our family Khamisa. My brother Juma is a very lucky man."

She smiled up at him and said simply. "Thank you my brother."

The term 'my' that she had just used elated him and gave him a pleasant feeling of bonding.

He followed Hamed from the marquee indulgently acknowledging and smiling at the women who playfully called to him. Before he ducked through the doorway, however, he looked back towards Khamisa hoping to see her looking in his direction. He was disappointed, her concentration was centred upon more people now being presented before her.

Outside once more the pair stood and scanned the throngs of people wandering around. Hamed was the first to spot Juma standing close by the cooking fires satisfying himself that all was going well.

"There," he said pointing and moved in that direction.

Mussalim caught his arm. "Wait," Standing at his side and looking very friendly indeed stood a man wearing a dark brown *dish'dasht* with ceremonial ammunition belts crossing his chest. Around his waist was a broad silver belt with a Khunja thrust in the front. On his head he wore a fawn-patterned shamag with dangling silken tassels. There was no mistaking the uniform of a member of the Sultan's very own personal guard. "We will wait a few moments," he said staring across the crowded area. As he watched someone casually strolling past acknowledged him and reminded him of his vulnerability. To stand there in full view and exposed to so many passers by might not be a good idea. "Come we will sit with our father while we wait."

✻ ✻ ✻

This was the best day of Juma's life so far and with the anticipation that from this day forward things would get even better. There was no doubt in his mind that Allah's blessing had descended on him and given to him a veritable jewel of a woman in Khamisa. He was, he knew, the envy of every man today who looked at his bride. Each sacrifice that he'd had to make paled to insignificance compared to what he now possessed as a result of those sacrifices. His main concern now would be to provided a home fit for his queen. He was also very aware that his family had suffered beneath the yoke of the marriage cost and he was determined that they would also be repaid.

He wandered along the row of cooking fires shaking hands and receiving the good wishes of everyone with Khaleef at his side. Khaleef was now a member of the Sultan's personal guard billeted in luxury within the high walls of the Salalah Beach Palace. It was, he said not only better living and better-paid but also greatly removed from danger. The only occasions when the personal guard ventured from their sentry duties in and around the Palace was to act as escort to the Sultan when he made the one kilometre trip to or from the Salalah airfield of his Air Force. After listening to his friend's attractive account of his new position Juma decided that sometime in the near future then he too would submit an application for consideration.

"Greetings," a grinning and almost toothless old man said holding out his wrinkled hand to be shaken.

Juma knew him only as one of his Al Hamer tribesman. "Greetings, *Shaffer.*" he replied taking the hand.

"Your brother's here," he informed him.

"Yes," he said patiently making allowances for what seemed to be dementia.

"No," irritated sensing his patronising attitude. "Your elder brother," and he pointed towards the main marquee. "He has just gone in there."

Juma glanced in the direction he had pointed then turned back to look at the old man still not sure if he had understood.

"Go, go," he said waving his hand dismissingly. Followed by Khaleef Juma hurried over to the marquee.

They stood for a moment staring at each other then reacting in unison they clasped each other in bear like hugs. It was the first time they had met since that day on the jebal over-looking Salalah when Mussalim had started his journey to join Sheikh Mussalim Bin Nufl. Even so the protocol of customary greetings had to be observed before they could settle and exchange their news. They enquired of each other's welfare and health then muttered praises to Allah for their good fortune. After that Juma remembering Khaleef standing quietly at his elbow turned and brought him into the conversation. As similar age and members of the same tribe formerly living in the same area they knew each other. While the brothers re-union was jubilant the greeting between these two was more restrained although polite. In his momentary elated mood Juma had missed until this very moment that he had just put together a PFLOAG Commissar and a member of the Sultan's personal guard. Two more diverse ends of the warring factions you could not get. The evidence of Khaleef's status was patently visible but did Khaleef know that Mussalim was a Commissar? He certainly knew Mussalim was his brother but had he linked Mussalim as the new Commissar on the jebal? Information is passed so readily that he probably had.

As Juma contemplated the potentially tricky situation it was Mussalim who provided the opportunity to detach himself. "Brother I have to talk to you privately," he said. Juma nodded his assent and as he started to lead the way Mussalim turned back to Khaleef apologised for leaving him so quickly and then magnanimously wished him the protection of Allah.

With Mussalim's arm draped affectionately across brother's shoulders they left the festivities and walked a little way to the shade of one of the palm trees. As they walked Juma received Mussalim's exalted compliments on the elegance and beauty of his bride. His brother's approval was important to Juma and the tribute pleased him filling him with pride.

They sat cross-legged in the shade looking seaward across the deserted beach. Mussalim took from the parcel the last of his presents and handed to him a dark brown *basht*. It was a magnificent robe with silver embroidered trim in the collar and cuffs. Juma expressed his appreciation with a handshake then standing tried it on. It gave him a dignified feeling and well pleased with the gift he left it on.

"What are your plans?" Mussalim asked when Juma had settled once more.

"To live happily ever after," he replied with an easy grin.

"With a wife as fair as Khamisa, I'm sure that you will. But that's not what I meant."

His brother's face showed no particular amusement so Juma bridled his buoyant spirit. "I have rented a modest house in Salalah for the immediate future. But I have hopes of progressing on from that very quickly to provide something more suitable for Khamisa."

"Return to the farm. You could do that tomorrow."

"My original plan was to build a house for Khamisa there and I would spend my off duty hours there too." Juma shook his head slowly. "But it's impossible to do that now. An *askar* alone on Qara, I would be lucky to live three days."

"Then don't be an *askar*. Leave the Army!"

"Leave the Army?" Juma exclaimed staring at his brother. "Will you leave the Front?"

Mussalim looked puzzled. "No of course not."

"Then why is what I do less important than what you do?" Juma was irritated.

For a moment Mussalim was quiet then he softly replied. "I joined the Front for an ideal. You joined the Army for money. Money to buy yourself a wife. Now you have your wife."

It was true. Juma's ire evaporated. "I still need money," he said with a sigh. "I didn't build the house on our father's farm and I have no money left to buy building materials so I still can't build it. Nor is there room in his house. Therefore I have to stay in the Army at least for the foreseeable future."

"Join our cause," Mussalim replied. "You are a trained soldier, I could get you in as a paid regular immediately."

Juma stared at his brother in surprise. "I could never do that," he replied shaking his head.

"Why not?"

"I have seen the effects of your cause. It robbed our family and drove them from their home onto the plain. I have seen evidence of its brutal repression tactics as it imposes its will on the common jebally. I have heard of its property stealing policy disguised beneath the doctrine of communalism. And of its satanic anti-religion decree. All this in the name of freedom. That's not freedom, that's oppression," he scoffed.

Mussalim stared at his brother. "It's this selfish Sultan who is the real oppressor. You have been brain-washed by government propaganda."

"No it's you that is brainwashed by PFLOAG propaganda from Aden," Juma replied hotly. There was acrimony between them now and they both fell sullenly silent. Juma gazed seaward allowing the silence between them to extend and heal the tension.

"Who do you fight for my brother?" Mussalim asked after a time, his quiet tone reducing the heat further. "Look around and ask yourself how many of the Sultan's soldiers in Salalah are Dhofaris. Less than half?" he suggested an answer. "British Officers, British NCO's and men from the north, mostly Baluchi's. None have any stake or interest in this struggle other than the money it puts into their pockets."

"The Firqats are all Dhofaris," Juma countered evenly.

Mussalim shook his head. "The Firqats," he said derisively. "The Sultan's anti guerrilla squad. It doesn't work." They're small in number, untrained, undisciplined and lazy. They lounge around inside the safety of the Um Al Gharriff taking money and do nothing to earn it. When they are sent out to patrol the mountains they sneak out to their selected hide-outs where they hide for three or four days, let off a few shots in target practice and return claiming to have engaged the enemy in several places."

Juma couldn't deny that there was probably truth in what his brother had said.

"I had hoped that I could persuade you to return to the safety of our jebal home," Mussalim went on. "The Sultan is losing this struggle. His troops are penned inside this compound and when he eventually accepts that Dhofar is lost then he will simply flee north, The British and the northerners will return home leaving the few Dhofaris behind to face surrender. What then?" The question was allowed to ferment. "If you won't join us then at least leave the Army."

It had been such a long time since Juma had seen his elder brother and the last thing he wanted was confrontation particularly on this his wedding day. He sought a calm response that would not give offence "I am sorry my brother but I cannot join your cause. Even if I could ignore the PFLOAG past behaviour how could I ever shoot at *askars?* Many are my friends. Nor can I leave the Army, I need money just as badly as I did before to provide a home for my new family." He stared at Mussalim sadly. "Allah has placed us on opposite sides in this war for some divine purpose and we must both follow his will."

"Inshaalah," Mussalim agreed gloomily.

They talked just for a few minutes more keeping carefully away from the insurgency topic. But by his subdued body language Juma could sense his brother's gross disappointment at having failed to get his way. It was almost a relief to him when Mussalim declared that he had already stopped longer than was wise and that he should now leave. They kissed each other on the cheek and after a moment's hesitation Mussalim left.

As he watched his brother walk away down the beach Juma was reminded of the last occasion Mussalim had left him long ago and wondered sadly how long it would be this time before he saw him again. He appreciated the enormous chances that he had taken to make an appearance at his wedding, albeit brief. Obviously he had felt compelled to take the risk to satisfy a desire to share some of his happiness however, there was also an element of elder brother duty. Mussalim's argument for him to leave the army had revealed his genuine concern for his safety. He shook his head sadly, he was still playing the role of brother keeper. When would he realise that he was no longer little brother? He was a man now and a married man at that, responsible for his own decisions. More than that he was convinced that Mussalim hadn't got his own choices right. While there was a great deal wrong with the current establishment that kept a nation impoverished the one that now sought to replace it was probably worse. The certainty of the situation though was that both factions could not co-exist and one would have to destroy the other. By the way things currently shaped the liberationists might well be the party to win. That would place him in the exact situation that Mussalim had described. A Dhofari deserted by his army and left to the mercy of the PFLOAG forces. He was under no illusions what that mercy would amount to. With a sigh he pushed those dark thoughts aside, today was not the day for such thoughts. With a last glance at Mussalim's disappearing form he turned away and went to rejoin his wedding celebrations.

Mussalim left Salalah through the checkpoint at Al Dharitz uneventfully. He made his way across the plain towards the Arzat wadi his body rocking to the steady plodding of the camel beneath him. His visit had not been as successful as he had hoped. Nevertheless, now that he had safely left the Salalah precincts he felt that his reckless undertaking was vindicated. For the first time in an age he had seen his brother, more than that it had been on a special occasion. He had met his new sister and the vision of Khamisa's loveliness kept drifting across his thoughts. The only unsatisfying part had been his failure to convince Juma that he should leave the Sultan's Army.

Some of the things that he had said still irked him. There was no doubt that there were some atrocities committed by the Front forces but that could probably be said for the other side too. Juma had taken all the bad things that he had heard and had disregarded higher ideals of the end objective, Dhofar independence. He did not choose to see that he and other Dhofaris just like him who made up the Sultan's forces propped up and kept in place the corrupt regime. Juma had argued that the Firqats were made up completely of local men. Even though Juma was his brother he was also a Sultan soldier, therefore he couldn't tell him that there was a PFLOAG agenda to make the easy money that the Firqats collected look less attractive. In the near future when these men took their "picnic jaunts" into the mountains they were going to be targeted and engaged. The objective to inflict heavy casualties and persuade these men that the few rupees that they were paid was not worth the risks they took. The Firqats might then melt away and cease to exist, reducing still further Dhofari manning in the forces. That way the Sultan's Army, made up of Northern Omani's Baluchi's and Foreigners, would begin to look more like an occupying force.

When he neared the top of Arzat he turned west over the rolling *gatn* moorlands. Thirty minutes later he came to the upper reaches of Sha'ab Al Sheikh and using a well worn goat track picked his way down through the stubby *Ghaf* trees into the wadi bottom. He dismounted from his camel and pulled it slipping and protesting over the rounded white boulders, which formed the bed of a river that centuries ago had dried. Another thirty minutes or so he rounded a sharp bend between sheer rock walls where the boulders petered out to a flat sandy bed. He was about to remount when from a little distance away four children poured from the mouth of a cave shouting and waving to him.

They ran towards him shouting excitedly their clothes a tangled mass of filthy rags. Small dirty hands pulled at his white *dish'dasht* leaving black smudges as they tried to drag him towards the cave. They led him to the wide mouth of the cave. Its floor sloped upward and became gradually steeper towards the rear. In the entrance a fire smoked filling the air inside with acrid choking fumes. Two sick and withered cows their bones protruding starkly got to their feet and staggered unsteadily away from the cave entrance. He gazed after them thinking how much kinder the deed to slit their throats and end the animal's misery. The reality, however, was probably that these people needed the milk desperately, even the meagre yield that might be got from such diseased cows as those. Hundreds of disturbed flies, feeding on the cow dung that covered the floor rose in the air angrily buzzing as the children pulled him further up the slope and into the darkness. They pointed towards a bundle of dirty rags on a low rock shelf and then stood back in silence. As his eyes became adjusted to the gloom he could see the emaciated form of a woman lying very still amongst the rags. He placed his hand on her arm, it felt solid, and the flesh was cold. He bent over her and looked down into a gaunt strained face. Her mouth hung open, her eyes stared upward but saw nothing. She was quite dead. Another victim of poverty.

She wasn't very old but with the ravages of starvation and some associated disease even a guess at her age was difficult. He covered her face with one of the dirty rags and looked at the children standing silently watching. The eldest, a girl could not have been more than seven.

"Your mother?" he asked.

She only nodded. He shook his head sadly it probably meant that the dead woman was aged no more than early twenties. He led them from the smoke filled cave into the fresh air. "Where is your father?

"Gone to Salalah for medicine."

Feeling hopelessly inadequate he patted her head sympathetically. He looked across to his camel, which had settled beneath the shade of a tree and he thought of the string of figs in the saddle pack. At least he could provide them with something eatable even though it was a pathetic answer to the family's deplorable situation. He took the figs from the saddle pack and gave them to the girl. Her eyes shone with childish gratitude and she began to meticulously divide the fruit equally into small piles. She then handed a pile to each sibling. Unsure whether they were allowed to eat or not they waited watching their elder sister. When she began to eat they did too, ravenously.

The girl had already begun the role of mother, Mussalim noted. By tragic circumstances she would now be forced to assume that role and yet she was herself still at the age of infancy. The situation was depressing and beginning to have an emotional effect him but he was impotent to do anything more. He felt an urgent need to escape. Presumably, their father would return before dark and their plight was for him to deal with. He left the children water and gave to each one a Maria Therasa dollar attempting to ease his conscience. The children watched sullenly and in silence as he remounted the camel. He looked down at the helpless expressions staring back unblinking. He was deserting them he knew, but what could he do? Nothing, he excused himself.

"Your father will be back soon," he said as he slapped the camel down the shoulder. Then he re-started his journey back to the Raythut HQ.

He glanced back just once expecting to see precisely what he did see. The children stood in the mouth of the cave staring after him mournfully. The story was just too familiar, poverty, squalor, ignorance, and disease. Lives prematurely ended at a point where expectations should have just begun. He thought of the banquet being presently consumed at his brother's wedding. Just one of those carcasses would feed this family for a month. But he couldn't begrudge his brother that feast. It was after all, his first wedding and it had cost a lot of sacrifices in the preceding months to achieve it. He just wished Juma had been with him to see the pathetic misery of this family. It might have changed his mind about serving in an army that sustained this unconcerned Sultan. He angrily cursed Said Bin Taymour for his indifference. He did absolutely nothing to ease the hardships of his people. His intent was to solely fill his own coffers with the country's oil revenue while the poor of his nation died. It reaffirmed his own allegiance to the cause that pledged to rid the Dhofar of this despotic selfish old man. It confirmed in his mind that which he already knew. Despite Juma's scathing comments the cause he followed was just. One day this family and hundreds of others just like it would be avenged, he vowed.

~ 13 ~

July 1970 • On the morning of July 24th 1970 the people of Oman got from their beds to learn that they had a new Sultan. Prince Qaboos had led a successful coup against his father. By the end of the day Said Bin Taymour had flown out of Oman to London, where he would live the rest of his life in luxurious comfort, provided by his son.

The coup itself had been carried out the previous day and assisted by the British had been swift, efficient and almost casualty free. The only casualties had been a slave who had needlessly died and Sultan Said Bin Taymour himself who had accidentally shot himself in the foot whilst reloading his revolver.

The nation began celebrations instantly. The news of a new Sultan instilled hope into the whole nation that the future might bring improvements and sorely needed relief to the impoverished Omani. Before there had been only hopeless despondency, seemingly stretching on and on into foreseeable future. Certainly the poor could not possibly be any worse off, so there was a massive feeling that living conditions could only get better.

The celebrations though nation-wide were even more joyful in the southern region of the country. For the first time in its history the Dhofar had its own blood ruler. The mother of Sultan Qaboos, Queen Mizoon, was from the Darbat area and of the Mushani tribe within the greater Kathir. In the streets of Salalah spontaneous celebrations had begun immediately the news had started to spread. Bonfires were lit, feasts prepared and large processions wandered the streets chanting loyalty to the new Sultan and impromptu street dancing begun.

On the jebal where the PFLOAG held sway the celebrations were more guarded. Nevertheless for most jeballys the news was greeted with arcane delight and many families gathered and had celebrations of their own. Because of the nervousness of what the liberationist reactions might be they were kept at a much lower key. Even among the PFLOAG soldiers there was confusion on how the news should be greeted. Among the hard-line Communist element the news made no difference to the situation. Qaboos still represented the smug bourgeois establishment that fed richly off the masses while keeping them destitute. Besides that, this Sultan whoever he might be was just another obstacle to be overcome on the way to the greater objective. Others with lesser objectives in mind however, struggled with soul-searching questions on the continued validity of the war. Many began to wonder if hostilities should be suspended to await developments which might bring some of the changes that they fought so vehemently for.

With the first full day of Qaboos's reign very nearly over the revellers were rapidly thinning. The long day's jubilation was being overtaken by tiredness. Juma and Khaleef had wandered aimlessly round Salalah witnessing many of the celebrations and being made welcome at all. Now as the festivities began petering out they made their way back through the narrow alleyways to where Juma lived. Reluctant to let the day end even at this late hour Juma invited Khaleef his home to drink tea before he returned once more to duty inside the Royal Palace.

Khamisa waited alone for Juma to return and now she hastened to make the tea that would show her husband as a good host. The two men sat cross-legged opposite each other on the large carpet in the centre of the dimly lit room. Between them Khamisa placed the metal tray containing small handless cups and upright teapot and then she sat in background, as a dutiful wife should, quietly sewing. Although an incense burner smouldered in the corner of the room its fragrance was subdued with the more pungent smell of paraffin. Fumes escaped in tiny wisps of black smoke from two lamps that lit the room. A window shutter remained wide open to dispel the fumes, but this softened the smell only marginally and allowed the gnats of the night access.

Juma still found the events of the coup incredible. There had been not the slightest indication that anything of the kind was even remotely pending. When it had it happened it happened not only with stunning surprise but also quickly. Yesterday, inside the confines of the Palace walls Khaleef who at the precise moment had been on gate duty witnessed the arrival of the Prince at his father's door with his soldiers and British officers. All the guards standing duty at the time had been calmly ordered to lay down their weapons. Shortly after there had been some shots from within the Sultan's quarters but it hadn't been very long before they had received assurances that all was well. Khaleef recounted his story for the umpteenth time, for Juma's benefit.

"History repeats itself," he muttered thoughtfully referring to the similar coup that had displaced Sultan Taymour Bin Faisel as ruler by his own son Said Bin Taymour in 1932. "Almost as if Taymour Faisel was taking revenge on his son from the other side of the grave."

Khaleef grinned. "That's an odd thought."

Juma grinned too dismissing the thought. "What of the future? he asked on a brighter note as he handed Khaleef one of the cups.

"I am told that Qaboos is a clever and progressive man. The nation's future now looks hopeful. *Il hamdu lillaah,*" he praised God.

"*Il hamdu lillaah,*" Juma mumbled agreement and filled the cup that Khaleef held out. "I only hope that it has come in time. The war is spreading and the stories from Muscat last month were disturbing."

"NDFLOAG?" Khaleef enquired.

Juma nodded. "Yes. The National Democratic Front for the Liberation of Oman and the Arabian Gulf. The revolt is intensifying," he said before sipping the black sweet tea from his own cup.

"They are weak," he shook his head dismissively. "Reports say that the attacks that were carried out at Nizwa and Izki amounted to little more than dissension. They fired off a few mortar rounds, a few rifle shots then they ran out of ammunition. While they were withdrawing the government forces counter attacked and captured several including some of the leaders."

Juma didn't dismiss them so easily. "Maybe so," he said refilling his friend's cup. "But the front does still exist and leaders can always be replaced. It is reported also that the organisation is getting financial aid and support from Iraq. Maybe next time they won't be so easily repelled." He paused to refill his own cup. "The very fact that three small movements have amalgamated should be cause for concern. It means not only is the resentment growing up in the North too, but also that the protesters are beginning to get organised."

"Hmm, that's true," Khaleef agreed shaking his cup to indicate that he had had enough tea. "It does seem that this civil war is spreading. But what can we do?"

Juma shrugged nonplussed and stared gloomily into his teacup.

"We must place our trust in this Sultan. He will bring peace and prosperity to Oman, *inshaalah*." Khaleef offered the solution. "Now I must go," he said getting to his feet. "I have early duty tomorrow."

✳ ✳ ✳

August 1970 • It was not often that Abdulla's brother Fiad visited but this was one of those rare occasions. The two men sat beneath the corrugated tin of the crude veranda sunshade. However, there was no sun to shade from, this season's Khareef had clamped in with a vengeance at the very time of the new Sultan's ascendance. Now a month later both men stared out into the thick swirling mist and watched the rainwater drip monotonously from the edges of the sagging corrugated roof.

"How you can stay up here in this foul weather, I'll never understand. Give me the open *nejd* and it's permanent sunshine everytime," Fiad said.

Fiad's only interest in his brother's farm lay with the goat herd that they shared. Even here his interest was strictly limited. Many years ago both men had merged what stock of goats they had and because grazing was better on the mountain than in the *nejd* village Haluf, it made sense for Abdulla to look after them. Since that time Fiad's interest in the herd had been non-existent. It amounted to nothing more than the occasional harvest perhaps a couple of times in a year when a couple of dozen animals would driven to his home for on tap slaughter as required. Even these harvest visits did not normally feature Fiad, it was much more likely to be one of his three sons who came.

He had arrived this afternoon alone and riding a massive bull camel pulling three she camels behind him. It was typical of the man that even at his age he still chose to ride a strong and raucous bull instead of a milder natured cow. The bull, he said, had served all three cows, and he generously offered them as a present. Abdulla suspected strongly that they had been stolen during one of Fiad's wandering but nevertheless his need was such that he was prepared to turn a blind eye to that and accepted the gifts with gratitude. His stock of animals had been decimated at the time of Juma's wedding and the recovery was painfully slow. Three extra camels would immediately increase the camel herd to five and potentially eight when these three dropped their calves about a year from now. It gave him also the option to sell one or perhaps even two to buy cattle and increase his cattle herd, which now numbered an inadequate five.

"You must be proud of your son," Fiad said.

Abdulla glanced sideways at his brother, not sure which one he referred to. "I am proud of all my sons."

Fiad grinned a toothless grin through a mass of wild grey beard. "Mussalim," he said. "I mean Mussalim. Oh Allah if I were ten years younger I would be in this fight with him."

"Ten years?" Abdulla challenged looking sideways at his brother. He must have seen around sixty birthdays. Or would have if he had perhaps known when his birthday was.

"Hmm," he wobbled his head and screwed his lined face. "OK twenty."

"Better twenty-five," Abdulla muttered. "But Bin Taymour is history now," he went on. "What of the new Sultan? He might yet change things for the better."

Fiad snorted. "Brother, this is the fourth Sultan that you and I have seen. Has any one of them made changes that have affected our way of life one grain?"

Abdulla recognised the same hard line attitude present in his eldest son. He wondered if it were perhaps some genetic intolerance inherited from their father, Mussalim's grandfather. With no desire to argue the point he replied meekly. "Maybe this one will. *Inshaallah.*"

Jokha appeared in the doorway and announced that the food was laid out.

Both men got to their feet. "Go and find Hamed," Abdulla instructed her.

Fiad grinned at her saucily. "Jokha, Jokha," he said. "When my brother dies then you will become my favourite wife."

"Oh!" Abdulla said. "What if you die first?"

"Ah," he breathed sympathetically and placed his arm around his younger brother. "Then I can only leave you Yasmin. And I am afraid that I wore her out many years ago."

* * *

Hamed tugged on the rope turning the camel to examine it the best way he could. This one looked to be a magnificent animal too. He estimated that all three were aged about three or four with their prime years still to come. If they were, as he suspected, stolen then the owner would be infuriated and perhaps even now searched for them. He started from its neck ran his hands down the animal's rough fur from shoulder to rump, then finding nothing did the same on its other side. On its shoulder he found what he was looking for, the scar marks of a knife – two short vertical slashes with a third angling across. It was the branding mark of the Mahru tribe. It only confirmed what he expected to find. He turned the animal free and examined the other two at the same place. These bore the same marks.

He leaned back on the roundavaal picket fence contemplating the situation. The Mahru territory was far to the west spanning the Yemen border and far beyond. A small isolated pocket of Mahru had many years ago moved eastward and had settled in the area around Jibjat. Though not nearly as far away as the traditional territory that settlement too was a safe distance to the east of this farm. Fiad, however, would not have plundered the animals from there, he calculated. Almost certainly he would have taken them from the distant border areas. So there seemed to be no danger that the Mahru would actually turn up here looking for these stolen camels. If there were to be any future problems then that would come when they tried to sell, but that was unlikely to be soon. If the camels were pregnant then there would be a year before the calves were born and at about six months beyond that before the calves could be separated from their mothers. It was a problem in the distant future and he need not be too concerned at this stage. He would of course have to inform his father of what he knew but diplomatically, he would wait until his uncle had left. Jokha's long and shrill throat warble pierced the mist informing him that he should come.

✳ ✳ ✳

At that very moment, twenty kilometres away Mussalim was seated in the great cave in Wadi Risham. Despite the large fire that burned at the enormous entrance it was cold. The thick mist heavy with damp from the continuous drizzle swirled into the vast chamber and chilled a man's body. Mussalim had pulled an old cagoule over his shoulders and although it helped to keep his upper body dry it did little to retain warmth.

In reaction to the recent significant development the PFLOAG congress had called a meeting of all its lead members and influential tribal leaders who supported the cause. Everyone who was anyone of significance in the movement was gathered here. Mohammed Bin Talib as Commander of the central region had obviously been summoned and he had brought along Mussalim as his aid. They had arrived over an hour ago into an atmosphere that was more like a cheerful reunion than a war counsel. Mussalim had circulated, greeting and shaking hands with comrades in arms that he now called friends. Al Mushani was there, so too was Al Shibbam but the face he was most pleased to see was the scarred one of Suhayl. The fact that Suhayl had unconcernedly ordered him to be shot at that first meeting in Wadi Ghadun was forgotten as both men greeted each other as brothers.

They sat with their feet tucked beneath them and their backs against the cave wall exchanging their news. Suhayl still remained in the eastern region and boasted that mostly because of his group's activities no government traffic now moved along the road between Mirbat and Taqa. The only supply route left open to them was the sea, and if they could get their hands on floating mines then that route too would be made dangerous, he laughed. He went on to congratulate Mussalim on his appointment to Commissar and acclaimed his subsequent achievements and his growing reputation since his return to Qara.

Everywhere in or around the cave men stood or sat casually exchanging news experiences while they waited for the meeting to become organised. Al Ghassani was last to arrive accompanied by Abdel Tahir. Both men immediately positioned themselves to sit cross-legged close to the fire. Now that the General Secretary had taken his position and was clearly ready to start men began to shuffle into spaces sitting in a vague semi-circular to his front. Mussalim nodded briefly to Suhayl, got up and shuffled over towards Bin Talib and sat close behind.

Al Ghassani began addressing the meeting by giving an account of the impressive progress so far made by the Front. He then went on to chronicle the large areas under the Front's control that were effectively 'no go areas' to government forces. He exuded optimism that complete victory in the area was now imminent and well within their grasp providing that the pressure was kept up.

Mussalim quickly picked up on the last statement. It was the first indication of the congress's reaction to the news of a new Sultan.

"The replacement of one Sultan for another," he went on, "was a clear indication of the disarray and panic that the capitalists were in. It was a desperate attempt to deflect the PFLOAG and its supporters from the present strategy that had brought them to the brink of victory. Easing the pressure at this time," he said, "was precisely what they hoped to achieve and that it would be a grave mistake. The plan should now be the exact opposite – to keep the momentum going and to increase the pressure even more." He mentioned the new NDFLOAG that had been formed in the north and described how that effect had been to add further strain to the already over-stretched government forces. He then announced an intention to make contact with the new group very soon with the object of co-operation to mutual advantage. He continued by praising those tribal leaders present for their endorsement of PFLOAG policy's and the pledged support that the front enjoyed from their people. He ended by stating, "the message that should go out from this meeting must be one of confidence and assurance that victory was close. The change of one ruler to another should be ignored because that would have no effect on improving conditions for the downtrodden people of Dhofar."

There was a short silence after he had finished, then some low mutterings began as men turned to their neighbour and passed comments. The muttering withered away when a man at the back stood and began to speak. He introduced himself as Amr Qassim of Bait Umr a tribe from the eastern region of Qara. He claimed to be a tribal leader and he spoke on behalf of the tribe Sheikh who was one of several that found themselves confined within the precincts of Salalah. The purpose of these restrictions had been an authoritarian attempt by Sultan Bin Taymour to remove tribe leaders from their people and so reduce the chances of organised resistance. However, the Sheikhs, although essentially detached still attempted to manage tribal affairs through a series of third party delegates. Amr Qassim spoke up boldly and he dared to disagree with Al Ghassani.

"This was not the time to increase the war effort," he said, "instead it was a time for dialogue. With the accomplishments achieved they could negotiate from a position of strength and with a completely new administration to deal with all previous diversity could be forgotten and discussions could begin afresh. It was an opportunity to end the conflict and improve living conditions."

Abdel Tahir sprang to Al Ghassani's defence by rebuking Amr Qassim as a short-sighted man with only limited parochial vision. He reminded him of the Front's higher ideals, the liberation of the Arabian Gulf.

Unconcerned Amr Qassim accepted the parochial criticism and announced that it was only the Dhofar region that concerned him and in particular his own tribe people.

Abdel Tahir scorned him further with condemning taunts that he was a self-centred man who had no interest for the plight of other Arab brothers suffering hardships and degradation. Tahir supporters cheered while others disagreed and jeered.

During the commotion another man got to his feet and taking encouragement from the challenge by Amr Qassim he too voiced his opinion. Whilst he supported this fight against tyranny, he countered, that because of the dictatorial policies of the PFLOAG enforced by brutal repression they were simply replacing one tyrant for a tyrannical system. He claimed the democratic system of Sheikhdoms that had been in place for centuries and predominantly used throughout the whole of the Middle East should remain. It should be the Sheikhs who decided the policies.

This time it was Al Mushani who stood to reply. "It was," he said, "impossible for any nation to progress forward as a whole while the Sheikhdom system remained. In communal meetings when the Sheikhs came together from all tribes within the same factions they could not agree upon even the most basic of policies and no decisions were ever made. Even when a majority did manage to agree a policy then the minorities would simply choose to ignore it. The so-called democratic system of Sheikhdom was a myth and in truth only anarchy," he summed up disparagingly.

A man close by leapt to his feet. "No Sheikh ever ordered a man punished or killed for following his religion," he shouted at him.

"Oh no," Al Mushani replied calmly. "Not even a Christian?"

"Not even a Christian," he countered hotly.

"If you won't kill a Christian then you must be pro British." Al Mushani distorted the point.

The man stared at him for a moment with wild eyes then placing his hand on the khunja in his belt he cursed Al Mushani loudly. A friend at his side got to his feet and put a restraining hand on his shoulder.

"Friends! Friends," Al Ghassani said raising both hands in a gesture of calm. "The policy of continued aggression is the policy decided by the PFLOAG Congress and while it may be open to opinion it is not open to option. It is the decided way forward. What Commissar Al Mushani said about the Sheikhdom system being indecisive is perfectly true and that is the very reason why an enlightened congress must make an assertive decision for the good of the whole. We must all continue to work together and to follow the direction of the Congress. It has brought us to the very point of success and now is not the time to deviate from the strategy that has put victory within our grasp."

The group was silent, the dissenters had sat down, and the last word had been said. No further challengers came forward. Mussalim studied Al Ghassani and marvelled at the man's power to control his audience, he had charisma of that there was no doubt. Whether it was authority, persuasion, or simple fear he certainly controlled respect. The meeting continued in a more subdued fashion dealing with items of trivia in comparison with the main issue, the instruction to continue the war against the establishment.

It broke up a little while later leaving Mussalim in a pensive mood. He agreed a good deal with what Amr Qassim had said. It might be a good time to suspend hostilities for a short while and begin talks. It could perhaps even achieve most of what they fought for. On the other hand if there were nothing on offer or even if nothing came from negotiations then Al Ghassani's argument was valid. A cessation would give the government forces time to regroup and would work to their advantage. If they re-organised then it would most certainly mean that previous PFLOAG gains would be lost and that victory slipped further away. It might even disappear completely. Perhaps under the circumstances the Congress was right, the continuation of the war was the best policy, at least for the time being.

"The General Secretary wants to see you," Bin Talib interrupted his thoughts. He led him to where Al Ghassani sat with Abdel Tahir and Al Mushani. They sat down quietly and waited while he continued to discuss the meeting's dissenters.

"You will need to watch Amr Qassim closely. He could cause trouble," he warned Abdel. "In the absence of their Sheikh he is an influential man in his tribe. Find ways to discredit him if you can to make him lose some esteem among his people. I don't have to tell you just how important the tribe Umr is to our plans in the east. The last thing we need is a mass desertion of Umr men."

He turned towards Mussalim and smiled. "Commissar Mussalim," he greeted. "Have you met Abdel Tahir?"

Mussalim leaned forward and offered his hand. Tahir was not a very imposing man being only slightly built, however he had an air of confident authority about him. He had a swarthy complexion with wild unkempt black hair and beard. His PFLOAG

Commissar uniform was well worn and streaked green with faded dye. He studied Mussalim silently with dark expressionless eyes as he shook his hand.

"First let me compliment you on a job well done," Al Ghassani said. "Mohammed informs me that the network of militia that we needed in this central region is now in place. It numbers more than two hundred, is well trained and effective. From it Mohammed has been able to organise a quick reaction force that enables him to rapidly engage any trespassing soldiers into our area. It has worked out as well as I had hoped. The support that this region enjoys from the locals is also improved and is the best it has ever been. And, he places most of the credit for these accomplishments with you."

Mussalim was extremely gratified to hear such praise from the most powerful man in the movement though somewhat embarrassed. He muttered a few modest words of thanks.

"But it is now time for you to move on," Al Ghassani went on. "Leave your team with Mohammed to continue recruiting and training while you move to our eastern sector. I want you to do exactly the same job there. Form and train a militia and at the same time improve the aspect of loyalty from the locals. Whilst you will be under Abdel's command the same circumstances will apply. You will have my complete authority to take whatever action you see fit to achieve the same results that you have achieved here."

"What about men for my team?"

"I will supply you with the men you need," Abdel Tahir broke in to answer the question.

"I would like to take one of my existing team with me."

"Should be no problem," Al Ghassani replied glancing at Bin Talib. "Mohammed?" He sought confirmation.

Bin Talib shook his head.

"OK it's settled. You may find things a little more difficult than you did here. There are many conflicts, inter tribal jealousies, area disputes, and personal frictions. In addition there is a separate movement, the Dhofar Liberation Front operating quite independently. So far they have stubbornly refused to join us or even to co-operate in ventures. A man called Salim Mubarak is its leader. I am told that you are very persuasive," he went on glancing at Bin Talib. "You should try those powers on him, because if he doesn't agree to join us soon then I am afraid that we will be forced to destroy him and his movement." He paused for a moment. Any Question?"

There were none that Mussalim could think of at that point. "No," he replied.

"Abdel!" Al Ghassani invited his input.

"We are based at Jibjat. Report to me there as soon as you have wound things up at Raythut. I look forward to having your assistance," he added.

"OK." Mussalim nodded.

"Good luck and keep up the good work," Al Ghassani held out his hand to be shaken.

The three men were silent and stared at Mussalim indicating that the discussion had ended. He got to his feet and went to find Suhayl. He could perhaps give him some insight of the circumstances that he was likely to find in the eastern sector.

* * *

Early September 1970 • In the upper reaches of the jebal, patches of fog pushed by a light breeze rolled lazily across its exposed uplands. The changing shapes altered gradually as they revolved slowly onward like some cumbersome monster. Sometimes it blanketed thickly reducing visibility to a few metres and sometimes thin and wispy allowing glimpses of sunlight to penetrate. On the lower reaches where Abdulla and Hamed worked cutting the tall grass these fog banks hung above their heads in the form of overcast clouds. The leaden skies dulled the green and lush landscape with a tinge of grey. It was now early September and this Khareef season was rapidly losing its grip.

Abdulla stood up straight placing his hand on the base of his back trying to ease the pain that it had cost him to straighten. He glanced down the hill towards the farmhouse two hundred metres away. He could see. Or could he? Perhaps he couldn't, maybe it was just his mind psychologically re-assuring him that it was there. His eyesight was still deteriorating and he wondered how long it might be before he was virtually blind. Even an old pair of spectacles that he had bought second, third or maybe even fourth hand from the souk some time ago didn't help as much as they had in the beginning. When the day was bright objects, shapes and colours were clearly discernible up to about twenty metres although detail was denied to him. Faces however were just featureless shapes at more than three or four paces. By far the worst time for him was the evening. In the gloom he could identify very little. Only familiar objects that remained permanently fixed or a family member by shape or voice. He glanced in the direction where Hamed worked. He could see him, no not really. He could see a human shape that must be Hamed, but he couldn't really see him.

He worried about the future. When blindness did come then he would be nothing more than an additional burden to Hamed. So much now depended on that young man's shoulders. Mussalim was off who knows where, while Juma although married with his own family could not return to the jebal farmhouse in today's circumstances even if he had the desire to do so. He turned back to the grass-cutting task and committed the future to Allah's divine hand trusting that he would provide when the time came.

Fifteen minutes later Hamed called to him and waved an arm in the direction behind him. Abdulla turned but could see nothing but the shape of the distant hills and the greyer sky above.

"Someone comes," Hamed said moving to his side. "Six or seven Land Rovers are moving this way."

Abdulla screwed up his eyes and scanned the landscape for movement, but could see nothing.

"There," Hamed pointed. "They are soldiers," he informed him.

"Soldiers or rebels?"

"Government soldiers."

"Perhaps its Juma and his friends," Abdulla offered hopefully.

"Maybe. Let's go back to the house and find out."

By the time they had descended the hill seven Land Rovers heavy with armed *askars* pulled up at the house front. The men leapt out quickly and reacting to barked instructions from a sergeant they fanned out in front of the house. Two others manned the GPMG's mounted in the back of two vehicles and scanned the surrounding hillsides. Accompanied by a tall British officer the sergeant came over to where Abdulla and Hamed stood.

"Peace be with you," Abdulla gave the customary greeting and offered a friendly handshake.

The sergeant took the hand and returned the muttered compliment. When the handshake ritual between all four was completed Abdulla then offered his guests water refreshments. It was politely refused and the sergeant came to the point.

"We are looking for the home of Abdulla Bin Salim of Bait Al Hamer."

"I am he."

He turned and spoke to the British officer in English, which Abdulla did not understand. "We are looking for your son," he said after the exchange."

"This is my son, Hamed."

"You have a son called Mussalim, is he here?"

Abdulla shook his head.

More English conversation, then the sergeant barked instructions for the soldiers to search the premises. "Where is Mussalim?"

"I have no idea."

"No idea, perhaps you do but won't say."

More English conversation followed. "Are you an *adoo* sympathiser?"

"I do what I have to every day to live, nothing more nothing less."

Four soldiers invaded the house forcing Jokha out and she stood nervously on the veranda silently watching. Two others searched the old wood shed while more moved around the back of the house. The British officer meanwhile moved close to Hamed and peered at him hard while moving around him slowly. He said something in English. "Are you an *adoo* bandit?" the sergeant interpreted.

"No."

"Your brother is though."

Hamed looked at his father for guidance. "We work here as peaceful jebal farmers," Abdulla said. "We tend our stock and do what we have to do each day to survive. We are too busy scratching a living to get involved in the power struggles of others."

Another interpretation took place, which was followed by a protracted conversation while they waited for the result of the search. From the behind the house two soldiers appeared leading the three camels that Fiad had brought as gifts. The sergeant went across and examined the Mahru brand marks that they pointed at. When he came back he explained the significance of the brands to the officer. "Have you been to the Yemen recently?" he sneered. "Or have you been just too busy scratching out a living."

"We haven't been any where near the Yemen border."

"Somebody has. How else can you explain those Mahru camels."

"They were gifts."

"Gifts from your *adoo* friends no doubt," he sneered at Abdulla's reply. Then he reported to the officer once again.

Abdulla apprehensively watched the two men and listened intently trying to gain a glimmer of what they were saying. Throughout the conversation they both looked frequently in their direction with the majority of glances being directed at Hamed. Eventually the decision made the sergeant nodded assent. "You are to come with us for further questioning," he said. Then he gave instructions for both Abdulla and Hamed to be handcuffed. With their hands secured behind their back they were tossed unceremoniously onto the floor in the back of vehicles and with Jokha screaming abuse at the *askars* they were driven away.

The vehicles bounced and jarred over the uneven ground and Abdulla lying in the bottom was bounced and jarred with it. With his hands fastened behind his back he was unable to do much to protect his body from the jolting. His head and face suffered the most, banging continually against the metal floor. In the cramped space there was no room to turn but by twisting his neck he could just turn his face upward a little and in this position it was the back of his head that took the bulk of the battering. He hoped that Hamed was not suffering the same way but feared that his situation was probably the same. Just when he thought he could stand it no longer one of the soldiers sitting in the back grabbed him by the hair and lifted his head. He slid his feet underneath and then let go. To Abdulla it provided some relief in the form of cushion between his head and the hard floor. Whether the man had done it from compassion or whether he did it simply for his own comfort Abdulla couldn't tell but he silently thanked Allah for his mercy.

An hour later aching and sore he was hauled from the Land Rover inside the compound of Um Al Gharriff Army base. Half-stumbling and half-dragged he was taken into a guardhouse where he was uneremoniously pushed into a cell. The cell was small and austere containing only a small cot with a stained mattress. It was without windows and dimly lit by an in-built light just above the door. The solid heavy door slammed shut behind him and moments later the light was turned off. He listened as scuffled footsteps filled the corridor outside and another door was slammed. That, he assumed, was his youngest son being incarcerated too.

He called his name several times and listened intently against the heavy door for a reply. Once he thought he heard a muffled reply but it was never repeated. Dejectedly he wandered across to the cot and sat down. He looked round the darkened cell at the four bare walls. In a corner a tin mug with a jug of water while in the other a battered metal bucket for relief. With a heavy sigh he lay back on the yellowed stained mattress and stared through the darkness to the ceiling. Why had they been brought to this place? Why was he being treated this way? What was it that he was supposed to have done wrong? He asked himself over and over again without being able to think of an answer. Eventually he gave in and muttered, "*Inshaallah,*" allowing that Allah must have some reason for putting him here. Some time after that he must have fallen asleep.

When he woke he had no idea how long he had been asleep or whether it was dark or light outside. Guessing at the time he decided that it must be time for prayer. But which was the direction of Mecca? With only instinct to guide him he faced the direction he supposed and made his prayer. Afterwards he returned to lay on the cot just staring into the darkness and wondering when something would happen and what it was likely to be. He worried about Jokha and Lailla on the farm. How would they cope? What if some of those PFLOAG thugs came? That was unlikely, he consoled himself, they had experienced none of that thuggery since Mussalim's return to Qara. It was probable, however, that it was Mussalim's return and gained reputation that had put both him and Hamed in this predicament. He sighed gloomily at the paradox. If his eldest son had stayed away they wouldn't be here now in these cells, but they would still have been subjected to PFLOAG abuse. The vast majority of Dhofaris were stuck in the middle attending the immediate business of every day living and caught between two dangers. By not offending one they offended the other and when either of the warring factions were offended then there was little to choose between them. Merciful sleep eased his worries once more.

He was awakened when the heavy door creaked open. He swung his feet to the floor and sat up on the cot. One soldier stood in the doorway staring at him expressionless while another entered and placed a small plastic tray of rice on the foot of the bed.

"What is the time brother?" His question was ignored. "What about my son? How long will we be kept here?" But both men left closing the heavy door with a solid thump without answering any of his questions. During the endless hours this happened four more times. Each time he asked the same questions becoming more demanding, as he became more concerned. The response differed only slightly when he was told curtly "wait and see," or simply to "shut up."

He picked at the rice on the tray half-heartedly calculating that if he were being fed evening and morning then by now it was probably into the evening of the second day. He had eaten very little when the keys jangled in the lock and the door swung open again.

"Bring your slops," one of the soldiers said pointing at the metal bucket.

Abdulla did as he was told and he followed the soldier down the narrow corridor a few paces. The soldier stopped at a narrow tiled cubicle and drew back a curtain to reveal a sunken porcelain drain.

"Empty it," he ordered. "Now rinse the bucket," he said pointing towards a nearby tap. "Put it down and come with me," he said when the task was complete. He led the way to the end of the corridor and with the familiar slam of the heavy door he locked Abdulla in a different cell. This one differed from the other only by its furnishings.

There was no cot, but there was a table in the middle with three chairs on one side and one on the other. On the wall there hung two clocks, one indicated 9.45 the other 3.20. This only served to confuse him more, which one was accurate or indeed if either was he could only guess.

Soon after the door was opened again and this time four uniformed men entered, two British and two Omani *akars*. One of the *askars* took post by the door while the other three men went across to the table. Abdulla recognised one of the British as the officer who had led the patrol to his farm and seized both Hamed and himself. With an arm wave he indicated that he should seat himself in the chair on the other side. Abdulla sauntered across sat down and then watched as they took position opposite laying out files and note pads preparing for the interview. With a deal of chair scraping they adjusted their seats to be comfortable. The man in the middle, the second British, glanced quickly in both directions to assure himself that the other two were ready. He then opened the file in front of him cleared his throat with a little cough and said.

"Abdulla Bin Salim Al Hamer, is that you?" Abdulla nodded. "You have been brought here because you are suspected of having connection with the insurgents calling themselves the PFLOAG. Do you understand?" He spoke Arabic fluently.

"Yes I understand, but you are mistaken, I have nothing to do with the PFLOAG."

"Then how do you explain the Mahru camels in your possession?" The *askar* to his right asked.

"They were a gift from my brother."

"Where did he get them from?"

"I have no idea."

"Your son, Mussalim is a Communist Commissar isn't he?" The Brit spoke again.

"Yes I don't deny it."

"Then they were his camels."

"No. My brother brought them as a gift."

"Do you often accept Mahru camels, obviously stolen camels as gifts?"

I accept gifts from my brother and I have no evidence that they were stolen."

The two men scoffed loudly. The third man who did not understand the language now spoke, probably enquiring what had been said, Abdulla assumed. Then a conversation developed in English. The man in the middle then nodded agreement and continued the line of questioning.

"So your brother must be *adoo* too. Who is he and how can we find him?"

Abdulla had no intention of surrendering his brother. "His name is Fiad and he has no more interest in the rebel cause than I. I live a settled existence but he is not like me at all. He lives the traditional bedu life and wanders the desert where Allah may guide him. Only he and Allah know where he is at this time."

"Convenient," the *askar* muttered. "No matter, it's your son that we want. We know that he moves through the mountains preaching lies and organising treason. Tell us where he is and you and your other son can go."

"I don't know where he is?"

"You don't know where your brother is and you don't know where your son is. You don't know much at all do you?"

"Oh he knows alright. He's just not saying," the Brit interrupted. "Are you?" He glared at Abdulla and didn't wait for an answer. "If you ever want to get out of here you had better start giving us some answers."

"Perhaps you don't understand your situation," the *askar* said softly. "If this man thinks that you are PFLOAG or if he thinks that you shielding PFLOAG then he has the power to have you imprisoned for a very long time or he could even have you shot."

Abdulla raised his hands in despair. "I don't know where either of them are."

"OK," the Brit spoke again. "I can understand you not wanting to give up your relatives. So tell us where we can find a PFLOAG nest."

Now Abdulla was on the spot. Up to this point everything that he had said was true, but now he either reported the Raythut location or he lied. News spreads easily on the mountains and probably by now lots of people knew that a government snatch squad had seized him and held him for interrogation. If suddenly the PFLOAG base at Raythut was to be attacked then it would be assumed that he had informed. His life and perhaps the lives of his family would then be in peril. "These people move about so often. Who knows where they are one day to the next?" He evaded the issue with a shrug.

The Brit leaned forward aggressively. "You do," he said. "You know exactly where they hide. Your son is one of the leaders and probably your whole family's *adoo* too."

"Because my eldest son fights for what he believes, then you think we all have those same beliefs?"

"Damn right. You're his father aren't you?" The implication was clear; a father influences a son.

"Then what of my second son who serves here on this very base in the Sultan's Armed Forces?"

Surprise registered on the Brit's face. He leaned back and glanced at the *askar* at his side. "You have a son in SAF?"

"Yes."

A lengthy conversation followed in English while they brought this unexpected development to the third man. The interrogators where obviously off balance and it seemed to Abdulla that a degree of argument was taking place. As they talked regular glances came in his direction and he curiously watched as he waited for their concerted decision. Eventually they became silent and returned their attention back to him. "What is your son's name?" the *askar* asked.

"Juma," Abdulla gave it.

More English followed. Then the Brit began to gather the papers on the table and with a glance towards the man by the door he instructed him to return Abdulla to his cell.

He came across to where he sat and taking him roughly by the arm began to drag him away "What have you done with my other son, Hamed?" Abdulla demanded as he was pulled away. No one even bothered to glance in his direction.

Back in the same cell once more Abdulla sat down dejectedly. He was worried about Hamed. He had no way of knowing whether he had been questioned or not. By the way the interrogators had been tripped by the news about Juma he guessed that perhaps he hadn't. When his turn did come, as inevitably it would, he hoped that he would have the good sense not to reveal the location of the PFLOAG group in Raythut. If he did he would unwittingly place all of them in a great deal of danger. But locked and isolated in the cell then there was absolutely nothing he could do to warn him.

Several hours later he was brought once again to the interview room. This time there were only two interrogators, the non-Arabic speaking Brit was absent. He sat in the same chair and had to endure a protracted conversation in English while he was wholly ignored. Eventually the British man decided to address him.

"Well, Al Hamer Jabally," he said. "We have talked to your son Juma and we are almost convinced that you are not a PFLOAG sympathiser. But," he added firmly, "not completely. For the time being we are going to let you go. However, don't think that we are going to forget you. If we have the slightest reason to suspect that you are *adoo* then we will definitely come for you again. In the meantime you are to pass a message to your *adoo* son. He is to cease inciting treachery immediately and surrender himself to this base within twenty-eight days. If he does then we will be lenient with him. If he doesn't surrender in that time then he will be placed on our execution list." He waited allowing time for the last words to sink in.

"I may not see him in time," Abdulla protested.

Disbelief glinted in the man's eyes and he scoffed loudly. "Then you had better make sure that you do." He began collecting the papers together on the desk. "Twenty-eight days only," he warned. "Now go!"

Abdulla looked around hardly daring to believe that he had been dismissed, but the man by the door opened it and stood back. He got to his feet slowly. "What about my other son, Hamed?"

"He's gone," the *askar* informed him. "Left a couple of hours ago."

When he got outside the sun was high and the day hot. So successful had the disorientating tactics been that he had no idea even which day it was. He approached the chicaned barbed wire barrier at the entrance a little nervously, half expecting to be prevented from leaving even at this stage. But the guards in the sandbagged sangars watched only mildly interested and allowed him to pass out of the base without challenge. When a few metres clear, he glanced back. The distance although not great was still too far for him to see clearly. As far as he could tell, however, no one was coming after him. Just in case he hurried his steps.

Hamed called to him and he turned to the direction of his voice. Vaguely, he could see the shapes of two men beneath a nearby tree getting to their feet and coming towards him.

"Hamed?"

"Yes father."

When they were near he could make out his second son Juma as well.

"Juma," he said pleasantly surprised.

"Hello Father. Are you well?"

"*Il hamdu lillaah.*"

"What happened?"

Abulla shrugged. "At first they accused me of being *adoo* and then asked a lot of questions. But it was Mussalim they really wanted."

"Yes," Juma agreed. "They brought me in too and asked me where Mussalim could be found. I don't know where he is. So I couldn't tell them even if I had wanted too. Then they asked me when I had seen him last. The British man became very angry when I told that it was at my wedding six months ago. He said that I should have turned him in. How could I turn my own brother in?" he petitioned. "Besides that he was my guest and therefore I was his *Rabia,* so I could not. He didn't understand. I think the Omani officer explained our ways to him."

"They have no honour these Christians," Abdulla said shaking his head.

"Then the Britisher asked why I hadn't reported that my brother was a PFLOAG Commissar. Then they accused me of being a PFLOAG spy."

"Does this make trouble for you?"

"I don't know. Perhaps not, I think I convinced them that I wasn't a spy. They checked my record and found it good and then they seemed to accept my story that Mussalim is the only one in the family that is revolutionist. Especially when I explained that it was only since his return from Bahrain that he has become so radical."

"What about you Hamed? What did you tell them?" Abdulla asked anxiously.

Hamed shrugged. "Nothing very much. They asked where those camels came from."

"What did you say."

"The truth. They were gifts from Fiad."

Abdulla nodded with satisfaction. It corroborated his story.

"Then they asked if he were PFLOAG," Hamed went on. Then they wanted to know where they could find Mussalim. I told them that I didn't know, but I don't think they believed me. Then they asked questions about Juma." He glanced sideways at his brother.

"What sort of questions?" Juma asked

"Where you were? How long you had been in SAF? Why did you join the Sultan's army? Things like that." He looked at his father. "They said that you had told them where they could find a PFLOAG cell."

Abdulla shook his head. "I didn't."

"They asked me to tell them too, just to confirm what you had told them."

"It was a trick. What did you say?" Abdulla asked anxiously.

He shrugged again. "I told them that those people move around constantly and one never knows where they are from one day to the next."

Abdulla grinned with relief. It might have been a rehearsed answer. It was almost identical to the answer he had given to the same question. He glanced away across the plain towards the distant towering jebal. It would be a long and a tiring walk home. "We should start our journey home," he said looking at Juma. "It will be dark by the time we get home."

"Yes," Juma agreed.

"Is Khamisa well?"

"Yes she is."

"When will I become a Grandfather."

"Juma grinned. "Next spring I think."

Abdulla grinned also and hugged his son. "Jokha will be happy." Perhaps this was the very reason that Allah had brought him to Salalah, to learn this news, he thought. Certainly apart from the contemptuous treatment they had received and the inconvenience it seemed that no apparent harm occurred.

⁕ ⁕ ⁕

Two weeks later, however, Juma arrived at the jebal home with Khamisa and all their meagre belongings loaded onto three borrowed camels. Juma's sudden re-location to the remote outpost at Manston was imminent. Situated as it was isolated on the *nejd* midway between Salalah and the Yemen border the opportunities for him to return to Khamisa in Salalah would be strictly limited. He had, therefore, decided it was more desirable for her to move to his father's home than to remain in Salalah alone. Conditions would be cramped but that couldn't be helped.

His father and Hamed helped him to unload the camels and carry their belongings into the room in which Lailla and Hamed slept. Hamed moved his own effects to the dilapidated woodshed and his opinion of that imposition was transmitted in silent disapproval.

Abdulla sensing his youngest son's discontent looked for a way to placate him and new quarters was the obvious answer. The three of them now stood before the remnants of the original bucolic stone house. The walls, once a metre and a half high and sealed together with wet sand for mortar had long ago tumbled inwards and all that remained was a circular pile of stones and rocks. They gazed at the rubble pensively considering its merit. There was none. The unanimous decision was that there was no part of the original construction that could be recovered. If it were to be turned once more into a shelter then it would have to be completely rebuilt. The only consolation was that the stones and rocks were assembled in one place.

"Three weeks," Abdulla suggested glancing at Hamed.

He said nothing staring at the pile of rocks realising fully that it would be he who would have to do the major share of the work and this in addition to the usual daily chores that demanded his attention.

"At least it will give Khamisa some kind of home and a bit of privacy when you visit," he went on this time addressing Juma.

Juma shook his head sadly. "I can't see much chance of visits. This is PFLOAG country and I am an *askar*." He sat on a nearby rock dejectedly. He was in effect at the very point of becoming separated from his wife and for all of the foreseeable future. There was little doubt in his mind that his sudden posting to the remote outpost had much to do with the Army's discovery that his brother was a Commissar in the insurgent movement. He was probably considered to be a security risk, albeit unfairly. Someone had decided that it would be prudent to send him to the remote base at Manston where little of significance happened. Therefore there could be little of significance to report, even if there were anyone that he could find to report to.

He gazed despondently at the pile of rubble experiencing feelings of shame and inadequacy. Khamisa had lived in a pleasant family home before she married him. Not luxuriant but in comparison generally comfortable. Now to his shame he had brought her to this. A wall of circled stones with a roof of sticks and straw in the hoary style of a mountain home was the best she could expect. And worse he was about to desert her to this situation.

His first reaction to the posting had been that he would leave the army. But if he did, what then? He still needed money to improve their lot especially with a child on the way and the army was still his best chance. Khamisa had suggested that she return to her father's home while he was away. However, he had flatly rejected that, it was not an option. To him it would be the ultimate shame upon him as a husband. Having failed to provide for his wife he had then returned her to her father. Khamisa had then suggested that she sell her dowry of gold. But here again Juma had given the suggestion a flat refusal. That also would be an affront to his pride. As he saw the situation his best chance was to accept his lot no matter how distasteful and once again save his money diligently until he could afford the materials needed to construct a more suitable home. This whole situation, he thought angrily could be laid entirely at Mussalim's feet. It was his radical viewpoint, his revolutionary actions that were sending him to Manston. Perhaps if Mussalim did surrender himself over to the authorities then he might yet still avoid this 'sentence' to the wilderness. That was unlikely, however, Juma knew his brother too well. Having achieved such a prestigious rank then to tamely surrender would reflect an enormous loss of face. His pride would never allow him to accept it.

"Did you pass the ultimatum to Mussalim?" He asked his father, clutching for straws.

"We tried. Hamed and I went the next day to Raythut to see him, but we were told that he has now been sent east to the Samhan Mountains. We left a message with his friend Ali and he promised to get it to him."

Abdulla watched Juma dejectedly look away across the hills. His depression was evident. Abdulla, however, was hopeful that this situation could yet work in his favour and bring his second son home. With Khamisa living here and Juma estranged at

Manston with little or no opportunity to visit it may only be a matter of time before Juma decided enough, and left the army. 'Please Allah,' he added in thought. "We will start on the house tomorrow," he said placing a consoling hand on Juma's shoulder and glancing at Hamed for assurance.

Hamed said nothing but glanced back over his shoulder towards the sound of women's laughter. He felt the crushing burden of responsibility. His father's eyesight was getting worse and although still the head of the family he was now little more than his helper. Now the welfare of Juma's woman was about to be added to his load too. More than that he was the one shuffled out into the wood store to sleep. He felt singular unappreciated and he resented the selfish way that both elder brothers pursued their own interests leaving him with responsibilities which should be theirs. Nor had anyone even bothered to ask him how he felt about it.

Khamisa laughed with amusement at Lailla's antics and looked away towards the three men standing before the pile of rocks. Her husband sat with his back to her, his shoulders slumped betraying his melancholy. Her smiles faded as she empathised the disappointment that he was feeling as a result of his transfer from Um Al Gharriff.

She knew it was not so much the relocation that depressed him it was more that he was forced to abandon her. Faced with a long separation she felt precisely the same disappointment. However, at the same time she also felt exalted, for she had no right to expect her husband to concern himself so much over her plight. Her duty was simply to do as he said and wait for him to tell her otherwise.

Truly she had been fortunate in her marriage as not only did she have a young and handsome man for her husband but also one who was considerate and attentive too. Whenever he left her for duty she counted the hours into minutes waiting impatiently for his return. When he returned there was nothing she tried to do except to endear herself to him attempting to anticipate and satisfy his every desire. But when it was time to lay at his side that was the best time of all. The lust that she felt for his beautiful body could not be proper and was surely sinful, so she attempted to disguise it. However, by astutely holding her body to his and by subtle casual touches he was easily aroused and the lust seeming to be his sin.

She was more than a little nervous about being left here with people who were strangers to her and in an environment that she didn't understand. But if that is what Juma wanted her to do then she would do it and willingly. There was no doubt however that it was going to be hard. She was sure she would quickly relate to her new family, even the hostile and surly Hamed. The pending long separation, however, with no envisioned end was daunting.

~ 14 ~

October 1970 • A hot wind crossed the open *gatn* rustling the long narrow leaves of the large Zakir tree as it passed through its branches. The tree grew on the top of the hill overlooking the village Aqarhanawt and was the favourite gathering point for the villagers. Mussalim sat cross-legged in the shade of its canopy facing a circle of about thirty men. In his hands he held a Fabrique Nationale self-loading rifle. He examined it closely for comfort and balance before cocking it. Then squinting down its sights he squeezed the trigger. The hammer fell on an empty chamber with a loud metallic click.

"Nice," he said nodding approvingly as he handed it back to the man sitting at his side.

"We have many such weapons," Salim Mubarak, a leader of the Dhofar Liberation Front said as he took the weapon from him.

Mussalim glanced around the circle of men before him, every man possessed such a weapon. Only Musabbah and himself were unarmed having left their own Kalichnikovs secured in their camel's saddle packs. This was Mussalim's first meeting with the DLF and the task given to him by Abdel Tahir was to persuade its members to merge with the much larger PFLOAG. There had been several meetings in the past but the leaders of the smaller group had stubbornly resisted embracing the PFLOAG communist philosophy. The parade of so much weaponry, Mussalim appreciated, was intended to let the two PFLOAG men know that they were not defenceless and would not allow themselves to be intimidated.

It was now the autumn of the year and two months since Mussalim had moved to this eastern sector. This assignment was proving decidedly harder than his previous one. The situation in this eastern area was far more complex than the Qara. Abdel Tahir's task as commander of the sector was without doubt an unenviable one.

His headquarters were established at Jibjat, the very heartland of the Mahru tribe. These particular Mahru people had split themselves from their Yemen tribal area generations ago travelled east and formed an isolated island of Mahru on the open *gatn* right in the midst of Kathiri country. By now well established and accepted they were nevertheless fiercely independent and brooked no interference by any of the neighbouring tribes. Although mostly supporting the PFLOAG movement they insisted on appointing their own leaders and did not recognise Abdel Tahir, a man from a Kathir tribe as the area commander. Instead their leader had placed himself directly beneath Al Ghassani. Consequently if Abdel wanted the Mahrus to participate in any offensive then he had to approach tactfully and request assistance. If their leaders showed reluctance then he had to appeal directly to Al Ghassani and even then their participation might be less that enthusiastic.

Twenty-five kilometres to the south of Jibjat on the edge of the spectacular Wadi Darbat was the village of Al Haq. Al Haq was the centre of the Mashani tribe of the Kathiri. Queen Mizoon, Said Bin Taymour's wife was born Mashani and therefore her son Qaboos, now the Sultan, had roots in that tribe. The Mashani now saw themselves as related to the Sultan and as such they were now reluctant to continue this war against their number one son. Only the most ardent Mashani PFLOAG supporters advocated the continuation of hostilities.

In the east at the coastal town Mirbat and the Samhan Mountains above Bait Umr were the predominant tribe. Although they were still solidly with the movement at this stage their deputy leader Amr Qassim was advocating a wait and see policy to give the new Sultan time to implement some of the promises that he was making.

In the midst of all this were the remnants of the Dhofar Liberation Front, which had been founded by Sheikh Mussalim Bin Nufl at the very onset of the insurgency. They stubbornly followed their own policies and pursued their own objectives only occasionally joining the PFLOAG in joint operations.

Abdel Tahir it seemed presided over a crumbling incumbency. The only area that did not create headaches for him was in the far eastern sector of the Zalawt plain. His able lieutenant Qartoob Ahmed effectively controlled the whole area beyond Mirbat right out as far as the small fishing town, Sadh. The plains airfield at Juffar had long ago been abandoned by the Sultan's Air Force as undefendable and that whole vast sector then surrendered to the PFLOAG forces.

Surrounded by all this discord it was hardly surprising that Abdel had resorted to forceful and heavy-handed methods to impose PFLOAG discipline. Because of these parochial attitudes Mussalim's attempts to rally the different factions unreservedly behind the cause had so far been ineffective. The support for the main objectives was still undoubtedly there, however it was the perceived routes to achieve those objectives that wildly differed and obstructed any progress towards unity. Abdel Tahir's supercilious expressions and 'I told you so,' attitude did nothing constructive to help Mussalim. Abdel saw himself as a professional soldier and as commander expected instant obedience to his instructions, not open discussions. However, he got full support only rarely and basically he was powerless to impose his will on tribal leaders. So he took every opportunity to disparage un-co-operative leaders attempting to undermine their authority and hoping that eventually they would be replaced. Among the ordinary jaballys his heavy-handed methods and rule of fear commanded much more support. Loyal regulars and voluntary militia formed the backbone and iron fist of his constabulary. Other militia pressed to volunteer their services had done so because they feared the consequences of not co-operating. Even the non-combatant jabally's were expected to act as spies and front sympathisers. Tahir's hard-core lieutenants enforced his rule by delivering severe punishments for disobedience and concluded misdemeanours. Kangaroo courts dispensed physical torture and executions with increasing regularity.

Here also Mussalim's attempts to mediate some of these extreme actions had failed. Abdel's patience had long ago dried up and as far as he was concerned fear and repression were the only effective methods left. Therefore he not only supported these actions but he encouraged them. On the surface these methods appeared to be holding the order together, beneath the surface, however, resentment and discontent simmered.

Frustrated by DLF non-compliant attitude Abdel had decided to solve this particular problem by arresting and executing the movement's leaders. To this end his plans were well advanced. He calculated that by removing the stubborn leaders the rank and file would soon come over to the PFLOAG. He confidently anticipated that by witnessing their leaders executions, fear would influence their decision. However, he had been instructed by Al Ghassani to give negotiations one final try and Mussalim had been sent to persuade this voluntary amalgamation.

Salim Mubarak handed the rifle to the man at his side without taking his eyes off Mussalim. "Your reputation proceeds you, Crazy Man Mussalim," he said.

Mussalim cringed inside yet again at the tag. "The actions that earned that reputation have been greatly exaggerated."

Salim nodded understandingly. He was a man perhaps in his early forties with a lean and wiry physique, typical of a man who eked a living in the mountains. Except for a moustache he was clean-shaven, his face thin and harshly lined. "We also were at Mirbat that day," he said. "Some did not return."

It was Mussalim's turn to nod understandably. "Some good men died that day."

"Yes. And this is why we consider very carefully before joining in with any PFLOAG actions. We prefer to fight this war our own way."

"Which is?"

He shrugged. "Sabotage, hit and run attacks, those kind of tactics. Anything that will keep our casualties low."

"Unfortunately those kind of tactics will not clear the Sultan's soldiers out of Dhofar," Mussalim pointed out.

"It could," he replied. "If we hit them often enough and inflict many casualties then the Sultan and his men may decide that to keep Dhofar is just a too heavy price to pay."

"There is no guarantee that will work and even if it does it will take a very long time."

"No government can ever win against terrorist tactics. Sooner or later this government will come to the point where they will accept that and will be forced to negotiate and make concessions."

"Concessions will not bring liberation to Dhofar."

He shrugged. *"Inshaalah,"*

"The way of the PFLOAG is the better way." Mussalim said. "Consider the vast territory we now hold. Areas that government troops dare not move into. We are forcing them into ever shrinking pockets. It needs only an increase in the pressure to squeeze these pockets out of existence. Trap them all in Salalah and the complete withdrawal cannot be that far away. Even the troops are made up mostly from men from the north and Baluchis who have no particular interest in this region. If we make it unpleasant for them many of them will leave without waiting for a withdrawal. You have good leaders and many good fighters, you should join us and help hasten that day."

"Then what?"

"Then the region is free."

"Free?" he snorted. "What freedom is there under the PFLOAG?" He sighed and placed his hand on Mussalim's arm. "My friend. You have a reputation of being a fair man. What you achieved in the Qara is well known among all mountain men but we could never join your cause. We are good Muslims and dutifully make our prayers. To join your cause we would have to turn our backs to Allah or suffer PFLOAG consequences. What freedom is there in that?" He stared hard at Mussalim.

Mussalim didn't answer. Salim had unwittingly placed him in an area where he could not admit that there was personal agreement. The man's dark eyes seemed to pierce through to his innermost thoughts and read his most guarded secret. The silence protracted as Salim waited for him to respond. He flicked a glance towards Musabbah, then as if sensing Mussalim's predicament he went on.

"Our sole objective is the liberation of Dhofar and when that is achieved we will turn our energies to making it a better place to live. But the PFLOAG philosophy is completely different. This region is only the first step for you. From here your intend to press on northwards and take the rest of the country. Do you think the Sultan doesn't know that? He cannot afford to withdraw from here. He *has* to stay and fight. No my friend our way is better. Through negotiations he will eventually hand over independence knowing that he can safely withdraw northwards secure in the knowledge that we make no further threat. So you see it is PFLOAG who should be joining us."

Mussalim smiled inwardly, this man was a clever negotiator. He had outlined Mussalim's own personal philosophy. He too had no personal ambitions beyond Dhofar independence. They shared the same opinions and the same beliefs and it now occurred to him that perhaps it was he who should be joining the DLF. He liked this man but if he didn't win this argument then Salim and the rest of the DLF leaders would probably find themselves facing PFLOAG execution.

The discussion protracted into the afternoon with just about every man in attendance giving his point of view. Mussalim and Musabbah argued long and strenuously attempting to convince the members to come across to the PFLOAG movement. Mussalim realising that they were making no progress towards convincing any of them and so in desperation he suggested some compromises that he might be prepared to put before Al Ghassani for consideration. All to no avail. Eventually he was forced to accept failure.

Salim accompanied him as he left the *dirwain* and walked wearily back to his camel. "That was important to you wasn't it?" he queried as they shook hands.

"Yes it was."

"*Inshaallah*," he said. "You must learn to accept the will of Allah. If it not his will that the two movements unite it is because he has different paths for us to follow." Then with a departing grin he turned and walked away towards the village.

"We did our best," Musabbah said consolingly as they watching him walk away.

Mussalim sighed and looked at the man he had brought with him to the eastern region as his assistant. He would have preferred to have brought Ali but in the end had decided that Ali was the man that he could trust completely to continue his Qara initiative without making radical changes. "We did our best." he agreed. "But I fear the consequences of our failure," he added staring after Salim Mubarak.

Ten days later Abdel Tahir took a force of PFLOAG regulars to arrest Salim Mubarak and the rest of the DFL leaders. He was met with stubborn resistance and a bloody battle took place. Out-numbered and out gunned Salim and the remnants of his movement fled to the coastal town of Mirbat and surrendered to the government forces there. Although the offensive had not turned out quite the way Abdel had hoped he took consolation in the fact that he had removed an independent force from his area. In so doing he had removed a challenge to his authority and increased his own dominance.

Mussalim was angry, to him Abdel had completely neutralised an ally.

* * *

January 1971 • Juma sat in the front seat of the Land Rover between the driver and the snoozing British passenger as the vehicle bounced along the rough *nejd* terrain. The road he could see just a few yards to his right, but the whole of the small convoy ignored it. The driver concentrated on running in the tracks left by the vehicle in front, he knew there would be no mines there. Tucked in Juma's pocket was a seven day pass and permission to visit Salalah. It was his first time off the isolated Manston base, since he arrived there in autumn five months ago and he had managed to get himself a seat in this supply convoy returning to Salalah. He had been placed in this vehicle with the CAD logo written on the side.

What CAD stood for at that time he had no idea but during the first hour of the journey when conversation had been lively he had learned that it stood for Civil Action Development. The British man speaking excellent Arabic had explained it was a newly formed scheme by Sultan Qaboos to find ways of improving conditions for the Dhofari people. Many possibilities had been identified such as establishing clinics manned by doctors, wells to increase water supplies, markets for jebal cattle and veterinary services all free of charge and widely available. Every idea or suggestion was given careful consideration. The initiative was simple. Give the people what they wanted, better conditions and their reason for insurgency was removed. To this end construction had already began on a hospital in Salalah and clinics were established at Taqa and Mirbat. Wells on the Salalah plain, which Said Bin Taymour had destroyed as punishment, had been re-drilled and plans to establish government farms growing animal fodder were advanced. Things were on the move to improve living conditions in the area.

The major problem, however, was to how implement these improvements in the PFLOAG controlled no-go areas. For CAD teams to venture into jebal areas they would need heavy government protection. That protection would be unlikely to prevent attacks by the *adoo* forces who would certainly see it as invasion. Even if they were successful and managed to develop some kind of improvement it would in all probability be destroyed as soon as they moved on. For the time being CAD had to be content to chip away around the edges winning over the people dwelling on the perimeters of PFLOAG control.

Qaboos had demonstrated the sincerity of his intentions by issuing a decree of amnesty to all PFLOAG fighters who came in and surrendered to government forces. It was hoped that this along with the current developments and announcements of further improvements would satisfy the people enough to cease hostilities and to give him the opportunity to deliver his promises. The response, however, had so far been disappointing, only a tiny trickle had taken the offer. The reason undoubtedly was that once a man surrendered then he would be unable to return to the jebal and *adoo* areas. So in effect he would become imprisoned within Salalah precincts.

All this Juma had learned from the British man who seemed to have some organisational role to play in the plan. Now after exhausting the topic he had nodded off.

Left alone with his thoughts Juma went over his own plan once more. He had no intention of staying in Salalah for the duration of his pass. At this slow lumbering rate the convoy would arrive at Um Al Gharriff around nightfall. Then he would book in at the guardroom where he would be allocated a bed in the transit room for the duration of his leave. Tomorrow he intended to discard his uniform and journey home to be with his wife Khamisa. As a soldier of the Sultan it would be foolish to advertise his presence in *adoo* country so any contact with other people would have to be avoided as much as possible. Even after reaching home he would have to conceal his presence as much as possible. A well-meaning friend could pass a casual remark in the wrong company and bring a band of PFLOAG fighters down on him. Neither could he declare his intention to his own side, his superiors would certainly prevent him from going. It was a high-risk situation and he would be strictly on his own. He realised fully that it was a very foolish position in which to place himself but his desire to be with Khamisa was an all-consuming motivator.

The convoy did not stop and by mid afternoon it descended from the cliffs overlooking the sea to the long silver beach at Mugsahyl. From there it followed a laboured route eastwards a little way off the beach. By the time it reached the concertina wire of Salalah the sun had turned the colour of gold and was low in the western sky. Inside the relative safety of the town compound they picked up a little speed and soon arrived at the garrison.

The first thing that Juma noticed inside the garrison was a small tent city had sprung up just inside the gates since he left.

"BATT!" the British man said noticing his curious stare.

"BATT?"

"British Army Training Team," he explained. "Another Sultan initiative. He has asked the British to provide a specialised team to train his anti-guerrilla squad. The Firqats," he added seeing Juma's baffled expression.

Juma nodded understanding, Training was most certainly needed in that squad. The Firqats had been an ineffective force and seen as something of a joke among professional soldiers. Made up from jebally volunteers they did little to earn their pay mostly staying within the safe compounds of Salalah. Occasionally they would patrol in the jebal usually spend the time in hiding before returning to the comparative security of the garrisoned town. It had even been known for PFLOAG members to infiltrate the Firqats and this had resulted in at least one ambush of a patrol relaxing in hiding.

"SAS Special Forces and the cream of the British army there," he went on proudly his tone indicating that Juma should be aware of that.

Sitting as he was in the middle, the tents soon disappeared from Juma's view leaving him reflecting that they would need to be special if they were going to turn the Firqats into an effective force.

The next morning early, Juma left Salalah and made his way on foot across the plain. He wore an old faded *futa* wrapped around his waist and an old cloth slung across his shoulders. His feet were bare as was his head and his hair was rubbed down deliberately untidy. He carried only a cane. The type that any jebally would use not only to drive livestock but also as a walking stick. He intended to avoid any sort of human contact if he could but if he were spotted then he wanted to pass as just another jebally going about his business.

He rejected the Shair valley as his passage up onto the jebal reasoning that it was a well travelled route. Instead he took the large gaping ravine of the next wadi, Arbot. Because of its deep base and sheer sides this wadi offered few exit places so only people who needed to travel its long length used it. Stunted Ghaf trees thickly covered its base and even eked an existence in the lower reaches of the rock walls. A wildly meandering path wound through the trees along the wadi base. As a precaution Juma ignored the path picking out instead a concealed route among the thick trees well to the side and above. This route was considerably slower as rocks and trees barred his way continually, forcing him to either climb or to retrace his steps and find alternative paths.

Around mid morning he rested, gazing up at the sheer rock walls guessing at his position. They were significantly less high than they had been so he anticipated that very soon he would be able to climb out of the wadi and turn back to the south east which would take him home. It was then that he thought he heard voices. He listened intently and at first heard nothing then unmistakably he heard them again. He swung his feet over the rock on which he sat and crouched down behind. Gradually, the voices became louder as they drew nearer. Though a clear view was denied to him because of the thickness of trees he could see a small party of men leading two camels moving along the path a few metres away. Two or three of the men wore faded sand coloured jackets, part uniform of the PFLOAG and on one of the animal's back he caught sight of a wide metal tube. In all probability a mortar! Feeling vulnerable he clutched his cane tightly and wished it were a rifle.

He waited a long time after they had passed before he emerged from behind the rock. Then he still sat there hardly daring to move wondering if there was an even bigger party of guerrillas ahead. There was little doubt that the intention of those men would be to launch some bombs at a Salalah installation. Perhaps the airfield! Probably sometime last night under the cover of darkness they had crept to within range of their target laid down the mortar plate then hid it under sand or brush. Now they moved up the weapon and tonight some place would get shelled. The question was, as a government soldier what should he do about it? There was nothing he could do, he decided. If he re-traced his steps then there was a possibility that he might stumble into them, with dire personal consequences. Even if he didn't he had no idea where they were going to fire from and there would be some awkward questions to answer about being on the jebal alone after he had made his report. He consoled himself that in all probability they would fire a dozen shells at the most them make a hasty retreat before either the Salalah artillery found their position or quick reaction patrols fell upon them. At the worst there might be a few holes in the runway tomorrow morning. They wouldn't get near enough to hit the technical site or the accommodation area. To do that they would have to advance a long way from their jebal safe ground. Best thing to do was to ignore it, he convinced himself. Then with even more caution than before he continued his journey.

A little over three hours later he crested the hill and looked down on his father's farm. Except for the cattle grazing and moving slowly forward seeking tastier morsels nothing moved. Probably everyone was sleeping. A low circular building with stone walls and a thatch roof now stood at the side of the larger square one. His father and Hamed it seemed had completed the traditional style bucolic jebal house for Khamisa. His wife would probably be inside and she too might be asleep. He smiled to himself imagining Khamisa's surprise when he woke her. He descended the hill quickly.

He glanced towards the old wood shed as he passed, it had definitely deteriorated and looked in even more danger of imminent collapse that it had ever done. Hamed emerged from beneath its sagging roof, his arms full of logs.

"Juma," he said the surprise registering on his face. He glanced around as if expecting him to be accompanied by a small army.

Juma grinned at him. "Peace be with you Hamed," he said with a happy grin, but he made no movement towards his brother. Khamisa had emerged from the doorway of the circular dwelling staring towards him and he hastened in her direction. She was heavily pregnant, nevertheless as he neared she ran into his arms with a squeal of delight.

∗ ∗ ∗

Hamed stood and watched the pair as they hugged kissed and then entwined in each other's arms went inside their home. In his desire to be with his woman Juma had barely acknowledged him and he felt snubbed. Much more than that, however, the way Khamisa had thrown herself at him aroused a rage inside of him and jealousy burned in his chest. He let go of the logs he was holding and allowed them to spill on the floor. 'They could fetch their own logs,' he thought petulantly. He stared stone faced at the agrarian building that he had built for her. The blisters, the skinned fingers and the backache it had cost him. He thought that she had appreciated it and now she was using it as a nest of love for his brother. He knew his rage was unreasonable because they were husband and wife, nevertheless wasn't it he who had done everything for her these past months? Where had Juma been during this time? Following his own pursuits and neglecting her! It had fallen onto him to make her comfortable and to look after her. How quickly everything that he had done was forgotten. He imagined what was happening inside and he tried to think of some excuse to go into the house and interrupt their canoodling,

The first week she had been at the farm he had mostly ignored her, seeing her simply as yet another expectation placed upon him without any consultation. The fact that she slept in the house while he was evicted out to the woodshed amongst the cockroaches and mice did little to sweeten his attitude towards her. As far as he was concerned she was an unwelcome imposition, an addition to his burden.

He started work on building the house quite early on. However, it was not because he wanted to make things better for her it was purely from a selfish aspect. The sooner it was finished the sooner he could return to his own cot in the house. As he worked, however, Khamisa came to his side whenever she could to lend what limited assistance she could. Often she would rise early complete her domestic chores and spend her spare time helping. At the beginning she carried the rocks and laid them close by but Jokha scolded her reminding her of her condition and stopped that. She had then to content herself with passing things to him, holding things steady, and keeping him supplied with water.

Despite his early resentment he had very quickly warmed to her friendliness and genial personality. Seemingly genuinely at ease in his company she worked at his side wearing a simple cotton dress without any facial restriction. Instantly he was aware of her striking beauty and as he worked he watched her clandestinely. The graceful movements of her body stirred unfamiliar feelings in his stomach. Her long black hair teased by the jebal winds added fire to those feelings and the accommodating smile that put a twinkle in her dark eyes whenever she caught him watching her fuelled that fire. Later on when it was time to mortar all the gaps and cracks with wet sand they sat close together talking quietly as they worked. In these close moments he ached just to touch her and when he found the excuse to do so she didn't object. Thatching time to him was the best time of all. They needed to work in close harmony and physical contact was at its most. There were endless opportunities for him to touch her even on to lifting her occasionally to the apex to place brush and palms in position. The feel of her young thighs and ribs through the thin dress churned ravages of desire through his every fibre. Although he knew it was forbidden to covet his brother's wife, he wanted her and he wanted her desperately.

Too soon the house was finished. To prolong the intimate contact between them he then found a hundred minor improvements that needed to be done. She tried to repay his attention with kindness of her own, doing whatever she could to lighten his load not only with the house construction but also the routine work of running the farm. When the endless detail was eventually completed and she occupied the dwelling, he still sought ways to please her. He brought her fresh milk, stacked logs at her door, and even filled her water butt from the well. Woman's work!

Now she had forgotten so easily and his endeavours counted for nothing. Once again he felt himself to be just the general help around the place and singularly unappreciated. He decided to take himself away for a while. To retreat to his place on the plateau high above the pass and just leave them all to look after themselves. In a black mood he saddled the camel hastily. Then with a vicious slap with his cane down the animal's neck he drove it at a gallop up the hill. He crested the hill urging the beast to go faster scattering the rocks on his mother's grave as he galloped over it.

❊ ❊ ❊

Khamisa lay in the darkness listening to the quiet snores of her husband. His arm lay heavily across her shoulder and she clutched it tightly to her chest with a sigh. She tried to fight away sleep not wishing to waste a moment now that he was with her. She had missed him, his close attention, his concern for her happiness and most of all his tender lovemaking. The ache for him was permanent and it never went far away. The worst time by far, were the long nights alone in her bed and tears often sent her eventually to sleep. She cursed this war and prayed to Allah to end it. But the PFLOAG were winning and while Juma remained a soldier he could never return to Qara.

Everyone in her new family had been kind to her and there was absolutely nothing that she could complain of on that score. Jokha had readily accepted her as a daughter. She had been attentive and protective, although at times over fussy about her activities due to her condition. Abdulla had been more restrained as one would expect from the family head, however, he always made sure that her welfare was taken care of. Lailla was much more than a sister, she was her best friend too. They spent a lot of time together particularly in the evenings when Khamisa remained in her house. Indeed sensing that she was lonely missing Juma and in need of company Lailla often stayed the night there. Even the surly Hamed had warmed to her.

She had recognised that for a man so young he shouldered a great deal of responsibility. Realising that she relied upon him completely to construct her house she had felt morally bound to lend whatever assistance she could. Besides that, her help marginal though it may be, hastened the day she would move in and gain a degree of privacy. The project had been good for them both. It had broken down his barrier of resentment that she sensed toward her and developed a more familiar and harmonious relationship. Beneath Hamed's indifferent surly veneer she found a generous and accommodating side to his nature. She valued him greatly not only as a brother but as a caring friend too.

She smiled to herself as she felt the infant stir inside her, it gave her the excuse to wake her sleeping husband.

"Juma, Wake up." She pulled his hand down on to her belly. "Feel your baby moving."

Juma woke instantly with some alarm. "What's the matter?"

"Can you feel it?"

He raised himself on one elbow and felt the movement beneath his fingers. "Yes. Yes I can."

"That's your baby."

"Does it hurt?"

"Of course not, silly."

"What does it feel like to have something alive growing inside of you?"

Khamisa sighed. "Wonderful," she said. It's part of you in there and part of me. It's ours we created it."

He sniffed in the dark and she raised her hand to his face and felt a tear drop on his cheek. "What's the matter?"

"Nothing, I just feel – I don't know, humble."

"Humble?"

"Allah has bestowed all his blessings upon me. He gave you to me and now we are to have a child."

She pulled his head down to rest on her breast and pressed his hand on her stomach covering the infant within. Tears stung her eyes also, she felt exulted that her man valued her so.

✳ ✳ ✳

February 1971 • It was the first time Mussalim had ever been into Taqah. He stood with Musabbah on its hot dusty street and stared back towards the jebal eight kilometres away across the plain. Many times in recent weeks he had stood up there and surveyed the town. Uneven rows of square flat roofed buildings lined the street on one side while on the beach side, shanty dwellings. Now from much closer he could see just how squalid and overcrowded those dwellings were. Even the aroma in the air suggested destitution, rotting fish mingling with the stench of sewage and made the place a paradise for flies. Squatting on the rock above all this slum the Old Castle dominated the town with thug like authority. Taqah had many PFLOAG supporters and despite the presence of Government soldiers in the castle Front fighters needed only thin disguise to move around its streets freely. The town was a major food and medical supply source for the PFLOAG.

Mussalim's original detail to this eastern sector had been to implement a copy of the system that he had successfully constructed on Qara. However, Abdel Tahir saw little advantage in that kind of set-up and Mussalim's role had downgraded to little more than arms trainer. Because this did not keep him particularly busy Abdel also used him as general factotum. On this day he was to be spy. There had been reports recently of new British forces in both Taqah and Mirbat and Abdel had despatched Mussalim from his training task in Darbat to see what he could find.

They stood in the clearing beneath the Taqah castle and stared up the rock face. There was not a breath of wind and the Sultan's flag hung limp from the fat prismatic tower. If there were another force in Taqah supporting the one already occupying the castle then it seemed reasonable to assume that they too billeted there.

"What shall we do?" He sought ideas from Musabbah.

"We could knock on the door and ask how many men they have inside."

Mussalim ignored the sarcasm. "We had better split up and find people to talk to."

"What do we want to know?"

"If there is a new British force present in the town? If so, why? How many? And what's their objective."

"Simple, Musabbah said with an easy grin. "And if we ask the wrong person we could find ourselves arrested.

"Then we need to be careful who we ask.

Musabbah snorted. "Wish I had my Kalachnikov," he said.

Mussalim also felt vulnerable wandering around a government occupied town unarmed. "I know what you mean, but that would have been a dead give-away. We would already have been arrested."

"Yes," he agreed sullenly. "Which way do you want to go?"

Mussalim shrugged. "I'll go that way," he said indicating toward the west. He glanced across the road towards a large palm tree. "I'll meet you over there under that tree in about three hours."

Musabbah nodded briefly then turned and sauntered away slowly up the street. Mussalim watched him for a few moments before turning in the opposite direction. He hadn't gone very far when he came to a small clearing. At the end a large imposing house with coconut palms at its rear. On either side were two more large houses, not as imposing but still far superior to any of the other dwellings in Taqah. It was the Sultan's flag hanging lifelessly from the corner of one of them that captured his attention. It suggested to him that here was another government post. He studied the house for a moment. Large, square, two storied with a flat roof. A heavy carved wooden door in the centre with shuttered windows either side and above. It was not fortified. Hardly likely to be a soldier's billet, he thought. Outside the door a black shrouded woman sat on the floor with a very young boy standing by her raised knee. Above her head was a wooden notice board on the wall. This gave him the excuse he needed to get closer. As he neared the woman looked up at him and spoke.

"Mussalim?"

He glanced down. She was covered completely by the *abeya* and he had not the vaguest idea who it could be. Full of caution and not wishing to give himself away he didn't reply.

She removed the cover from her head. "It's me, Jumaia."

"Jumaia?" He said blankly. Then "Jumaia." as recognition dawned. "What are you doing here?

"I live here."

"Here," he said indicating the house.

"No not here. In Taqah. This is the clinic."

Mussalim looked up at the building, "Clinic?"

"Yes clinic. I am waiting for the doctor to see my boy." She indicated a red and angry weeping sore on the boy's leg.

He looked closely at the boy for the first time, he was a least four. "Your boy?" he queried. The last time he had seen Jumaia was the night he left Jibjat for Hauf after the battle at Mirbat. That was two and half years ago and Jumaia didn't have a son then.

"My husband's son."

Now he understood. "Hello – ?"

"Salim," she provided.

"Hello Salim."

The door in front of him creaked open and a tall British soldier dressed in dark green combat fatigues filled the doorway. "I thought I heard voices," he said in English. "What can I do for you?"

Mussalim looked at Jumaia, it was clear she did not understand. "The boy has a bad leg," he provided the answer for her.

He glanced briefly at it. "Please come in." He held the door open for them to pass. "In future don't wait out there in the sun." It was clear that he had mistaken Mussalim as the boy's father. "Come in and sit in there," he indicated a room just inside the door. However, he turned away from that door and led the way into the room opposite.

Mussalim stood back allowing Jumaia and the boy to pass ahead of him while he took the opportunity to look down the darkened passage into the open courtyard beyond. Six or seven more British soldiers lounged on long forms in the shade of the high walls. Some were scantily dressed but all wore at least remnants of green uniform. A couple busied themselves cleaning weapons while the rest just sat leisurely talking. All, it appeared, had a mug of tea. This could only be the new British force that had been reported.

Mussalim followed Jumaia into the room. The medic had already lifted the boy onto the stretcher in the middle of the room.

"What's his name?" The medic asked.

"Salim."

"What have you been doing, Salim?" He asked at the same time offering the boy a sweet. "Hmm nasty," he said to himself as he examined the injury. "How did he do it?" Now he asked Mussalim.

Warning bells went off inside Mussalim, he needed to be very careful. Trusting that the Britisher didn't speak Arabic he passed the question to Jumaia. "On broken glass," he informed him.

"You should have brought him much sooner." He centred his attention cleaning the wound. Mussalim clandestinely studied his regimental shoulder badge, a winged sword. He committed it to memory, it might be important.

When the man finished cleaning he then soaked a swab in a golden brown solution. "This is going to sting, better hold him," he said to Mussalim. He passed the message to Jumaia and she took hold of the child.

When the wound was dressed he warned Mussalim to keep it clean and covered to keep the flies out. Then he handed him a strip of tablets and instructed him to see that the boy took one morning and night until they were all gone. Now he stood back and fixed Mussalim with a curious stare. "Where did you learn to speak English so well?"

"Bahrain," he lied.

"What were you doing up there?"

"Working," better to keep it vague.

He nodded thoughtfully. "Haven't seen you around here before."

"I am Bedu."

He waited for him to expand but Mussalim had no intention of obliging.

"You wouldn't like to work with me as an interpreter would you?" Mussalim's face must have betrayed his surprise. "Join a Firqat company and stay here in Taqah. The Sultan pays good money," he went on pressing the point.

Ironic! Mussalim thought. "This man has just offered a PFLOAG Commissar a position in the service of the Sultan. If only he knew."

"You have heard about the amnesty?" He paused, then fixing Mussalim with a searching look. "The Sultan has offered amnesty to any *adoo* that wants to come across."

Mussalim was jolted, perhaps he did know. He couldn't, he was guessing he decided. Either way this was not a situation where he should stay. "I'll think about it," he said scooping the boy up.

Jumaia led him, still carrying the boy down the dusty street and past the shanty shacks almost to the beach itself.

Here the stench of rotting fish was at its strongest. Sardines littered the beach in shoals where they had been tossed to dry and become camel food. The flies here were at their thickest. In front of a stack of haphazardly placed rusty oil drums she stopped. Battered and worn pieces of plywood leaned against the drums and were held in place with pieces of driftwood that had been collected from the beach. Another worn and sagging piece of plywood was placed across the top and held down by rocks. She pulled back the rag that hung down the front and indicated that he should sit inside.

"You live here?" Mussalim asked with incredulity. She didn't answer, but clearly she did. "Where is your husband?"

She shrugged. "Disappeared a year ago. Some say he was killed in an accident on the jebal, others say that he was taken away by the PFLOAG."

"How do you live?"

She shrugged "I do whatever I can. Some of the people here are kind. Sometimes they give me work and pay me with food. And there is never any shortage of fish on the beach." Mussalim glanced beachwards and imagined having to eat rotting sardines or dead fish washed ashore. "Landen, Salim's real mother, often visits and usually leaves a few rupees." She carried on. "We survive, Allah will provide."

Mussalim ducked under the low roof and sat inside the hovel. Jumaia had tried to make it comfortable inside. An old threadbare carpet lined the floor and there was no shortage of hand made cushions. "Where is Landen now?"

"She found a man to take her and she is looked after." She poured a little water from a jug into a small cup and handed it to him. "But he is old and didn't want her son. That's why I look after him."

"Why don't you go home to your father?"

"My father died two years ago. For a while my mother and I lived with my brother. But he has little and with extra to feed the strain was too much. So he soon arranged a marriage for me and I came here."

It seemed as if Jumaia had reaped misfortune in hordes. "May Allah bestow only good fortune on you all of your life," he muttered.

"What?"

"That was the last thing I said to you that night in Jibjat when I left."

"*Inshaallah*," she said without bitterness.

They talked for an hour mostly about their experiences in the interim period. Despite the annoying flies and the odious conditions he found that sitting there in her company and looking out across the beach at the breaking waves wasn't unpleasant. At one time she moved her cramped legs to a more comfortable position and as she did her black *abeya* caught on her other foot and dragged away, momentarily baring a shapely thigh. The memory of that night long ago when he had rested his hand on that same thigh passed through his mind. He resisted the strong urge to do so again. Unaware she adjusted her gown and unwittingly removed the temptation. He realised it would soon be time for him to go so he questioned her about the British soldiers. She couldn't tell him very much other than they had been there perhaps two months and apart from operating the clinic they seemed to do little except talk with the Taqah men. With kisses on both cheeks and all the money that he could spare he left her and made his way back to the palm tree to meet Musabbah.

When he got there Musabbah was already there and snoozed with his back resting against the knobby tree trunk. He became instantly alert when Mussalim neared. He settled down at his side and the two men shared their information. Musabbah's contribution was that the small British force was there to recruit locals into the Sultan's Firqat. Those that had joined had been sent by Dhow further up the coast to Mirbat for training. Since he had himself been accosted as a potential recruit Mussalim was convinced. Jumaia's remark that these soldiers had been in Taqah for at least a couple of months suggested that there could be a force in position at Mirbat and by now fully trained. Tonight he would report his findings to Abdel Tahir, tomorrow he decided to go to Mirbat and find out what the situation was there. The Firqats had up to this point been an ineffective force now it seemed as if some attempts were being made to recruit, re-train and organise. Perhaps, Mussalim thought, there should be cause for concern. These men are after all Dhofaris unlike the majority of the Sultan's soldiers in the area.

As they left Taqah making their way north towards Wadi Darbat and the safety of the jebal a Muezzin in a Minaret wailed the call to prayer. At least here the people were free to pray without fear of reproach, Mussalim thought.

The sun hung in the western sky with perhaps two hours left to sunset as they walked towards the enormous Dahaq escapement. Two hundred metres high and more than a kilometre wide it towered above them and guarded the entrance to Wadi Darbat. After a wet Khareef or a period of heavy rain thousands of tons of water tumbled out of Darbat and cascaded over the lip to crash deafeningly onto the rocks far below. From there it rushed fizzing over the rocks down to the sea at Khor Rourri. Today no water spewed over the cliffs and no waters fizzed over the rocks and they picked their way along the dried riverbed to the escapement. Almost beneath its awe inspiring sheer face they climbed one of the steep hills that bracketed it on both sides. Now above those cliffs they found the low cave where they had hid their weapons.

The steep climb had taken an hour and so while they resting they checked their Kalachnikovs. One never knew if some insect might have crawled into the works and perhaps cause a jam at the worst possible moment. The sun now slipped towards its setting and reflected spectacular colours of orange and reds on the underside of the clouds. Mussalim looked back over Dahaq and followed the dried riverbed to the distant lagoon at Khor Rourri. The colourful sky reflected shimmering pictorial colours in the waters whilst on the lagoon's edge the ruins of the ancient city named after the Moon God, Sin cast lengthening shadows on the ground. Beyond the lagoon towering headlands protected both sides of the enormous curved bay from the open sea producing a natural harbour.

Faced with such stirring beauty of nature no one could doubt Allah's existence. He glanced at Musabbah and thought to say something but held his tongue. During the whole time they had lived and worked together Musabbah had never given him reason to doubt his absolute loyalty, but still he did not trust him entirely. He turned back to mentally digest the incredible view.

Musabbah nudged him in the ribs. "What's happening there?" he said pointing down among the rocks.

A small body of ten men made their way slowly towards the cliff precipice. Centuries of rushing water had worn enormous boulders smooth while the softer bed had washed away leaving deep crevices in between. The progress by the men towards the cliff edge was slow as they picked there way leaping from boulder to boulder. It was hampered even more by the fact that three had their arms tied behind their backs.

Mussalim watched baffled until with horror he realised the probability of their intention. He got quickly to his feet. "Come on," he said already scrambling down the bank towards the bed. His urgency was such that he left Mussabah behind. He reached the bottom of the hill and studied the boulders quickly trying to select a route which would take him directly to the party of men who by now were near the abyss. He leapt from boulder to boulder hastily but often forced to tack in a different direction seeking alternative routes when the gap was too wide to jump. The wind howling over Dahaq pushed against him and tore at his clothes hampering his progress. On the wind he heard a man screaming and he delayed his next leap to look ahead. One of the men still with his arm tied behind his back tottered on the edge while others prodded him backward with long poles. Mussalim shouted but his voice was lost on the wind. Then the man was gone, disappeared over the edge.

Two men ventured cautiously forward towards the precipice and peered over the edge attempting to see the result of their handy-work while two others dragged the next candidate to his feet as he squirmed and cowered in resistance. A burst of automatic fire from behind Mussalim cracked sharply above the booming wind. He glanced back to see Musabbah bring his Kalachnikov down from firing a burst in the air to level it in the group's direction. They now had their attention and they stood still waiting for both men to approach.

"What's going on here?" Mussalim demanded.

"Who want's to know?" one man answered in defiance.

"Crazy Man Mussalim!" One of the men who had peered over the edge provided his answer.

"Ziad." Mussalim said as he recognised the man. "I should have known."

"This is none of your business."

"I'll decide whether it is or not."

"It's a legal PFLOAG execution. Sentence decided after a proper hearing."

"And what have they supposed to have done?"

"We've done nothing," one of the prisoners cried. Mussalim glanced at the prisoner who spoke. He was an old man with a long grey beard. The other was much younger perhaps his son.

They're traitors. Reported informers." Ziad said.

"We are not informers," the old man yelled hysterically. "We never see government soldiers. We hardly ever leave this wadi. So how can we inform? Besides what do we have to inform about?"

Mussalim studied the pair for a moment. The old man was probably telling the truth. He had seen similar situations before. More than just likely it was a denouncement by another family attempting to exact revenge because of some long standing feud. . "Reported informers? Reported who by?" He demanded.

"By all their neighbours."

"Set them free," Mussalim decided.

"No," Ziad stood defiant.

"Set them free," Mussalim addressed the others. No one moved. He was not in uniform, perhaps they didn't know who he was. "I am Commissar Mussalim Bin Abdulla. Now set them free." Ziad cocked his weapon but because of his stiff arm he had to do it pointing the muzzle down. By the time he had brought it up to point at Mussalim's chest he found Mussalim's own weapon cocked and aimed directly at his own chest. Both men stared at each other fingers tense on the trigger in a stand-off.

Musabbah cocked his weapon also. He had previously been Ziad's comrade and Mussalim experienced a slight panic wondering where his Kalachnikov would point.

"If your finger even twitches on that trigger then you will be dead, Ziad," he said softly.

Mussalim felt relief flood through him, but they were not out of the wood yet there were still six other men so far uncommitted. If they stayed that way then they might still live. Bluster was the best tactic he decided. "I said set them free," he yelled.

At first no one moved then one man pulled a khunja from his belt, moved slowly to the prisoners and began cutting their bonds. As soon as they were free the two men began to make off as fast as they could. They fled across the wadi not even bothering to go and collect their belongings and probably never to return to Darbat either.

Ziad scowled and slowly lowered his weapon. "Abdel Tahir will hear of this," he warned. "He is not in favour of handling traitors feebly."

Mussalim still held his Kalachnikov at the ready. He had no doubt that Ziad would report back to Abdel and what he said about his attitude to dissenters was certainly true. But he would worry about that another time and there was probably no evidence that these men were dissenters anyway, otherwise Ziad would have produced it. The more immediate and important problem, however, was still before him. There was probable danger of a back shoot as they withdrew. "Where are you men from?"

"Darbat," one muttered indicating with his arm.

Mussalim nodded. "OK, put your weapons down and leave them here. You can collect them from me later. You will find me in a large cave about two kilometres down the wadi east side." One by one they put down their weapons and began to make their way back leaping from boulder to boulder.

Ziad remained his eyes burning hate in Mussalim's direction until he was the last man. As he turned to follow the others he turned back and said. "Oh Commissar Mussalim. I have a message for you."

Mussalim stared at him but said nothing.

"You have twenty-eight days to surrender yourself at Um Al Gharriff or else you will be placed on the government execution list."

"Where did you get that from?"

"From your Father to Ali to me."

"And when do my twenty-eight days expire?"

"Oh," he grinned. "Sometime last autumn." Then he turned and followed the others.

Musabbah moved close to Mussalim. "You know that one day you will have to kill him. He will kill you if you don't."

Mussalim nodded. This was the third time he had been under the muzzle of a gun held by Ziad. "Come, soon it will be dark. Let's get back to our camp."

"What about these?" Musabbah indicated the weapons on the ground.

"Leave' em. We will tell them where they are when they come later."

Most jebal wadis are covered thickly by the stubby Ghaf trees down the sides and across their bases, but Darbat was not like most wadis. Ghaf was thick along the upper reaches of the steep sides but the base was mostly open grassland around a long narrow lake. Throughout the Khareef, water would cascade down from the surrounding hills swelling the lake and eventually overflowing it towards the Dahaq escapement. When the rains had gone the lake would shrink and slowly retreat back down the wadi towards its blind end but it never dried out completely. Consequently, Darbat was a very fertile wadi. Mushani people lived here in their round thatched beehive-like crofts gathered into small family hamlets. Grazing was good for their cattle and goats and provided them with plentiful supplies of milk, feta, and meat. Each hamlet cultivated its own small orchards of dates, coconuts and olives. Around the edges of the lake giant fig trees provided shade to the millions of guppies that swam in the water. Because of the plentiful supply of these tiny fish flamingo's heron's and cranes patrolled the lakes. Birds of this size provided a luxuriant supplement to a family's diet while gerbils infested the hillsides providing an additional variation. For centuries the Mushani who lived in this valley had guarded it fiercely against envious neighbours becoming a segregated community even against other Mushani tribesmen.

But times had changed now. The PFLOAG maintained a heavy presence and with their superior weapons intimidated the local community. They dominated the valley forcing the young men into the militia and expecting to be pampered like guests. They took occupation of dwellings and demanded to be provided with some of the bountiful supplies of food that the valley provided. Mussalim had failed completely to impress on Abdel Tahir the obvious advantages of at least offering payment for food. Abdel argued that he had tried all the conciliatory methods and in this region they just did not work. So no one even bothered to offer payment to the people of Darbat, after all they had plenty.

It was dark when Mussalim and Musabbah arrived at the cave where they had set up camp only the day previously. A good-sized fire blazed at the cave entrance lighting the interior and providing welcoming warmth on a cold February night. They were greeted by a grinning Nasser the third member of their team, who thrust tiny tin cups in their hand and filled them with tea from the pot just resting on the fireside.

Mussalim sat down tiredly and sipped his tea, staring thoughtfully into the fire.

"You need to contact Abdel," Nasser said nodding towards the portable radio and sitting down by his side. "You are recalled immediately to Jibjat for a Congress meeting the day after tomorrow."

They had only arrived yesterday after Abdel himself had sent them here to carry out weapon training amongst new militia. "What's happened?" he asked.

"Something bad." Nasser filled his own cup and stared into the flames. "Seems as if a government force landed at Sadh a three of nights ago and by daylight had taken the town without a shot being fired. Now the Sultan's flag flies over the Wali's house."

"They will withdraw in a day or two," Musabbah predicted.

"Not this time," Nasser went on. "Reports say that they continue to pour in supplies and now the Sultan's Army have arrived to occupy the town."

"So who took the town if the Army has only just arrived?" Mussalim queried.

Nassau shrugged, "That's the confusing part."

Mussalim looked at Musabbah. "I think we know the answer to that."

"The Mirbat Firqat," he said quietly.

"Where was Qartoob Ahmed while all this was happening?"

"He was caught off guard. When he found out about the force in his area the town was already occupied. He began assembling his men in Wadi Jeeshjesh to launch an attack. Someone must have betrayed him. The mystery force swooped out of the night, captured him and two dozen of his best men."

"So the Far Eastern PFLOAG not only has the Government Army now on its doorstep it doesn't have a leader either." Mussalim summed up. The three men stared gloomily into the dancing flames a few moments then with a heavy sigh Mussalim cast away the remnants in his teacup and went to radio Abdel Tahir.

Long after the other two had rolled into their blankets to sleep Mussalim sat huddled, a blanket across his shoulders, staring into the embers of the dying fire. He reflected how he had tried unsuccessfully to impress on Abdel that they needed many more portable radios than they currently held. With radios and with a quick reaction network as he had set up on the Qara then perhaps tonight the Sultan's flag would not be flying over Sadh. Abdel Tahir was a short-sighted commander and tactically inept he concluded. It was all going wrong. Support from the people was not as it should be. Disregard for their circumstances and extreme incidents such as what happened today on the Dahaq abyss only angered people and sent them across to the other side. He wondered if he could muster the courage to suggest to Al Ghassani that Tahir be replaced. Perhaps a more enlightened commander might yet rally the people behind the cause and halt this trickle away from the PFLOAG and towards the Sultan.

He thought of the clinic in Taqah. He had seen nothing like that before. Perhaps this Sultan might after all prove a good Dhofari. The formation of a new Firqat trained by expert British soldiers illustrated the man's determination to fight back much more than his father had ever done. Perhaps he cared about the region and its people! Or perhaps he just wanted to crush resistance and then revert the situation back to as it had been before. He thought about the offered amnesty that would encourage many who felt aggrieved by the PFLOAG to lay down their arms, if of course they could find a safe haven after. From what Ziad had reported then he himself was listed as a state enemy and earmarked for execution if he ever fell into government troop's hands. There could be no amnesty for him.

He thought of Jumaia living in her squalor and struggling to survive every morning she woke. He had found her to be good company and sitting under her primitive shelter that glimpse of her thigh had roused carnal thoughts within him. His mind raced back to that night at Jibjat more than two years ago when he had made clumsy amorous advances. She had been an innocent young girl then and had rejected him. Now she had been married, she would not be so innocent and he doubted that she could afford to reject him. Tomorrow he must go to Jibjat, Before he did, however, he would return to Taqah and there he would collect Jumaia then take her back to Jibjat as his comfort woman.

~ 15 ~

May 1971 • Abdel Tahir had a big gun and he was determined to use it. It had been smuggled in at night by Dhow into Khor Rourri. The Dhow had stayed well offshore all day then came in under the cover of darkness. It was a 75mm recoilless piece of artillery and broken down in component parts was easily moveable by camel into Darbat. Although it was landed right under the noses of the government forces at Tarqah it had been a fairly risk free operation. The soldiers rarely ventured out of their area of security, particularly after dark.

Tahir's options were three. He could use it against Sadh. However, at this stage almost three months since the Sultan's men took the small town back he had accepted the loss. After its initial fall and with the far eastern sector leaderless and in disarray he had gone there and had personally taken charge. Although he tried to hit back the delay had been disastrous, as the defenders had used the time to considerably strengthen their position. The attacks that were mounted were minor and other than a considerable nuisance amounted to nothing more than token. He had appointed a new commander, instructed that he continue the pressure and then returned to Jibjat. To take his gun to Sadh would have certainly increased the pressure, however, the immediate surrounding terrain was open *nejd* and fairly flat. The gun would probably have been vulnerable not only to capture but also to air attack.

His second option was Mirbat. The gun could be positioned on Jebal Samhan at the top of its steep escarpment overlooking the town and brought to bear on both forts. Because of the steep escarpment it was probably safe from capture but again the open terrain made it vulnerable to air attack.

The third option and the softer target was Taqah and its castle housing government soldiers. The jebal overlooking the town was thickly covered by the stubby *Ghaf* and therefore with some skill the gun could be hidden from air attack. Nor would its capture be easy because those same trees could conceal a sizeable defensive force. However, the castle was in the midst of town and therefore shelling would bring inevitable casualties among the townspeople.

Casualties among the Taqah population were not a particular concern to Abdel Tahir. He wanted to use the gun and therefore Taqah became his selection. To Mussalim it represented another tactical error. The town had many PFLOAG supporters and to shell your allies could only alienate those supporters and probably drive them to the other side.

He had tried unsuccessfully to persuade Abdel that Mirbat should be the target. Both forts there stood clear of the town and therefore any danger to the townspeople would be from wild shells only. Besides which the developing threat to PFLOAG security was emerging from there. The squad of Firqat operating from Mirbat, were making lightening 'seek and destroy raids' into the Front's territory more and more frequently. It was rumoured that many of the ex-Dhofar Liberation Front, which Abdel had driven off the jebal, made up their number and this accounted for the increasing success of these raids. These men would know a great deal and it seemed to Mussalim that some kind of retaliation was necessary. But positioned there on the open terrain the gun's vulnerability from air attack was a genuine concern. Perhaps, Mussalim petitioned, there were some precautions that could be taken and he had offered to go himself and examine the area. Abdel, however, had made his decision and his mind was therefore closed to alternatives. Furthermore he had charged Mussalim with the gun's protection.

Through a pair of binoculars from Jebal Aram he now studied the Taqah castle, eight kilometres across the plain. After a little while he lowered the glasses and wordlessly handed them to Ahmed Hinna the gun crew Commissar. There could be no doubt, during the night the government soldiers had brought in and positioned an artillery piece at the east end of the fort. For more than two weeks they had been able to shell the town and apart from mortar fire, which fell woefully short, the defenders had been impotent to reply. With the positioning of this new gun they were not now quite as impotent.

Ahmed handed back the glasses shaking his head. "No problem," he said. "They don't know where we are. When they fire then they will fire right over us deep into the jebal."

Mussalim glanced back down the slope and into the natural basin. Ahmed had chosen the gun site well and despite aircraft patrolling overhead the Sultan's men had not been able to find the gun. It was positioned at the bottom of natural indentation in the land with a camouflage net stretched over it. Tree branches woven through the scrim camouflaged the net further. Even the gun's muzzle did not protrude from beneath its cover. Instead it was elevated to send its shells from beneath its cover just clearing the bank ahead on their way across the plain into Tarqah. Close behind the placement, the bank was at its steepest and was covered by dense *Ghaf*. This served to hide the propellant gases that were exhausted behind the gun when it was fired. The smoke and the dust cloud dispersed upward hidden among the trees and filtered through the branches to make it practically invisible from any distance.

However, they dare not fire when the aircraft were actually overhead, that would mean discovery for certain. So they waited for clear skies before they sent out bombardments. By now the Air Force were at a quick reaction state and they could have aircraft overhead searching the jebal within five minutes so these bombardments were restricted to short daily bursts of five or six shells. Even so, by now the gun crew was extremely confident. The aircraft had been unable to find the weapon around the jebal edge and they now searched much further in. Probably Ahmed's comment about that gun firing right over the position was justified. Even so Mussalim was uneasy. He knew that the Taqah soldiers would not be prepared just to accept the gun's bombardments no matter how sporadic or short their duration. Sooner, and much sooner, rather than later they would come out to look for it.

He had less than sixty men and he was stretched thinly. He had placed picket lines two kilometres east and west of the gun's position guessing that the threat would come from either Salalah in the west or Mirbat in the east. But just in case it was frontal direct from Taqah he had placed another half way down the steep incline. Still he fretted he was stretched too thin. From recent experiences he knew that they would come under the cover of darkness, move into position and at first light advance. His only advantage when that happened was that they would not know where the gun was so they might take a wrong position and advance in the wrong direction.

He had studied his map long and often trying to anticipate what they would do when they eventually came but there were too many alternatives for him to cover with the men he had. The highest point was the very tip of Aram two kilometres northwest of their position and at the northern end of his picket line. He placed three men on the top as an observation post hoping that an early warning would enable him to react effectively.

Not for the first time he wished that he had more radios. There was one in the centre of each picket line one on the observation post and his. Al Ghassani had promised him more but all that had so far arrived was the gun. They would, he thought gloomily, lose this war because of the shortage of the minor essentials.

Ahmed stared up into the blue and cloudless morning sky. "I think it's time to wake them up," he said meaningfully. He slid back down the bank to rouse the gun crew and make preparations to open fire.

Mussalim continued to lay on the bank and study the distant town through the binoculars.

※ ※ ※

Something significant was happening. Juma could see that the minute he arrived at Um Al Gharriff. He stood on the shade side of a long wooden barrack room and idly watched as heavily armed soldiers clambered aboard Bedford trucks. Others swung ammunition boxes up and into the back which were quickly dragged out of sight further into the cargo area. At first he had thought it was the routine supply run to Taqah and Mirbat. However, this was not so, he had been informed that these runs had ceased. Supplies now moved by the safer option of Dhow. No, this was a to be a big raid and rumours exploded instantly about its destination.

After a little while he tired of watching the activity and turned to wander away. Other than hoping for its success and that all his comrades returned safely, it did not particularly concern him. His own personal concerns were much more exciting. He had been granted seven days leave to meet his new daughter who was by now six weeks old. His father had got a message to him at Manston through Um Al Gharriff that he would be taking Khamisa and his newly born baby to Al Dharitz to meet the other half of her family and Juma had been given the time off to join them.

He sauntered away moistening his dry lips with his tongue as he did. He spat away the unpleasant taste of dust that he had brought into his mouth. Sitting in the rear of an open Land Rover in the midst of a convoy there had been no protection from clouds of thick choking dust churned up from beneath wheels. He had buttoned up his clothes tightly and wrapped his shamag around his head leaving just a narrow slit for his eyes. Even so thick desert grime not only coated his clothing it had penetrated inside attaching itself to the film of body sweat. He thought of the cool showers in the transit building and thought it irresistible. It was now early afternoon and Al Dharitz only about an hour's walk away. Allowing time for ablutions and a little more for refreshments he anticipated that he would be at Khamisa's side in little more than two hours.

In the event his eagerness was such that he arrived at Talib's house less than two hours later. His father was already there with Lailla and both greeted him warmly. However, the face that Juma most wanted to see was Khamisa's. She stood quietly in the background waiting for him to complete the formalities of greeting each family member in turn. When eventually he stood before her they touched fingers and rubbed noses shyly very aware that the whole family looked on. Then taking his hand she led him into the sitting room where Talib's wife seated on the large mat held the new baby. Khamisa took the infant gently from her mother and held it out towards him.

"Husband, this is your daughter," she said.

Holding her very carefully and with a deal of nervousness Juma gazed down at his daughter for the first time, then he glanced up at all the grinning faces surrounding him and he grinned also.

✳ ✳ ✳

It had been a very pleasant day and a particular agreeable visit. Talib was ever a good host and his company enjoyable. Abdulla considered him to be a good friend as well as a relative. Now it was time to make preparations for the long trip home, in fact it was past that time. Completely at ease and relaxed he had allowed the time to slip by and now it would be dark before he had got even half way home. He hauled both camels to their knees and as the beasts settled obediently to wait loading Abdulla gazed across the road to the nearby beach.

The sun hung over the western sky glistening a path of sparklers on a flat listless sea. The calm waters lapped the sandy beach like a millpond on a windless day. But for the rows of seagull motionlessly staring out to sea and two lonely figures sitting huddled together, the beach would have been deserted. Because of his poor eyesight the detail of those two figures were denied to Abdulla, but he knew that they were Juma and Khamisa. They had, as soon as the opportunity came, retreated to the privacy of the shoreline with their baby. He smiled to himself as he watched the tender scene of two devoted young people fawning over the fruit of their love. Their had been many sacrifices made by the family to bring about their union, but those who witnessed them together could not doubt that each and every concession made had been worth it. He thought of his elder son, Mussalim, his financial contribution to his brother's wedding had been significant not only by the money that he had originally brought from Bahrain but also his PFLOAG money that he had generously given. Juma had no idea the true amount of that contribution, Abdulla had kept the precise details from him. He considered the irony of the situation that PFLOAG money had contributed greatly to the happiness of a Sultan's soldier. He wondered with a wry smile just what Juma would say if he knew just how much he owed to the Communists. Probably he wouldn't care he concluded.

"Doesn't it stir memories in an old man's heart," Talib said moving up quietly behind him.

Abdulla glanced over his shoulder to see him also staring in the direction of Juma and Khamisa. "It has been a long time since our marriages were like that," he went on.

Abdulla nodded silent agreement although he actually doubted that his marriage had ever been like that. Even at the stage when youthful exhilaration filled each day with excitement and desire he could not remember sharing as much with Jokha as his son did with his wife. Their marriage had been arranged by both of their fathers. Of course he had been asked if he would accept Jokha, as his wife but even so it would have taken a flat and determined rejection to oppose his father's wishes. It had been almost the same for Jokha the only difference being that her opinion would not have even been asked. The reasoning of the arrangement being that the elders considered them to be suitably matched and therefore they would eventually grow to appreciate each other. And that was the way that it had turned out too. Or at least had, until he had taken Kathya as his second wife.

"Juma is a good husband," Talib said again. "Khamisa seems completely besotted with him. Truly Allah has been generous to my daughter."

"And to my son. *Il hamdu lillaah*," Abdulla praised Allah

"*Il hamdu lillaah*," Talib agreed. "But when will he leave the army?"

"I don't know," Abdulla replied motioning to Lailla that she should come and mount one of the kneeling camels. "Now that he has a family of his own I can see no reason why he should stay. But all my efforts of persuasion fall on deaf ears. It seems he is determined to stay in and with the money he earns provide the very best he can for Khamisa."

"Perhaps this war will end soon and then he can live where he wants to."

"With this new Sultan there is reason to hope," Abdulla said helping Lailla onto the animal's back.

"*Inshaallah.*" Talib committed it to Allah's will.

Abdulla slapped the camel on its rump and using its back legs first it got awkwardly to its feet. "One week from today I will return for Khamisa," he said mounting the second camel.

"We will look forward once again to your visit," Talib said as Abdulla used his cane to get the second animal to its feet. "*Masalaama.*"

"*Masalaama*," Abdulla replied as he drove the camel towards the beach to take his leave of number two son.

* * *

The sharp cracks of rifle fire invaded Mussalim's dream and sub consciously he tried to shut it out but it wouldn't go away. Then alarm scorched right through and brought him instantly alert. He rolled from his blanket into a breaking dawn and sat up full of alarm. The firing was distant and the battle sounds coming from the north west.

It was inevitable that the soldiers would eventually come looking for the gun and an attack was therefore fully expected. He had guessed also that it would be this time of the day when they would begin their search. It took no imagination at all to anticipate that the soldiers would come under the cover of darkness to get into position and as soon as it were light enough then they would fan out and begin the hunt. They had, it seemed either deliberately or unexpectedly moved against the western picket line.

He was on his feet and stumbling towards the nearby radio handset. "Ahmed, wake up, he said aiming a kick at the sleeping man's legs as he passed. His eyes opened instantly but he remained motionless as his confused wits struggled to understand what was happening. When all the wires eventually connected he leapt to action and began to rouse his gun crew.

By this time Mussalim was already using the call sign for the western picket line. The answer was almost instant but the information was scant. Other than there was exchanges of fire somewhere further along the line to the north the radio operator could tell him nothing. Next he radioed the observation post on the top of Aram. The operator there was in an agitated state of excitement and the information came tumbling over air in a confused state. Eventually after several repeats Mussalim was able to gather that there was a firqat force of around sixty strong just beneath their position to the south attacking the northern end of the picket line. At the same time a similar sized force of Sultan's soldiers were climbing the hill from the west and advancing on their position.

Even though they held the high ground Mussalim realised that there was no way that those three men would hold a force of sixty for very long. The government soldiers would soon seize that dominant ground. His next concern was the eastern defence line, so far all seemed to be quiet over in that direction and a radio contact confirmed that.

As he reached for his map he became aware that Ahmed stood just behind him awaiting a report and instructions. "Dismantle your gun Ahmed, we have to get it away from here."

"Which way should I go?"

"I don't know yet. Just get it dismantled and loaded ready," he replied tensely.

He spread the map and studied it. Two forces, one from the south another from the west was gathering to their north west at Jebal Aram's peak. So far the eastern picket line was quiet which was a good sign. If that had been under attack also it would mean that they knew the position of the gun and had it in between in a pincer movement.

He concluded that it was probable that they didn't know where it was and that the jebal peak was their assembly point. The crew could escape with their gun to the east, then when clear swing north and make their way to the security of Jibjat. His objective therefore was simple, he would have to prevent the invaders moving east until the gun was clear.

His mission now clear in his mind he recalled the handful of southern pickets halfway down the hillside and set them to work assisting the gun crew. He found Ahmed working to dissemble the gun and interrupting him he outlined on the map the escape route he should take as soon as he was ready to leave. The extra men that now assisted him he suggested he should take with him as additional protection, just in case. With the gun's evacuation aspect attended to he should now inform Abdel Tahir that they were under attack. He returned to the radio and used Jibjat's call sign. There was a little delay before a sleepy operator answered. Not fully alert the operator did not quickly grasp the situation and Mussalim was forced to repeat the message trying as he did to impress on the drowsy operator the urgent need to pass the message to Abdel.

He now forced himself to calm down a little while he considered what else he ought to do. For the time being and as a precaution he decided to leave the eastern defence line where it was just in case another attack should materialise from that direction. As he saw it all the arrangements for the gun's withdrawal were now in place providing an attack from the east did not materialise and cut off its escape route. Only the organisation of its rear guard remained. The sounds of gunfire to the northwest had not lessened in intensity and his immediate concern was what the precise situation there was. The circumstances now demanded his presence at that rear guard point. He fastened two ammunition belts around his waist and crossed two more over his chest, then hooking the radio handset over his shoulder he picked up his Kalachnikov and left towards the sounds of the battle.

Twenty minutes later with the sounds of gunfire very close he made his way through a *Ghaf* thicket cautiously. The intensity of the exchanges seemed to have lessened a good deal. Now a GP machine gun seemed to dominate, its operator repeatedly letting off short disciplined bursts with monotonous regularity. Mussalim reached the thicket edge and still within its cover he peered down into a valley. Sloping away beneath him open grassland with a dried rocky streambed winding along the valley base. On the opposite bank more grassland with the same *Ghaf* thicket on the top edge. Amongst the rocks in the streambed six of his men pressed themselves against whatever cover they could find while the machine gun from somewhere in the trees on the other side regularly raked their position.

Mussalim shook his head ruefully wondering how they had managed to get themselves pinned down in such a precarious position. He began studying the far side through binoculars trying to locate the machine gun. The merest wisp of rising smoke betrayed its position. He lowered his glasses and peered hard at the spot wondering how he could create enough pressure on the machine gun to allow the men to break out. The situation looked desperate. He could never keep up the pressure long enough for the men to make a dash up the open bank and into the tree cover.

In the event he didn't need to. Movement made him once again study the spot through his glasses. Unaccountably the machine gunners were withdrawing. He watched them go filled with curiosity why they should release their indomitable grip. Deeply suspicious he scanned the surrounding area looking for replacements but could see none. The men in the streambeds were now beginning to stir wondering themselves why the incoming fire had ceased. This was their chance. Mussalim emerged from the cover of the trees and called for them to fall back out of the valley and quickly. They hesitated, glancing nervously up towards where the machine gun had been. Then after a few moments one man broke cover and helping one of his wounded colleagues began to climb the hill towards Mussalim. The rest quickly followed his example.

Two of the men were from the jebal peak observation post, the third had been killed. The rest including the wounded man had been at the very end of the picket line. They related that one force had come from the southwest and had stumbled into the end of the picket line just as dawn was breaking. Another force had come directly from the west with the objective of occupying the highest point of Jebal Aram. Faced by much superior numbers they had retreated then linked and had then been forced back towards the valley. With no where else to go they had tried to cross the valley but before they had made it across the pursuers had trapped them in the bottom.

Mussalim looked over the valley towards the peak of Aram. That high ground was predominant over the area and it was, he guessed the mutual assembly point of the government forces. At this moment they were probably completing their rendezvous up there which explained the machine gunner's withdrawal. He studied the peak through his binoculars but could see nothing, any activity was hidden beyond the lip. It mattered not, he knew precisely what they were doing. His Russian trainers had taught him well the British weakness of predictability. The Army forces were led by loaned British Officers and SNCO's as were the firqat's, so reverting to installed tradition they were attempting to establish a secure base position. When they were all eventually assembled then the officers would call a meeting, the soldiers would busy themselves fortifying the area by building sangars and then they would have to drink tea. Mussalim smiled wryly to himself. He had at least one hour to get his men in position perhaps even two. And more importantly it was valuable gratis time for the gun's escape.

He spread his map once more and studied the land. He could muster around fifty men and although outnumbered at probably more than two to one if he took the right positions he believed he could hold these invaders throughout the morning and well into the afternoon. By which time the gun should be half way to Jibjat.

The Aram position was dominant so there could be no advantage taking position around its base. Instead he selected positions a little distance away in amongst the heavy thickets to the east, south and west in effect placing a rough U shaped cordon around the government forces.

He summoned the eastern picket line on his radio and to his relief learned that all was still quiet. There was no danger now of any attack from that direction, the threat was right here in front of him. He summoned the whole picket line to his position immediately. A line in the cover of the trees here would make the valley in front of them hard to cross. The remnants of his western picket line lay half a kilometre ahead and a little to his left. He raised them by radio and sent them to new positions to the south of Aram and to the west on the very edge of Wadi Hasheem. The line numbered only around twenty and would be stretched perilously thin nevertheless it was only delaying tactics that were needed. There was nothing he could do now except wait and hope that his men got into their new positions before the Sultan's soldiers came down from the peak. The men already close by should be in position easily within forty-five minutes he estimated. Those coming from the east would need more time perhaps as much as an hour and a half. He tried to think of ways that might delay the invader's descent. Once the south and west positions were achieved then they could lay down sustained mortar fire, that might disrupt activities on the peak. He settled down to an anxious wait.

With time on his hands he took the opportunity to report in to Abdel Tahir. He raised the same operator at Jibjat who could only inform him that Abdel had already left for Wadi Darbat to raise a reinforcing force to come to his support. Mussalim shut down the radio and tried to estimate when those reinforcements might arrive.

Because of the shortage of radios the normal method of assembling was by daily meeting points of both regulars and militia. At these meetings their leader would inform the assembly whether they were needed or not. Usually they were not and in these cases they were simply dismissed to return to the same place at the same time the next day. In the event of a situation where they were required they would then return to their homes to collect the equipment that they would need and report back to the same assembly point within one hour. From there they would move to a general assembly point where they would be joined by other splinter groups. Once assembled they could then expect to be organised and moved on to their objective. This took time and invariably meant slow reaction, particularly if the men had been dismissed earlier from their initial daily meeting. In those instances it probably meant that no force would be assembled until the next day. In this instance Mussalim anticipated that Abdel would have got the word out in time. Even so, by the time all were assembled, re-assembled, organised and moved to this area then it would be nightfall, at the earliest. By that time the fate of the gun would have been decided either lost or safe.

He still had Musabbah and Nasser located in Wadi Darbat and he thought to contact them. They might be able to gather a few men together and get help to him sooner. But even then they probably could not get here until the afternoon. Although he anticipated that the gun should be clear by that time he decided to make the contact, there was no way of telling for certain what the situation would be by then.

Although there was nothing for him to do except wait for everybody to get into position, he could not relax. Anxiously, he scanned the area with his binoculars for any sign of enemy movement. He continually changed his position trying to survey different areas in case the soldiers moved through the dead ground below hidden from view. But he saw nothing, which should have been comforting but wasn't. The wounded man was giving him cause for concern. The bullet entry point in his left side was small, swollen and bled profusely. Its exit on his back, however, had taken with it a great chunk of flesh revealing dark red inner organs. Mussalim doubted his survival but he could not spare a man for his evacuation.

The man standing by the radio came to find him and reported that his men to the south and west were now in position. Those coming from the east meanwhile had passed through the gun's position and would be here in about half an hour. The gun itself was now dissembled, loaded onto camels and Ahmed was about to move east. All was going smoothly, Mussalim reflected, then pessimistically, perhaps too smoothly. It was time to apply pressure and hamper the soldier's preparations he decided. He made his way back to the radio and instructed that mortar fire from both the south and west be directed on to their position on the peak. Before it could begin however, the crackling of intense firing erupted in the west. The battle had begun and his vital eastern flank was still open.

Mussalim was frantic to find out what was happening over in the west but he could not get a response by radio. Either they were under too much pressure over there to answer, or maybe the radio was out. Perhaps they had simply moved into a deep area where the signal was screened by steep landscape. The exchanges sounded intense which was encouraging because it meant that at least they were still fighting. Mortar fire had also begun, albeit somewhat erratic and not much directed against Aram peak. His consolation was that the fighting was over in the opposite direction from the by now, hopefully, retreating gun. But how long it would stay that way was his major concern.

He was fearful that his other force would not arrive in time to close up the open flank and he waited anxiously for signs of their approach. At his back was the thick screen of *Ghaf* so whether they were more than a kilometre away or as close as a hundred metres he could not tell. He had just picked up the radio to establish contact when his worse nightmare was confirmed. The sharp cracks of gunfire began in the south.

Hastily he scanned the valley below him, nothing moved. Somehow a force must have passed across his front probably in the cover of the trees that covered the opposite bank and had now come into contact with the line to the south. He gathered the five men with him and moved towards the gunfire. He abandoned the wounded man. It seemed callous he knew, but he probably stood a better chance of survival if the government forces found him. There was no field hospital for PFLOAG soldiers here.

Only a torturous overland journey of three days or more to Shershitta or Hauf awaited casualties. If this man could survive for that amount of time then the rigours of the journey would probably kill him anyway.

By the time they arrived at the southern point the firing had stopped and there was no obvious sign of a skirmish. At first Mussalim could not find his men. When he did they were few in number and had rolled away a short distance to the west. They had sustained casualties, two wounded, though neither particularly seriously and one other dead. One man attempted to carry out some basic treatment on the wounded while the other two just sat sullenly silent close by. Of the government soldiers there was no sign and when he asked for a report they gave him the worst possible news. A force of around thirty strong had broken through and had headed to the east.

He did a quick assessment of the situation. The firing over in the west had become sporadic indicating some easing of the confrontation. The mortar shells bombardment continued, however, which informed him that his force over there was still in combat shape. These particular men here were at this moment demoralised so he instructed them to go west into Wadi Hasheem and then to link up with the others over there. He then radioed the men coming from the east and turned them about to fall back to the gun's original position. There they were to dig in and stop the government soldiers going any further east at all costs. With a deal of concern and with no time to delay he gathered the five men that he had brought with him and set off in pursuit of the Sultan's soldiers.

Thirty minutes later his alacrity was very nearly fatal. He and his companions emerged from a tree line crossing open ground with much less caution than they should. The earth all around them began erupting in tiny spurts followed instantaneously by ear splitting retorts of rifle fire. With fright and alarm lending speed they sprinted back to the trees diving undignified beneath their cover. Mussalim lay there with his chest heaving for breath while he reproached himself harshly for his sloppiness. He rolled slowly over onto an elbow and looked towards his companions, incredibly and to his relief they had all made it unscathed. A GP machine gun now systematically raked the low branches above their heads back and forth showering them with leaves and splinters. After what seemed eternity it eventually ceased. In blind rage Mussalim cocked his Kalachnikov and sent a long burst aimlessly out towards the high ground to the front of their position. He had no idea if that was where the fire was coming from but it was a reactionary release of pent up anger and a gesture of defiance. His companions followed his example, which only provoked another sustained burst from the machine gun. Not having pinpointed the attackers, nor having the slightest notion of their strength Mussalim bridled his temper and prudently withdrew back through the trees as soon as the machine gun paused.

Moving much more cautiously now he led the way taking a wide circle to the south and moving along the edge of the escarpment around that position. Almost an hour later and approaching the original gun position they once again came under fire but this time it was the automatic fire of Kalachnikovs. They threw themselves behind the nearest cover and waited for it to cease. When it did he shouted his identity and he was allowed to pass through the line to link up with his men.

He slumped down tiredly on a rock close to the position where he had slept about seven hours before which now seemed to be a very long time ago. Someone handed him a skin of water making him realise as adrenaline ceased that he had a raging thirst. He glanced around at the destroyed site. Someone had attempted to burn everything and remnants of the camouflage net and its supporting poles lay smouldering in three blackened piles. Water barrels had been tipped while rice and flour had been spread across the ground and deliberately spoiled with dirt and sand.

"Government soldiers," the man who had handed him the water explained. "They got here before us and destroyed what they could."

"Where are they now?" Mussalim asked with alarm.

"Withdrew back to the west."

He felt a wave of relief. They had found the gun's position but instead of pursuing it they had withdrawn back to their base on Aram's peak. It was now getting close to midday and he estimated that the gun had left at least three hours ago. By now it should be well to the east and probably swinging northwards. Since no pursuit had materialised then the start that it now had probably made it safe, he concluded. His forces were scattered east and west and there had been casualties but his primary mission was achieved. He rubbed his tired eyes as tension release now unlocked exhaustion.

Someone kicked his feet waking him with a start from a fitful sleep. Musabbah grinned down at him. "Is that all you have to do? I thought you said you needed help."

He was alert immediately concerned that he had slept too long. He glanced toward the sun it was early afternoon and he guessed that he had slept for perhaps three hours. "You soon got here."

"We left almost immediately after your message." He squatted down by his side.

"How many men did you bring?"

"Myself, Nasser and nine others."

"Abdel Tahir?"

Musabbah shrugged. "He hadn't arrived by the time we left. But the word was out that he was coming. What's been happening?"

He held up his hand feeling the need to find out what was happening around Aram's peak before filling in the details for him. This time radio contact was successful. His forces over to the west reported that they had been forced back down into Wadi Hasheem and now apart from exchanges of mortar fire to and from the peak there was a comparative lull in the fighting. He was relieved, there seemed to be no immediate crisis so now he outlined the morning's events very briefly to Musabbah.

"So what happens now?"

Mussalim shrugged. He could see no reason to continue the fight now that the gun was safe. If they were to simply melt away then in all probability so would the government soldiers. But that was not his decision to make. "I suppose I contact Abdel and get further orders."

Abdel Tahir was still in Wadi Darbat and now that the gun was safe he decided that he would remain there for the time being. His instructions were that hostilities should continue and make the soldier's occupation unpleasant forcing them to withdraw. If they hadn't retreated off the jebal during the night then tomorrow he would himself lead the Darbat men onto Aram and launch an all out offensive to make sure they did.

Mussalim replaced the radio receiver a little dispiritedly. He felt sure that having dislodged the gun and achieved their objective then the Sultan's men would withdraw during the night and there was therefore no need to continue fighting. But he had his orders and so he had no alternative but to instruct the men in Wadi Hasheem to continue hostilities while he moved these men westward once more in support. He passed the word that they should be ready to leave in one hour.

The sun was low in the western sky when Musslaim found a position to the north of Aram's peak that suited him. The peak itself was banana shaped, long and narrow basically running northwesterly from the south. Wadi Hasheem wrapped itself along its western side and curved behind in the north as it petered out to the open *gatn*. The site Mussalim had chosen was on high ground along the very lip of the wadi with open ground falling away in front of him before it began its steep climb up towards the peak. The position was mutually supporting to the men in the wadi to the west. If either force came under serious threat then the other could move along the wadi using the steep incline as dead ground cover to assist. It was not however PFLOAG normal strategy to stand and fight unless they really had to. They used true guerrilla tactics of strike and strike hard then when the counter attack came to scatter re-group and strike somewhere else afresh. This left the enemy frustrated and chasing shadows unable to come to grips with an elusive foe. This position complimented that tactic because it offered two back door escape options. To fall back and either cross Hasheem or to go along its base, both alternatives had thick *Ghaf* cover.

He had deliberately left the area south of the peak open inviting the soldiers to withdraw directly towards the escarpment onto the plain and back into Taqah. He expected with a good deal of confidence that under the cover of darkness that was precisely what they would do. But just to give then a little nudge he decided to lay down mortar fire into their position from here. This would advertise PFLOAG presence on their northern side as well as on their west flank and so encourage them to move south. Now without delay he despatched half a dozen men down the wadi to collect one of the two mortars from the men in the west. With luck they would be back within two hours and the bombardment could commence.

However, when the sun rose the next day and despite the persistent mortar fire from north and west the government soldiers still occupied the peak. Indeed the rate of mortar they had returned indicated their determination to defend their area. Mussalim sat perplexed and a little way apart studying the peak long and hard through binoculars. He could see nothing, any activity up there was hidden beyond the high edge nevertheless he continued to scan hoping for the slightest inclination of a clue. Now that they had cleared away the threat to of the gun on Taqah he could think of no particular reason why they remained.

"What now Commissar?" Musabbah asked coming up behind him quietly. He sat down at his side and handed him a small brass cup of weak coffee and a piece of stale bread.

Mussalim allowed the binoculars to fall hanging from his neck as he took the breakfast. Bewildered he shook his head. "Why are they still here?" He asked though he did not expect an answer.

Musabbah only shrugged.

He took a large bite of the bread tearing it with his teeth and continued staring towards the high ground afraid to take his eyes away in case something significant happened while he wasn't watching. "There is nothing here of importance now," he thought aloud.

"Who knows why they do half the things they do? I sometimes wonder if they know themselves," Musabbah said dismissively. "Remember Tawi?"

Mussalim softened the stale bread in his mouth with the coffee then glanced sideways at him. "Yes," he drawled understandingly. That incident two months ago had also seemed meaningless. Under the cover of darkness a large force of Firqats led by their British Army trainers had left Mirbat and scaled the sheer face of Samhan. Having achieved the summit they then dug in to wait nightfall. Under the cloak of night they advanced northwest to occupy an isolated high bluff to the south of the village Tawi. Once there they fortified the area as best they could and waited to be attacked. And attacked they were, ferociously from three sides. With helicopter support supplying their needs they held what amounted to an irrelevant position and under intense fire for four days before withdrawing back the way they had come. After the event no one within PFLOAG had been able to offer a satisfactory explanation for the operation other than to suggest that it was perhaps some kind of extreme training exercise.

"One day they will come and they won't go away," Mussalim forecast tossing away the stale bread.

"Perhaps this is that time."

"No," he shook his head. "They are not strong enough. And they will need easier supply lines than through rough terrain like this."

"Then why are they here?"

Mussalim took a last swig then cast away the remainder of the coffee. "I wish I knew," he replied getting to his feet. "I suppose that I had better inform Abdel Tahir."

Abdel sounded exasperated that he hadn't managed to force the government troops to withdraw and declared his intention to bring up the Darbat force and to personally take charge of the situation. He estimated that he would arrive at the eastern side of Aram around early evening. Mussalim was, he instructed, to continue the pressure and stand by for further instructions. He shut down somewhat irked by Tahir's supercilious attitude.

Throughout the morning Mussalim tried to maintain pressure by the use of mortar bombs, but as stocks began to dwindle he was forced to reduce the barrage to around just six in an hour. The men in the west were faring a little better being closer to a supply cache in the next wadi, Aythawn. Nevertheless, with an eye on the diminishing stocks and having no idea how long they would need to maintain this attack they too prudently cut back.

By early afternoon the exchanges amounted to little more than token and the whole confrontation settled into lethargy. It seemed to Mussalim that both sides had become content to accept a stand off situation for the time being. This misconception was very nearly his undoing and it was only by luck or a degree of alertness by one of his men that prevented a disastrous situation. He spotted a group of men moving stealthily along the wadi base in their direction and he let off a prolonged burst of automatic fire in their direction.

Mussalim's first reaction was that the man had fired on a party of his comrades coming from the other group. That notion however was instantly rejected when concentrated fire was returned. In his complacency he had almost allowed himself to get outflanked with his escape routes into the wadi cut off. But that danger still remained. If he allowed them to get in position behind then he would be forced to withdraw over the open and exposed *gatn*. Taking cover behind a rock he scanned the wadi through binoculars. The men wore *futas* with bits of uniform identifying them easily as Firqats. They had advanced in an orderly line across the base but now they had been spotted they hesitated and had gone to cover. He realised that to take advantage of that hesitation his reaction needed to be instant. He rolled away from the rock looking for Musabbah and calling his name. He came quickly keeping low.

Mussalim instructed him to take half the men and using the tree cover advance to a position halfway down the hill. When he got there he was to direct heavy fire at the Firqats while he advanced with the rest of the men through his position and into the wadi bottom. With a series of leapfrog advance and cover movements he intended to get his men across the wadi to the safety of the opposite side. As soon as the covering fire was intense enough Musabbah set off. The crossing was easily made and casualty free because under the intense fire the Firqats withdrew back down the wadi before the manoeuvre was even half completed.

Standing on the other side of Hasheem Mussalim looked across to his abandoned position and contemplated whether he should perhaps go back and re-occupy before darkness fell. He still had had no word from Abdel and could only guess at his intention. He pulled out the map and studied it carefully. Assuming that Abdel did arrive around the time that he had estimated then the Darbat force of perhaps sixty strong would be in position east of Aram in about four hours. He was currently to the northwest above Hasheem while the rest of his force was further down the wadi to the southwest. He decided the best thing for him to do was to link up his divided force.

That would give Tahir two forces of similar strength east and west of the government soldiers. There was no way of knowing how far those Firqats had withdrawn, so to move down Wadi Hasheem might be to risk ambush. Just a kilometre across the *gatn* behind him was the great Wadi Aythawn, which ran south and linked to Hasheem just before it opened onto the plain. That route should be safe.

His men sat around casually resting in the shade of the trees passing out food and water. He decided to allow them a little longer to rest and let some of the scorching heat fade from the day. It would be getting dark by the time he linked up with his other men so it would therefore be wise to radio ahead and warn them of their arrival from the direction of their rear. After he had done that he contacted Abdel's group and learned that they had just left Darbat and expected to be close to Aram around sundown. If it was his intention to mount some sort of attack then it would appear that he had timed it to take place in the dark.

An hour later they moved out across the *gatn* to Wadi Aythawn. So that they did not blunder into an ambush, Mussalim posted a party of six to move forward some way ahead of the rest. Aythawn was wide and deep though not particularly steep and they did not immediately descend. Instead they walked along its winding upper edge until it narrowed and the sides did start to become steep. At this point they descended into its base and continued on until they reached the point where Hasheem branched off away to their left. The derelict remnants of a small abandoned hamlet nestled at this junction. The crude thatched roofs of the houses had long ago collapsed in and now the circular rock walls were going the same way. Mussalim decided that it was a good place to take a short rest and he called a halt. While the men rested he didn't. He scanned the surrounding upper edges of the wadi through binoculars nervously. Although he believed that they were probably too far west of Aram's peak to be in any danger of attack he could not relax his vigil. After allowing just a few minutes he sent out his scouts again and a short while later he roused the main party to follow. They now left Wadi Aythawn into Hasheem cutting sharply back northeast. One hour later as the sun disappeared they linked with the other front fighters.

Hostilities by this time had petered out completely and as men now relaxed they took the opportunity to refill their magazines and ammunition belts, some slept while others just sat in small groups quietly talking. Mussalim had taken the precaution of posting sentries on the high ground both sides of the wadi although he thought it unlikely that the Sultan's men would come out looking for trouble in the darkness. All he could do now was to wait for Abdel Tahir to declare his intention and issue instructions.

It was a clear night and millions of stars in every corner of the heavens glittered with awe-inspiring resplendence. Mussalim stood under the trees a short distance away from the camp staring up into the constellation deeply appreciative of the vista of Allah's creation. The spectacle graphically placed into perspective the real insignificance of this particular conflict compared to the awesome magnitude of time and space. It did not really matter whether a man died at this moment or forty years from now in either case his life was as the merest immeasurable part of a moment compared to the longevity of the stars. In veneration of Allah's glory and unsure of his own immediate future he shrunk back further under the trees and clandestinely made his prayer.

His prayers were interrupted when gunfire erupted with ferocity renting the tranquillity of the night violently. He leapt to his feet in alarm and then realised that the gunfire was not actually directed in their direction. In the still and quiet it sounded close but it was in fact a little distance away to the east. He guessed that Abdel's attack had begun. But still he was puzzled there had been no radio contact, no instructions. Surely he didn't intend to make the assault alone using only the Darbat force. Unless the radio was out! He ran back to the camp.

Men were on their feet shuffling around in mild confusion. Some stared into the darkness towards the sound of the gunfire as if expecting the fighting would come into view at any moment. Mussalim tried without success to call the Darbat men over the radio. Either they were not receiving the signal or were at that moment too busy to respond and judging by the fire concentration that was a definite possibility. Obviously there was a battle raging over there in the east and whatever the situation was he could still lend support by starting the mortar salvo onto the peak once again. He instructed a nearby man to keep trying to contact the Darbat force on the radio while he went to direct the mortar teams.

It took a few minutes for the two mortar teams to get organised and they had just begun lobbing in their bombs when the firing in the east died away as quickly as it had started. Mussalim was now utterly bemused and could not even begin to guess what was happening over there. He glanced at Musabbah who flashed a grin and gave a prolonged shrug indicating that he had no opinion to offer.

It was then that the radio operator called to him, he had made contact. With relief he went quickly over to the radio and it was with dismay that he learned that Abdel Tahir had stumbled into an ambush. Now with dead and wounded they were falling back.

"Falling back to where," he asked.

"Darbat. I think," was the vague reply?

"Darbat?" he sought confirmation and got it. He shut down the radio, exasperated at their easy capitulation. "Abdel walked into an ambush," he informed Musabbah.

"Imbecile!" was all Musabbah said.

Mussalim did not contradict him. To him it seemed that to have Abdel Tahir on your side was a definite handicap but to have him actually in charge was a positive liability. "Cease fire," he shouted to the mortar teams.

By now he and his men had been fighting for around forty hours with only minimal time to rest. In view of Abdel's quick withdrawal he decided that these men deserved sleep and rest time, at least. That derelict hamlet in Aythawn seemed to be a suitable place to pull back to. It was far enough away to be reasonably safe but close enough for a quick return if renewed operations were required. He had expected the soldiers to withdraw last night and they hadn't but perhaps tonight they would, particularly if there didn't seem to be anyone for them to fight. He ordered their evacuation and infuriated with Tahir's performance he didn't even bother to inform him.

A large moon had risen by the time they reached the hamlet bathing the deserted ruins with an eerie pallor. Mussalim looked around the surrounding hills assessing its security critically. Behind the ruins the hillside rose steeply a hundred metres while a wall of rock almost as high dominated this side. This wall formed an acute corner and guarded one side of the entrance into Hasheem. On the other side of this entrance, another steep hill but in comparison to the surrounding landscape, dwarfed. Dominated as it was by the surrounding high ground caution warned him that he should reject the ruins as a campsite. A large dark patch halfway up the hillside caught his eye. It might be a cave!

"Is that a cave up there?" He asked of no one in particular.

"It is," someone replied.

"Then that's our camp for tonight."

He didn't rouse the men early the next morning, he didn't really see the point. If the soldiers were still on the peak then they would be there all day and if they had gone then his men would be stood down until the next time they were needed. He took Musabbah, descended the hill and crossed the wadi. A little further up Aythawn they found a goat track that wound its way steeply up the rock face to the top. It was a sharp and exhausting climb but thirty minutes later they stood on top. Away from the shelter of the surrounding hills the wind here was rough and they leaned forward into it as they walked along the top towards the precipice. They stood above the sheer wall with the wind flapping their clothes and looked down to the rubble that had been the hamlet, from here it looked tiny. To their right Wadi Aythawn with its spectacular rugged landscape wound its way north. To their left Wadi Hasheem cut northeast with the same awesome magnificence. In front of them the smaller hill that formed the opposite entrance to Hasheem and far beyond that the backdrop of brown coastal plain stretching to the azure coloured sea.

Through his binoculars Mussalim studied the castle at Taqah. As far as he could tell there seemed to be no activity, at least none on the outside. The flat ground in front was deserted and the gun to the side was covered and idle. Only the flag on the tower struggling vigorously at its restraining ties showed any movement. There was nothing to suggest that the jebal force had withdrawn during the night. He scanned the plain in between and apart from some wandering camels that too seemed tranquil.

"Can't tell," he said handing the glasses to Musabbah for his opinion.

"It's too quiet," Musabbah said after a few moment's study. "There should have been something." He lowered the glasses and handed them back. "They must be on the peak still."

"Looks like it," Mussalim agreed.

They turned and walked over to eastern edge and examined the Aram peak. Whoever or whatever was on the top, if anything, was hidden from their view well beyond the lip. They sat for a while in the morning sun watching the high ground looking for some telltale sign of activity. Movement along the edge, smoke from a campfire or anything that would inform them that the soldiers were still there. After a while they gave up and discussed their options. In the end they decided that there were realistically only two. To send out a reconnaissance patrol towards the peak or to toss in some more mortar bombs. In the end they decided on the second option. If the soldiers were still there then they would presumably retaliate and that was less likely to sustain casualties than a foraging patrol.

The sharp and piercing crack of a single rifle shot shattered the tranquillity. "What now?" Mussalim muttered getting quickly to his feet. That single shot provoked scattered replies and then the firing began to rapidly increase. It was coming from the direction of their campsite.

Stooping low so as not to expose themselves they peered over the edge of the rock wall into the wadi. The fire from their campsite halfway up the steep hill was intense and directed down at the ruins of the hamlet. Taking cover amongst the rubble and doing their best to return fire was a handful of Firqats. More firing came from the smaller hill behind as the main body of Firqats tried to put pressure on the hillside camp and give some covering fire to their trapped comrades. The position of the men among the ruins was desperate and more so than they yet realised. They were pinned down not only by the fire from above, but Masabbah and Musallim were high above them in the rear and able to direct fire in over their right shoulders.

Before they did however they decided it would be a good idea to build themselves a covering sangar. They worked frantically piling rocks into a low crude wall along their front. This created some protection from the fire that would inevitable come from that smaller hill once their presence was known. It took only a few minutes and when they were ready they settled down behind their screen and in fully automatic mode opened fire raking the trapped Firqats position mercilessly.

The surprise and shock of the trapped men was evident as they looked about in alarm, searching frantically to find this new threat. They began leaping around the ruins in panic attempting to find new positions that gave protection from both directions. There had been casualties too, perhaps even fatalities because some had to be helped or dragged to new positions.

On the hill opposite the Firqat's comrades quickly located this new threat and a GP machine gun opened up on their position. The fire was impressively accurate smacking forcefully against the rocks and sending splinters flying in the air. Musabbah instinctively ducked his head beneath the protection of his arm but Mussalim ignored the flying flints and carried on his fusillade uninterrupted. All the anger and pent up frustrations that Musallim had endured recently was released and became directed against those objects cowering amongst those ruins. He no longer saw them as men, just targets and obstacles that must be removed. He emptied his magazine quickly, replaced it with his spare and emptied that too. He snatched off his ammunition belts and tumbled in haste to refill one. Then he slammed it into place and emptied it quicker than he had filled it.

"You will soon be out of ammunition," Musabbah shouted in his ear.

Mussalim glanced down at the stocks, he was right. He reined in his wild temper feeling contrite and realising that he had been temporarily out of control.

"I can see why they call you Crazy Man," Musabbah said, shaking his head with a degree of astonishment.

Mussalim looked down into the ruins. Fire came from there no longer. Under the intensity of the onslaught from both directions the trapped men had stayed beneath their meagre protection. He switched his weapon over to single fire – it only needed sniping to keep them trapped until such time as they became desperate enough to make a run for it. Although the Kalachnikov is a superior weapon as an automatic as an accurate single fire for sniping it is not so good. But then in this instance it didn't need to be.

"It's going to be a long long day for those men," Musabbah predicted.

Mussalim nodded agreement. He was right. Unless desperation took over then it would be only under the cover of darkness that they would be able to get out. He rolled onto a shoulder and began filling his spare magazine.

There was a deep double boom in the distance followed by the increasing whisper in the air of an approaching artillery shell. It grew louder until with a deafening and earth-vibrating explosion it crashed to ground sending a massive splash of rock and earth skywards on the hill above the main PFLOAG position.

Mussalim glanced at Musabbah in stunned silence – he had not anticipated that. A few seconds later the double boom was repeated and the next exploding splash came lower down the hill close enough to shower the men with rocks and debris. As soon as the raining debris stopped men deserted their positions in a desperate scramble to reach the security of the cave. A third shell exploded in almost the same position as the previous one. There was absolutely nothing that they could do to prevent the in-coming shells and they were forced now to endure the treatment that they had imposed on Taqah over these past three weeks.

The next whisper of an approaching shell grew louder until it became a hiss obliterated all other sounds and then it thumped heavily into the ground causing an earthquake under Mussalim's belly followed instantaneously by an eardrum-shattering explosion. Deadly missiles of shrapnel and rock were flung with enough ferocity to pass through a man and were quickly followed by equally dangerous large falling debris. The falling stones and boulders thumped into Mussalim's back and legs driving away breath and leaving him numb from the blows. There was just enough time for him to take stock and to convince himself that he wasn't dead or dying when the terrifying hiss came again. Another heart stopping explosion and the deadly flying missiles peppered their position once again. Hardly daring to move they waited tensely for the next shell. The unnatural silence protracted, perhaps the firing had ceased.

Mussalim slowly lifted his head and stared into a thick swirling dust. Painfully he moved his battered body checking his injuries. Although bruised and here and there bleeding nothing seemed to be broken.

"Are you alright?" he croaked dryly to Musabbah.

"Oh Allah," he groaned stirring to roll on his back. "I think so."

Even in his agony Mussalim could not help a wry smile. "Oh Allah?" he mocked.

The thick cloud of dust driven by the strong wind was clearing quickly. Mussalim looked down into the wadi, which now seemed to have settled into a stunned silence. The previously trapped Firqats now boldly walked away carrying their wounded or dead with them.

"The bastards!" Musabbah exclaimed raising his Kalachnikov to open fire.

Mussalim put his hand on the muzzle and pushed it down. "Let' em go," he said. The message sent had been abundantly clear and understood. "Let them go or we'll blow you to pieces."

The wadi became quiet once more as if nothing had happened at all. They scanned the hill beneath them for any sign of movement but could see nothing. However, there could be a hundred men hidden amongst the thick *Ghaf* down there. But then they couldn't stay around here all day particularly since their position was known and those artillery shells could start again at any time. They needed to move out. Mussalim had no choice but to gamble that the Firqats had withdrawn.

They descended the goat track quickly into the wadi bottom and stood staring towards the hill for any sign of the Firqats. They could see nothing, but that still did not inspire confidence. If they were still there then it was not likely that they would obligingly wave. With a glance at each other and a tentative last look towards the hill they ran half expecting to feel the thump of a bullet, but none came. They made the comparative safety of the trees on the other side and began to climb towards the cave. Men sat in and around the cave mouth, silently watching their approach with stunned expressions on their grim faces. Although it wasted valuable time, protocol demanded that he walk among them, shaking each hand and enquiring about their welfare. Although shocked and dispirited, incredibly there had been no casualties, only superficial wounds from flying debris.

"How did they pinpoint our position so accurately?" Nasser asked.

Mussalim pointed towards the radio. "By radio!" He turned and indicated the Firqat position. "From that hill they directed the shells right down our throats."

"Oh I almost forgot," the mention of the radio reminded Nasser. "Abdel Tahir was in touch and his orders are to continue with the attacks."

Mussalim could not help scoffing. He had no intention of continuing the attacks at this time. In view of recent events and Abdel's much too ready withdrawal from the battle he felt no contrition disregarding that order. The village Aghatad was little more that a kilometre away to the west. Even if their presence there were known it was unlikely that the Taqah gun would be directed against a village full of innocent civilians, it would be a safe haven. Ironically he was banking on the man commanding the Taqah castle to have more scruples than Abdel Tahir. He set about urging the men to gather their equipment quickly and then without delay they moved out.

They climbed out of the wadi onto a clear stretch of ground and moved west, every stride taking them further away from Aram and the enemy. He was he knew, deserting the position to them. But what did that matter? If he had his way then he would have done that on the first day as soon as the gun was safe. Sitting up there on the peak with no one to fight then they would probably have soon gone back to Taqah satisfied that the gun had been removed. Instead the fight had gone on and people had died, probably on both sides. Even now he still could not really understand why the Sultan's soldiers were still on the jebal. Their main objective would have been to remove the gun, their second probably to capture it. Within hours of the first day they had achieved their first objective and any chance of their second had disappeared. So why had they stayed three days? Perhaps to prove they could, he concluded.

Without doubt the Firqats under their British Army trainers had shown that they had evolved from an insignificant outfit to an efficient and organised combat force. Nor could the PFLOAG claim that it was an imported alien force of Northern Omani's and Baluchi's since apart from its trainers it was made up entirely from Dhofaris. Worse still, it was rapidly growing in strength as more men flocked beneath its banner. To Mussalim it signified the growing satisfaction at the improvements and progress that Qaboos was making and more significantly their dissatisfaction with the stringent autocratic conditions imposed by the PFLOAG. If Al Ghassani and the General Command didn't do something soon to reverse that trend then they would lose the campaign of popularity and with it the support of the people. The tide of the war was perhaps beginning to turn against them, he thought gloomily.

It was while relaxing in the village later that afternoon that he received word that the government forces could be seen withdrawing from the jebal. He walked with Musabbah and Nasser the kilometre to the edge of the escarpment and gazed out across the plain. More than a hundred men could be seen walking slowly towards Taqah. Although their lines were ragged there was still an obvious element of discipline in their spacing. A spot on mortar shell would not be able to claim more than one casualty.

"And that's that," Musabbah said.

"Until the next time," Mussalim replied. "One day they will come and they won't go away."

"As you have said before," Musabbah replied.

"I think it is inevitable."

"What do we do now, Commissar?" Nasser enquired.

It was pertinent question. Now that there was no longer the gun to protect he was temporarily out of duty. He was therefore free to return to his recruiting and training role. "Tomorrow, you two can return to Darbat and continue your work there."

"What about you?" Musabbah asked.

"Me? Well I'll join you in four or five days. In the meantime I'll return to Jibjat and my sweet Jumaia."

All three men smirked saucily at each other.

~ 16 ~

June 1971 • Khamisa left Lailla sitting with the sleeping baby and followed the path that Hamed had taken a few minutes before. Since her return from Salalah a week ago he had virtually ignored her and she found it difficult to cope with his bewildering mood swings.

Most of the time his attitude towards her was that of a caring brother. The burden of having to run the farm fell, for the most part on him, but despite that he managed to keep a watchful eye on her welfare. In a busy day he still seemed to find time to carry out small helpful tasks for her benefit. Unlike Jokha, she rarely had to collect her own milk from the drum in the woodshed and there was ever kindling wood and logs at her door. Hamed was perhaps a little too serious to be really enjoyable company but then, she allowed he did have a lot to contend with. This week, unaccountably those small kind acts had stopped. At first she thought it was simply nothing more than he had become very busy and she made no comment. It was after all not much trouble to get her own milk and logs. Soon, however, it became obvious that he avoided her also and on the occasions when they did come into contact then his attitude was stony, almost disregarding her.

His initial resentment of her presence had been obvious from the onset but she had overcome that when they had worked harmoniously together to build her house. Then three months ago after Juma's surprise visit it seemed that she had to start from the very beginning again when he once again became aloof and indifferent towards her. But by going out of her way to be as pleasant and as helpful as she could she had gradually restored the relationship back to what it had been. Now it seemed his odd inconsistent behaviour had re-occurred again this week. From her doorway she had seen him herd the cattle over the hill in the direction of a nearby valley where the grazing may be fresher. She recognised this as an opportunity to get him alone and talk to him. She decided to follow him and daringly for a woman, she intended to confront him with his irrational behaviour.

She walked slowly along the winding hillside path rehearsing in her mind what she would say when she caught up to him. Thin wisps of low clouds hung motionless in the sky, the first signs that another Khareef was beginning to gather. Although they filtered the sun a little it was still oppressively hot and the merest whisper of a breeze brought no relief. She wore nothing more than a loose green cotton dress that stretched down to her bare feet and a large black scarf that covered her head. The cotton of her dress stuck uncomfortably to the sweat that moistened her back and just for a moment she longed for the cool sea breeze that would be fanning the beach of Al Dharitz right now.

The week that she had spent in Al Dharitz had been a wonderful. Her own analysis of the visit to her family roots was as a triumphal return. Now that she had a child of her own and a husband that would make other women envious she considered that she was fulfilling a woman's role in every way. Before her marriage her place had been with her sister and other young maidens. But with the evidence of her own child she was fully entitled to join the *dirwain's* of those knowing and mature females experienced in the ways of men and families. But the satisfaction that she felt from all that, even with a degree of smugness, simply waned to inconsequential when she lay with Juma. The kisses and caresses and his gently lovemaking sent her to pinnacles of pleasure that she never ever guessed might exist. So much was the craving for his hands to fondle her body that when they were close and he did not touch her she felt neglected and ached for his attention. There was nothing more that she could ever want from her life than to be permanently by her husband's side. This war, however, prevented it and she hated it vehemently. If Juma were here now to look after her then she would not need his churlish brother and there would be no necessity to placate him.

On the crest above the valley she stopped and scanned its base. It was mainly open and rolling grassland but here and there small clumps of trees broke up the regularity. The grass around her feet was as straw, brown scorched and lifeless. In the valley it fared little better although with perhaps just a molecule of extra moisture down there then was a hint that the grass was less brown. The cows she could see contentedly grazing but of Hamed there was no sign. The trees provided shade from the scorching heat of the day so it was a fair assumption that he would be somewhere beneath the cover of a canopy. She picked her way carefully over the uneven ground down towards the bottom.

In the third copse she searched she found him. She almost didn't. Where the wind had shepherded a low pile of taupe coloured grass seeds against a hefty sized rock, he lay stretched out. She didn't disturb him instead she stood for a few moments looking down on him as he slept. She smiled very briefly, "perhaps he wasn't quite as over-worked as she believed after all." He wore only a *futa* around his lower body while his upper was bare with no trace of manly hair on his chest. A small pool of sweat had gathered in the small hollow of his chest and she watched fascinated as it ebbed and flowed in time with the rise and fall of his chest. She studied his face searching for some similarity to his brother but could see none. Juma had a full round handsome face with a straight nose and white even teeth. Hamed's face was pinched thin with a typical Arabian hooked nose and uneven teeth. His hair was frizzed identical to his father's while Juma's was a shock of curls. For two men sired by the same father there was little resemblance.

She sat by his side in the deep pile of grass seed and placed her hand on his shoulder. He awoke with a start sitting up in alarm. She giggled at his expression of shock dispelling his alarm.

"What are you doing here?"

"I came to find you," she replied.

He looked around probably expecting to find Lailla close by. "What for?"

"I want to talk to you," she said brushing the grass seeds off his shoulders.

"What about?"

"I want to know what it is that I keep doing that upsets you."

"Nothing," he replied just a little too quickly.

"Nothing! Then why have you ignored me since I got back from Salalah?"

"I haven't. I've been busy."

She knew that he lied. She guessed the he probably now felt a little contrite and embarrassed by his recent behaviour. "There is something. Tell me what it is." But he didn't reply instead just stared straight ahead across the valley. "It was just the same a couple of months ago after Juma had left. You had exactly the same reaction." Suddenly, she linked Juma to all three incidents. "Oh Allah," she exclaimed. "You're jealous."

This time he didn't deny it instead he stared at her with a forlorn expression.

She sniggered and placed a consoling arm across his shoulder. "You don't have to be jealous. Juma will always be your brother and he will always love you even if he is married to me. I am not going to take him away from you."

"You have it the wrong way round," he said hoarsely

She stared at him puzzled trying to make sense of the last remark.

Suddenly he was leaning on her, kissing her face hungrily. His weight forced her back onto the cushion of seeds and through the cotton dress she felt his hand moving along her thigh. She grasped it firmly preventing its progress. "Hamed, what are you doing?" She asked alarmed but he didn't answer instead he wrenched his hand free from her grasp. "Don't do this," she pleaded. But she felt his hand once more moving along her thigh but this time beneath her dress. He touched her where none but Juma had and she felt an involuntary shiver as she responded, spreading her legs. He rolled on top of her and began fumbling with his *futa* as he prepared to couple with her.

"No, no," she said, struggling to control her own carnal lust and Hamed's frenzied desire, but it was too late. Juma was betrayed.

He felt like a bull camel inside her, making her wince in pain. In his urgency he was clumsy and much too exuberant. Despite that, she was unable to stop herself responding; she felt the need of wanton pleasure and tried to co-ordinate with his unrhythmic movements, but it was impossible and eventually she gave in, allowing his wild energy to work for her. He was insatiable and made up for lack of expertise with an astonishing virility. His ardour went on and on, unceasing in either appetite or energy. Long after she was spent and exhausted Hamed still continued thrusting at her zealously. Now she began to feel less than human, just an object to be pummelled. The pleasure had been fleeting and now gone, only enormous guilt remained and she lay perfectly still, her mind drifting into a world detached from what was currently happening. Hamed, either unaware or unconcerned by her unresponsiveness, continued unabated in relentless self-gratification. To Khamisa time no longer mattered, she was completely numb, this had now become unending punishment and the punishment was all that remained. She accepted it passively for it was well justified because of her infidelity.

At some point in never-ending time his furious fervour was eventually sated and her ordeal of degradation ended. For a few moments she lay in stunned silence, then she got to her feet and fled. She heard Hamed call her name, twice. But intent on placing as much distance between her and her humiliation she didn't look back.

* * *

Hamed stood on the edge of the copse and watched her until she disappeared from sight over the hill. With a contented sigh of elation he turned and returned to the scene of his triumph. A few metres from the rock he paused and stared at it, marking it as a shrine and burning the scene into his memory. This had been his first time and he could not imagine anything in this life more thrilling than that. He could now understand completely his young Bedu friend's preoccupation with the subject of sex. For almost an hour the most beautiful woman that he had ever seen had been beneath him submitting herself completely to his pleasure. She had been his possession and his alone and nothing could ever change that moment.

He walked over to the bed of seeds where her scarf still lay. He sat down and picked it up. It was gossamer light so characteristic of Khamisa and he pressed it to his face smelling her perfume. The same fragrance had been in her hair and he relaxed back onto the cushion of seeds basking in pleasure and re-lived each exhilarating moment. The fact that he had taken his brother's wife should have provoked some kind of remorse but it didn't. In his mind he already began to plan and fantasise for the next time. She would, he anticipated, make those same attempts to reject him again, but he would again sweep those rejections aside, masterly. Her rejections would after all be only token and not really resolute just the same as this time. The pit of his stomach churned with desire as he relived the way she had opened her legs invitingly to him. Two or three times more and even the pretence of reluctance would be dropped and she would then be his absolutely.

But what of Juma? When he returned then he would have to surrender her back to him. That was not a pleasant thought and rancour began to stir in his stomach as he imagined his brother doing to Khamisa precisely what he had done a few minutes ago. Juma was her husband and therefore had first call of her favours. But then he was here all the time and Juma only occasionally so he would have by far the most access to her body. That thought, however, didn't console him – he didn't want to share her. Juma was a soldier he thought, which is a perilous occupation. Perhaps he might yet be killed.

* * *

Khamisa's baby was stirring and Lailla sat up in her cot sleepily. It was not yet crying, just making those sounds that babies make before they began to scream for attention.

The room was dark though not completely because outside the morning had already broken and sent shafts of light through the gaps around the doorway and chinks in the roof thatch

She sat up and glanced across the room towards the baby's cot close by Khamisa's bed. Not surprisingly Khamisa slept on and didn't hear her daughter. Lailla often spent the night with her sister-in-law mostly to keep her company during the lonely evenings. But last night had been a little different.

After she had returned from her afternoon walk her behaviour had been strange. She had rushed in and wordlessly sat herself down in the middle of the house staring at the door as if expecting a *djinn* to follow her. Lailla's enquiry "What's the matter?" had prompted only a curt, "nothing." Then she had leapt to her feet pulled off her dress poured a bowl of water and bathed, scrubbing herself with vigour. After that she had woke the baby and held her as if fearful that someone would take here away from her. From then on and through the evening she had been quiet and withdrawn so unlike her normal self. Her behaviour had been so strangely out of character that Lailla had decided that she should stay. Then all through the night Khamisa had cried until at some point towards dawn she had eventually fallen asleep.

Lailla got up went over to the baby and, trying not to wake her sister, gently lifted it from the cot. Resting the baby over her shoulder and patting its back she carried her to the other side of the room. Cooing gently to the infant she then changed her and placed her quietly back in the cot. For a moment she stood and looked down at the sleeping Khamisa. Most of her face was hidden beneath the mass of long black hair but even so she looked so lonely and vulnerable. Lailla had no idea what it could be that had frightened her in the afternoon but she could guess the root cause for her odd behaviour was the ache she had for her husband to be near. She wished Juma were at this very moment standing at her side. If he could see his wife as she now saw her then he would quit the Army immediately and never leave her again. She felt inadequate and at a complete loss what there was that she might do to help Khamisa handle this separation. Jokha was the wise one and today she would talk with her, she decided. Perhaps there was after all something that could be done, certainly if Khamisa's latest behaviour was any indication then something needed to be done.

She moved away from the bedside and picked up a jug to fetch the milk for the baby's feed. There was no need, however. As soon as she got outside she saw placed in front of the door a pile of kindling wood, a jug of milk and Khamisa's black headscarf neatly folded. She smiled to herself, at least Hamed was trying to make life a little easier for her!

* * *

Mussalim stood outside the flat-roofed stone built house that was Al Ghassani's office and stared across the dazzling white sands to the blue sea. His thoughts were in turmoil. He felt that he had become the scapegoat for the poor performance of the militia in the eastern sector. In his hand he held the report that the third general meeting of the congress committee had put together after three days of deliberation. It contained twenty-nine points that were designed to seize back the initiative from the government forces. Sitting in the General Secretary's new office at Raykut he had been allowed barely a couple of minutes to hastily scan the document. Then Al Ghassani impatiently drew his attention to paragraph seventeen. This paragraph contained severe criticism of the eastern militia. It cited its lack of commitment and attributed that to insufficient indoctrination and its poor performance to inadequate training. Both areas were Mussalim's responsibility and Al Ghassani asked for his explanation.

Mussalim could not deny that motivation among the militia was poor but he blamed that entirely to the fact that most of the men recruited were pressed involuntarily into service through fear. A man forced in the firing line could never be as motivated as a man who wanted to be there supporting a cause. He pulled no punches and laid the blame entirely on that policy, without actually naming Abdel Tahir as the policy-maker. But that instantly rebounded when Al Ghassani argued that better indoctrination would convince unmotivated men that the PFLOAG way was the only way to independence and their own eventual prosperity. Then he had been astounded when Al Ghassani told him that it had also been reported that his support to the sector Commander was less than it should be. Mussalim pressed him to reveal who it was that had reported that but he had declined to answer. However, Mussalim could easily guess that it could only be Tahir himself, perhaps trying to shift blame. From then on he had received the classic textbook reprimand. His performance was laid open and severely criticised, so much so that he began to think that he was about to lose not only the job but his rank as Commissar also. After that the motivation rebuild had begun and Al Ghassani highlighted his previous glowing performances. Then came the vote of confidence. He was sure, he said, that if he applied himself in the way that he knew he could then the eastern sector militia would become efficient and another Mussalim Abdulla success. It was right at the end of the interview when the good news came. Abdel Tahir was moving to Raykut to become Al Ghassani's assistant and his new commander would be Mohammed Bin Talib who would take over the eastern sector. After that he had been dismissed.

Still seething with injustice he walked onto the deserted beach not keen to be in anybody's company at this very moment. Now he could also understand Abdel Tahir's remark after he had told him that he was to report to Raykut for an interview with Al Ghassani during the Congress meeting. He had told him that he should take all his belongings with him because he might be re-assigned and not return to Jibjat. Obviously Abdel had voiced his own version of the militia problems and as a result he expected Mussalim to be replaced. In the event it was Abdel who was being replaced.

There were special problems in the east that he had not faced on Qara but for all that he had tried hard to implement the same successful plan. On Qara Bin Talib had initially been sceptical but he had left Mussalim to do things his way, content to allow him stand or fall by the results. The results had been an effective force that had enabled Bin Talib to disperse his regulars as leaders among a trained militia expanding the web of his forces and enabling quick reaction responses. In the east however, Tahir had interfered almost from the onset showing no patience with Mussalim's conciliatory approach to recruiting. Instead he preferred the power of fear as persuasion implemented by his hard-line lieutenants. This meant that men went to battle not only reluctantly but also silently resentful. This sometimes had the counter effect of driving them to join the government Firqa. If they were forced to fight then they may as well fight for the side that took only volunteers, after all they could just as easily un-volunteer. As Mussalim saw the situation now, he was castigated for Tahir's incompetent tactical awareness.

He remembered the document in his hand and sat on the sand to study it more closely. It was a lengthy statement with many obscure references. It made a frank admission that the PFLOAG was losing the war of popularity because their current methods alienated the majority of the people and it set out a list of accepted proposals to reverse that trend.

The impromptu courts were to be abolished and replaced by a minimum of eight convenors drawn from regulars, militia and civilians. In future a proper trial would be conducted and less severe punishments would be dispensed on the guilty. Trained medical soldiers were to be recruited and placed strategically in the region to help the populace. Schools too were to be opened. All soldiers would offer to pay for the food that they took from the people and the forced labourers on the model farms would now receive payment. To Mussalim all these points were welcome and significant improvements but the next statement came as a complete surprise. "Although Islamic religion should not be actively encouraged it would now be tolerated." That issue had probably been the biggest point of contention between the Communist doctrine and the Dhofari masses. For the party leaders to now relent on that point indicated the depth of their concern over the drift of support away from the PFLOAG. Obviously all of these proposals were designed to counter the popular effects of the new Civil Action Development Plan by Qaboos.

To swell the shrinking combat force a six-month amnesty was offered to all those ex-PFLOAG who had gone over to the government and now wished to return. Women were also to be recruited and trained as militia, and the widow of a man killed in action would receive a pension. The statement ended with the usual rhetoric. "A protracted stubborn people's struggle was the only way to liberate the Arabian Gulf."

Mussalim dropped the paper to his lap and gazed out to sea. Much of his ire disappeared. These proposals were big improvements and would make the Front much more people friendly. His only regrets were that they should have come more than a year ago as a new initiative and not as now a reaction to the Sultan's popular schemes. His fear was that it might be too late to make a difference.

He folded the paper realising that perhaps he should not have taken it away and that he should return the document. He made his way back towards the tight cluster of dwellings that was Raykut village. Most of the houses were empty, only those that were occupied by Front personnel were not. All the villagers had left deserting their homes and abandoning the entire village to the Front forces. Al Ghassani had moved his headquarters to here from Hauf claiming that it was now appropriate to locate the movement nerve centre in the heart of the "liberated area." The village lay in a small cove surrounded by towering hills with wild undulating country beyond that, so strategically it was secure. Geographically however it was a poor choice for it was difficult to get to.

The house chosen as home and office by the General Secretary was long, narrow, one storey and situated on the very edge of the beach. It contained one door in the middle with rooms to the left and right, each room leading to another on the inside. Mussalim handed in the document to a secretary who sat at a wobbly collapsible table just inside the door. As he was about to leave Al Mushani emerged from Ghassani's office and seeing Mussalim he greeted him warmly. As good friends they sat outside in the mid morning sunshine looking out at the sea and exchanged their news.

Al Mushani had been given a new assignment – he was to go north to the capital Muscat. There he was to forge the emerging alliance with the NDFLOAG. He would act as their advisor and help to re-activate their flagging initiative. His main objective would be, he explained, to restart their campaign of violence against the government, which would then open up another front and relieve some of the pressure on this area.

He enquired why Mussalim was here and grinned when he explained that he was here purely to be reprimanded. "Don't worry," he explained, "they need to find someone to blame if things aren't going well. Otherwise they would have to admit they got their policy wrong. And for the Congress Committee to admit that would be a tremendous loss of face and many would have to resign. Much easier to blame some foot soldier somewhere."

Put like that, it made Mussalim feel much better and he grinned also.

"I hear that you have brought a lovely young woman with you!" He continued the light-hearted vein.

"Jumaia? Yes."

"She must be something really special if you can't leave her behind for a few days." He teased.

"I was told to bring everything I owned because I might not be going back. I own her. So I brought her." He preferred to dismiss the tease easily rather than admit that over the past four months she had become something special to him.

For an hour they sat and talked until as the sun got higher its heat became fierce and Mussalim made an excuse to leave. He declared that now he had received his reprimand there was no longer any reason for him to stay and he would begin his return to Jibjat soon after midday. They wished each other good fortune as they shook hands and Mussalim left to find Jumaia.

He walked through the eerie deserted streets towards the small house that he had temporarily seconded. As he picked his way over the uneven and rocky ground his thoughts drifted to Shamel. The last word he had heard was that she had moved with her brother's family to Raykut. Perhaps she had even lived in one of these very houses.

Or maybe she was still here somewhere providing comfort for one of the fighters. He reached the house and found it empty. Their belongings were laid out tidily on the floor in preparation for his arrival back. He thought to begin gathering those belongings together in preparation for the journey then rejected the idea. He would find Jumaia and instruct her to do it. Outside in the desolate street he paused and looked round wondering where she could be. The beach had been empty, so he turned in the opposite direction. A small shallow river trickled down from the surrounding hills spilled into the cove and cut it into two halves as it leaked into the sea. Seduced by its cool clear water Jumaia might be somewhere along its bank playing with young Salim, her ward.

Half a kilometre around the bend and just out of sight of the village he saw her. She stood in the river, the water barely reaching her knees but soaking her full black *abeya*. She held Salim flat trying to teach him to swim in less than half a metre of water. She didn't see him approach and he settled down beneath the shade of a nearby tree to watch. The scene was peacefully pastoral, a mother teaching her offspring to swim in a slow flowing river against a thick background of green shrubs with the ocean's roar numbed at this distance to a gently snore. He could hardly credit that this tiny tranquil spot was the very nerve centre of the Liberationist's war effort. He studied Jumaia closely. She was very young, no more than sixteen and at least ten years his junior. His first impression that night three years ago in her father's house that one day she would become a beautiful woman was proving correct. She still had more development to come but she was at this early stage, a lovely young girl. He began tossing stones in the water close to her and it took a little while before she noticed the little splashes. When she saw him her face lit to a happy smile and she waded towards him leaving Salim to play alone.

She wrung the water from the bottom of her dress and then came to settle close at his side leaning on his shoulder. He placed his arm around her and folded her hair back from her face trapping it under his hand

"We have to go soon," he said.

"Ah," she groaned disappointedly. "Do we have too? This is a lovely place."

"It is," he agreed but we have to go back to Jibjat."

"Right away? Can't we stay just another night?"

He was comfortable. It was truly a lovely peaceful place and it was only his own urgency that sent him back to Jibjat. It would take three days to get there anyway. "I suppose we could," he relented. "Perhaps," another thought occurred to him. "We could visit my father's farm on the way back. It's almost on our way."

"You are going to show off your Mahru comfort woman to your father?"

"Hmm."

"Perhaps we should get married and then you wouldn't have to be ashamed of me."

He sniggered. "As you say. You are Mahru and I am Al Hamer Kathiri, your Mueller would never agree."

"I have no family ties except maybe my married brothers and since you have already taken me as your woman they wouldn't object. And your Mueller can become my Mueller. Besides that, Allah may have blessed our union despite our tribal differences."

"Oh. What makes you think that?"

She took his hand and pressed it to her stomach. "It's almost nine weeks since I had my monthly malady."

✳ ✳ ✳

A shadow fell over the bowl of curd that she was draining surplus fluid from and Khamisa turned to see Hamed framed in the doorway. She experienced a moment of panic as she found herself trapped in the woodshed. She turned back to the task pretending no concern and muttered a restrained greeting. For a week now she had kept close company with someone, anyone, to avoid any possibility of a one-to-one situation with him. Her first unguarded moment and she was cornered.

She had recovered some shreds of composure from her experience of the previous week but very little self-respect. There was no doubt in her mind that she had betrayed her husband. She reproached herself intensely for not doing more to stop Hamed, in fact her problem was that she considered that she had in fact done very little. She had badly wanted the physical thrills and pleasure that she always got from Juma's love and she had given in to curiosity to see if another could supply it. It had proved to be a sour and unpleasant experience and her guilt was now a bitter pill to swallow. She had prayed fervently to Allah to forgive her moment of weakness vowing that it would never happen again, and she begged that Juma would never discover her adultery. It would take only his simple declaration to the Mueller and she would be his wife no longer. She would be shamed in the eyes of all and more, if he were to denounce her publicly then she could even be imprisoned. Nor was her secret safe, because one other shared it and because he was a man the consequences to him practically insignificant. The disapproval of his family, the disgust of his brother, all of which would probably diminish in time and the blame laid directly upon her. She had therefore to rely on Hamed not to give her away by word or by deed. She was extremely vulnerable and could not afford to even upset him. Inside she was wretched and extremely miserable.

He moved up behind her and put his arms around her waist.

"No," she said squirming away.

He grinned confidently at her as if expecting that. "That's what you said last week but you didn't really mean it."

"Well I do now. It will never happen again."

"That would be a pity. It was the best moment of my life."

"It was the worst of mine," she said softly trying to reveal her deep regret and with a hint of sympathy to placate him.

He laughed easily. "I don't believe that."

"You must believe it. It was very wrong and it must never happen again."

"You would have to say that wouldn't you? I mean in your circumstances." He put out his hand and stroked her arm but she lashed out pushing it away. He looked at her with a puzzled expression on his face. There were sounds of excited voices coming from outside and with people close by she recognised her chance to escape. She moved past him but he caught her arm. "There will be other times, Khamisa!" Whether it was a plea, a question or a promise she didn't know, she broke free and fled through the door.

❋ ❋ ❋

Mussalim had dismounted from his kneeling camel and had just hauled the second one down for Jumaia to dismount when the door opened and his whooping sister Lailla ran out. She leapt at him straight into his arms almost catching him by surprise. He laughed at her excitement pleasured by such a warm boisterous welcome. Over her shoulder he saw his mother and father standing in the doorway. As soon as he could he manoeuvred her gently to one side and moved to greet his parents. As he did Khamisa burst from the woodshed hurrying towards him and just for an instant he thought she was about to do the same as Lailla. But she stopped sharply and stood perfectly still staring in his direction. He hesitated a moment, grinned at her and was about to wave when Hamed appeared in the doorway behind her. He made his wave two handed to greet them both then carried on towards his parents. He hugged his mother and father giving and receiving kisses on both cheeks in the customary manner. After that he went to greet his younger brother, who by now stood at Khamisa's side. He hugged and kissed him in the same manner and then stood before Khamisa. Here he was unsure, he had only met her briefly as a bride and had no wish to appear over familiar so he cautiously leaned forward and kissed her once lightly on her cheek. He stared into her face, even without a bride's finery and the jebal wind raking her hair wildly she was as beautiful as he remembered. Just for an instant he thought he saw a hint of sadness in her eyes almost appealing for help and then it was gone replaced with a warm welcoming expression.

He remembered Jumaia still waiting on the camel and went to help her off the beast. Sensing her nervousness he gave her a brief encouraging smile and led her by the hand first to his parents and then to the others in turn. The welcome was genuinely warm but tinged with a good deal of curiosity, as all eyes looked first at her and then at Salim, the small boy at her side. Feeling somewhat guilty about the embarrassing situation that he had brought her into he introduced her as his betrothed. That caused another excited stir and some surprise for Jumaia as she glanced sharply at him wondering if the claim was genuine or just convenience. Then it was appropriate to explain the young boy's presence as her ward since all the curious stares became directed towards him. After this, and to Mussalim's silent gratitude, Lailla enthusiastically took over whisking her, the boy and Khamisa away to Khamisa's house to show off Juma's new daughter. He watched them disappear inside the low doorway presumably to do what all young girls of similar age do when they assemble privately away from their elder's eyes.

He sat with his father and Hamed beneath the tree close to the house and exchanged news. It had been some time since they had last met and there was a great deal of catching up to do. Not least were the events of Juma's baby daughter and his enforced isolation to Manston. Eventually Abdulla moved the topic to Jumaia. Mussalim knew he would, it was inevitable but he didn't relish the topic for it was fraught with potential disapproval.

"She's a Mahru woman?" Abdulla exclaimed in amazement. Mussalim only nodded. "How can you consider marrying a Mahru woman?"

"Why not? The old ways are changing, did not Juma marry outside our tribe?"

Abdulla nodded. "He did but Ruwas are at least Kathiri."

"But not in our faction of Kathiri. Ruwas are Hinawi," he argued.

"That is different. Kathiri and Mahru are traditional enemies. What does her father say?"

"Her father is dead. That is why she was married so young."

"She was married?" He exclaimed. "Then where is her husband?"

"Disappeared. Probably dead also."

"Probably?" Abdulla sighed heavily after Mussalim's affirming nod. "Oh Mussalim," he breathed. "You intend to take a Mahru woman as your wife whose husband may or may not be dead. Let me remind you a man can have three wives, a woman can have but one husband."

"I know."

"Then why not select another?" He appealed. "A young virgin from within our tribe or at least within our faction of Kathiri."

"Jumaia will be whatever I want her to be. If I want her to be Al Hamer then she will. Only her brothers or her Mueller can object and her brothers won't, I am sure. As for her Mueller I will take her away and not even ask him. People are people and what tribes they are born into is purely co-incidental."

"You echo the very words of your brother," Abdulla said tiredly.

Mussalim glanced towards Khamisa's house. "Did it not work out for my brother?"

Abdulla followed the direction of his gaze. That he could not deny, he had never seen two people so happy together and judging by Khamisa's recent attitude, so miserable apart. "It did," he admitted. "But what if her husband turns out not to be dead?"

"Then I will kill him."

His father stared at him in horror. "You would kill a man to possess his wife?"

"I would have no choice." Mussalim stared back holding unrelenting eye lock. "She carries my child."

"Oh Allah!" Abdulla groaned and the argument was ended.

✳ ✳ ✳

Hamed had listened intently to the argument throughout and he empathised completely with his eldest brother's statement. His situation was similar the differences were that in his case the husband was his own brother and that the woman did not carry his child. Then the thought occurred to him. What if within Khamisa Allah had guided his seed too? Then he might also have justification to kill her husband.

Later Abdulla instructed Hamed to slaughter a young goat and in the early evening they dined royally on goat meat, rice and fruit laid out on a large platter. Afterwards Abdulla and Hamed left to shepherd the returning cows into the stick woven rondaaval. Now it was the women's turn to eat and they gathered around the platter to finish what had been left. They were in high spirits and even Jokha joined in with the girlish giggling. Mussalim was particularly pleased at the way Jumaia had been accepted and she appeared to be completely at ease in their company. He watched Khamisa for a few moments noting that she was perhaps a little more reserved than the rest but he thought nothing significant of that. It was probably her normal manner, he concluded.

Left alone for the moment he climbed the hill above the farm to watch the sun set on what had been a pleasant day. He re-arranged some scattered stones and rocks around Kathya's grave and then settled to stare at the western sky's nightly kaleidoscope of colours. Tomorrow he would have to continue his journey to Jibjat and return to the seemingly never-ending struggle for independence. It was very nearly three years since he had left the farm to join that struggle. At one point a little over a year ago it seemed that victory had been within their reach. Apart from isolated pockets they had controlled the vast majority of the region and with the support of the majority of the people it had only remained to squeeze out those pockets one by one. Elusively, it had slipped away. The front still held the vast majority of the region but the people support was unmistakingly weakening, while the support for the new Sultan was strengthening. So too were his forces. He sighed heavily, anticipating that there would be a long struggle ahead to get back to that position and once more to the brink of victory. Within his family too, much had changed over this period. In fact it seemed nothing had remained the same. As he looked around the effects of those changes were patently obvious. For a start Juma was no longer here. He was an *askar,* which back then had never been his remotest intention. More than that he was now a father and with a charming wife. He glanced at the pile of stones by his side, his second mother's grave. She had gone, her life cut short in its middle and a victim of indifference by an uncaring ruling class. His father was now a virtual invalid, his eyes so bad that even with the aid of a second hand pair of spectacles that he had bought from the souk he was more a burden than help to Hamed. He recognised the burden of responsibility that had fallen on Hamed's young shoulders and it seemed that he had measured up admirably. He had it seemed matured into a responsible and dependable young man. Lailla too had grown so very quickly. She had developed into a young woman full of exuberance and it was time to begin considering her future. Some unsuspecting young man somewhere would very soon find himself encumbered with a lively wife, he thought with a smile.

Almost on cue the sounds of Lailla's happiness drifted towards him interrupting his thoughts and he looked back to see her and Jumaia hurrying up the hill towards him cavorting with Salim as they did. Khamisa followed a little way behind ascending the hill in a more dignified manner. Mussalim watched her closely and wondered if she was always so introverted.

The boy was first to him and threw himself onto his back flinging his arms around his neck and Mussalim wrestled him head first over his shoulder into his lap. One by one the girls settled around him as he moved Salim to a more comfortable position sitting on his lap. The continued with their happy banter and Mussalim unable to join in listened with benign amusement. As if by signal the jovial trivia suddenly ceased and an unnatural silence descended.

"Lailla has something to ask you," Jumaia said cautiously, resting her hand on his arm.

He looked at his sister. "Not me, Khamisa." He turned his attention towards his new sister but it was Lailla who spoke. "She wants to know if you can persuade Juma to leave the army and come home?"

He shook his head sadly. "I have tried. On your wedding day I tried but he would not even consider it. The sacrifices that he is making he sees as necessary for your future comfort." He shrugged resigned.

"I care nothing for future comforts just to be with him is all I need. I would willingly sell my gold dowry to raise the money that he thinks we must have." Her eyes appealed sadly.

He studied her silently for a moment. She was desperately unhappy that was obvious and he wondered what made her this way. She had shelter and was accepted and revered by the family around her. She even had her own house that Hamed had built for her albeit very basic. The thought of Hamed emerging from the woodshed behind her after she had run out crossed his mind. Could it be that he was being too familiar? Whether that were so or not, he instantly recognised Khamisa's unhappiness as a powerful persuader to get Juma back home and out of the army. He nodded slowly "I will try again," he said. "Tomorrow, early, I will leave for Manston and I will speak again with my brother. I will do my best to persuade him to come home."

"He cannot live here on the jebal," she said. "A young man and an ex-*askar* he would have to join your movement or be killed by your comrades."

Mussalim shook his head and unclipped the little red Commissar star from his shirt epaulette. "I will be his *rabia*," he said handing it to her. If anybody tries to interfere then show that and tell them that Commissar Mussalim Bin Abdulla, Crazy Man is your protector and no one will dare to disturb you."

She clutched the tiny star tightly as if it represented a lifeline and it was only on Lailla's insistence that she opened her hand again to show her. Seeing his sister's admiration Mussalim unclipped the other. "And one for you too," he said handing it to her. He waited patiently for the excitement to die. "Now would you please leave us, I would like to talk to Khamisa alone," he said lifting the boy and handing him to Jumaia.

As soon as they were out of earshot he turned his attention to Khamisa sitting opposite and looking at him with an apprehensive expression. "First I would like to welcome you to our family. Your presence does us all honour by your beauty and your virtuous demeanour. *Il hamdu lillaah*," he praised God. "My brother truly is among Allah's favourites and long may he remain so." Seeing her embarrassment he paused allowing her a moment to recover. "My father grows old, his eyes are bad and if it is Allah's will then soon he will have no sight at all. I am the eldest and even though I am absent for long periods it will fall to me to be the head of this family. The time has come for me to begin to take up some of those duties." She looked at him curiously unsure where this was leading. "As your family head, is there anything that you wish to tell me?"

She looked away towards the figures making their way down the hill, avoiding his gaze. He waited allowing her time to gather her thoughts but when she looked back with eyes glassed by tears she shook her head slowly. He had nothing substantial to proceed with, only a suspicion that Hamed was perhaps imposing on her a little too much attention.

"Hamed is a young man with immature feelings and no experience of the proper protocol in the company of women. Mostly he has seen only his second mother and his sister on this farm until you arrived. You too are his sister, but then you are not his sister and perhaps his feelings are confused. From tomorrow you must wear your complete *abeya* at all times and find a *yashmak* to hide your face behind. Jokha will give you one, if you ask. If anybody asks why you have started to wear whole covering you can tell them that it is my will that you do. When Juma returns, then you can wear whatever pleases him. Until then, my sister you must not present yourself as temptation to Hamed.

One day perhaps this war will be over and we will all return here to live happily, *Inshaalah*. Until that time all of us rely on Hamed to keep the farm operating ensuring that we have a home to return to. Tomorrow, early, I will leave to find your husband but before I do I will talk also with Hamed."

He waited for her comments but received only her nod of compliance. He felt a degree of satisfaction and was convinced he had interpreted the situation accurately. "You may go," he said with an assuring smile. "Jokha probably tires of nursing your infant."

"Thank you brother," she muttered as she left. Mussalim watched her go but *he* thanked Allah for guiding him to the farm so timely and preventing possible family conflict. Now it remained only to convince Juma to return; not only would that problem be cured completely but it would also ease the weight of responsibility imposed on Hamed.

The next morning while it was still dark he enlisted Hamed's help to saddle two farm camels. He decided to leave behind his own two camels to rest, in favour of two camels Fiad had given Abdulla. They were fine animals and would get him to Manston and back quicker. He tethered one to the other. When he was a little distance from the farm then there would be no need of the tether, the loose animal would obediently follow the ridden one. He brought the lead animal to its knees in preparation to mount. He had struggled to find the best way of approaching the topic of Hamed's attitude towards Khamisa and had so far thought of no easy way. Now was the point where he had to say something.

"What do you think of Khamisa?" he asked tentatively.

"She's nice enough," he replied indifferently.

"She is a very comely young woman, don't you think?"

"Yes I do."

"Is she too much of an extra burden on top of everything else you have to contend with."

"No, not at all. I am pleased to do extra things for her."

"Could it be that you do too much for her?"

For the first time concern showed on Hamed's face. "What do you mean?"

"She is our brother's wife and perhaps you are doing more than she welcomes."

"Why do you say that?" Now there was the hint of hostility.

"I saw her run from you out of the woodshed yesterday. Perhaps you overstepped the mark and were too familiar with a woman who is after all married."

Hamed scoffed. "You are hardly in position to say that to me. You who have taken from another man's wife everything that she could possibly give. And more, you have even planted your own suckling in her belly."

Mussalim looked hard at his young brother. "I have taken another man's widow," he corrected firmly. "Jumaia is free to become my wife and very soon. Khamisa is the property of Juma, our brother and you should not take liberties with her in his absence." In his mind his suspicions had been confirmed, his unwanted attention was precisely what disturbed his sister-in-law. "Hamed," he said petitioning "Khamisa is unhappy she longs for her husband. Don't make it worse for her."

"She is not unhappy," Hamed contradicted. "You see her for barely half a day and you can decide that. I have seen her every day for months. She works, she plays and she laughs all the time, I see that you don't. There is no need for Juma to resign from the army yet."

He didn't have time for an argument that would obviously lead nowhere. In any case it was not a point for debate. "I think there is," he said mounting the camel, "and I go now to tell him so. In the meantime as your elder brother I appeal to you for everybody's sake be prudent in your actions and do not impose yourself on Khamisa. Do you understand?"

Hamed said nothing and stood back from the animal as it got to his feet. He watched his elder brother ride the beast up the hill, the rear camel tugging reluctantly at the tether. He wished that Mussalim would mind his own business and leave things as they were.

Mussalim headed north keeping to the high ground across wildly undulating country until he reached the open *gatn*. With no deep wadis to avoid he angled a little more westerly until he came to its edge and overlooked the barren *nejd*. He descended the steep escarpment and turned directly west. By noon he reached the ruins of the ancient frankincense village at Hanoon. After a very short stop he changed to the second camel and continued west, following the route of the old Dehododa frankincense trail. The heat was frazzling but he didn't stop to shelter, instead he swathed himself completely in robes and rags leaving only his eyes peering out from beneath the shroud. By late afternoon he was just north of the Al Hamer tribal village, Haluf. He had many relatives there and it should have been the ideal place to spend the night. However, there still remained at least four hours of daylight so he pressed on continuing westward. He was very aware of his recent reprimand and he was determined to keep his tardy return to duty at Jibjat as minimal as possible. He kept the animals' pace above their normal sedate plod, though not at a rate that would prove exhausting. He travelled light carrying only water skins and his trusty Kalachnikov. Mindful that he was going to an area of Army activity he had taken special care to make sure that it was well hidden.

Alone on the long journey he had only his thoughts for company and he perused a wide range of subjects. The war situation as it stood and its possible outcome. His role in that war and what his own future might be, whatever that outcome He was a listed man in the government books so there could be no amnesty for him, Ziad had made sure of that. The tide of war was gradually but perceptibly turning against the PFLOAG and unless the trend was reversed his own future looked dour. If that were so, then what of Jumaia? If he took her for his wife, or if he didn't take her for his wife she looked destined to be alone again. In that event if she were his wife then she would automatically become the responsibility of one of his brothers. The thought of yet another burden on his young brother had caused him to smile wryly. If however he could persuade Juma to return to the farm then he was sure that Hamed's load would be greatly eased and many of the problems present and future would disappear. Not least those concerning Juma's wife. All were potential dilemmas for the future and none that could be solved by a decision at this moment. Better, he decided to solve each problem as it occurred and leave the future to Allah. His immediate concern was to convince Juma that he was needed at home. Nor was it entirely for the benefit of Khamisa that he made this journey. She was after all a mere woman and she was expected to make the best of the situation in which her husband had placed her. However, she was the tool, and a powerful tool that he would use to get his younger brother not only back on the farm where he was badly needed but also out of this conflict. The war was about to become much more intense of that he was convinced.

He didn't particularly choose a campsite for the night instead he pressed on until it was too dark to see and bedded where he stopped. The animals he turned loose to forage for themselves among the scraggs of greenery that eked out an existence in the crevices and gullies where a minuscule of moisture lay. With his foot he scraped a small area to remove any stones then wrapped in the same robes and rags though now to keep him warm, he laid down to sleep. Tomorrow at around this time, he estimated, he should arrive at Manston.

It was close to sunset the following day when Manston came into view. The countryside had for the last hour been steadily altering in appearance as he got higher. No longer was it *nejd* nor was it *gatn* more a mixture of both. There was still hard-baked sand underfoot but the landscape was more akin to gently undulating moors except the grass was brown scorched and patchy. The Army Base itself was remote commanding the high point in the midst of vast open ground, like an island above rolling seas. He dismounted, wrapped his Kalachnikov carefully in cloth and then buried it beneath a pile of rocks. After marking the spot in his mind he re-mounted and rode on towards the camp.

Soon he was confronted by a double row of concertina wire one twenty metres inside the other creating a sterile area. The inner row was two coils high and double the height of the outer while inside the compound tall machine gun towers strategically placed dominating the perimeter fence.

Mussalim made his way along the wire fence looking for the way in. He came to the outer gate, a simple wire chicane manned by three guards, one behind a GP machine gun peeping out from behind a sandbagged sangar. Inside the chicaned entrance a well-worn track led across the sterile area to the heavily guarded more substantial inner gate. For a moment he experienced a moment of panic. He was a noted Commissar in the PFLOAG and about to present himself at an army camp gate. It was unlikely that he would be recognised, but not impossible. Additionally Juma had been posted here because his brother was a Front leader and it may be that was common knowledge. If it was he could only hope that nobody suspected that he was in fact that brother. He hesitated steeling himself against what he must do now. He slid off his camel without making it kneel and approached the guards cautiously. Still several metres away they ordered him to halt. Aware of the rifles pointing at him and the machine gun, he stood still and called to them that he carried an important message for Juma Bin Abdulla Bayt Al Hamer from his father.

They made him leave his camels and approach with his arms raised. He was then searched and when they were sure that he carried no weapon they searched his camels. He was relieved that he had had the foresight to hide his Russian weapon. Satisfied that he was no threat they asked him again what it was that he wanted. One of the guards then used the field telephone to contact the main gate. They were about to eat and as is Arabic law of hospitality they invited him as visitor and traveller to sit and eat with them while someone sought Juma. According to Arabic law of hospitality Mussalim accepted.

The man in the sangar remained at his post while the three of them sat around a platter of rice and fish talking as they ate. The situation was bizarre but only Mussalim knew it. A Communist Commissar sitting and eating in social harmony with *askars* of the opposite side. He learned that both men were of the tribe Al Rashid from the central part of the country. They were therefore neither Dhofari nor Northerners and both had joined the army for no better or no worse reason than the money that they were paid. That money they explained simply meant the difference between their families eating or going without. Mussalim could not hate these men for doing the best that they could for their families. Then the seemingly innocent questions were directed at him making him instantly cautious and ill at ease. Staying as close to the truth as he dare he described himself as a simple Jebal Qara farmer. They were well aware that Qara was the very heart of PFLOAG occupied country and they asked about that. He shrugged non-committal and said that they came and went. Next they asked about the forced recruiting of the militia. He thought it might seem strange if he were to deny any connection so he fabricated what he thought would be a believable story. He admitted being forced into the militia but claimed disinterest. He reported each day and was usually sent home. On those occasions he wasn't they gave him a gun and took him off somewhere. Once there he fired off a few rounds when the others did, advanced and withdrew when he was told and then went home until the next time. What else could he do? He appealed. He had simply described the predominant attitude of any forced militiaman, so it had to be believable. The two men shook their heads in sympathy and promised that one-day the PFLOAG would be forced away from his jebal.

A few minutes later Juma came to his rescue. Obviously shocked to see his *adoo* brother sitting eating with two of the Sultan's soldiers he was at least quick-witted enough not to give him away. They wandered a few metres away to talk privately. Mussalim glanced back to the *askars* feeling no animosity at all towards those men, his enemy. In fact quite the contrary, they were simply ordinary men that found themselves in a conflict situation due entirely to their own circumstances without any stake in the outcome or any personal hostility towards their opposite contemporaries. He wondered again how it always came to be that the gullible masses allowed themselves to be duped into fighting and dying to protect the realms of the rich and powerful while they themselves managed to stay well away from areas of danger.

"What are you doing here?" Juma's urgent whispered demand.

" We need to talk."

By now it was quite dark and the perimeter lights had been switched on. Juma led him further away from the gate to sit on a large rock at the very boundary between light and dark. "You must be mad to come here."

Mussalim smiled. "That's why they call me Crazy Man, I suppose." Juma only looked puzzled. "How are you my brother?"

Juma relaxed a little now and clasped Mussalim's hands. "It is good to see you."

They then spent a little while trading news and pleasantries before Mussalim congratulated Juma on his new daughter, which brought him appropriately to the reason for his visit.

"Your wife is very distressed. Your presence is needed."

"Khamisa?" he said concerned. "What is the matter with her? She was alright last week."

"Well that was last week when you were with her. But this week you are not with her and she isn't all right now. She is very unhappy."

"What can I do? I can't have leave again so soon."

"Why do you stay in the army. You only reason for enlisting was your craving to possess Khamisa. You have achieved that, but still you stay in even though it now robs you of that which you craved. It makes no sense."

Juma sighed. "We have had this conversation once before."

"We have. And on that occasion I accepted your reason that you wanted only the best for your woman. But then you were at least together while you accumulated those things. Now you are separated and have not the slightest idea when you will even see her again."

"That's true," Juma agreed wistfully.

"Then resign," he urged. Besides all that your presence is needed at the farm. Hamed needs help."

"Then you help him," he countered, a little hostile.

Mussalim realised that was the wrong tact. "What is it you think you need to make your woman happy?" he reverted to the original line.

"All the things she deserves. A fine home, fine things, fine clothes."

He put his hand on Juma's shoulder sympathetically. "She doesn't want any of those things. She wants only you. She gave me a message for you. She said, she would willingly sell her gold dowry to raise the money that you think you must have."

"You know I could never take an ounce of her dowry."

Mussalim nodded agreement, it would be below a proud man's dignity. "The point is she doesn't want those things you speak of. She would give all just to have you with her."

"I know," Juma replied softly.

"Then resign," he urged again.

"Perhaps I will,"

Mussalim was elated the trip and the associated risks had been worth while.

" The Commanding Officer here says," Juma went on, "that when I have been here one year I can apply for a posting back to Um Al Gharriff. In less than three months my year will be completed. If my posting is refused then I will resign."

His elation was short-lived. "And if your request is granted?"

Then I will take Khamisa back to Salalah and all will be as before."

It was not even close to what Mussalim had hoped to achieve and momentarily he thought to raise the issue of Hamed's close attention to Khamisa in hopes of a more powerful persuader. He rejected it instantly. It would probably create more problems than it solved. In any case he believed that he had solved that issue, so he held his tongue. Three months was not long to wait and there was, at least reason to hope that he wouldn't get that posting. If he did, however, it meant that he wouldn't be back on the farm or even out of the war. But it would take Khamisa back to Salalah, which in effect would reduce Hamed's responsibility by one adult and an infant. It would also remove the object of his temptation too. It was a compromise and like all compromises it fell short of the desirable but it was an acceptable solution.

"Three months one way or the other?"

"Agreed."

"Now for tonight!" he thought aloud. He looked over his shoulder into the darkness. There would be no way that he would find his Kalachnikov tonight. "I had better find a campsite close by."

"I will stay with you," Juma decided. "It has been many years since we camped together like we did as boys."

"Yes," Mussalim grinned, "that will be good."

~ 17 ~

October 1971 • Juma tossed his bergen into the back of the truck. The flat nosed Bedford was just one of many that lined the road inside Manston. He took a last look around at the camp that had been his home for a year and then grasping the helping hand he was hauled up to join his pack. Six other of his comrades were already in there and they began to make themselves as comfortable as possible for what was to be a long and rough ride.

Last week and twelve months from the very day since his arrival at Manston he had submitted his application for a posting back to Salalah. However, the very next day it had been returned to him and he had been told it wasn't necessary, he had been assigned to Operation Jaguar. He was therefore confined to camp and on forty-eight hours alert.

Operation Jaguar was a top-secret operation that everybody in the region had known about for weeks. As soon as the Khareef mists had cleared from the jebal then there was going to be a major offensive against the PFLOAG. Only the operation's objective and actual timing was unknown. However, because of the massing of arms and forces at Taqah and Mirbat even the objective could be confidently forecast. It could only be a sortie into Wadi Darbat to clear out the large cell that was stationed in there. It was likely to be a bloody encounter because the highly visible build up would not have gone unnoticed and the *adoo* forces were going to be ready and waiting.

Led by a Saladin armoured car to clear the way in case of mines the convoy set off. It didn't head in the expected direction, however. Instead it went north east along the rough track which only barely passed as a road, towards Mudhai. They bounced and lurched over ditches and potholes following the track as it bent and twisted wildly along the contours of the high ground. The terrain was wild and spectacularly rugged with deep and wide barren wadis falling away steeply either side of the road. In the bowels of the truck and beneath its covering tarpaulin Juma clung to the frame until his hands ached trying to ride some of the buffeting. The convoy ground on painfully slowly through the morning until by midday it reached the tiny settlement at Mudhai. Here on the high ground above the village they made a brief stop.

Thankful for the respite Juma leapt down from the truck and went to join a group of men gathering on the top lip of a sheer rock face. From this vantage-point he looked out towards the village a little distance away. It nestled in an expanse of flat ground surrounded by brown rocky hills. Herds of camels meandered, or in the midday heat just squatted, behind the cluster of rudimentary village dwellings. Directly beneath him a large and deep semi circled *falaj* captured the water that trickled from a crack somewhere in the rock face on which he now stood. A crude wooden sluice gate allowed the water in the *falaj* to overflow and create an area of bog beyond in which a small forest of date palms grew through a carpet of green bog sward. Bright coloured dragonflies skittered low across water while birds flitted among the date palms, giant fronds. The green of the oasis contrasted vividly with the surrounding harsh barren desert while the sounds of trickling water supplemented a serene pathos. It had been many years since Juma had been to Mudhai but as in all remote settlements like this one they are timeless and little changes. There was no war here. These villagers remote and detached as they were, grew their dates and raised their camels seemingly indifferent to the conflict that raged through the region. Most of Juma's comrades were Northerners and Baluchi's and he wondered what they thought of this apathy. They themselves had for whatever reason come far to fight in this war and here in the very middle of Dhofar was a pocket of people who seemed untouched and unconcerned.

Bread, fruit and water was handed out and taking refuge in the tiny slivers of shade that the trucks provided they ate. Soon after they were on their way once more. From this point on the *nejd* became a good deal flatter and the road conditions improved so their progress was quicker. Two hours later they arrived at Thamrit and the isolated Air Force base Midway.

Inside the security of its compound and away from spying eyes it was an area of intense activity. Not only was there a sizeable force already massed but it was swelling every hour. A Caribou operating a continuous relay from Salalah flew in more men while the Skyvan fleet brought in equipment and ammunition.

The trucks pulled up in the front of a sizeable Tent City and the organisers waiting to meet them walked down the row of vehicles banging on the sides demanding the passengers inside come out. They removed their bergens from the trucks and tossed them into a pile nearby. Then as the trucks left deserting them the organisers succinctly allocated them to tents in groups of twelve.

With nothing left to do now, except to try and satisfy his curiosity Juma walked around the rows of tents. If the activity on the airfield side was intense here it wasn't. Men sat around talking idly or cleaning their already spotless rifles waiting. Waiting for what? Juma wondered. It had to be that Operation Jaguar was being launched from here and not as was commonly believed from Taqah and Mirbat. And the objective? It could not possibly be Darbat from this location, he concluded. They were more than forty kilometres north of the jebal on the *nejd* while Darbat was on the southern coast side and very much further to the east. The make up of the force too was diverse indicating that it was a major joint operation. About half were Firqats with at least a hundred of their British SAS trainers. The rest were drawn from different platoons of the Sultan's regular army. The total number, he estimated was over six hundred. Occasionally he recognised some of his old *askar* colleagues from Salalah and passed some time exchanging news and speculating what the objective could possibly be from here. Although Operation Jaguar itself was probably the worse kept military secret ever, its objective was not and only opinions and guesses were put forward.

The next morning early they were all assembled and instructed to gather their equipment and move it to the front of Tent City ready for loading. The trucks had returned and were parked in Indian file ready. Juma's section was assigned to three trucks and they loaded their bergens then sat around once more waiting. All the Section Commanders had disappeared inside the long metal shed opposite to receive the operation briefing. The outside of the building showed only inactivity actually looking deserted and belying completely the significance of the operation being outlined in there.

Eventually the briefing ended and the officers emerged to outline the framework of the plan to their own sections. Juma listened as their young *Naqeeb* revealed the objective. They were to be carried by truck east to Wadi Halit, then south down the wadi to the very foothills of the jebal. When the trucks could go no further they would go on foot climb onto the jebal and continue south. Their objective was to occupy and secure an old disused airfield at Lympne and that had to be accomplished by daylight tomorrow morning. Once the Airfield was secure then the Air Force would begin to fly in more equipment and men to fortify Lympne as a permanent base. Once Lympne was established then phase two could begin which was to expand outward establishing more permanent bases. The Operation Commander was Lieutenant Colonel John Watts of the British SAS who would lead the assault personally.

They clambered aboard the trucks and a few minutes later the vehicles began to roll, led once again by the Saladin armoured car. They bounced and lurched east ignoring the road in case of mines. Time was precious there was far to go and much to achieve before tomorrow's dawn so despite the rough terrain beneath the wheels the pace was forced. Yesterday's journey was as a mere float on a millpond compared to this one. Juma was buffeted, tossed and thrown about wildly in the back of the truck. A little respite came when they arrived at the wadi and turned south. Here the wadi was shallow and the drivers able to drive along the rocky walls just above. It's not possible to bury mines in rock so they could confidently follow the road picked out by previous drivers. It wasn't to last very long, however, because soon they came to the deserted drilling station at Barbazum where the rough road ended and they were then left with only a cross-country route down the wadi itself. From here on the Wadi Halit became deep and narrow hemmed in on both sides by sheer walls of rock as it snaked wildly on its way towards the distant towering jebal. As the wadi began to rise the route became more difficult and by mid afternoon the trucks could go no further.

Juma watched a little forlornly at the rear of the last vehicle disappearing around the rock outcrop on its way back to Midway. Now they were committed. They always were, but the departure of the trucks brought home the stark reality of the situation. They were now abandoned to see the plan through to its conclusion whatever that might be. At least they were more than six hundred and that was formidable but the *adoo* would not simply allow them to move in and take over. He checked his water supplies and calculated a rough programme to make sure it lasted then took a long drink. He glanced at the frazzling sun, its heat baked the rocks which in turn re-radiated multiplied heat. It would be a long and exhausting march. He adjusted the straps on his heavy bergen to a more comfortable position and set off to following the enormous snake of men clambering through the uneven and rocky terrain.

The sun was setting by the time they reached Mahazair Pools deep in the confusing labyrinth of lofty blind canyons. Here they were told to rest while the guides scouted ahead to find a route that would lead them from this maze and onto the *gatn*. The water in the pools was green and scudded with brown scabs floating on the still surface. Through the long hot march Juma had used half his water supply and had only one and half canteens left. Despite the water's un-appetising look he filled his empty canteen and marked it. He was wise enough in desert survival to know that in dour circumstances water was essential no matter its taste or appearance and this canteen would be his emergency supply.

Two hours later and now in the dark they were moving again. From this point on the climb became much steeper and the going harder. The sun's unmerciless heat had gone but the night was hot and body fluid and strength was lost in profuse sweating. Each hour short breaks were called and Juma rationed himself to drinking only then. As men became weaker their Bergens became heavier and during these breaks much lightening of loads was carried as many began to discard the things that they now considered to be frivolous. After all when conflict actually starts all a soldier really needs is ammunition and water.

The sun had risen and cleared the demarcation line of land and sky by the time they reached Lympne and despite their daylight arrival they were still undetected. Gratefully, the men released themselves from their loads and flopped down tiredly. But there was to be no respite yet. The Op Commander, Col Watts, with tireless energy now began dispersing men to perimeter defence. To him it mattered not whether the man was Firqat, British or *askar* all were simply soldiers with the collective aim of protecting the Airfield. Juma was despatched to the eastern side and once more he lifted his bergen onto his back and wearily set off.

The area of *gatn* was a little undulating and not ideally flat, it was however open. Only scattered mounds of giant anthills more than two metres high disrupted a clear killing area outside the intended defensive circle. Low ground hugging shrubs and thin tufts of scorched grass spread sparsely marked this terrain as the transition area from barren to fertile. The runway itself had at some time been well graded, but now through neglect and nature's reclamation attempts it cultivated sporadic vegetation. The ground itself was a hard baked crust, basically sand compacted into rock that crumbled on impact.

Juma and two comrades were able to scrape out a small indentation and build up the sides with rocks to form a horseshoe shaped sangar. When they were satisfied that the bunker provided at least effective protection, Juma looked at the line of sangars to his left and right. The line faced out from the airfield towards the east and stretched for about half a kilometre at even spaces of around thirty metres. He cocked his FN rifle, fixed the safety catch and laid it carefully on the wall at the ready. He was sure the *adoo* would arrive eventually. It was three hours after sunrise and now that all was ready there was time to pay attention to less important things such as hunger. He began ferreting inside his bergen to see if on the gruelling climb to this plateau there were any rations that he hadn't discarded. The three men combined what they had and shared the contents. The only water that they had was Juma's brackish emergency supply. He laid the canteen out for general use in case re-supplies were not issued and the thirst situation became desperate.

As they ate dried biscuits and chocolate the noisy high pitched whine of a Skyvan's twin prop engines grew louder. It passed low over the runway looking like a pregnant flying fish before with a loud groan it banked steeply away to the north. They watched it grow smaller in the distance as it made a wide sweep before turning to go around again. Now the loud unmistakable thumps of helicopter rotor blades could be heard approaching from the south-west until it was so loud that the ground beneath their feet vibrated in time with the rapid relentless knocking. Four Hueys swept in low and fast then pulled up to hover well inside the protecting circle. Their noses tilted upward before they slowly settled to the ground behind a cloud of thick rising dust. Juma grinned at his two comrades, the arrival of artillery pieces, mortars, ammunitions, water, rations and reinforcements had begun, and so far the *adoo* had not yet put in an appearance.

✳ ✳ ✳

In the house that PFLOAG had annexed as its regional headquarters at Jibjat Mussalim began making his plans to visit Al Haq. The visit would not be without a certain amount of risk, so he considered his options carefully. The militia at Al Haq had collapsed completely and some kind of resurrect mission was therefore necessary. Because of Operation Jaguar threat he wasn't able to go before but now that threat seemed to have diminished there was no longer any reason to put it off.

Al Haq was at the very heartland of the tribe Mushani and because of their perceived relation to the Sultan their desire for insurrection had all but evaporated. Worse, it was a significant source of haemorrhaging away from the Front and into the Firqa. Mussalim's re-indoctrination mission might conceivably result in a seizure and his possible hand over to the authorities. For his own protection he planned to increase his usual training compliment of three to round about ten. He would of course take Musabbah and Nasser but in addition he would send for Ali and his small Qara team to join him from Raythut.

This morning's news from Bin Talib had cheered him and put him in a good mood. Acting on intelligence received Bin Talib had gathered a considerable force locally and moved it east anticipating that Operation Jaguar's thrust would be against the PFLOAG detachment in Darbat. This additional force had doubled the strength of that detachment. Then yesterday the Mirbat spy network relayed the information that a force of over a hundred *askars* and *firqats* had moved onto Jebal Samhan and were moving rapidly west towards Darbat. Bin Talib moved out from the wadi to intercept it and late yesterday a fierce battle was fought south of Tawi which went on through the evening and into darkness. Under the cloak of night the government troops had broken off the engagement and withdrawn presumably back into Mirbat. So much for Operation Jaguar!

He heard the distinctive and instantly recognisable thump of helicopter rotor blades approaching rapidly and the noise grew to earache proportions. Curiosity got him swiftly to his feet and outside just in time to see four pass directly overhead very low and very fast. He went around the side of the house and watched them fly northeast straight as arrows and out of sight. The more casual drone of a Skyvan's engines could now be heard but this time he had to search the skies before he found it flying high above and well out of range of small arms fire heading roughly in the same direction. There had never been this kind of activity in this area before and an uneasy feeling began to stir inside him.

A small group of other curious watchers had gathered close by.

He sauntered over to where they stood. "What's over that way?" he asked.

Shrugs, head shakes and bemused expressions. "There used to be an airfield over there. Lympne! " An old *Shaffer* offered. "But that was a long time ago."

That uneasy feeling increased. "How far?"

A shrug. "Six, seven kilometres."

Mussalim stared into the distance hoping for more clues but there was nothing, just the rolling *gatn* disappearing beyond the skyline. He had no option but to go and investigate.

He went back to the HQ house where he found both Musabbah and Nasser waiting for him. He instructed Musabbah to stand by the radio then he told Nasser to go arm himself and be back in ten minutes.

He hurried the few metres to the house where he currently lived with Jumaia. She watched with growing alarm as he looped two ammunition belts across his chest. "It's probably nothing," he placated her. "Just something that needs to be investigated." She was now approaching the halfway point of her pregnancy and despite the loose robes her condition was becoming obvious. He smiled at her trying to induce a calming effect. "I'll be back by noon," he squeezed her shoulders reassuringly then patted her swollen belly affectionately. "Take care of my boy," he said, then he picked up his Kalachnikov and left.

Before he and Nasser had travelled half the distance Mussalim's worse fears were just about confirmed when two more Skyvans flew in low and very obviously landed somewhere not too far ahead. They crested the rise and from more than a kilometre away they could clearly see three Skyvans and four Hueys parked on the ground. For a few moments they stared gloomily at the scene realising that this was a serious and significant invasion into PFLOAG territory.

They climbed onto a tall anthill and took turns to study the situation through binoculars. The extended row of sangars around the perimeter could clearly be seen and beyond that a hive of activity around each aircraft. Groups of armed *askars* and *firqats* stood around in close vicinity, presumably having just got from those aircraft. Even as they watched the high pitched whine of one of the aircraft's engines increased and it began to taxi away for take off. From here there was no way of accurately telling how many men were hidden in those sangars but disregarding them he could presently see at least two hundred. Assuming therefore that two men manned each sangar and the ring extending right round the airfield he calculated gloomily that there could be as many as seven hundred men currently occupying Lympne. Worse it was strengthening in both men and armoury with every aircraft that landed. Clearly this was Operation Jaguar and they had been completely fooled by the diversionary actions in the south-east. But what was he to do about it?

Using the radio handset he reported his findings back to Musabbah to relay on to Bin Talib. Then contemplatively he stared across the open ground towards the invaders. Now that they were established and in such numbers it would be difficult to dislodge them, if not impossible. Even if they were to assemble every regular and militiaman in the area it was unlikely that they could match their number. The only hope was that it was just another sortie and that within five or six days they would be gone, but the evidence of the build up indicated that hope was remote. He had known that one day they would come to stay and it looked very much as if this were that day.

The Skyvan's engines revved noisily and the aircraft began speeding down the runway on take off leaving dense clouds of dust behind. Perhaps, Mussalim thought, something could be done about damaging the runway and at least hamper the build up. A short skirmish might also give some indication of the invader's strength, which might be vital information for those who must decide what the PFLOAG reaction should be. The only possibility of any kind of attack force lay very close by at Jibjat with the Mahru. Their leaders however did not welcome interference from any Kathiri and it was they who decided what parts they played in any engagement. There was no other alternative but to approach their leader and ask if he would lead an attack on the runway. However, he decided, that it would be prudent not to reveal the size and strength of these forces or they would not even consider it. They made their way back and Mussalim went immediately to find Rabih Bin Aziz, the leader of the Mahru fighters.

The sun was close to setting by the time they launched the attack. They approached from the west with around thirty men and sent over rockets and mortar in the general direction of the runway. The response from the perimeter defence was furious drawing fire from not only their front but to their left and right also. The handful of men were hopelessly outnumbered but for a while they matched the onslaught with rapid fire from their Kalachnikovs and Russian light machine guns. Mussalim lay on an anthill studying the defence positions through binoculars gauging the invaders' strength. They used tracer, which not only told them exactly where their bullets were going but it betrayed the location where they were coming from. They were strong and well entrenched and it would take a lot more than the Front could muster to force them out, Mussalim concluded. After twenty minutes the Mahru wilting under the onslaught and sustaining casualties, began to withdraw. How much damage, if any, that they had managed to inflict on the runway he couldn't tell but the probing had given some indication of their strength and it seemed to be awesome. Sometime tomorrow Bin Talib would be back with his force and perhaps with two forces co-ordinating a series of attacks the outcome might be more effective. They would still be utterly outnumbered but with typical tactics of strike and withdraw they might be able to keep their casualties low and the pressure on the defenders high.

※ ※ ※

Apart from that skirmish over on the western side towards the end of yesterday aircraft had relayed men and equipment into Lympne uninterrupted. The force by now had built to around eight hundred strong, was fully equipped and just about invincible. However, under the heavy traffic of aircraft the runway was starting to break up. Now they had been told to get ready to move on to Jibjat. The ground there was firmer and a more substantial runway could be established. An advance party of *firqats* a hundred strong had left three hours ago to seize the area and they waited now only the word that the mission had been accomplished.

So far Juma had not yet fired a shot and that surprised him. He had expected stiff resistance from the Communist insurrectionists but the operation had been accomplished practically unopposed. As he crouched behind his sangar gazing out at the stretch of land that by now he knew far too well he wondered if the PFLOAG threat had been over estimated. If this resistance were any indication then it seemed that it had. He began to hope that if they were to spread outward from here with the same results then the war might be over within weeks. With the war ended he could locate his Khamisa anywhere it suited him and in an army that did not have to fight then the money paid looked easy earned. Movement began to spread down the line and the word came to destroy their sangars and gather their equipment, they were moving west to Jibjat.

They set off advancing west in long lines and several metres apart. Juma's position on the eastern perimeter meant that he was among the last to start and was among the rearmost lines. Soon Jibjat came into view on the top of a low hill on their left. Its houses were clustered together tightly around the hilltop leaving the lower gently sloping banks clear. The advancing column did not angle in towards it instead moved straight on ignoring it in preference for the flatter ground directly north of the village. The advance party of Firqats had already built their sangars around the secured area and as the last of the men passed through their positions Juma saw a banner announcing that the Firqa Khalid Bin Waalid had done the fighting for them.

The area was a hive of intense activity as the protection of the ground that was to be the new airfield began all over again. This time Juma was sent to the northern end and on the edge of the deep winding Wadi Salaafan was instructed to build his sangar. It was a commanding position with the side of the wadi falling away steeply below. The row of sangars along this edge could dominate completely anybody or anything that attempted to move along its barren base. He set to work with the same two comrades to construct their bunker. The ground here was hard and flinty impossible to scrape away. There was, however an abundance of rocks and stones so the walls could be made higher and solid. When it was finished there was nothing left to do except to take turns watching the wadi below while the others passed time lazily watching the runway clearing activities. It was a reassuring feeling knowing that not only was the company strong enough to withstand any *adoo* attack but also once that runway was clear then supply deliveries would start again strengthening them further.

✳ ✳ ✳

His brother also watched the runway clearing activities but from the edge of Jibjat village. His feelings, however, were entirely opposite to Juma's and a lead weight of depression settled on his stomach. Clearly this occupation was intended to be permanent and there could be no way to move it except by a long campaign of attrition. Regular perimeter raids, bombs, mines, sabotage and sniping until the occupation became untenable. Victory that once seemed so close now seemed to be years away.

Rabih Bin Aziz stood by his side. "For us the war is over," he said quietly.

Mussalim looked at him sharply. "We can move them," his words belied his feelings but he had to maintain motivation. "It may take a little time but we can force them away, eventually."

Rabih shook his head. "If we continue to fight they will drive us from our homes. What then? We are Mahru in the middle of Kathiri lands. We have nowhere else to go."

"Perhaps the Front will relocate you."

"No," he smiled wryly. "For us the war is over." He stood gazing across at the intense activity only a kilometre away. "We must begin to hide our weapons right away. Very soon they will come to search the village."

That was true, Mussalim silently agreed. Once they were established over there then their eyes would turn to the village on their doorstep and they would need to confirm that there was no threat. He thought of the weapons stored in Jibjat which they would need to be moved and quickly. "You will give me some men to help move the weapons?

Rabih nodded. "I must go, there is much to do."

Mussalim stood a few moments longer watching the government soldiers getting established and pondering Rabih's situation. He was probably right he admitted to himself. If the Mahru did continue to fight then they would undoubtedly be overwhelmed and driven out of Jibjat and there was nowhere else that they could go. He was also right that there was much to do, he reminded himself. Not only were there vital PFLOAG arms to be moved but also there were important papers to be destroyed in the headquarters. He went to find Musabbah and Nasser.

Using the southern route from the village and out of sight of government troops he began moving the supplies away. He used camels and drovers in small groups of three or four. Not only was this less noticeable but it also it reduced the possible extent of losses in case of any interception. It went smoothly and by the end of the day he had successfully moved all the arms and himself back to Qardhayt in Wadi Jaloob where he linked up with Bin Talb moving up from the south.

Bin Talib did not have with him as many men as Mussalim had hoped. That diversionary force in the south east had not returned to Mirbat, instead it roamed the area on a series of seek and destroy missions. Bin Talib had been forced to leave the full Darbat contingency in pursuit.

After receiving Mussalim's report about Jibjat he agreed with his assessment that by this time the soldiers there were immovable. However, assuming that they would act with the usual predictability he anticipated that very soon they would start to sortie out from their secure base. That would be the time to strike with a series of well-laid ambushes and together they studied their maps attempting to second guess the potential objectives and have pre-set traps waiting. The next problem was that they didn't have enough men so Bin Talib got busy on the radio summoning additional forces from other parts of the region. The damage had been done by the surprise occupation but he was determined to make any sortie out by the invaders a hazardous venture.

* * *

Two days later Watts went into phase two of the operation and sent a sizeable force south east on a seek and destroy mission attempting to clear that area. The following day they linked up with the diversionary force roaming the southern area and now vastly superior in numbers turned to fight the pursuing PFLOAG. A vicious and bloody battle took place often at close quarters before the *adoo* broke off and retreated back into Darbat. Attempts to follow them into Darbat had to be abandoned, it was too stoutly defended and casualties would have been high.

Juma watched the casualties from the battle arriving back at Jibjat that night and made a re-assessment of his previous opinion of the Liberationist resolve. Perhaps it had not been over-estimated after all. He turned away thoughtfully, tomorrow it would be his turn to find out. He had been assigned to a force detailed to move directly south. Its initial objective was to secure the water hole at Ain denying *adoo* access and then to move on to Al Haq. Since Al Haq was the very heart of Mushani territory it was appropriate that the Mushani *Firqa* Khalid Bin Waalid should be part of the detachment.

They moved out early the next morning around one hundred and forty strong, with the *firqats* skirmishing ahead to prevent the main force stumbling into any ambushes. Around noon the main column caught up to the *firqats* who waited for them at the head of the deep valley where the water hole was located. The valley was straight and narrow more than half a kilometre long and disappearing around a sharp left hand bend at the other end. The pool itself was situated at that end and extended out of sight around the corner. The sides of the valley were steep and covered thickly by *Ghaf* and thorn bushes. A better place for an ambush could not have been purposefully designed, Juma thought gloomily.

While he waited for the officers in charge to put together a plan he scanned the valley carefully looking for some betrayal of occupation. Nothing stirred except that which could be accounted to the wind funnelling down the narrow gorge. Still he was uneasy as were many around him, he could tell. Eventually the plan decided was that the *Firqa* would lead the descent into the valley to the water hole. They would be followed closely by the main force of soldiers. To provide overall cover the heavier weaponry GP machine guns and mortars would be dispersed along this end bank ready in the event of trouble. An hour later the emplacement of those arms were in position and the descent began.

Juma cocked his weapon and keeping a wary eye on the dominating banks he followed his comrades down the hill into the valley bottom. The move along its base was tense and painfully slow with the *firqats* at the head inching forward cautiously reluctant. Half way to the objective the *Firqa* went to ground taking cover behind rocks and stones leaving the main body halted in confusion and completely exposed. All eyes anxiously searched the banks above apprehensively wondering what it was that had sent the *firqats* to cover. Just to add to the confusion they did not respond to their call sign, instead they waved the main body on to continue to the pool through their position.

With no alternative the *askars* began once more to move forward. As Juma passed the men crouching behind their cover he thought of the boastful sign that he had seen five days earlier, 'Firqa Khalid Bin Waalid has done the fighting for you!' Some fighters he thought disparagingly.

A minute after that the valley exploded with simultaneous gunfire the sharp ear-splitting retorts echoing back and forth across the steep sides. For a moment Juma froze confused wondering where exactly the fire was coming from. The men around him scattered like a bomb burst in all directions galvanising him to move also. He threw himself down behind an inadequate rock and pressed himself hard against its meagre protection. The incoming fire was intense and as far as he could tell coming from three sides, both edges and the end of the valley. They were caught in a well-sprung trap and there was nothing they could do except stay hidden. When under fire from above on three sides really effective cover is difficult to find. Juma was more fortunate than some of his comrades, he was well over to one side and under the lea of the nearest bank, therefore out of sight and in the dead ground from that direction. Nevertheless, he was receiving fire from his left as well as his front. The sustained fire from a heavy machine gun raked the top edge of the rock inches above his head him blasting him with flying splinters. Instinctively he crouched lower and cringed further back and in so doing he exposed himself to a different direction. The earth around his feet began erupting with deep thuds. He pulled his legs in tight to his chest turning himself into the smallest cube size imaginable. He could do nothing but pray and wait.

The support fire from the British SAS at the head of the valley began pouring into *adoo* positions bringing a little respite but no lasting relief. Juma saw the lines of tracer passing overhead speeding on somewhere towards the *adoo* areas. Soon mortar shells began splashing on the hillside too as the operator began to locate their exact positions. Juma was selfishly thankful that he wasn't getting the undivided attention of that heavy machine gunner, he had many targets to choose from. Even so he regularly shattering the rock lip just above his head with short taps to let him know that he had him marked in his position. Juma and the men around him were taking no part in this fight they were helplessly pinned down unable to move more than an inch in any direction.

To the trapped men time wore on painfully slowly, mere minutes seeming endless as battle raged all around and over their position. It seemed to have been a longer period than normal since the last burst from the heavy machine gun had splintered the top edge of his rock, Juma thought. He realised that its unmistakable hammering had at some point stopped. Cautiously he uncoiled himself from his tight ball and risked a glance. The enemy on the hillside was now taking less interest in the trapped men beneath them and concentrated much more on returning the intense fire from the opposite end of the valley. Tracer streaked backwards and forwards in both directions like a spectacular firework display. Temporarily forgotten, Juma scanned the hill in front and listened for that machine gun. He could neither see nor hear it. Either it had been knocked out or withdrawn. In any case it gave him the opportunity to move around the rock and open fire on the hillside opposite. Eventually the firing began to subside until only the occasional defiant round split the extending silence. The *adoo* it seemed had gone. It was still some minutes before the men began to emerge nervously from their cover and begin to make an inventory of the cost. Despite the almost perfect ambush the casualties were comparatively light. No fatalities and only a mere handful requiring airlift evacuation. But it seemed that the waterhole was taken and all that remained now was to occupy the positions that the PFLOAG fighters had just deserted and the use of Ain waterhole would be denied to them.

The next day an additional strengthening force arrived and after leaving a securing squad at the pool the main body pressed on to Al Haq. The village with its lime washed houses stood on the highest ground in open rolling countryside. The column moved in extended lines up the hill from the north-east into the village. They were greeted in a carnival like atmosphere, as the Mushani people greeting their own *firqa* the Khalid Bin Waalid like a liberating army. Juma was not Mushani, neither were the majority of the men, but nevertheless the happiness of the occasion was contagious and all were affected by the villagers' exuberance. Clearly the imposed ideology and stringent policies of the PFLOAG were not welcomed here and Juma felt the smug satisfaction of a deliverance hero. If there were any lingering doubt that what they were doing here on the jebal was against the people's wishes it disappeared right here at Al Haq.

* * *

November 1971 • Mussalim approached Jibjat from the south. He wore a simple *futa* round his waist and a grimy sun protecting cloth across his chest flung casually over his shoulders. On his head he wore a dirty shamag with the lower end wrapped over his mouth hiding the lower part of his face. He was bare-footed and led an old and scrawny camel. To anybody who cast a brief glance at him they would see a simple impoverished jebally, and probably not spare him a second glance. At least that is what he hoped. Although he thought there was very little chance of him being recognised should the Sultan's men confront him, a thin disguise was advisable. It had been four weeks since Operation Jaguar when he had fled Jibjat leaving Jumaia behind. Today he pampered to a desire to be with her and see to her welfare.

The fighting had during this past month been ferocious and bloody. Many good men had died but the government forces had undoubtedly gained the upper hand. They were firmly established with large bases and active airfields at both Jibjat and Al Haq and they controlled most of the area's water holes too. Despite the many successful ambushes that the Front had carefully laid and executed they had not managed to discourage the Sultan's men from sallying from their secure perimeters. They had driven a wedge across PFLOAG territory from Jibjat in the north, to Al Haq in the centre and Tarqah in the south and many points in between. Not content with that they patrolled out from these bases almost daily on seek and destroy raids. To the PFLOAG the campaign this past month had been intense and costly not only had they sustained casualties that they couldn't replace but stores of arms and ammunition had withered away to acute shortages. The urgent priority was to re-supply and until then they were practically reduced to hiding and defending themselves the best they could when discovered. The Front was definitely now on the defensive.

Bin Talib had wanted to withdraw back to the Qara region and abandon this eastern area. That would he argued create recognisable boundary lines of conflict. Al Ghassani and the General Council, however, disagreed. The strategy was to be flexible. Which in effect meant nothing more than disorganised bands wandering around the area launching impromptu attacks on the government positions. That would it was hoped keep those positions heavily manned with no spare resources to begin the spread westward. Even that reasoning now looked suspect. More bad news had recently been received that the intended revival of the NDFLOAG and hostilities in the north had failed and Al Mushani had been apprehended. This set back in effect meant that the large surplus of soldier and resources in that area were not committed and could be used to reinforce this area if need be.

Mussalim walked down the side of the village tugging at the reluctant camel. Before he visited Jumaia he wanted to see the extent of progress made by the soldiers. He gazed across the flat area to what had been until recently just an extension of the featureless landscape. Today it was very different. The whole area was compounded by double rows of concertina razor wire inter-spaced by stubby machine gun towers. Inside the compound were myriads of tents in regimented straight lines and behind them rows of construction vehicles. Over in the far corner at the furthest extremity construction of a large building had already begun indicating that occupation here was intended to be permanent.

He turned away and shuffled into the wide main street. A group of men sitting beneath the shade of a veranda stared at him mildly curious about the jebally stranger in the village but soon lost interest. He turned into a narrow street and passed the house that had until a month ago been PFLOAG HQ for this area. It was empty and looked as if it had been well and truly ravaged. The doors were gone, most of the window shutters had too and those that survived hung askew on twisted hinges. He carried on the few metres to where Jumaia lived. Did live or had lived? Only now did he realise that she may not live there any longer. Still he wouldn't know that until he opened the door.

In the event he didn't have to. Before he had secured the camel she burst from the door.

"Mussalim," she exclaimed grabbing his hand and looking about her in some fear. "What are you doing here?"

He pulled the shamag clear of his face. "Do I need a reason to come and see you?" he said grinning at her.

"You shouldn't be here," she said without humour and dragged him urgently inside the house. She glanced both ways down the street before closing the door. "They are looking for you."

He shrugged, "They have been looking for me for a while now."

"Yes but here anybody can give you away."

"No, they wouldn't."

"Yes they would, you don't know how things have changed. The day after you left the Mahru *firqa* A'asifat came into the village and were greeted as liberating heroes. Even the previous Front fighters greeted them with hugs and handshakes. Then they denounced the PFLOAG as thugs and bandits, handed over their weapons and joined the *firqats*. After they had been questioned the soldiers came and acting on the information they had been given they worked their through the village searching houses and taking away other people for questioning. They came here and questioned me for an hour about you. They even asked Salim questions," she indicated the infant sleeping contentedly on the cot. "You are in great danger here. Because of all their promises there are no Front supporters in Jibjat at all."

"Promises?"

"School and clinic within six months. Cattle trade with the government. New wells. Everybody's pleased."

Why wouldn't they be, he thought. "Rabih Bin Aziz?"

She nodded. "He was the first to surrender. Smiling and shaking hands and blaming the PFLOAG for all the misery in the village."

For the first time Mussalim realised what a dour situation he had walked himself into and now his survival instinct began to work. Anyone who recognised him and most could, would turn him in quicker than a heartbeat. It was possible also that Jumaia was under surveillance as the authorities might have anticipated that one day he would return. Even a neighbour curious about a visitor was a serious threat. Nor did he have a weapon for protection. First thing to do was to move the camel since it noticeably advertised a visitor. He immediately sent her to take the animal outside the village, hobble its leg so that it wouldn't stray too far and leave it. He was now imprisoned inside the house at least until dark. When she got back he questioned her about her normal daily activities. Around this time each day she would normally be at the village sump doing the laundry. It was a communal meeting point for the women and her absence just might arouse curiosity so he decided that she should go. He hid in the second room while she woke Salim and left. He couldn't trust the four-year-old Salim not to unwittingly give him away so it was better that he didn't know he was there.

After she had gone he berated himself for getting into this situation. He had thought it would be convenient to leave her here for a while. She was among her own people and with comfortable accommodation. Jibjat had been a Front stronghold and he anticipated that providing he kept a low profile from the government troops then he could come and go reasonably safely. Under these circumstances Jumaia was accessible for conjugal visits when the opportunity arose. However, he had miscalculated the situation completely and because of that, and to satisfy a desire to be with his woman he had placed himself in peril.

But then how could he know that the Jibjat people had been won over by the government promises? Nor could he blame them, clinics, schools were some of the very things that he was fighting for. If Sultan Said Bin Taymour had offered these things four years ago then he would never have taken up the struggle. It was also doubtful that in those circumstances the PFLOAG would have even been born. Then again Bin Taymour had never had any intention of making any such offers and if he had still been Sultan then the people would be exactly where they were then. So by that confused reasoning it was the rise of the PFLOAG that had been his downfall and placed his son as Sultan. Perhaps violence should have been suspended then and Amr Qassim the Bait Umr deputy leader had been right that day in the Wadi Risham cave 'It was time for dialogue, and to give Qaboos the chance to make changes.' However, the

PFLOAG could never agree to that. Incited by Communist countries their eyes were set on more ambitious goals than just the Dhofar region.

It was around midnight before Mussalim dare venture on the village streets. He found the old camel not far from where Jumaia said he would and he brought it back to the house. They hastily loaded their belongings onto its back and then with Mussalim on foot tugging the rein and Jumaia riding, holding the sleeping Salim, they journeyed west.

Because of the aggressive raids by the government forces the Front men were being kept constantly on the move. To remain in one place in any significant numbers for very long invited attack by the *firqats*. These *firqats* being mostly local men were soon informed of any PFLOAG presence and with superior numbers and at present superior weapons they quickly and confidently swooped. The only really secure place in the eastern area at this time was in Wadi Darbat with its well-guarded narrow entrances and its high towering sides. But Mussalim was not located in Darbat, his place was in the wider area among what tatters remained of any militia. In these circumstances it was not feasible for Mussalim to keep his pregnant woman with him. Since Jibjat was also denied to him then his only alternative was his father's farm and that was where he was now taking her. He realised that he might be imposing yet another burden on his luckless young brother, Hamed but he had hopes that by now Juma having not got the posting he wanted would be back on the farm too.

He led the way directly west keeping to the open *gatn* because progress was quicker along this higher ground than the deep and winding wadis. After two hours they were well clear of Jibjat and beneath a large and lonely looking Bedam tree he decided it was now safe enough to rest. He turned the camel loose not bothering to unload allowing it to simply crouch down on its belly to take its rest. With his back propped against the tree and Jumaia snuggling close against his body for warmth and the boy crushed between them he waited for daylight. His mind was active pondering many possible scenarios and sleep did not come.

He was tired and disillusioned with the war. In his heart he knew it was lost and only the forlorn and pointless struggle to its bitter conclusion remained. Even the motivation was gone. Under Sultan Qaboos the people were beginning to get some of the things that had been denied to them, things that every human being had a basic right to. What therefore was the point of the war? He wished that he could just walk away from it all, take Jumaia to the farm and just stay there with her. But he was a Commissar and for more than three years he had taken communist money and now that he was required to actually earn that money they therefore had a right to expect his loyalty. Besides that, he was a listed Commissar and wanted by the Government. He despised Rahih Aziz for his hypocrisy, an influential Commissar one day then a *firqat* soldier the next, but at the same time he envied his ability to simply make the adjustment seemingly oblivious to the enormous loss of honour. In the end it would be people like Rahih Aziz who would get positions somewhere inside the government while he himself would get the executioner's bullet if indeed he survived that long.

The woman sleeping on his shoulder stirred in her sleep sighed contentedly and slept on. She perhaps didn't realise it yet but her future too was bleak. She would soon be married to a husband whose life expectancy was limited. He could only survive as long as the war did and perhaps not even that long. What was her future then? She was yet another burden that he would impose on one of his brothers. Even the PFLOAG proposed widow's pension was valueless. The pension would last only as long as the Front remained in Dhofar, when they were eventually forced out then that communist money would go with them. It would be much better for her if they didn't marry and he gave her instead to Hamed. His baby that was in her belly would at least be brought up by its uncle. He sighed with sadness. He didn't want Jumaia to be with any but him, but he knew that this was something that he must do. Tonight he would speak to his father about a wife for Hamed.

Abdulla had listened to his son and now he was thoughtfully silent. He had to admit that it was a sound and safe solution with a very courageous and self-sacrificing decision. It gave Hamed the wife that he was now old enough to need and it gave the woman, her offspring and her ward a reasonably secure future. Only Mussalim was the loser and as he put it his own future was limited anyway. It was typical of his oldest son's selfless and caring attitude.

"What about you?" he asked.

Mussalim shrugged.

"And the woman, what does she think?"

"I didn't ask her."

"Does she give you pleasure?"

"Yes, she does. In many ways."

Abdulla sighed and stared at him. "Then keep your Mahru woman. Keep her as long as you can. Sometimes in this life we need to act selfishly and take our pleasures, there would be no enjoyment in living it we did not. Allah intends for us to be happy and to thank him every day for that happiness. If it is his will that soon you will be taken from us then I, or Juma if I too have gone, will with Allah's guidance decide the future of your woman. Perhaps then it will be appropriate that she does become Hamed's wife but that is for Allah to decide."

Mussalim looked at his father seeking sincerity in his face. He wanted to keep Jumaia but her secure future was more important to him than his own selfish pleasure.

As if reading his thoughts his father chuckled. "She will be my daughter, how could I not provide for her?"

"If I had listened to you four years ago, father then I wouldn't be in this situation now. You were right."

"No I was wrong. It needed people with courage to stand up and protest. You had that courage I did not. Instead I advocated letting others do it for us while we got on with our lives and waited for them to win the improvements. The path you chose may have been the wrong one, there should have been a better way. But nevertheless you made your protest and now things do begin to improve." He paused, his voice softening. "You are a good man, my son. You struggle and fight for the benefit of others." He shrugged resignedly. "You keep company with thugs and murderers but even so your ideals are noble and the ultimate benefit of the impoverished is your aim. Allah will recognise that. He will not desert you."

He thought of the day that Mussalim had returned to the Qara from Yemen, from the west. From the first day he had relentlessly pursued his objectives but had instantly taken a stand against the cruelty and atrocities committed by his comrades against the ordinary people. He could only guess at the difficult situation that had placed him in. It must have taken an enormous amount of courage to stand in direct opposition to the uncompromising authority of his uncharitable masters. But stand he did and with good effect because for the simple Qara Jeballi things did improve.

The words of that fortune-teller that day so long ago in Salalah reprised through his mind. 'A man will come from the west who will pursue his own mission tirelessly and as he does the results will be that he will ease not only your burden but also others like you.' That man had proved to be his own son. But the man also said that he would unintentionally add great tragedy to his load. Perhaps it was Allah's will that he would not survive and that would certainly bring sorrow into his life.

"Take your woman, my son and be happy while you can. She will always be safe here." He offered his hand as his bond.

"Thank you my, father," he said grasping it.

The sound of laughter attracted his attention and he looked in that direction to see on a blurred background the vague shapes of the three young women somewhere near Khamisa's round house. "I think that the three young women will all be happy here."

"I hope so," Mussalim muttered. "I had hoped the Juma would be here to help Hamed and to make Khamisa happy."

"So did I, but he has not come yet. Perhaps soon, *Inshaalah*."

"How is Khamisa? Is she any happier?"

He shrugged. "She is withdrawn but I suppose happy enough. Now tell me," he asked curiously. "Why did you instruct her to wear a *yashmak* and her *abeya* at all times?"

Mussalim hesitated and looked a little uncomfortable. "Because, although Hamed is her brother he does not look on her with a brother's eyes."

"Ah, he said understanding. "Allah gave man the gift of a brain, he also gave him the gift of a *zube*. Unfortunately he failed to give him enough blood to use both at the same time."

~ 18 ~

July 1972 • The relentless drizzle ran down the rocky face and raindrops dripped off the top edge of the cave's enormous mouth. This cave, one of many in Wadi Darbat was not deep but it was high and it was long with a mouth that extended its full length.

Beyond that the mist eddied sometimes thick with visibility down to ten metres sometimes thinner and visibility better than thirty. At both ends large fires burned with tongues of flame that danced sometimes two metres casting brief grotesque shadows and shapes on the rough rutted walls and roof. Many men crowded together inside the shelter the sombre expressions on their faces made more austere by the shadows from the flickering light. The target would be Mirbat, again. That was well known only the plan was left to reveal and that was why they were now assembled.

Mussalim stood to one side with Musabbah and Nasser and he scanned the gathering of around one hundred and seventy. The faces were mostly of newer recruits and unknown to him but here and there, a familiar one. Bin Talib, Mohammed Ishaq, Suhayl, who flashed him a brief crooked grin from his disfigured face as their eyes met and the malicious Zaid. Even Yaqub the young man who had cracked under the stress of his first conflict at Mirbat four long years ago. Now he looked battle hardened and fierce with a stubbled chin and long wild hair. In fact, Mussalim reflected the whole band looked cold-blooded and barbarous. There was no militia here in this mob. That had all but melted away in this area, either into dormancy or recruited into the *firqats*. Only PFLOAG dedicated regulars filled this cave.

These past eight months, since Operation Jaguar had not been good for the Front. They had been hounded and hammered by the Sultan's men. The Government forces had established a network of secure bases throughout the eastern area and patrolled out from these bases on unrelenting seek and destroy missions. Desperately short of arms and ammunition the PFLOAG fighters were forced continually to cut and run with no ability to sustain any sort of a stand. Any kind of attacks that were launched against the soldier's secure bases was sporadic, uncoordinated and short in duration amounting to nothing more than token sabre rattling. Essentially though the pattern was familiar and unchanging, discovered, defend then disengage. The thick blanketing fog of this new Khareef now provided some badly needed relief from this consistent harassing and an opportunity at last to conserve ammunition. The re-supply of crucially needed munitions from the Yemen to this area had been depressingly slow, hampered considerably by the establishment of the Leopard Line.

The Leopard line was constructed thirty kilometres west of Salalah and its sole intention was to cut the PFLOAG supply routes. It was a narrow strip of mined ground between two wired fences and was heavily patrolled. It ran south to north in three stretches starting at Jebal Aroomq across the *gatn* to Jebal Qaftawt. From Qaftawt it continued on northwards down the mountain and out onto the *nejd*. Although some determined suppliers did manage to cross, it was decidedly dangerous and most preferred to go around which pushed them far to the north out onto the open and more exposed *nejd*. With constant air patrols overhead these supply caravans were often spotted and then acting on the relayed information the Kathiri *Firqa* Al Nasr operating from Al Donib raced to find and intercept. The Leopard Line did not completely cut the supply route but it did effectively slow the flow right down.

Now at last there was considered to be enough reserve stocks to mount a significant offensive. A victory of some sort was desperately needed to kick-start the movement's flagging fortunes back into life. Four years ago the attack on Mirbat had signified the move from civil disobedience to organised revolutionary violence and after that the Front's strength had flourished. Where better to start again than back at that beginning?

Today there was no Al Ghassani, he was, it seemed, away soliciting funds from the movement's communist supporters. The plan was outlined by a man unknown to Mussalim, Zahir Ali Matar of the Central Committee. Although the man was unknown the plan wasn't. It had a familiar slant to it in as much as it was very similar to the Al Ghassani plan of four years before.

The first objective was to take out the northern outpost before daylight. Then supported by mortar fire from the foot of Jebal Samhan to advance to the perimeter wire and engage both the hill and the beach forts. The main thrust, however, would be from the east up the hill to the very walls of the hill fort. It was from here that the plan differed. Since that day four years ago an old Second World War twenty-five pound artillery gun had been positioned on the north-west corner of the fort. It dominated the northern approach and the wire. However, with the fort at its back it had a blind side and was ineffective to any attack from the other side. Masked behind the walls the attackers could move to within a few metres of the gun pit and the first objective was to take that gun. Once captured it could be turned inwards and onto the fort itself. From point blank range shells blasted into and through the heavy wooden doors would be devastating. Not only would it rapidly disintegrate the doors but also shells passing through the interior would wreak incalculable damage. The fort would soon fall and after that the gun could be turned to other targets. First the building on the edge of the town that was BATT headquarters, British Army Training Team, and then eventually to the beach fort. After all those buildings had been reduced to rubble it remained only to spike the gun itself and then to withdraw in triumph.

After the brief came the questions, "When?" Tomorrow night they would move into position and attack before dawn the next day. "What about the threat of reinforcements?" From where? Zahir Ali countered, the Government troops were fully stretched and widely dispersed throughout the region. "How many men currently manned both forts?"

From information received no more than seventy in total. "What about the threat from the skies?" He shrugged there was not a lot that could be done to prevent that except hope that the mists were thick enough to limit the aircraft's effectiveness. The memory of those aircraft swooping over the defenceless men below and the devastation that they caused that day was still vivid in Mussalim's mind and he was filled with foreboding. Then followed the rhetoric how important this victory was and what it would do for the PFLOAG cause.

Mussalim had stopped paying close attention, he looked out into the swirling mist hoping that tomorrow it would be similar. The mists down on the plain were invariably thinner than up in the mountains but then a really thick mist would be a handicap to the attackers also. It needed to be just thick enough to prevent aircraft intervention. If it weren't, then those aircraft would come for certain. There would be losses that was inevitable, but if there were aircraft hunting in the skies overhead then the casualties would be considerably greater. Perhaps if it were Allah's will, then he would be one of those casualties. He considered that likelihood and was surprised by how little it worried him. Perhaps that was because he had already accepted that his time was limited. Whether his last day was to be the day after tomorrow or next year it did not matter that much. Then he thought of his infant son of three months whom he had seen only twice and his resolve stiffened. No, he would not die at Mirbat, whatever the outcome of this battle he would survive. Every day that dawned he would fight to survive for as long as he could and when there were no days left then he would struggle each hour down into minutes just to see his boy grow for as long as he possibly could.

✳ ✳ ✳

Juma walked from the gates of the beach fort into a grey misty morning and for a few moments he stood staring out at the agitated sea. It reflected the colours of the cloudy sky as it rushed huge rollers towards the shore. These rollers arriving at the beach clashed with a deafening crash against the waters being sucked back, then with an angry hiss ran up the sand until its momentum was gone. He had just finished a twelve-hour duty and his eyes felt raw and swollen through lack of sleep. The rest of the day until sundown was his and his intention now was to catch up on some sleep.

He turned to walk in the direction of the tight cluster of houses where Khamisa would be waiting for him to arrive home. Six months ago he had managed this posting from Al Haq and a month later he had brought Khamisa from his father's jebal farm to live in a modest home in the middle of Mirbat's tight narrow streets. Her attitude since her arrival here had greatly improved and she seemed to have recovered much of her previous vitality. The time she had spent on the farm had not been good for her and on the face of it she seemed to have experienced a good deal of unhappiness. From her previous open and cheerful disposition she had changed to become quiet and introverted. He had wondered how much of that could be attributed to the insistence by his brother Mussalim that she must wear the full *abeya* and the ugly *yashmak* at all times. In the farm's isolated location there seemed to be no valid reason why she should. Particularly when considering that he had his own woman, Jumaia, living there for two months before Khamisa left and he hadn't imposed the same regulation upon her. It could only be that his elder brother did not welcome Khamisa onto the family farm. He resented that and resolved that the next time they met he would confront him. He had said as much to her, but she had insisted that Mussalim had shown her nothing but kindness. However, when he asked, how did she account his attitude to her dress? she couldn't. He felt that she was being dutifully compliant for the sake of family harmony.

He passed close by the BATT house and waved to the two Fijians sitting outside cleaning a GP machine gun. He would never understand how those two men from Fiji half the world away from Britain came to be serving in the British SAS elite force. But soon they would be going home. Only yesterday they had received word that the new replacement G Squadron, a hundred men' had arrived in Salalah. These men would be given three of four days to acclimatise to the conditions and then they would start to replace the existing SAS men scattered throughout the region. When they were in position then this B Squadron would leave Oman.

He made his way down a street that was little more than a narrow alley between high sandstone walls. The ground beneath his feet was uneven and compacted down hard by countless feet over aeons. He continued through a labyrinth of identical streets until he came to the rusty wrought iron gate that was his. Inside, a small barren compound fronted the flat roofed house. Although it was modest consisting of only two rooms one each side of the heavy ornate carved door it was greatly superior to the rustic jebal beehive style that Khamisa had been forced to live in for more than a year. Even so, he saw this as temporary and a mere stepping-stone onto better things for her.

Now that the communist inspired insurgents had been forced on the defensive and were being systematically cleared from their previous strongholds then, in his opinion, it could be only a matter of time before they were gone. This Khareef he saw as a temporary hindrance. When eventually it cleared away then the campaign could be renewed. The PFLOAG would be soon cleared from this area and probably by the time the next Khareef came they would have been rolled back all the way into Yemen. Then without war, a full-extended career in the Sultan's Army in a peacetime situation looked attractive. It would provide a regular and secure income for as long as he wished and that would give him the opportunity to obtain all the things that he wanted for Khamisa and his baby daughter, Tuful. For the first time in his life he could map out his own future and the prospects looked bright. He was of course turning his back on his father's farm, but then Hamed was currently running it and he considered that he was fully entitled to it, if he so wanted. The only complication to that would be Mussalim and here was the only blot in his otherwise optimistic outlook. His circumstances were tied to the PFLOAG fortunes, which were rapidly shrinking and looking increasingly bleak. Even here, however, he could find reason to hope. Mussalim may be forced into exile in Yemen for a while but then with a passage of time and the healing of wounds there would come a time when it would be safe for him to return. This dilemma apart, things were looking good. He had the thing that he wanted most in life, Khamisa and their future looked very rosy indeed.

❋ ❋ ❋

Khamisa stood quietly in the darkened room and looked down on her husband asleep on the cot. She would like to have lain at his side to be close to him, to feel his protecting arms around her but Tuful needed attention and a watchful eye. Their baby was a little over a year old now and she was at that curiosity stage when everything that attracted her attention required investigation. She disliked these night duties that kept Juma in the fort and out of their bed at nights. However, that duty came around only one week in four and was therefore bearable. Their current situation living as family in Mirbat was inestimably better than being separated for those great swathes of time when she had lived on the jebal. Now under Juma's protection and away from the lustful eyes of Hamed she had learned to relax once more and felt happiness returning.

She still felt an enormous burden of guilt for betraying her husband but now that she was away from the farm and that situation she had begun to hope that her indiscretion would never be revealed. She also relied on Hamed not to betray her secret and she would have to rely on his silence for the rest of her life. She was therefore still very vulnerable but with each day that passed she felt just the tiniest bit more secure.

She felt immense gratitude to Mussalim for his intervention. His instruction to her to keep herself covered provided her not only with a refuge where she could hide from Hamed's wanton glances, it also relieved her of the necessity to explain why. It was a simple, "Mussalim wishes it," reply. Hamed had still pursued her and had sought to get her alone several times but from behind the *abeya* and *yashmak* she found it easier to deal with the situation or perhaps it was that he found it restrictive also. Mostly though she had avoided being alone in vulnerable places. The arrival of Jumaia to live in the same house had also helped. It added yet another person besides Lailla where she could get refuge by keeping in their close company. To have been constantly on her guard had been an unpleasant and stressful situation for her and she had never been so pleased in all her life when Juma eventually arrived to take her away. Her joy however was tempered by concern that perhaps after her departure Jumaia may become the object of Hamed's desire. She was an attractive young girl and although heavily pregnant when she left, she would not always be so. She handed her the *yashmak* on that day and although Jumaia had accepted it she had looked at her enquiringly. "Beware Hamed's lustful eyes," was all she dare say and hoped it would be enough.

The Mirbat houses were bucolic and packed much too close together and even among these modest dwellings their particular home could not be remotely considered among the better ones. There was also a heavy stench of fish that hung permanently in the air attracting flies in their thousands. Despite all this, to Khamisa Mirbat was a paradise. She was at her husband's side enjoying his close and tender attention. It seemed to her that Allah had looked mercifully upon her, forgiven her indiscretion and had allowed her to continue as Juma's wife. She sighed contentedly and left her husband to his rest.

＊ ＊ ＊

Along with a hundred and twenty men Mussalim crouched in the bottom of a shallow wadi a hundred metres away from the eastern perimeter wire. They had crept cautiously forward an hour ago and now waited only the signal to advance to the wire itself. He looked at the men around him and even in the darkness he could see the tension mirrored in the faces. Each man knew well the role that they had been detailed. Most here would on a given signal advance up to the fort on the hill. Others armed with RPD machine guns and RPG rocket launchers would remain on this wire to make life difficult for the defenders on the ramparts to fire down on the attackers. He looked to the eastern sky searching for the any sign of the redness that would mean sunrise was coming. But there was nothing only blackness, sometimes he could see the stars clearly and sometimes not at all. Driven by a stiff breeze off the sea the mist drifted towards and over them sometimes thick some times thin. It carried with it the hint of a spray that added dampness to the uncomfortable cold edge that wrapped around the waiting men. When the sun rose he expected that for a short while the mist would thicken and that was good. As it got higher the cold would ease also and that too was good, but on the other hand the mist would then thin and that was not so good.

For the hundredth time he nervously went through his checks. He removed the magazine and checked that it was full before putting it back without slamming it into place. A loud click in the stillness of a pre dawn would carry far. Then he checked his two spares before fingering along the ammunition belts that crossed his chest to make sure each loop housed a bullet. Next from the sheaf on his hip he eased the knife to be ready for a quick draw if things became up close and personal. Then he felt round the opposite side to be sure that the two grenades were still clipped there. For the hundredth time things checked out perfect.

He turned craned his neck and peered over the wadi lip towards the fort on the top of the short steep hill. It stamped black against a dark grey background, large, square and bulky with a tall round tower in its north-east corner. It looked formidable and defiantly challenging them to attack at their peril almost as if it were alive and knew that they were there. Somewhere around on the opposite side would be the gun, the twenty-five pounder that was to be their first objective.

"Allah Fiih Akhbar," an off-key wail suddenly without warning penetrated the stillness. Somewhere within the town a Muezzin from a Mosque Minaret called the faithful to prayer. "Allah Fiih Akhbar," it came again.

It was, Mussalim decided, a good time to pray and beg Allah's protection.

✻ ✻ ✻

Juma heard the call lying on a cot in a small windowless chamber inside the beach fort, it seemed that he had only just closed his eyes. He had finished his last guard patrol less than an hour ago and he had attempted to steal a few minutes sleep. He glanced around the dark room at the other beds. The motionless bodies of comrades, either sleeping or pretending to be, occupied four. Beyond the solitary empty bed he could see Malik standing motionless facing the west wall his head bowed deep in concentrated prayer. He threw the blanket back swung his legs to the floor and slipped his toes through the thongs of his flip-flops. Even though he was fully dressed the cold of the morning air made him shiver. He grasped the blanket wrapped himself completely in it and quietly shuffled from the chamber.

The chamber was one of a pair either side of the great fort doors. He swung the heavy pivoted wooden bar which held the gate shut and opened one of the giant doors just enough to allow him out. This fort had been built many years ago to protect the town from raiding pirates and faced westward out to sea. He crossed the crude road and holding the blanket tightly together across his chest he walked onto the beach. He watched the frothing growling seas hurling agitated breakers onto the beach while he urinated. The bodily function completed, he cleared his mind and turned to face the west and prepare himself to pay homage to his maker. He sank to his knees, pressed his forehead into the sand in servility and oblivious to the forces massed in attacking positions around the perimeter wire made his first prayer of the day.

He had not finished his prayer when the sound of distant gunfire echoed from the jebal, disturbing his concentration. He listened intently then after two or three minutes the firing stopped. It was he decided, only another minor exchange, probably between the outpost and some small meandering group of rebels creating mischief. Apathetically, he dismissed the event and re-asserted his concentration. What he couldn't know was that the first phase of the PFLOAG plan had been successfully accomplished and the outpost had fallen. His prayers finished Juma remained on his knees staring westward in a placid mood listening to the oceans relentless repetitive roar.

Thump, thump, thump, followed by as many sudden explosions shattered his calm mood with a heart-arresting start. He leapt to his feet, thump, thump it went again and mortar shells exploded somewhere inside the defence compound. The mortar fire intensified and in the dark to the north he saw flashes around the base of the jebal. This was not another one of those half-hearted reminders that the PFLOAG was still active, this was shaping like a full and determined attack.

He dropped the blanket and ran back to the fort. The door was still slightly ajar just as he had left it. He squeezed through pushed it shut and swung the heavy pivoted bar into position. Inside the fort all was confusion as men poured out of their complacent night havens to face this surprise threat. Juma ran into the now empty chamber where he had been trying to sleep only minutes before and pulled on his boots and grabbed his FN rifle. He took a few seconds to check the magazine before returning to the outside confusion. Men were already on the ramparts taking positions to repel any attack that might develop. It seemed the thing to do so Juma decided to join them. The way up there was by a series of stout wooden pegs driven into the wall each about one foot above the other. He slung his rifle over his shoulder and climbed. As he reached the top a helping hand hauled him onto the narrow ledge. The loud hiss of a passing artillery shell followed by a loud explosion somewhere in the direction of the town shattered his nerves and filled him with concern for his wife and daughter in among those houses. Keeping low he ran along the ledge and took the next position along the extending line. He sat down breathing heavily his back against the wall and his rifle between his raised knees. Malik ran past him and took the next position. The hiss of another artillery shell passed overhead followed by another deafening explosion, but this time nearer. They exchanged a brief wordless look, then as if by signal both fed a round into their rifle's breach turned around and peered out from between the castellations. Juma faced east and peered into the misty darkness across an open expanse of barren nothingness up the hill towards the other fort. Behind it the dark sky shaded red with the first signs of a new day.

✳ ✳ ✳

Away in the east Mussalim still crouched in the wadi listening to mortar explosions and waited for the signal to move forward. Most of the shells were landing a good way from their position between the two forts. With a flash like lightening the darkness momentarily vanished as a launched rocket from an RCL exploded against the fort tower tearing a gaping hole. The defenders were now beginning to get organised and responding mortar fire had started to explode in the foothills along the jebal base. A few minutes later small arms fire began much of it automatic indicating that the men at the northern wire were moving into position. Now the deep earth vibrating booms of the gun at the front of the fort were added to the noise as it opened up on the men arriving at the northern wire. The battle was escalating.

The signal was given and a ragged line of one hundred and twenty men got from the wadi and moved cautiously towards the eastern perimeter wire. Incredibly for more than fifty metres they advanced before the defenders spotted them and opened fire. Caught in the open there was now no need for caution and Mussalim started to run towards the wire setting the precedent for those around him. Halted by the wire men began to loop ropes through it and drag it away into single strips making it easier to cut. The machine gunners who had also moved forward selected their positions and now began to give some covering fire as they raked the ramparts of the fort.

Mussalim tore furiously at the razor wire ripping his hands on the wicked barbs. All around him was a crescendo of noise and he glanced up at the lines of tracer flying backwards and forwards in seemingly every conceivable direction. The air all round must have been full of invisible projectiles of instant death. But there was no time to think of that now the men to his right were through the wire and had started up the hill. Two men close by went down one with a short grunt followed by ominous silence while the other writhed and groaned on the ground. The wire in front of them was proving stubborn and standing before it they were all sitting ducks. Something needed to be done and quickly. He waved those closest back, while he planted one of his grenades and then retreated himself. With a deep dull thud the grenade exploded showering them with stones and debris when the dust cleared the wire lay mangled and twisted but dispersed. He picked his way through it and started running, driving his aching legs up the steep incline. The vast majority of attackers under intense fire angled towards the north-east corner and the tower. He and a few others went instead towards the opposite corner and wider where they didn't seem to command as much attention. On the southern side running parallel to the fort was a low crease in the ground that would provide some meagre cover and Mussalim led the dash to its protection. With a heaving chest that felt on fire he threw himself at the bottom of the paltry bank and took a minute to recover.

The sky in the east was rapidly lightening preparing the way it seemed for the first glint of the sun on the horizon. The shadows had all but disappeared, only the murky grey mist hampered good visibility. Mussalim couldn't see over the hill to the north to so he had no idea what was happening there. The crescendo of noise coming from there, however, suggested that was where the bloodiest and bitterest part of the battle was being waged. He watched the endless streams of tracers passing across the front of the fort heading to the north wire coming from the British SAS GP machine gun in the BATT house. He could feel the earth's shakes as well as hear the twenty-five pound gun's double boom as it belched destruction on the northern attackers. He could do nothing about the gun at the moment but he might be able to reduce the intensity of the fire from the British. He shouted to the men around him to open fire on the BATT house.

The line of tracer soon altered direction to begin speeding in towards them as the machine gunner changed target and raked their position. The bank gave meagre cover from the fort above them but they were fully exposed to fire from the southern direction of the BATT house. They were forced to abandon their position and to pull back.

✳ ✳ ✳

The men in the beach fort had held their fire even though incoming regularly sent flying debris of sandstone erupting along the ramparts. Now with the sun growing on the horizon the light was improved and the order to open fire came. The men in the beach fort joined the battle.

Juma peered between the castellations into the murky morning. The gun on the corner of the hill fort pointed northwards and belched a puff of smoke, which was instantaneously followed by its deep double boom. He followed the direction the gun was pointing and saw the shell splash the earth on the wire where the shadowy figures of many men tried to breach the coils of concertina wire. They were his targets and he added his contribution to the airborne missiles of dissolution flying in that direction. Just as it had been that day at Habrut in that cross border incident this too was impersonal. The men on the wire were mere targets and not to be associated with human beings that might also have families. Nor could he know if any of his bullets actually found their mark, it was just speculative fire that would hopefully eventually persuade them to stop this madness and go back to the jebal where they had come from. But they didn't, they determinedly pulled and hacked at the wire even though the throaty thud and canon splashes of the gun continued to apportion death and disfigurement.

He changed his magazine and watched the trailing smoke of a rocket hurl towards the other fort. Lines of racing tracer criss-crossed in all directions. The main element of the battle was between that fort and the northern wire and it seemed to Juma that nothing out there that was exposed could possibly survive. The wire was breached and men now started uphill towards the gun. Down they went, filling Juma with hopes that they were halted, only to get back to their feet and advance a few more metres. It was only the sheer weight of small arms and machine gun fire that hampered these men and kept forcing them to the ground, they were now beneath the gun's range. The gun itself continued to blast the men that still remained on the wire but very noticeable with reduced regularity.

✳ ✳ ✳

Mussalim crawled forward to take up position once more under the meagre protection of that shallow bank. This time he was alone, the rest had joined the main group moving toward the tower on the other side. Unobserved he crawled on to find another shallow indentation that offered protection on two sides instead of one. Just ahead of him to the front on the south-west corner of the fort was a machine gun sangar. It was silent and looked strangely deserted. Could it possibly be that it was unmanned? He rolled onto his back, removed his magazine and began refilling it with bullets from his belt while he thought about it. If it was, and he could get in there, then he would be in a protected position only a few metres behind the gun. The gun crew with fire from behind would have to stop firing, take cover and deal with the new threat. He had no doubt that he could get in there with a quick dash, but was it actually empty? And more importantly once in would he then be able to get out alive. He would be trapped until his comrades actually captured the gun and if they didn't then he was as good as dead. He rolled over and glanced back hoping to see some support but saw nothing, he was completely alone.

He was still pondering the dilemma when he saw two British soldiers scrimmaging towards him covering around ten metres at a time before dropping into cover. Mussalim eased himself into position and sighted them. They were unaware of his position and were running right down the barrel of his Kalachnikov. Then they were spotted and intense fire was directed at the two men. With no alternative now they began a reckless sprint towards the fort. The ground around them seemed to be alive with small eruptions and moving earth as bullets slapped and ricocheted on the stony ground. But they disregarded the missiles of death all around and pressed on bearing down unwittingly on Mussalim's Kalachnikov. It seemed impossible for them not to be hit but still they determinedly ran on. Briefly he lowered his weapon and looked with incredulity, such bravery deserved good fortune and he hesitated to be the one to end it. As they neared his position those eruptions and ricochets began all around him and he was now in danger of becoming a casualty of his own comrades' wild shots. Crazy Man Mussalim he might be, but he was not as crazy as this pair and he shrunk back under the cover of the ground hollow. When the fusillade had passed over him he looked up once more to see both men disappearing around the corner of the fort wall. Incredibly they had safely made their objective.

Whilst he readily acknowledged their incredible bravery he cursed himself, he knew should have stopped them. It was too late now, or was it? Perhaps he could yet redeem himself and he made a dash for the fort wall. Here on this side there had been a short squat tower added, much more as an afterthought on the original design. It was the same height as the battlement above but protruded out like another square fortification bolted onto the corner. Its sharp deep corner provided a safe haven and undetected from above Mussalim made its cover. With his back to the wall he inched along until he got to the south-west corner. The machine gun sangar was now only seven or so metres away and easily achievable. He peeped out along the fort's front to the gun pit. The fighting here was ferocious and at close quarters.

The gun was silent, what remained of the crew plus the two who reinforced it were too busy fighting for their very lives. The attackers from the north still inched up the hill and were bearing in. The attackers from the east had made it under the fort walls and from the comparative shelter of the north-east corner were also pouring in fire. From his position fifteen metres away, Mussalim could hear the repeated raps of bullets on metal as the gun's shield was pounded. Realising their desperate situation the defenders inside the fort ignoring the extensive fire from the wires stood boldly exposed to fire down at the men beneath their walls. Five desperate and hard pressed men in the gun pit was all that stood between the first objective.

Mussalim leaned back and coolly rested his Kalachnikov against the wall. He took the grenade from his belt. A well-aimed grenade right into the gun pit and the gun would be theirs the rest then would topple like well placed dominoes. He composed himself, so much depended on this throw. He took a deep breath, pulled the pin and counted. "One, two, three, four." He stepped boldly out, paused a moment measuring the distance and hurled it towards the pit. He watched as it fell short two metres bounced onto the very lip, then rolled in. He didn't even bother to retreat back to cover. Instead he watched and waited and waited and waited. Nothing happened.

He ducked back to cover cursing the unreliable Chinese grenades. His only alternative now was the sangar in front of him. But since the attackers were all around the gun and closing it didn't now seem to be such a 'blind alley' situation to get in. He collected his weapon and prepared himself to make the dash. Before he did, however, two Strikemaster Jet Fighters with deadly spitting cannon screamed in low from the sea just skimming the top of the fort.

* * *

Juma had watched the fight for the gun with increasing concern, he knew well the gravity of the situation if it were to fall into *adoo* hands. That suicidal dash by the two SAS men from the BATT house had raised fleeting hopes that it would stay in the very capable hands of the British soldiers. However the PFLOAG men seemed to have it surrounded and were slowly tightening their circle. From this fort they could do little to help except to keep pouring into the men moving up the hill now so very close to the gun. The situation was desperate.

The sudden terrifying whoosh of maximum pulled jet engines passing low above his head shocked him. With huge relief he watched both aircraft streak away from him and begin to empty their cannon into the attackers. One flew directly over the men on the hill while the other just a little off the leader's port wing blasted along the northern wire. Just beyond the fort both aircraft pulled up sharply and were instantly lost in the very low cloud. Seconds later they reappeared in Indian file this time flying along the eastern wire spitting destruction. The upward racing tracer lines from the machine gunners on that wire indicated that the low passes were not without an element of high risk. The twenty-five pound gun temporarily forgotten, the attackers broke and fled seeking what protecting cover they could. Despite the lines of tracer and rockets that chased them all over the sky the aircraft continually swooped and twisted, relentlessly strafing all the pockets where the attackers now cringed for cover. But no cover was adequate protection against the 500lb bomb that each aircraft carried and both of these were unloaded too. Being directed from somewhere on the ground they then flew towards the mortar lines and slammed in rockets before returning once more to pulverise the men in the open. Flying through curtains of lead it was inevitable that eventually one or both would be hit. During a low pass along the wire by one its tail section suddenly disintegrated and the fighter wheeled upward struggling to gain altitude and the safety of the low clouds. The remaining Strikemaster made two more passes before its cannons were exhausted and that too disappeared into the mist not to return.

A stunned silence descended over the battlefield while the *adoo* waited uncertainly until they became convinced that the aircraft had actually gone. Seconds stretched to minutes and cautiously the attackers began slowly and raggedly to rise from their cover and begin to mount another assault. The momentum, however, was lost they moved more tentatively this time their original enthusiasm diminished by heavy losses. Shocked and stunned, some seemed to be content to continue the fight from their cover or at least from nearby. They had no appetite to get caught again out in the open if the aircraft were to return. Others moved around in aimless groups engaging the fort defenders then after a short exchange content to withdraw and seek different targets.

Although concentration on the main objective had disappeared and with it the whole point of the attack this new phase actually posed a more imminent personal danger to Juma and his colleagues inside the beach fort. The main thrust had been against the hill fort and the beach fort had been of only secondary interest at that stage. Now, however, this fort was the softer option. There was no particular danger of it falling but its surrounding approaches were less exposed and provided more cover for these aimless groups. With attack ambitions no greater than simple sniping it was less hazardous than assaulting once more up that exposed hill.

Juma needed to stay alert, these attackers had a distinct advantage. They moved around, small groups appearing and disappearing continually in different positions. Sometimes on his left, sometimes to his right and often the first he knew they were there was when bullets began to disintegrate the sandstone ramparts around him. The fort defenders on the other hand were static and were easily found.

The heavy thumping sounds of helicopter rotor blades passed low overhead. Juma instinctively glanced up but in the low cloud it was hidden. It could only be the arrival of help either in the form of munitions or perhaps even men, he thought.

* * *

Hidden unnoticed in the relative safety of one of those deep corners beneath the fort wall Mussalim had listened to the sounds of havoc being administered by the two aircraft. Although from his position he could see nothing of what was actually happening, memories of the carnage four years previous made it vividly imaginable. He appreciated too that these jet aircraft were much more deadly than those old pistoned engined Provosts of that time, therefore the extent of devastation would be much more lethal. He slumped down to gloomily wait out the air raid. After what seemed an interminable amount of time they were eventually gone and an unnatural silence descended over the battlefield.

Soon ragged small arms fire began again gradually building in intensity. Fight still lived in some of the Front fighters. He got to his feet and moved cautiously once more to the south-west corner and looked to the gun. It was not at this moment under attack, which was a pity because its defenders were in no shape to repel. Of the five men only one moved freely, two were propped painfully nursing wounds while two others lay stretched out motionless. It was still there for the taking if he moved quickly. Four years ago the Sultan's Air Force had only those two fighter aircraft in Salalah to call upon. Today this Sultan had a full squadron therefore he could expect with certainty that more aircraft would arrive very soon. The gun, however, was too close to the fort for them to risk bombs or rockets and even strafing would require precision and might be considered too risky. If they were to take the gun then they could still get something from this attack. He needed a couple of dozen men and quickly.

He set off at a run back towards the eastern perimeter wire where he hoped to find help. As he did the thumping sounds of helicopters rotor blades passed low overhead, but out of sight in the low cloud. He found around thirty men on the wire milling around in some confusion unsure whether to end the attack or to renew the assault back up the hill. Most had opted for something between and settled down to fire on the fort's defenders from cover.

Mussalim moved among them motivating and gathering them for another assault. The machine gunners on the wire had sustained casualties and damage from the air raid but they could still render some support. Mussalim briefly outlined his plan to go back up the hill once more and move down the fort's southern wall. He explained that only one fit and two wounded men manned the gun therefore one more determined attack but this time from the other side of the fort would overwhelm the crippled crew. Having then taken the gun they could still inflict telling damage before withdrawing. Many stared across the open ground and up the hill towards the fort, the reluctance showing on their faces. Mussalim sensing the unwillingness, assured them that the gun was theirs for the taking if they would muster just one more effort.

"Wait," one man said. "Some more men are coming."

Mussalim looked in the direction that he pointed. From the south forty or more shadowy figures moved through the murky mist towards them. He tried to find a reason why Front fighters would have held a position that far south and he couldn't. These men advanced in straight and disciplined skirmish lines, that was strange too. Then he remembered the sounds of helicopters passing low overhead going in the direction. He raised his Kalachnikov, pushed the lever to rapid fire and sent a prolonged burst in their direction. "They're British he shouted."

The gun's capture now relegated to secondary the group began dispersing immediately to face this new and more immediate threat. Before most could find suitable cover, however, a Strikemaster at almost zero feet came streaking out of the mist with cannons booming. It skimmed along the wire towards them with instant eruptions of stone and gravel carving a double path along the ground ahead. Mussalim was caught in the open and could only throw himself down. Moments later he was pelted with flying splinters of stone as canon shells carved a channel in the ground either side of him. The next moment his eardrums were blasted even more as the aircraft at little more than four metres passed right over him pulling maximum G's from its engine. For an instant he felt the scorching hot blast from the jet's exhaust pipe and then it was gone pulverising further along the wire.

He rolled over wondering how he had survived and tried to control shaken nerves that had been shattered as much by the noise as by the exploding cannon shells. His head hurt and his fingers came away sticky with blood as he tentatively dabbed his forehead. There seemed to be no other injury so he supposed that a flying splinter must have cut him. He started to take an interest in the men around him. They were beginning to stir checking themselves for injuries but ominously in a couple of places they did not stir.

They just did not have any answer to air attacks and it was sheer madness to expose men to it, he concluded. It seemed that lesson had not been learned from the other time four year's ago. But then, he thought uncharitably, these attack organisers were not the men actually exposed to it.

He got to his feet. The British soldiers were still sweeping forward and closing on their position, two aircraft were plunging mercilessly on the vulnerable attackers, casualties were mounting and the attack had lost direction, it was time to withdraw. He began instructing the men to fall back carrying the dead and wounded with them. They needed no further encouragement. He found a temporary position that he could hold while he covered the withdrawal and opened fire again on the advancing soldiers. The soldiers' advance faltered and they went to ground. However, these men were seasoned and determined professionals and both flanks began to curl in on his position. With men to his front and closing in from both his left and right he couldn't hold the position very long. His escape route to the north after his retreating comrades was cut off and he was forced to abandon his position in a westerly direction.

❊ ❊ ❊

One persistent sniper had found himself a good position and was being particularly troublesome. He had been there a little while now and harassed the whole east wall single-handed. An exposed head attracted his fire instantly with a short controlled burst from his automatic. That made it difficult to even locate his position. The reinforcement arrival of the fresh-in-country SAS G Squadron from Salalah, which now swept methodically across the battlefield clearing the area didn't seem to faze this man either. His comrades now streamed northwards in full retreat but not this man, fanatically determined he stayed.

Juma thought he had a rough fix on his position. He was somewhere in the narrow ditch sixty metres away below him and a little to his right. Every time he raised his rifle to point out from between the castellations, however, the flying sandstone deluge forced him back down as bullets tore in.

This was becoming personal and he moved to a new position on the other side of Malik. Removing his shamag Malik placed it carefully on the barrel of his rifle and then with a grin at Juma he moved to the place where he had just come from. Juma nodded that he was ready and Malik cautiously raised his rifle with the shamag on the end. The reply was instantaneous with a short staccato of rounds ripping through the shamag. Juma raised himself quickly peered out. In an instant he spotted the sniper in the ditch then he dropped back quickly as the bullets then ricocheted from the wall where an instant before his head had been.

"Got him," he said to Malik easing back the breech a little to check that he had a round beneath the hammer.

❊ ❊ ❊

Musallim meanwhile had retreated away from the battlefield and been forced into refuge in Mirbat's narrow streets. His route to safety and the security of the jebal was north back across the battlefield. With the soldiers sweeping across and gradually securing that area he was in grave danger of being cut off completely. He arrived at the rough track that was the main access road from the town. It cut a path between the two forts to the chicaned entrance on the northern perimeter wire more than half a kilometre away. It was fully exposed and he would have little chance of making it safely across. He ignored it and carried on in hopes that he would have a better chance of escaping along the beach. Before he got there, however he spotted a better possibility. A shallow wadi cut from the somewhere in the east along the front of the town and into the sea. Just before it opened to the sea, however, it curved a little way north before straightening back east. If he followed that and deserted it at that point then made a dash across a short piece of open ground he could gain the cover of a shallow ditch that did run north. This would carry him perilously close under the wall of the beach fort and then beyond. If he made it that far then it would be another risky dash to the far wire and the safety of those rocks beyond. Those rocks he knew well because it was from that position that he had taken part in the Mirbat attack four years previous. After that he could follow the same escape route past the tomb of Mohamed Agyl just as he had that day. It was a risky way across but his only alternative.

He dropped down into the shallow wadi and crouching over made his way cautiously to the point where he would have to make his first dash. There he took a brief moment to steel himself. If he were spotted from the fort then his dash to the ditch would border on suicidal. Even if he made it and they were aware that he was in the ditch then he was still in deadly danger. Everything depended on him arriving at that ditch unobserved. From his position he could see the lines of soldiers already sweeping down the hill away from that fort and angling in his direction. He could not afford to delay. Gritting his teeth he leapt to his feet and started his sprint.

Almost immediately gunfire came spurring him on to even greater speed. Before he made the ditch he realised that the gunfire was not directed at him at all, but came instead from the ditch and was directed up to the fort. He reached the edge and with a long stride leapt into the bottom. Miraculously he seemed to have made it unobserved. Taking just a moment to recover he then began to crawl along its winding bottom more than a little curious about why some had remained behind to lay siege to the fort. Surely they were aware of the soldiers moving in this direction? He crawled around a corner and was further surprised to see five or six metres away just one man, Ziad. He lay against the bank elbow resting on a ledge just below the lip cradling his Kalachnikov. He concentrated heavily peering along his sights lightly feathering the muzzle backwards and forwards along the fort ramparts above him. He was so intent watching for the slightest glimmer of a target that he was unaware of Mussalim close to him.

"Ziad," he said startling him.

Ziad rolled back away from his position. "Crazy man!"

"What are you doing?"

"Killing *askars*."

Musallim peered along the ditch. "Are you alone?"

"Not any more."

"You can't stay here," Mussalim said. "There are British soldiers sweeping forward." He waved his arm in their direction. "They're going to be here in about five minutes."

Ziad craned his neck slightly and peered in the direction he had pointed. "Then you go," he said flatly and turned his attention back once more to the fort.

✳ ✳ ✳

Malik raised the shamag on the end of his rifle once more but this time it didn't attract fire from the sniper. He looked at Juma puzzled and shrugged. Juma hesitated a moment wondering if it were a trap then screwing up his courage cradled his rifle and rolled quickly into position. In an instant he squinted down the sights and found the position where he had last seen the sniper. There was no sight of him. He waited concentrating on the spot but still nothing happened. Uneasiness began to grow inside him. Perhaps at this very moment while he concentrated his attention on this spot he was now in a different position and about to squeeze his trigger on his exposed head. He took tight control of his nerves and made himself wait a few moments more. Then he was there, right in his sights moving back to position. He held his breath and gently squeezed the trigger.

The man was jerked to his feet, staggered backwards and lay motionless on the far side of the ditch staring up into the grey morning skies with sightless eyes. Juma lowered his rifle slowly and stared at the body. It was perhaps not the first man he had ever killed, but it was the first man he had witnessed as a certain personal kill.

"Good shot," Malik complimented, but it did nothing to appease the growing feeling of abhorrence as he stared at the lifeless body.

Men around him began to cheer as now free from the sniper danger they could safely look out at G Squadron sweeping across the battlefield and clearing the area. Groups of PFLOAG men could be clearly seen streaming away ignominiously back towards the jebal. Juma could see all this and the all events unfolding around him but his eyes were continually dragged back towards the corpse and the life that *he* had ended. He should have felt the relief and the buoyant spirits that his comrades did, but an enormous guilt complex suppressed it.

Malik hauled him back from between the castellations and hugged him in frenzied delirium. All around him he could see happy and grinning faces as the men celebrated their deliverance. The happiness was infectious and Juma began to recover from his guilt complex. He stood at full height and looked out from the ramparts at the scene of carnage before him. At least twenty bodies were draped across and around the northern wire. More lay in the killing area between the wire and the hill fort. He couldn't guess how many had died outside the area killed by those Strikemaster's deadly passes. He glanced once more at the body of the man he had shot still laying where he had fallen and realised that except for Allah's mercy he himself could have been one of those fatal casualties. For the sake of Khamisa, Tuful as well as for himself he was very glad that he survived. He turned his back on the carnage and joined in the celebrations.

✳ ✳ ✳

Musallim stared at Ziad's body with shock. One instant he was alive the next he was dead. Killed by a single shot that punctured a tiny hole in his right temple. He looked towards the fort in time to see the barrel of the weapon that had killed him being withdrawn. He crawled three or four metres further along the ditch to a better position and then looked again. He could now see clearly the back of the head of Ziad's killer covered by a camouflaged shamag. He pushed the lever to single fire and took careful aim.

✳ ✳ ✳

Searing hot pain passed through the back of Juma's neck. Numbing completely the right side of his face where the bullet exited. He felt as if he was floating but he knew he was falling. When he stopped, he lay, unable to move, just staring at Malik's feet. The tingling numbness in his arms and legs began spreading inwards towards his core. Shocked and frightened, he lay helplessly paralysed. He knew he had been hit, he wondered how badly? A question began forming in his mind. 'Was this...?' He never finished the thought.

CHAPTER 19

Mussalim glanced over his shoulder at Zaid's body. He would shed no tears for his death and he wondered if there would be anyone who would. The Front, however, had lost a fearsome fighter but at least it looked as if he had managed to exact a one-for-one price. He looked beyond that away into the thinning mist. The soldiers were very close now and it was time make good his escape.

He crawled on hands and knees keeping close to the edge of the ditch. When at last it petered out he was clear of the fort. The next hazard was an open hundred metres sprint to the wire and the safety of the rocks beyond. Hooking his Kalachnikov over his back out of the way he set off running hard. If anybody saw him then they either watched mercifully or apathetically because he made it to the wire without a shot being fired at him. The wire before him was gapped and mangled showing evidence of the twenty-five pounder's barrage and he picked his way through easily. When he reached the summit of the hill above the rocks he paused and looked back. People moved around inside the defence compound re-securing the area and checking the wounded or dead. No one pursued him, no one was interested and it looked as if his escape was now a formality. He descended the hill on the other side towards mausoleum and the beach. An hour later he arrived at rolling sand dunes and here safely hidden he stopped to rest.

Mirbat had been another defeat. But this time it had been so very close. As close in fact as a single dud grenade that he had thrown. If it had gone off properly the gun crew would have been dead or wounded and out of the battle. The gun then would have been taken and the outcome would have been different. Even the intervention of the aircraft though deadly and damaging could not have prevented the gun from being taken. The gun could have then been used to inflict serious damage and a victory of some sort could have been claimed. In the event, however, it wasn't the aircraft or the dud grenade that was the most significant factor in the battle it was the unexpected intervention of those extra British soldiers. Once again it seemed to Mussalim that the PFLOAG spy capabilities had fed back wrong information and let them down.

But, what of the PFLOAG future? It now looked very bleak indeed. The gamble to restore credibility in this eastern area had been lost. The government would claim another victory and probably attract even more Dhofari men under its banner. He could easily guess the future. It seemed inevitable that the Sultan's soldiers would spread their web more and more across the mountains winning over the people as they did with Civil Action Development. As they grew stronger they would push the Front further and further east until they eventually ran them out of the country. All that would be left after that would be small groups reduced to carrying out terrorist activities until they were either caught or just got tired. It was only a matter of time.

Now he began to question his own ethics. What was he now doing? In the beginning he had been struggling against oppression to bring to all Dhofaris that which every human being deserves. Freedom from want. Now with Sultan Qaboos that freedom was beginning to happen and the only thing slowing it down was the very cause in which he now fought. He couldn't understand how the side of right and without any significant change in policies had now become the side of wrong. Had he been wrong from the very beginning? No, he decided. Four years ago there had been no other way. But what should he do now?

Nothing! He was a noted and wanted man in the Government files and there could be no amnesty into the *Firqats* for him. Even if there were, would he be able to turn his gun on people like Ali and Musabbah who had been his friends? He shook his head slowly, wishing that he could simply throw his Kalachnikov away and return to Jumaia and his son on his father's farm. He sighed heavily, getting once more to his feet, neither side would let him do that.

It was well after sunset by the time he got back into Darbat, the darkness brought on quicker by the thick wet mist. He could not be bothered to report to the cave over the other side of the wadi where Zahir Ali and the Mirbat survivors would assemble. He would go there first thing tomorrow. But tonight he was tired and disillusioned and not in the mood for any post-mortem, that could wait until tomorrow He made his way to the cave that he, along with Musabbah and Nasser used when operating in this wadi. He had hoped that one of them at least would be there and a warm cheery fire might welcome him. But it was dark and empty. It took an hour before the fire was burning hot and fierce and he sat before it staring into the hypnotic flames getting increasingly concerned that his two comrades had not arrived back. He supposed that it was possible that they were over the other side with the main group or perhaps they would be back in the morning but he could not shrug away the growing foreboding. Eventually he stoked up the fire once more and wrapped in a blanket settled down to sleep.

He slept well until the fire dropped to ashes and then the damp and the cold rolled over him disturbing his sleep. For a while he tried to ignore it but eventually he was forced to give up. He re-lit the fire and on a stone on its edge threw on a piece of goat meat to cook. Ominously his comrades had still not returned and while hoping that he would find them a little later with the main group he began to mentally prepare himself for the worst. Then after first washing he turned roughly in the direction of Mecca and made his morning prayer.

In no particular hurry to link up with the assembly he ate breakfast leisurely looking out at the mist and the rain. Eventually he roused himself from his apathetic mood, girdled his ammunition belts, picked up his rifle and set off to cross the wadi and rejoin the war.

Even at this early stage of the Khareef the lake was swollen and had already begun to overflow into low areas further down the wadi. Another month or so at this rate and its waters would arrive at the Dahaq escapement and soon after that begin to spill over the abyss. He found a shallow place where he could wade across and made his way to the camp. The campfires shone like beacons through the mist guiding him directly to the massive cave mouth.

Men sat idling around fires in small groups while others wrapped in blankets still slept. Mussalim wandered around each group looking for Musabbah and Nasser, but couldn't find them. He checked among the sleeping; they weren't there either. He was told that there were fifteen or sixteen wounded men in the next chamber so he went to look there. He checked every pain-ridden face, offering words of encouragement to all. These men faced a long and torturous journey all the way back to the caves at Shershitta before they would receive any qualified help. If they didn't die from their wounds immediately, they might well die from the rigours of that journey. As a last resort he looked among the dead, sewn up in cloths and laid out in the rain, awaiting burial.

He returned to the campfires, asking if anyone had seen either Musabbah or Nasser but got only blank stares or shaking heads. At the third fire he received part of the news that he was by now expecting. Musabbah was dead, blown apart by a shell from the twenty-five pound gun, but of Nasser he learned nothing. The news of Musabbah hit him hard. In the very beginning he had started out suspecting him as a potential Bin Talib spy and definitely not to be trusted. But over the past two-and-half years his loyalty had been proved, repeatedly. Truly, he had lost a very good friend. Gloomily he sat down by the side of Suhayl.

"Crazy man, you made it," he said offering his hand to be shaken. "I had begun to think that you were dead too."

Mussalim looked around the gathering. There was probably only around half of the original number here. "Is this it?"

Suhayl shrugged. "Probably. They're may be some stragglers out there somewhere, but I don't think any significant number."

"What happens now?"

"Well. That seems to be an issue at the moment."

Mussalim looked at him quizzically waiting for him to explain.

"Opinion is split. Bin Talib wants to pull back to Raythut and defend the central region. Zahir Ali wants to stay here and continue the fight in the east."

"What does Al Ghassani say?"

"That's the problem, he's not even in the country."

"What will you do?"

"I like it here. I'll stay with Zahir Ali. What about you?"

A return to the Qara and his home region sounded very desirable to him at this time. "Maybe I'll go with Bin Talib for now and wait for Al Ghasanni's decision."

It was during the evening on the next day as he prepared for an early morning departure with Bin Talib that Hamed and Ali arrived. They had made a special journey just to see him. His joy at seeing his brother and his trusted friend was short-lived when Hamed gave him the sad news about Juma.

✳ ✳ ✳

Khamisa was numb, she felt nothing but an overwhelming sense of loss. She still could not really believe that it really was Juma that she had just left buried in the ground at Salalah. She had watched the impersonal black body bag being lowered slowly into the grave struggling to accept that Juma was inside. Now sitting quietly in a room somewhere on RAFO Salalah she waited to be put back on a helicopter to be returned to Mirbat.

Yesterday, only hours after the battle, two of Juma's comrades and a military doctor arrived at her house and broke the tragic news. At first unwilling to accept what they told her, she found reasons to hope that they had been mistaken. Even after their insistence that there had been no mistake she hung on to that hope; the reality was too horrific to accept. It was only when they had taken her to the fort to see his body and she was confronted by reality that she had been forced to accept the awful truth.

Overcome with grief she had then been heavily sedated by the doctor and placed in the clinic overnight. This morning still under the effects of sedatives and accompanied by a neighbour's wife she returned home to prepare herself for today's funeral. Through a bewildered haze, due to grief or the drugs, she prepared herself. It seemed to be of monumental importance, as a tribute to her beloved husband, that she looked her best for this ceremony. It was, after all, her farewell. When she was eventually satisfied with her appearance she had covered herself completely under the black *abeya*. From his place at Allah's side none but Juma would see beneath her mantle.

Soon they came to collect her and she was led slowly through the narrow Mirbat streets supported by that neighbour's wife. Silent sympathetic faces stopped and stared as she passed but in her trance-like state she didn't notice. She passed through a small guard of honour that lined the last few strides to a helicopter and had been helped into the back. A few minutes' later Juma's body was brought to the aircraft on a stretcher carried on the shoulders of six pallbearers. At the doorway they lowered the stretcher and slid it inside at her feet. One man then climbed in unzipped the body bag just a little and then he had waited motionless for a sign from her. One half of Juma's face had been covered to protect her from the shock of its mutilation. She gazed for the last time on his face. Even with the wax-like pallor of death and his expressionless features he was still very obviously handsome. She reached out and gently touched his hair then her courage had crumbled and she began to sob. The man slowly re-zipped the bag and climbed out from the aircraft.

There wasn't many at the funeral, Juma's father, mother and his brother Hamed. Her own father, Talib, was there too and Juma's friend, Khaleef. An *askar* officer, along with the same six pallbearers represented the Army.

After the simple ceremony Jokha had tried to persuade her that she should return to the farm, she was after all now her husband's family's responsibility. But because Tuful still remained in Mirbat being looked after by neighbours she was forced to return.

She stared out from the window across the flat expanse of the airfield towards the distant towering jebal, she had no particular desire to return to Abdulla's farm. Her stay there had not been a happy one, but then perhaps that didn't matter so much anymore. Her duty was clear and singular. The only function left in her life now was to make sure that their daughter grew up happy. As for herself she felt she would never be happy again, but that was no more than she deserved. Allah had not after all forgiven her disloyalty but had instead taken away from her the husband that she had betrayed. Clearly he considered that she no longer deserved him and perhaps the punishment was just. She accepted his will, her own happiness was no longer important.

A uniformed man approached her carrying a tall metal coffee-pot and one of those small handless cups. With a brief sympathetic smile he poured a little coffee and handed it to her. But her hand shook so badly that he had to take it from her and put it down on the small table by her side.

"Just a few more minutes and the helicopter will be ready," he said quietly.

❋ ❋ ❋

After the funeral Jokha took Abdulla, who by now was very near and limited sighted, to the new Salalah hospital. He had accepted that it was Allah's will that he would eventually be blind but he had allowed himself to be persuaded by Hamed to at least go and see a doctor. The building was one storey, flat roofed but large and sprawling with, 'afterthought,' bolt on construction still going ahead. Jokha, directed backwards and forwards, led him through a confusing maze of corridors until she eventually found the reception counter. Even then their wanderings were not at an end. A Filipino secretary thrust a piece of scribbled paper in her hand and directed her elsewhere. Once again they joined the throngs of bewildered people roaming the corridors. At last they arrived at the correct department and joined the queue of people sitting patiently on the corridor floor outside the doctor's door.

With nothing to do but boredly wait Abdulla sank deep into his thoughts. He had tried to blame someone for his son's death but it didn't matter from where he started he came back every time to himself. He could of course blame the unknown PFLOAG communist who had fired the deadly bullet, he was undoubtedly directly responsible. "God damn the man to purgatory." But even so he could never get over the feeling that Juma should never even have been at Mirbat in the first place. What was Mirbat to him after all? Probably nothing, a remote fishing village of Bait Umr people a long way from his own stamping ground. But it just happened to be a place where he could arrange to be with his Khamisa. Wherever he had been his only desire had been to be with her and this was why he now blamed himself. If only he had stood firm in the beginning and opposed the inter-tribal marriage. No one would have criticised him for it, indeed most would have approved. If only he had, then Juma would most likely be back on the jebal farm at this very moment and probably just as happily married to another woman. Memories of Juma and Khamisa on the Al Dharitz beach that day when he had first laid eyes on his daughter crossed his mind. He had never seen such a devoted pair, so perhaps he may not have been quite so happy, he allowed, but he would at least still be alive. It was such a heavy price to pay for fleeting moments of happiness stretched thinly over only two years. The marriage had been a high price and hard struggle to achieve right from the very beginning. As it had turned out his approval back then had been a bad decision with tragic consequences.

At last it was his turn to see the doctor and for the time being at least, he was released from his gloomy thoughts.

The doctor of Asian origin shone a bright beam and peered long and hard into each eye. Then wordlessly he moved back behind his desk and scribbled something on the piece of paper that Abdulla had given him. When he was ready he turned his attention back to him.

He rested his elbows on the desk and pressed his fingers to his mouth looking thoughtful as he chose his words. "Well – you have cataracts," he said opening his hands. "If you had come two years ago, then with a simple operation we could probably have cured them."

"Two years ago there was no hospital here," Abdulla reminded him.

"No, there wasn't," he agreed ruefully. "As it is now with an operation then we just might save a little sight in one eye. For the other it's already too late."

"Part sight is better than no sight. *Il hamdhu lillah.*"

"I said only might," he warned. "But the sooner we get you in here then the better our chances." He thumbed through a page weary writing book. "Can you come into hospital three weeks today?"

Abdulla nodded agreement.

"Good," he said making a note. Then he handed the book and the slip of paper to his assistant.

Jokha got up from the floor at the back of the room where she had been quietly sitting and took her husband's hand. It had been a long stressful day and there was still a homeward bound trek of more than four hours to undertake. It would be a mournful and taxing journey.

* * *

Two days later Mussalim arrived at the guarded chicaned entrance that was the entry inside Mirbat's compound. While he apprehensively waited his turn to be searched he looked around for evidence of the ferocious battle that had been fought there only three days ago. All the damage seemed to have been repaired. The debris was cleared away and the concertina wire replaced. There and here there was a crater, a scorch mark or two on the hill fort but other than that very little. Life seemed to have very quickly returned to normal. People followed their daily pursuits of trading, fishing or tending their everyday chores as if the battle was a distant memory and perhaps for most it was.

He wrapped himself a little more in the blanket and pulled the trailing end of his shamag just a little higher across his face. He didn't do it particularly against the cold and damp it was more to conceal as much of himself as he could. This was a very dangerous mission that he had imposed upon himself but he felt obligated to his dead brother to do this. The danger of him being recognised here was very real. The town would have many ex-PFLOAG whether among the *Firqa* or just refugees from the jebal.

Soon it was his turn and he dragged the two camels forward to the searching guards. Unlike all the other animals both his beasts were unladen. "I have come to collect my brother's family," he responded to the quizzical looks. They nodded and waved him forward to the entrance.

Two search guards stood a few paces in front of the entrance while four others behind two sandbagged sangars stood poised manning Browning machine guns.

"State your business," the guard said as he frisked him.

"I have come to collect my brother's family."

"Who is your brother?" He said it only half interested but Mussalim knew well the potential danger that lay in the answer.

"One who fell in the battle," he answered vaguely. But it aroused interest in the guard.

"Oh. What was his name?"

Mussalim could now only answer. "Juma Bin Abdulla."

"Ah yes, He was a good man," he said sympathetically and stood back to let him pass.

"What is your name?" The second guard who had stood back silent now asked.

"Hamed," he lied.

He studied him closely for a moment then nodded acceptance.

Mussalim made his way along the rough track midway between the two forts that was the road to Mirbat. It was an eerie feeling knowing that only three days before he was here for a very different reason. He had not known then that Juma was here too and he wondered if it would have made any difference to his subsequent actions if he had. Perhaps he might have warned him in some way and may have persuaded him to be away from Mirbat. He dismissed the thought instantly, as a soldier he could not have been absent even if he had wanted to. He would also have been compelled to reveal what he had known if he had a pre attack warning. No, at that stage the dye was cast and it was already too late. It was that night months ago when he had gone to him at Manston when the chance to alter things had been lost. He should have been much more insistent, should have laid it down thicker about Khamisa's unhappiness. But he hadn't. Then how could he have known what would happen? Only Allah had known and it had been his will. Sometimes the way of God is hard to follow, he thought with a sigh.

It took three or four enquiries before he eventually found his way to where Khamisa lived. She looked tired and strained when he found her but she didn't seem surprised to see him. He explained his reason for being there that he had come to take her and Tuful back to the jebal farm where she would be looked after. She nodded silent compliance seeming to have no particular interest. Every minute he remained in Mirbat was a minute longer in a vulnerable situation so he urged her to gather her things quickly and they would leave immediately after midday prayers.

He waited patiently outside in the compound and amused himself by amusing his infant niece as he did. His attention was focused on the baby and he took little notice of the voices in the street just the other side of the wall. A creak of the gate and he turned to see three men enter and point FN rifles directly at him. They stared at each other without speaking. The men wore *futas* so were not therefore soldiers, however they did wear pieces of uniform, which identified them as *firqats*. Mussalim was angry with himself it had taken just a moment's unguarded attention and he was a prisoner. Without speaking he slowly picked up Tuful and carried her to the door before moving away and well clear of the baby.

"Khamisa," he called. She quickly appeared in the doorway. "Take your baby inside," he said without taking his eyes off the pointed rifles.

"Nasser," the older grey bearded man in the middle called and Nasser appeared in the gateway. "Is this Commissar Mussalim Bin Abdulla?"

He nodded slowly. "Yes it is."

"Search him," the man instructed one of the others and Mussalim was frisked. When he was established unarmed the men relaxed and lowered their rifles. "Sit." said greybeard.

"This is not what it seems," Nasser said coming towards him and offering his hand to be shaken.

Mussalim ignored it. "I thought you were dead."

Nasser shook his head. "Taken prisoner."

"And now you have had me taken too."

"Not so," said the greybeard. "I am Omar Mohammed of the *Firqat* Al Umri and we are here to talk to you only. We have heard of you. You have a reputation of being a fearsome and determined fighter. But of those who know you, ordinary jeballys or SEPs, none speak badly of you."

"SEPs?"

"SEPs is what the British call ex-PFLOAG regulars or militia who now fight in the *Firqats*."

Mussalim nodded not really understanding but appreciating the British tendency to invent words. "How did you know I was here?"

"An alert guard on the gate was suspicious. Nasser here knows you well and so we brought him along for identification."

He looked at Nasser. "So, on whose side do you now fight?"

He shrugged. "I am just a prisoner under interrogation at the moment."

"We hope to place Nasser in among our *Firqa* eventually. But in the end it will be his choice."

"And what choice is that? Join or go to prison!"

Omar ignored the bitter remark. "Mussalim," he went on. "You have a reputation of being a fair man and a man on the side of the people. We know that you have stood against the brutality and excesses of some of the PFLOAG people. Fahud here," he indicated the man sitting on his left, "owes you his life."

Mussalim looked at the man but didn't recognise him. "He does?"

"Yes, the man said. "One day you rescued me and my father from being thrown over the Dahaq escapement."

Mussalim nodded, he remembered the day but still did not recognise the man.

"You are Dhofari jebally and obviously on the side on the Dhofari people," Omar went on. "Why then do you fight so hard for the party that seeks to oppress the Dhofari people?"

The very question that he had been silently wrestling with. "When I joined the PFLOAG then it was Bin Taymour who repressed the people through poverty."

"But now he has gone and this Sultan is very different. He is finding ways to help all his people not just Dhofaris. Things are getting better but they would get better much quicker if the Communist Front were gone. Come and join us and help us clear them back into the Yemen."

Mussalim looked at him without replying. His words made sense but there were still problems that he either hadn't considered or didn't mention.

"Just think of the impact it would have on PFLOAG propaganda if we were to announce that leading Commissar Mussalim Bin Abdulla, 'Crazy Man Mussalim,' had quit the so called Liberationists and now fought against them."

"I am flattered that you think I am that important but there are some things you are overlooking."

"What are they?"

"First, I am not of Bait Umr. I am Al Hamer of Kathiri."

"No matter. Many of different tribes serve in other *Firqa*. No one will object and to have such an influential ex-PFLOAG in our ranks would reflect some importance on our *Firqa* Al Umri."

"I am high on the Government's wanted list. They would not forgive me as easily as you do."

"Perhaps I can talk to a senior British SAS officer who might have some influence. The information alone that you could bring could make a case for a pardon."

The thought that they he would be expected to impart all his PFLOAG knowledge freely gratis did not rest easily with Mussalim. It would be bad enough changing sides but to deliver up classified information at the same time seemed to be a long way short of honourable. However, he passed no comment on that. Instead he said. "I could never fire on my friends who stay with the PFLOAG any more than I could my own brother. God rest his soul."

"If you come over, your friends might follow you."

Mussalim shrugged. "I don't know about that, I think you may be over-estimating my importance. But even more importantly is the situation of my family."

Omar looked at him quizzically.

"They live on a small farm in the Qara deep in secure PFLOAG territory. What do you think the consequences to them would be if I were to switch sides? They would be in danger for certain. The Front leaders would have to do something to punish me and to deter others in similar situations from doing the same."

"You could bring your family here to Mirbat to live among us."

Mussalim shook his head slowly. "I doubt very much that my father would desert his farm. It has been his life."

Here they seemed to have met an impasse and although they talked more they made no progress. Mussalim wondered now just what his own circumstances were. Was he this man's prisoner?

"What happens now?" he asked. Am I a prisoner?"

Omar shook his head. "I will be your *rabia* today, if you promise to consider the things that we have talked about."

It was an easy promise to make for the offer, despite all the complications attached, did not seem unattractive. "I will give it some thought," he agreed.

Two hours later and accompanied by Omar he arrived at the compound gate with Khamisa, Tuful and all their belongings on the two camels.

"You will give it some thought?" Omar sought confirmation.

"I will."

I'll be here," he said holding out his hand. "Surrendered enemy personnel!"

"What?"

"Surrendered enemy personnel. That's what SEP means. The British avoid using the word surrendered, they think it might offend. Of course you wouldn't be classed surrendered," he added hastily. "You would come across with honour."

Mussalim smiled at his attempt to moderate the term. "*Masalaama,*" he said taking the held-out hand.

It was getting dark by the time they reached the cave in Darbat. It had been a quiet and strained journey because Khamisa locked entirely in her own thoughts hardly seemed aware of what was happening around her. He had soon given up trying to make small talk and through the afternoon had led the camel on which she sat with the second tethered behind. Now as he nursed the kindled fire just inside the cave he clandestinely watched her. He doubted that she would have known if a hundred watched her as she stared out into the darkening mist nursing the sleeping infant with gentle rocking motions. Wrapped in grief she was almost oblivious to the living world. While he could empathise, for he too felt the loss of his brother keenly, he recognised the danger of allowing her to slip into self-pity and away from reality.

He allowed her that little time until the fire was hot enough to begin cooking. Then he laid out goat meat and rice from his pack then spoke sharply to her. "Khamisa. Put the sleeping child down and cook."

She did as he ordered and went through the motions woodenly. When the food was ready she woke the sleeping child and they sat in the firelight glow and in a subdued atmosphere ate from the same platter. Khamisa with little or no appetite picked at the tray feebly being more concerned that Tuful at least ate something. After they had finished eating she cleared up and wrapped the remnants away for another time. Then she bedded down the child and prepared to put herself once more into isolation by lying at her side. Mussalim however would have none of it.

"Come and sit here," he demanded pointing at the spot by his side in front of the fire. "Talk with me for a while."

His intention was to break into her introverted world and make her talk about her dead husband and to voice her concerns. It would be much better if she did rather than contain it all silently inside. He began with small insignificant questions content at this stage just to get her talking. When he had established two way communication he quickly moved on to re-assure her that she should have no fear for her own or Tuful's future. As Juma's eldest brother he was obliged to take over the responsibility for their welfare and he assured her that he intended to fulfil that obligation completely. He couldn't tell if his assurances had any comforting effects because her expression remained impassive leaving him with the feeling that perhaps she didn't even care. Deciding now to cut right to the very core he moved the topic on to his dead brother and he declared his own inner most feelings that he felt a good deal of responsibility for his death. In the past he should have been much more forceful with his persuasion that Juma should leave the army. He admitted to her that he had failed on at least two opportunities to convince him that he should. The first was on their wedding day and second on the day he had gone to see him at Manston. With both her and Juma unhappy at the enforced separation then the second occasion had been a golden chance and he should not have failed.

Khamisa shook her head slowly. "You shouldn't blame yourself," she said. "You undertook that long journey at a moment's notice and made a special effort. You did your very best and you could have done no more, therefore you should attach no blame to yourself at all." She bowed her head a moment then with eyes full of tears she looked at him and said. "The blame is mine. Allah took my Juma from me because I was a poor wife."

Mussalim was confounded. "Nonsense," he said. "You were a good wife. You gave Juma a fine daughter and brought him a great deal of happiness. What more could a husband ask?"

"Loyalty."

"Loyalty?"

"I was deceitful," she said dropped her head. "I have known his brother Hamed," she whispered.

Mussalim was confounded before, now he was absolutely astonished and his stomach jolted with shock. "No," he said involuntarily. But she continued to look down unable to meet his gaze.

He got to his feet walked from the cave into the wet misty night his stomach churning in revulsion. A few paces outside he leaned against the wet rocky wall and stared into the slow rolling dank mist not noticing the rain that ran down his face and soaked his clothing. The rage blazing inside of him twisted and knotted at the thoughts of Juma's betrayal and by the one closest to him. How could she do that to him? And with his own brother, Hamed too. What a repulsive pair and Allah be praised that Juma never knew. His imagination was uncontrollable and the apparition of them together in the physical act burned through his mind nauseating him and caused him to retch.

*   *   *

Hamed cut down the goat he had strung up and slaughtered in the Hilal way then began the gory task of skinning it. He sat the in doorway of the dilapidated woodshed just under its cover from the persistent drizzle. The rolling mist varied from thick to even thicker. Soon the light would begin to fade and navigation across these mountains would go from difficult to impossible. If Mussalim and Khamisa didn't arrive soon then they would not arrive until tomorrow. It didn't matter, in this cool weather the goat meat would easily keep. He could not even see the house only a few metres away never mind the round rustic one beyond where Lailla, Jumaia and Mussalim's brat lived. Soon there would be Khamisa and her brat living there too. The welfare of four adults and two children had once again been loaded onto him without any consideration of his opinion.

His feelings about Khamisa's imminent return were confused. Part of him was pleased that she would once again be close and excitement quickened his pulse. Perhaps this time with Juma gone she would be more receptive to his advances. The other part of him however was shrouded in guilt. He had wished his brother dead and that wish had come true and now that it had he deeply regretted even thinking it. It was almost as if he had caused it and every day in the form of his widow he would be reminded of it. He did not know where to direct his anger. Should it be against himself for wishing Juma dead? Should it be against the man who had fired the bullet who could never be identified? Should it be against the PFLOAG on whose behalf that man had pulled the trigger? His elder brother was part of that organisation too, so perhaps he should be accountable in part also. He pressed the curved knife with anger across the dead animal's neck severing the head and wished he could severe his connection with this farm and his family as easily. The possibility of escape perhaps just for a while seemed to be an attractive solution. If he could get away, perhaps he would be relieved of all these responsibilities that were imposed upon him. At the same time away from all the constant reminders he might also be able to escape these incessant thoughts of guilt that blackened his mood.

He slit the carcass from throat the length of its belly and began with his hands to tear the skin back. Perhaps, he thought, if his father's operation were a success and his eyesight improved just a little then maybe he could just like his elder brothers rid himself of the yoke of family responsibility and leave also. He too wanted to do other things, see other things and feel new experiences. His brother's death had revealed the true extent of human vulnerability and life should not be wasted on a continuous daily existence cycle of mediocrity. He felt trapped in an unsolicited obligation to other people's responsibilities.

With a final tug the skin came away from the carcass. He used dry straw to wipe away some of the blood that spattered his hands and arms then picked up both pieces of the goat and moved back further into the wood shed. He dropped the meat on a crudely constructed table, slammed the curved dagger into the wood by its side and carried the goatskin over to a woodpile. With the inside facing upward he draped the skin out to dry and turned back to find Mussalim standing in the doorway silently staring at him.

"Mussalim, I didn't know you had arrived." He didn't reply, instead stood silently in the doorway and stared at him solemn faced. Hamed hesitated and waited. "Is there something wrong?" he asked eventually.

Wordlessly he moved towards him and then menacingly grabbed him by the clothing at his throat. "I want to talk to you," he growled and Hamed found himself lifted back against the far wall.

"What about? What's the matter?" He had never seen his brother like this before.

"You. You and Khamisa."

"What about me and Khamisa?"

That seemed to enrage him more. "You know what about," he shouted.

"Let me go," Hamed demanded. " I don't know what you're talking about."

His head was jerked backwards and forwards as Mussalim began to shake him. "You own brother's wife," he spat furiously.

Hamed's instinct for survival took over and unable to break free he drove his fist into Mussalim's face. Far from stopping him it enraged him even more making him shake harder. He gathered himself again and drove it in once more but this time with all the strength that he could muster. Mussalim staggered backwards and still holding on to him dragged him with him. Now on the floor with Mussalim beneath him all that pent up anger found a release and he began to flay his fists wildly seeking any target that was his brother. Most of the blows found only arms and shoulder and his attack was so furious and unbridled that soon he began tire. Mussalim now rolled him over and then dragged him to his feet then with an enormous shove he hurled him across the shed. He fell against the table, which toppled over beneath his weight. On his thigh he found the dagger and he got to his feet with it in his hand. "Come on you murdering PFLOAG bastard," he snarled. "I only took his wife. You and your kind took his life. Now I'll take yours and then I'll take your wife." He lunged forward wildly swinging the knife. Mussalim leapt clear then stood warily waiting his next lunge. Hamed recovered his balance quickly and turned, now he moved forward more cautiously. He leaned forward this time with a much more controlled lunge only to find himself blinded by the goatskin that Mussalim swung and wrapped over his face. He felt his hand grab the wrist in which he held the knife then he was falling as Mussalim's weight sent him sprawling. Locked together they crashed against the doorframe, which collapsed with a loud crack and a shower of mud. They rolled in the mud outside all their concentration and strength focusing on the struggle for control of the knife.

Hamed still held the knife but now his hand was being continually pummelled against a partially buried rock. Somewhere a woman's voice was screaming for them to stop. He heard his father's voice gruffly ordering them to stop also, but tenaciously he held onto the knife. The pain though was increasing with each smash against the unyielding rock until he could hold it no longer and it slipped from his fingers. He was hauled to his feet the skin pulled from his face then pushed clear. Blood pounded in his ears and his chest heaved as he stood and glared at his brother who watching him warily about four metres away.

"What's all this about?" His father demanded. Hamed stole a quick glance in his and Jokha's direction. Further back on the edge of the mist he caught sight of his three sisters watching also. As his temper began to subside, embarrassment began to grow.

"Why do two brothers fight with a knife?" His father demanded loudly with a degree of alarm.

He looked down at the knife close by his foot then he bent down and casually picked it up. Everyone waited to see what he would do next. In that instant he thought to throw it at Mussalim and to bury right in the middle of his chest. He flicked it around to hold it by the blade, drew back his arm and sent it spinning towards him. It thudded with a little shudder into the mud at his feet. "Ask him," he spat. Then considering that he had recovered face by having the last word, he turned and stormed into the mist and away from his embarrassment.

Abdulla watched his blurry shape fade further into the mist. "Why did you two fight?" he asked Mussalim.

Mussallm turned to face him but didn't answer. He was just too far away for Abdulla to read any expression that he might have so there was no clue possibility. He bent and retrieved the knife from the mud at his feet then came much closer.

"I'll talk to you later, father," he said softly, handing him the knife. Then he moved past him and went towards the young women. Abdulla turned and screwed up his eyes trying to see what he did next.

"It's not good two brothers should fight with a knife," Jokha said softly coming up behind him and slipping her arm through his.

He nodded agreement and she started to move back towards the house. He understood that the arm-lock was not merely a show of affection but also subtle way for her to guide him while leaving him the dignity of independence. He glanced back over his shoulder forlornly hoping that he would see Hamed re-appearing from the mist and following. Even if he were he would have needed to be in close proximity for him to have seen him. "He's gone," Jokha said, guessing the reason for his look back. "He'll be back later."

What had caused the two brothers to fight so bitterly and so intensely that a knife had been pulled? Anger such as that often meant a woman was involved somewhere and he wondered if this were the case in this instance. He thought of Mussalim's words when he had questioned him about his reasons for instructing Khamisa to wear the *yashmak*. "Hamed does not look at Khamisa with a brother's eyes," he had said. Perhaps in her absence Hamad's eyes had turned on Jumaia and that was why the two fought. But also on that day Mussalim had unjealously offered his Mahru woman to be Hamed's wife, so that thought didn't quite make sense. Perhaps Mussalim had now come to see the Mahru as his sole property and a man is less than a man if he does not protect his property from thieves. That must be the reason, he concluded. If Hamed had looked covertly first at Khamisa then at Jumaia then it was the basic human instinct for a man to know a woman that tormented him. He was now into his twenty-second year and perhaps it was time that he sought a wife for his youngest son.

Later that evening in the house after the women had retired to bed leaving them alone, he asked Mussalim again why he and Hamed had fought. Then he had to patiently wait while his son worked his way verbosely towards the point. When he eventually arrived at the sole reason for his anger Abdulla listened impassively. As full brothers little more than two years apart, Mussalim and Juma had grown up together happily wandering the hills facing fanciful childhood dangers and adventures. As they had grown older the bond between them had grown stronger and even for brothers they had shared a special relationship. As young men and despite long absences they had still retained that devotion for each other. He could therefore well understand the reasons for Mussalim's outrage. To him it was a huge and bitter double betrayal of Juma. Firstly by the one person in the world who had been even closer to him than he himself, Khamisa. Then secondly by another almost as close, Hamed.

But taking a more dispassionate view Abdulla could easily understand how it would have happened. Hamed, a young inexperienced man at his sexual peak had been put in a situation where he was expected to watch over an attractive woman of the same age and for a long period. It would have been unnatural if there hadn't been some basic urges aroused. Nevertheless, because the woman was his brother's wife, Hamed should have controlled those urges. Much more blame however, could be laid at the feet of the Ruwas woman, As a wife she should have never have allowed herself to get into a position where she would have been tempted into adultery. Thinking on a little more charitably, he thought that perhaps a portion of the blame could be his. If he had been more aware, more observant then he might have taken steps to make sure that the pair didn't spend much time alone together. His main excuse, perhaps feeble, was his failing eyesight, which had not alerted him to any visible signals.

The light from the fire had faded to little more than a dull glow as the last tiny flicker of flame died. Through the gloom he watched Mussalim as he stared preoccupied into the ashes of the dying log fire. Despite his cool and controlled temperament he knew that inside he felt the loss of his brother as sharply as a stomach full of thorns. In his absence he undoubtedly saw himself as the last defender of his interests. The welfare of Khamisa clearly would have been Juma's major concern and so Mussalim had made it his priority also. Only to discover her infidelity and he probably found that to be a very bitter pill indeed.

"Allah works in mysterious ways," he said breaking the contemplative silence. He had no idea if Mussalim had even heard for there was no reaction at all. "No one. No one at all must know of this business," he went on. "No good could come from it. It would bring only shame on Juma's memory, his wife, your younger brother and this house also."

"And so it never happened," Mussalim muttered bitterly without taking his eyes away from the diminishing glow of the embers.

"To the four of us that know, it did. But to the rest it never happened. And since Hamed has known this woman and she is now widowed then as soon as it is proper to do so, he will marry his brother's widow."

It seemed the perfect solution. Hamed knew her body, she had known his and with the passage of time it would not matter so much that they had transgressed before they were sanctioned. It provided Hamed with a wife and the family responsibility of providing for a son's widow would be also be accomplished. Only the dead son's honour was not satisfied.

* * *

In the dead of night, in thick swirling mist, Hamed crept back past both the main house and the round 'beehive' type. When he reached the stick-woven rondaaval fence that quartered the livestock, he paused and looked back. He could only just make out the darker shapes of the buildings against a black background. He listened intently but only the steady drizzle hissing softly on the ground broke the silence of a murky night. He moved the bar that was the gate and scattered the snoozing goats as he moved among them. Four camels squatted on the ground close together and watched him unconcernedly as he approached. From the three fine animals that his uncle had stolen from the Yemeni Mahru he selected the best. Kicking it to its feet he led it out of from the enclosure.

He stared once again in the direction of the houses, wondering if he dare walk the animal past them. He decided against it. He couldn't be sure that everyone was asleep and it might take only a complaining bellow from the animal to bring someone out to investigate. He guessed that Lailla and Khamisa would be in the beehive, while Mussalim would undoubtedly be lying with his woman, probably in the main house, or perhaps lying with both Jumaia and Khamisa, he thought bitterly. That would account for his rage earlier this afternoon. Pulling on the camel's halter, he led it around behind the enclosure and approached the woodshed from the opposite side of the houses. This was as near as he dare take the animal, so he tethered it to a low branch of a tree and went on foot to the woodshed to get a saddle. The door frame hung lopsided and the roof above was poised ready to fall; a testament to the struggle that had taken place there earlier. That was no longer his problem, someone else would have to repair that he thought as he ducked carefully inside.

By now all the family would know what he had done with his brother's wife and the shame he now felt made it impossible for him to face them. He did not really feel any remorse for the deed itself, in fact he still remembered it with a great deal of pleasure. The shame he did feel was because now all knew how he had cuckolded his own brother. It was far better that he should run away rather than to face their disapproval. But more than that, his shame was compounded by an additional guilt. He had wished his own brother dead and now he was. Perhaps this desire had in some way contributed to it. He carried a saddle over to where he had tethered the camel and began saddling up.

All through the evening he had sat gloomily moping beneath a shallow rocky over-hang attempting to shelter from the cold and wet of the Khareef. This was when he had made the decision that it was much easier to run away than to face disgust of his family. Having made up his mind to escape from his ignominy his problem was where could he go? The only alternative that he could think of was to join the Kathiri *firqats* Al Nasr. Here his choices were two. Sheikh Mussalim Bin Nufl the original founder of the organised resistance who had fled to Saudi when the movement had re-structured to become the PFLOAG had returned from his exile and sworn for the Sultan. He now roamed the *nejd* to the north with a small band of Al Nasr attempting to seek and destroy Front supply lines. To the south-west Sheikh Mussalim Bin Tufl with the far greater force was more static and patrolled the Leopard line, therefore he would be much easier to find. After checking the girth he hauled the camel to its knees and mounted.

He glanced back towards the darkened homestead. Nothing stirred. There was no one to see him go, or to wish him good fortune. In all probability no one cared. All his past loyalty, all his sacrifices counted for nothing. Well, so what? They would struggle without him, he was sure. Perhaps after he was gone they would begin to appreciate the contribution he had made. But for now it was someone else's turn to take on the responsibility. He was free of all that and free at last to do only what Hamed Bin Abdulla wanted to do. And what he wanted to do most was to kill *adoo*. Juma was worth any ten of them and that included his brother Mussalim. To kill ten would avenge Juma and at the same time might appease his own guilt. If Allah was kind he would even guide a bullet into the black heart of the man who had killed Juma. He slapped the animal down the neck and headed it south-west into the wet rolling mist.

~ 20 ~

January 1973 • Hamed's departure had a serious effect on the family's welfare and in the six months since he had left, things had gradually deteriorated. Despite his operation that had for the time being saved the sight in one eye, Abdulla's sight was still very poor and he was badly handicapped. So much so that his contribution was restricted almost entirely to an advisory role and he could milk the animals providing they were penned for him. He also had to make all the trips to Salalah to buy and sell because women could not do so alone. But he was nothing more than a token male figure to whomever that led him and more of a hindrance than useful.

With no one else Lailla had taken on the major responsibility for running the farm and she took on the more demanding role of tending the cattle. Each day she would herd them across the hills seeking decent grazing. It was January, the Khareef was long past and the grass on the mountains was now scorched tinder dry. When it had been lush and green Abdulla and Jokha had been absent due to his operation in Salalah and the responsibility for hay harvesting had fallen on the three young women. They had done their best but because of their lack of strength and the fact that both Khamisa and Jumaia lacked experience the amount of hay stored was only moderate. Lailla had been reluctant to break into that stock for a long time but with the cows rapidly losing weight and the milk yields only meagre she was forced to begin using it. Her calculations indicated that there was nowhere near enough to sustain the current head of cattle until the next rains. The herd that by now had grown to more than twenty head would need to be reduced considerably. The positive side of that was that due to Civil Development the Dhofar Cattle Company had been formed in Salalah and provided a ready cattle market and the effect of that was that cattle prices were rising. Their cattle however were in a lean condition and that would obviously affect the price. She had decided that it would therefore be better to use the remaining stock of hay to fatten the animals and get a better price. This would enable them to buy more fodder to sustain the rest. At the same time there would be a little surplus money which was badly needed for their own welfare. But she would have to convince her father that it was the right policy. He was firmly against downsizing the stock fearing that it would create a spiralling downward trend until eventually there would be no cattle left to sell. But the feeding problem was present now and very real.

Khamisa and Jumaia were both restricted with small children but they did the best they could to help. Their major contribution was to manage the goatherd between them. They would take it in turns to wander out daily with the animals foraging for decent grazing while the other acted as babysitter. From the surplus milk Jokha had taught them both to separate the curd and whey. The whey was used for drinking while the curd was placed in the sun to heat and form cheese. Some of this cheese was used right away as a cream cheese while the rest was put aside to ripen and then sell. However as the milk yield reduced, the surplus became less and another potential income was disappearing.

For her part Jokha's contribution was limited, due entirely to Abdulla's handicap. Although he tried to be independent he relied on her greatly and consequently she could never be very far from his side for very long. But she did what she could which amounted mostly to woman's domestic work extended to help all.

Mussalim was now based in nearby Raythut and visited as often as he could, but his visits were infrequent and irregular. When he did come he would stay a day or perhaps two and make some attempt to carry out some of the maintenance repairs that were beginning to pile up. However, the greater amount of his visit time was devoted to Jumaia and his infant son whom they had called Taimul. 'Taimul Bin Mussalim Al Hamer.'

At the tender age of eightteen and a mere woman as well Lailla had become the hub at the centre of the family's welfare and she revelled in it. It had given her more status than she could have ever aspired to. Her opinion was valued and in all cases except where her father was concerned her decisions unquestionably accepted.

This morning she had driven the cattle a little further than normal into the wadi Theydawt. At its head where the Khareef rains create a cascade it floods into to a small pool, she was pleased to find some traces of the pool still remained. Very shallow and reduced to only a few metres across it nevertheless still supported a wide band of greenery around its edges. The cattle moved forward eagerly to stand in its muddy perimeter and munched contentedly on the sward. Here was good grazing that would not only help to replace some of the meat on the animal's bones but also preserve the farm's hay stocks. She found a shady spot and settled to spend a long and boring day allowing the cattle to gorge.

Just a few metres away a rusty old oil drum lay on its side by a small pile of stones that had once been a fire circle. Lailla stared at it, her mind swelling with a flood of memories. It had been three and a half years since she, hidden in yonder nearby thicket, watched her mother Kathya assisted by Jokha perform that strange beauty treatment. She had watched curiously as her mother had first immersed herself in the water heated by a fire beneath the drum and then plunged into the cold water of the pool. Driven by curiosity she went across and stood the drum on its end. Her mother's fingers had once gripped that edge and she ran her fingers sadly along its rusty edge feeling an urge for this flimsy contact. With this battered and rusty old oil drum the contact to her deceased mother was strong. She had been the last person to handle it and Lailla felt her presence all over it. She looked slowly around the lonely wadi. Its steep sides and top edges were covered thickly by stunted *ghaf* shrubs, while on the more exposed cascade face long ropes of twisted vines hung. The lazy breeze funnelling along the sides of the wadi teased the leaves of the *ghaf* gently while high in the blue sky two black crows circled casually on a rising thermal. The cows with their heads down meandered slowly among the sward, nothing else moved. She was completely alone and she was tempted to try the treatment that she had witnessed her mother performing. Once again she scanned around wondering apprehensively if she dare take all her clothes off in the middle of a wadi. First, however, she needed to make a fire so it was not a decision that she had to make at this moment.

She gathered kindling wood and with plenty of tinder like grass available she soon had a fire burning strongly. Now she rolled the drum into place and using a rusty tin that she had found she begin to fill the drum with water. The tin wasn't very big and so the task turned out to be a long and laborious one, but eventually the drum was almost half full and she decided that it was enough. She continued to feed the fire until the water was hot. Now it was decision time. She sat down nervously and keenly scrutinised every bush and rock that might conceal a watcher. She could see nothing that remotely suggested that she was not completely alone, but still she hesitated. In the end she decided upon a compromise. She dowsed the fire and with one last look around she removed her long dress but left on her under-shorts.

It made her gasp when she lowered herself into the hot water and she could not stay in very long. She clambered out with difficulty and ran through the mud into the pool. It was shallow and she had to lie on her back to submerge herself. This water wasn't really cold it was tepid but nevertheless the temperature change from hot to tepid was enough to make her skin tingle with invigoration. She also felt the thrill of exhilaration from her daring sensual deed adding greatly to the pleasure. She found herself beginning to hope that perhaps some young and good-looking young man was watching and she squirmed provocatively in the water. She imagined that her mother had felt all these things too and here in the exact same place with everything else identical she felt close to her spirit. Several times she went from the drum to the pool until the temperatures between the two became close together and there was little difference and so the exercise was ended. Now full of daring and confidence she pulled off her wet under-shorts and stood for a few moments exposing herself fully to those imagined eyes of that good-looking young man watching her from somewhere in the bushes. Then almost reluctantly she pulled her dress over her head and allowed it to fall very slowly depriving him gradually of the forbidden view of her naked body.

She scanned the steep banks around her but nothing had changed and she wasn't now sure if she were relieved or disappointed. With a sigh she picked up her underwear and laid it out in the sun to dry. Something red and bright lay amongst the grass tufts and caught her attention. She picked it up, it was Mussalim's little red Commissar star that he had given her. She treasured it and kept it with her at all times, it was after all his gift of *rabia* for her protection. It must have fallen from her pocket when she had taken off her dress and she had come very close to losing it. She must take much better care of it, she scolded herself.

* * *

Where the mouth of the Wadi Nahiz opened out onto the Salalah plain Musallim stopped and used his binoculars to scan the area ahead. He was on foot and probably one hour ahead of the small caravan that followed. Here the road from the jebal crossed very close to the wadi mouth before running off straight as an arrow to Salalah. This part was easily the most vulnerable and it was important that he was sure the caravan could move to its position unobserved. He studied it long and hard and didn't like what he saw. The road was too close.

The small caravan following consisted of eight PFLOAG fighters of the Bait Gatun tribe, four donkeys each were carrying two Katyusha rockets and a camel toting the two launchers. The target for all eight rockets was the Air Force's technical site on the far side of the airfield. The plan was after clearing the wadi to turn westward and find a suitable concealed position among the undulating foothills and unleash the deadly rockets in quick succession and then to beat a hasty retreat back up Nahiz.

He squatted down on his haunches, rested his Kalachnikov across his knees and stared thoughtfully towards the road. Anyone moving along that stretch would very likely spot them. It was a no go and he needed an alternative. He glanced back over his shoulder the way he had come. Nahiz was narrow and steep, its sides climbing almost vertically upward. Its base undulated wildly and was clenched within the towering walls as it twisted its way northwards gradually ascending into the jebal as it did. Through its every elevation the awesome ravine was cloaked beneath a dense carpet of *ghaf*. He considered if it might be possible to fire off the rockets from within the safety of its thick mantle of green cover. He looked towards the direction of the airfield but a towering peninsula of land away to his right jutted out onto the plain and hid it from view. They would be firing blind so he rejected it. A few minutes earlier when he had moved down the Wadi he had crossed a steep canyon running off to the west and he wondered if there might be a way to climb out from there. If there were then it would take them in the right direction and divert them well away from any curious eyes that might be encountered close to the road. It was a possibility that needed to be checked. His mind made up he got up and retraced his steps. When he arrived at the canyon he settled down to wait for the caravan to catch up.

It was closer than he thought and within only a few minutes he heard it approaching through the trees. He got up and took an intercepting course into the middle of the wadi. Because of the tree density, it was very close before he actually saw the party. The wild looking Yaqub his long unkempt hair blowing across his heavily bearded face led it and he greeted Mussalim with a grin when he saw him. Briefly Mussalim outlined the problem and then leaving the rest of party resting beneath the shade of the tree canopies he and Yaqub left to explore the adjoining wadi. Physically it was identical to the main wadi but only short and although the sides were steep the end leaned away slanting upward. The two men surveyed it and agreed that although it would be a steep climb it should be possible to get the animals up on to the top. Mussalim began the ascent while Yaqub went back to fetch the rest of the caravan.

On top it was clear of trees and more exposed and high above the flat land he had a clear view across the plain towards Salalah. He was on the highest point of that peninsula of land that jutted out onto the plain and a descent down the other side would be completely hidden from the road. He glanced back hoping to see the others starting their ascent. If they were then they were concealed beneath the layer of tree branches. He crossed the hilltop to the opposite side and soon found a well used goat track that wound down that side of the hill. That would, he decided, do nicely.

A couple of hours later and by now late afternoon they were located in a near perfect position in the base of a hollow among the undulating hills that were the mountain foothills. Two kilometres to the south-west the edge of the airfield, beyond that the runway and further away in the distance the buildings and tin hangars that was the Air Force's technical area. The mouth of Wadi Nahiz was not too far behind them and easily accessible. On their retreat it mattered not if they were spotted from the road so they could take the quickest and most direct route. Once in the wadi and amongst the thickets they would be comparatively safe. The Government soldiers might pursue them a little way but they would be very reluctant to go too far into a wadi where potential ambush places were plentiful.

Mussalim and Yaqub climbed to the upper lip of the basin and lay on the bank studying the airfield through binoculars. They were in no particular hurry to begin the barrage, one hour from sunset would be ideal. The light would still be good enabling them to see where the rockets landed and adjust the range if need be and darkness would fall soon after they had fallen back into the wadi deterring further any pursuit.

Mussalim looked back over his shoulder into the base of the hollow. The men had unloaded the animals and were now beginning to position the rocket launchers. The rockets themselves, as long as a man was tall, lay in a tidy row looking somewhat innocuous. However they were fearsome weapons, screaming in with the sudden nerve-shattering sounds of jets and delivering the explosion wallop of a 200lb bomb. Those airmen over there were in for a very nasty experience. He turned back and once more studied the target through the binoculars.

He heard the distant deep boom of the Um Al Ghariff artillery gun and even at this distance felt the slight vibration in the ground. He lowered the binoculars and waited for its impact. The hissing of the shell grew louder as it came in their direction and with an ear splitting boom it shattered the earth a hundred and fifty metres to their right. He hunched his shoulders as some of the lighter furthest flung debris rained down on them. He glanced at Yaqub, whose face betrayed astonishment. Mussalim shrugged, he wasn't unduly worried, undoubtedly it was the routine random barrage that was supposed to act as a deterrent to would-be attackers like them. It seemed, however, that by pure luck they had chosen the right location. But from that explosion they might drift further away or even choose a different site completely. Soon after he heard the expected second boom and once again the hissing shell came in their direction. This time it exploded in one of the hollows close behind their position. This time the surrounding banks absorbed the shock. However, its closeness eroded Mussalim's previous confidence. Was it pure luck or did they somehow know that they were there? The third growling boom indicated another shell was on its way. This time Mussalim held his breath.

It came in with its hiss growing louder into an ear-aching whine before the ground all around him shook violently and the earth close behind erupted. Air was forcibly sucked from his lungs and he felt himself lifted and flung skywards like flying debris from a volcano. Something drove in hard against his ribs when he landed and then he was heavily peppered by falling shards. He lay paralysed on his back staring up into a web of dark shapes and a thick enveloping dust. The unrelenting high pitch whistling in his ears blocked out any other sound as he lay stunned gaping upwards and watching the web of dark shapes gradually reforming to be tree branches. Slowly the pinkish tinted dust began to settle and blue sky began to filter through. He began to wonder how badly hurt he was. After a few moments he found that he could at least move his arms and he tried to push himself to a sitting position. He gasped the moment he moved his torso as indescribable agony raked across his ribs. Even the gasp with its sharp intake of breath cost him some pain and he lay back once more waiting for it to ease. When it did he rolled slowly away from the pain onto the other shoulder and looked back up the hill to where only a few moments before he had lain surveying the target. The shell had been a direct hit or at least close enough to be just as effective and he wondered now if there were other survivors.

Something caught by the low sun glinted brightly halfway up the jebal face well above his position but it did not arouse his curiosity until it disappeared. Something up there had moved? From beneath the trees branches he watched the spot until the glint returned. Then a figure emerged from beneath the thicket and through binoculars scanned the position were the PFLOAG men had been. He wore a camouflaged uniform and even from this distance Mussalim could see by his size and cut the man was not Omani. He had to be a British Special Service soldier. The significance of his presence quickly dawned upon him. He had guided the artillery shells right down in amongst them and had been placed there for just that specific purpose. If there was one then there were very likely others and probably this whole face of the jebal was covered by clandestine observers. This was a serious development and it was imperative that it be reported as soon as possible.

He waited only four or five minutes after he had disappeared before he tried to move. He dare not wait longer – soon a patrol would arrive from Um Al Ghariff to inspect the results of the destruction. Gingerly, he moved to an all fours position then steeling himself straightened up slowly. That wasn't too bad. The pain came when he got to his feet. Even though he pressed his arm stiffly down his side and clutched his ribs tightly with his other hand it eased nothing. Gritting his teeth and taking only shallow breaths to avoid expanding his rib cage he staggered slowly back up the hill.

It took only one glance down into the hollow to see the effects of the shell. What remained of bodies, human or animal, lay thickly covered in dust where they had been flung. It seemed as if he was the only survivor. Unless? He wondered now where Yaqub had been thrown. Checking back down the hill, he saw his body laying face down and motionless close to the tree from where he had just come.

Moving downhill was even more painful than going up as each step stretched muscles in his torso that he didn't even know were there. Yaqub wasn't dead and was beginning to groan recovering consciousness when Mussalim sunk to his knees at his side. By the opposite angle of his foot he could immediately see that the man's leg was broken. Yaqub rolled over and contorting his face in pain clutched his broken leg tightly with both hands just above the knee as he sat up.

"My leg," he groaned. "Look at my leg, it's broken." Panic was starting.

"We can't stay here, the soldiers will be here soon." Mussalim ignored his anxiety. "Can you move?" He asked but he already knew the answer. Just getting Yaqub to his feet was agony for both of them and he fell to the ground immediately he tried to move forward. Somehow he was going to have to be carried, Mussalim concluded gloomily.

He grunted with pain when he took the weight of Yaqub on his back and a black border floated around the periphery of his vision as he struggled to stay conscious. He steeled himself and glanced towards the mouth of Wadi Nahiz. It seemed to be a very long way away but gritting his teeth he planted one foot forward and began to stagger towards it. Each step seemed to jolt his ribs and the weight on his back multiplied that jolt several fold. The physical exertion of the extra weight also increased his demand for air causing him to draw deeper breaths and that intensified the pain even more. Twice before he even reached the wadi he was forced to stop as the pain induced vomiting, The deep stomach retching only amplified his agony further. Eventually he reached the wadi mouth but now dazed and numb with pain he was oblivious to the physical torment and continued trance-like to just concentrate placing one foot ahead of the other. Stumbling and staggering but relentless he blundered onwards until completely exhausted he went sprawling. He heard Yaqub shout in agony as he hit the ground but Mussalim had agonies of his own to worry about. He screwed up his face and gritted his teeth as he lay there unable to move just waiting for the waves of excruciating pain to recede back to the agony that it had been before. Gradually the pain eased a little and he was able to roll onto his good side into a more comfortable position. Clearly he couldn't go on this way and the information that he had to pass on was important. Reluctantly, he decided that he had no alternative but to abandon Yaqub. Looking back he tried to guess how far they had progressed into the wadi. Any pursuit would depend on whether they had been seen escaping from the scene. If there was a pursuit then those chasers might by now be very close.

The sun had set and dusk was descending, soon the light would begin to fade which increased their chances of escape. He stared through a gap in the foliage towards a clump of heavy fig trees screening a sheer rock wall. Through its branches he could just make out a blacker patch imprinted in the rock. Could it be hole or perhaps a cave?

He struggled over to it and found at around chest height a cave entrance. Although the mouth was a not particularly large it opened out inside to a deep and spacious cavern. Any pursuing soldiers just might miss it and pass by. Although he dare not take a chance on that for himself considering the information that he needed to pass on it might do to hide Yaqub. It would have too. He hoisted Yaqub into the entrance and left him to drag himself further inside through the guano as hundred of bats flitted above their heads and out into fading light of early evening. Then after promising to send help to collect him Mussalim continued on his way up the wadi towards the village Nahiz.

Although each stride was still painful without a man's weight upon his back it was not nearly so bad. In fact he found that by striding forward with his right foot then bringing his left up to it and no further the stretch of his chest muscles down his left side was greatly reduced. Nevertheless it had long been dark by the time he stumbled into Nahiz village.

Gradually he surfaced to consciousness and reluctantly opened his eyes. Not daring to move he lay motionless on his back and stared up to the thatched palms that was the low roof. The room was dark and small, big enough only for the two cots. Yaqub with his leg heavily splinted lay sleeping on the other, proving that at some point his hysterical ramblings must have made sense to someone.

Stumbling exhausted into the village last night was just a vague memory. Half delirious with pain he had tried to pass on the news about the soldier spotters on the Salalah side of the jebal and of the injured Yaqub hiding in the cave. The villagers trying to understand his ramblings were more concerned with the fate of the rest of the party who were after all relatives and friends. Whether they actually made sense of his ramblings or whether they just set off to find the answers for themselves he didn't know but he had been carried into one of the rustic bee-hive style houses and laid on the cot. Despite the pain his exhaustion was such that he quickly fell into a sleep of sorts. It was a fitful sleep. Any movement of his torso or any deep breath sent waves of pain across his chest jolting his brain awake. Even when not aggravated by these stabs of agony his mind was tormented by the nightmares of the exploding shells and dismembered bodies. Through dreams bordering hallucinations he vaguely recalled somebody placing wet and cold compresses upon his chest, soothing away some of the throbbing heat.

But now lying perfectly still the pain in his ribs throbbed gently but he knew that movement of any sort would instantly multiply that. He felt physically battered and pulverised as if he had been trampled over by a herd of stampeding camels. Even so he could not just lie there, there was important news that must be passed on before he could rest. Grunting with pain he struggled to a position sitting on the edge of the cot and then after steeling himself to the agony that he knew would follow he got to his feet. He swayed unsteadily and was forced to hold tightly to the central pole that supported the roof until the wave of pain down his left side became bearable. When it did he took stock of his physical condition. He was naked and the whole of his left rib cage swollen and bruised deep purple with yellowing around the edges. Broken ribs for certain, perhaps that whole side of his rib cage. He looked around for something to cover his nakedness. A grimy cloth covered the cot on which he had lain. Gritting his teeth and swallowing hard to control the nauseous feelings he turned and gingerly picked it up. Carefully, he wrapped it around his waist the best way he could and then shuffled towards the doorway.

He emerged into the brightness and heat of the hot afternoon. A woman sitting cross-legged by the doorway began to insist that he return to his bed. She had, he guessed, probably been his nurse through the long night and morning. He silenced her abruptly and demanded that she help him to the radio. She stared at him a moment then ducked beneath his left arm lifting it slowly and resting it across her shoulders. Then putting her arm around his back she acted as his crutch as they made their way slowly to the building where the radio was hidden. He sank down heavily onto a crude form grateful that the ordeal of actually moving was over at least for the moment. The woman placed everything he needed in front of him and then went over to the furthest corner and squatted down watching him while she waited for him to finish.

He radioed region headquarters in Raythut, now commanded by Zahir Ali. The former commander Bin Talib had two months previously been sent north to the Muscat region. He had been despatched on another attempt to organise and martial the resistance there and in so doing perhaps relieve some of the pressure being applied here. Perhaps this time Bin Talib's attempts would be more successful than the unfortunate Al Mushani's twelve months previously. That had resulted in his capture.

It was a radio operator who replied to Mussalim's signal and he asked to speak directly to Zahir. The operator said he wasn't there and that he would take a message and pass it on. Mussalim, reluctant to entrust a message on this particular issue to an apathetic sounding operator instructed him to have him found and to contact him urgently. Exasperated he broke the contact. To make the painful journey back to his cot and then to return when Zahir Ali did radio back was not an option he decided. All he could do was make to himself comfortable right here and wait. He licked his dried lips with a dry tongue trying unsuccessfully to raise moisture in his mouth to relieve a rampant thirst. He eased himself around and looked at the woman, she stared back with a bland expression.

She was a comely woman with features betraying ancestral African origin. She wore a long grey robe and on her head, a large brightly patterned headscarf. A pearl studded either side of her nose, which suggested to Mussalim that she belonged to someone. It was unlikely that a maiden would be so adorned. Under his glance she lifted one end of the scarf to modestly cover the lower part of her face. He hid a smile, since she had in all probability spent the night over his naked body applying cold compresses to his injured ribs this modesty seemed somewhat absurd.

"Fetch me some water," he instructed her quietly.

It took only a few minutes before Zahir Ali called him back and he was able to report the important news about the spotter situation. However, Zahir's cool, seemingly unconcerned attitude to the news perturbed him. Had he failed to realise the importance of the information or the probable hazards connected to any further such attacks? Mussalim stared at the radio set thoughtfully as he shut down. He shrugged helplessly, perhaps it was his own imagination and Zahir had appreciated the situation without getting excited about it. Either way he had done all he could do at that stage and he relaxed a little. Gratefully, he allowed the woman to help him back to the cot and to rest once more.

The rest of the day and through the night he lay there restricting his movements as much as possible. This time except for being spoon-fed early in the evening he was unattended. Yaqub drifted in and out of sleep but during his conscious periods he was in little mood to talk. It didn't matter, Mussalim's mood was precisely the same. Except to struggle outside on a couple of occasions to relieve himself he stayed as immobile as possible.

Early the next morning men came to prepare Yaqub for the long trip to Shershitta where he would get his broken leg reset. Placed on a litter and dragged behind a camel it would undoubtedly be a very long and a very painful journey. Mussalim decided in his own circumstances that it was far more desirable to return to his father's farm. It was considerably closer and Jumaia was there, she would pamper and nurse him to recovery.

He waited out the heat of the day getting as much rest as possible before starting the ordeal of the journey. In late afternoon two men came for him bringing with them his Commissar uniform, which had been washed. They waited while he slowly and carefully dressed then helped him to his feet. Outside three saddled camels waited and he watched as one was hauled to its knees ready for mounting. One man then held the tether making sure the animal didn't try to rise while the other helped him into the saddle. He gasped as he was jerked forward and then back when the kneeling camel got to its feet. Both men hesitated staring up at him obviously wondering if he was going to be able to ride. Reading their thoughts he forced a grin to reassure them that he could, he was determined to get home even at the cost of extreme discomfort.

One man led the way out of Wadi Nahiz at the slow plodding camel pace while the other behind Mussalim brought up the rear. They set an easterly direction keeping to the high ground but forced often to snake north and south to avoid dropping into the deep wadis. The rocking motion of the animal's long neck and each plant of its big hoofed feet nudged Mussalim's spine causing a jerk across his rib cage. He gritted his teeth against the pain and forced his mind away from his discomfort until numbness set in and he drifted into a hypnotic-like trance. It was getting dark by the time the men delivered him to his father's farm.

* * *

She was close enough to Mussalim to blow gently into his ear. But Khamisa resisted the temptation instead standing slightly behind him and looking over his shoulder she clandestinely studied him closely. How very much like his brother, Juma he was? Except for Mussalim's beard they were so alike that they could have been mistaken for twins. The same handsome features, the same unruly shock of black hair and the same dark eyes that seemed to penetrate into one's very thoughts.

It had been six months since Juma's death and she had at last begun to come to terms with his passing. However, she didn't want to and she felt only guilt that she had unavoidably begun to accept it. Her guilt was compounded by the fact that she was struggling to even remember the detail of his face. In quiet moments at nights or out alone with the goats she forced his image into her mind trying to brand each detail into permanent memory but each day it seemed his image faded just a little bit more. She was in dread that one day soon it would be gone and he would then be lost to her memory also. But here so close to Mussalim it was reprinted in every stark detail. He would be a constant reminder and the memory of Juma's face could be permanent.

He sat straight-backed and perfectly still on a form while she moved around him applying strapping around his rib cage. She had torn up the *Basht* that Mussalim had given Juma on his wedding day and now as she encased him in his brother's coat it was if she were wrapping him in his identity also. She passed the loose end across his chest and as she reached around his back with the other hand her face was so very close to his. She could feel the hammering of her heart as it quickened with desire for Juma and she held that close position as long as she dare. Straightening up she brought the end to her and all that remained now was the last tightening. She placed her hand upon his bare shoulder savouring the feel of his hot skin then gave a little tug on the material with the other. He gasped sharply giving her an excuse to gently touch his hair in sympathy. Now she secured the material in place and the strapping was finished. But she didn't want it to be finished. The close physical contact to Mussalim's body brought a tenuous contact with her departed husband and she fiddled frivolously with the strapping to extend the task as much as she could. Eventually fearing her prolonged fiddling would betray her passion for Juma's substitute she stood back.

"It is finished," she said placing her hand once more on his bare shoulder.

For a moment he looked around at all the anxiously watching family faces, then he stood up slowly. He hesitated a moment before moving a couple of paces towards Jumaia. He grinned at her before turning slowly around to look at Khamisa. "Yes," he said. "That's much better. Thank you sister." Then he came to her, took her hand and kissed it.

Khamisa wanted more, she wanted his lips but oblivious to her desire he went back to Jumaia.

"Perhaps now you will give up this madness," Abdulla chided. "It was a warning from Allah."

"Maybe so," he muttered, then he reached out his hand towards Jumaia. "Come," and in an instant she was on her feet and at his side.

Khamisa watched sadly as Jumaia stole her Juma and led him into the other room. Could he make love to her with such tender ribs? She was sure they would find a way. She swallowed hard, fighting back a lonely tear.

February 1973 • Hamed climbed into the back of an Army Land Rover that was already overloaded with men. At last he might get a chance to kill some *adoo*. Almost five months he had been on this outpost on the Hornbeam Line and so far he hadn't even seen any PFLOAG men.

The Leopard Line concept of creating a mined and patrolled barrier to hamper the PFLOAG supply caravans was a sound idea, however, its weakness had proved to be in its positioning. The Jebals Qaftawt and Aroomq where it had been laid were subject to Khareef fogs and under its cover supply trains had easily slipped through. So a new line was being constructed further to the west where it avoided most of those Khareef mists and had been called the Hornbeam Line. This line started at the coastal village Mugsahyl and when it was eventually complete would stretch for more than forty-five kilometres directly north to the village Ayon. Every five or six of kilometres a fortified outpost was created. Electronic sensors placed in the fence alerted these posts if the wire was cut. Hamed's small group of Al Nasr Firqats and Government soldiers was responding to such an alert right now.

The line of battered vehicles stripped right down to their basic shell enabled an extra fully armed man aboard. Eight vehicles all driven by regular soldiers and each carrying at least seven Firqats now began to move off, heading directly south along the wire.

On his initial arrival six months ago at Al Nasr headquarters at Adonib at the very western edge of the Salalah plain, Hamad had been greeted somewhat suspiciously. He had been interviewed straight away and then although made welcome and fed was left for some days to do nothing. It had been almost a week before he had started on another series of interviews being processed from one person to another. The point of issue was his notorious brother Commissar Mussalim and his application to join Al Nasr was treated dubiously. However, his deceased brother's good reputation in the Sultan's Army eventually countered this and satisfied his interrogators.

From there he had been taken to Salalah where along with several other new recruits he was taken before the Sheikh of the all the tribes of the southern Kathiri and the leader of Al Nasr, Mussalim Bin Tufl. Hamed was a little in awe of this legendary Sheikh who many years before had led the Englishman Wilfred Theisiger on an expedition across the vast mountainous dunes of the *Ramlet*. But Bin Tufl was a slightly built man with the typical wiry physique of the Kathiri Bedouin and to Hamed it distorted his own version of what this man should look like. They all sat crossed legged around a large carpet sipping tea while the Sheikh exalted Sultan Qaboos and the emerging new Oman. He promised a future of prosperity for all Dhofaris once the country's evil enemies and the misguided had been defeated. He went on to explain the role that Al Nasr would play in clearing away the nation's enemies and assisting Civil Development. He went on to stress the importance of their current role of strangling the *adoo* supply lines and the impact that would have on the PFLOAG's ability to continue hampering the Dhofari people's path to prosperity. Hamed had left the *dirwain* in a highly motivated frame of mind, as had been the intention.

The next two weeks back at Adonib he had undergone some weapon and tactic training from the SAS men of the British Army Training Team before being sent up to the northern extreme of the Hornbeam Line. That had been five months ago and since then the line had extended much further north and well out of sight leaving behind at this outpost a small mixture of firqats and soldiers. This location was on a featureless land that was neither *gatn* nor n*ejd*. The outstretched fingers of any Khareef would reach this far west only occasionally and when it did it was weak. Consequently, although there was enough annual moisture to just hold back the *nejd* there was never enough to sustain any greenery. The undulating land was barren and flinty with scattered tufts of wiry brown grass. Nothing of any significance happened and that motivation planted by Bin Tufl had soon withered beneath boredom and inactivity. The main event of a week usually turned out to be the arrival of supplies and mail. Even the mail aspect was denied to Hamed since he wrote and read only poorly and he had not written to anyone, therefore none of his family even knew where he was. Nor was he sure that any of them even cared, which was another reason why he had not made the effort.

The small convoy of vehicles ground and bounced slowly over the uneven ground. Even at this painfully slow speed, clouds of thick choking dust were thrown from beneath the wheels forcing each driver to fall back from the vehicle ahead and soon they were well strung out. The men inside the open vehicles wrapped themselves completely from head to foot pulling their shamags over their faces leaving only the narrowest slit for eyes, but still the dust seeped through irritating skin and drying throats. It wasn't very long before the lead vehicle arrived at the point where a hole that had been cut in the fence. Although the wire was constructed and the sensors in place the laying of the landmines was proving slower and along this sections they had not been placed. Notices had been posted warning of mines but it seemed that in this instance the smugglers had not been fooled.

Taking advantage of a break from the jolting Hamed climbed from the Land Rover. He leaned on its carrier tray sipping water as he watched an Army officer, the Firqat leader and some of the soldiers study the tracks of the camels that had passed through the wire fence. He was too far away to hear what was being said but by the gesticulating arms and gestures he could tell that they believed the caravan had gone east bending slightly towards the south. He glanced in that direction. For many kilometres the landscape was unaltering but in the hazy distance the landline rose steeply. If this supply caravan could make it to there it could disappear in the mazes of deep and thickly wooded wadis and would be comparatively safe.

It was just past noon and seemingly in no particular hurry to start the pursuit the army officer leading the patrol decided to call a break to eat and for those who wished, to pray. It was February and the cooler season just ending but even so by midday the temperatures soared above the hundred degrees fahrenheit mark. The sun at this time of year was not yet too high in the southern sky and the vehicles afforded a tiny sliver of shade on their northern sides. Hamed found himself a space among the men crowding into this narrow shade and ate the bread, feta and fruit that had been handed out. This would be his first engagement and this delay only triggered the chance to dwell on what it was that he might be getting himself into. He began to feel apprehensive about the uncertainty of the situation and its unpredictability. Juma had been killed in confrontation with men such as these so they should not be under estimated. His British trainers who were experienced top of the range soldiers had also emphasised that the PFLOAG fighters were very determined and formidable men. This hold-up and his thoughts were increasing his tension greatly. Perhaps the time would be better spent first in prayer asking Allah for his protection and secondly in a more earthly practical action of servicing his FN rifle.

He got up and using a small amount of his water supply washed himself the best way he could. Then he wandered off a little way, turned roughly in the direction of Mecca and began the off-key chant to attract Allah's attention. "*Allah Fiih Akhbar,*" he sang. "*Allah Fiih Akhbar.*" Soon men began to fall in behind him content to allow him to lead the prayer. He stood head bowed muttering his prayer and then sank to his knees and pressed his head to the ground in servitude, while the small group behind followed his every action.

When his prayers were finished he climbed into the rear of the Land Rover and began dismantling his rifle. Using a tiny piece of four by two cloth moistened with oil he pulled it through the barrel then carefully cleaned out the tiny particles of sand and dust that had inevitably found its way into each movable part. By the time he had finished the camp was beginning to break and men were getting back into the vehicles. Some of the more seasoned firqats had special home made cloth sheaves to wrap their weapon in, probably made by wives or mothers. He didn't but he could now appreciate the wisdom of that and he determined that when he got back he would somehow get himself some kind of wrap. For now however, the best he could do to protect it from the inevitable clouds of dust was to stuff the barrel end with the spent four by two and drape the part of his *futa* over the firing mechanism as it rested across his knees.

For well over an hour the vehicles bounced and jarred slowly across the rough terrain swirling up thick clouds of dust as they did. Almost imperceptibly the landscape began to change, its undulations becoming more pronounced into much steeper hills and wadis as the jebal got gradually nearer. Still some way from the jebal the lead vehicle breasted the top of a hill and abruptly stopped. One by one the following Land Rovers drew alongside and the men in the rear stood to peer forward. The vehicle in which Hamed rode was in the middle of the line and when it stopped alongside the others he too stood and stared down the hill into a large basin.

In the bottom was a herd of thirty or forty camels and all still burdened by their packs. Some squatted on their bellies while others meandered around casually feeding on barren scraps of foliage. A little way off beneath a lonely clump of scraggy wind distorted trees a campfire burned its thin wisp of smoke winding lazily upward in a windless day. A dozen men or more beneath the low branches sheltered from the relentless frazzle of the sun at its hottest. Some reposed horizontally and some sat in a circular huddle talking while two or three others stood close by. Those that were not asleep now stared up the hill in the direction of the new arrivals. Hamed looked towards the jebal beyond perhaps an hour away and found it almost incredible that these men had been so complacent that they had been caught completely off guard taking shelter from the hottest part of the day with comparative safety not far away. He could only assume that those men knew nothing of the sensors in the line wire that alerted the nearest outpost when it was cut.

A shouted warning and all eight vehicles sped down the hill into the basin taking full advantage of the element of surprise before any resistance could be organised. The men did not move as the vehicles stopped in great clouds of dust close by and forty-eight soldiers and firqats leapt out pointing weapons directly at them. The men seemed unfazed by the sudden arrival of government troops and relaxed instead into the traditional Arabic custom of politeness and they invited their captors to join them as guests. Even more bizarre, the army officer after first directing some men to inspect and seize the cargo still loaded on the camel's backs accepted their hospitality.

Hamed helped search the cargo and it was quickly confirmed that it did indeed contain weapons and munitions. Then the freight was roughly inventoried and a sergeant reported the findings to the officer, who in company with the Firqat leader and some of the soldiers still sat beneath the trees in social discord with the prisoner's. Seemingly still unconcerned the officer then ordered that each of the prisoners weapons should be gathered up. Then for the next two hours and through the heat of the afternoon they continued to sit beneath the trees talking with the men as if they were all caravan travellers that had crossed paths in a chance meeting.

There was not enough room beneath the trees shade for all and most of the Firqats had to find or create their own shade. Hamed crawled beneath one of the vehicles and out of hearing range he lay watching the inactivity of the party beneath the trees. He was bewildered this had been easy, so easy in fact it seemed almost contrived. It was far too friendly belying completely any suggestion of hostility. He had expected at least some token resistance but there had been no reaction at all. Was this how it was always? In the heat his eyes grew heavy and flicked closed several times before bored he lapsed into a light level of sleep.

Much later things started to happen and men began to stir. He crawled from beneath the vehicle and stood idly by with most of the other Firqats waiting for someone to explain what precisely was happening. In the end it was the Firqats own leader who came over.

He confirmed what they all knew that it was *adoo* supply train and that the weapons had been confiscated. The caravan had come from the supply dump at Shershitta and was destined for a cave in Wadi Risham. All the men were arrested but only four were PFLOAG regulars, the rest claimed to be simple drovers who were working the caravan train just for the money it would bring. The four regulars were to be taken back to the outpost in the Land Rovers and then flown out by helicopter to Salalah for further interrogation. Meanwhile the Firqa, which he would himself lead would accompany the caravan back to the outpost on foot. After their arrival the drovers also would be sent on to Salalah for further interrogation. Not considered to be as important as the PFLOAG men they would be sent by road sometime within the next day or two. He went on to heap congratulation and praise on his men for a job well done. Then he left once more to receive any final instruction from the officer who by now was making preparations to leave with his four prisoners.

Hamed watched the drovers as they obediently packed up their camp intending full co-operation with the surrender and transportation of Front weapons. He looked at the PFLOAG men sitting meekly in pairs in the back of two Land Rovers accompanied by two armed guards. This was not what he had expected at all. He had come on this patrol expecting an element of danger and a probable chance to kill some *adoo* exacting as he did a molecule of revenge for Juma's death at their hands. But it had proved to be a massive anti-climax. These men, it seemed, were not dangerous at all, just mild mannered petty criminals! The tension and apprehension that he had experienced had been completely groundless. His British trainers had warned him that the *adoo* were formidable and extremely determined fighters but none of these men remotely showed any of those qualities. Their threat, it seemed had been grossly over-exaggerated and he felt nothing but contempt for men who surrendered so easily. He recalled that day when the PFLOAG men had come to their farm arrogant and brash and the unpleasant Ziad had pushed the muzzle of his gun against his father's head. It's easy to bully defenceless people but when confronted by someone of equal strength they were obviously no more than contemptible cowards. Perhaps one day he would have the opportunity to confront that particular man on equal terms, *Inshaallah*. He had no doubt that if he did he would also prove just as gutless as all the rest.

* * *

It had been three weeks since Mussalim had arrived back at the farm. At first the recovery from his injuries seemed slow but over the last ten days the tenderness had cleared rapidly. Now it was only if he directly pressed his ribs that he experienced discomfort. He knew that he should rejoin his unit at Raythut but his enthusiasm for the cause had waned a great deal.

PFLOAG co-ordinated resistance had all but disappeared. Replaced by tactics termed as 'a strategy of flexibility,' by the General Committee. In effect this meant that small groups of fighters had splinted off independently from the Regional Commands. These splinter groups operated more as opportunists' carrying out impromptu acts of terrorism when the opportunity presented itself or when the fancy motivated them. Consequently, without specified objectives the movement had lost direction and Zahir Ali as Commander of the Central and Eastern Area was little more than a figurehead. Many of the previous members had become content with the Sultan's policies of improvements and the progress made towards achieving those goals and no longer saw any reason to continue the opposition. The supporting militia had faded away completely, leaving behind only the hard line PFLOAG regulars to continue the fight. Even among these radicals there were daily desertions.

Back on the family farm with his son and his Mahru woman those soul-searching questions that had haunted Mussalim before now returned even more persuasive than before. Disillusioned with aimless policies and the seeming lack of ideas Mussalim's motivation was practically zero. Recovering gradually from his injuries he had taken more interest in the daily routine farm activities. Jumaia delighted to have her man close and attentive was happy and her happiness was infectious. The natural bonding with his infant son was growing stronger each day, as was his relationship with Jumaia's stepson, Salim. In simple family life he had found the contentment that his father had years before tried so hard to convince him existed. At that time his anger and resentment against poverty and oppression had deafened him to such words. Now, however, with a family of his own and the rapidly improving living standards of the ordinary jeballly the war seemed almost pointless. But he knew that if he didn't return to his unit at Raythut soon then they would out of curiosity come looking for him.

Omar Mohammed's offer to join the *firqa* Al Umri haunted him and he wondered if the offer still held. If it did then it might be a way out for him. It would mean that the family in its entirety would have to give up the farm and all move under *firqa* Al Umri's protection at Mirbat and remain there until the Front had gone from Jebal Qara. The cattle could all be sold which would, in view of the rapidly rising prices give them a sizeable dividend that could support them for a while. However, it was these rising prices that would almost certainly work against them. At some future date when they wished to restore their life on the farm then they would not have the amount of money required to buy more cattle in any significant number. Additionally there would of course be the problem of persuading his father to leave also. He would be extremely reluctant he knew. There was much to think about and much to discuss. However, before the subject was even raised he needed to know if Omar's offer still stood.

To find out he had two days ago written a letter and sent Jumaia to carry it to her brother at Jibjat. There she was to persuade him to deliver it to Omar at Mirbat. Then she was to wait until his return and bring his reply back. He had not told her the letter's contents only that it was important that she keep it safe. He expected her to be back in one week and that was, he estimated, as long as he could reasonably expect his absence from Raythut not to arouse curiosity.

This day he had set himself the task of repairing the shed doorway that he and Hamed had damaged when they had fought last summer. As he worked he wondered where his young brother might be. He pondered the accuracy in the story some passing travellers had related last week as they stopped and accepted his hospitality. Hamed had they said, been seen in the company of Sheikh Mussalim Bin Tufl. For him to be in such exulted company could mean only that he had, or was, attempting to join Al Nasr *Firqats*. Mussalim shook his head ruefully at his thoughts. Had Hamed not learned the lessons from his two elder brothers' poor examples? He wished that he were back where he belonged on the farm. His father's solution that he should marry Khamisa as soon as it was appropriate to do so seemed to reduce his and Khamisa's appalling betrayal of Juma to less onerous proportions. After they were married then it could become forgivable.

His musings were interrupted when he realised that someone from a distance was shouting his name. He turned to see Khamisa running towards him agitatedly waving her arms. He frowned and wondered what it could be that had alarmed her.

"Soldiers. Soldiers are coming," she shouted from a distance.

"Soldiers?" He muttered to himself and scanned into the distance behind her looking for them.

She was closer now and she waved her arm towards the valley away to her right. "Soldiers in Land Rovers," she called. "Coming this way."

If they were in Land Rovers then they could only be government soldiers. Whether they were coming purposely or by chance made no difference, they could not find him here. The immediate area around the farmhouse was open and exposed he would be spotted making a run. He scanned around quickly looking desperately for somewhere to hide.

"Here," Khamisa said and grabbing his arm she led him running away from the shed. "Under here." She lifted the edge of the sheeting that covered the remnants of the hay.

Mussalim crawled under quickly and buried himself further in the hay. It was not a particular good hiding place but it might do if they were just a roaming patrol. Doubts invaded his mind, patrols were usually *firqats* on foot, not soldiers in vehicles. His confidence was jolted. Could it be his presence had been reported? If so then this was probably a snatch squad looking specifically for him. He might very well be in deep trouble. Suddenly he felt very vulnerable and the situation desperate. If discovered he had no escape route, not even a weapon with which to defend himself. The only thing that he could do was to wait and hope.

Time dragged on and even though he strained his ears he could hear nothing. Perhaps they had gone? Or perhaps they had gone straight past? He dismissed both thoughts instantly, Khamisa would have fetched him if they had. Maybe they were just sitting talking, drinking tea perhaps. His father would be obliged to offer them refreshments, it was customary. Still nothing happened and he had just begun to hope that he was safe in this hiding place when the covering sheet started to move. Instinctively he buried himself deeper as it was slowly dragged away. Now he could hear voices and he thought he heard one man suggest burning. If they set the hay alight then he would be forced out. Minutes later his worse fears were realised when unmistakably he smelled the smoke. He could hear the loud cracks indicating that the dry hay was burning fiercely. He could hear his father's voice protesting that it was his winter cattle fodder they were destroying. The flames fanned by the jebal breeze soon began to lick all around him curling the hay into scorched black fibres as it burned. Without an alternative he was forced to get to his feet. There was choking black smoke all around him and as he stumbled clear of the burning fire one of the soldiers shouted triumphantly, "here he is." Instantly pointing rifles surrounded him.

Mussalim looked dejectedly at the impassive faces all about him. More soldiers who searched in different areas of the farm responded to the triumphant shout and hurried over to stare at the captured PFLOAG Commissar. Though no one spoke all the expressions were smug. Someone at the back growled at the soldiers to be let through and a thickly set sergeant elbowed his way through the circle to stand directly in front of Mussalim. He was taller by far and much heavier. He had a deeply lined face with beard streaked grey and he fixed him with a hard stare.

"Commissar," he said mockingly with a slight Baluchi accent. Without warning he lifted his rifle and with the speed of a snake rammed the butt into the side of Mussalim's face. Mussalim staggered backwards and fell to the ground. "*Adoo* murderer," he spat staring down at him venomously.

Mussalim carefully touched his numb cheekbone and felt wetness of blood on his fingers. He looked up into the man's merciless expression just in time to see his face twitch as he swung his heavy boot. It crashed into his tender ribs sending instant pain through his whole torso making him gasp and catch his breath. Somewhere a woman was shouting hysterically. He thought it was probably his mother but locked in waves of pain he couldn't be sure.

"That's enough of that sergeant," a calm voice said and a young man wearing epaulettes of officer rank appeared at the sergeant's side to stare down on Mussalim. "Get him up," he instructed no one in particular and rough hands dragged Mussalim to his feet. He stood unsteadily when the hands released him. For a moment the officer stared curiously into Mussalim's glassy eyes as if looking for some abnormality that made a man *adoo*. "Where's that uniform?" he asked turning away from him. Someone handed him Mussalim's uniform that had been lovingly laundered by Jumaia. "This is yours, I presume!"

There was no point denying it but Mussalim still suffering waves of pain in his ribs did not reply.

"You are Mussalim Bin Adbulla Al Hamer?" Whether it was a question or a statement he wasn't sure but it didn't particularly matter. Obviously the officer knew precisely who he was and more than that had known that he would be found here. Undoubtedly somebody had betrayed his presence to the authorities. He took Mussalim's silence as confirmation. "You are arrested in the name of the Sultan." He waited just a moment for his reaction and when none came he nodded briefly then said. "Tie his hands."

With his hands tied securely behind his back Mussalim was tossed unceremoniously into the back of one of the vehicles. Nor was he allowed the dignity of a seat. Instead he was pushed to the floor and the four guards sitting above him rested their feet on his body. Jokha still shouting hysterically, clung to the vehicle as it began moving away until as it gathered speed it pulled her over and she was forced to let go.

As soon as they were clear of the farm the small convoy of five vehicles swung to the north-west not as Mussalim expected in the direction of Salalah. As the pain in his ribs faded his wits began to function. He could not imagine where they might be taking him but he didn't dwell too much on that. In the bottom of the vehicle he lay on his back with his hands beneath him out of sight of his captures. He began working his wrists to loose the rope binding his hands. Somewhere before their destination was reached he might just get a chance to escape and if he did he wanted to be ready. To make sure his guards didn't notice his struggling against the rope he tried to restrict the movement in his arms as much as possible. Thankfully the vehicle bounced wildly over the rough terrain bumping and jolting all inside and this helped considerably to disguise his attempts. The rope wouldn't slacken and the only result was sore scraped skin around his wrists. But desperation is a powerful motivator and despite the pain he persevered. He had to, there was simply nothing else. Gradually almost unnoticeably the rope began to loose. Just the slightest movement at first and then little by little it began to loosen until he felt his hands almost free. Now the problem was the opposite and he had to hold the rope in place until the right moment presented itself.

The vehicles ground slowly on bouncing over the uneven terrain still heading in a north-westerly direction. Lying as he was in the bottom of the vehicle beneath the feet of four armed soldiers Mussalim could not see how an escape opportunity was going to present itself. His thoughts performed high-speed acrobatics as he tried to think of a way where he might possibly make an opportunity happen. But nothing other than wild or hopeless possibilities came to mind. There was absolutely nothing he could do but wait and hope. Even the bouncing stopped as they reached a road of sorts and the speed instantly improved. As the speed improved so did the clouds of dust from beneath the wheels and the soldiers wrapped their faces beneath their shamags for protection.

The small convoy progressed uneventfully onwards getting ever nearer to the destination wherever that might be. Mussalim by now was despairing that there would be any change at all in the situation when a sudden deep resonating thump shattered the air and nerves. The vehicle swerved violently to its right and stopped. The soldiers were on their feet and staring forward towards the front of the convoy. There was a lot of shouting from that direction and Mussalim heard the words land mine several times. One of the vehicles he guessed had run over a mine. Their misfortune might just be his luck and he prepared himself to be ready for any chance that came.

He was dragged from the vehicle to stand at its side while two *askars* covered him by pointing their FN rifles directly at his chest. Most of the attention was centred at the head of the convoy where what was left of the lead vehicle lay upside down in a tangled mass of scrap metal. Small groups of men centred their attention on the scattered bodies of dead or dying while others still searched the area for other missing comrades.

Mussalim began to assess his possibilities. He had his back against the next to last vehicle. The rear vehicle had a mounted browning in the back and was manned by an alert soldier who scanned the surrounding landscape for any sign of danger. That was not good! The two other vehicles were just ahead and empty. They were on a road that was little more than well-worn tyre tracks cutting along the hillside of a wide rolling valley. The ground to his front was open exposed and sloped upward steepening towards the hillcrest. He glanced casually over his shoulder where the ground fell away. It sloped gradually at first then fell into a deep gully in the valley bottom. He followed the route of the gully as it wound through trees becoming deeper as it headed towards a more significant deep wadi. If he could make it as far as that wadi then he would have a good chance, he concluded. However, the wadi was a full kilometre away and the cover in the gully not particularly good. Worse, the cover between here and the gully was non-existent. He glanced to the sun. Three hours at least to sunset, four to darkness. Darkness would improve his chances considerably but would the soldiers stop here for the night? He doubted it, particularly if some of the casualties were still living. Wickedly, he wished for all their deaths. That might improve the chances of the soldiers staying here till the morning, particularly if they thought that there would be more mines in the road. They wouldn't be keen to press on into darkness.

He became aware of the hostile glances from the men tending bodies. Did they blame him for the mine? They might, he was after all PFLOAG. He watched carefully as the small groups started gathering together passing obvious messages with gloomy head shaking. As the groups grew in size some arguing broke out and more glances came in his direction. He began to become concerned, they were obviously discussing him. It was desirable that he make his bid to get away very soon, but one look at the two rifle muzzles aimed directly at him from only a couple of metres warned him it would be suicide.

Eventually after some heated discussion three men split from the group and came in his direction. Mussalim did not like the look of the situation and he was further dismayed to see that one of the men was that thickset sergeant.

"We are going to string the bastard up," he said to the men holding the weapons but the remark was directed straight at Mussalim. "Five dead and one, who will be very soon," he went on.

Mussalim looked around desperately seeking that officer who had come to his rescue before. But he could not see him and assumed that he must have been one of the men in the lead vehicle. He glanced back to the sergeant who at this moment held his destiny in his hands. There was only hatred in his expression and he knew that he could expect no mercy.

From somewhere inside the vehicle one man produced a towrope and began making it into a noose. Mussalim struggled to control the rising panic. The guns still pointed at him but he was at the point where it didn't matter, he had to do something and do it now.

"There are some trees over there." The noose maker said and nodded towards the gully in the valley bottom.

"That'll do," the sergeant agreed and rough hands grabbed Mussalim's arms and tried to frog-march him down the hill.

A glimmer of hope. They would be escorting him across the open ground toward the gully. He still held the ropes in place that wrapped his wrist and now was not the time to reveal his hands were free. Even though a man either side dragged him towards the cover and a potential chance he fought every step by planting his feet firmly and leaning steeply backwards. That was what was expected, but he was alert and cool now waiting, waiting, waiting. The man with the rope led the way while the sergeant and another on the other side dragged him struggling toward the trees. The two men with the rifles followed close behind. No one else seemed inclined to either interfere or to join in. Even the soldier manning the browning had relaxed his vigil to watch.

The man with the rope selected a stout bough, threw the free end over then adjusted it so that the noose was at the right height. Then taking a firm hold of the rope he called to one of the men holding a rifle to come on that end also. Clearly the intention was to put Mussalim's neck in the noose and then those two would haul him up. The man propped his rifle against the tree trunk and took hold of the rope. Mussalim was dragged to the noose. It was now or never. One man a couple of metres to his front still held a rifle, the sergeant and another still held his arms and two men were braced on the rope end behind him.

He rolled his head about making it difficult for the sergeant to slip the noose over. Then he let the rope fall from his wrist and with all the strength he could muster swung his arm around behind the sergeant. Taken completely by surprise he stumbled across the front of him. He swung his other arm up behind the smaller man and found he had his head beneath his arm in a headlock. The man with the rifle raised the weapon to fire. Instinctively he released the headlock and hauled the man across his front taking refuge behind. Two sharp ear-splitting cracks and the man slumped. Mussalim felt the thud of the bullets entering the man's body, but with the strength of the desperate he held him up as a shield. Gathering himself he stumbled forward at the weapon still keeping the human shield in front. When he collided with the rifleman he allowed the stricken man's weight to fall on him sending him falling to the ground beneath his dead weight. Spread-eagled beneath the dying man he still held the rifle in one hand. Mussalim placed his foot on his wrist and wrestled the weapon from his grasp. The sergeant head down was charging towards him and almost upon him. Mussalim held the rifle by its muzzle and could only swing it upward. Even though the situation was still desperate he felt enormous satisfaction at the sickening squelch when the up swinging stock disintegrated the man's face. The man on the rope end now raced towards his rifle propped against the trunk. Mussalim spun the weapon in his hands and with two squeezes of the trigger shot him dead then turned the muzzle at the noose man. Not so smug now his face betrayed his fear and he quickly raised his hands in meek surrender. Mussalim glanced quickly around. The sergeant on his knees pressed his hands to his face, blood trickling through his fingers. The other man struggled to a sitting position trying to escape from beneath the body. There was no immediate danger from any of these three. However, a row of erupting earth moving quickly towards him and the sharp chatter of that Browning was the new danger. Time to go. He dodged behind the tree trunk for cover grabbed the other weapon as he did and ran for the nearby gully.

He ran down the gully heading for the cover and security of the deep wadi little more than half a kilometre away. Once in there and beneath the canopies of its dense shrubs they would never find him. With two weapons in his possession would they even want to look for him? He doubted it. But this had been a close thing and he had been very lucky. One thing that was now certain though! The soldiers' version of what had happened back there would probably not reflect the true events. That, coupled with two dead from the incident meant there could be no amnesty for him now.

~ 21 ~

October 1973 · With the sun rapidly disappearing beneath the western horizon Hamed clambered apathetically aboard one of the Land Rovers. It promised to be another of those uneventful nights silently waiting in ambush for the PFLOAG to creep forward to sabotage the wire of the Hornbeam Line. He anticipated that it would be as all the other ambushes he had been on, uneventful. He didn't doubt that somewhere along the Line's thirty-kilometre length an attack would be made but almost invariably they managed to strike where the ambushes were not. He stifled a yawn as he waited for the vehicle to fill with his comrades. The party of around twenty men, *askars* and *firqats* were heavily armed with mortars, grenade launchers and general-purpose machine guns as well as their personal weapons. Any *adoo* that did blunder beneath their guns would have the devil to pay. If tonight's sortie followed the usual routine then they would travel two or perhaps three kilometres from their base and set up position. It didn't particularly matter if they went north or south it would be somewhere that they had been before. The advantage of this was that it would already have sangars and fortifications built.

The Communist Front was focusing a lot of attention on attempting to destroy the Hornbeam Line. This only emphasised how successful it had become in restricting the movements of supplies to their hard-pressed forces in the central and eastern region. Attacks on the actual outposts were unusual, however. When they did come they came in the form of not very accurate artillery fire from a recoilless gun. This tactic enabled the PFLOAG to stand off without committing men they could not afford to lose. These attacks were always short in duration because within minutes Strikemaster aircraft from RAFO Salalah were in the sky overhead seeking the gun as a target. This was why these bombardments invariably came at sunset. Around sunset it was still not dark enough to see the flash that would pinpoint the direction of the gun but it was close enough to darkness to make it difficult for searching aircraft pilots and also to deter a patrol from setting off until first light. This gave them the opportunity to withdraw under the cover of darkness to a new position. In the main the sabotage of the wire was made between the outposts. It was a softer and less hazardous alternative to place explosives in these unguarded spots. These attacks were always made under the cover of darkness so that by the time the soldiers' pursuit started the next morning they had long made good their escape. It was not particularly successful in making lasting breaches in the barrier because repairs were very soon carried out. However, it was effective to some degree. The irritating and constant repairing had the effect of slowing down the Line's completion dramatically. Now in the autumn of 1973 and a year after it had been started the Line still had not reached its northern end objective at Ayon. These nightly set ambushes by the government forces were an attempt to deter the PFLOAG from these sabotage attacks.

Hamed slid further along the seat allowing room for two more of his *firqat* comrades into the back. Lal Baksh gave him a grin revealing yellowed and crooked teeth as he sat down heavily at his side.

"Tonight we'll catch some *adoo*," he said optimistically.

He didn't draw much encouragement from his remark because Lal possessed the permanent optimism of the very young but was not often right. "Perhaps," he muttered with a shrug.

Lal pulled back on the lever of his FN rifle working a round into the breach then he slipped on the safety catch. "Now I'm ready."

Hamed glanced at the young man at his side, he could not be more than eighteen years old. The faintest wisp of facial hair down his chin betrayed that he was not yet able to grow a man's beard. Although Hamed had not particularly encouraged it Lal had for no apparent reason virtually placed himself under his protection. They were not of the same tribe. Indeed Lal was not even from a tribe in the Kathiri group. He was of Bait Khawar, a tribe whose tribal area straddled the southern end of the Yemen border. Perhaps it was just that Lal saw him as an elder brother. Or perhaps it was that as a Khawar in the Kathiri *firqa* he found himself as something of an outsider and in Hamed's moody introverted nature he recognised another lone figure. A kindred spirit! Whatever the youngster's reason he had attached himself to Hamed and he found the situation of being looked up too like an elder brother quite pleasing.

The last glint of sun had just slipped beneath the horizon leaving a western sky of red, orange and pink when the small convoy of four Land Rovers set off. They followed the well-worn tyre tracks that ran a few metres parallel to the line. The line itself was not particularly substantial consisting of six foot pieces of angle iron concreted into the ground as posts and chain link fencing attached. On the face of it, not much of a barrier but the implanted sensors alerted the nearest outpost of any breach and it was that quick reaction that made it effective. Moving slowly over the undulating flinty ground, with a man sitting on the bonnet of the front vehicle scanning the ground ahead for potential planted mines, they headed south towards the not too distant jebal.

"Wadi Disht!" Lal predicted after a few minutes. "We are going to Wadi Disht."

Hamed looked forward towards the jebal. Wadi Disht carved a deep groove from the mountains far out into undulating landscape. The line of wire cut right across it. It rather looked as if they were in fact heading in that direction. Ambushes had been set there many times and so by now the sangars constructed there were quite substantial. It was a secure and safe location and also well known to the *adoo*. So the chances of a trap actually being sprung was slim. It was promising more and more to be yet another uneventful night. Although this time Lal might be right about their destination he would be wrong about catching *adoo*.

Since the chase last February that had resulted in the capture of the gun runners and their armaments Hamed had not even sighted the elusive *adoo*. His burning desire to avenge his brother Juma had withered beneath a lack of opportunity and endless days of boredom. Since that chase day this particular section of the wire had been breached three times but on each occasion it had been simple sabotage. Other than one occasion when the outpost itself had been briefly shelled, life had been an endless cycle of routine boredom. Basic sentry duties and regular wire patrols punctuated long periods of sleep and trivial pastimes. Most of his comrades had managed some periods of relief by taking home leave but Hamed had not. Apart from two brief spells in Salalah he had remained on station in the line for a year now. Lately however thoughts of home had begun to haunt him and he wondered if sufficient time had elapsed to lay a coat of forgiveness on his indiscretions. He supposed that his family had somehow managed to continue to run the farm although without his presence he could only guess to what degree. If things were as bad as he guessed they might be then that would add fuel to his case for forgiveness. But unsure of the welcome he would get when he sheepishly arrived at his father's door it was still an ordeal he did not relish. What he could expect when, or if he did return was that Mussalim would not be there. In the earlier part of the year he had heard the news of his seizure and his subsequent quick escape. For Mussalim to return to the farm or to spend any significant amount of time there now would be foolhardy. And he certainly was not that. So he would be spared the embarrassment of facing the brother who he had tried to stick a knife into. One humiliation at a time would be enough.

Lal was telling the other two men in the Land Rover about the situation in his home village, Sarfait. Hamed looked out across the featureless terrain and despite the conditions Lal was describing he thought that he would prefer to be there rather than here. At least something happened there. Sarfait was a sizeable village on elevated ground coastal side of Jebal Sayq right on the Yemen border itself. Until earlier this year it had been occupied by the PFLOAG. However, the Sultan's Army had arrived in force and taken it back. Now according to Lal it was subjected to almost daily bombardment across the border from the PFLOAG training camp at Hauf.

"Why doesn't the Army fire back?" one of the men asked.

"The Sultan won't let them," the third man answered for him. "He doesn't want to cause an international incident."

The man tutted loudly. "The *adoo* don't seem to be worried about that."

The third man shrugged. "The last thing we need right now is to give the Yemenis an excuse to come in on the side of the *adoo*.

Hamed as Lal's friend had heard about the Sarfait situation so many times. He sighed quietly to himself through boredom and returned once more to his own thoughts. There was no doubt the monotony of an unaltering schedule was beginning to wear him. The previous every day routine of the farm seemed positively capricious compared to this life on an isolated outpost. The army officers told them almost daily that, "Their presence on the Hornbeam Line was making a great difference," and he didn't doubt the truth of that statement. However, after more than a year on the line he felt that he had done his part in full. Perhaps it was time for him to face his shame, return home and test his family's reaction. If it proved to be unfavourable then he could always return to Al Nasr. At least then he would know exactly what his situation was. He thought also of the money he had accumulated. Receiving pay regularly and hardly leaving the outpost he had a considerable wad stashed in his bedroll. He had never in his life had money of any consequence but now he had and he would miss those paydays for certain. On the other hand the amount he could hand over to his father should go a long way towards moderating any anger that might remain. His mind was made up and he now began to plan when. There was no reason that he could think of to delay so next week would be as good a time as any, he supposed. Tomorrow upon his return to the outpost he would make the arrangements.

The vehicles curved away and stopped when they arrived at the steep edge that overlooked Wadi Disht. In no apparent haste men began to slowly dismount from the vehicles. Hamed wandered away a couple of metres and looked across the wadi. The sun had disappeared from view leaving an angry red on the undersides of the darkening clouds. The sky above had turned the colour of purple bruises and the first of the evening stars were just visible. The wire fence that was the Hornbeam Line ran to the edge of the wadi and holding no respect for the contours of the wadi continued on down its steep side across the bottom and up the other side. Centuries ago a wild river must have rushed along the wadi for large smooth boulders completely covered its base. These boulders bleached white by the frazzling sun across hundreds of years now cast a peculiar glow in the fading light. Disht had been a well-known route for arms-carrying caravans in the past. Hidden from view these caravans had followed the bed across the *gatn* and right up into the comparative safety of Jebal Qaftawt. That was the very reason for the regular trap set along its top edge.

"Hamed," Lal called.

He turned to see Lal staring in his direction. He was fully laden with a grenade launcher across one shoulder and an ammunition box under his other arm. "Which one?" he nodded towards the row of sangars that were constructed along the edge overlooking the wadi.

Men had gathered around the four vehicles and were beginning to get busy unloading the weaponry. The drivers meanwhile still sat behind the wheels watching and waiting patiently for the unloading to be finished. When it was they would be free to return to the outpost abandoning the ambushers until morning.

"You choose," Hamed replied moving towards the vehicles. It was time for him to help. He claimed a box of ammunition also and a veri pistol. That would be a necessary piece of equipment. Soon it would be as dark as a slaver's dungeon in the wadi bottom and if saboteurs did foray down there then illumination would be essential. He waited until the man at his side moved then reached across to grab a handful of flares to go with the pistol. He never actually managed to grasp them.

A deep resonating thump vibrated the ground violently and shattered nerves with its sudden deafening crash. He hunched his shoulders as flying debris peppered his back fiercely. Instinctively he sank to his knees at the vehicle's rear his thoughts racing in alarm. Something metallic clattered to the ground close by and bounced on another couple of metres before coming to rest. He glanced unseeing at the bent and twisted object wondering if they had just been blasted with an artillery shell. But he dismissed it he had not heard any incoming hiss. The flying debris ceased and he looked behind him to see a cloud of smoke and dust drifting lazily away from the wadi lip. Someone somewhere muttered booby trap and with that prompt his mind recognised the twisted metallic object. He glanced back at it and although badly mangled he could now identify it as a grenade launcher. Lal had been carrying a grenade launcher.

He got to his feet quickly looking for his friend among the slowly stirring men but could not see him. He hurried the few metres to the slowly dissipating cloud calling his name. Where seconds before there had been a solidly built sangar there was now only a shallow crater. Somebody prevented him from jumping in the hollow to look for Lal. As he was being restrained he heard in the background a warning cry being chorused to keep out of the sangars. Over the man's shoulder several metres away Hamed saw what looked like a half-butchered cow. Even without approaching the bloodied bulk shape he knew that it was Lal.

He watched as two men approached the shape and stared down at the bloody mass. One of the men cautiously touched the body with his boot and shook his head sadly. Hamed was led away while others organised a cover of sorts for the remains of Lal. Hamed slumped to sit on the ground and resting his back against the Land Rover wheel he sipped water from a canteen that someone had handed him.

It could have been anybody who had stumbled into the booby trap, but it had been *Allah's* will that it should be Lal. It seemed to be such an incredible waste of a very young life and he wanted answers, why? His stomach churned with anger against the unseen assassin who had indiscriminately killed his friend. It was so easy and the very pinnacle of cowardice to lay a killing trap and then to run away. He was filled with loathing for such contemptible objects of humanity. He though also of Obiad his former Bedouin friend who had lost a leg in similar circumstances. The debt of revenge that he was owed was mounting considerably. Juma, Obiad and now Lal. He took another drink from the canteen swilled it around his mouth before squirting it out. Trapped in this mundane duty on the Hornbeam Line he didn't see how he would ever collect on that debt. But his anger demanded payment in full.

＊ ＊ ＊

Abdulla stared hard at the indistinguishable shape standing six or seven metres away. He was the right height and shape to be Hamed but the detail of his face was denied to his failing eyesight. Jokha left his side and with an excited greeting hurried across to the man and threw her arms around his neck. She kissed him on both cheeks before linking her arm through his and led him closer. Abdulla stood beneath the shade of the veranda and waited.

"Hello Father," Hamed said quietly.

There was no mistaking the voice and Abdulla with a welcoming grin went over to his youngest son and hugged him. Then with his arm across his shoulder he led him into the house.

Jokha fussed backwards and forwards laying a platter of tea and fruit between the two men while they sat cross-legged and talked. At first the talk was superficial enquiring politely about each other's health and then moved on inevitably to the events of their past year. Hamed related his experiences how he had joined the *Firqa* Al Nasr and moved out onto the Hornbeam Line. He recounting the daily unaltering cycle of boredom that was punctuated occasionally by periods of fear. He scorned the cowardly tactics of the PFLOAG who sought to maim and kill with long-range shelling and indiscriminate booby traps while avoiding contact at all costs.

Abdulla listened quietly and did not interrupt although a question burned within. When Hamed had finished it was then his turn to account the farm's condition. Even with his poor eyesight Abdulla did not miss Hamed's smug grin when he was forced to admit that because of his absence things had deteriorated badly. The maintenance repairs were neglected, the goat herd was shrinking and the cattle herd had dwindled to less than a dozen heads. Because of his very poor sight Abdulla excused himself but he praised the efforts of all three young women. However, they were after all only women and could not be expected to achieve what a man could. Then he tried to guide the conversation so that he could ask the burning question, "Are you finished with soldering?"

"Well – " Hamed hesitated, "I can't go back onto the Hornbeam Line. The boredom is just too much."

Abdulla considered his answer. Was it deliberately vague while he waited to see if he was welcome to stay on the farm? Or perhaps he had some other plan? He decided to ask outright the question. "Are you back to stay?" Sensing again his hesitation he added quickly. "Son, you are needed here."

"Perhaps I'll stay for a while."

"For a while?"

He shrugged, "I do have some unfinished business."

Abdulla waited then when he didn't expand asked. "What business is that?"

"I want revenge for Juma's death. I want revenge for my friend's death. I want revenge for all the indignities that we have suffered these past five years."

There was so much anger in his reply and Abdulla was taken aback. "You would kill for this revenge?"

"If *Allah* is good to me he will put these murderers in my sights and guide my bullets right into their black hearts."

"And if you should happen to fire on your brother?"

"Or he on me," he evaded the answer. "He chose the side of the *adoo*."

Abdulla shook his head slowly. "Five years ago your brother did what he thought was right. He took arms to oppose oppression and tyranny and who knows at that time he may have been right. When he returned to the area he had some influence and he used it when he could to mediate some of the Communist's brutality. He is not a bad man, you know that. Now he is locked in the Revolutionary Cause with no way out."

"He can always surrender to the authorities."

"He tried." Hamed's silence indicated his surprise. "He sent his Mahru woman with a message to discuss his surrender. But before she returned the soldiers came and dragged him away."

"And he escaped killing two as he did." Hamed added bitterly.

"He did. But did you know they were trying to hang him when he did?" There was stunned silence. "It seems that one of the patrol vehicles ran over a mine and some were killed. Some of the soldiers decided to take their personal revenge."

"How do you know this?"

"Mussalim told us himself."

"He is still here?"

"He is still in Qara somewhere and from time to time, under the cover of darkness he comes and leaves the next morning before daylight."

"How will he respond to the news that I am back?"

"He is your loving brother. He will be happy that you are safe and have returned."

"He was not my loving brother the last time we met."

Abdulla grinned. "All families quarrel and sometimes they become a little over-heated but things usually cool and mend with a little time. I know that he bares you no grudge. So stay here where you belong. Forget these unhealthy thoughts of revenge." Hamed was silent and Abdulla decided that now was time to offer the carrot. "Hamed, stay here on the farm, and I'll give you Khamisa for a wife."

Hamed was stunned. Khamisa as his wife! Such a jewel among women would be a wife that all young men would envy and her possession was offered to him. Only in his wildest fantasies had that been a possibility. He relived in his mind the day in the copse when she had surrendered to his urgent desire. He could smell again the fragrance of her hair and the strong odour of the dried grass seed upon which they had lain. His stomach churned with desire as he remembered the exact moment of penetration and the triumphant thrill that the moment brought. Now her beauty, charm and body could be his and all he had to do was agree to stay home on the farm.

But what of the rage for revenge that burned within? To make someone pay for the death of his brother and his friend, could that be quieted? To possess Khamisa, probably! But here was the paradox. Without Juma's death Khamisa would not have been offered to him. Why then should he burn for revenge? He remembered with enormous feelings of guilt that he had once wished him killed by the *adoo* and *Allah* had granted that wish. But still he felt that someone should be made to pay for his death. When that anger was eventually satisfied and laid to rest then so too would his own feelings of guilt. Then there was his young friend Lal Baksh recently blown apart by a booby trap carefully laid by a coward. A coward who dare not even be close when his foul handiwork dispensed death upon any unfortunate who stumbled into it. He deserved revenge, indeed cried out for it. For the sake of possessing his brother's widow could he really appease that fury? But then did he have to? Perhaps there was a way to achieve both.

"If I agree to stay when will the wedding take place?"

"Since Khamisa is a widow and no dowry is involved then there is no need for a large ceremony. You can be married before the Mullah within two months."

"Two months?" His father nodded.

Two months! He could afford to wait that long. Two or three weeks after he was married he could still return to soldering. Though not with the *firqa* Al Nasr and back to the Hornbeam Line. Next time he would join a *firqa* operating west of the line and in closer contact with the *adoo*. This would be where he would gratify his need for revenge. Then with the vendetta satisfied and all guilt appeased he would be free to return to the delights of his new wife.

"I agree," he said firmly.

✳ ✳ ✳

Khamisa sat in the dappled shade of a small copse gloomily watching the goats milling aimlessly around tugging at scant bits of scorched vegetation. She had learned the news only last night that she was to marry Hamed and the news horrified her. Since the day he had forced his attention upon her she didn't particularly want to even be close to him and she wasn't pleased to see his return yesterday. Without her husband the farm existence held little attraction but although it was a hard struggle to exist it did at least provide food and shelter for her and Tuful, Juma's daughter. With Hamed's desertion a year ago any worry about his unwanted attention went with him and therefore farm existence was bearable. But now it seemed that he was back. Worse, Adbulla's decision that they were betrothed not only gave him a right to pay her close attention it actually encouraged it. She felt that she was being forced to be disloyal to her dead husband. Her immediate reaction had been that she would rather die than go through with this marriage but she had quickly dismissed that thought, she had a solemn duty to be a devoted mother to Juma's daughter. Next she thought to take Tuful and flee. But where could she go? She could go to her father, he would not turn her away, she was sure. However, a widow is the responsibility of the dead husband's family

– she was after all bought and paid for. Abdulla would be morally bound to send someone to look for her and her father's house would be the first place he would look. In that event he probably would not want her back, perhaps he would even be pleased to be relieved of her responsibility. Most certainly, however, he would demand his son's daughter and that was an alarming thought. If she was to run then she needed a less obvious place to run to than her father's house. As a war widow she did have a modest pension and she still had some gold from her wedding dowry. Juma had tried to ensure that she kept that intact and it might now be very useful. Perhaps she could go back to Mirbat and establish herself from the dowry then live off that pension. It would be a struggle but it was a possibility. But word travels around freely among Dhofaris and she was known there. So how long would it be before searchers heard the word? Not too long she supposed. To run meant that almost certainly she would have her daughter taken from her eventually. Under no circumstances could she ever be separated from Tuful. She was trapped with no possible escape.

Weighed down by the hopelessness of her situation her eyes flooded with tears and began to trickle down her cheeks. In his wisdom it seemed that *Allah* had decided that she would become the woman of the man with whom she had been adulterous. It seemed that he still punished her for her betrayal. So be it, *Inshaalah*. In the meantime she would retreat back behind the *abeya* and the ugly *yashmak* until a wedding gave Hamed the right to stare lustfully at her person.

※ ※ ※

December 1973 • From the crest of a small hill Mussalim scanned both directions of the road through binoculars. To the north it wound its way along a wide ridge between two wadis while to the south it descended into a tree line in a valley bottom. Beyond the trees it re-appeared climbing steeply out of the valley. Other than a few grazing cows and pair of crows wheeling lazily in a thermal above nothing moved. He sat down making himself comfortable while he waited a few minutes to see if anything would emerge from the hidden tree area. When it did not he looked back down the hill behind him where six men with two camels waited. He waved them forward to plant their mines in the road while he stayed in position watching in both directions.

The government forces by now had them almost completely encircled and the main objective of the PFLOAG forces in the central region was to keep them out of the Jebal Qara. An impassable Salalah, Midway road across the jebal was a vital part of that objective. Mussalim had made PFLOAG domination of the road his own personal mission. With the liberal use of mines and ambushes he intended to make the road far too hazardous for government forces to even consider using it. To this end he had based himself in the village Nahiz where he could rely absolutely on the support of the Gatun tribe. Although fiercely independent and with their own leaders they accepted Mussalim as a valuable advisor. His reputation almost assured that.

His arrest and subsequent quick escape in the early part of the year had rocked his confidence and warned him that to remain in one place for very long was decidedly risky. The government by now had the support of the vast majority of the Dhofari people. The man that welcomed you to his campfire and fed you could be potential enemy. He might report your presence to the authorities as soon as it was safe for him to do so. But among the Bait Gatun tribe was one of the few places where there was security. By enlarge they were still wholly loyal to the Front.

Government forces had established strongholds along the whole northern edge of the jebal. From Jibjat in the east they had soon progressed forty kilometres westward along the open *gatn* to secure Zeak. From Zeak they continued on west and new posts at Qaroon Hairatti and Hagif were also being secured. Qaroon Hairatti was a particularly important location because the jebal road ran right through it and only three kilometres beyond it descended into the pass that led out onto the *nejd*. The northern line was completed in the west at the village Ayon and when the Hornbeam Line creeping from the south eventually reached Ayon then the portal for the whole of that side would be closed. In the east Wadi Darbat was still a strong Front reserve but Al Haq and Tawi Atteer were government positions sandwiching either side while Tarqah in its south stared right down into its throat.

From all these bases regular patrols acting on information received chased and harassed the dwindling PFLOAG forces. For PFLOAG members to stay in one place very long was decidedly risky. The deserted village of Raythut remained the central hub for the area but Mussalim suspected that by now it was well known to government intelligence sources and it was therefore a matter of time only before the soldiers swooped. There were persistent rumours that a mass of foreign Iranian troops had just arrived in Salalah and if true Raythut might be one of the targets.

From his own point of view he was happier to stay in Nahiz, he felt much safer. Even so it was clear that the life was being slowly and systematically strangled out of the Front. He personally doubted if there were as many as two hundred active supporters left in the whole region. Even the leadership seemed to have given up. Since their declaration of "a strategy of flexibility," no other guidance had been issued. Although Al Ghassani still held the office of General Secretary it seemed that he now pursued a more self-centred political career. No one had stepped into the void to fill the role that he now neglected. But while the Front still held the jebal road the Qara could still be considered a PFLOAG area.

From the hilltop he watched Yaqub as he took control and organised the small party. He swung his leg rather stiffly as he moved about suggesting that its reset at Shershitta had not been an unqualified success. Selecting four places either side of the rough uneven road he instructed that the mines should be laid there. When they had and he was satisfied with their concealment he indicated another should be placed in the very centre of the road. Then waving all the others back he carefully brushed away the sand until its mechanism was just visible. Mussalim permitted himself a wry smile, understanding completely his tactics. From that day at Mirbat more than five years ago Yaqub had clearly progressed from that frightened trembling novice to become a real professional. The idea was that a vehicle grinding cautiously along the road with a sharp-eyed lookout watching for concealed mines would spot that one and detour from the road to go around. Unwittingly he would be directing the vehicle right into the mini minefield.

He waved briefly in Mussalim's direction indicating that the task was complete. He got to his feet, acknowledged the wave and with a quick glance up and down the road he turned and descended the hill. That was the second and it would be the last trap they set today. It was mid afternoon and as he waited for the men to join him he contemplated the evening ahead. It promised only dull routine sitting around a Nahiz campfire discussing the same topics that they did most nights. On the other hand a mere two-hour walk away the delights of Jumaia and his infant son promised much more interest. For security reasons he kept his visits irregular and infrequent but it had been almost three weeks now and he felt that he could take the chance tonight. Two hours from now the sun would only just be setting but he could find a copse and wait for the cloak of darkness before he actually went in. The long hours of darkness at the December time of the year meant also that he would not have to leave too early in the morning. His mind was made up.

When he came in after dark he stopped by the side of the rondavaal fence and listening intently as he scanned the darkness for any signs of danger. Close by was the beehive styled house where the young women slept and a little further away the main house. He could hear only the soft rustling of animals stirring in the pen while the only movement appeared to be a smoking chimney in the house. When the sun left the sky at this time of the year it took with it all the warmth of the day and he shivered as the teeth of the wind cut through his flimsy clothing.

As he always did he gave a couple of low whistles and then blew hard into his cold hands while he waited for a response. When none came he tried again, he would go no further until someone came. This served not only to warn them of his approach but more importantly it allowed an escape option if something was wrong. This time the door of the round house opened and a dim light from within cast a framed shadow in front of the doorway. Jumaia hurried into the darkness coming in the direction where she knew he would be. Mussalim smiled to himself, everything was all right, and there was no danger. Delighted to see her man she smothered his face in kisses then looping her arm through his she led the way back to the house.

A small paraffin lamp served not only as the light source but also as the heater. All the women were heavily wrapped indicating the heat inadequacy but for him coming from the outside cold its warmth was welcoming. His unexpected appearance caused excitement among the children and the three women were forgotten as they clamoured for his immediate attention. Eventually satisfying the children's demand he was able to greet his two sisters and it was Lailla who gave him the news of Hamed's return a week ago. Elated by the news that he had at last returned to the farm he went immediately to the main house to greet him.

In contrast this room was warm, heated effectively by a brightly burning log fire. Hamed sat cross-legged one side of the fire while his father was on the other. Both looked up with an element of surprise by his sudden entrance. Jokha who sat near the door was first to react struggling a little clumsily to her feet to greet her son. Mussalim then greeted his father with a handshake and a kiss on each cheek before turning towards his brother. Just for a moment both men stared at each other a little uncertainly then with a smile Mussalim held out his hand and as Hamed took it he clasped him in a warm brotherly embrace.

By the time he returned to the other house it was late and only Jumaia waited for him. Because this house had only the one room there was no privacy, nor could they talk without disturbing all the others who slept. So despite the cold they went outside and sat huddled together beneath a blanket.

It was a clear sharp night with a moon that was almost full. Its wan light turned the night a watery blue grey and cast eerie shadows along the ground. The heavens were filled by a million visible stars while the bitterly cold wind whispered softly as it hurried its way south. At first they hardly spoke, both contented by the close physical contact beneath the blanket while they stared in appreciation of *Allah's* wonders. Despite the covering blanket Jumaia began to shiver and Mussalim felt the trembling of her delicate body on his chest. He turned towards her and wrapped his other arm around her holding her closer. He felt the urgent desire churn in the pit of his stomach and received the reply from her body as she responded to his carnal signals. She pulled him down over her writhing her pelvis sensually against his as she did. He felt her lift her hips to welcome his rampant need and felt the warmth of her body as he coupled to her. Now there was no cold wind, no silvery moon, nothing only themselves and the all consuming desire to give and take of each other. When their passion was spent Mussalim still did not move away, instead he lay above her providing the protection of his warm body from the cold night.

They talked of their children and the heartache of separation. She appealed to him to take her with him wherever it was that he went. He considered it far too dangerous and told her that it was just not possible. When that appeal failed she used their children in the argument, both the boys needed a father, she said. He didn't doubt it but still not only were they all safer on the farm she was needed here also. They talked of the hardships on the farm with only their handicapped father at its helm. They considered the differences that it could mean to have Hamed's full support once more. Jumaia went on to tell him of the despondency Khamisa felt at becoming Hamad's wife. But he dismissed her dejection. It was, he said, the perfect solution. It secured her and Tuful's future and gave Hamed a wife he deserved. She would get used to the situation, he added. He didn't mention the other reason for it was better that only he and his father knew of their transgression against decency. In truth he had little sympathy for Khamisa's feelings. If Hamed was good enough to sally with behind her husband's back then he was most certainly good enough to be her husband. Besides that Khamisa was probably better off than Jumaia because Hamed was a better prospect for a husband than he. They were losing this war, he knew and his own future looked very uncertain. Death seemed to be the likely outcome for him, or at best exile in Yemen. In the more optimistic event of exile it would probably be possible for Jumaia to join him. In Southern Yemen she would at least be in her ancient Mahru tribal area. He then made her very happy by telling her that she and he would stand before the Mullah with Hamed and Khamisa in a double wedding. Then once more they made love.

He left before daylight the next morning. The ground beneath his feet was wet and the trees heavy with dripping dew it would need another hour before the sun crested the eastern sky and brought some warmth to the morning. He was feeling on good terms with himself. His announcement of their wedding day to Jumaia had at least secured some kind of future for her. As his wife she would become the responsibility of his family in the event of his death. So, although it might be an additional presumptuous burden that might one day be placed on his luckless brother he felt self-righteous. It was the correct and moral thing for him to do. With his Kalachnikov slung lazily over his back he walked westward keeping to the high ground above Wadi Theydawt and one hour later just as the sun made its first glint against the lightening sky behind him he started to descend into Wadi Arbot. It was as he climbed through the thicket of trees that lined the opposite side that he heard distant voices drifting on the morning air. Unslinging his rifle he proceeded cautiously to the edge of the tree line. Before him open ground stretched steeply upward to the road above. The road was hidden from his view somewhere beyond the crest of the hill but the voices were coming from up there. Staying hidden inside the tree line he turned north intending to circle wide of the unseen voices and then continue on west to Nahiz. However, only a few minutes later he had a clear view of the road ahead as it swept down into a long shallow valley and up the other side. There were several army vehicles parked in a tight cluster on the side of the road. He rested his rifle against a tree and settled to study the campsite through binoculars.

He counted ten vehicles, a mixture of heavy trucks and Land Rovers. At least forty soldiers busied themselves building sangars and strengthening their position. In the middle, nailed to a makeshift pole, the flag of Iran.

He lowered the binoculars and stared thoughtfully towards the distant camp. Could these be the Iranian soldiers that were rumoured to have been in Salalah? It rather looked like it. But what were they doing camping by the roadside? With growing alarm he raised the glasses and studied the camp again. There was no doubt that these men were preparing for a long stay. He thought of the voices he had heard a little way back and wondered could there be another roadside camp there? There might even be another beyond that and perhaps another after that. There might even be a camp every two or three kilometres all the way along the road right through the mountains. If there was then the road had been occupied during the night. He lowered the glasses once more and dejectedly stared at nothing in particular. The more he thought about it the more sense it made. It was now perfectly clear why a mass of Iranian troops had been brought to Salalah. While he had been gratifying himself in his woman's arms the Iranians had it seemed occupied the Salalah Midway road unopposed. He should have been more concerned about those persistent rumours and much more watchful. If he had then perhaps he might have done something to make the task harder for them, at least. His feelings of guilt were compounded by anger against a Sultan who was now prepared to use foreign troops against his own people. And more, they were non-Arabic troops too.

He picked up his weapon and continued northwards as far as the tree cover would allow. By the time he had reached the open *gatn* and could go no further he had seen two more such camps confirming his worst fears. Knowing for certain what he would find he turned and retraced his steps checking the road to the south. By the end of the morning he reached the edge of the jebal overlooking the Salalah plain and had counted seven others. Physically tired from the long march and mentally dispirited by this significant turn of events he slumped down beneath a tree to rest.

Government posts surrounded the Qara and now it seemed they had established a line right across the middle dissecting PFLOAG territory still further. The region was as good as lost with the remaining Front forces reduced to small independent bands operating in isolated sections. Even these sections could not remain static for very long as the 'seek and destroy patrols' foraged into the shrinking areas. The Qara was being systematically carved up and the hiding places becoming not only scarce but more accessible to the Sultan's forces. Inevitably these pockets of resistance would be gradually destroyed and because they could not be replaced the resistance would slowly fade. One week from now and the road would be clear of mines, regular patrols would secure the stretches between the guard posts and the road would be open for government business. His days in the Qara were definitely numbered perhaps measured by days rather than weeks. To stay must mean eventual capture. Very soon he would have to retreat west of the Hornbeam Line.

❋ ❋ ❋

At the top of the hill Lailla turned and glanced back to the farm's houses. She could see Hamed industriously working repairing the weak places in the rondavaal animal enclosure. If she had been concerned that his return would diminish her leading role in the daily routine then she was mistaken. Apart from two trips into Salalah he had not left the farm in the two weeks he had been there. Maybe it was just that there was much repair work to be done but she suspected it had much more to do with just being close to Khamisa. Certainly he paid her so much more attention then he did anyone else. The jug of fresh milk that greeted them each morning on their doorstep was intended more as a consideration to her than anyone else. When it was Khamisa's turn to stay close and look after the children, as it was this week, then the attention those children received from Hamed owed much to the fact that it gave him an excuse to be closer to her. His fondness for her was apparent for all to see and it augured well for her future as his wife, she would have a considerate husband.

However, Khamisa's attitude towards the coming marriage was much less enthusiastic. She had taken once more to the full covering *abeya* and hid her beauty behind the stiff ugly black mask of the *yashmak*. It was as if she hoped that Hamed would be put off and eventually reject her as a wife. Indeed in the evenings when the children were asleep and the three of them were left to talk she had made no secret of her reluctance to the marriage. But Abdulla and Mussalim had made the decision in her best interests and as mere women, who were they to question their wisdom?

But if Khamisa was in the depths of dismay Jumaia was at the pinnacle of happiness about her pending marriage. Her regular recounts that once upon a starry night many years ago at Jibjat she had suggested that Musallim should take her for a wife had started to become a little tiresome. She recanted endlessly that after he had left her that night she thought she would never see him again and now after all that had happened she was to become his wife! She never stopped marvelling at the wondrous ways that *Allah* performs his wonders.

Lailla turned away and followed the cattle who had left her a little way behind. By now the animals knew the way to the regular grazing area and she had no need to drive them, only to follow. More than three months after the last Khareef the pool in Theydawt would be rapidly shrinking but the grazing was good and there was drinking water available. She thought that she might go through the bathing routine today, but then after considering the cool edge on the northern wind, perhaps she would not. Her thoughts turned again to the pending marriages and it generated a little envy inside her. She wondered when it would be her turn? Her thoughts turned fanciful as she imagined what her husband would be like. The only boy so far who had come close to her had been Gheer and that had been such a long time ago when she and Hamed had camped with the livestock on the Salalah plain. She remembered how she had daringly permitted him to touch her thighs and bare arms and she wished that she were going to meet him today. In truth she hardly remembered what he had looked like but it was the fantasy of secret romance that provided excitement and an escape from the mundane. Now starting her twentieth year and well into womanhood she considered that her time for romance was long overdue. Jumaia, who was the same age, had been married previously had a son, a stepson and soon a second husband. In comparison to her she was naive and felt that she were missing out on life's experience. Perhaps it was time for a more bold approach with prompting reminders. Maybe she could ask Khamisa or Jumaia to mention it to Jokha who could in turn mention it to her father.

She flapped her arms at one of the cows in front of her as it dawdled to graze on something sweet that it had found. It promised to be just another lazy day in the wadi patiently waiting for the mid-afternoon return time while the cows grazed. Good grazing meant not only fat cattle but also good milk yields so she appreciated that it was a necessary chore but still she felt that her young years were being wasted. She wanted excitement. She wanted romance.

The opening of the mountain road had brought a buzz of excitement and an air of anticipation to the jebal. To many in the region the war was as good as ended. Only pockets of hard-line extremists were left and they could create little but an aggravating nuisance. Now that the road was secured by soldier-manned stations the Civil Action Team could move in and civil development could at last begin. The talk was of strategically placed permanent posts along the road containing clinics, schools and even shops. The people of the Qara could look forward to enjoying facilities that had never, throughout its history, been available. Perhaps with many more travellers along the road and these posts acting as sorts of communal centres then life would become less insular. That would provide opportunities to meet other people in her age group. She certainly hoped so for stuck in her current situation she felt that her adult life as a good-looking young man's wife and mother of his children could not begin.

~ 22 ~

Late January 1974 • There was an emergency Congress meeting of the Central Committee at Raykut and Mussalim had been recalled to hear the results of that meeting. He had arrived yesterday to find the small coastal village full of PFLOAG members and most of the houses occupied by early arrivals. Normally this would not have bothered him but on this occasion he had with him his new bride and their two children so for their sakes he needed to find reasonable shelter at least.

When he had learned of his recall he had relented almost immediately on his previous decision that Jumaia and the boys should stay on the farm. Jumaia had formed an affection for the village during the short time that they had stayed there once before. The place was still considered to be "the capital of the liberated area," by the PFLOAG and as such it was probably the safest place to be at the moment. Additionally by taking Jumaia and the two boys away from the farm he considered that he had also lightened Hamed's responsibility. He had his own new wife, Khamisa, Tuful her infant, his sister, Lallia and two parents to worry about as he ran the farm, and that was enough. Instead of leaving for Raykut as soon as he received the call Mussalim waited four more days for his wedding ceremony at the tribal village Haluf. He left immediately after the double ceremony but the delay and the fact that he was forced to take a route arcing well to the north to avoid government positions meant he had arrived three days late.

It had been his old comrade Ali who had come to his rescue and surrendered the small two-roomed house that he had previously claimed for himself. Mussalim's gratitude was waved aside with disdain and remarks like, "I can easily move in with another comrade or sleep on the beach if necessary. But a family couldn't do either."

In fact the house itself was little more than derelict. Rubbish littered the floors to ankle depth and in one room part of the roof had collapsed. The local people had long ago abandoned their village to the occupying PFLOAG forces and their homes had through neglect and the ravages of nature soon deteriorated. Nevertheless, Mussalim was delighted with Ali's gesture and had been pleased to accept the shelter. After all Jumaia would soon clean the place to a habitable standard and it was to be only temporary accommodation anyway. As soon as the conference finished then many of the Front fighters would return to their previous stations, wherever that might be. When they had then he would soon be able find more suitable quarters for he had been told that his new duties meant he would be staying in the area.

Soon after he had arrived yesterday the meeting of the Central Committee had finished and broken up. This morning many of the delegates would depart, leaving behind just a couple of members to brief the rest of the assembly on the decisions made. Now in the cool of a January morning he made his way casually to the meeting point.

A place just outside of the village and beyond the noise of the sea's crashing breakers had been chosen. Not sure of the precise location Mussalim followed a small group of men as they ambled along the riverbank. They in turn probably followed another group a few metres ahead. He glanced up the towering hills that surrounded the village assessing the defensive merits of the bay. After five years of conflict such appraisals had become an unavoidable habit to him. Although this village seemed idyllic with its steep scenic hills encompassing the sandy bay and a freshwater river slicing right across to the sea it would be a bad place to get trapped. Defensively the line along the top of the hills would have to be held at all costs for any fall back down into the bay would leave defenders completely dominated on three sides with only the sea behind as an escape route. For the time being however he could dismiss such thoughts. This was PFLOAG country and for the near future at least would remain so. Many kilometres of the harsh mountainous terrain of Jebal Sayq formed a barrier between the coastline and the more vehicle friendly inland. Any advance into these mountains and penultimately onto the village would have to be cautious and on foot because there would be a hundred ambush places along the way.

Where the river valley began to narrow and by the road that was the only land route into Raykut, men had begun to gather beneath a large wind contorted Bedam tree. He paused a few moments and surveyed the gathering mass looking for a familiar face, he could not find one. A few metres away and suitably isolated, was a twisted spiny acacia shrub. He shuffled across to it and sat in the sparse shade of its low branches quietly watching the gathering steadily grow.

Here and there were old gnarled faces and some faces not so gnarled but generally the number of fresh youthful faces in attendance surprised him. He wondered the motivation that brought so many youngsters beneath the PFLOAG banner. Perhaps it was opposition to despotic oppression by what was their idea of an uncaring ruler? But if so their ideas of an uncaring ruler were misguided, because compared to his father Qaboos certainly was not that. Indoctrination of the Marxist ideology to remove all the privileged rich from positions of power? More likely! Brainwashed fanatics! But then, that would not apply to all. The answer, he concluded, was probably much more simple. Bravado of the inexperienced coupled with the excitement that goes with it. That disturbed him and filled him with apprehension. In a battle a soldier needs to be able to depend on the comrades around him. Bravado and excitement are likely to soon disappear in the face of the fear. And fanatics were probably worse because they were unpredictable. There was just no way to anticipate what a fanatical crazed mind might do.

He saw Ali arrive and just as he had done himself a few minutes before he stood looking around the gathering for familiar faces. Mussalim waited until he looked his way and then waved to attract his attention. Ali acknowledged his wave, shuffled over and sat down by his side.

"Who will be addressing the meeting?" Mussalim asked after they had shook hands and passed the obligatory Arabic greetings.

"Zahir Ali and Abdel Tahir."

"Where's Al Ghassani?"

Ali shrugged bemused. "Word is that he's further up the Gulf somewhere trying to raise money or bolster support."

Both men were thoughtfully silent for a minute then Mussalim nodded towards the main body of the gathering. "There seems to be lots of young faces in our revolution these days," he said.

"And not many familiar," Ali added.

"Where are they all?" Mussalim asked softly.

"Dead, surrendered, captured or just simply quit. You heard about Bin Talib I suppose."

"He went north to organise the NDFLOAG."

"Yes and soon after he got there he suffered the same fate as Al Mushani. Taken prisoner along with just about the rest of the whole movement. A dozen were executed and the rest, about another seventy imprisoned. There is no NDFLOAG any more, it was smashed."

Mussalim was not surprised and took the news philosophically. He was used to bad news these days. "And now we have to rely on men like these," he said indicating the increasing gathering. "Novices and hotheads."

Ali laughed easily. "Hotheads? So no more 'Crazy Man?' Perhaps we should rename you Family Man Mussalim."

Mussalim glanced at him sharply, nettled by the insinuation, but he let it go. "There never was a 'Crazy Man.' That moment of foolishness was greatly exaggerated because it suited propaganda purposes at the time."

"Yes there was," Ali disagreed. "In the beginning you were a hothead with a blazing anger burning inside. You fought for the cause with a reckless passion. But because Allah willed it you survived long enough to learn that if you didn't bridle that anger then you wouldn't live through to the end."

"*Il Hamdu lillaah*," Mussalim muttered grudging agreement.

"*Il Hamdu lillaah*," Ali praised Allah also.

Zahir Ali and Abdel Tahir were last to arrive and picked their way through the men sitting cross-legged on the ground to stand beneath the trees shade. After a few moments Zahir Ali began to address the meeting.

First of all he welcomed the Front members to the meeting and then went on to give a brief outline of the current situation as the Committee interpreted it. He described a situation that had undeniably seen a significant reduction in the Front's dominance of the area. However, he offered in mitigation vastly inferior resources of weapons, men and money. Nevertheless, under the circumstances the fighters should be proud with what that they achieved. He pointed at the recent substantial influx of foreign soldiers as an indication of just how hard pressed the Sultan's Forces really were. Although vastly superior in both numbers and weaponry they had been unable to press home their advantage and had been forced to resort to Iranian help. At this point he introduced a note of optimism. This recruiting of non-Arabic forces would backfire on the Sultan and prove his undoing, he predicted. There was a protest, he said, that was quickly gathering momentum from neighbouring Arab Countries. They objected to Qaboos' use of non-Arabic troops to vanquish brother Arabs. Moreover those condemnations were compounded by the fact that these particular Arabs were his very own subjects.

Then Zahir Ali announced that the PFLOAG, the Popular Front for the Liberation of the Occupied Arabian Gulf had ceased to exist and had been renamed the PFLO, the Popular Front for the Liberation of Oman. Here he was forced to stop and wait until the murmur of surprise that rose immediately from the listeners had ceased. This renaming, he went on, meant that the new objective was the Liberation of Oman only and that they no longer intended a threat to neighbouring regimes. This would encourage neighbour countries to lend immediate support to the new PFLO against this blatant warfare on all Arabs. Then he explained the General Secretary's absence by accounting that Al Ghassani was at this very moment touring these countries soliciting both practical and political support.

Then followed a succession of diatribe against the establishment berating the government for its self-centred policies. After this he went into the motivation phase praising and encouraging those fighting in the eastern and central regions to continue the successful "strategy of flexibility." In the meantime here in the west they would continue to hold in check the government force's attempts to invade into PFLO territory.

After that questions and opinions of little significance came from the audience. Mussalim felt that many of those who did speak spoke only to satisfy their own need to bring attention to themselves. Young men just trying to make an impression. Abdel Tahir who had glanced in their direction several times during the meeting now got to his feet and leaving Zahir Ali to deal with the prosaic remarks and questions came over to where they sat.

Customary polite exchanges were made before he sat himself down cross-legged directly in front of them. He expressed his delight and admiration on hearing the news of Mussalim's magnificent escape from capture. He complimented him on how he continued to set a shining example of tenacity and dedication in the interest of the cause. His example, he said, provided a spur and excellent motivation for many of the younger members of the Front. Mussalim sat listening without comment feeling somewhat hypocritical. He wondered what Abdel would say if he knew that but for the intervention of that snatch squad he may well have been sitting in Mirbat at this very moment as a member of the Bait Umr *Firqa*. If Abdel noticed his lack of response he ignored it continuing his rhetoric as if it were rehearsed.

"Because of your renowned reputation and because of your previous recruiting experience the Central Committee has decided that you should lead the team assigned to aggressively recruit men to the new PFLO throughout this Western area. Young men will listen to the words of 'Crazy Man Mussalim' veteran of many campaigns and scourge of the government soldiers. A man who cannot be stopped by government artillery shells nor it seems held after capture. Words from such a man will influence many into the cause."

Mussalim looked at him impassively. It seemed that yet again his reputation was to be inflated and used in a propaganda exercise to attract new recruits and motivate those already enlisted in the Front. This would do nothing to assist his desire to simply fade out of the spotlight and assist his disappearance when the inevitable government victory came. Quite the contrary, it would highlight his role and place him once again near the top of their most wanted list. It could only be a matter of time before the government launched a determined assault into this area. The Hornbeam Line sealed the PFLO in the west while the rapidly strengthening base at Manston in the north pushed them south. This area of Jebal Sayq in the south west corner was the last bastion of the Liberationists. He had no doubts that when his forces were strong enough and ready then the Sultan would launch a strong and determined advance. Trapped in this corner and in this thickly wooded and rugged terrain then fierce and bloody exchanges would follow. But with superior resources and manning the eventual outcome would be assured. After that there would be only another "strategy of flexibility" left. Pockets of saboteurs continuously running and hiding until they were grubbed out one by one. Where could a "most wanted man" hide then?

Because of his pre-occupation with his thoughts he had missed part of Abdel's continuing verbose and he became aware that he now addressed Ali. He it seemed came in for similar flattery and at the end of it he was informed that he would once again become Musallim's assistant. Abdel stood to leave instructing them both that Zahir Ali would talk to them later. Then as he shook hands with both men he expressed confidence that they would accomplish something equally as successful as that which they had created in the Qara.

Both men watched in silence as he made his way back over to Zahir Ali's side.

"Well old friend, it seems that we are once again to be partners," Mussalim broke the silence.

"Good," Ali replied a little flat. Then after a pause he asked softly. "Don't you sometimes wish that you could just go home?"

He thought of his family, Jumaia, his son and stepson, Taimul and Salim and of the simple pleasures that came with them. "All the time my friend, all the time," he replied.

Khamisa pulled the *futa* out from the wooden tub of water and swung it forcefully against the large flat rock that had been placed there for that very reason. Again and again until she was satisfied that it had been pulverised enough then she dropped it once again back into the tub. It was her husband's *futa*. Not Juma but her new husband Hamed.

It had been one month since the wedding ceremony in Haluf and in complete contrast to the other bride of the day, Jumaia, she had been wretchedly miserable about the whole situation. After the ceremony she had gone to the wedding bed like a condemned prisoner walking to the gallows. The experience though bitter had not proved to be as unbearable as she expected it would be. She had surrendered herself to thirty minutes of humiliation obediently excepting Hamed's right to her body detaching her mind as much as she could throughout. Afterwards he had quickly slipped into a contended sleep while she lay awake silently pleading understanding from the spirit of her dead husband.

Since then and despite not wanting to admit it to herself Hamed had so far proved that he was not at all a bad husband. He never beat her, never raised his voice to her and so far had treated her with every consideration. His expectations were patently obvious and therefore un-decreed, he wanted only that what any husband has the right to expect. His only proclamation so far had been that she did not wear the *yashmak* unless he ordered her to do so. But then since she was now his possession then there was no point in her hiding from him behind its ugly mask. Each night in their bed he still exercised his conjugal privilege but with each occasion the dutiful acceptance of his demands became just a little easier. She had told herself that so long as she submitted and did not welcome his advances then there was no betrayal to Juma's memory. After all what choice did she have? Even so she could not help but compare and she kept her opinion of Juma's superiority her smug secret. Where Juma had been unhurried, caring and accomplished Hamed's performance was callow enthusiasm and virile energy. Even so a couple of times recently she had found herself beginning to respond to the base physical gratification. However, she had been strong willed enough to detach her mind far away just in time to control her emotion. To accept the bodily pleasure would be Juma's betrayal and the guilt unbearable.

She glanced at the sun halfway down the western sky, Hamed would be home soon from Salalah and there was still much to be done before her husband's return. She wrung each garment from the tub and then added them to the rest already draped across the line. She emptied the water into the animal drinking trough and looked beyond the washing line down the hill. Jokha was returning making her way back slowly with Tuful clutching onto her long black *abeya* and the goat herd meandering in their wake. Today to give each other a break they had swapped their usual routine. In Khamisa's mind there was little doubt that tending the goat herd was the easier task. In itself the daily routine family chores were not particularly arduous but the constant interruptions that were necessary to assist the near blind Abdulla added a frustration element. Understandably with very little that he could do he sought company and being conscientiously forced to provide at least a little of that company from time to time it added a serious handicap to progress.

Jumaia's contribution had been markedly emphasised since her departure. The chores that she normally undertook were now shared and added to those of Jokha and herself. Not that Khamisa minded that so much, adjustments are quickly made. It was her bright effervescent company that she missed. Her contented and happy nature had been good for everybody's morale. But then she had the man that she wanted and her adoration of Mussalim was patently obvious for all to see. Therefore why wouldn't she be happy? In her mind's eye she saw again Mussalim's smiling face. How so very much like her Juma he was? Even his mannerisms reminded her of him. So much so that she often found herself watching him so closely that on occasions and to her embarrassment she had been caught blatantly staring. A shadow passed across her thoughts as she thought of Mussalim's situation. He was in constant jeopardy nearly blown to pieces by an artillery shell and then his capture and subsequent escape emphasised just how vulnerable he was. Both incidents had been so very close to disaster. She hoped most sincerely that it was not Allah's intention that he should suffer the same fate as Juma. Jumaia would be distraught if that were to happen, just as she had been by her own loss.

The rising smell of bread reminded her that she should check its progress in the oven. She went across to the crudely constructed mound of boulders and peered into the blackened cave-like chamber. The round flat cakes of dough were almost ready. Using the long handled shovel made specially for the task she flipped each one over and then just to ensure that the heat did not drop she tossed another small log into the fire chamber below. Dusting off her hands she planned what to do next. It was now time to put the bowl of rice over the fire, then after that she could cut the curd that by now had set into small squares of cheese.

✳ ✳ ✳

It was dark when Hamed made his way from his father's house to the small conical one nearby where his wife waited for him. There was much to do before dawn and not least was to gluttonise his appetite for Khamisa's body before he left. It might be a year or more before he returned.

During the time he had spent in Salalah earlier in the day he had made the point of reporting to the army base Um Al Ghariff and declared his intention to return once more to the *firqats*. Although his return to Al Nasr would be welcomed and could be easily accomplished he had flatly rejected the offer. He had no desire to spend the rest of the war idly sitting on the Hornbeam Line. That would not achieve his need to kill *adoo* and avenge the deaths of his brother and his friend Lal. Instead he declared that he wished to join the *Firqa* Tariq Bin Zeead who he knew were heavily involved in the fighting in the south west, which was after all part of their tribal area. His declaration had been greeted with surprise. Why would an Al Hamer of the greater Kathiri wish to join a Mahru *Firqa*? Nevertheless, he was adamant and not wishing to discourage a volunteer, particularly one already trained it had been agreed to at least transport him to the far western base at Manston where he could make his own application direct to the leaders of Tariq Bin Zeead. The arrangements were that tomorrow morning he must report to the Air Force base where arrangements had been made for him to be transported in a helicopter due to fly direct to Manston that afternoon.

He had spent the evening with his father in quiet trivial conversation. Several times the opportunity had arisen for him to inform him that he was once more leaving. However, as each chance rose he let it pass lacking the courage to declare his intention. He knew that he had deceived his father by allowing him to believe that if he gave him Khamisa then the bargain was that he would stay. But he had never intended to stay. He had stayed only to possess Khamisa and then tarried a little longer to take full advantage of the delights she brought. He had achieved both of those desires and now it was time for him to satisfy his need for revenge for both of those murders and all the atrocities and humiliation that he felt the *adoo* had imposed upon him. Lacking the courage to face his father's anger he decided not to tell him, it was easier instead to sneak away before daylight and leave Khamisa to inform him that he had gone.

He ducked through the narrow doorway into the dimly lit room. Khamisa sat in the centre beneath the murky light of the small paraffin lamp sewing. She was wrapped in a heavy blanket and glanced his way and without speaking gave him a brief acknowledging nod. For a moment he paused staring at her remembering the time Juma had arrived at the farm unexpected and he had watched Khamisa, then heavily pregnant, run squealing with happiness into his arms. There was never such a greeting for him and he felt irritation rising. He bit his lip and controlled it warning himself that it was patience that was needed. Perhaps one day she would run to him with the same unrestrained happiness. He sighed quietly to himself, she didn't know how much he longed for it? But for now it had to be enough that she was his possession.

He began gathering some things that he would need. Three or four *futas,* a couple of *shamags,* a *dish-dasht*. It would be little enough but the lighter his load the better, the army would provide the rest.

"What are you doing?" she asked after a few moments.

"Gathering a few things," he muttered continuing the task. Then turning and looking directly at her, he said. "I'm going away." Just for a moment a confused look crossed her face then it was gone. Was it concern or was it relief? He couldn't tell. Probably relief he concluded and turned back to his task. She was at his side now and reached to take the items from him.

"Where are you going?"

"I am going back to the *firqats*." He let her take the things from him.

"When will you go?"

"Before daylight."

"How long will you be gone?" She carried the clothing over to the old chest.

He turned and picked up an old and ragged duffel bag. "A year, maybe more," he said trying to sound matter of fact. He watched her foraging inside the chest.

"Do I not please you," she asked without turning.

"And there you have it," he thought. "She is more concerned on the shame that it might reflect on her. A newly married husband deserting his bride because she couldn't please him." He carried the bag over to where she stood and as he handed it to her said. "You please me in so many ways, Khamisa. To have a wife as you makes me the envy of all and increases my prestige a thousand fold."

She turned and looked directly at him with a misty sort of sympathy in her eyes. "But still you go!"

"Yes."

"I'm sorry that I cannot be the wife that you want. But I try to be a dutiful wife."

"A dutiful wife," he scoffed. "It's a loving and dutiful wife that I want. I want to see that same sparkle that shone in your eyes when you looked at Juma. All I see is dull indifference. I want to get inside your shield and feel some of that happiness that you and he gave to each other."

"It's not there, Hamed and I can't make it be there," she said sympathetically. "I'm sorry."

"Sorry? Don't keep saying sorry," he blurted angrily walking away. "A wife should not say such things. She should be happy and praise Allah that she has a good husband."

"Yes," she agreed and went quietly back to packing his clothing.

He stood above the cot that they shared and stared down at it gloomily. At least he would possess her body if not her love he thought angrily. Then as his temper cooled he sat down and watched her carefully pack his things in the bag. Just as a considerate wife would, she began to put in little extras, a *mafoof* to tie his hair, rub root to clean his teeth, figs and pomegranates to eat. "My leaving has nothing to do with you Khamisa," he said relenting. "This is something that I have to do for me. For a dead friend and for Juma,"

"Juma?" she said surprised and stopped what she was doing.

"Yes. It is the ways of the old ones, someone must pay for his death too."

She sighed and pulled the drawstring on the duffel bag. "Still, it won't bring him back."

"No it won't," he agreed. He watched as she placed the bag handy against the door the task completed. Perhaps a year away would be good for them. When he was gone she might realise what a good husband he was and appreciate all the little things that he did for her. In fact all the things that he did for everyone. Perhaps then when he did return she might even be pleased to see him, maybe he would even see a sparkle in her eyes. Maybe? Then again maybe not and he sighed once more. For tonight, however, he would be content that she surrendered her body.

He got from the cot and went over to the paraffin lamp. "Tomorrow you will tell father that I have gone."

She nodded compliance and he indicated that she should get into bed. She lifted the blanket from her shoulders went over to the cot and spread it over the top. He waited a few moments more while she slipped out of the loose dress and slid into the bed. Then he turned down the lamp making the room as dark as his mood.

✳ ✳ ✳

Lailla tested the water in the old metal drum. Satisfied that it was warm enough she splashed cold water on the fire underneath putting it out. She glanced across to the rapidly shrinking pool. By now it was very shallow. This would probably be the last time that she would be able to do this until the next Khareef rains again replenished it. She wasn't sure what value if any the exercise actually was as a beauty treatment but that didn't matter. She found it very pleasant to simply bathe first in the hot water and then in the tepid water of the pool. Then there was the added excitement of daringly exposing herself in the open wadi. There was something safely erotic about the whole operation. She could be almost certain that no one would come into the wadi but at the same time there was just a glimmer of a chance that someone might. It was this tiny chance of danger that added excitement stimulating her imagination into fantasies of romantic encounters. Besides that it helped to pass on the long boring day as the cattle grazed.

She wore a loose full-length green dress with an embroidered yellow pattern on the chest and sleeve cuffs. As she always did Lailla looked carefully around for any sign that she might not be alone. Without even the merest whisper of a breeze all was still, not even a leaf quivered on the shrubs that thickly lined the wadi sides. Still she examined every bush, tree and rock meticulously. It was one thing to fantasise about being watched but it would be enormously embarrassing if she actually were. She saw nothing that suggested she was not alone but she continued to scan around as she undid the buttons around her throat and wrists. One last look around, still nothing so she pulled the dress over her head. From the remnants of the old disused goat compound close by she had over the past weeks constructed a rough stairway alongside the drum to help her get in and out. Clad now only in thigh length shorts she climbed the wobbly stairway and then lowered herself into the hot water.

It was hot enough to make her gasp but as her skin adjusted she relaxed and felt the soothing qualities of hot water cleansing her opening pores. She bent her knees as much as she could to allow the water to envelop her body up to her shoulders. Wedged comfortably against the drum by knees and back she allowed the water's penetrating warmth to soothe her into a mellow trance. In this relaxed state she stayed there much longer than normal and it took an effort to eventually rouse herself to climb out. She picked her way carefully across hard baked ground made uneven by cattle footprints when the pool edge had been mud. The pool by now was so shallow that she had to lye flat on her back to submerge herself. After the first shock of temperature change she adjusted and found the cooling effect just as relaxing as the hot water. A colony of zebra finches skimmed across the pool chattering noisily as they passed a mere metre over her head. Careful not to move and frighten them off she watched as they drank from the water edge until by some communal signal they took immediately to wing and continued on their way. Only dragonflies flitting between the tufts of marsh grasses and the cattle contentedly grazing broke the stillness in the wadi.

She closed her eyes thankful that she was here in this complete tranquillity and not at home close to her father's anger. Perhaps by the time she got back his fury would have cooled. His immediate reaction this morning to Khamisa's news that Hamed had once more left to rejoin the Firqats was disbelief. That was soon followed by furious anger at his youngest son's sheer irresponsibility. To abandon the farm in the hands of a man near blind and three women showed a complete disregard for the welfare of his family, Adbulla had raged. Then because she was there and her husband not, his fury turned on Khamisa accusing her of driving him away. She had taken his scorn with bowed head wordlessly accepting his wrath. Lailla had been pleased to escape with the cattle soon after that. While she agreed with her father's understandably rage towards Hamed to lash out in sheer frustration at those that remained was grossly unfair. She knew, however, that time would cool his anger and when it did he would regret his outburst, even if he never said as much. After that he would consider the new situation and adjust the daily work plan accordingly. But until his anger did cool then away from the farm would be the best place to be.

Deep in thought she stretched contentedly and allowed her hands to float on the water surface until a giggle shattered her reverie. She turned her head sharply and was horrified to see half a dozen soldiers standing by the drum with another dozen moving up behind. They were not Omani soldiers, the uniform they wore was different. These men wore dark green soldiers' uniform of Iran. Her first reaction was to duck beneath the water before they saw her but in the same instant she knew it was too late. They stared in her direction with lewd grins on their faces then one or two began calling to her. She didn't understand the language but by the arm waving she understood that they wanted her to come out of the water.

"What do you want?" she cried hysterically. "Go away."

But they had no intention of going away instead they began to make themselves comfortable sitting on the ground around the drum. She glanced the opposite way and thought to make a dash to the trees over on that side of the wadi. But almost naked it would be embarrassing and what if they followed her? She would have to hide and hope that they couldn't find her. Even if she managed to hide from so many searching men she would still have to wait until they left because her dress was over by the drum. She was in a sharp panic frantically seeking a possible solution. One man slowly approached the water edge calling to as he her held out her dress inviting her to come and collect it.

"Put it down and go away," she shrieked desperately.

He only grinned and shook it, tempting her to come and get it. Something fell from the pocket and tumbled over his hand distracting him to glance down and look to see what it was. He bent down picked it up and for a moment he studied it. Then he glanced in her direction but this time with a much more serious expression before he turned away and retraced his steps back to his comrades. Several of the men gathered round while he showed them the object. Lailla watched as their mood now turned serious. One man pointed towards her and uttered some curt instructions and three men began running towards her. Now the issue forced and with nothing to lose she struggled to her feet and began to run in the opposite direction.

The water dragged on her legs slowing her down and even without turning she knew the men were closing. She cleared the water edge and stumbled in the uneven ground but drove on as fast as she could. She could hear the cheers or jeers of the men on the other side. The thump of running feet were close now and she took a terrified glance over her shoulder in time to see the man closest reaching out to grab her. She managed to swerve back and away to her left avoiding his despairing grab but straight into the arms of another. They fell to the ground as she struggled to escape. But with the other two pursuers joining in she was quickly subdued. They hauled her to her feet and spoke in a language she did not understand but by their lewd grins as they ogled her half-naked body she could guess what the remarks were about. She continued to struggle until one of the men lifted her legs and the three of them carried her still squirming back across the pool. They dropped her on the ground right in the midst of the group. Surrounded by silent staring male faces she bent over hunched her shoulders and used her arms to cover as much of her nakedness as she could.

A pair of booted feet appeared directly in front of her and she looked up at a large framed man towering above. He had broad sergeant's stripes upon his sleeve and his face was the pale face of a foreigner He stared down at her impassively. Wordlessly he held out his hand in front of her face then slowly uncurled his fingers. In the palm of his hand he held the object that had fallen from her dress pocket. It was the little red Commissar star that Mussalim had given her. Now he began a torrent of angry abuse and the only word she could understand was 'adoo.'

She shook her head vigorously "Not adoo." she said desperately. "Not adoo." But is served only to annoy him more. She tried to explain it had been a rabia protection against adoo abuse. But these men were Iranians and even if they understood her language they probably did not understand the Arabic code of rabia.

He used the sole of his boot against her shoulder to push her backwards and silence her desperate pleadings. Then he said something to the men around him and some sort of argument broke out. Cowering prostrate and propping herself up on an elbow Lailla knew they were arguing her fate. She studied the faces above looking desperately for allies and mercy. She knew that she had been tried, found guilty and only her sentence remained. The sergeant was dominant and his dictatorial attitude was beating down any resistance. As they succumbed to his argument men began drifting away until only five remained. He glanced around at those who remained and shrugged. Then he took the pistol from its holster hanging on his hip and looking in the direction of the dozen men that had moved away, he shouted something derisive at them. He looked down to Lailla leaned forward and pressed the barrel of the pistol against her forehead.

"No, no," she pleaded and began trembling violently.

He only laughed and in the palm of his hand he held out the Commissar star close to her face. He screamed something at her, which she didn't understand and that served to agitate him even more. Tears flowed down her face as she tried pleadingly to explain that she didn't understand. Then exasperated he handed the pistol to another man and grabbing her by the hair he forced the star into her mouth with the other hand. Then he shook her head violently before forcing her mouth open to make sure that she had swallowed it. Satisfied, he stood back and looked down at her with a smirk. Then he muttered some instruction to the men around him.

With the pistol pressed against her temple she was too afraid to move or even resist as she was held down and her shorts, the last vestige of her modesty, were ripped away. The sergeant now with a big grin on his face knelt between her outstretched legs and began undoing his belt and fiddling with the front of his trousers.

"No, no," she pleaded as she realised what was about to happen. It wasn't supposed to happen like this and she glanced to the small band of men standing a few metres away. Most seemed unconcerned almost as if nothing of any importance was happening. But here and there a sympathetic face stared back giving her the merest vestige of hope. "Help me," she sobbed, "please help me." But no one moved. Her distressed scream echoed across the granite walls of the wadi until a rough hand across her mouth muffled it.

Time was meaningless as she lapsed into a protective state of semi-consciousness. She was aware of brief respites as each gratified man moved away to be replaced by another. In between these pauses unbearable degradation and the stench of sweat, bad breath and seemingly endless grunts as they used her with less regard than an animal. Eventually the man that moved away was not replaced and although her physical ordeal had ended the mental defilement was overpowering and she ached for the finger twitch on that trigger that would release her from her humiliation. But there would be no release, the pistol was gone also so she coiled herself into a tight ball for feeble protection. If she could perhaps stop herself from breathing then she would induce a merciful death. But you cannot stop breathing any more than you can stop your heart beating so her traumatised body reacted in the only protective thing it could do. She slipped into the oblivion of unconsciousness.

In dreams she was a child again and her mother Kathya came to the pool to be with her. They gathered balsam by the armful and laid them out on the ground to form a sweet smelling bed of pink. She heard once more her mother's laughter as they sat together on that bed twisting the stalks to form laurels to place on their heads. Soon it was time for Kathya to go leaving her behind and alone once more. She called for her not to go but her mother only smiled and waved as she went away.

She woke with a start, then instantly froze her movements. She dare not move fearful that if she betrayed her returning awareness the men would come back again.

Someone had covered her with her dress and she clung to it tightly and strained her ears attempting to establish were they where. A breeze had risen its hot breath rustling the leaves on the trees and somewhere close by a crow squawked. She slowly raised her head and seeing nothing other than the wadi tranquillity she sat up and looked around. She was alone, at some point while she slept they had gone. For a moment she hoped it that it had all been a nightmare, but her nakedness, the pain in her abdomen and the smell of men all over her betrayed the awful reality. Her immediate instinct was to wash away every trace of their very existence from her body. Wincing with pain she stumbled slowly back into the pool and then began frantically trying to wash away every last hint of her violation. She scrubbed her skin until she was sore but still the smell of men would not go away. It was branded into her memory and its taint would not leave her nostrils. Eventually she gave up and accepting that it was probably just imagination, she pulled on her dress.

She glanced at the sun, it was time for her to go home and that would be another ordeal to be faced. How would her father react? How could she bear the shame? Then she realised that it was entirely her own fault and she could not tell him. Wasn't it she who bathed near naked in the wadi? No one had forced her, therefore it was she who had laid temptation in the way of those men. She could never tell anyone, nobody must ever know, she decided. Her shame that several men had known her body was immense but for others to know also would magnify it tenfold. She could never be the same again for she was soiled now, but it must be her own secret. And so they were to get away with it?

Anger churned and knotted in her stomach causing her to clench her teeth and roll her hands into fists. She had been subjected to humiliation, degradation and trembling fear. They had laughed at her pleas and then wantonly violated her body. No, she vowed, they would not get away with. They would die for what they had done to her this day. She didn't know how yet but the red mist of fury demanded revenge.

✳ ✳ ✳

Early February 1974 • Jokha watched thoughtfully as Lailla drove the cattle up and out of sight over the hill. There was no doubt that she was taking Hamed's departure very badly. Since his departure three weeks ago there had been a remarkable change in her attitude. The effect seemed to have been a fundamental character change. From a bright and cheerful young girl she had become very quiet and gloomily morose. Nobody was particularly pleased that Hamed had undercover of darkness slipped away without a word seemingly abandoning his moral responsibilities. However, of all the people who remained behind she would have thought that Lailla would be the least depressed. It seemed that she had revelled in the responsibility that had fallen on her young shoulders when he had left previously. Perhaps she had been mistaken after all and that she had been pleased to be relieved of that responsibility when he had returned. Now with his departure the responsibility had been re-imposed. She shook her head and sighed, admitting her bewilderment, then went back inside the house.

Unless he planned to go to Salalah Abdulla didn't rise very early these days. Why should he? There was very little he could do. His only useful task around the farm was to milk the cattle and goats each evening and even that job had to be laid out for him. If it wasn't some animals would not get milked and others he would try to milk twice. If it wasn't so demoralising for him then an element of humour might have been found in that. But sometimes it frustrated him almost to the point of tears. She laid out his breakfast so that it would be ready for him when he did decide to rise. It was only a little cold rice and goat meat from the previous night that had been left over. She couldn't stay here and wait because she had things to do, so she did as she did every day and placed it in the exact same place so that he could find it. After wafting away the flies she covered it with a cloth.

Today she intended to go to the nearby village, Shair. There was a surplus of whey and cheese that she might be able to sell. She would have to carry the produce and when she got there she would then simply sit patiently in the middle of the village, spread her goods on the ground before her and hope that somebody would buy. She had instructed Khamisa to remain close to the farm this day in case Abdulla needed anything. The goats would just have to spend most of the day in the pen. Perhaps if she were to get back early then Khamisa could let them out for a short ramble later. Certainly with just the three women running the farm and one of them locked to Abdulla's side they were definitely struggling. She wished that Jumaia had not left. Her contribution right now would be invaluable. But then she could not begrudge Mussalim his woman, she obviously made her eldest son happy and that pleased her. If only there were some way that he could escape from this war then he would be back here on the farm with his family straight away, of that she was quite sure. That would make life so very much easier for everyone concerned. She compared Mussalim's circumstances to Hamed's. Unlike Mussalim he did have the opportunity to be on the farm with his woman and yet he had chosen to go. Perhaps it was as Adbulla had said. Khamisa was a poor wife and did not welcome Hamed into her bed. He certainly could never have applied that suggestion to her where Juma had been concerned she had been as his willing slave and he hers. Perhaps in the circumstances it was only natural that she was a little withheld. But Khamisa is not a bad young woman, she allowed, and given time she might come to appreciate Hamed more? Young people today were becoming more independent, she concluded with a sigh. More inclined to follow their own opinions and Abdulla just did not understand this. The ways of the old ones are fading and perhaps this war was contributing to those changes. But only Allah knows what lies ahead and in the end it will be he who decides. "*Inshalaah,*" she muttered to herself. "*Il hamdu lilaah.*"

Lailla stood on the upper lip of the Wadi, the strong wind ravaging her long hair and billowed her loose dress like a boat's sail. Behind her the open rolling *gatn* while to her front the deep and wide ravine of Wadi Aydaas. Not a particular large wadi, Aydaas was nevertheless spectacular. Its base and steep sides thickly covered by the bright green *Ghaf* shrubs contrasted vividly with the golden scorched grasslands above. Along its top edge thorny shrubs heavy with tiny balls of yellow flowers was savaged by the breeze and tainted the air with the heavy aroma of mimosa. The wadi was shaped as a giant 'Y' its horns climbing almost sheer to an abrupt end where the *gatn* began. Its trunk ran southwards steadily deepening until after only four kilometres it spilled into the greater Wadi Nahiz. From her position at the very end of one of the horns Lailla could follow the path that the deep chasm had carved in the earth. Where the subservient wadi opened into the greater one she could see the dwellings of Nahiz village from this distance little more than a cluster of miniatures.

She scanned the scene carefully, her eyes taking every detail. It was not the panoramic vista of Allah's creation she studied, it was potential hiding places. Once Mussalim had hinted that an arms cache was hidden in Aydaas and if it was still here then she intended to find it. To kill Iranians then bullets and bombs were required and she had an all-consuming need to kill Iranians.

The hiding place might well be a cave. Many caves littered these wadis. Or perhaps a derelict building somewhere in the base hidden beneath the heavy leaf canopy. It might even be something as small as a narrow cleft scarred in the steep walls. Whatever and wherever she would search until she found it no matter how long it took. She planned to work methodically, first to search this element of the 'Y' then the other and finally the trunk down towards the village itself. That, she estimated, would take three days and if she hadn't found it then she would start again. If it were still there she would find it.

She had made provision for the cattle by herding them into a short blind canyon. She had discovered a suitable place a week ago and had spent the intervening time building a rough barrier across its narrow entrance. That would keep them in during her long absence. So today having penned them in and leaving them unattended for the first time she was now free to look for the killing equipment she needed.

From where she stood three caves were very apparent and fairly close. The first was almost beneath her just a little to her right. It had an enormous entrance promising a fairly deep depth. The second right over to her right was even closer to the top and looked more like a small tunnel cut into a mound. The third was furthest away and more than halfway to the bottom. From here it looked little more that a horizontal slit in the rock wall with a protruding hood. She planned a route that would enable her to search all three as she made her way down into the wadi bottom.

Although it was close beneath her by the time she had found a way down and worked her way back almost an hour had passed before she approached the gaping mouth of the first cave. Even then it had a very steep incline up to its entrance. It was unlikely this would be a hiding place, she decided it was much too difficult to get to. Nevertheless, she persevered because it needed to be eliminated with a degree of certainty. Eventually breathless she pulled herself over the last lip and into its yawning mouth. It was damp inside and it wasn't as deep as she had expected. Although there were some unusual ferns and plants enjoying the dank dark environment a cache of arms there was not. She looked out from its jaws straight down the valley. It had taken an hour to investigate the first possibility and she was only a few metres below the spot where she had started. This section was not going to be covered in a day, she concluded.

The second cave she also eliminated in her mind as she neared. This one was too open, the top of the mound almost breasting the very lip of the wadi with a clear view down inside its throat before you even got close to it. It would not be a very secure hiding place.

She found a winding goat path that would lead her down to the bottom bending roughly in the direction of the third cave. As she worked her way down she lost sight of the cave and had to pause to try and establish its position. She glanced back towards the end of the wadi and the yawning mouth of the first cave she had investigated. From that she guessed that although she perhaps had not gone far enough into the ravine she was too far down and the cave now above her somewhere. However, she continued along the track that continued roughly in the right direction although still downward. Very close to the bottom it joined another, this leading up from the bottom. The new one was wider and better trodden with camel tracks. This in itself although encouraging was not necessarily significant because camels loose in a wadi use the same tracks to follow the same foraging trails.

Emerging above the shrub line she came upon it abruptly. An innocuous looking horizontal cleft in the rocky wall, it looked as if part of a sandy seam had crumbled and tumbled away. The remnants above formed a protruding overhang and at first glance it looked to be nothing better than perhaps a comfortable shelter for some wild hyena or some similar animal. Forced to duck her head to move inside she found that although at first glance the crevice appeared shallow in fact it had a small cavern leading off. Doubling up even more to move along this low tunnel she found that after three or four metres it emerged into a larger cavern the size of a modest room.

It took a couple of minutes for her eyes to start adjusting to the darkness but as they did gradually the shapes of boxes and packages began to form. Her hopes began to rise it seemed that by pure dumb luck she might have already found the arms cache she sought. As her eyes became used to the darkness she could see more clearly. However, things were not quite as she expected. The boxes and packages were tossed around haphazardly, scattered, broken and tipped over. She moved among the litter and that was precisely what it seemed to be.

Ammunition boxes, packing crates with foreign writing on and oily green polythene wrapping paper indicated that it was or had been some kind of weapon-store. Deeper in she found a long unopened crate raising hopes that perhaps there was something here that she might be able to use. She tried to drag it clear from the craggy wall but it was heavy and she gave up. She had no tools to break open the lid and briefly she tried another piece of wood as a prise, but unsuccessfully. Having no patience at this point she decided that she should look around to see what else there might be and return to this crate later. Most of the packages were empty but among the debris she did find some weapons Wrapped in oily green polythene she found a dissembled machine gun of sorts and in another box with metal latches, hand grenades. The gun would be no use to her but the grenades certainly were attractive. She continued searching until she came across half a dozen opened boxes stacked together. When she looked inside she found, to her delight, round oval shaped mines. She was elated, these were the ideal ultimate weapons. With these she could plant instant death beneath Iranian feet. Even better and with Allah's help they might not kill but instead disfigure a man by blasting away the bits between his legs that made him what a man is. She could think of no better revenge than reducing a rapist to a eunuch with a lifetime to live. With her stomach churning again with anger and hatred she continued her search but there was nothing more so she returned to the crate. It was a struggle but eventually she got part of the top off. Wrapped in the same oily green polythene she found AK 47 Kalachnikovs. She didn't know how to use one but she decided that it might pay to fiddle and practice with it until she could. However, even though she searched again and thoroughly she could find no bullets to load it with. With a Kalachnikov beneath her dress fastened against her leg, two grenades in her pockets and two mines in her arms she emerged from the cavern. She glanced back into the dark tunnel, as an arms cache its stocks were woefully inadequate. However, there was a useful supply of grenades and mines and as she needed more then she could return to get them. Providing of course the stolen weapons were not missed! Probably the cache belonged to the Liberationist men of the tribe Bait Gatun from Nahiz and possibly several had access. With any luck they would assume that any missing items had been taken by other comrades. That is what she hoped!

For now however, she was well pleased with the day's work. As she began to descend the path she permitted herself a wry smile. She had the means to kill Iranians and needed only a plan and they would start to die. A slight stab of conscience suggested that she might kill innocent men, but she dismissed it easily. Even while she was being abused others had stood by and watched unconcerned. They were as bad as the actual rapists and deserved to die also. To her all Iranians were exactly the same.

~ 23 ~

April 1974 • Lailla was two months into her private war with Iranians and although she had seen evidence that she had at least caused damage she was not satisfied. Her feral rage demanded to know if Iranians had bled and died and only then would she feel any satisfaction.

She had made rudimentary provision for the cattle security during her absences. She could not leave them at the farm because she still needed the chore of tending them in order to have the excuse of spending full days away. Nor could she simply abandon them while she pursued her own vendetta. So she herded them each day away over the hills and inside that rough barrier that she had constructed across the entrance of a short canyon. Once they were penned in, she was assured that she could find them upon her return. There was a little concern that in her absence they might be vulnerable to wolves or hyena, however, she dismissed it and didn't allow it to prevent her from pursuing her objectives. Disregarding her responsibilities lightly, she was free to spend time observing the Iranian security posts along the jebal road.

The posts on the *gatn* she ignored because they stood in open and exposed landscape. It would not have been long before somebody noticed her watching. She also ignored the two posts at the other end of the road, one at the foot of the jebal on the Salalah plain and the one on the top. From her brother's experience with the artillery shell she knew that army observers clandestinely roamed the mountainside and she didn't want to find herself confronted by any of these soldiers. Even without these it still left her with four potential targets.

It had quickly become patently obvious that all these security posts had similarities. All were positioned on hilltops overlooking the road and all had built a circle of sturdy sangars around the top to fortify their positions. Around the bottom of the hill they had positioned a double row of concertina razor wire to create a sterile area in between. There was only one entry point in the wire and it was manned during daylight hours by three guards. Two regulated the traffic while the third manned a GP machine gun from behind a sandbagged sangar. Not that very much regulating was being carried out by the sentries because the traffic coming and going was mostly from within their own compound and rated only a cursory glance before being waved in or out. Each post seemed to be operating from the same set of standing orders also. These small convoys of Land Rovers seemed to come and go twice daily and at roughly the same times, presumably patrolling their own specified stretch of road. Lailla soon appreciated that this predictability was a probable weakness and it could perhaps be turned to her advantage.

Just inside these entrances, very much in evidence were barbed wire barriers and these she assumed would be dragged into position to close the entrance. Did this perhaps mean that the circle of wire was closed at the end of the day and the Iranians retreated to the hilltop behind the security of their sangars? To check out this notion she had on three different nights waited until her father and Jokha slept and had then stole from the house and approached each position. It was as she suspected, they did indeed desert the first line of defence. She also learned something else on these reconnoitres. The Iranians were very nervous soldiers, they let off long bursts of gunfire directed at nothing more than night noises and shadows. Just to approach the wire itself in darkness was a very dangerous task. Because she didn't observe every day it took around a month to gather the information and then she went into the planning stage to decide how she might use the information to exact retribution.

Her first plan, to plant a booby trap had been simplicity itself. She had selected at random one of the outposts and under the cover of darkness she crept forward to its entrance. Then she taped one of the hand grenades to one of the angle iron posts that were driven into the ground securing the razor wire in position. After that she tied a small piece of string around the release pin and attached it to the barrier. The next morning the barrier would be dragged away and so would be the release pin, seconds later the grenade would explode. The next day she had hurried to see the results and from her concealed position she was elated to see the evidence of an explosion by the twisted and broken wire. However, by that time there was no indication of death or injury so she had to content herself with the hope that someone had been close enough to pay the penalty.

Fearing that the word would have been spread and that the Iranians would be much more vigilant for a while she had waited two weeks before renewing her campaign. The next time she selected a different target and planted a mine. She could have planted a mine anytime anywhere along the road and hoped that one of their patrols stumbled onto it but that wasn't precise enough for her. Besides that anybody on the road might step on it. She watched carefully and it soon came to her that the only ground that the patrol vehicles used consistently was where they passed through the narrow entry points. Once again under the cover of darkness she crept to the wire. On this occasion she had to press herself flat to the ground when loosely directed machine gun fire raked her area after she made a little sound as she scraped out a hole to bury the mine. But the job was soon accomplished and once more she melted into the night and returned smugly home to her bed. The next day as soon as she could get… she went again to the post to see the results if any of her plan. Once again there seemed to have been some success. This time the remnants of a small truck had been dragged off to the side. Its carrier part at the rear seemed intact but the front cab was collapsed and leaned heavily to one side. The door swung loose attached precariously by one hinge only, while rubber hung in shreds around what was left of the wheel rim. Once again although she derived great satisfaction from the evidence she felt a little cheated because she could not be sure that someone had died.

To satisfy her need to actually witness her revenge she considered ways that she might modify her plans. With limited resources of landmines and grenades and only one each of those left she was puzzled how she might achieve that.

✳ ✳ ✳

In the south west of the country Hamed had been accepted in the *Firqa* Tariq Bin Zeead and this morning he stood with around forty-five of his comrades watching the vehicles disappearing northwards on their way back to Manston. It was still early but already the sun poured relentless heat down on the undulating flinty land. To the south the green mountain ranges of Jebal Sayq and Jebal Altim towered above their position. Those mountains were strong *adoo* country and just about their last refuge. The company of *firqa* stood on the road which ran straight as a flighted arrow west to the Yemen border. This road roughly marked the unofficial boundary between the two forces. The greater expanse to the north was firmly government held, while the shrinking *adoo* forces with only the sea behind them hid themselves in the peaks and valley of the mountains.

The Tariq Bin Zeead carried out regular sorties into these ranges on seek and destroy missions. Sometimes they acted on information received and moved to engage *adoo* positions. However, they were rarely in time because either the information was days old and the Front forces had moved on or they had got wind of their advance and had melted away. But usually they moved to set ambushes around villages, wells, and waterholes where *adoo* were known to frequent. Often they would lie in wait for days before fruitlessly withdrawing. Just occasionally though these traps were sprung but they were never devastatingly successful as the PFLO were soon eager to disengage and melt away after only brief skirmishes. The fact that the *firqats* could quickly call upon air strikes to beat up on the enemy positions made it rather foolhardy for them to stand and fight for any length of time.

Today the Tariq Bin Zeead reinforced by half a dozen of their British SAS trainers were to move to the village Seefeer in between Altim and Sayq where it was reported that some members of 9th June Regiment, the last complete PFLO regiment, were recruiting and training. They were to advance from the north west while another force of similar size moved from the north east. It would be a forced march with both jaws of the pincer to be in positions in early afternoon. The co-ordinated strike would take place soon after when it was anticipated that the *adoo* would be resting and off guard.

The order came to move out and men began a little unenthusiastically to gather equipment and lift it onto their backs. A couple of minutes to adjust their loads to more comfortable positions, tighten the straps and they moved out on their way directly south. At first the ground before them sloped gently upward but soon became steeper as they got nearer the mountains. Two hours of hard upward slog later the first halt was called but as they temporarily eased themselves of their burdens they could look back down the mountain side knowing that the worst of the climb was over. Ahead although the terrain undulated wildly many of the climbs could be avoided by keeping as much as possible to the higher ground. It meant that an indirect meandering route would be taken but in the end it would be less energy sapping. Avoiding as much as possible the bald open mountaintops they continued on, keeping as much as possible amongst the stubby *ghaf* that thickly lined the hillsides. These shrubs, only as tall as a man and thinly leaved, gave practically no shelter from the frazzling sun as they relentlessly stumbled on in Indian file. After another two hours the line began to extend as men started to flag, so the second halt was called.

Hamed dropped his burden then sank to the ground resting his back against his pack. Then he watched the *firqat* leaders and the British soldiers discuss the next phase while he sipped water from his canteen. They were situated on a hillside that fell away to the front into an expanse of plain in the bottom of a wide valley. This flat plain interspersed only by shrubs dotted here and there was exposed and seemed to be giving the leaders some cause for concern.

"How far are we from the target?" he asked the man sprawled near by.

"One hour," he muttered pulling a face and very obviously guessing.

Hamed gazed out across the plain. By the time they had descended the hill and crossed the open ground one-hour would have just about passed. So unless Seefeer was just over the hill on the other side the guess was unreliable. One thing on which he could rely, however, was that by the time they got to Seefeer then he would be exhausted. Then he would probably have to fight and perhaps for his very life. This was nothing like what he had expected. On the Hornbeam Line his perception of exacting revenge was to chase the *adoo* in vehicles, arrive at the scene fresh and then to kill them unless they surrendered. After that all that was left was to ride back in comfort. Humping twenty-five kilos across rough terrain beneath a blazing sun before you got in position to fight was earning his money the hard way. He pulled his shamag over his face. Better he snatch a few minutes sleep while the experts decided how best to cross that open ground.

In the end they divided into two groups and well spaced out they advanced in two rows. Hamed was in the front row and when they were within two hundred metres of the rising ground on the other side they came under intense machine gun fire. Caught in the open Hamed hesitated, not sure which way to run. Thirty metres forward of his position was a circular clump of low shrubs. Its centre was deadened and charred black by the sun, but both ends were healthy and thick with greenery. It would offer little protection to bullets ripping through but it did offer a hiding place. At this instant that was all he could see and so he ran to it as hard as he could. Cover was sparse and he was not the first to get to it, nor was he the last. The arrival of a handful of men in bushes that were no higher than a man's waist had not gone unnoticed by one or two alert ambushers and the length of the thicket were systematically raked by automatic rifle fire.

Hamed pressed himself down into the hard baked ground and listened to the cracks and thuds all around him as bullets tore through the brush and hammered into the ground. It seemed impossible that he would not be hit but he wasn't and to his immeasurable relief the sweep moved away from him and onto other comrades cowering in other bushes. But soon it came back reversing the sweep. This time his leg took a hit, he felt it involuntarily jerk over his other but surprisingly he felt no pain. The fusillade died away as the rifleman moved on to a fresh target. Hamed rolled over to his back to inspect the damage. The thick heel of his boot had been ripped away and flapped loose, it was this that had actually taken the hit and not his leg. Reaching down and pulling it off completely he glanced along the bushes to see how his other comrades had fared. Others had not been quite as lucky. One groaned as he writhed around while another sat squeezing his thigh with blood stained fingers. The fourth was mobile though his face was also blood stained. He glanced at Hamed and then moved to help the man who seemed the worst hit. Hamed followed his example and crawled to the other man. He looked at Hamed, cursed and grimaced with pain then he opened his hands for a moment allowing Hamed to see his wound. A large splinter from dead bark had been torn away by a bullet and had buried itself into the man's leg. Driven by instinct Hamed pulled the man's hands away from the wound and with a jerk dragged the splinter out. As he did it started to bleed more profusely. Having nothing to bind the wound with he tore off the sleeve from his shirt and used that. Before he had finished however, the *adoo* rifleman returned his attention to the thicket. Once again they were forced to cringe into the ground as he raked again letting them know that he hadn't forgotten them.

Hamed looked around in some desperation, their position was poor but then there seemed to be nothing close by that would afford better protection. If the *adoo* continued to rake this thicket then it seemed inevitable that even though they fired blind they would eventually find their mark. He realised fully that he and the men with him were in grave danger. The *firqats* were now beginning to recover from their initial shock and starting to return fire. While the men in the front row had been caught fully exposed and been forced to whatever inadequate cover they could find the following second row had gone to ground in the shelter of a shallow gully. They were organising quickly, forming a line from which they could fire. A few moments later they began laying down intense covering fire into the trees on the overlooking hill. The fire from above had not ceased but it was certainly now less intense as some switched to return fire towards the gully.

Some of the more experienced men saw their opportunity and encouraging those around them to follow they began dashing back towards the organised line and the comparative safety of the gully. Hamed glanced towards the bloody-faced man tending the stricken colleague.

"Let's go," he shouted.

"He can't make it." Hamed stared at him confused wondering what to do next. "You two go," he made up his mind for him. He hitched his rifle across his shoulder ducked beneath the arm of the other man dragged him to his feet and they set off running as hard as the man's injured leg would let them. With great relief they sprawled into the shallow bottom of the gully.

A few minutes later two Strikemaster's roared overhead and thumped several rockets into the hillside leaving rising pillars of smoke drifting away on the wind. Twisting and turning in the blue sky they made a wide circle and came round again. Passing low over the heads of the *firqats* they repeated the attack. With their payload of rockets exhausted they were still not done. This time they flew along the hill strafing the *adoo's* last known positions. Then with victory rolls they passed over the *firqat's* heads once more before disappearing east back toward Salalah. With their departure the hills once again became pacifistically serene basking in the scorching sun. Apart from the smoke clouds dissipating casually in an otherwise cloudless sky there was not the slightest evidence of the fury that men had just inflicted upon each other.

The *firqats* now began counting the cost of the ambush. They had taken several hits, two or three serious and they would need to be evacuated by helicopter. They reported in by radio and a few minutes later the attack on Seefeer was abandoned. Carrying their wounded they withdrew back over to the far side of the valley to await the arrival of the helicopters.

Hamed sat slightly apart from the rest in reflective mood. He gloomily inspected his heel-less boot realising how easily it could have been a fatal disaster. There was PFLO here all around him but they were as a will-o-wisp and impossible to get to grips with. However, their capacity was a very real and present danger. Unlike the Hornbeam Line where the role was defensive here it had to be offensive and there are more risks involved when attacking. This had been his first real taste of PFLO determination and his previous conception of cowards setting booby traps and running away or capitulating as soon as they were confronted had taken a severe jolt. Here in their own territory these men had no intention of giving in, they would fight to the very end even unto death and they would not die easily. The blood repayment that he sought demanded its own price.

❊ ❊ ❊

For two days Mussalim and Ali had rested in Wadi Al Shawq. Not that they had any particular business there other than curiosity. Three days ago they had delivered the sum of their three months recruiting drive, eight men only, to Seefeer for training. Their duty for the time being then ended and with Wadi Al Shawq less than ten kilometres away they had decided to visit the Headquarters of the notorious 9th June Regiment. It was the oldest regiment in the Communist Front being named to mark the formation of the first Congress Committee in 1965. The Committee's objective had been to co-ordinate and organise the resistance to Sultan Said Bin Taymour's despotic regime. On that day the Congress had issued its first manifesto statement calling for all Dhofari's to support the new party, to destroy all imperialist presence and to destroy Said Bin Taymour's regime. The movement had called themselves simply 9th June. Since that day the movement had undergone many changes and its ideology bore very little resemblance to its original ideas. However, the day had been an historical one and the Regiment still symbolised the day by its name.

The wadi cut through the land that was neither *gatn* or *nejd* but an arid blend between the two. The wadi itself ran off the high ground cutting a deep wedge northwards until it spilled out on to the *nejd* below. The opposite end was the more fertile with scattered fig, bedam and date palms eking out an existence from the invisible underground moisture. In the middle a well had been sunk and gathered around this in a desultory fashion was a series of buildings some substantial some not.

More than two hundred fighting men lived here although Mussalim was surprised to see that around half were soldiers of Peoples Democratic Republic of Yemen. No attempts were made to disguise their presence. They openly wore their uniforms sporting the shoulder flashes of the Hadhramaut Bedouin Legion. They were a complete self-supporting detachment with their own officers and facilities.

The self-styled 9th June leader who had given himself the rank of Brigadier General made Mussalim and Ali welcome. Despite the exalted rank he entertained them dressed in a simple *dish-dasht* in an open fronted Bedouin tent and seated cross-legged on an impressive Persian carpet. Minions hovering in the background serving tea while they discussed the war situation. Although attempting to emulate imperialistic behaviour by keeping lackeys patiently waiting to serve he paradoxically orated Communist diatribe against the Omani ruling classes. Mussalim glanced at the servants standing watching dispassionately and despaired that this man who obviously knew so very little about socialist philosophy had gained such a position of influence. In his narrow world he simply wished to exchange places with those already holding privileged positions. After an hour or so he handed his two guests over to his adjutant and excused himself. To Mussalim this came as a relief because he did not know just how much longer he could suffer his pomposity without retaliating against such absurdity.

Despite the Brigadier General's facade of prosperity it was soon apparent that here it was as throughout the western area, food was short. The meal served at night among the soldiers consisted of little more than small portions of bread and rice. Perhaps it was that the Brigadier General privately fared better. Mussalim found himself resenting the man and perhaps a little unfairly, after all he didn't know whether the man was eating better or not.

During the rest of the time they passed among the soldiers socialising. They didn't find anyone who had been with the company since its onset in 1965 and indeed they couldn't even find any that had been in the movement as long as they themselves had. Mostly the men were newer recruits and full of confused ideals. Here and there they did find a veteran of around four years who had a better understanding of the principles for which they fought. But even in these cases Mussalim could sense that much of the motivation had blunted, undermined by the Sultan's pacifistic development policy gradually granting the things for which they had originally gone to war to achieve.

Among the Yemeni soldiers there was even less understanding. The poor economic situation in South Yemen was having disastrous effects on its own population and many men came into the Army simply because there was no other way they could obtain money to feed their families. They would do precisely as they were told and without question, for if they didn't then their families would suffer starvation. They knew only that there was a wicked Omani Sultan that should be deposed. Beyond that they had no other interest.

Now this morning as Ali and Mussalim saddled their camels to return to Raykut, they were happy to leave.

* * *

Four months Khamisa had been married to Hamed and for almost three of those, he had been away. But still she was pregnant and she resented this child in her belly that was not Juma's. She knew that she was not a good wife to Hamed and he didn't really deserve her rejection but she could not give what she did not have.

Shortly after he had left she had come to terms with the fact that for as long as he wanted then she would be his wife. With that eventual acceptance there had come a little easing of the bitterness she felt and a realisation that since she did not have a husband who would treat her severely then perhaps she ought to be a little more grateful. Most certainly she could have been much worse off. However, as this new situation developed and her suspicions became reality all those resentments returned. Before, she had convinced herself that her body was temporarily loaned for his pleasure and in return she and Tuful would have shelter and be well treated. But now with his child inside her, her body was possessed completely. Her first instinct had been to try to find a way that would make her miscarry, but that was a sin against humanity and against Allah himself. If she did miscarry then it would be by Allah's will and not by anything that she did.

She went over to the cot where Tuful lay sleeping peacefully. She gently brushed back her black hair and covered her shoulder with the blanket. She was a happy child with a natural inquisitive mind chattering away incessantly through all her waking hours. Now very nearly three years old Khamisa wondered what her father would have thought if he could see her now. She was sure that Juma would be very proud of his daughter. Just for the briefest instant she wished that she were a son, that would have made him prouder. But she was a girl and still he had loved her from the instant that he had first seen her. She remembered that day in Al Dharitz at her father's house when first he had met the delicate fragile bundle that was his daughter. That may have been the happiest moment they had shared amongst so many moments of happiness, she thought. 'Why did you have to take him away from me?' she silently asked her God. But she already knew the answer. It was her own sin that had been punished and similarly it was Hamed's punishment too for he was burdened with a wife who did not want him. But unjustly the punishment was imposed on Tuful also, she would never know her father. Only a year old when he had been killed Tuful could never remember anything about him, but even so she would at least know all about him. She would make certain of that. Now it seemed that soon she would have a sibling, a little brother or perhaps a sister. It would only be a half sibling though and it would be the nobler half that would be missing.

She pressed her hand on her stomach looking for the first signs of swelling. It still seemed flat, aligned perfectly with her thighs. For a moment she wondered if there could be some other explanation but she knew there was not. But just in case she would wait a little longer before telling Jokha.

As she moved to turn down the paraffin lamp she heard the footsteps outside. So she waited a few moments with her hand poised to turn down the wick, but no one entered. Driven by curiosity she lifted down the lamp and went outside. Lailla walked up the hill away from the farmhouse and just the same as the last time Khamisa had seen her stealing away into the darkness she was again dressed as a man.

Where did she go when she sneaked away into the night? She supposed that there was a boy involved but if that were so there could only be one reason she went clandestinely at night and that was very wicked. But why dressed as a man? She had been behaving very strangely these past few weeks but a secret lover probably would explain it. However, that was a very dangerous game to play. Perhaps she should talk with her very soon, she thought. If she could gain her confidence then she could warn her of the potential consequences.

✳ ✳ ✳

Lailla reached the intersection of the Midway road and the track that led west towards Nahiz and here she paused. Her heart thumped wildly in her chest because on what she was about to embark – it had good cause. She took a couple of minutes to compose herself and as she waited her common sense told her that she didn't have to go through with this reckless plan. But the ferocious hunger for revenge overruled and told her that she must. She glanced towards the moon just into its last quarter and wished it were less. But it wasn't and her impatience would not allow her to wait just five or six days.

Beyond the next rise would be the hill on which the Iranians had built their fortification. Like all the others it was situated on a hilltop overlooking the main road and had been prepared in exactly the same way. The difference between this one and the others along this stretch was that a clump of wizened acacia grew to one side of the hill and nature had seeded the occasional offspring even onto the hilltop. By using the clump of trees she could approach from the blind side almost to the wire itself. She wore an old pair of sand-coloured pants that Mussalim had left behind and a dark brown *firqat* shirt of Hamed's. For the umpteenth time she patted all the pockets to make sure they were empty. They were all except one. In that one she had a rusty old penknife and even that was wrapped in a piece of cloth. It would not do to allow something metallic to betray her position by clattering against a rock. She slipped the sandals from her feet and placed them by the side of the road where she could find them later. From here on she would go barefoot.

She eased the landmine she carried from beneath her arm and set it on her lap. It was not heavy but its flat oval shape made it awkward to carry. She thought it looked quite harmless, however she knew that when the lock pin was removed it required only that the top plate contacted the plate beneath to complete the circuit and it would explode with devastating effects. She couldn't read English but she could recognise it, and the writing on the mine was English. The irony of the situation was that a mine made in England by allies of the Sultan would be set to blow up Iranian allies of the Sultan, somehow it seemed remotely appropriate.

She moved on down the road bolstering her courage by telling herself that she could still withdraw from this action at any number of points yet. A long prolonged burst of machine gun fire shook her, making her start with fright until she realised that it couldn't be directed against her, there was still another hill between her and the post. It would be just another nervous soldier firing off at shadows, she told herself. But that only added to her fear. Those jumpy Iranians were likely to fire off long and hard at the slightest noise.

The road bent around the side of the hill and at this point she left it, angling off at a right angle seeking the clump of acacia. She moved slowly placing her feet carefully and stopping often to peer into the gloom ahead. The trees she could see a few metres ahead stamped black against an inky black skyline. She made the trees without incident and more confident in their cover she approached the wire. At the edge she paused looking for the razor wire. It was in exposed ground about twenty metres from where she stood but it looked more like a hundred. Once again she warned herself that she could still abandon the plan and perhaps take an easier option, but the need for retribution burned stronger. She imagined the shock a man would experience at the instant he knew that he was dying and the alarm that it would spread among his fellow contemptible swine. That was all the incentive she needed.

Feeling fully exposed she crawled very slowly forward to the razor wire. The barrier wire was in continuous coiled pieces about one metre high and on the bottom a double row. On these bottom coils another piece rested on top and all was held in position by angle iron rods driven into the ground. Every few centimetres wicked barbs were twisted in the wire and pointed outward waiting to tear a man's skin. On her belly she crawled along the wire looking for a place where it might be stretched just a little more creating a wider gap between the coils. But there seemed to be little difference. Resigning herself to a painful passage through the wire she pushed the mine as far forward as she could and then followed it inching forward on her shoulder into the coils. The first barb painfully punctured her arm and as she squirmed to take the weight off her clothes became snagged and that set the pattern for the whole operation. Picking her way through delicately centimetres at a time she carefully un-snagged clothing and ripped skin as she went. The whole time she could hear the blood throbbing in her ears as the stress sent her heartbeat soaring. Another burst of gunfire while she was stranded halfway through did nothing to lower her heart rate. She lay unable to move and in complete terror until she realised that it wasn't directed towards her position. When it ceased and just for that instant she thought to go back, but now that she was halfway through the wire she rejected the thought. Eventually she made it through and as she pulled her legs clear she rolled over onto her belly. Now she was inside and past the point of backing out.

Twenty metres to her left and now sealed for the night was the entry into the outer compound where the guards usually stood. Just a few metres beyond that one of those single acacia trees that seemed to have got away from the main clump behind her. This was her next objective. She collected the mine and began crawling towards it agonisingly slowly, fearful of making a slightest noise. Trapped inside the wire there could be no escape if discovered.

Beneath the tree with its thin trunk between her and the sangers on the upper lip of the hill she took a moment to relax. Surprisingly she realised that her thumping heart had slowed and now she felt quite composed. She set the mine to one side and with the penknife she began to quietly scrape away at the hard baked ground. At the speed she worked it took the best part of an hour before she had a small hole deep enough to sink the mine in. She placed it carefully and removed the locking pin. It would require now only a little pressure on the top to push the contacts together. Carefully, she pushed back the covering soil and scattered the surplus. Then crawling back feet first she smoothed the area she was leaving with her hands to obliterate any sign of the mine laying operation.

When she was clear of the tree she turned and took the same route and painstaking method back to the razor wire. Picking her way back through the wire was even worse than coming in. Every centimetre took her closer to safety and the massive temptation was to hurry and then dash to safety. Acting very professionally she controlled that urge and took as much care to make no sound as before. She safely negotiated the wire and then set off for the trees but this time her control broke. Halfway there she got to her feet and stooping over hurried beneath their cover. With a huge sigh of relief she retraced her steps the way she had come and with every step taking her further from danger and closer to safety feelings of incredibly elation quickly grew.

As she made her way home she smugly considered what she had achieved. She had invaded right inside the Iranian's area and planted a mine where complacently they would never expect a mine could get placed. That would be an awesome blow to their confidence. Tomorrow when the sun got hot these predictable soldiers would do precisely what she had witnessed them do many times. They would move away from the sun-exposed area of the entrance and stand watchful a few metres away beneath the shade of the tree. There was a very good chance that at some point one of them would step on the mine and by that time she would be there to see it. Despite the cuts all over her body from the wire's barbs, her skinned knuckles and broken finger nails from scraping out the hole she was well pleased with her night's work.

The sky in the east was just beginning to suggest that the sun would soon exert its influence and start to chase away the darkness with a new day when she crept through the door. All was still, her father and Jokha still slept. With a satisfied smile she turned away to the end room that was hers, she might even get an hour's sleep.

Despite the fact that she only catnapped during that hour she was soon up. The adrenaline of her night-time achievements would not allow her mind to relax. She was anxious to be on her way back and find a comfortable position where she could secretly and safely watch one or more Iranians pay the full price for the callous degradation they had subjected her to.

She ate a little bread, drank a little milk and was filling her goatskin with whey when a bleary eyed Jokha emerged from the other room. She was not surprised by her early start, Lailla could see that. But then why would she be? There had been so many these recent weeks. Nevertheless, she insisted on packing a little fruit and a little dried goat's cheese to take with her before she would let her leave. The morning sun was still low in the sky as she drove the cattle up the hill.

When the cattle were safely penned in the makeshift corral Lailla was free to witness some of the revenge that she was entitled to. She cocked an eye at the sun trying to gauge how long it might be before the guards sought the protection from its fierce rays beneath the tree's canopy. Fearing that it might possibly be sooner than she anticipated and that she could miss what she fully deserved to see she hastened her step.

The forced rate that she imposed on herself only made her hotter. As she climbed yet another steep hill she could feel the sweat oozing from every pore drawing in the loose dress she wore and sticking it like plaster to her body. She told herself that it was the pace she set that made her so hot and she knew that it was true. Even so, she could not get from her mind that if the guards were only half as hot they would even now be shading beneath the tree. Fearful of missing her moment of revenge she pressed on unrelenting. Eventually as she topped the steep bank she reached the jebal road and the Nahiz track that led off. The post was just beyond the next rise and only minutes away. Now she could relax a little and seek a good observation spot. Perhaps that clump of acacia might be suitable. She followed the road as it bent around the hill and rejected the copse as soon as she saw it. In the daylight it was not only too close it was also too thin. She hesitated wondering if she should go back and climb the hill from the other side and seek a vantagepoint on the high ground.

Half a dozen Land Rovers overburdened with men came towards her and were less than a hundred metres away. Of course she should have been aware, she scolded herself, it was around the time for the patrol to go out. There was nothing for it but to stand aside and behave as unsuspiciously as she could. She covered her face with the corner of her headscarf as they drove slowly past. One or two shouted things to her but she didn't understand what it was that they said. By their carefree expressions she could guess, but more importantly it also indicated that nothing had yet happened to deflate their spirits. She permitted herself a grim smile beneath the mask as they passed leaving her in a cloud of dust, soon they would not be so happy.

She stood gazing after them waiting for the dust to settle. Would they associate the girl at the roadside with the mine when it went off? Probably not! Not this time, anyway. But if she were to be seen in the vicinity on other occasions suspicions might grow. She resolved to be more careful in the future.

Turning in the wake of the vehicles she retraced her steps around the bend and climbed to the top of the rise. On the breast of the hill not far from where she stood was a low clump of camel thorn clustered around a large boulder. She gazed down the hill and across the top of the acacia copse into the sterile area of the post. That clump of camel thorn might do if she could find a place inside where she was sure she would not be seen suspiciously watching. In the end it proved to be admirably suitable. Masked behind the thorny shrubs she could lay on the rock peering over its edge and through the screen of tiny leaves right down to the guarded entrance. The guards still stood too at their posts. One inside his shaded sangar behind a GP machine gun and the other two with an air of boredom at the wire's entrance. All that she could do now was wait and hope.

An hour later with the sun beginning to assert its intensity there had been no change in the situation. The guards still meandered boredly at the entrance while the man in the sangar had mostly disappeared from sight, just occasionally did she catch a glimpse of him. Meanwhile the rock upon which she lay was beginning to get hot as it absorbed the sun's heat and it was she rather than the guards who was getting uncomfortable. She had begun to consider altering her position to somewhere that was perhaps a little more sheltered when three men left the hilltop citadel and walked slowly down to the entrance. A guard change was about to take place.

The six men stood for a few minutes talking before the three that were relieved made their way casually back up the hill. It took only a few more minutes before the two men who did not enjoy the cover of the sangar wandered casually over to the tree and stood in its dappled shade. Lailla watched intently waiting for an explosion but it didn't happen. Both men then settled to sit on the ground with their rifles propped inside their bent knees. While they sat then there was no danger of them standing on the mine. She tried to gauge roughly where it might be but things look so different in the dark and she could only estimate roughly. The sun's heat was building and she realised that in her position exposed to its increasing strength and upon a rock that was beginning to re-radiate magnified heat she would not be able to remain there much longer. She began to look around for an alternative. That was when she saw the patrol making its way slowly along the road back towards the post. Until it was safely settled in the base and out of sight then it would not be a good time to leave cover. She settled back and watched as the patrol passed to her left and beneath her position. The six vehicles rolled on towards the outpost sedately. The two guards got slowly to their feet and began moving to the entrance making some sort of show that they were at least prepared to go through the motions of security.

When it happened its deep thud startled even her. She stared at the spot where moments before the two guards had been and now only a cloud of dust and smoke. She waited for the dust to clear and couldn't repress a grin of satisfaction, someone had made a payment to her vendetta. As it cleared she could see that both men were down. One lying prostrate waved an arm in a slow arc and was then still. The other on his back tried to sit up then fell back with bent knees and rocked slowly in pain. The vehicles stopped at the entrance and men stunned by the unexpected explosion jumped out but hardly daring to move lest they too trod on a mine stood close by. She had seen enough, it was time to go just in case they thought to search the surrounding area.

She made her way back to where she had left the cattle softly humming to herself. The night's work though extremely chancy had paid dividends and the enormous risks she had taken were completely vindicated. The bonus was that she had witnessed the results of those labours and tasted the pleasure of vengeance at the actual point of retribution. Part of the sentence had been carried out and she hoped that one or both of the victims were the actual guilty swine that had raped her. Perhaps it was that neither of those victims had anything to do with it but she felt no qualms about that at all. They were Iranians and the guilt as far as she was concerned was collective and so therefore was the punishment. When will the hatred be finally satisfied she asked herself? When they are either all dead or gone was the resolute reply.

Those pigs would be horrified that a mine had been placed right inside their protected compound and beneath their very noses. However, to rattle them further then the pressure should be kept up. But her arsenal was now depleted down to a single hand grenade. So there was no time to be lost and tomorrow she would go again to that cave in Wadi Aydaas. Perhaps by now it would have been re-stocked in which case she might even obtain some bullets for the Kalachnikov as well as more mines and grenades.

~ 24 ~

July 1974 • Despite her resolve to keep up the pressure on the Iranians things didn't work out the way Lailla had hoped. Soon after her successful attack she had gone again to the cave in Wadi Aydaas and had been disappointed to see that it had not been re-supplied. In fact the situation was the opposite, it had been very much depleted. Only a small supply of grenades remained. Although it was the mines that were more attractive to her she stole another two grenades anyway. Frequent subsequent visits since had brought only the same disappointment. It seemed that the arms cache was now hidden elsewhere. She knew of nowhere else to look so without alternative she had continued as a routine to keep checking just in case.

Many weeks had passed and the obvious signs of the approaching new Khareef hung over the jebal. The clouds were gathering and as they thickened they got a little lower each day. Some days it seemed they hung so low across the high *gatn* that they were little more than just above head height. The moisture trapped in the slowly churning clouds added the slightest hint of spray on the wind's breath. Soon the peaks would be shrouded and the mist would roll down to the lower reaches bringing with it the persistent drizzle that would eventually become hard rain. Hidden in this mantle where visibility would often be as little as three or four metres even in the brightest part of the day the opportunity to strike at Iranians was golden. But without the means Lailla was powerless and she feared that the opportunity would be lost.

To add to that frustration the Iranians were slowly being relieved by the Omani Army one post at a time. Where the foreign soldiers were disappearing to she knew not but she considered that they still owed a big price and her irritation was enormous. Time had laid a dampening blanket over her wild anger and it had faded from an all consuming obsession to a more reasoned calculated hate. The events of that day and the over-powering humiliation that she had been subjected to still burned across her mind in every detail like a persistent re-occurring horror. However, much of her rage along with the momentum of her private war had faded. Nevertheless, she was determined that before they disappeared completely more payment would be made for her degradation, somehow.

But time was running out and the posts that the Iranians now manned had whittled down to just three. Two on the *gatn* and the other on the high flat plateau at the extreme northern end of the mountain road. The position of this last one was strategically significant, situated as it was high above the narrow gorge that was the pass from the mountains to the barren *nejd*. From its position it completely dominated the road that snaked along the base between towering sheer sided walls.

However, it was not impregnable and the posts on the *gatn* were far too exposed, so Lailla had marked this one as the easier target of the three. To its front it towered resolute above the pass and the *nejd*. But at its rear the approach was across gently rolling hills and it was only where it climbed two hundred metres steeply onto the plateau itself that presented difficulties. The network of gullies that interlaced the hills behind and presented better cover along which to approach and escape after a strike singled it out as the easier objective.

Anxious to hit before they withdrew completely she considered what she might achieve with what she actually had, three grenades. To actually toss them and run was not an option, she would undoubtedly be caught. That left booby traps as the only option. But her problem was how too accomplish that? The inner compound out of sight on the plateau was well guarded and protected the Iranian soldiers inside. The previous trap where she had fastened the release pin of a grenade to the barrier seemed to have worked but there was no opportunity to repeat that here. A narrow track had been cut climbing steeply up the side of the hill and the entrance into the fortified camp was at the very top. The top was a veritable fortress with the barrier entrance heavily manned and well illuminated. To scale the hill at a different point was not an option either. The upper edge of the plateau was completely ringed by sangars and it would be suicidal to attempt any breach there. The only possibility that she could think of at this time was trip wires on that hillside track. If she could rig the grenades so that passing vehicles pulled the release pin that might cause an explosion. However, it was more than likely that by the time the delay period expired then the vehicle would be clear of the explosion anyway. Unless there was a convoy of sorts in which case the lead vehicle might trigger the grenade and a vehicle following a few seconds behind could pay the penalty. She was not entirely happy with that scheme, it relied on too many eventualities. But she was desperate to achieve something and so she was forced to consider ways to develop the plan.

Three weeks later in the early evening and the Qara very definitely in the grip of the new Khareef Lailla walked away from the farm. This time she made no attempt to leave in secret; she did not any longer see the point. Another visit to the cave in Aydaas had revealed yet another disappointment and she had accepted now that for whatever reason that particular arms cache would not be re-supplied. In all probability this would be her last opportunity to kill Iranians and she would deal with the consequences of her night's absence upon her return. She knew that Khamisa believed that when she sneaked away at nights that it was a boy she went to meet. She had said as much weeks ago and warned her of the possible consequences. Lailla had not denied it because she preferred her to believe that rather than confess that it was killing she was about. If she did she would then have to reveal the reason why. But for tonight she had a plan and with the cover of the rolling mist thickening the darkness and with the addition of a little luck this last strike might have gratifying results. In her pockets she carried the three grenades and a length of string while in her hand she carried three short pieces of barbed wire. That was all she would need to set the booby trap that she had in mind.

It was a long walk from the farm to the village on the northern edge of the *gatn*, Qairoon Hairatti. The night's rain and cold clammy fog did nothing to make it pleasant. Soaked to the skin and her teeth chattering with cold she thought enviously of the warm and dry alternative that she had left behind. But her grim determination coupled with the knowledge that this was in all probability the last sortie, made her continue. Her feet were cold and numb soaked by the wet emerging new grass. The legs of the trousers she wore were heavy and dragged on her legs as water absorbed to knee height. Across her shoulders the soggy shirt stuck to her back dribbling water to gather around her waist belt. Her hair she had coiled up onto the top of her head and covered it with a tightly wrapped turban. Water dripped from the edge of this soaked turban adding to the rivulets that ran down her face. She hoped that the results of tonight's strike would be worth all this discomfort.

She angled much more northerly than normal and it took three hours before she came to the jebal road. When she did she could not identify her position, but she knew that she had to turn north along the road and follow it until she came to the pass. After a short walk, a thick clump of tall Zakir trees emerged from the mist and she recognised the landmark as the Hagif road junction just outside Qaroon Hairatti. Now she paused, she had to plan her route carefully. She did not want to enter the village – a stranger and a woman at that, walking the jebal on a night like this would be bound to arouse curiosity. To the east was a well-established *askari* post and she didn't want to stumble into that either. To circle west of the village was the obvious alternative, however here too there was the need for caution. If she went too far beyond the village she would stumble into the Iranian outer defences. To protect the plateau fortification from a possible rear attack across the hills they had strung out an outer defensive line. Very soon after clearing Qaroon Hairatti she would need to turn sharply east and in effect move across the front of this line. The blanketing mist although essentially her cover might also be her undoing if she went too far or not far enough. She needed to proceed with a lot of caution.

The best part of an hour later and now north of the village she arrived uneventfully back at the road, which meant that she had successfully circled the village and made it through the gap. She crossed the road to put a little distance between herself and the end of the outer defensive line and looped around its end. Here on the edge of the high ground overlooking the *nejd* the rain was reduced to fine drizzle and the mist was thinner With the visibility improved a little she looked for the rocky wadi that cut a deepening chasm across the landscape and ended abruptly beneath the plateau hill. Its location was made easier by the flares that regularly lit up the area fired off by the nervous Iranians from their fortifications. In the light cast by one of these flares she was able to spot the gorge and trace it right back to the road.

Hidden in its depth she made her way along the bottom of the wadi to its end. Taking a few moments to rest she contemplated the steep climb before her. There were a hundred metres to be climbed before she was out of the wadi itself and with much loose rock and shale it would need to be slow and careful. In the silence of night sound travelled far! After that, immediately to her front was the steep hill that was to be negotiated and another hundred-metre climb to the track. Although the climb was steep she had chosen the spot well. Its very steepness meant that until she actually got onto the track then she was in dead ground and out of sight from the sangars above. The only danger through this stage would be her own carelessness. She needed to be as quiet as a desert fox as she picked her way upward. She guessed that there were still about two hours to midnight and she was well within her time plan so she need not hurry.

Concentrating hard on the ground immediately in front of her and selecting carefully the firmer underfoot places she picked her way upward. Twice during the climb she paused for breath and both times she was pleasantly surprised by the progress that she had made. Arriving just beneath the track quicker than she had expected she stopped to rest and compose herself for the next and more risky stage. While she rested she peered into the gloom along the track edge hoping to see a stout shrub or a rock that would suit her purpose. Unable to find what she had hoped to see she became restless and getting to her feet once more she began making her way along the side of the hill. She was careful to keep hidden from the sangars above by staying beneath the track's lip. Once she had to stop and quickly push herself hard against the rock face when a flare right above her head turned the night to day. She watched helpless as it fizzed high into the sky and then lazily looped to descend in slow motion disappearing somewhere into the rocky wadi directly beneath her. Then the night was plunged once more into darkness seemingly darker than it had been before. Breathing a sigh of relief she once again resumed her slow climb. As she followed the road she was getting steadily higher and the lights at the barrier entrance were beginning to get uncomfortable close. She stopped and stared towards the yellow glow diffused through the misty gloom wondering if she should turn around and try in the lower stretches of the track. But then on the very edge of the track silhouetted by the glow she saw a low stumpy grown shrub that suited her purpose admirably.

She crawled very slowly to the track and allowing only her head and shoulders to show above its lip as she wedged a grenade beneath a heavy rock. Then she tied the string to the release pin and moved along the track playing the string out as she went. After around ten metres she placed a second grenade beneath a rock and after gently tugging the string until all the slack had gone she tied it around that pin also. Then she repeated the operation with the last one and now that she had all three pins fastened to the same piece of string it would take only a sharp tug to pull all three at the same time. Next she twisted the three short pieces of barbed wire together into a rough pyramid shape and fastened the end of the cord to it. Now came the most dangerous part she had to leave cover and crawl fully exposed onto the track itself. She looped the cord around the shrub's trunk to act as a pivot point and then gathering her courage crawled to lay the wire in the middle of the track. She squirmed back quickly after she had planted it. Then she took a just few moments to re-check the trap and consider its merit. In the morning when the vehicles started to come down from behind their secure compound the first driver would grind slowly down the track. He might even see the innocuous piece of wire lying in the road but hopefully would pay it little regard and unconcernedly pass right over it. It was just high enough to become snagged somewhere beneath the vehicle and be dragged along for a little way at least. If it did the string would then tighten around the pivoting shrub's trunk and pull all release pins at the same time. Hopefully the driver would not have cleared the last grenade before it exploded. If it was Allah's will then there will be more than one vehicle involved and those following would be blasted also. Satisfied that it could work she decided to withdraw and to make good her escape. Relieved that the hard part was over she began her descent back into the bottom of the wadi.

This time she didn't stay in the wadi until it petered out at the road, instead she angled across to her right attempting a shortcut. As she increased the distance from the *nejd* the rain became heavier and the fog thicker but this time she didn't mind the conditions so much, each step took her closer to home. Suddenly out of the fog a fence of razor wire barred her way? She stared at it for a moment wondering what had happened, then she concluded that either she had left the wadi much too early or her angle across to find the road had been too acute. Usually supporting such a fence soldiers lurked behind sangars, care was needed here. Making a quick about turn she retreated away from the wire. When the wire was out of sight she angled back to her left. After only a few paces she was once again confronted by the razor wire. Now beginning to panic a little she retreated quickly once more. This time, when she was clear she tried to think rationally and she decided to retrace her steps back to the wadi and start again. However, after walking for longer than she expected in the direction where she thought the wadi was she still hadn't found it and consternation was growing. A distant flare lit the sky above but to her complete surprise it was in almost the opposite direction that she would have expected. Could she be that disorientated in the fog? She supposed that she must be! Dubiously she accepted it as a marker and she re-adjusted her direction. A few more minutes and she knew that wasn't right either. Although she could see little beyond six or seven metres she knew instinctively that she was in a valley between steep hills and when she was again confronted by barbed wire she knew that she was hopelessly lost and in deep trouble. Again she questioned the marker and realised that the flare might have been from the outer defence line.

Even as she thought about it another flare fizzed into the sky almost directly above her head. In the instant it lit the area she could see that she was indeed in a narrow 'U' shaped valley with steep hills all around her The wire fence in front of her coiled around the bottom of the hills following the contours. In almost the same instant she noticed the rock built sangars along the top edges. She was completely surrounded! Desperately she looked around for somewhere to hide but it was too late a burst of machine gun fire split the night's silence and ran a row of tiny eruptions along the ground in front of her. Her assailants kept the sky lit with a succession of flares while the slightest movement from her prompted another burst from the machine gun. She was caught.

Well covered from above by all the men in the sangars eight armed men approached her. Surrounded by pointing rifles she stared silently at the hostile faces. One man spoke harshly to her but she didn't know what it was that he had said. This seemed to infuriate him and he shouted the instruction again. Laillia just shook her head bewildered. The man closest grabbed her arm roughly and put her hand on her head. Now she realised what it was that they wanted her to do and she stood there meekly with her hands on her head. That man now began to search her and when he patted her chest her hesitated taking a moment to confirm his suspicion then withdrew his hands is if they had been burned. He muttered something to the others then pulled the turban from her head releasing her long hair to tumble onto her shoulders. There was a gasp of surprise as they now realised that she was a woman.

With a man either side holding her upper arms roughly she was half dragged, half frog-marched up the hill towards the sangars. At the top she was pushed forward to jump down into a narrow trench and then with a man in front and another behind she was led along the trench which meandered along the hill crest. The trench proved to be a means of moving between sangars while keeping under cover. She passed through several heftily constructed sangars receiving bland and curious stares from the men that manned them. Eventually she was told to stop and while an armed guard stood nearby she was made to sit in the trench bottom with her hands and feet bound.

Her situation was dour she knew and she could see no way out. Her only chance it seemed was to lie but she struggled to put together a believable story. How would she account her presence wandering about among an Iranian security position in the early hours of the morning in such foul weather? And if her booby trap was sprung in the next few hours then even a plausible lie would become completely unbelievable. In total contradiction to her night's effort she now hoped that her trap did not work. Her future looked dejectingly bleak, in addition sitting in mud made sloppy by busy feet she was wet, cold and dispirited. Even so despite her situation the exertion of her night's toil began to tell, her eyes grew heavy and she surrendered to the overwhelming tiredness.

Someone kicked her foot waking her. She had no idea how long it had been but her neck ached with the angle at which she had slept and her legs tingled with pins and needles. Her feet were untied and she was hauled to her feet and with her legs unable to support her so quickly she was virtually dragged by two men into a covered sangar.

Inside it was small and pokey lit by a battery powered light fastened to a pole in the middle. The air was thick with the stale smell and grey haze of tobacco smoke. A thickset man sat at a foldable table while a smouldering cigarette hanging loosely from his lips added to the foul air. He continued his pre-occupation not even sparing Lailla a glance as she was pushed roughly to the ground by the side of the heavy curtain that acted as a door. When he finished whatever it was that he was reading the thickset man closed the file and placed it to one side. Holding the cigarette carefully he took a long pull before adding it to deep pile of stubs already overfilling a deep tin lid. Now he turned and lowering thick lensed glasses to the end of his nose he peered at Lailla over the top.

"What are you doing here?" he asked in flawless Arabic.

"Your men brought me here," she replied evasive.

He nodded patiently and re-phrased the question. "What were you doing down by the wire?"

"Looking for my goats."

"Looking for goats at this time of the morning," he sneered. "Then why are you dressed like a man?"

"It is better in this weather."

He said something in a language she didn't understand to the two men who stood by waiting. By the amusement it caused she guessed he had said something sarcastic about her replies. "Who are you?" he turned his attention back to her.

"Laila Bint Abdulla."

Her pushed his glasses back to the bridge of his nose, turned to the table and wrote it down. "Tribe?"

"Al Hamer."

"Where are you from?"

Now she had problems. To tell him would reveal how far she had come and no one would come so far without a specific purpose. Neither would goats have wandered that far. To lie and claim that she came from nearby Qaroon was easily verifiable in the morning. "We are Bedu and my father camps not far from here," It seemed plausible.

"And your goats wandered away during the night!" He scoffed.

"Yes."

He took off his glasses and rubbed his eyes tiredly. "How did you know that your goats had wandered off in the night? Are you in the habit of getting up to check every few minutes?"

Lailla nodded and said nothing. The story was weak she knew.

He looked at the other two men and said something. She was dragged roughly to her feet while he replaced his glasses and began once more to read the file. Then he came over to where she was held between the men and stood so close that she could smell his cigarette reeking breath. Using the flat of his hand he measured the top of her head against his chest then stepping back he nodded knowingly. A short conversation then followed before she was again pushed back down to the ground.

"Have you been planting land mines?" he asked directly looking down on her.

"No."

He sat once more and stared silently at the ground. The silence protracted as he continued unmoving seemingly lost in thought. Then still without moving he said quietly. "A woman has been seen several times in the past weeks watching and studying our bases. And after, some of those bases suffered land mine or booby traps attacks." He sighed and looked at her. "You fit the description. I think you are that woman."

Lailla stared back evenly and shook her head slowly. What else could she do?

"You are PFLO aren't you? And you have been planting mines tonight haven't you?"

"No," she denied firmly.

He shook his head and said something angrily to the men. She was roughly hauled to her feet. "You will be moved to our citadel on the plateau where you will be interrogated further," he said. Then after a look of disgust he turned dismissively away from her.

Her feet were bound once more and with the same man guarding her she was made to sit again in the mud in the trench bottom. She had lost track of time completely and she looked from the trench to the darkened sky. It still rained and the mist still drifted slowly across driven by a lazy wind but through it she could see hundreds of stars, dawn was not imminent. If she set off now then she could still be home before her parents woke and they would know nothing of this ordeal. But she wouldn't be setting off for a while if at all and she wondered what they would think when they discovered her absence. What would they say when they found out that she had been killing Iranians? Most certainly they would want to know why. How could she give them a reason? She would be too ashamed. Cold, wet and trussed as a goat awaiting slaughter she lay in mud in the trench bottom feeling absolutely miserable while a bored guard watched indifferently.

The deep muffled thud of an explosion or was it three, in quick succession, caused some excitement in the trench. Men hurried backward and forward stopping sometimes to peer out into the thick fog in a vain attempt to find out what had happened. Lailla knew her trap had been sprung and her fate was sealed. Now they would know what she had been doing in their area.

It took about thirty minutes before word was received of what had happened presumably by radio or perhaps field telephone. But Lailla knew the instant they knew because men gathered around glaring at her menacingly and discussing her in agitated fashion. A rope was looped around the ties that bound her hands and she was hauled to her feet and suspended by her arms with her toes only just touching the ground. One man more irate than the rest pushed her causing her to swing back then as she came forward grabbed her and screamed abuse in at her his face only inches away.

"Rapist," she shouted back defiantly. She didn't recognise him but he was Iranian and to her there was no difference.

Whether he understood or not she had no idea but he drove his fist into her ribs twice, using her like a punch bag before gathering himself to time a full blow into her stomach as she swung gently on the rope to meet it. The air was driven from her body and she had never felt so much pain as her stomach muscles collapsed inwards emptying her lungs. It took a while before the contracted muscles began to relax and allow her lungs to suck badly needed air. It ended the crisis need for air but brought only multiplied griping pain in her stomach.

Vaguely she heard a calm authoritative voice speak and the gathering began reluctantly to saunter away.

However, she wasn't cut down, instead was left hanging rolling her head and grimacing with pain. Eventually the stomach pains did ease but were soon replaced by increasing pain across her upper arms and shoulders as the weight of her entire body hung on those muscles. She tried to ease the weight by standing on toes that just reached the ground but after a short time that was worse. For a while she tried short spells of each but eventually half delirious with agony she hung on arms and shoulders that became torturous lumps. Soon the upper muscles in her chest began to add to her agony and it became difficult to draw a decent breath. To avoid that pain she began to restrict herself to shallow breaths. But later swelling chest muscles began squeezing up her windpipe and even shallow breaths were becoming difficult. She had no idea how long she actually hung there but when somebody eventually cut her down and threw cold water over her through hazed senses see knew it was daylight.

A little while later she was given some water to drink and her legs were untied. The water she needed badly but because of swollen chest and throat muscles it was painful to drink and she could only sip. Then she was hauled to her feet and found that her legs had been re-bound but this time by loose cord that permitted her to take a short shuffled step. In the midst of six armed guards she was lifted from the trench and indicated to follow the two men in front. Doing her best to keep up she half stumbled and half-shuffled after them.

With daylight the rain had eased to drizzle and the fog thinned to a visibility of around a hundred metres. She was on the top of a series of small winding hills with steep sided valleys between and on the edge of visibility was the road. Despondently she realised that last night she must have been walking parallel to it and perhaps less than twenty metres away. The flare had confused her and she had turned right moving away from it and straight into this blind valley below her. Left instead of right and she would have been on the road in a few paces and by now safely at home; such a huge price to pay for a tiny mistake.

She stumbled on over the flat ground towards the high plateau with two guards ahead, two behind and one wide on each flank. Still unable to draw a deep breath because of the lumps of agony in her chest her breathing was laboured and shallow and even at the slow pace they allowed it was an ordeal. Breathless, in pain and thoroughly demoralised she was in no condition to make a running bid to escape even without the restraining ankle ropes. Soon they began to climb the track that led to the plateau and the going for her became tougher. Towards the top she saw the results of her night's work. So successful had it been that there was now a gap in the road making it impassable to vehicles. She glanced down the steep drop as they picked their way across what remained of the track and saw with grim satisfaction the remnants of two vehicles far below in the wadi bottom. Whether they had tumbled down there as a result of the explosions or whether they had been pushed to clear the way she had no way of knowing but by the mangled condition they were in she could guess that some Iranians had made ultimate payment towards the dues.

Though not at all pleased to be on the plateau, she was nevertheless relieved when at last the climb was ended and they arrived on the top. Five guards still surrounded her as they stood waiting for the sixth to make enquiries about where she should be delivered. As she waited she looked around at the activity and was amazed by the remarkable changes. She knew this tabletop well as one of the places where Hamed liked to come to be alone. As a child he had brought her here several times and they had sat on that far edge just gazing into the distance over the vast *nejd*. It was been a remote and lonely place with only the whispering wind to disturb the absolute silence. Now that quiet was shattered. Many pre-fabricated buildings clustered in the centre on an enormous flat concrete area. Beyond that ugly square concrete pillboxes lined the far lip of the plateau and they in turn were defended by coils of concertina razor wire. Vehicles of different shapes and sizes clustered in a car park over to the side while along this near edge a row of rock made sangars were filled with men. The whole site seemed to be a hive of activity as men busied themselves doing whatever it was that they were supposed to be doing.

The guard returned accompanied by a uniformed officer who stared at her hard before barking some instructions to her guards. She was prodded with the butt of a rifle to follow the officer. He stopped at the entrance to a large canvas tent and waited for her to catch up. When she did he seized her savagely by the arm and dragged her inside. Its spacious interior would have been empty but for the five silver body bags spaced out on the ground. Still grasping her arm firmly he spoke over his shoulder to one of the guards who moved over to the first bag and knelt by its side. Slowly he unzipped a corner and folded it back to reveal the impassive wax-like face of a moustached young man.

The officer shook Lailla angrily, making her teeth clatter. "That man has a wife and three children," he said in broken Arabic. Lailla shrank back and stared at the corpse; she had never considered these Iranians would be family men. The officer spoke again to the kneeling man. He unzipped the next bag to reveal the stony face of a mere boy. She was dragged closer to the body to get a better view. "He was little more than eighteen," he growled pushing her closer still and holding her there. Then after he was satisfied that she'd had a good look he pulled her away crudely. "*Adoo* bitch," he spat.

For the first time the enormity of her deeds was driven home, this close-up view of death was not detached; it was personal. Neither of these men had done her harm, it was only her wild frenzy that someone must pay for her degradation that had blinded her to justice. She still held loathing contempt for the rapists and for those who had stood and watched but she had exacted the ultimate payment against the oblivious innocent. How many blameless men had suffered for the offence of the others, she wondered? Had any of the actual guilty been made to pay? She would never know the answers to either of those questions. For the first time she began to feel the pangs of remorse. After that more anguish was piled on as they took her to the clinic where she saw three surviving casualties one of who had lost an arm. All three stared at her silent and expressionless with languid eyes. Lailla said nothing as she was taken away, there was nothing to say. It was far too late to even express regret. She was taken across to the far side of the plateau to one of the concrete pillboxes and without ceremony pushed inside. As she stumbled to the ground in the darkness gently hands helped her to sit up and brushed her mud caked hair back from her face.

"You're alright now," a sympathetic voice said.

The pillbox no more than three metres square and even less in height was built from substantial concrete blocks with a small entrance that turned a sharp corner. The light, such as there was, came from a long narrow slit that ran the complete length of one side. As her eyes became accustomed to the darkness she made out the figure of the young man kneeling at her side. He was around her own age, perhaps slightly older with an untidy black beard and wild unkempt hair.

In the darkness he found the cords that bound her wrists and began untying them. "What is your name?" he asked. "And what have you been doing to end up in here?" he asked after she had told him her name.

"It would seem that I am an *adoo* bitch," she replied

He chuckled and began to gently untie the cords about her ankles. "And are you?"

"No. Not really." Even in her pain and discomfort she found something sensual in the way he caressed her sorely chaffed ankles.

He moved over to the corner and she was immediately sorry that he had stopped. But soon he was back and this time with a tin jug of water. "This is our ration of drinking water," he said pouring a little into a tiny tin cup and offering it to her. He waited until she had finished and them moistened the corner of the shamag that draped loosely around his shoulders. With the dampened end he began washing the mud from her hands and arms. Mystified by his actions and a little mesmerised by his touch she meekly allowed him to do it. As he worked he talked telling her his name was Yaqub of the tribe Gatun from the village of Nahiz. He admitted to being an active member of the PFLO for six years up to the very brink of victory and through on to today where defeat now stared them in the face. He went on to explain his presence in this pillbox that was their cell while he turned his attention to wiping the mud from her face. He had been caught by an Iranian patrol actually laying mines in the jebal road. She relished his hands gently touching her and imagined that this was how it should feel. She imagined that this was how Jumaia and Khamisa felt when touched by their husbands. Too soon he had finished leaving her flesh tingling but feeling deserted and disappointed.

She couldn't prevent a gasp of pain as she moved to rest her back against a wall. He stared at her questioningly without speaking. "They strung me up by my arms for a long time," she answered the unasked question.

He came and sat by her side once more. Where does it hurt?"

"Everywhere," she answered flippantly. "Mostly here," she said rubbing her upper arm. "And here," she indicated her shoulders and neck. "It even hurts my chest to take a deep breath."

He moved behind her and to her secret delight his hands were once more upon her, this time gently massaging her shoulders and arms. 'Tell me how you come to be here, Lailla," he said.

"Because I needed to kill Iranians."

"Did you kill any?"

She nodded. "Yes I did," she said and for the first time with a hint of regret.

"How many?"

"I don't know. More than I should have."

"Why?"

Whether it was his relaxing massaging fingers or some need to confess now that there were regrets she didn't know but this quiet stranger placed a confidence in her and for the first time she related the whole story. At first she was nervous dreading that he might pull away in horror when he learned of her polluted condition. But he didn't he listened quietly sympathetic while all the time his fingers soothed her aching muscles.

He gasped with surprise when she explained about the Commissar star *rabia* symbol because then he realised that she was Mussalim's sister. Then it was her turn to be surprised when he explained that they were comrades and that he was the other survivor from that near fatal artillery shell.

She went on to reveal how she had set traps to kill Iranians and got a gasp of admiration when she revealed how she had penetrated inside the secure area of one outpost.

"Where did you get the mines and grenades," he asked breaking her story and chuckled when she told him. "You stole from the Bait Gatun cache," he declared.

She continued her story while all the time his soothing hands wore away the aches and pain leaving only the sensual pleasure of his touch. Under his gentle massaging she drifted pleasantly into a state of relaxed drowsiness. It had been a long and eventful night and feeling completely secure in his arms she fell asleep. It was very much later when she woke afraid that she was alone, but as she stirred to a sitting position he was re-assuringly at her side.

"How long did I sleep?"

"Nearly all day! Come," he said taking her hand and leading her to peer out from the firing slit. "Isn't that beautiful?"

From their position high above the pass they commanded a spectacular view across of the *nejd*. The sun had sunk onto the horizon with the resplendent glow of burnished gold. Scattered clouds hanging thinly above reflecting a myriad of reds and oranges while the sharply peaked hills cast long dark shadows across the barren landscape. Closer in drifts of mist edged pink by the strange light settled into the wadis and gullies like blankets of cotton wool. Lailla had seen many sunsets but the awesome beauty of this one seemed like none that she had ever seen before and she was glad that she shared it with this particular man. She looped her arms around his affectionately and held it tightly against her while they silently absorbed nature's sensational splendour.

The sun had sunk from sight when the guards brought food. From large containers they ladled a pile of rice onto tin plates and then poured a curry of sorts over the top. They ripped off chunks of bread from a large loaf and abruptly left.

"What will happen to us, Lailla asked as they settled down to eat.

Yaqub shrugged and pulled a face. "They will probably hand us over to the military authorities in Salalah."

"When?"

"Soon. Tomorrow probably."

"And then?"

"Then interrogation and I suppose after that we will be sent for trial. Then after a short pause he said gently. "I expect there will be time in prison. But don't worry," he added re-assuring. "You tell your story just as you told me and you ought to get leniency. Maybe two years, perhaps less."

Two years? The thought appalled her. How would she be able to survive two years in prison?

"It won't be so bad," he said reading her thoughts. "You can get used to almost anything and two years will soon pass."

"What about you?"

"Longer. Much longer."

"If I am out in two years, then I will come and visit you every week."

"I would like that," he said softly.

After the sun had gone the light very quickly followed and the temperature dropped rapidly. With the cold came the damp and with nothing else to do they huddled together in the darkness for warmth and talked. He encouraged her to tell him more about herself and Lailla began filling in some of her background. She told him of her family the farm and how they survived. She mentioned her absent brothers and how that affected the role that she had been forced to play. She talked of her dead mother Kathya and Juma her dead brother. She told of Khamisa's unhappiness and how her father had secured her future by marrying her to Hamed. She chattered about Mussalim and Jumaia's shared happiness and her own fear for their future. She mentioned a host of trivia that she suspected that he could not possibly be interested in but she didn't want to stop because it kept her mind from brooding about their uncertain future. Eventually she did stop and wanted him to tell her all about himself.

He began by describing his green and spectacular wadi, Nahiz where he was born and lived. Of a happy boyhood he had spent within its fertile ranges. It was only when he grew older, he said, that he had started to become discontent and started to demand that the wealth that the Sultan set aside for his own comfort was distributed more fairly among the people. He told how he had embraced the communist cause as a means to that end. He related some of his escapades while fighting for that cause and admitted that even though he now probably faced a long prison sentence he did not regret being part of the Front. He enthused over the qualities of her brother 'Crazy Man Mussalim' and the fervour he had put into the fight.

With his arm around her and her head on his chest she felt secure and warm as she listened silently to his soothing voice. She believed that at long last she had found what she had craved, a man who she could easily learn to love. She hardly dared hope that he could feel the same, but his every kindness every gentle gesture suggested that he might. The anger and hostility of the world outside no longer mattered here and now was all there was and all that mattered. His quiet voice had a sedating effect and as her eyelids grew gradually heavier she slipped into a contented sleep.

It was so much later in the night when he woke her and came to her in urgency. At first alarmed and confused she stiffened as memories of her previous ordeal swamped her mind causing a brief moment of panic. But his soft voice and gentle touch calmed her fears and even though she was not his wife she did not reject him. For tonight only they would be together and there would be many years before they could share another such moment. She gave herself to him and discovered that to give pleasure unselfishly returned ecstasy in bountiful dividends. She knew now how it should be between a man and his woman.

The sun had just risen when the guards came for them. They bound their hands behind their backs and tethered their legs with loose cord so that they could take only short steps. Despite the ordeal to be faced Lailla was not afraid, she had the strength of Yaqub's love with her and she need fear no one. Even the probability of prolonged separation did nothing to daunt her spirit. They had promised to wait for each other and for as long as it took they would wait. One day for it was Allah's will she was sure, they would eventually be together. One of the guards indicated that they should move outside. They shuffled out into the early morning sun and waited somewhat bemused for the next instructions. Outside eight armed guards leaned apathetically on the side of a Land Rover waiting for someone in authority to bring some organisation to the procedures

Lailla surrendering to an impulse to touch Yaqub leaned backward onto him. She tingled with pleasure at the feel of his chest in her back and his breath on the top of her head. Once again they looked out over the awe-inspiring *nejd* but this time in all the glory of sunrise.

Someone was barking instructions and as she glanced back to look her heart took a jolt as she recognised the sergeant taking control of the actions. He was the same one who had led her multiple rape.

Yaqub felt her stiffen. "What is it?" he asked.

"He is the one," she said staring at the man wide-eyed and afraid.

"Courage," he said as someone took them by the arm and led them around to the other side of the pillbox. "He can't hurt you now."

The sergeant stared at her and recognition dawned in his eyes. He sauntered slowly across as the armed guard behind him began to assemble themselves into the semblance of a line. Staring hard into her face he leaned close and said something in derisive manner then made a crude gesture with his hands. She shrank back away from him but as his face started to split to a grin Yaqub leapt at him butting him in the face. With a curse he staggered back and two men jumped forward to restrain Yaqub. Then a short and furious argument broke out among the Iranians before the prisoners were stood back against concrete wall of the pillbox.

"Lailla," Yaqub said quietly. "Look at me and don't take your eyes off me."

Confused she glanced around. The soldiers were now lined across their front facing them and in an instant she realised what was about to take place. "No. No, not now," she cried. It could not be so. It was so unfair, just when she had found the perfect mate.

"Lailla," Yaqub said again.

With eyes filled with tears she looked beyond the soldiers towards her beloved Qara but shrouded in thick grey Khareef mist the view of its peaks were denied to her. Everything it seemed was denied to her including the normal happiness that every woman has a right to expect.

The sergeant gave the order and the line of soldiers raised their rifles.

"Lailla look at me," Yaqub demanded firmly. She looked into his dark eyes and he nodded slightly with satisfaction and he even managed a slight re-assuring smile.

She felt as if she had been kicked in the chest by an angry camel. She staggered back against the wall behind her and then fell forward onto Yaqub's still body. Her body demanded air but without lungs to suck she could not supply it. The pain increased as her body now screamed for air. She opened her mouth wide hoping that air would somehow find a way inside. Writhing, as the agony became unbearable she tried to call to Yaqub but could make no sound. In front of her eyes she saw the muzzle of a hand pistol and just for the merest flicker of an instant she felt a thud in her forehead.

✳ ✳ ✳

This was the sixth day Lailla had been missing and Abdulla sitting alone in the shelter of the veranda felt absolutely helpless. The first day she was missing Jokha and Khamisa had searched the nearby wadis. But with Jokha old and Khamisa eight months pregnant he guessed that the search could not have been very thorough. He knew that his own near-sightedness would have proved a further hindrance to the two women so he stayed home and waited with increasing frustration. On the second day his concern was growing and it was then that Khamisa had tried to ease his fears by revealing that Lailla had been in the habit of slipping away into the night after dark. Probably to meet a boy she speculated. This did not ease his mind instead it sent him into a fit of rage that she would do such a shameful thing and his anger became directed at Khamisa for not reporting it to him.

The next day he had saddled two camels and guided by Jokha had gone to the village Haluf to seek his brother's help. Fiad still lived the ways of the old ones roaming the *nejd* and Empty Quarter stealing livestock from other tribes. But he had found him home and Fiad had gathered his group together and the next day they set off to search while Abdulla had returned home to wait.

For two days now he had sat on under this veranda listening to the rain water drip off the corrugated sheets and staring hazy-eyed into the swirling mist. Fiad and his friends were skilled in the ways of the Bedu and they would find this boy if he indeed existed. If not and some injury or something prevented Lailla from returning they would still find her. Dead or alive. He wasn't sure which he preferred. If she had taken up with some boy out of wedlock then his shame would be enormous and he would be faced with no alternative but to save face and disown her or worse. If she were lying injured then by now her suffering would be great but to him it was marginally preferable.

The camel in his pen sensed the approach of another beast and bellowed a greeting long before it emerged from the mist. Abdulla sat forward and stared hard but he could see only the vague shape against a darker grey background of grey mist as the rider drew closer. He called to Jokha inside the house and she came instantly.

"It's Fiad," she informed him

"Is he alone?"

'Yes."

"What news brother?"

He didn't reply instead he brought his camel close to the house and guided it to his knees. He didn't look in their direction as he slowly and deliberately dismounted. "The news is bad," he said eventually then approached the house. He dragged a battered cane chair over to Abdulla and sat by his side. He placed his hand on his brother's shoulder and after a glance at Jokha he revealed the news. "Lailla Bint Abdulla Al Hamer along with Yaqub Bait Gatun was shot by the government forces six days ago."

"Oh no," Jokha gasped.

"It is said they were enemies of the state," he went on

"Enemy of the state?" Abdulla queried incredulously.

"It is claimed that they were active members of the PFLO."

"Ridiculous."

"It seems there was irrefutable proof," Fiad went on.

"What does Lailla care who should have materialistic wealth and who shouldn't? That has never interested her at all. So why would she be a member of the PFLO?"

"I don't know," Fiad said meekly taking his hand from Abdulla's shoulder.

"It was that boy," the thought occurred to Abdulla. "She sneaked away at nights to be with him and it would have been he who involved her in that nonsense. May he rot in hell," he spat venomously. "She has paid the price that all the deceitful pay." He gritted his teeth, set his jaw and stared out silently angry into the mist.

"Allah have mercy," Jokha sobbed as she retreated to cry in the privacy of the house.

Long after Fiad had left, Abdulla still sat there staring sightless into the gathering gloom of evening. He was angry but he didn't know precisely where his anger should be directed. Should he be angry with Lailla for her deceit? Or should he be angry with that unknown man who had obviously influenced an inexperienced girl to follow him into disaster. Should he be angry with the soldiers who it seemed had acted extremely heavy-handedly and without sufficient enquiry into the circumstances. But mostly he blamed himself for his pathetic inadequacies. Had it not been for his failing sight then he would have taken a more active part in the day to day running of the farm and he would have been much more alert to the circumstances. Wherever he directed his anger he recognised that it would not help the desperate situation in which he now found himself.

He heard all the time about the improving conditions on the jebal but none of it seemed to be effecting his circumstances in fact it seemed as if the opposite were true. The jebal road outposts were rapidly being turned into permanent fortresses. Large concrete bases were laid and surrounded by sturdy walls four metres high with castellated upper edges. Circular squat watchtowers protected each corner of these mini forts. The main objective of these forts was to ensure the continued security of the road but it was the popular additional benefits that civil development brought that would ensure these fortifications would stay. Inside the precincts there was not only billeting for the soldiers manning the forts there were also clinics and schoolrooms and even a shop for the locals to use. This string of forts not only provided security and brought stability to the area they became posts more akin to community centres. For the first time the jebally farmer had protection and medical cover for his family. He had schooling opportunities for his children and a shop where he could trade essential food items without the long trek to Salalah. The conditions and prospects for the mountain people were improving rapidly. But not it seemed for Abdulla, his prospects looked bleak.

While he could undoubtedly make himself useful achieving minor chores he was physically incapable of running the farm, he accepted that. Jokha was old and mostly committed to his welfare while Khamisa besides being about to have another child was only a fisherman's daughter and knew little about farming. With Hamed and Mussalim away pursuing their own madness a lot had rested on Lailla's young shoulders. Now she like Juma and Kathya was gone too. He could not see how he could continue to sustain a living from the farm and he feared that the time was very near when he would be forced to give up.

The livestock he could sell and with the rapidly rising price of cattle he could anticipate a decent price for the few head he had left. However, they could never be replaced because the continued upward price would spiral beyond his reach and his funds would dwindle the opposite way. He could see little alternative however and at least the revenue would sustain them for a while. But what about after that? The choice was either Salalah or back to the tribal village Haluf. In either case the burden of family support would fall on Hamed because he accepted that Mussalim could never return. The choice would have to be Haluf, at least there they would be able to keep the goats and that would help a little. But Haluf was from where he had started so many years ago and after a lifetime of hard work he would be right back at the beginning but this time without the strength of his youth. His life's work amounted to nothing.

~ 25 ~

December 1974 • The fish had bit well this evening but as the tide turned the fish had gone with it. Still the catch in Mussalim's basket numbered more than two dozen good-sized bream. He was thankful that he had learned the skill well from the fishermen during the time he had spent in Dalkut six long years ago. Because the deliveries of essential food supplies had become very slow to arrive, fish had become the mainstay of their diet through these past months. From what he had learned from those fishermen he had recognised the potential of this spot right away. The tide running into the bay at Raykut carried masses of plankton right into the cliff face. Trapped beneath the lea of the cliff it could only bounce and rebound on the rock wall until the tide turned and began sucking it away. The fish following found a feast of plenty just ebbing and flowing but going nowhere and could gorge themselves without effort. Mussalim found a shelf on the cliff face just above high tide mark and with nothing more than a hand line and a piece of red cloth for bait hauled in fish. The waters were clear and from his position he could see the shoals. It took only a swing, a good cast right into their midst and then to reel back in. Hungry fish attracted by the bright coloured rag fought each other to bite.

Now that the fish had gone there was little point in continuing. He wore an old *futa* pulled from the back between his legs to form pantaloons. He loosed that piece to form the traditional long skirt and gathered in his line.

Rivulets of sweat ran down his bare chest and the taste of sea salt was thick on his lips. As he dropped the line in the basket he glanced towards the river that split the bay. Though shallow and little more than knee deep it was nevertheless fresh water and it looked inviting. He picked up the basket and decided that he would yield to its invite and wash the salt and sweat from his body as he made his way home.

Although the catch was good he knew that Jumaia would not be particularly overjoyed to receive it. A continuous diet of fish soon becomes boring and dulls the appetite. Without spices or any other ingredients to add variation then what she could invent was limited. The essential supplies of food items that were supposed to be delivered into Raykut had become more and more infrequent and when they did arrive then the amount delivered had become less. The crisis had become so acute that the food when it was received was rationed and supplied to PFLO members only. There was no surplus for member's families nor for any comfort women. Consequently supplementing sources needed to be found and the bountiful fish supply was an obvious alternative.

Raykut was still considered to be the 'capital of the liberated area' by the PFLO even though there were less than a hundred men stationed here. That was a dwindling number too as men bored with inactivity or through simple hunger left for destinations unknown. Since most of them disappeared during the hours of darkness Mussalim suspected that most were probably deserting back to a previous life. Nor could he find it in his heart to blame them the momentum behind the party manifesto had come to a halt and the war seemed as if it were simply fading away. Even the Central Committee seemed to have slipped into apathy and offered little motivation. The Front had been without a recognised leader since the early part of the year when Zahir Ali had gone to Beirut for special training and there had been no deputy appointed. The Committee's vague policy of 'freedom of action devolved to regional leaders' simply meant that scattered isolated groups were left to their own devices. There was no longer any recognisable co-ordination or any clear objectives.

Mussalim had also been gripped by this apathy. He and Ali had throughout the spring and summer roamed the area unproductively recruiting. There had been little interest in joining a movement that was clearly on the verge of defeat. Thirty Omani Rials per month was the going rate and that didn't compere with the fifty that could be had by joining the Firqats. So for less money and with a probability of eventual defeat and all the consequences that brought there was no incentive for young men to join. Only the men who were too old to join the Firqats showed any interest and their motivation was based entirely on money. Because these men were not only too old to fight but would also be a liability then Mussalim had rejected almost all. Eventually discouraged and without any encouragement from anywhere Mussalim virtually gave up. Occasionally he and Ali would go out to at least demonstrate some resemblance of performing their duty but even these trips were getting less frequent.

Now as he made his way across the bay in these idyllic pastoral surroundings he pondered the possible outcome of the war. Perhaps everyone would become tired of fighting and gradually it would just peter out. If that happened then perhaps he would be left alone to eke out a living here in this village. Then maybe after a while he might be able to return to the family farm. He snorted derisively to himself because of his fanciful thinking. War was still being fought around the edges of this area. Cross border shelling from Hauf was directed almost daily against Sarfait and it couldn't be too long before the Sultan was forced to do something about it. Probing sorties were made constantly by the government soldiers along the northern edges of Sayq and Altim. Attempts to discourage these probes were made by the means of ambushes but still they came with increasing regularity. Sooner or later those probes would become a major offensive. He knew this stand off was only temporary and as soon as the government forces felt themselves strong enough they would come.

In the Eastern and Central part of Dhofar the PFLO had been effectively strangled and only isolated pockets of guerrillas remained. Even these were rendered almost ineffective by the Front's inability to keep them supplied with weapons. The effect of the Hornbeam line was to divert arms shipments much further to the north into the *nejd*. Even then there was still a gauntlet to be run. Government posts commanding the high ground above the desert at Ayon, Hagiff, Qaroon, Zeak and Jibjat commanded excellent vantage points with panoramic views from which to watch. Large caravans coming in towards the mountains across the exposed desert could be spotted. Consequently shipments were restricted to five or six camels approaching under the cover of darkness attempting to sneak between these post's, usually between Zeak and Jibjat where the gap was biggest. Even so things would be very much settled and peaceful back there, he imagined. Perhaps it had been a mistake to bring his family here after all. From a purely selfish attitude it was nice to have his wife and boys close by but the severe food restrictions and the certain knowledge that one day the government forces would arrive with guns blazing placed them in dire circumstances.

He laid his basket on the ground and waded into the cool river. Sucked by the retreating tide the river's water tugged at his legs and lower part of the *futa*. When he reached the middle he sat and began splashing the salt from his upper body then he ducked his head beneath the surface to do the same for his hair. Seduced by its cooling effects he indulged himself stretching out to enjoy the feel of the water flowing over his body as it hurried seawards. His thoughts returned once more Jumaia and his family.

He knew that he ought to overcome his own selfishness and find a way of returning them back to the comfort and security of his father's farm. But unless he risked all by taking them himself them he couldn't see how he was going to achieve it. He smiled to himself as he imagined Hamed's irritation when he was once again burdened with looking after his family. But now with a wife of his own perhaps he had mellowed a little and maybe had become a little more tolerant. It was early December and was a year since they had left and as things never stay the same then it might be that Hamed had a son of his own by now. Now that was a thought! He chuckled to himself as he imagined his surly brother as a doting father.

"Something amusing?" He looked round to see Ali sitting on the riverbank by the side of his basket. "Good catch," he said prodding around in it.

"Not bad," Mussalim agreed getting to his feet and allowing the water to drain off his body before wading across to where he sat. "Take a couple of big ones for yourself."

Ali nodded briefly a little unenthusiastically.

Mussalim studied him, he seemed more withdrawn these days and very unenthusiastic about everything. It seemed as if he had been greatly affected by the present lack of direction within the cause and the boredom of inactivity had blunted his spirit completely. He wondered if he should suggest that tomorrow they go out recruiting. That might break the tedium a little. But then the disappointing results that they would almost certainly achieve might add to his malaise.

"Have you heard the news that came in this afternoon?" He asked.

"No."

"It seems that soon after his return from Beirut Zahir Ali managed to get himself shot."

"How do you know this?"

"Radio message from Hauf."

"What happened?"

He shrugged vaguely. "It seems as if he was in a vehicle at Rustaq with four others and it was stopped by the soldiers. Gunfire was exchanged and Zahir Ali was killed. All the others escaped. So it seems we will still have no leader."

Mussalim was puzzled? Rustaq was in the Muscat area far away in the northern part of the country. "What was he doing at Rustaq?"

"Who knows? Who knows anything any more? Why did he go to Beirut?"

"He was in special training with the Palestine Popular Front."

"Lot of good that did him," Ali said sarcastically. They fell silent for a few moments then Ali said. "I won't be needing your fish." Mussalim glanced sideways at him and waited for him to go on. "It's over and I'm leaving tonight," he added. "I'll be sorry to leave you stuck here but this fight means nothing to me anymore. It's time I got on with other things."

"Like what?"

"Like putting a family together like the one you have for a start. I envy your happiness and I want to experience something like that for myself."

As a Commissar Mussalim knew that he should stop him from leaving but as a friend he knew that it was the right thing to do. To stay would only mean death or imprisonment or at the very least exile. "Where will you go?"

He sighed heavily. "I don't know. I could go back Hagif where I lived before. But I am well known there, everybody knows that I left to fight for the PFLOAG. But now there's an established military post there and someone might report my return to the soldiers. If that happened almost certainly I would be arrested. Even if no one gave me away then I would be uneasy all of the time just waiting for the soldiers to come." He shook his head dubiously. "It will be better if I go somewhere else."

"What about Haluf?" Mussalim suggested the traditional Al Hamer tribal village.

Ali shook his head. "There is nothing in Haluf for me. Perhaps I'll go to Hayla, the village of my grandfather. That's much further into the *nejd* and well out of the way of any interest to the soldiers."

"When will you go?"

"Later tonight."

Mussalim was silently thoughtful. "Ali," he said after a while. "I want you to do something for me."

"What is it?"

"This is no place for Jumaia and the two boys. Food is scarce here and one day soon the soldiers will come." He glanced round the picturesque bay. "There is no doubt that this place is beautiful but there is a better and a safer place for them than this. I want you to deliver them to my father's farm."

"You would deprive yourself even of that happiness?"

Mussalim nodded. "I must."

"Even though you might never see them again?"

"Yes."

"Come with us," he urged.

"And face a firing squad?"

They were silent again and then Ali said. "I will do it. I will deliver them safely to your father and from time to time I will visit just to make sure they want for nothing. And one day if it is Allah's will then you will be together again."

It was in fact the next morning before the sun had actually risen when the small procession of three camels left. Ali was on one camel with the eldest boy Salim and Jumaia on another with Taimul. The third carried their meagre belongings, but among those belonging Jumaia would eventually find a thick wad of money that he had secretly put in there. Reluctant to let them go easily Mussalim accompanied them a little way. Just outside the village the road split in two opposite directions, one to climb the steep hill to the west while the other scaled the hill to the east. At the top of the eastern hill they made their goodbyes and Mussalim sat gloomily staring after them long after they had disappeared from sight among the twisting hills and thick *ghaf.* He wondered if he would actually be able to keep the promise that he had made to Jumaia last night that one day when the war was over he would come for her whatever the circumstances were. Jumaia was a dutiful wife and despite pleading to be allowed to stay with him she would do precisely what her husband instructed. She would go to the farm and she would wait there until he came no matter how long it took. Secretly he feared that he might never see them again and he felt almost bereaved. But Ali was a good and faithful friend and he knew that he could rely on him completely to look after them.

Two days later he knew that the sacrifice that he had made was the correct decision when the rumble of heavy guns was heard in the north. It seemed that the soldiers were coming. The guns rumbled and boomed right through the morning and fell silent around midday. In the evening the news began to filter through of a great PFLO victory.

It seemed that Iranian troops had massed at Deefa and the PFLO forces anticipating an attack on the supply caves at Kharfat had taken position in the mountains above the open *gatn.* As the Iranians advanced towards the mountains they were caught in open and pinned down. In the cover of the trees the PFLO were able to move their positions easily to create different attacking angles spreading alarm and confusion among the forces below. Eventually the rout was completed when through confusion or indiscipline some troops withdrew while others stayed. Then PFLO fighters came down from their positions flanking the remaining troops and inflicted heavy casualties almost unopposed.

News of this badly needed victory was received joyously rekindling hopes that perhaps all was not yet lost and the end result may not after all be a forgone conclusion. In Raykut existing food supplies were pooled to create a feast of sorts and dancing and singing went on into the night. At the end of the celebrations Mussalim went home to the house that he had shared with Jumaia. He was struck instantly by its awful echoing emptiness. Where there had been laughter there was only silence and where there had been love there was now nothing. His buoyant spirits were immediately deflated.

✳ ✳ ✳

Ali was in no hurry and Jumaia was pleased about that, with two small children regular stops were very necessary. Because of the Hornbeam Line he was forced to take the coastal route and that too was agreeable. Not only was the azure coloured sea delightful but more importantly its cooling breeze kept the temperature at a comfortable level. Before dark they had reached the pass at Wadi Afel but instead of descending into its deep bottom Ali decided to stop for the night on the cliff tops. He found a large shallow cave that would provide some shelter against the plummeting December night temperatures and lit a fire just inside its entrance. They ate dried fish wrapped in flat dough cakes and watched the sun set below the sea's horizon. They talked about Mussalim and the predicament that he was in. "I am sure," Ali had said, "that he would be here with us at this moment if he could." Jumaia knew that what he said was true but at this time she could see no way that he could alter his situation. She feared that eventually she would lose him and so while she still could, she wanted to be at his side. But he had ordered her away to a safer place and for the children's sake she knew that it was the right decision. However, from a purely selfish point of view she feared that she might have already lost him and that it was sooner than she needed to.

The next morning they descended the winding road into the pass and climbed the steep banks on the other side. From there the camels plodded along the cliff tops at the same monotonous but relentless pace until they arrived at the steep descent into Mugsahyl Bay. Mugsahyl was the coast end of the Hornbeam Line and there was a heavily armed checkpoint here. At the bottom of the cliffs they were directed towards the beach and into a compound with other travellers to wait their turn to go forward to be searched.

Ali did not immediately join the queue, instead he tethered the animals a little aside to the others. Then he led the way over the rocks to show the children the fascinating 'blow holes.' Beneath the expanse of large flat rock on which they stood was a honeycomb of caverns all below sea level. When the tide pushed in and drove the waters against the rock it compressed the water that already filled these caves and forced it under pressure through holes in the cave roofs. This produced instant fountains all over the top surface of the rock. The two boys now aged eight and two, shrieked with laughter as they ran through the fountains trying to dodge the sprays.

Jumaia watched with amusement and wished Mussalim could be here to see this. She watched the older boy Salim as he peered tentatively into one of the holes watching for the water to gush up. He was very much a son to them both but she supposed that one day he would have to be told that Mussalim was not his biological father, nor she his mother.

A man travelling with a woman and two children do not attract very many question's the assumptions that are made are obvious. Although the packs on their camels were searched they themselves provoked very little interest and they were passed through the checkpoint fairly quickly. It was now mid-afternoon and there was no chance that they could arrive at Salalah before nightfall. So Ali decided to stay the night on the silver sands of the long bay. As he slept away what remained of the afternoon Jumaia stood knee deep in the breakers still wearing her long *abeya* and watchfully supervised the children as they played in the waves. She looked the length of the bay and watched the rollers running towards the dazzling sands. The ocean's roar subdued all other sounds as easily as the scene denied the conflict that she had left behind. Tomorrow they would arrive in Salalah, the next day they would climb Qara and would arrive at the farm. She wondered how long she would have to wait there before her husband came for her? She couldn't prevent the dark thought that he might never come.

✳ ✳ ✳

Jokha sat in the shade around the back of the small flat-roofed house at Haluf. The view across flat scrubby sand to the barren brown hills beyond did not compare to the mountain home that they had left. There was no greenery here, only solitary dust covered Frankincense bushes and scattered desert weeds eking an existence broke the monotony of sand and brown colours. From the other side of the house the views were worse! The house was on the edge of the village and faced inwards on an irregular complex of typical *nejd* built houses. The houses built from the countless rocks that littered the ground and mortared together by wet sand followed a simple basic pattern. Square, flat-roofed, a door in the middle, two rooms with small barred portals that acted as windows. Only the sizes varied and here and there, seemingly as an afterthought, crude extensions had been added. Several had surrounded themselves with low walls to create a zone between their door and the avenues that tangled throughout. Many houses stood empty and derelict either abandoned by families who had moved away or by families who had simply rebuilt at another spot within the village. There is no such thing as plot ownership; the earth belongs to Allah and all may use it. The house where Abdulla and Jokha now lived was one of these abandoned houses.

Jokha worried about Abdulla. Since that day five months ago when he had been told of Lailla's fate he had become very withdrawn and uninterested. With no one to look after the cattle he had sold them straight away. The price that he had received looked to be very fair. However, these weeks later with the price continuing upward it didn't now look quite as good. Hardly moving from the house he had stayed on the farm just one more month until Hamed's son had been born. Whether he had been waiting for the baby to be born or for Hamed to arrive she wasn't sure. She suspected the latter because soon after he had arrived to see his new son Abdulla announced that unless Hamed intended to stay then they would be moving to Haluf. With a son as well as a wife to support Hamed was reluctant to give up the Firqat pay that financially rewarded him far better than his time on the farm ever had. However, before he returned to his duties at Manston he helped with the move to Haluf. His own wife Khamisa was also brought to this village but Hamed housed her separately although close by. But Abdulla's spirits were low affected by the loss of the farm. He slept late every day then sat around bored until evening. After eating he would wander off tapping the walls with his knuckles as he went confirming where he was finding his way to an old man's *dirwain*. He would stay there all night returning in the early hours of the morning. Then the cycle would be repeated the next day.

It was a mistake to come here she concluded. Because of his limited eyesight there hadn't been much that Abdulla could do on the farm but here in this village there was even less. Also that farm had been his life's work and therefore he had a keen interest in its future. He had no stake in this village, he hadn't even built the house in which they now lived so there was no particular interest. She appreciated too how inadequate he might be feeling not only with his physical handicap but also mentally. After a lifetime of hard work he had ended with very little and he probably felt something of a failure. How could she make him see that he wasn't a failure? Fates had conspired to send him naught but bad luck and perhaps a lesser man would have capitulated sooner. It was not his fault that each of his children for their own specific reasons had turned away from their livelihood and involved themselves in the war that had raged in the region. Mussalim for his socialist beliefs and Juma to possess the woman he had loved. Their reasons were clear. Hamed's reasons were a little more obscure to her. He had left initially to escape some mysterious conflict with his elder brother and after that had been resolved he now stayed away for money, or so it seemed. Some unknown young man had been responsible for Lailla's fate. It had been he who had influenced her down the same perilous road as Mussalim. In each case there seemed to have been no way that Abdulla could have prevented it. He had been God fearing and worked hard throughout his life, he deserved much better. She sighed saddened by the unfairness of it all, perhaps even now things would get better and one day they would be able to return to their home in the mountains. That would in all probability depend entirely on Hamed, it was he who had become the key to the family's future. Because of his role in the PFLO her own son Mussalim could return only after the passing of many years if indeed he managed to survived the conflict.

In the meantime until such times as things changed, if indeed they ever did she had to try and hold things together. Khamisa would be here soon. She visited every day bringing with her Tuful and her new baby son Mubarrak. She got up from the shade, it was time that she got on with her chores. First she would need to round up the goats.

Every day they were turned out of the crude pen that she had constructed using battered and rusting corrugated sheets and old discarded oil drums. Foraging around the edges of the village the goats had to search much harder for less fodder than they had been used too in the mountains. Consequently the milk yields were very much poorer. Even so the small herd was worth the effort of keeping as it would provide meat to eat.

* * *

Khamisa had found a degree of independence that she had never expected and this had made her a little more content. There were no demands placed upon her other than those she willingly self-imposed to take care of her two children. She virtually lived alone in a modest house in the village and she was forced to admit, adequately provided for by her husband. Away from the jebal farm there were no routine tasks that ever required attention and she enjoyed a more stress free style of living. Nor was she subjected to Abdulla's authority. She wasn't sure whether it was because of his near blindness the short distance between the two homes was too much for him to cope with, or perhaps it was that he no longer saw the necessity. Whichever, he attempted no control at all and left her very much to her own devices. Her situation was that she was the mistress of her own house and she could please herself entirely what she did and when she did it. She enjoyed a degree of autonomy that few women could even aspire too. Living alone her only duties were to attend the two children and to reflect only credit upon her absent husband.

Soon after the news had reached him Hamed had returned to the jebal farm to see for the first time his new born son. She had been surprised by the genuine display of affection he immediately showed towards the baby. At first afraid of his own clumsiness he hardly dare hold him. Khamisa had found herself sympathetic to his nervousness and showed him how a baby should be handled. Then to bolster his confidence she left him for short periods in his care. He had soon gained confidence and she found then that on occasions she had to almost demand that he be returned to her for feeding.

But that was perfectly understandable she allowed, not only was he the father but the infant was a bonny little baby seemingly taking an interest in everything around him. She hadn't particularly wanted Hamed's baby and when he was born she couldn't help a stab of disappointment that it was a boy. It seemed to her that she had done much better for Hamed than she had for her beloved Juma. However, one cannot stay angry very long with a helpless new born particularly this one who noticed everything and seemed to smile a lot.

Shortly after they had left the farm and moved to Haluf, Hamed had returned to his unit at Manston. However, not before he had attentively seen his wife and son settled in comfortable accommodation and given Khamisa a generous amount of money for their welfare. Then with a promise to return after four months, directed more to the baby than to her, he had ridden away to rejoin his unit. As she watched him go she found herself becoming more amiable to accepting him as a husband. Juma he could never be and what they had shared she would never share with him but nevertheless for a husband she could do very much worse, it seemed. His physical demands were salacious and much less than sophisticated but since she only responded dutifully perhaps part of the blame was hers. Her feelings were thickly entwined with strands of guilt. He had shown her only consideration and perhaps she should do better, particularly as for long periods he was absent. She acknowledged a little contritely that it was only right for him to expect that during the periods when he was in the marital home she would be an appreciative and respectful wife. Next time she would have to try harder to please him.

✴ ✴ ✴

As they neared the farm Jumaia was experiencing mixed emotions. There could be only sadness returning here while leaving her husband behind and not knowing when or indeed if, she would ever see him again. Yet in contradiction she looked forward very much to seeing Khamisa and Lailla after a year. A year? She realised that their circumstances might be very different to the last time they had met. Of course Khamisa was now married and their roles would be completely reversed. Last time it was she who had her man with her where as Khamisa had been a widow. Now, at least for the time being, it was she who to all intents and purposes was the widow. And Lailla? Well, she might possibly be betrothed! She was close to twenty and almost the same age as herself but unlike Lailla who was still a maiden she'd had two husbands already. It was definitely past the time that Lailla had a husband. She wondered if it were possible that she might even be married. Surely not, Abdulla would have found some way of notifying Mussalim of a wedding she was sure. The train of three camels began to climb the last knoll in single file. Soon she would have all the answers.

At the top of the hill Ali stopped hooked a knee over the saddle stool and waited for her to catch up.

"Is that it?" he asked nodding towards the settlement at the bottom.

She glanced down at the two rude dwellings, the rondavaal fence and the tumbling store shed. "Yes that's it," she replied and then stopped to stare curiously.

"Looks deserted," he remarked concurring her own impression.

"Perhaps they have all gone to Salalah." Even though she said it she found it unlikely that all would go. But there would be some explanation, she thought.

Ali slapped his cane down the neck of the beast setting off down the hill, the pack animal on the end of a tether following.

As they got gradually nearer, however, she began to have doubts about that explanation. The roundavaal fence was in need of obvious attention and the roof of the *beehive* styled house had collapsed in on one side. There were no animals to be seen nor any evidence that there had been any about for some time. More ominously no one came to greet them when they approached the house. Ali had already slipped off his kneeling camel and he was helping Salim off by the time she reached the house front.

Reining her animal to a halt she looked inquiringly at the house. One end of the roof over the veranda had collapsed giving more evidence of dilapidation and the front door hung half open. Ali was immediately at her side hauling on the animal's halter wordlessly bringing it to its knees. The beast went down awkwardly front legs first snorting and bellowing as it did. That noise alone would have brought out any occupants if there had been anybody about. After Ali had lifted Taimul to the ground he then helped Jumaia off too.

Then with a look back over his shoulder at the house he said. "There's no one here!" She didn't answer instead she searched the surrounding hills hoping to see someone, or something. "I'll look inside," he added.

She watched as he went in but even before he did she could tell by the undisturbed layer of sand in the doorway that no one had been in or out of that door for some time. 'What could have happened that had caused them to desert the farm? Where had they gone? When did they go? And where were they all now?' Questions tumbled rapidly through her mind each unanswered question prompting another. None of this made any sense at all.

Ali emerged shaking his head. "Nothing!" He looked around obviously wondering what to do next. "I'll take a look around," he muttered.

She nodded but she knew that he would find nothing because there was nothing here. He walked away to go through the motions of checking the other buildings. Driven by curiosity she went into the house. Not everything had gone, here and there scattered items of abandoned belongings littered the place. However, there was nothing of value and that suggested that at least the departure had been organised and not hasty. She went back outside and sat on the step waiting for Ali to complete his search while the two boys played nearby.

Eventually he returned shaking his head. "Nothing," he said sitting by her side. "What will you do now?"

Jumaia shrugged. "I don't know."

"You can't stay here."

"Mussalim said that I was to wait here for him. So I must."

"He didn't know that you would find the place deserted when he said that. He would not expect you to stay here alone."

"What else can I do?"

He shook his head bemused. "I don't know. But a woman alone, here? And with two children! You couldn't survive?"

He was right but she didn't know what else she could do. Perhaps she could go back to Jibjat? But how would she get there and what would she do when she did? There were also her two children to be considered and that was a crushing responsibility. She felt enormously vulnerable and she wished that she had the reliable protection of Mussalim wrapped around her and the children at this moment. She stared depressingly at the abandoned farmhouse buildings and felt just as abandoned. In addition, however she was frightened and very lonely.

Ali glanced sideways at her, she could not stay here, there was no question about that. But what was he to do? He had promised Mussalim that he would look after her and his children. Therefore, there was an obligation to his absent friend. But it is one thing to promise when there is the expectation that there is someone to whom you can hand over that responsibility, quite another when that responsibility unexpectedly becomes solely yours. How long would that responsibility last? Until Mussalim returned? If indeed he ever did! That was not probable either! So for the foreseeable future and far beyond that he could expect to burdened with another man's family. It was not that she was unpleasant to be with and neither were her two boys. It was more that his future was just as uncertain. He had little idea how he was going to survive himself but to add the crushing liability of three others and helpless others at that, would make his survival that much harder. He didn't need this added disadvantage at this time.

~ 26 ~

January 1975 • Although the Iranians had been comprehensively defeated on their sortie into Jebal Sayq they had not gone away. They had fallen back only as far as Deefa to reform. Consequently PFLO forces had been placed on a state of alert with the expectation that eventually they would try again. The continued build up of Omani forces a little further north at Manston only added to this fear. Raykut as the "Capital of the Liberated area" had been listed as a potential target and the forces there had been instructed to prepare its defences.

Surrounded as it was by cliffs overlooking the bay it was a bad place to defend. With only one road in or out of the village there was no escape alternative either. The only option was to take positions in the hills surrounding and defend to the bitter end because to retreat back into the village would be to enter a trap from which there could be no escape. A force holding position on the cliff tops could pulverise those below mercilessly and at their leisure.

Outside the village the road split in two and climbed the steep hills to the east and west while the river valley cut a furrow in between. The road to the west meandered along the top edge of an acute ridge and would be the easier of the two to defend. The ridge ran parallel and close to the cliff tops before it ended abruptly above the bay. At this point the road turned sharply inland and descended into the valley below. With cliffs on the left flank and the land falling steeply on the right only the road and its edges needed to be fortified. Mussalim established a chain of sangars manned by RPD machine guns right across. The next problem was the cover that the thick growth of dwarf shrubs provided. Leaving the sangars hidden in among the *ghaf* an area of about one hundred metres to the front was cut to provided a sterile killing area.

The eastern side was not as straightforward. The road tacked up the hill and when it reached the top it continued straight on dipping and rising across an expanse of shallow valleys. The attack potential was across a wide front. To fortify a straight defensive line was to invite an attacker to go around the flanks. Mussalim had the sangars built in a flattish arrowhead formation with the outer tips on the brow of the hill. If the attackers did go around the ends they would find themselves on the steep hill below the defenders. Here too *ghaf* was thick providing excellent approach cover and the solution was the same, chop it down to ground level.

He pushed the men hard to finish the work fearful that an attack might come before they were ready. To act as an early warning of any advance he had posted men well forward in the hills and as the work neared completion he began considering moving the defence line further out to those positions. In effect that would make these established lines as a second line defence and create a fallback position if required. However, while he still considered it a gun ship arrived in the bay and stationed itself well offshore.

Everyone watched the boat curiously as it just sat on the water holding its position. It made no attempt to come closer or to move away. Speculation ranged from simple reconnaissance to an intended landing. The latter was wild conjecture because the boat was a Corvette and hardly big enough to carry a decent sized landing party without men over spilling onto the decks and there was no evidence of that. The morning wore on and the boat still held its position spreading apprehension among the PFLO defenders. Through binoculars the men on shore studied the sailors while the sailors studied the shore. Mussalim climbed the hill to the west and took a position on the cliffs to overlook the bay. With an overview down onto the Corvette's decks there seemed to be little activity of any significance.

It had double cannon in its stern and mid-ship with a machine gun mounted at its bow. Reconnaissance was the most likely reason for its presence there but Mussalim was uneasy. There were four small dilapidated boats on the beach left behind by the village fishermen after they had left. If these boats could survive a short trip then there would be some means of escape for a few in the event of Raykut being overrun. However, positioned as it was, this boat barred the way to any sea escape. Mussalim studied it pensively and the more he thought about it the more he began to fear that was the very reason for its arrival. They had no way of knowing that there were only four boats left in the village, possibly they believed that there could be many more. If that were so then they were sealing up the 'back door.' If they were sealing the door then the expected attack was imminent. Probably even now government soldiers advanced towards the village. He made his way back to the command sangar and used the radio to warn everybody to take position and be ready for an attack.

Just after midday gunfire started over in the east in its forward position alerting the defenders. As if by signal the boat in the bay began to hurl shells from its guns into the village. Within thirty minutes the main defence line on that side of the hill was engaged and the hills echoed with the sounds of gunfire. Soon the splash of mortar shells peppered the defender's lines. The defenders retaliated with RPG anti tank rockets driven low through the trees in the direction of the attackers.

Mussalim watched anxiously through binoculars from his position in a sangar that he shared with the radio operator and one other. The fighting on that hill was obviously intense but other than that he could see little to re-assure him that the defence was holding. But neither could he see anything that suggested that it was not. He wished that he were over on that side, at least then he would have a clearer idea of what the situation was. He wondering if he should hurry across and he began to estimate how long that would take him when gunfire started from the forward position on this side. The government forces were advancing along this road too. It was a two pronged attack definitely planned to cut off any escape route for the PFLO.

Within a few minutes the forward placed men retreating before the soldiers appeared in the sterile area and hurried towards the security of their defence lines. Mussalim pumped his first round into the breach slipped his Kalachnikov into automatic mode and with an encouraging nod at his two companions waited for the first of the soldiers to appear.

He didn't have to wait long before there was movement in amongst the *ghaf* as the soldiers moved forward cautiously. At the edge of the clearing they came under intense fire from the men in the sangars and they began to hastily withdraw back out of sight. By the dark green uniforms that they were wearing that brief glance had told Mussalim that these soldiers were Iranians.

It didn't take the attackers long to get themselves organised and mortar shells soon started to rain into the defenders' position. However they were indiscriminate and wild because hidden amongst the shrubs the Iranians could not fasten their position. Nevertheless the weight of fire coming in was much heavier than the PFLO men could hope to match. With only around one hundred and forty defenders and two thirds of those on the hill opposite they were heavily outnumbered. But the defensive positions were well prepared and so far there was little evidence that the attackers could break the line. The crescendo of noise was immense and frightening. The deafening cracks of rifle fire stung eardrums while the deep boom of exploding mortar vibrated the earth. The sudden angry hiss of anti tank rockets punctuated the ear-aching din as they fizzed across to the thicket on the other side of the clearing. Smoke and dust drifted across the battle hampering visibility and sometimes blocking out the brightness of the day as it washed over the sangars. Mussalim could hear the branches snapping all around him as bullets tore through the shrubs while tiny eruptions in the ground to his front indicated that not all was passing overhead.

After a few minutes the Iranians massed and began an advance through the trees. When they reached the clear area they began to run towards the defence positions firing blindly as they did. Mussalim pulled the trigger back on his Kalachnikov and held it there fanning the area to his front with a wild spray. Soon his magazine was exhausted and he slipped back beneath the sangar's protection while he pulled off the spent magazine and replaced it. When he got back to his position the advance was already floundering as the Iranians still short of half way and taking casualties, hesitated. Panicking slightly he began fanning in their direction once again. There was little time to aim at selected targets the priority right now was to force them back and a continuous hail of bullets seemed the best persuader. There would have been little point squinting down the sights anyway because the short barrel was so hot that rising heat shimmered the vision. Helping their wounded and dragging their dead the Iranians began to fall back. Mussalim ceased firing and slipped lower into the sangar's cover. He became aware that his heart thumped wildly in his chest and his breath was coming in short gasps. He blew out through puffed cheeks releasing the tension.

Although the mortar shells had started again there was a comparative lull. Mussalim gathered the empty magazines that littered the bottom of the sangar and after passing some to his two companions began to hastily refill. This fight was a long way from decided.

Masked by the noise he had missed the thump of rotor blades until with a loud engine groan a Huey helicopter passed low across their front. It sped on over the cliffs and over the sea it arced steeply to make a re-run. This time it came in behind their position and much slower. It slowed right down to hover while a soldier in its open doorway with a bird's eye view of their positions raked the sangars with a GP machine gun. Mussalim lay with his back against the inner wall and sprayed bullets upward in the direction of this new threat. Whether this singled him out for special attention or if it were just chance he had no idea but the immediate area around him erupted into impact thuds and clouds of dust as the gunner directed his attention on his particular sangar. Instinctively he rolled away, he could just as easily have rolled into a bullet but miraculously as the thuds stopped and the dust continued to rise he found that he was not hit. Someone fired an anti tank missile at the Huey. The aim was poor and it hissed harmlessly wide. However, the point was not lost on the pilot and he immediately heeled over his machine and sped off over to the other side of the valley.

Now that the noisy rotors had gone Mussalim heard once more the cracking of smashed twigs as sheets of bullets once more came from the Iranian soldiers. "All – ah," he involuntarily muttered cringing under the intensity of the incoming fire. The radio operator shook his shoulder and shouted something to him then dabbed his pointing finger several times in the direction of the opposite hill. Mussalim did not understand but looked in the direction he pointed. Rising smoke and bursting mortar splashes on the top of the hill was all he could see. Obviously they were taking as much fire if not more than they were on this side. Both attacks were mercilessly intense.

The radio operator leaned forward again and shouted once more in his ear. "They are withdrawing. They can't hold them over there."

Mussalim looked back hoping to see evidence that it wasn't true, but beneath the cloud of drifting smoke he could see nothing. If it were true then their position on this hill would be compromised too. They could be faced with Iranians at their front and also coming up the hill on their right flank. Behind them and on the left flank were only sheer cliffs. They had no alternative but to withdraw before they were cut off at the road junction. But withdrew to where? To fall back into the village was sheer folly. A desperate alternative occurred to him.

He grabbed the operator by the arm. "Tell them to a hold position at the bottom of the hill," he shouted

After the radioman nodded that he understood, Mussalim set off running low and hard to each sangar instructing the men to withdrew back down the hill. None needed a second instruction. Abandoning the dead and carrying the wounded they gathered their equipment and set off down the hill using the thick *ghaf* as cover. With a nervous glance across the sterile area Mussalim followed the last of the men. He knew that it was a good position that they were deserting and there was nothing as good to retreat to but unless he wanted to be marooned up here then he had no alternative. It would not be long before those soldiers realised that they had pulled back and would soon be in pursuit, they barely had minutes start.

When they reached the bottom of the hill and the road junction Mussalim was dismayed to see the procession of PFLO fighters streaming back towards the village. There were barely two dozen with enough faith to trust him. He called desperately to those within hearing distance to return and although some did others ignored him. He stared despondently after them. They were putting themselves into a trap where their eventual alternatives were limited to two, surrender or die. There was nothing he could do and no time to waste. At this very moment it was likely that soldiers were advancing down both hills. He waded into the shallow river and waved the men past indicating that they should make their escape up the river valley back towards the hills.

While the main body retreated up the wadi he stayed to organise the rear guard. It was a leap frog action with two defensive lines, one falling back through the other to form a new line for the other to pass. At first there was a pursuit and skirmishes developed but as the wadi became deeper, steeper and much more rugged the soldiers eventually broke off to return to the main objective to seize Raykut. In the upper reaches of the wadi the river had become nothing more than a trickling stream and the small band of around three dozen waited to reform. They had successfully escaped but there was no elation. Some attended the wounded but most sat stern-faced and silent listening to the sounds of battle. The double booms of the Corvette's guns continued to pound the village while the low bumps of exploding mortar shells mixed with the endless crackle of rifle fire. By now the soldiers would control the road out of the bay and those PFLO men who had retreated into the village were now effectively bottled up. Raykut was lost and no longer could it be considered the "Capital of the Liberated area."

There were comfort women and even some families in that village and Mussalim wondered how many of these men had left something like that in the village. He was very glad that last month he had sent Jumaia and the boys to safety. With no danger of pursuit and now in comparative safety Mussalim decided that it was a good idea to allow these men an hour's rest. After that the obvious alternative was to move on to Dalkut and link up with other PFLO fighters.

✳ ✳ ✳

At that precise moment Hamed was in a small clearing less than four kilometres away. The *Firqa* Tariq Bin Zeead led by their British SAS trainers had joined a sizeable Army Force mounting an assault on the main *adoo* supply depot at Kharfat. The column had left Deefa in the early morning and headed south passing well to the west of Wadi Kharfat. Later they had bent back to the east curling in behind to a position south of the wadi. As they neared the track that the PFLO used to move shipments in and out they came under intense machine gun fire. However, it was only a delay. The government forces pressed forward determinedly and their number superiority eventually forced the *adoo* to withdraw further into the wadi. Having seized the clearing they then threw a cordon of defence around and secured the area. This was to be the base of the operation and now that it was secure helicopters began to shuttle in the heavy supplies that would be needed for the main assault.

Hamed pulled his shamag tighter across his face and turned his back as the pilot of the Huey increased the rotor speed hurling clouds of dust and grit all around. The aircraft slowly rose from the midst of this dense cloud like the Phoenix emerging from its own smoking ashes. It then pivoted around to face the right direction and headed north back to the safety of Manston. Hamed enviously watched it growing smaller in the evening sky that was the last delivery of the day and despite the battalion strength around him he could not help but feel somewhat abandoned. Tonight under the cover of darkness the *adoo* would return. They had to they could not ignore a large force gathered close to the wadi mouth.

Although everybody was stood too for the night he was not actually allocated a post. So free to tend his own needs within the defence perimeter he settled cross-legged in the circle of his *firqa* comrades listening to their opinions while he cleaned his FN rifle. Not that it needed cleaning, it hadn't fired a round since he had cleaned it last night at Deefa. Wrapped in the dust protecting bag that Khamisa had made for him it had even been protected from the dust kicked up by hundreds of feet during this morning's advance.

For a moment he examined the bag. Made from a light nylon material neatly stitched together with his initial embroidered on it had coloured knitted tassels dangling from its bottom edge. It was these tassels that pleased him the most. Although superfluous and over elaborate it indicated to him that Khamisa had put in that little extra effort to please him. Perhaps it was an indication that she was beginning to warm to him. What else could it be? Certainly on his visit last month she had seemed to be less withdrawn and a little more eager to please. Before he had felt that she performed her wifely duties because that was what she had to do, but this last time there was just a little more piquancy in her attitude. Or was he finding something that wasn't really there simply because he wanted it to be there? He fingered the tassels again. No, this was an indication that she was beginning to do a little more to please. Certainly she was a wife whose beauty brought him prestige and increased his reputation. Away from the farm's isolation and in the village community of Haluf her demeanour would be more evident and his reputation better advertised. If only she would show the same unconstrained affection that she had openly poured on Juma then all would plainly see that she was happy and privileged to be his wife. His reputation would grow even more but that would be nothing against the delight of possessing her love completely. Juma had it and he wanted it so badly.

He still experienced mixed emotions about Juma. Killed by some repulsive *adoo* his ghost still cried out for revenge. At the same time he had wished him killed so that he could possess his wife and he had been granted that wish. Sometimes he appeased his guilt by telling himself that he hadn't really wanted that. But when he thought of Khamisa the guilt would not be silenced. When Juma's death had been truly avenged his ghost would rest, and then these feelings of guilt that tormented him would disappear. He wondered how he would ever avenge his brother's death. So far he had been involved in many skirmishes and possibly he may have killed *adoo* but he didn't know for certain and this did not satisfy him. He needed to see at least one man die by his hand and before his eyes. That was the way of the old ones, "an eye for an eye." His stomach knotted with anger and frustration. Tomorrow there would be a huge battle and perhaps somewhere in its midst then his need for revenge might be appeased. He suddenly realised that deep in thought he was twisting the rifle cover that Khamisa had made for him. He let go instantly and smoothed it out. Fortunately it was undamaged so he folded it carefully and stowed it away in his pack. Tonight after he had finished cleaning his rifle he wouldn't put it away in the bag he would keep it close and readily available. He was certain that he would need it.

Soon after it was dark and before the moon had risen the *adoo* came. With the advantage of knowing precisely where the soldiers were they crept forward through the thick cover of the trees to the very edge of the clearing. Although they fired blind into the defence cordon the fire was heavy and with the number of men inside they could not help but inflict casualties. The intense fire from automatic rifles crackled ceaseless and anti-tank missiles came angrily hissing before their deafening explosions lit the night with blinding orange flashes. Mortars were tossed in indiscriminately their dull thuds adding to the noise and mayhem. The soldiers returned fire with GP machine guns blindly spraying the darkness among the trees. The volume of these bursts made sure that in the tree line was a very dangerous place to be. Hamed could do little except take cover and pray that Allah spared him. To add his own fire into the darkness would only jeopardise the perimeter defenders. A bullet in the back from one of your own side would not be an auspicious way to die. Eventually the attack momentum dwindled and the firing gradually faded to sporadic and then ceased altogether. In the darkness both sides were left to count the cost and tend their casualties.

✳ ✳ ✳

A little further to the south Mussalim led the stragglers from Raykut through the deserted village of Umbaraaf on their way to Dalkut. They heard the gunfire to their north and speculated on what was happening. There was little doubt in Mussalim's mind that it was the supply caves in Kharfat that was under siege. With the advance on Raykut and the simultaneous attack on the supply depot it seemed to him that the government forces had launched a determined initiative to smash the PFLO. Herded into and then virtually sealed in this south western corner of the region it was inevitable that one day they would. It seemed that the day had arrived and he wondered, could this be the beginning of the end?

It was very late when they descended the cliffs and onto the beach road that ran into Dalkut. Even so a large bonfire burned in the village and attracted as a moth to its flames Mussalim led the group towards it.

As he approached he could see a dozen armed men keeping a waking vigil on the edge of its light. Faces marked more austere by the shadows and flickering flame stared seriously at the fire as if hypnotised by its dancing flames.

They didn't cause much of a stir when they walked into the firelight it was almost as if they were expected. Places were found for them when they declared who they were and where they were from. Then bread, dates and scented tea was handed out as the men listened stoically to the stories of the newcomers. The news of Raykut's fall surprised no one, somehow the news had proceeded them, probably by radio Mussalim guessed.

He knew he should report to someone and Mussalim asked who was in command in the village. No one at the moment one man informed him. The new Commander, a Yemeni, had left early in the evening taking with him every man that could be spared to reinforce the Kharfat defence. A large government force at least a battalion strong had gathered south of Kharfat and with the daylight it was expected that an attack would be made on the supply depot. A bloody battle would be fought because Kharfat was well manned and heavily armed.

It had been a long and arduous day and even though Mussalim was tired he stayed there with these men just staring gloomily into the flames. The flames dwindled and the fire collapsed into several smaller sub fires then died. The embers glowed then became covered by grey ash only glowing red when the fresh breeze off the sea fanned back some life. The voices ceased to make sense and gradually faded to low murmuring then he fell asleep.

✳ ✳ ✳

Although the sun had not actually risen it was lighting the sky when the first two companies left the operation base. They were to move directly north under the thick cover of *ghaf* and establish positions on the high ground directly north of the supply caves and another south west. When they were in position a third company, which included Hamed's own *firqa* would move directly up the wadi to the caves. Although the fighting would undoubtedly be fierce under fire from the front, rear and to their right the *adoo* would eventually be overwhelmed.

Hamed watched them go hoping that the plan was as good as the planners had made it sound. Even if it were it was likely that there would be lots of casualties. There would be another four hours before his company moved forward, he decided that the time would be well spent checking his personal kit. He took hold of his rifle and began stripping away its moving parts, even though he had cleaned it twice in the last twenty-four hours without firing a round it wouldn't hurt to do it again. A breach jam in the very midst of a battle was not desirable, it might even cost his life.

It was a large force that moved forward in the mid morning made up from the Firqa Tariq Bin Zeead, their British Army trainers and the Sultan's Army. Progress up the wadi was handicapped by a series of steep escapements like crude steps in some mythical giant's garden. However, a track well worn by thousands of animals' feet looped up and around each escapement, which helped to keep the column moving. Hamed looked forward and back to see the column moving along the track like some enormous thin snake. He was pleased to be in its middle and not towards the front, those men were particular vulnerable. In a narrow column only four or five men wide they would be the first casualties if they came under fire. Not only that they would have difficulty returning fire only the front three or four rows would be able to respond.

Surprisingly, however, they progressed steadily and without any resistance. It was by now well past midday and the sun was at its hottest. It poured heat into the wadi, and trapped it in there by its steep sides. The rocks absorbed the relentless energy and re-radiated the heat magnified. It was only the shade of the trees that thickly covered the wadi base that made it bearable. Hamed began to resent the British officers that led this assault. "Didn't they know that it was wise to rest during such heat as this? After all energy sapped to the point of exhaustion takes three times longer to replace." The track began climbing steeply coming out of the wadi's base and when they reached the top a rest was called. They were still among trees, not as thick or tall as they had been in the wadi bottom but nevertheless they still afforded welcome shade. Hamed gratefully sank down in the shade, his clothing soaked in sweat and sticking uncomfortably to his body. He watched as the assault leaders went into a huddle consulting maps. It almost seemed as if they didn't know where they were? Too tired to be concerned he closed his eyes, better he snatch a few moments sleep if he could.

Too soon the column was on the move again, continuing to follow the track this time along the wadi top. Its steep edge to Hamed's right fell away out of sight and he glanced towards it curiously. They were above the wadi but the plan had been to advance up it? Within minutes the column halted again when they arrived at an exposed clearing. The track that they had been following cut across this bottom corner and turned sharply to the right to disappear once more beneath the trees over on that side. Seventy or eighty metres directly to their front the ground rose steep and was covered thickly by trees. The column fanned out into line as they prepared to cross the exposed area.

They left the tree cover and started across. Hamed fixed his eyes firmly on the high ground opposite searching for tell tale sign of *adoo*, this seemed to be perfect ambush territory. And so it was, before they reached half way the whole hillside erupted with machine gun fire, mortars, rockets and automatic small arms. Men were cut down like stalks of hay above a swinging scythe. Exposed with very little cover the line broke like a bomb burst; some sought what scant cover there was while others simply ran in blind panic. It was a long way back to the tree cover and the casualties among the runners was heavy. Hamed threw himself to the ground and looked around desperately for something to hide behind. Not far away, a cluster of low rocks beneath a lonely windswept tree. That would do! The main attention of the ambushers was for the moment centred on the runners. Risky though it was there would not be a better opportunity. Panic driven he crawled on all fours at sprint speed to the rocky cover. Several others sought the same protection and soon a dozen had gathered in its shelter.

He had no idea how long he and the men around him cowered trapped among the rocks but the fusillade was relentless. Their position as a shelter for a dozen men had been well marked by the ambushers. The situation looked desperate and he began to wish that he had taken a chance and made the risky run back to the safety of the trees. Gradually however, resistance began to become organised and the trapped men started to receive support from the high ground behind them. Tracer from machine gun fire began speeding its way into the *adoo* hillside that was soon followed by splashes of mortar shells. Now that the *adoo* fire was divided the trapped men were able to start adding their own fire to that of their supporters. Hamed now began to hope that he might after all survive this. Minutes later artillery shells presumably from Deefa also began to burst on the PFLO position leaving pillars of smoke to drift slowly across the hillside. But not to be outdone the PFLO retaliated with their own artillery, pounding the hill position behind Hamed. Minutes later air support came in the shape of two Hunters. Pulling maximum revs on their engines they screamed low across the battle before wheeling to begin their strafing runs. In the confusion and the closeness of the conflict they strafed the wrong hill and were then sent away.

That kind of intensity could not be maintained and gradually the firing began to ease then soon after faded to sporadic. At first the trapped men stayed in their positions unsure whether the battle was running down or had just entered a pause. Soon one or two began to break cover and fall back, others quickly followed their example and eventually gathering their wounded all the trapped men left the clearing and reformed back in the trees.

As the sun dropped to another resplendent set the column retraced its steps tiredly back down the wadi to the operation base secure area. Men straggled in through the defence cordon dispirited and disillusioned and counting the cost of heavy casualties. All this without actually launching the offensive against the supply caves itself. They had been successfully halted short of their objective. Hamed was too tired to care. He had survived and that hadn't seemed likely at one point. Soon he would make his prayer and thank Allah for his deliverance. His personal quest for vengeance was proving much more difficult than he had ever imagined. These PFLO men were as illusive as shadows but as deadly as the *djinn of death*.

No further open assaults were made on the supply depot. Instead three days later the army moved to a new higher position on the edge of the wadi and brought up two artillery guns. Then for a week they hurled shells into horseshoe shaped canyon where the caves were located. A week after that the forces withdrew completely back to Deefa. Whether the shelling was effective or not, didn't really matter, it recovered vestiges of pride and exacted some revenge for the defeat. However, it did not prevent Radio Aden exalting the victory of the gallant PFLO at Kharfat, although it did neglected to report that the 'Capital of the Liberated area' was now firmly in government hands.

✳ ✳ ✳

"Hey Jebally," Someone kicked his cot. "Wake up. Are all Jebally's as lazy as this?"

Mussalim peered out from beneath his blanket and looked up into the twisted grinning face of Suhayl. "What are you doing here? he mumbled groggily.

"I would ask you the same thing. Except I already know." He went over to the other side of the darkened room and released the wooden bar that held the shutters together. Mussalim moved to a sitting position on the cot then had to shade his eyes when Suhayl dropped the shutters allowing the morning sunlight to sweep through the room. He looked around the bare room, a collapsible cot, a rocky cane chair, an old cupboard and a dirty rug on the uneven floor. "You do well Commissar!" he said sarcastically.

"It'll do," Mussalim made no apology. "Last I heard you were over in Darbat." He got from the cot and went over to the cupboard. From a battered tin jug on the top of the small cupboard he tipped water into an equally battered tin bowl.

"You know me, where the fighting is hardest!"

Mussalim nodded before bending over and splashing water in his face. As he dried himself on a dirty old *futa* he looked at Suhayl. "So what are you doing here?" he asked. He hadn't noticeable changed in six and a half years. His hair was still long, unkempt and tied with a headband above his ears. His facial scar still made him look frighteningly villainous. He wore a Commissar's uniform but it was crumpled and dirty looking as if it hadn't been off his back in a very long time.

"Temporary Commander," he answered.

"Ah, the Yemeni. Of course," Mussalim connected the remark of the man by the bonfire when he had arrived here three weeks ago. "When did you get back from Kharfat?"

"An hour ago."

"What was it like?" It was a stupid question, he already knew that it had been intense.

"We made them pay dearly for their audacity. They won't come back in a hurry," he said casually.

"Perhaps not in a hurry but they would be back," Mussalim thought but he said nothing. "I'm sorry I can't offer you refreshments," Mussalim started to apologise for his inadequacies but Suhayl raised his hand silencing him.

"As soon as I heard you were here I came to find you. Join me for breakfast in my quarters in one hour. Do you know where that is?"

He did, and so he nodded. It was in the same house that Hemel Al Shibam had set up as the Front headquarters so long ago and where he himself had lived for a while with Shamel, his comfort woman.

"One hour then," he moved towards the door and then paused. "Crazy Man, I have a new assignment and I need a good man to be my second in command. So I was delighted when I heard that you had stumbled in."

"What's the assignment?"

"One hour," he said and left without answering.

One hour later Mussalim made his way through the village. The houses were dilapidated and mostly empty only those containing PFLO fighters were occupied. The villagers had long since moved away driven away either by the hardship of the government stranglehold or the excesses of the PFLO themselves. He looked beyond the enormous bay to the rugged beauty of the rocky coastline, its green and fertile cliff tops contrasted against a blue cloudless sky. The sea reflected the sky except its depth marked it darker while its swelling rollers ran up towards the golden sand beach. Here was simple beauty and pacifistic peace and now one of the last remaining strongholds of the movement. It was true that Kharfat had been held, for now, but Raykut had been lost and gradually the government stranglehold was tightening. This might be where the final battle was destined to be fought and a more inappropriate place to fight a battle he could not imagine.

Breakfast was simple fare but far better than most could aspire in the chronic food situation. They sat cross-legged facing each other and ate pitta bread and cream cheese from a large brass tray placed between them. They black drank sugarless tea from handless cups and made superficial conversation. Inevitably the talk was of the dour war situation and its possible outcome. Suhayl although not optimistic was a good deal more hopeful than Mussalim. He thought that with the Yemeni's help, his fellow countrymen, they might yet still secure this area and the Sultan might abandon it to the PFLO. Mussalim could not help but compare his new more modest aspirations against his "Free The Arabian Gulf," tirade on their first meeting so long ago in Wadi Ghadun when he had virtually been his prisoner. However, he passed no comment. Naturally they mentioned missing colleagues, particularly amongst the elite in the movement. Al Mushani, Bin Talib and Zahir Ali, all killed by government forces. When Suhayl questioned Mussalim curiously about Ali he became evasive and with a vague shrug said, "the last time he had seen him was at Raykut." That was true! However, he allowed Suhayl to believe that he had been left behind during the recent battle.

Eventually the topics dried up and Suhayl came to the reason he was here. "The Central Committee has a plan to keep the government forces out of our area," he said pushing the breakfast tray aside. Reaching behind him he dragged a rolled up map to him and spread it out between them. He used the dirty cups on the map edges to stop it re-rolling. "The soldiers have established a forward base here at Deefa," he said dabbing the spot with his finger. "Every strike is launched from here. Both the attacks against Raykut and Kharfat," again he dabbed the map, "came from here. Instead of dividing our forces and trying to make so many defensive positions around possible targets, Raykut, Dalkut, Kharfat, and others we should have made a strong united line just south of Deefa. Then we would have had a larger force barring their way before they even moved into the jebal. Well it's too late for Raykut and for the time being we will have to suffer its loss. However, if we establish a line here," he dragged his finger in an arc beneath Deefa, "we can prevent them from moving south into our area. At the same time we can throw in a few shells and make life very uncomfortable for them, perhaps we can even make it so uncomfortable that eventually they will withdraw."

Mussalim dragged the map closer towards him and studied it a few moments. It made sense, however there were flaws. "What if they launch from here?' he asked pointing at Manston further to the north east. "There would be an open door all the way south and then behind our line."

Suhayl shook his head. "They would have to come through here," he said pointing at Wadi Al Shawq on the map. "And we have our 9th June Regiment in there."

Mussalim was still uneasy. "It still leaves us very exposed behind the line if most of our forces our concentrated in that line."

"Good point," Suhayl allowed. "However, we can expect some help from the Yemen Army. They have agreed to place troops in some of the villages that we have to leave undefended."

That put a slightly different slant on it. "It could work," he allowed. Certainly it was much better than just sitting there waiting for the government forces to gradually gnaw away at the edges and slowly shrink PFLO territory.

"I am allocated this section here," Suhayl went on pointing at an area south west of Deefa on the northern side of Wadi Sayq. I need a number two on who I can rely. And that's where you come in. I want you as my partner."

❊ ❊ ❊

Late February 1975 • A month later in mid February Suhayl's detachment was in position and well establish south west of Deefa on the northern side of the deep and wide Wadi Sayq. They had fortified themselves on the high ground in tree cover overlooking the open *gatn* below. Any advance from Deefa in this direction would have to be across this exposed ground and with fire from above there would be little cover. Although it was essentially a good position it did have a potential weakness. Little more than ten kilometres in their rear was a government held position at Sarfait and the possibility of an attack from the rear did exist. The likelihood was slim because it was not a strong force and it was under pressure from Hauf with constant shelling. However, it would have been foolish to ignore the possibility so Mussalim and Suhayl had split their force and placed part of it on the opposite side of the wadi to protect their rear.

Meanwhile from north of Kharfat the centre position kept Deefa under pressure by regular shelling. Locked in its own perimeter the government post was a static and well located target and although the soldiers did their best to return fire they were not sure where the fire was coming from. Consequently they mostly fired blind. The most effective way of hitting back was from the air. Marauding Hunters would scan the hills trying to locate the guns positions but the guns were well back and hidden and difficult to find. Nevertheless the aircraft did have some successes and when they found a position they struck hard.

But by-en-large the half circle PFLO line south of Deefa was having an effect. Several times strong patrols had tried to break out and drive south into PFLO territory and in all cases they had encountered fierce resistance and had soon retreated back to their base.

Mussalim stood in the shade of a tree studying Deefa through binoculars. The distant rumble of guns could be plainly heard and occasionally borne on the wind the sounds of battle. But Deefa seemed inactive the battle was not taking place there. He lowered the glasses and shook his head. "I don't know," he said handed the glasses back to Suhayl. "It's much further to the east. Perhaps the eastern flank is under attack."

Suhayl didn't reply but with the glasses to his eyes scanned into the distance. "Maybe!" he allowed dubiously, lowering the glasses. "But I think it's even further than that."

Mussalim pulled the folded map from his pocket and without opening it fully studied the two half pages. "Then the only other place that it could be coming from is Wadi Al Shawq," he said after a brief study.

"Hmm," Suhayl responded thoughtfully. "I wonder if the soldiers are attempting to come south from Manston and outflank us? Perhaps they are?" He agreed with his own query. "If so then they have probably been stopped by the 9th June Regiment."

Stopped? Mussalim hoped so. He traced a route with his finger on the map. If they weren't then they could continue south and either link up with the Iranians at Raykut or swing west behind the PFLO line and drive right through to Kharfat.

"Lets go and stand by the radio. Perhaps some news will come through eventually," Suhayl suggested.

But though they stood by the radio nothing was reported and it was more than a week later when the news started to filter through by word of mouth. Government troops had suddenly arrived in force by Huey helicopter at Wadi Al Shawq and the regiment 9th June had been routed and overrun.

This news had Mussalim reaching for his map and studying the implications. It was not good. In effect it had opened the way for a line to be established in the east from Raykut towards Manston. Soon after that there were reports that construction of a new line copying the Hornbeam Line had been started. This line, the Demavend Line, had moved the eastern frontier forward considerably and cramped PFLO forces in the region even more. The eastern part of the PFLO line now exposed and vulnerable to outflanking had curled in behind the centre and turned to face any threat that might materialise from the east.

October 1975 • It had been a long summer with both sides entrenched and determined to hold what they had. The PFLO still held their lines below Deefa and did their best with Katyusha rockets to make life untenable for the government soldiers on the base. The soldiers however were equally as determined and would not be driven away. To show their defiance they would occasionally break out and probe away aggravatingly at the *adoo* defences. In the east the Demavend Line had been completed. Wired and mined it ran north from Raykut across the mountains to the *gatn* and manned by the trigger happy Iranians it effectively sealed the PFLO into this small south west corner. Now with autumn well advanced and the summer mist over the mountains cleared both sides prepared themselves for the next inevitable stages. While the government forces planned and prepared for the final push to clear the *adoo* away over the border the PFLO dug in and fortified to hold.

Hamed had very recently returned from leave. The time he had spent with Khamisa as far as he was concerned had been real quality time. She had it seemed continued to mellow towards him and had begun acting as a model wife should. Gone was her shroud of unhappiness replaced by a quiet submissive acceptance of her situation. He knew that he would never command the unbridled devotion that she had lavished on his brother Juma, but he too had accepted that he would have to settle for less. His son Mubarrak was a year old now and tottered around unsteadily as babies normally do. Even so he had filled with pride at his every little achievement and found immense pleasure in the boy's dependence and attachment to his father.

As always personal survival is paramount whatever the circumstances but now that he had a real family of his own it became even more important. From a selfish point of view he wanted to live to enjoy the luxury of his woman and the pleasure of his son. From an unselfish point of view they depended on his survival for their welfare and his protection. The talk around the base here at Manston was that before the coming winter had ended then the PFLO would be smashed. He sincerely hoped that was so because to continue to draw firqat pay when there would be no fighting or dying would be comparatively easy money. Additionally and just as attractively wherever he was located during peacetime then there could be no reason for him not to have his family with him. The only thing standing between those halcyon possibilities it seemed were these last few *adoo*. Even the need to avenge his brother had paled to be less important. It was no longer an all consuming anger but more of a hoped for opportunity. This conflict had dragged on and on and for far too long more than anything now he wanted it finished so that he could begin a new life.

Manston was teeming with troops. The recent arrival of Jordanian troops to take over the security of the Salalah Midway road had released hundreds of Omani soldiers and they had been sent here to strengthen the western forces. The troops were massing and the anticipated offensive could not be long coming.

Mussalim listened in the darkness to the thump of rotor blades as yet another helicopter passed over their position. At first he hadn't been too concerned but now it was happening every few minutes. It had started as soon as darkness fell and he guessed that either supplies or men, perhaps both, were being ferried southward.

"What do you think?" Suhayl asked.

"They are building up their position at Sarfait."

"Yes. I think so too. That can only mean that they're about to break out."

Mussalim nodded and stared out through the darkness towards the other side of Wadi Sayq. "If they come north they will soon be in among our men over there."

"Yes. Take some men from here and go over there to strengthen the position."

"That will weaken this side, So what happens if they come out from Deefa and attack here at the same time?"

"We'll hold."

He probably would. Dominating the flat open ground to their front would take fewer men than the thicker covered ground on the other side.

Could this be the start of the offensive that they had been expecting? Almost certainly it would have something to do with it. The struggle was likely to be long and intense and the best the PFLO forces could hope for at the end of it would be to still hold what they had. There was a feeling that if the government forces were to be beaten back then they would simply cordon off the area and abandon it as too costly to take back. However, with the superiority of equipment and numbers then beating them back would be mighty task. The most likely outcome would be that they would eat away at the edges pushing the Front fighters back a little at a time until they were pushed right into Yemen. He guessed that Suhayl thought along those lines too even though he hadn't confessed as much. During the time they had sat talking away the long nights he had begun to reminisce about his own Manahil tribal area. It seemed he had accepted that he would be there soon and that he was looking forward to returning after such a long absence. Mussalim considered their opposite circumstances. The consolation of defeat for Suhayl would be that he would go home while defeat meant to him exile in a country he did not know. The flat barren *nejd* lands of Yemen did not compare in the slightest to the rolling greenery of his beloved Qara. Perhaps he could get used it although he had doubts. Maybe after a little while he might be able to have Jumaia and the boys join him. That might soften the misery of expulsion a little. However, there was no doubt in his mind where he would much sooner be.

The sounds of another approaching helicopter grew gradually louder interrupting his thoughts. With its sheer sides and wide base it would take at least two hours to cross the wadi. He had better get started.

∗ ∗ ∗

Hamed tumbled from the Huey and shivered slightly. For a mid October night it was quite cold. Perhaps it was the height of the Sarfait location almost a thousand metres above sea level or maybe it was the wind that rose directly off the sea only seven kilometres away. He and the dozen men that he had flown in with were moved quickly away from the aircraft and were shown into a long narrow trench. It was full of earlier arrivals huddling together just waiting for the rest of the force to assemble. Even before they had found a niche for themselves the helicopter behind them lifted off on its return to Manston to collect more men. Most of the men in the trench were soldiers but they were well supported with the Tareeq Bin Zeead *firqa*.

The citadel up here was generously littered with many sangars and all robustly constructed. They had to be because artillery shells from Hauf only eight or nine kilometres away over the border blasted this position daily. Its height made it an impregnable bastion however in the very heart of *adoo* country and within easy range of those guns it was not a coveted post. Strategically however Sarfait was a good position to hold. It not only provided a good base from which to launch strikes at the soft under belly of PFLO held territory but it was also a major source of irritation. The *adoo* could not afford to ignore it and were therefore forced to maintain some fighters in the area at least.

An hour later and still two hours to midnight they moved out. They moved in two columns a few minutes apart heading west towards the border. Before they reached the border they descended into Wadi Sarfait and turned south descending off the high ground and onto the coast. Using this 'back door' route off Sarfait they reached the coast unopposed and began to deploy in positions to create a skirmish line. Soon a third column moved off Sarfait to reinforce these positions and by daylight the soldiers were well dug in. With the daylight the priority became to strengthen the hastily built defences in preparation for the inevitable retaliation.

Hamed found himself manning a position a little way from the sea and beneath the lea of steeply rising ground. He and four others worked feverishly to establish a sturdy sangar stacking the rocks double thick in a narrow 'U' shape. Then they scraped out its inside to a depth of a metre and used the soil to pack the rocks into place solidly. Satisfied that it would stand all except a direct hit from an artillery shell they dragged their equipment into its cover and settled down to wait for the attack. Hamed looked out across the flat ground towards the sea. Only a few metres to his front was the road that had carried the PFLO arms from their Hauf base to their supply depots in Shershitta and Kharfat. This line effectively cut that route and the certainty was that the *adoo* could not allow this situation to stand without stiff opposition.

The heat of the day coupled with the sleepless night began to tell on Hamed and stretching out best he could in the cramped position he attempted sleep. His sleep was restless haunted by uncontrolled thoughts of angry charging *adoo* attempting to dislodge him from the sangar. Through sheets of bullets they charged relentlessly forward the gap narrowing rapidly. He fired as fast as he could and fanned wildly trying to force them back but they would not be repulsed. They bore down upon him

– now at point blank range he increased his fire even more but still they would not go down. It took a sudden and earth shattering explosion before they disappeared. He woke with a start, the explosion was not part of the nightmare.

It was the start of a long and intense barrage as shells rained in on their new positions from Hauf across the border. Everything they had it seemed was poured onto their position, the PFLO were not about to tolerate this new line cutting off their fighters. All through the day Hamed cowered in his sangar with his four comrades as explosions randomly erupted geysers of earth all around the line. The only consolation seemed to be that the shells were poured in blindly but even so there were inevitable casualties. After sunset the shelling eased a little dropping to a rate that was monotonously frequent. If its intention was to deny the soldiers sleep then the tactic was successful as ground-shaking explosions occurred every few minutes. Hamed's eyes felt swollen through lack of sleep while his stomach churned nauseous in sympathy with his body's exhaustion. Despite the explosions he did drift into a sleep of sorts. Each blast roused him to a temporary wakeful state but he immediately settled back into the level between sleep and consciousness. With the daylight the intensity of the barrage was stepped up again and without any lessening in the onslaught throughout the long day. It seemed that the options forced upon the government forces were two. Withdraw or be annihilated! Meanwhile their own guns positioned on the high ground at Sarfait were silent. They were forbidden to retaliate across the border into Yemen.

It was at dawn the next day when the Sultan rescinded and ordered his Air Force to launch an attack to silence the guns at Hauf. Hunters and Strikemasters struck in waves slamming in rockets and bombs before wheeling to strafe the camp for good measure. When their payloads were spent they returned to Salalah to re-supply but were replaced instantly by the next wave of aircraft pulverising the PFLO base. When eventually the last of them flew low over Hamed's position performing their victory rolls Hauf had disappeared beneath an enormous rising column of thick black smoke and the guns were silent.

✳ ✳ ✳

The PFLO were under enormous pressure. That morning Mussalim had listened to the distant sounds of exploding bombs in the Hauf direction and the absence of any gunfire afterwards was ominous. But the problems hadn't ended there. Now it seemed the Iranians had moved off their Demavend Line and advanced towards Kharfat. The eastern flank had engaged them and for the time being was holding. The centre with its eyes on Deefa was now forced to pull back to Kharfat and turn to face this new threat. Meanwhile the position that Suhayl and Mussalim held to the south west of Deefa at Wadi Sayq had become obsolete and so they too had been ordered back to Kharfat. The supply depot was vitally important for the Front's continued struggle and it must be held at all costs.

The word had been received around midday to move to Kharfat in all haste. However, by the time they had gathered their equipment and destroyed all the fortifications that they had painstakingly built it was mid afternoon. Satisfied that all was ready at last Suhayl led his men east. With a forced march they should reach Wadi Kharfat around midnight.

Mussalim stood watching the sombre faced men burdened with their equipment file past. There was no trace of that optimistic spirit that the fighters had carried into battle in the past. In those days, based on previous successes, expectations had been high. Now that the actual successes were few and far between those expectations had suffered many disappointments and they had all but withered and died. An air of morose silence and an acceptance of inevitability seemed to be all that remained. The look of defeat was in their eyes.

He glanced towards Deefa. For eight months now they had kept the soldiers more or less bottled up in there. As they now withdrew the door would again be opened for them to come marauding south. But then Kharfat had to be secured for without arms and ammunition the fight could not go on. Lose this battle and the war was lost with it. The first priority was to hold the supply depot, later they could perhaps return.

It was after midnight by the time they reached Kharfat and they were soon sent to a position to the south near the deserted village Umbaraaf. As the dawn broke and the Front men began to dig in and build their sangars

Mussalim gazed east through binoculars looking to catch a glimpse of the wired fence line of Demavend. But he could not see it. It must be positioned beyond the distant hills. Probably it would look deceptively innocuous he speculated. However, it would be very effective, that he did not doubt. The much larger and longer Hornbeam Line had proved the proficiency of these barriers. Heavily mined and fitted with sensors that alerted the manning troops of any breaches it was a formidable blockade. Here in this spot, somewhere opposite Demavend they had to create their own line and it had to be just as effective.

With the supply of plenty close at their backs the PFLO forces began to pulverise the Iranian positions trying to force them away from Kharfat and back behind their own Demavend Line. Guns positioned on the high ground above the caves hurled shells into their positions while the men facing added Katyusha and anti tank rockets to the bombardment. But after three days the Iranians still held.

Mussalim had been growing increasingly uneasy, there was something unsettling about the way they held. Although they replied to the bombardment they made no attempt to either advance or fall back. As evening fell on the third day he looked for Suhayl. He found him in one of the sangars in a forward position.

"This is not an attack," he said voicing his concern. "It's more like aggravation. They moved up which forced us to respond and now it seems that they intend to stop there just to make sure we stay too."

Sahyl nodded agreement. "I have been thinking the same for a while now." He inched up the low sangar wall and stared through binoculars into the gathering gloom towards the Iranian position. He slid back shaking his head. "All quiet," he said with a shrug.

"There is something else happening," Mussalim said nonplussed. "This has to be diversionary."

"Yes you're probably right. But what can we do? If we move away then they will overrun Kharfat. They have us locked here."

"In the meantime at this very moment they're probably preparing another nasty surprise for us somewhere else."

Suhayl stared silently at him as he thought. Then after a few moments he grabbed his Kalachnikov and as he got up said. "Let's go and talk to the commanders."

They made their way up the wadi and by the time they came to the blind canyon at its head it had been dark for some time. The whole scene was a hive of activity as men moved stocks from the caves to stack in the flat area beneath towering rocky walls. Here men worked feverishly lavishing supplies on an impatient circle of men acquiring the needs for tomorrow's renewal of the bombardment. Ignoring that mayhem they made their way past to one of the caves. Just inside its enormous gaping mouth a circle of men sat around a large blazing fire argued furiously. Mussalim stood just on the fringe of the firelight listening with growing alarm. As he listened his suspicions were being confirmed. Now that the barrier below Deefa had been withdrawn a large force it seemed had moved out and now occupied Wadi Sayq. The arguments were all about what the intention of this force was and what should be done about it. The argument was split on whether it would continue on south and link up at Sarfait to form another line squeezing the PFLO still further or whether they would now move east to attack Kharfat on its the western side. Either way it was another serious development.

"You have your answer," Suhayl said. "That's your nasty surprise."

"The noose is tightening," Mussalim muttered.

"And there are two who definitely would not want to get caught in it," Suhayl said nodding towards the two men sitting at the head of the circle. "Isa Abdulla and Mohamed Adbulla Hussein, Central Committee Leaders!"

They gloomily made their way back to their position almost in silence. There was not a great deal to say. The PFLO main force were squeezed up in and around Kharfat, while the coastal villages were held by their allies the soldiers of the Peoples Democratic Republic of Yemen. In effect the territory now held by the Front had shrunk into the narrow shape of a backward 'L' and was surrounded on all sides.

Worse news followed a week later when the Yemen government, realising that their soldiers were all but cut off in Oman and not wishing the international embarrassment of Yemeni prisoners of war in a foreign country, ordered their troops to withdraw. By night they moved up through Wadi Kharfat then headed west back to Yemen. The Omani Army allowed them through unhindered.

Mussalim watched them go. That was it, with the PFLO fighters tightly bottled up around Kharfat the war was all but over. The next day the guns were silent, even the

Iranians it seemed were content to allow the fighters this time to consider their position. Men went into small huddles discussing what alternatives were open to them. Many had their minds made up for them when around midday the word was passed that the PFLO leaders had followed the Yemeni soldiers also and had retreated into exile.

"What are you going to do?" Suhayl posed the question that Mussalim had wrestled with for months.

"I don't know." He watched him gathering his few belongings.

"Come with me to Yemen."

He shook his head. "I can't. I don't belong to Yemen."

He stopped what he was doing a moment and looked at him. "You don't belong here either. You're an undesirable."

It was true. Exile was where he belonged but it wasn't home. Home was here but he did not belong here anymore. Still he would not go to Yemen. He could not live there enviously staring over the border towards his homeland. Instead he would take his chances on the Sultan's leniency. And if he demanded the ultimate price then death would be better than exile. He watched Suhayl go back to his packing and wondered what he would do. Almost all of his life he had been at war. First attempting to force the British out of Yemen and since then furthering the Communist cause in the Middle East. "What will you do?"

He shrugged and flashed him that crooked grin. "They say civil war is coming to the Yemen. I will fight for my homeland against the North."

"Another war! Don't you ever get tired of fighting?"

He had finished gathering his meagre belongings. "I don't know anything else," he said facing him. "What would I do?" He hitched his bag over his shoulder and picked up his Kalachnikov. "Change your mind Crazy Man and fight alongside me."

Mussalim shook his head. "No. But may Allah protect you."

He smiled crookedly and shook his head. "You never did give up your religion did you? I knew that. You never fooled me for an instant. But you were a good a soldier and to have you shot would have been a big loss to the PFLOAG."

They shook hands and he was gone. Mussalim stood and watched him climb the hill and disappear over its crest wondering if he would ever stop fighting or would it be that another bullet would next time get closer than the one that had deformed his face.

What to do now? Men streamed away in all directions, some heading for the border others of no notoriety simply going home. How he envied them. To be able to go back to his father's farm to Jumaia and the boys! Perhaps if the government were to send him to prison then after he served out his time it might happen. He didn't intend to stop here. To surrender to Iranians was not a desirable thing. He had heard stories that they simply shot ranking prisoners. He decided to go back to Dalkut and wait for the Oman soldiers to arrive.

✳ ✳ ✳

Early November 1975 • Hamed sat on a large rock and idly watched the circle of men sitting cross-legged in the shade of a large tree. His tribal ancestry as Al Hamer of the larger Kathir isolated him in this Mahru *firqa*. He would take no part in this conversation but he knew precisely the topic and exactly what it was being said. The *firqa* Tariq Bin Zeead being made up mostly of men from the area had now been detached from the army and sent out into the villages. With face to face contact with the populace they were able to pass on the word of the Sultan's civil development policies. At the same time they gleaned any information they could about any pockets of *adoo* that still skulked in hiding. Any news of this nature was passed on to Army Intelligence who then organised purging operations. These purging operations carried out by the army and using the local *firqat* men as guides were usually low risk affairs because any *adoo* that were found soon handed over their weapons. It was much more the case that they only waited for soldiers to arrive to give them someone to surrender to. However, a full-blooded cautious approach was always made because there were still some diehards around.

He could not believe it even now. Little more than two weeks ago he had been cowering in a sangar under intense shelling and now the PFLO had gone. More or less, anyway! He hadn't managed to achieve the blood payment that he had badly wanted because in his case face to face contact with the *adoo* had proved to be non-existent. In fact he'd had more actual *adoo* contact on his father's farm before he had become a *firqat*. But since he had been in a situation to retaliate they had maintained at least a shooting distance. As far as he was concerned it reflected a lot on the calibre of men they were. On the defenceless they swooped and demanded extreme tariff but give a man a chance to defend himself and they kept their distance. He consoled himself, however, with the thought that at least he had taken an active part in the Communist force's downfall. It was meagre consolation for Juma's death but it seemed that was all the recompense he would get. He would, it seemed, have to learn to live with that and his uneasy conscience too.

With the collapse and retreat of the PFLO he also wondered what had become of his other brother Mussalim, and his family. The last word that he had heard was that they were in Raykut. But Raykut had fallen to the Iranians in January and now it was early November and he hadn't heard anything since. For all he knew they could have all died there, however, he believed that was unlikely. Mussalim was a very resourceful man and it was much more likely that he would have got out with his family somehow. The probability was the he would have escaped to Yemen and he would even now be starting a new life there. He shook his head ruefully sympathetic as he considered where his eldest brother's radical beliefs had finally led him. At the best, exile in Yemen.

The war had very definitely shattered the family. Every member it seemed had suffered and those that had survived had come out of it rather badly. The one exception however, was himself. He seemed to have been the only one who had benefited. He had a wife and son that would be the envy of many, he had a paid position in the *firqa* and this had enabled him to escape the yoke of the farm. Such was his shattered family state he also held the most influential position. Now he looked forward to finishing this mop up process and then he would be free to transfer back to the Firqa Al Nasr in the Qara area. Wherever that placed him he would be able to settle and locate his wife and son with him permanently. That was his major desire. In view of his father's helplessness and his brother's exile, he would be forced to assume the role as the family head and consider the welfare of his parents. How he could appease his desire and that duty at this time he didn't know but he would have to find a way.

The men in the circle began to fidget, the meeting was breaking up. One or two even got to their feet, but even so these withdrawal activities might go on for a little while yet. It was well past the hottest part of the day and if they left in the next few minutes they would not be back at Sarfait before dark. It was always a risky business approaching a soldier's defence perimeter in the dark. He guessed they would probably move onto the lower reaches of Jebal Sayq and camp there until daylight and when it was light then they would report in. He wondered if there would be anything special to report. Twice this week already they had reported that there was still a strong pocket of *adoo* in Dalkut.

✳ ✳ ✳

December 1975 • For almost three weeks now Mussalim had waited in Dalkut for the soldiers to arrive. He had with him a contingency of around forty men. They had held long evening *dirwains* and all but a mere handful had decided that it was a hopeless situation – there was nothing to be gained by standing to fight. The handful that could not accept the ignominy of surrender had left to follow some other alternative. Each morning brought the expectancy that the soldiers would come and each evening had added another day's reprieve. There was nothing to do but wait.

Mussalim had taken one precaution. He had in his pocket almost a year's PFLO pay in Omani Rials and he knew that after his arrest the money would be confiscated. Possibly shared among the soldiers who actually arrested him. In all probability, he would not be able to even protest. They could deny its existence and who would care anyway? He was PFLO and had disqualified any right to any sort of consideration. So he had wrapped the money in a goatskin and hidden it amongst the rocks in the steep hills behind Dalkut. His own future was bleak if indeed he even had one, but somehow he might be able to get word to Jumaia where she would find it. How she would even get to Dalkut to find it he had no idea but it was the only legacy that he could leave her.

With a great deal of time to spend alone he could not help but contemplate his circumstances. His prospects seemed particularly gloomy. Although the possibility had crossed his mind that it was still not too late to make a run for the Yemen, it was never really an option. He would ache to return to the mountains of Qara and sooner or later he would give in to that ache and return anyway. The outcome in the end would be the same certain arrest. Therefore he considered that it was much better that he face his prosecutors now.

Today was the morning of December 1st in the Christian year 1975 and the soldiers had arrived in force. They positioned themselves along the cliffs looking directly down into Dalkut. As a warning they fired mortar over the village and into the sea. Then leaving that force in place as cover they advanced down the road and swept into the deserted village.

In a small but prominent clearing Mussalim, dressed in his Commissar uniform had the PFLO men sit unarmed in a wide circle adopting a quiet and non-threatening attitude. The Land Rovers drove through the deserted village streets until they saw the seated group. They stopped a few moments while somebody in the front vehicle stood and studied them through binoculars. Then seeing no particular threat the vehicles rolled forward once more. In a pre-determined fashion each vehicle pulled up creating a half circle around the seated men. About half had a machine gun mounted in the rear and with a man behind each, the weapons pointed threateningly.

Mussalim stood in front of the PFLO men with arms outstretched in a submissive manner. For a while nothing happened and then the soldiers responding to instructions got from the vehicles and with weapons ready formed a line beneath the protection of the machine gunners. When all seemed to be in position two officers each holding hand pistols and pointed loosely in his direction approached him warily.

Mussalim stood and waited until they stood directly in front of him. "I am Commissar Mussalim Bin Abdulla Al Hamer of the PFLO," he said. Then with a brief wave towards the men behind him he went on. "We are here this morning to surrender."

"Put your hands on your head," one of them demanded curtly. He did as he was ordered.

"Now tell your men to do the same."

After he had done that he was then unceremoniously searched while the other man continued to point his pistol directly at him. The searcher then waved three men forward from the ranks behind him. "Take good care of the Commissar," he instructed with a heavy hint of sarcasm. As Mussalim was led away he could hear the rest of the PFLO men being ordered to come forward one at a time to be searched.

With his hands tied behind his back he was kept for a long time sitting in the back of a Land Rover while three guards stared at him impassively. The rest of the PFLO men having been routinely searched were once more seated on the ground with a cordon of guards around them. During the next hour or so more men and vehicles continued to pour into the village and systematic building searches were carried out.

Mussalim could not help but compare this new situation to those days long ago when he had been located here under the command of Hemel Al Shibam. The PFLOAG had been strong then but perhaps even then he should have known that one day this would happen. The government with its superior amount of money and all the resources that it could eventually muster must in the end prevail. But then Bin Taymour's love of money prevented him spending it on such wasteful projects as clearing away the "trouble makers" that ravaged his country. It was only with the ascension of his son Qaboos that turned that self-centred policy into the inevitability it became. Without him the Communist doctrine could have succeeded and Oman might have become another Peoples Democratic Republic. What then, he wondered? Perhaps the Omani people would have been no better off anyway? It certainly had not worked for Yemen!

Eventually he was driven away and put in a room in a village house that had been selected as suitable for a cell. It was small, windowless and had one door leading off from a main room. Probably at some time it had been a family storeroom. He had no way of knowing how many guards were outside but he had one armed inside with him. He was not inclined towards conversation answering Mussalim's attempts to talk with only grunts and short bland replies. Eventually he gave up and with absolutely nothing else to do he tried to sleep. Sometime later the guard was changed and his response to conversation was no better. Mussalim by now had guessed that they had probably been instructed not to talk to the prisoner.

It was mid afternoon before he was collected and taken to one of the bigger houses in the village that had been set up as a temporary command post. Confronted by three seated on the other side of a long bench and one who wandered around restlessly behind him he underwent a vigorous interrogation. He answered each question the best way he could, after all there was no longer any reason why he shouldn't co-operate fully. After what seemed an age he was eventually taken back to his "storeroom cell." Later sometime after sunset he was given food and informed that tomorrow he would be moved by helicopter to Um Al Gharriff at Salalah for further interrogation.

~ 28 ~

January 1976 • Mussalim sat on the floor his back resting against the concrete wall and stared at the heavy metal door just three metres away on the opposite wall. Sometimes in his imagination that door grew so small that it looked impossible that he would be able to pass through when eventually it did open. Apart from the narrow collapsible cot down one wall the cell was bare with only crude graffiti on the walls breaking up the starkness. It was hot and rivulets of sweat stuck the threadbare prison boiler suit to his body like sticking plaster. The only hint of relief was the smallest breath of air that occasionally wafted through the bars of the narrow slit above his head. Even the cockroaches it seemed found somewhere else to be during the heat of the day. But at night they could be heard rustling around in the darkness on the uneven *bondhu* floor.

For a month he had languished in a prison cell in Salalah. Most of the time he was "banged up' like this with absolutely nothing to do. Sheer boredom turned each hour endless and even the degrading tasks of cleaning toilets and floors were welcomed. Exercise was limited to one hour towards the end of each day and consisted of all inmates just walking continuously in a circle around the small compound. Every once in a while in no set programme he would attend re-training classes. These were sometimes a classroom situation where as a group the prisoners would be instructed in the progress and the plans of the new Oman. Sometimes it would be in an interview situation where he would be questioned and encouraged to discuss his viewpoints on a wide range of subjects. During some of these interviews he had tried to establish when his trial might be. But the response had been vague and sometimes even discouraging when he had been asked, why he thought he was entitled to a trial?

Once he was presented with a grain of hope when he had been informed that the Sultan had granted amnesty to all PFLO members who had reformed, swore allegiance to the Sultan and intended to play their part in the building of the country. However, it was only a spirit breaking exercise. They soon told him that it could never apply to him. He was a much too influential figure to be released back into society. There were still pockets of resistance in the central area and a Commissar of his reputation could easily become the leader that united them. His contrite reply that he had no ambitions along those lines and that all he wanted now was to return to his father's farm and live a quiet life with his family around him, was received sceptically.

Nor could he learn news of his family. The first week after his arrest he had undergone a series of strenuous interrogations while being held at Um Al Gharriff. As a reward for his co-operation one of his interrogators had promised to contact his father and let him know that he was still alive and being held in the Garrison.

On the morning of the 11th December just before he was moved to Salalah prison he had been brought to listen to the jubilant Muscat victory celebration on the radio and the triumphant announcement which proclaimed. "SAF and irregular forces have achieved a decisive victory and eliminated the Marxist terrorist gang in the western area of Dhofar. They are now in full control of every inch of land that is adjacent to the border with the Peoples Democratic Republic of Yemen."

As he was being prepared to move he had been informed that his father's farm was derelict and looked as if it had been that way for some time. This puzzled and worried him enormously. He had over the past months complacently believed that life had gone on as normal in his absence just as it always had. But it seemed that something drastic had happened. The unanswered questions piled up. What had happened? When did it happen? Where had they gone? Were they still all together? Was the farm abandoned when Jumaia arrived? If so what had become of her and the boys? In his imprisoned situation he was impotent to discover any answers. Alone in his cell with long hours to think his imagination formed all sorts of horrors driving him to depths of depression and the point of despair. As the eldest son and his father physically failing he should have been there to make certain of their welfare.

When he had left two years ago he had left them all in Hamed's care and on the scant information he had it seemed that he failed them all. A year later he had entrusted his own wife and family to his care too! Perhaps in his anguish he was being uncharitable? Hamed had always been reliable and perhaps it was a situation beyond his control that caused the abandonment of the farm. It was possible that he had made other comfortable arrangements. But when? Had Jumaia arrived there before or after they had left? He was frantic with worry and his application for enquiries to be made on his behalf received only a tepid response. Someone would contact his tribal Sheikh to see if he had any information, they said. But as days had turned into weeks and no information had come back he doubted that anyone had even bothered to enquire.

For himself it didn't matter, perhaps he even deserved this treatment. But to think that his family might be suffering when he could possibly do something to help seemed an outrageous injustice. Sometimes his stomach knotted in rage against such a callous attitude, while other times in despair he was on the verge of tears. But he wasn't sure what it was that he would be able to do even if he did know their circumstances. Perhaps it was that they lived comfortably anyway and did quite well. Maybe the authorities already knew that and they kept that from him to use as a tool in these mind games they played. All these thoughts tormented him, tumbling endlessly repetitive through the long empty hours. By now he was convinced that it had been a grave mistake not to flee to exile, this was nothing like he thought it was going to be.

Mechanically and hardly aware that he was doing it he got to his feet and made the three strides to the opposite wall and back repeatedly. After a few minutes of this head-spinning turning and pacing he became aware of the heavy jangle of keys outside his cell door. He stopped and listened hard hoping to hear the sounds of the door being unlocked. His hopes were raised, perhaps it would be another re-training session or just some cleaning work. Whatever, anything was better then this mind crushing boredom. The sound of bolts being slammed back lifted his spirits. There was about to be some relief, no matter how small it was welcomed.

The door swung open and Mussalim, after a moment's hesitation went to stand in the doorway awaiting instructions. Two prison guards stood in the passageway either side of the door.

"Step out," one said.

Mussalim did as he was instructed. Then he led the way down the corridor after a wave of an arm indicated that he should. Near the end of the corridor outside the communal toilet he was stopped then directed in. Usually the place was crowded but at this time of the day with almost all of the inmates locked in their cells the place was empty. A row of hole-in-the-floor toilets lined one side while a narrow metal trough lined the other. Fastened along the wall at the back of the trough was a row of taps all with short flexible hoses attached. A strong smell of carbolic failed to mask the smell of urine. He stood in the middle of the room and looked at the guards questioningly.

One of them thrust a towel in his hands and a clean boiler suit. Then with a brief wave indicating towards the trough one of the guards said. "Five minutes only. You have a visitor."

Using one hand to direct the hose he showered awkwardly immensely curious of who the mysterious visitor could be. Who actually knew he was here? When he was finished he was led across the exercise compound into a large wooden building and shown into a room at the far end. Compared to his cell it was light, airy and cooled from the ceiling by a large electric fan spinning at aircraft propeller speed. It was furnished spartanly with just a wooden trestle and a chair on either side. Hamed stood to greet him when he came in.

Such was his relief to see him that Mussalim struggled to control a lump that rose in his throat as they embraced each other. He clung to his young brother until he composed himself and trusted his voice to speak. "*Il Hamdu Lillaah*," was all he could croak as he pushed him back to arm's length and looked at him.

The guard indicated that they should sit each side of the table and when they had, he retreated to one side of the room and stood watching impassively.

"You look tired my brother," Hamed said as they sat.

Tired? He was probably being kind Mussalim thought. Gaunt would probably be a more accurate description. Due to the harsh conditions and worry of the family fate he knew that he had lost a great deal of weight. "You look well," he replied. "How did you know that I was here?"

"Two day's ago our Al Hamer Sheikh informed father and he got a message to me. I came as soon as I heard."

Someone had it seemed at least made some enquiry. "Is everybody well?"

"Yes."

He had a hundred important questions and he struggled to select the priority. In the end he spread his hands inviting the flood of information. "What happened to the farm?"

Hamed hesitated not sure where to begin. "Well after Lailla's death father could no longer manage on his own."

"Lailla's dead?" Mussalim stopped him straight away.

"You didn't know?"

He shook his head slowly staring at him wide-eyed, the questions and confusion instantly multiplied "You had better start from when I left the farm two years ago."

He waited while his brother gathered his thoughts and then listened with mounting dismay at the events that had brought reversals of the family fortunes. He found all the old resentments rising against autocracy when he learned the alleged justification for his sister's execution. That had to have been a travesty of justice. He would never be convinced that she had become PFLO. She had no interests in things materialistic and was as naive as a child. Hamed listened to his protestation shaking his head sadly. There was indisputable evidence, he said, and it was probable that some Bait Gatun young man had influenced her. Even so Mussalim found it incredible that his baby sister was capable of violence and was still unconvinced. He sought somewhere to lay the blame for all the misfortune that had fallen on the family and his first target was Hamed himself. If he had stayed where he belonged carrying out his obligation to the family instead of returning to the firqats in all probability none of this would have happened. But then it was he who was the eldest son and the ultimate responsibility for the family's welfare was his. He had complacently believed that

Hamed would dutifully take over the responsibilities that he had so easily discarded. The shame was his and not his young brother's and the anger became directed inwards. He blamed himself.

He buried his face in his hands and stayed motionless for a moment. Then with a heavy sigh he looked up once more and asked quietly. "What about Jumaia?"

"Jumaia?" Hamed repeated with a puzzled expression. "We thought she was with you!"

"Well she was but I sent her back to the farm more than a year ago."

"A year ago?"

"Yes."

"It was more than a year ago when he left the farm and moved to Haluf."

"So where is she now?" Panic was rising in Mussalim's voice.

"I don't know."

"You have to find her. She has the two boys with her."

"Time's up," the guard across the room said loudly.

"I'll do what I can," Hamed said hurriedly. "But although I have moved back to the Qara with Al Nasr I'm currently stationed at Zeak."

Zeak was not that far away from Haluf but it was just far away to make things awkward for him. Mussallim gripped his hand across the table. "You have to find her."

The guard was standing above them and looking down at them impatiently. Mussalim knew the signals by now and got to his feet to placate the guard.

"I have applied for amnesty on your behalf this morning," Hamed said getting to his feet also.

Mussalim hesitated a moment as the guard nudged him towards the door. "I don't think you will get it," he replied thinking of what he had been told about being far too influential. But compared to Jumaia and the boy's welfare that was less important. "Brother. Find my wife," he said as he began to move to the door.

Back in his cell he had much to contemplate and he lay on his cot staring upward, lost in thought. At least he knew where most of his family were now, and that was a tremendous relief. They also knew where he was and that too was comforting. The whereabouts of his wife and children however was enormously worrying, but at least Hamed now knew that they were lost and he had to trust that he would do something about finding them. The news of Lailla both shocked and appalled him. He was convinced of her innocence or at the very least some mitigating circumstance for her involvement with this anonymous young man. The thought of her dying alone before a firing squad and surrounded by hostility overwhelmed him with a deep sense of sadness. She deserved to at least have someone with her for some degree of comfort. While she was standing alone looking down the barrels of rifles and indeed while all this misfortune was descending on the family he was busy pursuing his own quest. Could he have got out of that quest if he had really wanted? By that stage, probably not! But certainly he could have done much more to ensure his family's well being than he had. He felt largely responsible and a huge weight of guilt. If he could get his time over again then he would be a much more dutiful son and more protective elder brother. But what is done cannot be undone.

✳ ✳ ✳

Hamed rode away on one of his father's camels. He was happy to be leaving the prison. It was indeed a stark and depressing place. He had been surprised to learn only yesterday that Mussalim was being held there. He had assumed that he had fled to Yemen. He knew the Omani Army had stood aside and allowed Yemen forces and any PFLO who wanted to cross the border into exile to go unhindered. He had himself been very close to the gap that had been deliberately left open for that very purpose. Despite the certainty of imprisonment and perhaps even worse Mussalim it seemed had chosen not to go. The second he had laid eyes on his brother the physical cost had been very apparent. Lean and haggard he looked at least ten years older than a man in his early thirties should. Incarcerated in there he doubted that Mussalim would survive very long. He was so like their father's brother, Fiad the blood in his veins was Bedouin and the spirit in his chest needed the freedom of Allah's garden. That restlessness may have been a contributing factor to the course of actions that he had followed and had brought him to his present predicament. Whatever the circumstances that had put him there were irrelevant now, to leave him there would mean a lingering death.

There was however a glimmer of hope. In the interests of re-unification the Sultan had decreed that an amnesty be granted to PFLO members who swore their allegiance and genuinely wanted to be part of this new Oman. As soon as he had received the message at Zeak from his father yesterday he had been granted a leave of absence to see what he could do. He had returned home to Haluf and spent the evening in discussion. Without being too optimistic they had soon agreed that they should make the application to get him released back into the community. The war was over and only a few fanatical radicals remained. The task would be to convince the authorities that although Mussalim had been a highly respected Commissar in the PFLO he was not one of those fanatics.

He had left Haluf long before sunrise and arrived at the Wali's office in Salalah by mid morning. There he had patiently sat in a crowded reception hall waiting his turn for an interview. He hadn't actually seen the governor but he had explained to his secretary what it was that he wanted and together they filled out the application for his brother's amnesty. At the same time he had given him a pass into the prison to visit Mussalim.

His own situation was that Zeak was just a little too far away from Haluf for him to return between duty shifts. That meant unless he actually had two or three days between duties he could not be with Khamisa and his infant son. So although he was better off by far than he had been with Tariq Bin Zeead in the western area he did not have the family life he wanted. He could perhaps move Khamisa to the village of Zeak but that would mean that he more or less abandoned his father and Jokha in Haluf because he would have little reason to visit on a regular basis.

With this new development another possibility had occurred to him. If Mussalim could get his amnesty then he could pass the responsibility for their parents back where it belonged, with the eldest son. He could then in easy conscience move Khamisa to Zeak and Mussalim would have to look after their welfare. It was time that he did what he was morally obliged to anyway. For too long he had delegated his responsibilities easily. Now it seemed that he had managed to misplace his wife and two sons also. He shook his head ruefully, there would be absolutely no way that he would ever allow Khamisa and Mubarrak to be misplaced. But yet again the burden of responsibility had fallen back on him. "Hamed go find." Wherever was he supposed to start looking? And more to the point as a busy firqat, when?

He weaved the camel through the chicane that was the town gate and waved at the guards as he did. The barriers were still manned but now that peace had more or less broken out their presence was little more that token. Only occasionally when the fancy took them or if they became bored did they stop to search people and loads passing through the gate. Still it was an effective deterrent because no man could be sure whether his load would be searched or not.

He looked across the plain to the towering distant jebal. He would have to climb its heights and cross its peaks to the *nejd* on the other side and even though it was only mid afternoon it would have been dark a long time by the time he reached Haluf. Common sense told him that he should spend the night on Um Al Gharriff and leave first thing in the morning. But Khamisa was not in Umm Al Gharriff, she was in Haluf and so common sense did not win.

✳ ✳ ✳

February 1975 · After another featureless week the routine changed for Mussalim. He still had the degrading menial chores to perform, the hours of overwhelming boredom to endure and the routine exercise to undergo. However, another round of prolonged interviews had begun. But this time the difference was that there were two army officers present. The questions varied from each interview. Sometimes they would centre on his personal circumstances and sometimes the radical opinions that had taken him into the revolutionist movement. Sometimes it was the activities and experiences he'd had when involved in the actual fighting that interested them and sometimes there seemed to be little purpose or direction in any of it. He tried to be straight and open with all his answers even though he could see that some of the questions were designed to lead him to traps. There was no doubt in his mind why he was being intensely grilled and that the board were looking for a reason to deny the application for amnesty made on his behalf by his brother. He did not blame them for that it was only to be expected that they would distrust him. But he tried hard to convince them that his only desire now was to follow a quiet pastoral life with his wife and children. He'd had enough excitement and uncertainty these past seven years to last the rest of his life. If indeed he had a life to live.

Then came the day he had been expecting. The army officers began cross-examining him about the day he had escaped from capture when two soldiers had been killed. These would be the events, he knew, that gave them precisely what they needed to reject his application. Nevertheless, it did give him an opportunity to put the record straight because he was sure the reports by the soldiers that day would bear little resemblance to the actual events. He admitted that two soldiers had been killed that day but only one had died at his hands the other by one of his own comrades. He claimed self-preservation as the sole reason. The stark choice had been to be hung meekly or to fight for his life. When he had finished his account, by their dubious expressions he doubted that they believed his version. It probably didn't matter anyway, the events on that day were probably just the final persuader they needed.

After that the interviews stopped. At first he had waited to be summoned but as the days slipped to a week, then longer, he realised that they would not be coming again. That last interview had probably killed off the last flicker of hope. With this realisation came another fit of depression. He had warned himself that it was unlikely that he could get the amnesty but as the last vestige withered he realised that he had nevertheless still hoped. With nothing left to hope for and still no date set for a trial he was stuck in limbo.

He tipped a bucket of water into the sunken metal toilet basin and then swished the mop around slapping the water to all corners. He went through the motions as slow as he dare and glanced briefly to see if the guards had noticed. Even this degrading task was much better than the endless hours locked inside his tiny cell and so he attempted to prolong the chore. He shared the ablution cleaning task with three others while two disinterested guards half supervised the work party. If they had noticed the men worked slowly then it did not bother them. Perhaps it was that they were almost as bored.

A third guard came into the ablutions glanced towards the work party and then spoke to the other two. One of them nodded then pointed at Mussalim.

"You," he barked. All four prisoners looked at the new arrival. "Yes you," he indicated Mussalim. "Come here." Mussalim put down the mop and went obediently over to the guards. "Mussalim Abdulla?"

"Yes."

"Commissar Mussalim Abdulla," he sneered. He was a heavy-set man with a large belly, a fat neck and several flabby chins.

"I am no longer a Commissar,"

"That's very true," he agreed. "You are nothing. All those illusions of grandeur, all those little red stars you pinned on yourself amounted to this. A mere toilet cleaner."

Mussalim did not reply. What was there to say?

The guard leaned forward his face close to his. "You're a toilet cleaner aren't you?" He shouted at him. "Aren't you?" he demanded.

He felt like driving his fist into his fat face but instead meekly nodded.

That wasn't good enough for him. "Say it," he demanded.

Mussalim swallowed his pride and agreed. "I'm a toilet cleaner." And you're a fat pig, he added in thought only.

"And that's too good for a PFLO Commissar," he muttered. "You're to come with me."

Mussalim was marched to the interview room where he found both the Army officers waiting for him. They waved him to sit at the table and to Mussalim's satisfaction they off-handedly dismissed the fat guard. He sat a little apprehensive half expecting some repercussions as a result of the last interview when he had conceded those two soldier deaths as a result of his escape. However, the atmosphere was different, almost cordial as they asked him some more questions about his actual combat experiences. Then as the questions dried up they looked at each other with some sort of agreement.

"Mussalim," one began. "Our intelligence have gathered quite a dossier on you," he said tapping the closed file on the table. "And I have to say that not all of it is bad. It would seem that you are quite an accomplished soldier, even formidable."

This was almost flattery and he wondered where he was going with it.

"We – er," he hesitated. "We think we can offer you an amnesty under certain conditions."

An amnesty? That was all he had heard. To get out of this awful place and then to be free to start all over again with a clean slate! For this he would be the best-damned subject in this Sultan's realm. Conditions? What conditions? Warning bells. "What conditions?"

"We want your special talents as a soldier. If you agree to join the army we will recommend an amnesty."

On the table before him was the amnesty that he never thought he would get and all he had to do was join the Sultan's Army. He should have been delighted but still he had reservations. He was tired of fighting and wanted no more of it. He just wanted to be left alone to find Jumaia and his boys and eke out a living on the jebal farm. From their point of view he could see it as the perfect solution to their dilemma. Perhaps they were not sure of his sincerity and to release a Commissar back onto the Qara where isolated pockets of die-hard PFLO still remained was an enormous gamble. To place him in the army where he would be under constant surveillance minimised the danger greatly and at the same time they could take advantage of his expertise and experience.

"You're less than enthusiastic," one observed.

"Yes I am," he admitted. "I want this amnesty more than anything in the world. But for seven long years I have been fighting and I'm just very tired of it all. I only want to go home and be left alone. I would take your offer with gratitude rather than stay rotting in this hellhole but there would be no enthusiasm in my contribution. I would be going through the motions and counting the days until my release." Had he just wrecked his chance for release? He feared that he might have.

"We thank you for a truthful answer and obviously a very sincere one." They glanced at each other. "We will talk again, perhaps in a couple of days."

It was three days later when the guards fetched him and walked him to the ablutions. Still wondering what it was that was about to happen Mussalim showered and was even more mystified when one of the guards handed him a clean white *disht-dasht* and a red and white chequered shamag to put on. From there they took him to the same room in the same wooden building where he once again found Hamed waiting for him.

His brother greeted him with a huge grin and got to his feet immediately. After the customary hugs and greeting Hamed turned away, picked up a piece of paper from the desk and held it up. " Good news brother," he said waving it about. "You have an amnesty."

Mussalim stared at the paper in his hand hardly able to believe what his brother had just said. Wordlessly he took it from his hand and began to read it.

"We have to go from here to the Wali's office where you are to swear allegiance to the Sultan," Hamed went on. "Then you will be released under my guarantee to do whatever it is you wish. Within the bounds of your parole of course."

He was talking but his words were not registering with Mussalim. He stared only at the paper that said he was forgiven his treason and he could return to society and take his part in the rebuilding of Oman. For him the war was at last over and all that resentment that he had harboured in the beginning could now be completely discarded. The society that the new Sultan strived to put together meant that there would be a place for all and all were important. Hamed's words eventually pierced his thoughts. He was to go to the Governor's office! Then he would be free to do whatever he wished! Parole? What was that about parole? He looked up at him.

"Parole?"

"Yes the usual conditions. You're to take no part in subversive activities and so on." He shrugged. "You just have to behave as a model subject. And you have to report to Um Al Gharriff once weekly until further notice"

"What for?"

He shrugged again. "Re-training, I suppose. And of course it helps them to keep track of your movements. I don't think there is anything particularly unusual to worry about."

It was only to be expected Mussalim conceded and it was a small price to pay anyway. The important thing was that he was to be freed and very soon he could look for Jumaia and the boys. "Did you have any luck finding Jumiai?"

Hamed shook his head. "No. But I haven't really had much opportunity to look," he confessed. "Soon you'll be able to do it for yourself," he said re-assuringly. "Come, father, mother and Khamisa wait for us at the Wali's office."

They were taken under guard by military Land Rover into the centre of Salalah where they were shown into the reception hall of the Governor's building. Although the hall was spacious it was crowded with many people all waiting their turn to be received by the Wali. Even so and still under guard Mussalim was taken to a spot just outside the heavy ornate double doors that was the Wali's office. He had a few brief moments to greet the rest of his family. Jokha looked particularly well but his father did not. The ravages and strain of the recent years had taken its toll and to Mussalim he looked old and frail. Nevertheless, he seemed visibly lifted at the prospects of his eldest son's imminent return. Khamisa also seemed to him to be less tense than he remembered from the time just before she and Hamed were married. Perhaps it was that father's solution to that particular distasteful situation had been a wise remedy. At least it seemed so anyway! Then after he met their son, Mubarrak, for the first time he recognised the binding bond and he was sure.

The interview was brief. The Wali asked polite superficial questions about Mussalim's desire to return to society as a Dhofari citizen as if re-assuring himself about his sincerity. But Mussalim knew that he was going through the motions only, the decision had been made elsewhere and required only his approval. Then he read out the terms of his parole before Mussalim swore the oath of allegiance to the Sultan. He was told that he would have to repeat that oath in the presence of Sultan Qaboos himself sometime soon and of course at his majesty's pleasure. Then he was dismissed and when he stood once more outside the double doors the Wali's secretary gave the two guards the nod that all was as it should be and they too were dismissed.

He wandered outside into the early afternoon sunshine and gazed across the walled courtyard garden. Beneath tall shading palms multi-coloured bougainvilleas covered the ground each side of the wide gravel path. At the end of the path great wooden gates yawned open inviting him to walk out into the world beyond. He was free.

Free to return to normal life. But what was normal life. Life had never been normal for him since he was a young boy. His desire for something better had driven him to Bahrain and there the comparison between what was possible there and what wasn't possible in Oman had nurtured his anger. That anger had festered into hatred and pushed him into a crusading war against oppressing poverty. Then trapped by his own aptitude, as a skilled soldier of the revolutionists there had been no way out. Until now! Now because of the magnanimous generosity of the man he had fought against for more than five of these seven years he had been granted the opportunity to start all over again. And he would! He would find his wife, his two boys and return to the jebal farm. His father and Jokha too would be much happier back where they belonged. It had been his father's lifetime's work and there was no earthly reason now why it should be wasted.

The farm was derelict but with a little effort he could restore it. There was still that money hidden in the rocks at Dalkut and with that he could buy two, perhaps even three cows. In one year with breeding there would be six, in three more than a dozen, in five two dozen. Lots of hard work lay ahead but the opportunity was there and it was entirely up to him now. For his children there was promise of schooling and the security of health care for all. These were the very objectives for what he had fought and in the end how he had found himself as part of the barrier to those constitutional rights he still did not understand. But these advantages were there for all and now he would work to ensure that the Sultan's Civil Development Programme worked and at the same time reap its benefit for himself and his family. If any nation were to threaten that then once again he would take up arms and this time it would be in Qaboos' cause that he would fight. The prospects for all Omanis beneath this benevolent Sultan looked bright indeed.

His first priority, however, was to find Jumaia. Ali was a good friend and reliable he would not have abandoned her without doing something to ensure her welfare. Perhaps he had returned her to Jibjat back with her Mahru people. Or perhaps he had kept her with him. Find Ali, that would be the starting point. If he had Jumaia still with him then that would be the ending point too. Unless? A dark thought occurred to him. What if believing that he would not return or perhaps that he were dead he had taken her for his wife? After all that had been the very circumstances under which he himself had found Jumaia in Tarqah. Ali had also openly stated just before he had left Raykut with Jumaia that a wife and family just like his was his desire too. If he had taken her for his wife then when he did find them he would have no option, he would be forced to kill him in order to get his family back. He fervently hoped that he would not find that situation. After all Ali had proved to be his best friend.

The rest of his family now waited for him on the beach on the other side of those gates. With only that remote possibility to blot his high spirits he went with a spring in his step to find them and to let them know of his decision to re-start the family farm. That news would be well received of that he was sure.

✻ ✻ ✻

Abdulla wandered a few yards down the beach towards the barrier that was the Sultan's Salalah Palace. The wind off the sea had a cold edge to it even for February but the sun was warm and the day was pleasant. It would not have mattered to him if the weather had been really bad, Mussalim had an amnesty and was home to stay. Even better he had only a few minutes before declared his intention to move back to the farm. Abdulla had no doubts of his eldest son's capabilities; he was a very determined character and would make it a success. However, it certainly would not be easy because he would virtually have to start from scratch. Although there was still a small goat herd wandering around Haluf all the cattle had gone. He still had a little money left from that livestock sale but during their time spent in Haluf it had dwindled considerably. That coupled with the continuing spiralling cost of cattle meant that its buying power was greatly reduced. Mussalim would certainly need Allah's special help.

At sunset he would make a special prayer asking that he look favourably on his son's new struggle. At the same time he would express his own gratitude because now he would be able to return to the mountains he loved and spend his remaining days amongst its peaks. Also he would have a legacy to leave when his life was ended, his life's work had not after all been in vain. *Il hamdu lillaah.*

The war had ravaged his family Kathya – Juma and Lailla all gone. Two as a direct result of the conflict while the third as a result of a complete absence of medical amenities. However, with the conflict all but ended and a more liberal attitude from the Sultan-led government uniting a divided nation the future looked more far secure than at any time during in his long life. Perhaps that fortune-teller he had visited almost seven years ago had been right after all. A bright sun was rising on a new Oman and there would be peace and prosperity for all. And that man that he had predicted would come from the west pursuing his own mission and at the same time easing his burden and other jebally's had been Mussalim. But the fortune-teller had been wrong about him unintentionally adding a great tragedy to his load. The biggest tragedies that had befallen him after that 'telling' had undoubtedly been the death of Juma and then later Lailla. By no stretch of the imagination could either of those be attributed to Mussalim. So perhaps the predictions owed more to luck than real authenticity.

He arrived at the barrier that prevented him wandering onto the beach in front of the Palace and he squinted his eyes trying pick out its detail. But all he could see was the blues of sea and sky, the gold of the glistening sand and the tall imposing shape of the palace. He felt no jealousy in comparison with his own modest farm. This Sultan was a great man and a great man deserves great status such as fine Palaces. Unlike his father Qaboos was a liberal man willing to share his wealth with his subjects. He recognised that a nation's greatness lies not with its ruler but with its people. If a nation is to become great then it is the total sum of its people's effort that will make it so. He wondered what would have been the outcome today had not Qaboos ousted his father? He shuddered slightly as he thought of the bullying and forcing tactics of the men of the PFLOAG who had controlled the mountains at that time. It could have been that not only Dhofar would now be under their firm control but perhaps also the whole country too. But Allah in his wisdom had known what was best for his people and thwarted that by removing a selfish intransigent ruler and replaced him with an enlightened man for the benefit of all. Another reason to recognise Allah's greatness.

As he stood before the barrier staring at the kaleidoscope of colours Jokha moved quietly to his side and took his arm. "What do we care for Palaces?" she asked guessing at his thoughts.

"Yes you're right. A Palace can never really be a home."

They were silent a moment then she said. "We have to go now if we are going to make it home before dark."

"Home?"

"Yes home. Our farm."

Abdulla glanced once more towards the shape that was the Palace and even felt a little sympathy for the man who had to live there.

"Then let's go," he said, turning away.

End

Appendix

This story is based inside the framework of events of the Dhofar Insurgency. These events and their sequence provided perimeters beyond which, in the interest of credibility I could not stray and it was these perimeters that presented me with the biggest challenge, I had to control my wayward imagination. The only place in the story that I have knowingly deviated outside this framework of facts is when in the interest of continuity of my story I placed Hamed on the Hornbeam Line in Autumn 1972. The Hornbeam Line construction did not start until the following spring.

The basic story is of course fictional and all the lead characters are figments of my imagination. However, there are characters on the periphery of the story that did exist and in some cases still do today.

His Royal Highness Sultan Qaboos most certainly exists, and today he presides over a progressive and devoted nation. His late father was indeed Said Bin Taymour. While Sheikh Mussalim Bin Nufl and Sheikh Mussalim Bin Tufl of the greater Kathiri also exist and are both to this day loyal subjects of his Majesty. Also Salim Mubarak was a leader in the dwindling Dhofar Liberation Front that was driven off the eastern jebel by the PFLOAG in autumn 1970. He and his band were forced to surrender to government forces at Mirbat. He became a founder member and an influential leader in the Firqa Salahadin before his untimely death six months later in spring 1971.

Other characters Ahmed Al Ghasanni, Abdel Tahir, Mohammed Bin Talib, Salim Al Mushani and Zahir Ali Matar also existed on the Marxist side. Al Ghasanni was indeed the General Secretary of the PFLOAG and Abdel Tahir his trusted lieutenant. The other three were members of the Central Committee and active leaders in the Front. However, I have no evidence of the actual roles they played and the roles that I have placed them in this story are imaginary and I claim only that they could have played similar roles. It is true, however, that Salim Al Mushani and Mohammed Bin Talib were both arrested around the capital area on separate occasion whilst attempting to incite the National Democratic Front for the Liberation of Oman and the Arabian Gulf to more active and greater rebellion. Later Zahir Ali, after a training spell in Beirut with the Popular Front for the Liberation of Palestine, suffered a similar fate upon his return to Oman. He was killed at a military checkpoint near Rustaq after a shoot out.

Many bloody and bitter skirmishes took place during this conflict and I have conveniently placed my characters in some of them. There was a great deal of self-sacrifice and many heroic deeds performed during these actual skirmishes and on both sides. It is not my intention to detract or be-little these acts of courage in any slight way. Indeed I hope that I have been able to clarify to the reader the situation as it was at that particular point in history and present a viewpoint from both sides albeit through the minds of fictional character. If I have accomplished that in any small way then perhaps it may be that I have emphasised the brave acts of many.

The battle at Mirbat in July 1972 has been well documented in the annuls of the British SAS. On that day the best courageous traditions of the SAS were upheld. Capt Kealy was awarded a Distinguished Service Order and Trooper Tobin a posthumous Military Medal for their suicidal dash across the battlefield to re-activate the silent 25-pounder gun. Corporal Bradshaw's actions also earned a Military Medal while Trooper Labalala received a posthumous mention in despatches. Both he and Trooper Tobin died from wounds received at that gun. There is no doubt that these citations would have received higher accolades and much more publicity had it not been for the fact that to the world outside, British forces were not in action in Oman. A secret situation that in today's sophisticated media communication links would not have been remotely possible. In his book Tony Jeapes quotes the words of the Commanding Officer of the Northern Frontier Regiment and I can do no more than re-iterate that passage.

"It may appear that an unusually large number of names have been recorded. This is because there were, on the 19th July, an unusually large number of gallant actions at Mirbat."

To say that the Mirbat victory had been a very close call could not in any circumstances be considered an under-statement. Other acts of valour included the Air Force pilots who flying almost blind and at zero feet hampered the *adoo* advance sufficiently long enough to allow G Squadron to move into the battle theatre. Mike Kealy did indeed owe his life and the security of the 25-pounder to a hand-grenade thrown into the gun pit that failed to go off. What the potential implications would have been had that gun been seized by the attackers can only now be conjecture. However, it is safe to say the impact would have been serious. But by far the largest slice of luck was the relieving SAS G Squadron, which had landed in Oman only a couple of days previously. If the attack had been carried out before their arrival then there would have been no reinforcements to deploy. In those circumstances the eventual outcome can only be speculated.

By far, however, the most influential event throughout the whole period of the conflict was without doubt the bloodless coup by Prince Qaboos to remove his father as Sultan. There is no doubt that at that point the communists were in control and perhaps on the very brink of victory in the Dhofar region. Upon ascension Qaboos immediately put into place more popular liberal policies and effectively removed many of the reasons for revolution. Then in order that these policies could be implemented he determinedly set about removing the communist elements that barred the way to progress. It is true that Said Bin Taymour lived only another two years after being de-posed but if Qaboos had waited till then it would undoubtedly have been too late. The next domino to fall would have been Northern Oman and with the narrow Straits of

Hormuz under communist control then the passage of oil supplies to the west would have been in garrotting stranglehold. In that event what a very different place the world would have been today. Today as all the populations of the western world accept without a second thought all the benefits that oil brings the irony is that very few could tell you who Sultan Qaboos actually is? They are blithely oblivious of the enormous dept that they owe.

The people of Oman today enjoy a prosperity that compares favourably with all the countries of the Middle East and in some cases their living standard is better. Its splendid capital city Muscat has few equals either in or outside the region. Certainly its traffic roundabouts of imitation forts, waterfalls, clock towers and desert scenes etc, all lovingly maintained, leave me envious when I compare them to the dull unimaginative roundabouts in the UK. The progress this nation has made in recent years is absolutely astounding. When Prince Qaboos became Sultan Qaboos essential amenities were non-existent. For instance there were hardly any schools and precious few iron roads, none at all outside Muscat. In a country the size of Great Britain there was only one hospital and a poorly equipped one at that. In a comparative short period of thirty-one years Sultan Qaboos has hurled his nation from its backward mid nineteenth century standard right into the modern twenty-first. He is revered by his populous, and justifiably so.

Hill Fort at Mirbat – see Chapter 18.

Wadi Aydaas – a typical Qara Wadi in Oman.

Wadi Sheetah – a typical desert wadi.